Publisher's synopsis

In a story that creates what George Bernard Shaw termed "a very strong and very painful impression of evil," Mabel Blair Steering follows young Gwendolyn as she encounters the tragedy of hijacked human goodness and its effect on its victims. This novel, locally amusing but globally disturbing, has already brought into public discussion a deepening moral failing of our time—a problem born of our collective drive to make ourselves believe we are good, a problem nourished by our lack of will to identify evil in those who thrive by exploiting others.

Sustenance Through Starvation is fiction—but only if George Orwell authored fiction. It is satire—but only if Franz Kafka wrote satire.

Judge for yourself.

What do the critics say?

"Through the tale of Gwendolyn, the guileless daughter of the head of the world's largest charitable organization, we are led to coming to terms with the grim reality of our 21st century world. Our young heroine, selfless and brave as well as being somewhat naïve, is decidedly driven by the will to help the real other... by going right there, where hunger thrives and disease spreads. So she sets off, heart brimming with enthusiasm...

"In a style that takes on a strong didactic dimension but without lacking the emotional depth and richness that makes a good novel, *Sustenance Through Starvation* leads us behind the curtains of what "charity" can be in a world in which our sustenance is their starvation. Yet far from being an incentive to be passive, this novel spurs a strong feeling of indignation regarding our unjustly double-tiered world: *Sustenance Through Starvation* can be read in a plush armchair with a comforting hot chocolate in hand, but once the last page is turned, the chair will feel outrageously too plush, and the chocolate taste appallingly too sweet."

Rating: ★★★★   —The San Francisco Book Review

From the reviews on Amazon

★★★★★ *Lighthearted, cynical, and brilliantly absurd*
It's one of a few books that have regularly made me both laugh and think hard on the same page… What draws people to charity? Wanting to help people is a strong motivator, but is it all that's at play? This book will make you think twice… I walked away from the book with a number of mental images that still make me chuckle against my will. In all, this is a must-read for the reader who loves to mix critical thinking and pure entertainment.

★★★★★ *Worth the read on a number of counts*
Thought provoking book with a rare combination of wry writing (the mere phraseology will bring a smile) and engaging character development. The scenes of natural disaster leave the reader on edge. The writer does not feel the need to spoon feed the reader…

★★★★★ *Enjoyable, Relatable, and Thought-Provoking*
As you question Gwendolyn's choices, you also question your own idealistic thoughts. The characters of the novel are very well-developed. Gwendolyn's interactions with all of these characters are intriguing… Overall, this book has it all—it's a very powerful and insightful look at the relatable idealistic young adult facing the realities of the world…You would be wise to make it your next read!

★★★★★ *Intriguing Warning in Story Form*
A hilarious expose and a warning… I did not know if I should laugh or cry after most of the chapters. This book is a quick read with realities to ponder.

★★★★ *Charity Corruption on Display*
I was intrigued by the subject manner and how the author was able to craft the different levels of the charity world in a fashion that opened my eyes… Technical yes – humorous yes – worth the read yes yes.

★★★★★ *Entertaining, Alarming! Humorous and educational*
Although the setting and characters are clearly fictional, the story may be "ripped from real life."

SUSTENANCE THROUGH STARVATION

Mabel Blair Steering

SUSTENANCE THROUGH STARVATION

— Scales Dropping —

Krakatoa Classics

An imprint of Duxbury & Gloucester

Published by Krakatoa Classics,
an imprint of Duxbury & Gloucester

Publisher's Cataloging-in-Publication data

Steering, Mabel Blair.
Sustenance through starvation : scales dropping / Mabel Blair Steering.
p. cm.
ISBN   978-09888242-5-6

1. Corruption—Fiction. 2. Charities—Corrupt practices—Fiction.
3. Charities—Corrupt practices—Africa—Fiction.
4. Political corruption—Economic aspects—Fiction.
5. Universities and colleges—Fiction. 6. Young women—Fiction.
7. Bildungsromans. 8. Capitalism—Fiction. 9. Satire. I. Title.

PS3619 .T442 Su 2013
813/.6—dc23   2013952323

Second Edition
2 4 6 8 7 5 3 1

Manufacturing information is available on the last page of this book.

Contents

Preface

If this story, with all its absurdities and written using only the least subtle of colors, stimulates nontrivial discussion on how those we choose to trust must live up to that standard, I have succeeded.

Dinner at the Mowk

What have we created?

"There's no shame in changing your mind, sweetie." Dr. Kingman Q. Dressel-Meier's attention was ostensibly consumed in carving his steak as he tried another tack in the conversation with his daughter. A detached observer would perceive that something in his mannerism conveyed awareness of extant defeat despite his continuing participation in the verbal battle. Gwendolyn was not really listening to her father. With her gaze on the scenery outside, she could hear the rest of the family exchanging content-light babble over the dinner table. Tonight her mother's voice was unusually sparse.

The hastily scheduled gathering was an unusual off-cycle meeting. The family had spent two weeks together in Bermuda last month, and their next scheduled get-together was not until the holidays. But Kingman wanted to meet with Gwendolyn and work through his current disagreement with the headstrong girl, so he called a board meeting and brought the rest of the family across the continent. And here they sat.

Gwendolyn was looking out the window surveying the darkling city almost twenty storeys below. She always enjoyed her perch in this restaurant crowning the hotel on the most famous hill in the city. The family had been situated here at a floor-to-ceiling window many times since she was a little girl, and she loved the vantage point, from which she could view the busy town with its hills and sleek buildings. The place was truly a living work of art, ablaze with action. Nowadays Gwendolyn lived near enough that she could come here any time she wanted, but she never came alone or with friends. It was a family favorite, and they all called the place the 'Mowk' in honor of her attempt to pronounce the hotel's name when she was a toddler.

The girl had grown weary of squabbling with her parents about her intentions. She was tired of arguing this evening. She was tired of arguing this month. She was tired of arguing this year. As the glow from the sunset warmed the western sky she admired the silvery-grey colors of the hills, speckled with their lakes and inlets. She watched the motion of boats on the bay and cars on the bridges. She turned her eyes down and examined the hive of activity on the gridded, sometimes obliquely sliced streets that marked San Francisco. Impatient clumps of cars tested their constraints, seeming to navigate by near-braille. The cheery lights of shops and restaurants and nightclubs festooned the wharves and streets at the water's edge. She quietly imbibed the beautiful visual music, letting Kingman's words echo soundlessly and meaninglessly in her mind for a bit. Then she allowed them to drip from her consciousness as tangential irrelevancies.

Kingman worked his delicate filet with powerful authority. He was an impressive, dark-haired and bearded man, impeccably dressed in a dinner jacket that could have been a uniform, and he had never quite gotten comfortable with situations he did not control. And now he was faced with his daughter placing herself outside the command structure. He dramatically but unconvincingly concentrated on his food, trimming the steak as though he planned to enter it in a sculpture contest.

Gwendolyn turned back from the window, and the genial murmur at the table quieted down. Her mother looked at her with trepidation, then quickly looked away to her two older sons. Handsome and well groomed in their suits, they were the picture of their father: trim figures, straight backs, dark hair. The younger of the two, Hunter, was even considering growing a beard like his father's. Handsome people often look younger than their years; the brothers were under thirty, and nothing in their behavior contradicted an impression of immaturity. Gwendolyn's looks took after her mother—lighter hair, average build, less striking than the males in the family. Winifred sat next to her husband looking quite elegant and somewhat older than him, though in fact they were the same age.

Gwendolyn knew she had no allies in the conversation. So far neither Marshall nor Hunter had spoken up in her support, even in the most philosophical of tones. Marshall, the eldest, always followed his father, and Hunter usually coasted along whatever tack seemed easiest. In truth neither brother cared very much about their little sister's plans, which were the subject of the discussion between the girl and her father. Gwendolyn and her mother were the only ones giving no visible attention to the fine food on their plates, but for all his theatrics, Kingman was uninterested in the steak he so carefully manipulated. Gwendolyn inhaled, tensed, straightened and prepared to resume battle.

Kingman spoke again, returning to his more conventional lines of argument. "I can tell you there's nothing to see over there. There are lots of these groups, and I know all of them to one extent or another. You're better off staying at Stambridge and getting some credentials people will respect." He paused, giving her a chance to speak as he deftly worked to excise a string of fat from the edge of his expensive meat. "You'll do more for the world by staying here." He suspended his surgery to glance at Winifred. His wife was listening, nodding. He looked at his daughter with a resolute but neutral frown. He sipped some wine without breaking his stare, and Winifred and the boys each took a drink as though on command. Then Kingman turned back to his food, speared a piece of steak and chewed it slowly, allowing plenty of time for his daughter's response. Nothing emerged.

He surveyed the food on his plate as he spoke up. "Hunter and Marshall, I'm sure, had the same sort of restlessness when they were your age. Get your degree. You'll be better off for it." The boys' eyes went to each other's quizzically; their shoulders exchanged surprise and confidential denial. "They stayed focused, and I don't see why you shouldn't. You know what your mother and I think. Stay in school. Stay here." Winifred nervously fingered her necklace with one hand and nodded to her daughter as her husband spoke.

Gwendolyn had heard the part about doing more good by staying at the university so many times that it was trite. And she was not distracted by the absurd picture of her older brothers as focused scholars during college. She spoke up. "You don't see it, Daddy. I'm not looking for what makes *me* better off. I'm looking for what makes *them* better off. And besides, I'm not talking about dropping out, just stopping out for a quarter or maybe two. I promise I'll get my Stambridge degree." She was done arguing. She turned back to the window in resignation. There had been no surprises today, and there was no chance that being stressed would change the conversation, so she tried to relax. She reminded herself that this was just her parents' latest attempt at dissuading her, and that she knew she would win—her father had implicitly recognized that in earlier rounds of the contest. She had no doubt whatsoever that her father would commit the Foundation's financial support to both Stambridge and the Wholesome Globe Project if she went to Swazizibia to work with the Project for a while.

Kingman looked at his sons, eyeing one then the other briefly. "What do you think about it, boys? Will Swazizibia be good for Gwendolyn? Or should she stay here?" He took a determined drink of wine and returned his apparent concentration to carving his food. The brothers sat in clumsy silence, each seemingly on the verge of making a sound but gridlocked until the other spoke; both were gesturing negative agreement with their father.

Winifred's head traveled inches forward and, still fumbling with her necklace, she broke in, "For goodness' sake, Gwendolyn. Why in god's name do you want to go over to that terrible place and get mixed up in all that? Starving people! Let those missionaries and doctors over there deal with the situation. We can send them some money." She glanced at Kingman, whose focus was seemingly on his steak. "If you insist on helping." She shook her head. "You don't know anything. What can a twenty-year-old girl do that they're not already doing? Won't it help the world more if you just finish school and take your place in the Foundation? How many times has your father told you that's how you can really do good? What does he say? 'Move the needle. Have a stronger impact on the bottom line.' That's what we do in our family, the Foundation. We help people, really help. For heaven's sake, they didn't even ask you to come. They want donations, not people. They all do."

The words about the Foundation's mission were familiar. Gwendolyn had heard them often. "No, Mother," she said. "Yes, they certainly want volunteers too. People are dying over there. How many times did you tell me 'every little bit helps' when I was growing up? Sure, I don't know how to kill infections or set broken bones. But I know how to care, and I'm going to show that. I care about every one of them. All the children. All the older people too, not just the kids. Everyone suffering over there. I've showed you the pictures. You've seen those children." She paused and drew a breath, aware of the escalation incipient in her next words. "And I don't buy the message on the Foundation's stickers and trinkets. Most people do care, they just can't do anything but maybe give money. I'm different. I can go over there. And I'm going for those starving people, and I'm going right to where they need help. I'll hitchhike if I have to."

Her slight referred to the stylish trademarked 'IDIC' logo: the four bold black letters in a light green oval. In jewelry it was realized as raised or engraved letters in gold, always gold. It was her mother's conception, but it was Kingman's genius for marketing that had made the symbol a stylish and popular meme that elevated awareness of the Foundation among the general public. He had positioned the logo to signify the humanity and highly evolved social conscience of its bearers. Many celebrities had been spotted sporting it these past few years, and it was salient on all of the best college campuses. The Foundation made the trademark freely available for educational institutions, movies and celebrities. They licensed it for appropriate fees elsewhere. Bank headquarters buildings displayed it prominently in their lobbies, as did the home office of most large American corporations. Societies fighting all sorts of diseases used the logo in their materials. And just a month ago the United Nations had accepted the Foundation's offer of a mammoth sculpture of the IDIC symbol for its new building. The emblem decorated cars, from smoke-choking buckets of bolts plastered with 'be-good-to-the-planet-and-coexist-and-visualize' stickers to astonishingly expensive machines whose finish was marred only by the sleek gold IDIC emblem itself.

'IDIC' means "I'm Different—I Care."

The Foundation sold items with this logo and also awarded them for donations. Stickers and key chains bearing the image were found in the checkout lines at exclusive stores and country clubs. A few hundred dollars' donation to the Foundation garnered a matching pair of fine polo shirts with beautiful four-letter embroidery spelling out the message in gold thread. A trophy with the logo above a pewter base engraved with the donor's name, date of donation and numerical rank for that year could be obtained for a mere ten thousand dollar contribution. It was a beautiful artifact, with the gold IDIC logo held by the spread arms of a silvery nude woman with wings. The prize was suitable for display in the office along with a benefactor's diplomas, hundred-year-old Scotch whiskey and golf trophies. Grander symbols were available through negotiations with Kingman or one of his sons. As an example, they had supplied a few large metal logos, robustly plated to withstand sea salt spray, for use on yachts in marinas on both coasts.

Winifred was hurt. "You're going for yourself. You are being selfish, young lady." Her mother's harsh voice bit into the girl, making her consider regretting the affront to her mother's symbol. Winifred was still unconsciously stroking her necklace, a necklace terminated in a jeweled, golden pendant engraved with the IDIC logo. "You're not going for them. Your father and I will suffer for it." She writhed in a cold shiver and took a sip of her Drambuie to warm herself. Winifred never drank wine, regular hard liquor or heaven forbid, beer. Her drink, regardless of context, was the royal cordial. In establishments that did not have any Drambuie in stock, the management always found a way to procure it for her.

Kingman reached over, took his wife's hand in both of his, and patted it. He nodded to the waiter as the man silently questioned whether Kingman's wine should be replenished; the gesture implicitly included instruction to bring another drink for his wife as well. The waiter picked up the bottle from the table, poured wine into Kingman's glass and turned around. Winifred put her cordial glass down, and just then the waiter emerged from his smooth spin with a full cup of the liquid treasure for her.

Hunter had been quietly sipping his brandy all this time, but now he wiggled as though he had gas pains. A thought was forming. "Ginny, actually aren't you hurting the world by taking a year to empty bedpans and clean up vomit?"

Gwendolyn shuddered at the question, but quietly awaited whatever would gurgle forward next. Hunter was forming his coming words and growing proud of the new wrinkle he figured he was bringing into the discussion, though it was just a restatement of his mother's comments of a moment before, wherein she restated her husband's position. "Doesn't it just delay the things you can really do by a year? Or however long?" Hunter had not listened closely enough to know how much time was being discussed. Their older brother, Marshall, was listening now, and he was slowly processing the familiar idea, nodding. Their father seemed impressed by the tack as well; it clearly made sense to him, and he was happy to have a non-parental ally speak up.

Marshall had something to add now. "And since you'll be closer to the money it's more impactful. I've seen it myself. Always keep your nose near the money. We've finally started getting real statistically important results from my program in Outer Cryptonesia. The machinery's been going for almost three years now. Women who need abortions get them in most any town in the country for free. It's actually easier than getting a tooth pulled. And remember this is one of those places where abortions have been a superstitious religious taboo forever. Our program doesn't just help those women themselves; it's going to start decreasing the overall population in the area. It's a small step to improving the global environment over time, granted, but a real one." He paused for a sip of Scotch, glancing to assess his father's reaction to his offering. Kingman assented smilingly.

Continuing, Marshall said, "Now *that's* what the Foundation does. Not just feeding another hungry wight, not just scraping pus off another wound.

The area is lush with jungles and species you can't find anywhere else. Those people aren't improving that part of the world, that's for sure. Or the rest of the planet. If truth be told, it would be better off deserted."

Hunter added a small joke, eyebrows momentarily arching, eyes rolling across the dome of their orbits to Marshall as he leaned toward his brother, "And it's still unacceptable to achieve *that* in the most straightforward way." He chuckled at his clever joke, but just as Marshall was about to join him, his mother's glare demanded attention, joined by an even more severe glower from Kingman. The parents were not so much in disagreement with the sentiment, but they were afraid this sort of talk would not put their young daughter in the mood to be persuaded of anything. Hunter could only suppress the outward aspects of his amusement; deep within he continued to laugh at his witty remark.

Marshall took back the floor and spoke to Gwendolyn. "What I'm saying is, if I had just put on sandals and mosquito nets and gone into the jungle villages there and eaten the vermin and sticks they call food, we'd never have been able to set up the system. Sure, I visited a few villages, you have to do that. But anywhere like that, the real business has to be done in the capital. Where the rules are made. Where the money changes hands. If I had just gone there for, say, a year, to live with them and 'help,' women there would still be prisoners to nature. We all want to be on the 'front lines' like the jungles in Cryptonesia, or the desert or whatever at your place. I denied myself that satisfaction, and I did it for a good reason." Kingman was visibly nodding, looking at his daughter. "You need to listen to Father on this. You need to summon up the self-discipline to do the right thing. Believe me, I understand how you feel. You need to get past the emotional delusion."

Marshall understood nothing of Gwendolyn's thoughts or feelings.

Kingman was satisfied and even impressed; Marshall could seem very convincing advocating something a listener already firmly believed, and the young man was pouring it on now. Besides, his argument was logically impeccable.

Kingman's mind wandered now. He looked at Marshall, then at Hunter. Both of his sons were brutes. No, not brutes. Both of his boys might could be considered brutes if they weren't so damned attractive and harmless, perhaps if they weren't so impeccably dressed and groomed. Whatever their genus, Kingman had always assumed that Marshall would be the one to run the Foundation someday, suboptimal as that plan seemed. You see, none of his children were what one would call brilliant. The boys had no inner drive beyond satisfying their immediate desires. And Gwendolyn, ingenuous as she was, certainly had the greatest intellect in the group, and she was certainly the most fearlessly obstinate in pursuit of her own desires. But she had never shown signs of the toughness she would need for that sort of job. Kingman could not picture her resisting anybody who claimed any sort of need. He looked at her and wondered if having spoiled her was coming home to roost. In all probability she would become a nursery school teacher or some social do-gooder, and there was likely little Kingman or Winifred could do to change that now.

Marshall was talking, "… looking to expand the abortion program to other places where people are so marginal. My point is this: there will be a lot to do where you can make big decisions. Don't kid yourself with this 'front lines' babble. Stick around here like Father says." He took a satisfied, tinkling hit of his Scotch on the rocks as Hunter nodded.

Things became quiet, and Gwendolyn felt the intense focus of Kingman's silence as he directed its full force at her. Winifred tagged along, expectantly looking at her daughter. As for the brothers, Hunter was enjoying rolling his brandy around in his mouth and Marshall was basking in the afterglow of a brilliant speech.

Now, thinking about distant results was never Gwendolyn's strong suit. She was more oriented to the concrete, the 'here and now.' *Could they be right? Could I just be trying to make myself feel better? Will I really help more if I don't go?* The argument made some sense to her, but as the baby of the family she was accustomed to being bamboozled by the others. It had happened all her life. When she argued with Kingman, she usually finished in agreement with him. *Of course. How could I ever have seen things differently?* But every single time, with speed proportional to her distance from her father, her prior convictions reasserted their grip on her mind afterward.

Gwendolyn forced herself to remember how she had set her resolve back on campus: *The decision has been made. We've talked about it till we're blue in the face. He has rhetorically stated that the decision is mine. And I am going to help those people.* She worried about letting her commitment flag yet again, which she knew would only be a temporary relief from the controversy; it would spawn another bout of argument over the project. Her prior discussions with Kingman had often included his commitment to provide financial support if she really was to go. But they all ended with his assertion that she saw the light of his argument, or at the very least, that the matter was not closed. *Oh, but if only today were just like any other Thursday. Right now I'd be volunteering at the soup kitchen down the peninsula, helping people for real and not having to fight with anyone.* He had worn her down tonight, and she wanted to escape the discussion. She had some temptation to tell her father she would think about it some more.

No. This beast must be slain; it had survived too many woundings. She would deal it a death blow or die trying.

Gwendolyn had stored away a trick, a tool to stiffen her resolve if things got too pressured. She reminded herself of a few inspiring lines she had memorized long ago. Some old and insignificant poet had written a rambling poem about how to live life. When she was thirteen she had an English teacher partial to the verse. As with all her classes in school, she remembered almost nothing of that English class. But she remembered the last few lines of the poem. She had adopted the lines as a sort of motto over the years.

> *You author your story. The future's at stake.*
> *You're sure to construct it. Which path will you take?*
> *The wind or the feather? The golf club or ball?*
> *In living your life the game's winner take all!*

She actually heard the poem in her own voice when she recounted the words silently, and it cheered her. She found that Marshall's little speech had also in some way helped stiffen her resolve—that he considered some people pollutants of his planet demonstrated that his words had no relevance to her. She discarded his whole argument as the blather of someone to be ignored; if they were that far apart on something so simple, how much could he have to tell her on a complicated decision like traveling to Swazizibia? And the seeming concurrence of her parents bothered her.

Gwendolyn took a breath and spoke up in a verbal hurricane. "Daddy, I love you, but I'm going. I feel like I'm the one starving, not those piteous people over there. Starving for meaning, contribution. I need to help these people or I'll … waste away and die. I can't just stay here, going about my daily pampered-student existence. It's not even a choice. I have to go. Can't you see? It's like a hunger. When I tamp it down it wells up again like… like… haven't you ever had to sneeze and you try suppress it? You're stuck with this weird pressure feeling and tickling and a sneeze that won't bloom, and you can't move on, can't really do anything till it's consummated. You can hold it in for a while, you may think you have it beat. But you don't. It gets you eventually."

She paused because her nose tickled; maybe she had to sneeze. She sat perfectly motionless, her mouth open. She rubbed her nose. It was a false alarm, and the sensation subsided. Mostly. Kingman and Hunter massaged the bridges of their noses as well. Kingman thought to himself, "Well, I can't vouch for the syntax, but I think her time at Stambridge has at least been good for her vocabulary."

"That's what this is like for me, Daddy. I've been thinking about this for a long, long time, and I have to go. I couldn't live with myself if I didn't." She appropriated one of Kingman's favorite unoriginal lines: "What good is it if I just talk the talk and I don't walk the walk?" Her father stirred, his mouth starting to open, but she continued. "I just can't do what you want. I can't ignore them and stay here in school until I get my degrees in sociology and political science. Like I said, it's not a choice." She turned and looked at Winifred. "Mother, I will be very careful, and I promise I'll return intact," she said without moderating her speed.

In truth, though he did not realize it, Kingman had long understood where the discussion must end. A man without the ability to read people would never have been able to found and grow a meta-charity into one of the largest economic concerns in the world. Still, reading people and understanding or influencing your own daughter are quite different subjects, so up until now he had held out hope. It did make him silently bristle that she almost seemed to be crediting her choice of majors to him—why not major in ancient Javanese mythology? From his perspective it would be equally valid. He would have preferred she study economics or business, but he loved his daughter and understood her feelings about the more rigorous majors. At least she had not enrolled in Stambridge's Grievance Studies major.

As a father he was compelled to push one more time. "Well, princess, it's your decision, as I've always said. You think it through, and let us know what you decide. If you want to know what I think...." The finish was for show; he did not complete the sentence. Winifred, who had genuinely thought they may sway her, maintained a worried forehead, attention frozen on her daughter, but she was silent.

How do I point out that I know he knows the decision has been made? Well, actions speak louder than words, as they say. Gwendolyn suppressed her desire to assert and said politely, "Of course, Daddy." She looked over to Winifred and nodded.

Around the table nobody misled himself with the possible exception of Winifred, who held out an infinitesimal hope that her daughter would come to her senses. Kingman knew better. It is impossible to say for certain by observing the uninterested brothers guzzling their drinks and quietly fooling around, but they probably knew as well.

Kingman returned to his steak, but the effort was a feeble pretense. He was not hungry, and he soon laid his fork and knife in the 'take my plate' position. He momentarily lifted his spirits by glancing at his reflection in the now-darkened window. The trim face, the strong jawline supporting the cropped beard surmounting his tailored clothing—all this made for a truly enjoyable visage, a refreshing boost.

Gwendolyn pushed her luck a bit, pulling her father back into the conversation, "So, if I decide I'm certain I am going, do we still have to take our exploratory trip first? Why don't we just..." She sneezed suddenly and consummately.

Kingman's head turned toward her, at first without his eyes, which were anchored till the tethers broke. He looked directly at his daughter and shook his head. "Gesundheit. No, I want to see the place before you go. I want you to see it. We will still take the trip." His voice was powerful and certain. He glanced at Winifred, who returned a worried look. Gwendolyn nodded. She had been careful to use the word 'if,' but was happy to hear him use more certain phrasing in his response.

Gwendolyn had been stressed all day, knowing what dinner would be like. Now the big confrontation was over, and she was determined not to allow it to reopen. After a few more minutes she was able to eat. Her parents sat quietly, and the three siblings talked and visited, Hunter and Marshall over refilled drinks and Gwendolyn over her fine, now-cold pasta meal. Kingman rolled his wine in his glass, not once looking at his reflection, and watched his daughter fondly. He realized she was growing up, and he missed his little girl. In truth his thinking lagged reality; progressive tense was invalid—he should have thought in past tense.

Marshall asked his sister, "So, Ginny, what did we miss today?" He was referring to the fact that the entire family had intended to be in the audience for an interview of two men that afternoon in San Francisco. Drs.

Wilbur Buffaloon and Bob Gaines were as different as two unathletic white American males who were among the richest men in the world can be. They had one similarity, however: two silent letters in their surnames. The 'i' and the 'e' in Bob's name were as silent as the second 'f' and the 'a' in Wilbur's. Friends—true friends—are hard to find for those living in the lonely and stratified habitat of the super-rich, and these men were the best of friends.

Wilbur Buffaloon was seventy-eight years old and had grown up on an old tobacco farm, the only child of a United States senator. Bob was forty-four years old and had spent his formative years at the country club being beaten at tennis by the offspring of every one of his father's colleagues; his father was the president of a large bank.

The two men had converged on San Francisco earlier that day to dedicate a new museum. The project had been in the works for a decade. The committee had worked long and hard to take possession of over five hundred acres of public parkland that had been a Navy base not far from the Golden Gate bridge. When confiscated, the property still held many historic buildings which were all knocked down; the first of a collection of planned modern edifices was now complete. The beautiful structure was to be the main gateway to a large complex. It stood at the entrance to the whole estate, an entrance enhanced over the past year by massive landscape surgery. Bob Gaines had endowed this first building and the museum's collection within. The grand opening was today.

The function of the new museum was unique: to display artifacts from the lives of the wealthiest people in the history of the world; to give the common people some level of understanding of the complexity of the lives of those at the top of the social pyramid. The first building would open with an assortment of items owned by Andrew Carnegie, David Rockefeller and a few kings and emperors.

Gaines and Buffaloon had deeded much of their personal property to the museum with the proviso that ownership, and certainly display, must be delayed till after their deaths. The humble men thought it unseemly to allow earlier exhibition; some people would probably consider it a form of braggadocio. The two luminaries had made one concession to satisfy the grateful museum committee: they allowed construction of a statue in their image. It was a beautiful thing, and visitors encountered the artwork as they first entered the estate. Buffaloon's likeness was sitting on an elevated throne-like seat, and Gaines stood behind, one foot on top of a globe on the ground at the side of the throne. Buffaloon was pointing northeast with stately grace, and Gaines's gaze followed. The statue was larger than life, constructed at a two hundred fifty percent scale, and it comprised fifty tons of metal. It was gold plated for durability. The charter documents required refreshment of the eight thousand microinch plating every other year.

The sculpture resided in the center of an oval garden directly in front of the entrance to the new main building. Its design and placement guaranteed that on a clear day it was plainly visible from far across the Golden Gate bridge. Careful landscaping and a tad of excavation ensured its visibility from many points on the hills of the city as well. Nearby was a small outdoor amphitheater, and the men's heads could be seen from every seat within it.

There had been a few hasty changes made to the care of the artwork and the surrounding landscaping recently. Within days after the statue was first placed, the director of the museum, walking by admiringly, was horrified to see two filthy birds comfortably perched on Dr. Buffaloon's extended finger and two more on the corners of Dr. Gaines's spectacles. We need not mention the corresponding messes on Buffaloon's lap and both men's shoes. A hurried cleanup was ordered, and starting the next day, a twenty-four hour guard was posted at the statue to preclude further infractions of this sort. The requirement for this position, designated the 'tattie-bogal,' was quickly codified in the charter documents of the museum complex. As a further precaution, instituted in consideration of Dr. Buffaloon's balding pate and the other top surfaces of the sculpture, all tree limbs in the region were chopped off fifty horizontal feet from the men's likenesses. This, also, was entered as a requirement in the legal documents.

Today the two wealthy men had dutifully attended the museum's grand opening. They were unaware of the bird situation, and as he entered, Dr. Gaines cluelessly remarked on the ugliness of the lopsided trees in the vicinity of the museum entrance; Dr. Buffaloon agreed. Nobody picked up the thread of conversation, and soon they were all inside and everyone could exhale.

Kingman was well acquainted with both the philanthropists. He had some long-term agreements with each man involving funding for his Foundation. Both men knew him by name, and he chatted with them for a few minutes after the museum dedication.

Soon after the ceremony Dr. Gaines departed, and presently Dr. Buffaloon was interviewed by his niece's daughter, a woman who had recently entered the broadcasting field here in San Francisco. Kingman's family was invited to be present at the interview, but Marshall and Hunter missed the event, an occurrence they blamed on their pilot. He had failed in his duty to have the airplane ready when they wanted to leave New York, because neither brother had bothered to notify him of their plans to fly. They had departed late and missed both the museum ceremony and the interview.

"I really wanted to meet those guys," Marshall said, Hunter agreeing alongside. "So, what did they say?"

Gwendolyn had attended only because her father had demanded it. Things in which she was uninterested included history, politics and money, but Kingman had admonished her to make a good impression when she met the men and to pay attention during the interview. She had succeeded on both counts. Possibly as a defense against tedium, she had actually taken notes.

She said, "Well, it was pretty boring, actually." Her eyes darted to her father, then her mother. Kingman was looking at his reflection in the window, and Winifred listened expressionlessly as she sipped her Drambuie. "Dr. Buffaloon looks like everyone's old crotchety uncle. Bob Gaines looks like everyone's geeky cousin." She giggled. The boys chuckled.

Gwendolyn pulled out her GVCD and looked at her notes. "Dr. Gaines didn't stick around for the interview like he was supposed to. He just left. Dr. Buffaloon talked about himself and his history. He made a fortune in heavy industry and progressed to working in what he called 'financial-legal engineering.' He said he went from wealthy to super-rich due to one event when the worldwide markets crashed, and then jumped, crashed again and recovered again, all within two weeks. He made his money because he was ready for that second bounce. He seemed pretty proud of the fact that he became one of the richest people in the world in one day.

"He said he owns two thirds of the freight hauling capacity inside the country, and one large shipping line that works mostly between eastern Asia and North America. He went on and on with percentages and different things of his. I got a lot of them but not all. He owns power plants and hospitals. He says soon he will possess the two largest hospitals in each city in the country—well, the few hundred biggest cities. Dr. Buffaloon said his holdings include most insurance firms and the biggest reinsurance firm, whatever that is. He said there is only one big life insurance company he doesn't own. And they will soon have announcements about some large retailing move and some more international shipping things."

"Sounds pretty boring," Hunter said. Marshall shushed him.

Gwendolyn nodded as she continued. "The guy's quite a salesman. He seemed quite proud of his accomplishments, and he was always interjecting what a good deal his companies can give, especially to the government. When he was talking about the government it came up that he has the biggest single piece of what he called the 'broadcast, connection and access to information' segment of the economy. He would not say what fraction when the girl asked him. He made a joke about having to keep that secret, and said he had to make some calls to people in government to stop troubling him about it, but then it seemed like he was especially careful to call out for more legal limits on what his own companies are allowed to do! I didn't get the logic there. Oh yes, he said he owns sports teams in almost all cities. That's cool. He's moved some around, and a bunch of towns are building new stadiums for the teams.

"Dr. Buffaloon said he's been on government panels constantly for decades, involved with tax policy and issues related to the public good. He contracts with the government and gives the taxpayers a better deal than anyone else. One thing he said was that all these companies work closely with the government, and that it would really be better if after he is gone he could just give them all to the government but that he can't do that for some reason. He did gripe about having to deal with so many state governments and said things should be streamlined for companies like his, companies big enough and dispersed enough that they should not have to deal with individual states' meddling. I wrote down that he said that's one of the things that is keeping him out of the electricity distribution business, though I don't get it—he said he has power plants. He just said it is the biggest industry in the world, and he would get into it, if he could make sure he would be able to get the right position in the markets."

Hunter's attention had departed already. Marshall found Gwendolyn's answer a bit long-winded as well. "Did you get to meet Bob Gaines?"

"Yes. I met him before Dr. Buffaloon's interview. Daddy introduced me to both of them after the dedication. I really just said hello, but he talked a little. He said Dr. Buffaloon is like a second father to him. Bob Gaines said he gives a huge amount to charity through his foundation. He mentioned that three or four times. He smiles a lot more convincingly than Dr. Buffaloon. He looks a little goofy. He was nice and said he liked my outfit. He said we should all be proud of Daddy." They glanced at Kingman, who turned from the window, his eyes still focused at twice the distance to the glass, and nodded to his children.

Marshall said, "I'd like to have heard what old Buffaloon would say about the bitching that people are doing about transportation, freight rates. They've gone pretty public with their complaints, and they're accusing him of antitrust, theft, being a bum, whatever. Some of my old classmates are pretty vocal. They're all over the place with it, they won't shut up. I've seen a couple of them on the news, and when I've talked to them the conversation always gets around to how shipping is twice as expensive as two years ago. The wry joke is that they may have to start making things right here in the U.S. rather than just brokering deals with the Orient for a living."

Gwendolyn answered, "Oh, that came up. His niece asked him about it since it's been in the news. Mr. Buffaloon smiled and said it is not news. He quipped that she'd not heard it on any of his news stations. They laughed about it. He told the lady that he was absolutely certain he had not been proven to have broken the law in any significant way. Then he said that whatever they do could not be illegal anyway because all of his air and ground freight lines are legally separate entities, and so are the ocean shipping companies. They make decisions on their own based on only general guidelines from the central office, and their officers only talk to each other about corporate stuff, not the real operational business. He said they've had their lawyers carefully involved, especially since he bought his last two railroads last year. He says there are other hard-to-specify outside factors putting pressure on those prices and pushing them way up. He talked about how much unfair crap he has taken recently. He didn't seem too concerned, but it sounded like we should feel sorry for him and his companies, like they were barely making it."

"I wish I'd been there." Marshall said. He took a sip of his Scotch. Hunter matched him with his brandy. Kingman was listening from across the table. He had never seen his daughter pay this much attention to anything beyond brushing her dog's fur, and he found it interesting to observe her.

She went on, looking at her GVCD. "At the end Dr. Buffaloon said a couple of strange things that weren't about questions—they were a solo performance he said he wanted to get out to the world. He said that taxes should be higher and mentioned two pieces: first, nobody should be able to pass something on to their children without most of it being taken in taxes. That distorts the life insurance market, which is about life, the most important thing to every American. Second, and pretty weird, he said people as rich as him should be forced to pay more taxes. And he said everyone should give more to charity and the tax thing would help that, so long as the system is structured right."

Hunter broke in. "We've all heard that pay-more-tax hobby horse of his before. He writes about it all the time. But I never got it; he brags that he's always fighting the IRS aggressively. And his net worth is growing by billions every year, but his taxable income is a few percent of that, so even if he paid it all in taxes, he wouldn't pay on ninety-seven percent of what any rational person would call income, unless I don't understand accounting."

It was quite likely that Hunter did not understand accounting. He had many classes in the subject on his university transcripts.

Hunter continued, "I don't get it. But as of now he's right about the charity thing. Higher tax rates would redound to the benefit of the Foundation, that's for sure, but who knows when that next won't be true?"

Marshall agreed. Kingman was quietly proud to see Hunter making the case that two plus two equals four, though his words were pretty unclear on the ninety-seven percent stuff. He was also pleasantly surprised that Hunter seemed to verge on detecting the slickness under Buffaloon's avuncular veneer. Kingman's younger son may have more potential than he had been crediting.

Gwendolyn said. "Yes. Well, then she asked why he doesn't give to charity. He said when he dies all but a few billions of his money will go to charity instead of paying taxes. He seemed fixated on taxes, I have to say. The few billion is for his kids. He said he can't leave it all to them, or they'll never know the value of hard work. When his niece pressed him on the charity thing he said he's keeping his money not for himself, but for the good of the charities. He thinks he can make it grow into more money, because he's the best in the world at that sort of thing. He said if he dies, he'll have more to give. It made sense, I guess. Dr. Buffaloon worked hard all his life, and I think he's proud to make a sacrifice for other people."

Wilbur Buffaloon's youngest child was fifty-three years old.

"He said *if* he dies? Not *when* he dies?" Hunter asked, smiling. Marshall grinned too.

"Yes." Her expression agreed. "It sounded strange enough that I wrote it down with the quotation marks. Whenever he spoke about being gone, or dying, he was always smiling. Odd, huh?"

Marshall elbowed Hunter, "Yeah, yeah. He really doesn't think he's going to die, ever." Hunter chuckled. Gwendolyn gaped. Winifred grimaced. Kingman glared.

Then Gwendolyn said, "I guess I took down a lot more than I thought, huh?" Kingman was happily surprised to see that Gwendolyn had exercised her note-taking ability instead of just letting her GVCD record, sort, prioritize and present the information. He nodded proudly to her and took a sip of his wine.

The three younger family members sauntered into a relaxed and meandering conversation, with the parents as background decoration. The boys addressed the backlog of teasing and horseplay that had built up since they last tormented their sister. The three discussed current events and gossip from their lives, girlfriends and so forth. It went on for a little while.

After a time Gwendolyn remembered she had been bothered by something, and she turned to her quiet father. He was relaxing looking at, but not out, the window, holding his wine. "Daddy, there is something I wonder about. Can I ask you?"

"Sure, princess. Anything." His voice was tender, friendly. He looked at her as though she were boarding an airplane to China. He would miss her when she was gone.

"Some of the kids at school keep saying that I'm filthy rich, or rather, that you are. I tell them we aren't poor, but we're pretty much like everyone else. Actually lots of my friends are pretty rich themselves, but a few are really poor. Anyway they all talk about the size of the Foundation and how you're in charge of it. I tell them the Foundation is all about getting money to other people, not us. But they don't believe me. And you know, I guess I don't know. I never thought about it much. I know we don't live in a mansion like some of them, though. You should see Millicent's place. She was in my dorm last year. She lives just up the road from school. Anyway, lots of my friends here haven't ever traveled around the world. Some have never even been out of the country. And they think that only rich people travel around like we do. They say we're rich."

Kingman and Winifred listened patiently. Each took a sip of his drink. Kingman contemplated how he would answer when the question came.

"And a few tell me their parents are always fighting about money. One girl claims her parents got divorced over money. It all seems so unreal, so absurd. But I've come to realize there's a lot I don't know. When I volunteer in East Altos Flats I feel like I've been transported to another planet. My friend who usually works with me there tells me that money is not the whole problem for those people, but it's a real big one. I've started to realize that maybe I don't know much about money. That has to be it. So tell me two things. How important is money? And are we rich?"

Kingman was momentarily distracted by the idea of Gwendolyn volunteering in the slums with her friends. It alarmed him, and glancing at the darkened window, he made a mental note to find out more about it, which he promptly forgot. During Kingman's absence Winifred delivered some stern motherly instruction, brow creased, well-groomed eyebrows almost touching above the bridge of her nose, voice at once pitched and lusty and low. "Gwendolyn, dear, I am shocked at you. You know better than that. Here at dinner asking about money. Your father has been trying to have a conversation with you. We are here to enjoy ourselves, and you are a guest at a Foundation board meeting. Don't be vulgar."

Her head shook itself in disgust. "But as to your question let me say this. Your father does not take a cent in salary. We own almost nothing. Dressel-Meiers rich! I know all about it. They talk that way at the club, those women married to profit-hounds. The technology bigots' wives are the worst. Or maybe the surgeons' wives." She fully committed to a wrenching, closed-eye shudder. Kingman again took hold of her hand and patted it to calm her.

He said, "Princess, you know what I do. You know I created the Foundation many years ago, and that its budget would make it one of the few hundred biggest companies in the country."

In fact Gwendolyn was surprised at the magnitude of the organization, and she knew very little about this. The Foundation just existed, to the best of her knowledge. She nodded nonetheless.

Kingman suddenly dropped his wife's hand, turned to look at the boys, and said, "That reminds me, boys. This is a board meeting, and we have to transact some level of Foundation business or it's just a vacation trip. We should do the name change thing now." The brothers shrugged and nodded, Hunter following Marshall's lead. Winifred bowed her head once in agreement as well.

"So moved," Winifred said.

"Seconded," Marshal pitched in.

"All in favor, all opposed, the motion carries," Kingman said in one smooth breath, almost as though he had done it many times before.

Gwendolyn did not know what was going on but did not ask anything, as it was not unusual for her to be dropped from conversation like that by her father.

Just now they had authorized him to rename the Foundation, which had always been named the 'American Worldwide Foundation, Un-Limited.' The reason for the change: detractors had concocted the obvious acronym for the organization. Kingman, who never liked acronyms anyway, was mostly uninterested when this was pointed out to him, and refused to consider changing something so important as the Foundation's identity in response to sophomoric giggling. But as years went by more and more professional-looking spoofs appeared. Even neutral outsiders and news organizations eventually started referring to the Foundation by its bastard acronym. Hunter and Marshall finally convinced him to acquiesce to a renaming. Kingman himself had developed the new name. Tonight the vote gave him the authority to go through with the renaming. Sometime soon after tonight he would attend to the legal details of changing the name and unveil it.

The new name he had chosen to solve his problem was: 'Worldwide Transformative Foundation.'

None of the other board members knew the name yet, and they all forgot to ask about it. Kingman turned back to Gwendolyn. "Sorry dear. Where were we? Most everybody else running such a large economic entity gets millions of dollars every year. And I will tell you that running the Foundation is far more difficult than running even the largest company— certainly tougher than running a university. So it would be easy to imagine that I pay myself millions each year."

She was listening raptly, disturbed by none-too-quiet clowning around of her brothers, and she shot them a disapproving glance. They responded by dampening their antics marginally. She was trying to process the idea about her father paying himself. What could it mean?

Kingman continued, "Obviously you know that you and your brothers have been well cared for, and I've given the family a good life. So you may be forgiven for suspecting truth in what your friends so enviously surmise. But they're wrong.

"Now, I'm happy and proud of what I've done over the past three decades. The Foundation indeed directs a huge amount of money each year. We put it to charitable purposes. To help people. If you go through with your little adventure in Africa, for instance, we will be donating heavily to both the Wholesome Globe Project and to Stambridge. The Foundation, on your behalf, will be spending at least eight times the amount the average American family earns next year. And from that, what? I imagine they will give you a room and food to eat. I want you to know we put our money in good causes.

"And it is not quite true what you mother said," he smiled at Winifred and patted her hand in his. "What is true is this: I do take a paycheck, it is actually minimum wage, the lowest salary legally possible. It technically puts us below what the government calls the 'poverty line' or some other moniker of the day. However, I donate every cent of my salary to charity. I just give most of it right back to the Foundation directly. A little bit goes elsewhere. But I give it all away. I make this sacrifice because it is the right thing to do as a leader. I don't want to alarm you, sweetie, but your mother and I have almost no assets. I don't know if you know exactly what assets are. They are wealth. Zero wealth. We have almost nothing to our name beyond some of our clothes and the few pieces of inexpensive jewelry your mother owns."

Gwendolyn involuntarily looked over to her mother's earrings, her necklace and other jewelry, her fine jacket. Kingman noticed and said, "No, not that stuff. That belongs to the Foundation. It's necessary for us to be well-appointed in public. In fact, if truth be told, most of her clothing and quite a bit of mine technically does not belong to us.

"The only thing your mother and I could consider a noticeable asset is not even available for me to use. Someday if I get sick, or when I am so old I can't any longer carry on the fight to help people, I'll have an income, really for the first time. If I die, it will be there for your mother." Kingman was unemotional as he mentioned his death; Winifred was doubly so. "This is simply in place to make sure your mother and I don't end up penniless after decades of selfless work."

Gwendolyn must have been alarmed at the thought of her father dying. She shifted in her seat. Her father addressed it, eyes closed, one hand held up. "Don't worry. That day is not soon. I plan to live to be one hundred ten years old, and I won't drop out of the Foundation till I'm a doddering old fool." The girl was relieved and suppressed a laugh at the unlikely picture of her father as anything but an invincible warrior. She envisioned a Rip van Winkle, beard to his waist, struggling along with a cane.

"Your mother is going to live longer and dodder even more." He and Winifred looked at each other, smiling. He patted her hand. Winifred closed her eyes, pursed her lips and nodded slowly and deeply in affirmation, pulling down the corners of her tightly closed lips.

Kingman had not mentioned the size of his future annuity, but his tax-free retirement income was headed for easily twenty-five times the annual household income in the country; he would not be at a loss for a few perks like transportation and paid speaking engagements in attractive locations if he desired them.

Gwendolyn had been listening, somewhat confused by how Kingman's picture could represent the world she knew, with the family so comfortable. No money at all? She bounced a glance off Marshall and Hunter who were just now caught up in some private joke that provoked all-consuming but quiet laughter in both of them. She thought about her mother's fine jewelry, the wonderfully tailored suits the whole family wore. Their cars. The limousines. The vacations. Even her allowance, her tuition. Puzzlement showed in her eyes. Was none of it theirs? She asked, "What about all the things we have? What about paying for us to go to school? Everyone knows that a year at a school like Stambridge, or Halford and Darthmoor where the boys went to school, costs more than most entire families earn in a year. I don't know much about money, but I know that much. I know the boys both went to graduate school. I know you guys had a great time." She looked at Marshall, then Hunter. Under normal circumstances neither brother paid attention to her voice, but tonight both faces indicated that the comments had triggered some fond memories in each. "Quinston and Pennumbria—they're expensive too. Where do you get all that money if you have nothing? What about the cars? How exactly did I buy this dress?"

"Stop it, Gwendolyn, right now." Her mother angrily interrupted. "Everything is always about money. Don't be like them all." Winifred looked down, shaking her head. Furrowed brow, pinched lips—her face was the prototype of authentic disgust. "It's sickening the way people are always talking about it." Surely revolted by the vile topic, she found some consolation in giving this solid correctional instruction to her daughter in a time of obvious need. She quietly sought a further increment of comfort from her Drambuie.

Kingman delivered patience to both females. He nodded to Winifred, then continued. "You asked a lot of questions there. I see we didn't raise a dummy." Without intent his eyes made a quick trip to the older brothers and back. "That's a good example. Your clothes, sweetie—they don't actually belong to you." He smiled and drew a sip of his fine wine.

I'm here in somebody else's clothes? "But I bought this outfit myself, with my own money. I choose all my own clothes."

Kingman had started to roll his wine around his mouth. He swallowed and answered. "It makes no real difference. You buy things with your allowance. This is an expense of the Foundation. It is all quite complex, and you can do what you want with your clothes, but technically they're all owned by the Foundation. Now, understand that the Foundation has no use for them other than dressing the daughter of the executive director. They won't be taken away. It's so complicated it's best to think of it simply: you essentially own them; there's just a meaningless paper trail saying otherwise."

The brothers were quietly chuckling about something again, leaning together, joking, and Hunter broke out in a laugh. Kingman glared in their direction, and they silenced. He glanced at his reflection briefly as he turned back to Gwendolyn, who was listening. He stroked his hair, putting a tuft back in place behind his ear. She said, "But Daddy, how?"

"Well, you remember the papers I have you sign every year now that you have turned eighteen, don't you?"

Gwendolyn disremembered. She shook her head as she searched inside it. Finally she recalled: once in a while he presented her with a stack of papers to sign. Lots of pages. Legalese, disclaimers. *Notwithstandings, heretofores, irrevocables, fine print.* The lawyer was always present. It was such a non-event that she almost did not have a memory of it. She nodded.

"Well, you're an employee of the Foundation! You have been since you were a little girl. You don't make much money, of course. We've taken care of it; your mother controls your money. That's why it seems like your allowance comes from us. And oh, by the way, I should tell you: you donate all your spare money back to the Foundation. You really don't have any money of your own. Of course now that you're grown, we could let you change things around if you choose."

Gwendolyn was nonplussed. She thought she had been spending her family's own money. "Wow! No, no, let's just go on with whatever you have set up. I've been doing fine. But what about the schools?"

"We didn't—we could never pay for any of that. I told you we don't have any money. That's all paid directly by the Foundation. You should be grateful to them."

"Yes. I'm grateful for everything. So are Marshall and Hunter," which she doubted, if only because she could not imagine that particular emotion was in the repertoire of either. "But our house? Daddy, I mean, ever since

I was a little girl being punished for drawing on the walls, I thought it was ours. Don't we own that, at least?" She realized that without ever thinking about it, she had always assumed she would bring her children back to visit the house where she grew up.

Her father answered, "Princess, it's a little complicated. But don't worry. Everything we have is not really ours, yet it can never be taken from us, and we will never have to pay any form of taxes on it. After your mother and I are gone, one of you will be able to live in our house forever, with the exact same arrangement. And you can pass it down to your children. And on and on. Of course, Hunter and Marshall will probably never want to move out of the big city." He glanced at his sons. Neither said a word. They had never thought about these things.

"Believe me, I've set things up this way for a reason, and it's done right. Everything comes from the Foundation. I do mean everything. Your riding and dance lessons. The boys' dental work. Your mother's plastic surgery. Our club memberships. Our cars. Your schooling at the Maple Day School. Stambridge. We ourselves could afford none of it. You can honestly tell your friends that we are actually not un-poor."

Gwendolyn was troubled, mostly because she was accustomed to knowing things like which way gravity pulls, whether the sun will rise tomorrow, how many moons there are...

"I am not trying to make you anxious. We're never going to run out of funds, though we have none. We're not like your friends at school, the rich ones or the poor ones. Most of them are, in one way or another, seeking personal gain, like canonical good Americans are expected to do. We have a higher calling—the not-for-profit version of a life goal. We seek nothing but good for others, and yet want nothing. Think of it as: 'Nothingness as a bookkeeping tool allowing us to put service to others before our own needs and wants.' It's all okay."

The girl was trying to understand and accept all this. "It sounds complicated, as you say. Really, it even sounds so complex it can't be right. Is it worth all the trouble? Is it honest?" *Are we crooked? Am I part of a family of thieves or saints?*

"Honest? Absolutely. I have paid huge amounts of money to the best accountants and legal experts in the country. The arrangement has been challenged by the government, mostly just to pacify outsiders I suspect, several times. It is completely in keeping with the letter of the law. And we have well paid people in Washington constantly watching and perhaps nudging things to keep the law itself honest—you know, there are always attacks against people like us, people who live only to serve others. I think it's some guilty psychology thing. Honest? Yes, it's honest. As I said, perfectly within the legal system. You can't get more honest than that.

"As for the other part: Yes it's worth the trouble. Sure, if I took a salary from the Foundation, I suppose I could have a bank account. We could own the house, vacation houses and nice cars. And the government would get a huge bite of it, something like half. Still, I'd pay myself enough that we'd have it made. But who needs that? I didn't go into this for personal gain. I went into it to support others, less fortunate people. I should take you down to South America next time there's a volcano eruption and let you look into the faces of the people we help. I've seen pictures of them. It would tear your heart out."

Gwendolyn had slowly slipped into a rapt silence, hands on her lap as she listened. This good man had navigated the complex legal system and created something of value to the world. Her questions had been answered and the doubts eliminated. The family was intertwined with the Foundation and had been making sacrifices all along, sacrifices well worth it to help others.

Kingman delivered a conclusion, "Yes. It's worth it. Basically you could say I have taken a vow of poverty. It has its own rewards." He paused, took a sniff of his wine and rolled some in his mouth, savoring.

Winifred followed suit with her Drambuie, enjoying the strong liqueur. "And, we're living up to that vow in the best way we can," she said with a serious expression after swallowing.

Just then Hunter slapped Marshall's shoulder, and the two roiled in laughter, catching everybody's attention. The boys recovered, straightened up and attended to the rest of the group. Gwendolyn sipped her mineral water. She said, "Thanks, Daddy. Thanks, Mother. I never know what to think about it all, and this helps me understand. What I like most about our family is how everyone is working for the good of other people. We don't just talk about it. It's the biggest part of our life, and I'm glad."

Kingman smiled proudly. Tears welled in Winifred's eyes. A few minutes of quietude followed in which Kingman was inscrutable. Three sat pensively, and the brothers interacted with each other in great spirits. Finally, it was time for the family meeting to adjourn. Kingman settled up with the waiter then all rose, took the elevator downstairs and approached their waiting limousines. They said their goodbyes, Winifred kissing each of the children. Kingman held his wife's hand as she stepped past the waiting driver and into their vehicle. Then he walked over to Gwendolyn's limousine, leaned in, gave his daughter a hug and kiss and said, "Listen, this poverty thing is not really so bad, sweetie. And think it over and call me when you decide about your little project." She nodded and mentally declared victory over him regarding the Africa trip as he walked away.

Gwendolyn had the chauffeur drive back and forth along the waterfront and across the bay bridge so she could enjoy the city lights. After a while she pulled out her GVCD and woke up Alitisha back east. She knew it was late, and she also knew Alitisha would never pass up a call, and she slept near her own GVCD.

"Hello?" Alitisha wiped her hair back from her face as she yawned.

"Well, I think I've had the last argument about going to Africa."

"Gwendolyn!" Young people sometimes wake up quickly, and Alitisha was now sentient. "I've heard that before. So, when did you tell him you'll go?"

"Well, we're going to take a trip out there early next year. We didn't talk about the date. I'll take care of that."

"I thought you would get him to drop that. Anyway, you want to hear something fun?..." Yes, Alitisha was awake now. The girls gossiped and giggled for half an hour as Gwendolyn had the driver take the highway along the hills so she could enjoy the glimpses of lights below as they cruised back down the peninsula to her Stambridge home.

Cecilia, the Birds, and All That

How big is 'Larger Than Life?'

"How old are you, Cecilia?" Gwendolyn kept her eyes on her task of cutting as she continued wielding her knife, slicing up the chicken pieces.

Cecilia, working at her side, said without slowing down her identical task, "Old enough to know better." She paused. "Too young to resist." Her thin cheeks lifted her wide-lensed old lady glasses as her smile asserted itself.

The two females hailed from opposite sides of the continent. They stood working side by side as colleagues, one merely twenty years old and the other possibly four times that. One quite average in build with flowing, dirty-blonde hair and a sweet disposition, and the other barely achieving five feet and ninety-five pounds, with salt-and-pepper hair and a strong, optimistic personality.

The older, faster-moving woman had come to enjoy these Thursdays when she worked with Gwendolyn. Through her amused smile, without diminishing her production lead over the girl, she said, "I've logged more score than you have decades, honey," She continued with a pause in her work, "Okay, enough clowning around. I'm sixty-seven. What do you think? Have you ever been this close to anyone that old?" Cecilia had a mild, almost permanent grin, but not a foppish or silly one like most such things. Her smile varied in form depending on circumstance and view angle, but persisted most of the time—its deep roots were anchored in her soul.

Gwendolyn was not surprised. The woman's hair and skin, not to mention her powerful wisdom, disclosed that she was pretty old, and she knew the woman had been coming here for several decades. But Cecilia's energy level and general comportment was more that of an impatient twenty-seven year old, and that complicated the computations. Gwendolyn would have accepted any age from forties to maybe sixties; within that age range she had little resolution. She had a vague idea that 'old' started somewhere below the fifties. Above seventy or so, she would confidently identify one as 'ancient.'

The two were contentedly fixing food for the hungry at the Helping Ministry of East Altos Flats. They met there the better part of a year ago. This was a poor city just on the border of several fantastically affluent neighborhoods on the California peninsula. Cecilia was attracted to the Helping Ministry because their outlook was straightforward. They had one simple criterion for serving food: it went to people who said they needed it. Most were not lying, and if one applied the softer definition of 'need' none were lying; they were all hungry when they came in. Gwendolyn liked the place just because it helped people. She had chanced upon the organization last winter as she looked for a volunteer opportunity, and she met Cecilia when they both showed up on the same day. She felt she had struck gold by meeting her—the older woman was everything Gwendolyn admired.

Cecilia was unusual. She was the Supreme International Commander of the Saving Arms. She held the top position in a worldwide charity with tens of thousands of employees and volunteers. She spent her days inspiring her organization and attending to logistics. It was a demanding and exhausting job that could easily have taken over her whole life, but she had always lived up to one personal rule: every single week she donated some of her personal time and effort for a good cause outside the organization. On the first and third Thursday of each month she came to the Helping Ministry at four in the afternoon like clockwork. She prepared food, served it, cleaned up and unceremoniously went home to bed. Gwendolyn came every Thursday after her classes. The two had become friends, and she looked forward to the evenings when Cecilia was working. The girl admired Cecilia, and in turn the older woman cared for her and had come to worry about her.

Gwendolyn said, "I always go home so energized when we work here together, Cecilia. I really have fun here with you."

Cecilia kept working, nodded silently, and said, "We're not here to have fun, sweetie. You're coasting." The spanking was deserved. Gwendolyn looked down and noticed that she had all but stopped her work. In some way glad that she had suffered the mild rebuke for the transgression, she turned her attention back to working on the task in her hands.

Eventually they finished the last increment of chicken parts. They rolled the huge vat down the hall and handed it off to others who would cook the pieces throughout the mealtime. Cecilia poured two cups of coffee from a beat-up steel tank. Tired, the two climbed onto nearby stools and sat for a coffee break after more than two hours of work. In Cecilia's case these were the eleventh and twelfth hours of overall work that day; her workday normally started at six o'clock in the morning, and it was now just past six in the evening. Gwendolyn, as a Stambridge student, had a less brutal schedule, but she was perhaps equally weary owing to physical differences between them.

"We're all done with the planning for the symposium," the girl said as Cecilia handed her a cup of lukewarm coffee. On her own, Gwendolyn normally drank fancy espresso mochaccino. But she always remembered the tepid coffee here as the best in the world, a perception anchored in warm memories of first and third Thursdays. She smelled the weak liquid and sipped slowly as they talked. "I've told everyone they're going to love you."

Cecilia took a drink of her black coffee. She paused for an animated gesture, rolling her eyes good-naturedly, stretching her mouth downward in a tight circle. "Oh, just wonderful, Gwendolyn! So they'll love me! They think I'll be great entertainment." She smiled more seriously. "I'm not a showman. I warned you. I can answer questions, and I can state facts. If I were you I'd've gone for somebody else." Her bony shoulders delivered a shrug.

"No. The students have to meet you. Really, don't you see? All the others are the same as each other. Don't you think all my life I have had to have tea and lunches with these people?"

Cecilia indeed knew what she meant, of course. But she did not answer.

"They're so...formal. So polished. So... perfect."

The friendly older woman feigned indignation with a whole-body display. She leaned back with her hands thrust forward and down, coffee cup and all. Her head was turned forty degrees and tipped back twenty. Her lips were pulled into a fake frown as wide as her thin face could deliver, and she looked at Gwendolyn askance through her slitted eyelids. "What? I'm not perfect?" She held the pose till the unnatural frown exhausted itself and cracked into her genial smile. She relaxedly dropped her shoulders and morphed back into the real Cecilia. She sipped quietly.

The fished-for protest arose on schedule. "No, no... Yes, of course... No. You know... c'mon Cecilia. But don't worry. It's just you and Dr. Hull.

She's confirmed, so the professor disinvited the others. She says that the two of you on the same stage covers the range of the whole universe. I don't get that... but it's going to be a great night!"

Booking Victoria Hull would not have happened without Gwendolyn's extraordinary connections, namely her father. The woman was famous and always kept herself in the news. The Glowing Circle was one of the world's most celebrated charitable organizations, and Dr. Victoria Q. Hull was its executive director and its public face. Until recently she was just Victoria Hull, but she became Dr. Victoria Hull with a doctoral degree awarded from the Stambridge School of Service last year, a year or so after her organization had consummated a multi-year agreement with Stambridge. The two institutions cooperated on lofty and vaguely specified things, with financial transfers for support of graduate students as well as 'facilities, management and initiatives.' Also included were consulting contracts for Stambridge faculty. Everything, of course, contained friendly provisions for what the school termed 'overhead recovery,' a subject in which the school had made a name for itself.

Gwendolyn herself had concocted the idea of a seminar for Stambridge students where Cecilia and some other leaders of local public service organizations could describe life in their organizations. The goal was to help students understand whether they wanted to make a career of helping others. She had not set out to get a national superstar to share the stage with Cecilia, but her faculty sponsor, the dean of the Stambridge School of Service, had suggested that Victoria Hull was the leader the students should see. Gwendolyn's father had some ongoing transactions with Dr. Hull's organization, and Kingman was the one who obtained the woman's commitment.

Cecilia sipped quietly. She was not surprised they got the Glowing Circle to participate—she understood that certainly the organization would be in some kind of financial partnership with Kingman's Foundation. Many, probably most, huge international charities had such arrangements with what would soon be publicly known as the Worldwide Transformative Foundation.

The older woman was not looking forward to this colloquium at Stambridge. It would be an evening meeting, two weeks in the future. The title of the meeting was 'Your Future in Charity Work,' and she felt uncomfortable going to a school and encouraging the students to work in the field—or any field, for that matter. She was not against the career choice, but she herself was in her late thirties when she took a job working in the charity organization. She was thrilled to have settled herself in this career, but it seemed presumptuous to pitch the career choice to students just because she herself found it rewarding.

"But you're not pitching. The students are making decisions about their futures. They go to all sorts of these things. It just gives them information so they can make decisions," Gwendolyn had told her many times.

Cecilia Strong was the leader of a massive charity, arguably the most efficiently run of such establishments on the planet. But she felt aloof from most of the other charities. In her opinion the industry had strayed, a feeling she had never discussed with the younger girl. She steered the Saving Arms away from what she perceived as the corruption of those whose occupation was charity. The woman was uneasy in recognizing that charity could even be called an industry; somehow that seemed to connote something cold, mechanical. But there was not a more accurate word in the English language, the only one she knew.

She was troubled by what she had noticed as the charity world evolved during her three decades at the Saving Arms. These were decades of the 'professionalization' of the industry. Many organizations, and the great majority of the large ones, had changed direction way back in the latter twentieth century. Cecilia saw that they had morphed into self-serving institutions; certainly their executives had progressed into elite financial status. Cecilia had worked very hard to keep the Saving Arms as true to its original nature as changing times allowed. The woman had resisted the pressure to join what she perceived as the interlocking network of symbiotic, favor exchanging, mutually justifying institutions comprising the nonprofit sector of the economy. It was a system that included what she called the tera-charities, along with the major universities and tangent government agencies. Even the business world perceived it to be in their best interest to be seen as aligned with the network, and the corporations with the most 'pull' populated government committees and directorships of universities and large charity organizations.

So long as Cecilia was its leader, the Saving Arms was going to work independently and right down here on the ground with people who need help. She was all in favor of effective cooperation with other organizations, but resistant to assimilation into the cabal.

Cecilia Strong was an unusual leader with an unlikely history. Her personality ran more toward production than ostentation or presentation. She had started working as a paid employee of the Saving Arms decades ago. She had an accountant's eye for detail, an engineer's disinterest in trivia and a mammoth's capacity for work. She harnessed all this through a driving passion for helping people. She had always lived and worked here in the bay area, and never aspired to do more than to help people. The woman was childless and long ago widowed.

Through a sequence of improbable events she rose through successive decreasingly local positions in the organization. At each step of the ladder she had been reluctant to take the higher-level position, and in every case she had made concrete suggestions of two or more others who were qualified for the job. "It was destiny, I guess," she had told Gwendolyn when the girl asked how she became the top person in the Saving Arms. In truth, she was not sure she believed in destiny as anything other than a metaphor, and certainly did not understand how she had been nominated for repeated promotions. She felt the organization should focus solely on its work; if any criticism of her were valid, it would be that she did not promote the organization much. She had no interest in grandstanding or traveling around the world and 'showing the flag' to the overseas operations. She just had a focus on results, a key sense of people, and a need to serve.

So here she was. She found herself International Commander of Saving Arms. And twice per month she found herself packing chicken or slinging hash here at the Helping Ministry in East Altos Flats with Gwendolyn, feeding people a few miles from where she was born.

The two sat on their stools and sipped their coffee. Without provocation Gwendolyn burst out with a laugh. "Remember Professor Stumpf? She really couldn't figure you out." She was referring to Dr. Brunhilda Q. Stumpf, professor, dean of the Stambridge School of Service. Dr. Stumpf was Gwendolyn's faculty sponsor for the upcoming presentation. She was a natural professional fit to be the girl's advisor; her expertise was in the ecology of charitable organizations in the economy. She had practically invented the academic discipline. She came from Europe but had no accent. Her close friends called her Hilda or simply Dr. Stumpf; a few called her Brunhilda.

Along her career Dr. Stumpf had met the leaders of all of the largest charities in the world except Cecilia, who lived here locally. She was looking forward to enhancing existing entanglements between the Glowing Circle and the School of Service. But the Saving Arms, which Gwendolyn had proposed, gave the dean pause. For one thing, it was nominally a religious organization. Secondly, Cecilia was publicly perceived as eccentric, almost a hermit. Dr. Stumpf insisted that they meet beforehand if Cecilia were to address the Stambridge community. The professor was pretty sure that the religious aspect was just a tax dodge of some sort, but she wanted some personal assurances from Cecilia. She required that the colloquium, intended to benefit the students, not turn into some kind of recruiting for Jesus.

As they sipped their coffee, Cecilia answered, "I do find it a bit awkward talking to people like that. I'm just me. Remember I didn't even want to do this; I am doing it as a favor to you. I'm not convinced the students will get anything positive from it, but I will try to give them something."

Three weeks earlier, when Gwendolyn was setting up the symposium, Cecilia had visited Stambridge to fulfill the professor's demand for an audience. The meeting between Cecilia, Gwendolyn and Professor Brunhilda Stumpf had gone something like this:

> *Dr. Stumpf:* So you're the head of the Saving Arms. I'm pleased to meet you finally. Gwendolyn tells me she knows you from the Helping Ministry in East Altos Flats. (The professor tips her head toward Gwendolyn, whose contribution to the discussion is now finished.)

> *Cecilia:* Yes Ma'am.

> *Dr. Stumpf:* You live here don't you?

> *Cecilia:* Yes, Ma'am. You could say I work remotely from my apartment and my office right here in Mountain View, and from my car, driving around the bay area. I have lived there since long before I became the commander. Of course the organization has to be based in Washington, but I never considered living there. I grew up here.

> *Dr. Stumpf:* Let me understand. You're the worldwide head of the Saving Arms. You volunteer your work outside the organization cooking dinners? In East Altos Flats with Gwendolyn? Is it some kind of publicity generator? Is the Helping Ministry affiliated with your organization?

> *Cecilia:* Yes, Ma'am. Yes, Ma'am. Yes, Ma'am. No, Ma'am. No, Ma'am. That's my separate, personal thing. I've volunteered there for many years. They help people too.

I have not promoted this within the Saving Arms,
though it's not really a secret.

Dr. Stumpf: But I've been asking Gwendolyn, 'Why East
Altos Flats?' Don't people all over need some help?
Monta Loma? Limerick? It's such a dangerous area. I
worry about her every week when she goes. (This last
was an untruthful flourish—Professor Stumpf hardly
knew the girl and certainly was not capable of caring
about her.)

Cecilia: They really need the help, and as for safety, it's not
that dangerous. I've been going there at least once a
month for years. I usually leave in the dark, and I've
never had a problem. Yes, it's a bad, very bad area.
Lots of violence and drug problems, and I am not going
to say anything so corny as that the criminals will credit
good intentions and cut us any slack. But look at the
numbers: You could walk every day in the most pover-
ty-stricken neighborhood in the country, and on average you would have a robbery or violent encounter
once in eighteen years. Poor people are not bad people.

Dr. Stumpf: (Displays an unconvinced look)

Cecilia: Have you ever even been to East Altos Flats? (It
was a preposterous question to ask someone who chairs
the public service department of one of the world's leading universities, given that the Helping Ministry was
exactly two and a half miles away from the professor's
office at the university in Mountain View.)

Dr. Stumpf: "Of course I've been there." (An odd pause
emerged, followed by a stutter.) You can't get to the
bridge without driving through East Altos Flats.

Cecilia: (Shoots a quizzical glance at Gwendolyn but the
older woman is alone—she sees that Gwendolyn may
as well have heard the professor say 'the weather is
nice today.')

As that discussion progressed, Dr. Stumpf had made it clear that she
would be the subject of professional ridicule among her peers at Stambridge

if she were seen as allowing Christianity into the symposium. Once Cecilia understood this, she agreed not to bring up the subject of Jesus Christ, the true savior of man. She had no interest in making her host uncomfortable.

The chicken pieces were now well into their cooking cycle in the other room. And Cecilia, it seems, had arrived at the maximum time she was able to sit still. As she hopped off the stool, an act that only slightly increased the distance between the woman's head and the floor, and drained the dregs of her own coffee, Cecilia pointed to Gwendolyn's drink and said, "Better finish that." The doors would open up for the hungry folks in just a little while. There was preparation to do.

Imbroglio at Stambridge

Who are these people?

T he day of the symposium came. Gwendolyn took her limousine to pick up Professor Stumpf, and the two went to the airport to greet Dr. Victoria Hull. As they traveled back toward Stambridge Dr. Stumpf seemed in especially good spirits, and the two older women chatted agreeably. The professor artfully mixed a few drinks as they discussed high-minded things—their discipline, the stamina needed to continuously be of service to others, the grand and parallel sacrifices made by those in their two professions. They commiserated over the low level of compassion and the general stinginess of the population at large, over how most people seem too busy to concern themselves with their fellow man. It's hard to say whether the conversation made the drinks seem sweeter or more bitter as the vehicle glided down the peninsula.

The doctors were acquainted with each other but not really familiar, a situation that stimulated a confusing combination of atavistic and highly evolved social protocols for interpersonal posturing and calibration. Gwendolyn felt most of the conversation existed in a dimension orthogonal to her life experience. The language and customs of the two senior participants bemused her and only occasionally intersected the realm of her understanding. The girl's reaction was to enter the lifelong mode of operation she had for such situations: she spoke politely when spoken to. Her mind wandered as she watched the hills amid a pleasant background of warbling, occasional titters and various species of nods. The doctors' incessant and enthusiastic chatter gave her the impression that the professor and Dr. Hull were nurturing a relationship that could last a long time.

The limousine took the elders to the faculty club where they would dine before doing nine holes of golf. Gwendolyn went back to her room. She tried to do some homework but was too restless. She could not get this evening's colloquium out of her mind. She tried and failed to contact Cecilia. She went running around the loop. She read from some old-fashioned book. She practiced the lines she would deliver at the start of the meeting. When dinner time came she skipped it due to butterflies in her stomach. Bored and nervous, she sat with her stuffed animal, but Pyratticus Julius wasn't communicating today. She read the book some more. She dawdled until early evening.

Finally the symposium was ready to start. Professor Stumpf stood at the podium as Gwendolyn and the two guests sat and quietly exchanged niceties. Gwendolyn had worried that she would set up this important presentation, and when the time arrived nobody would come, but she was thrilled with the large turnout. Charity work was not historically high on the list of top careers for Stambridge students, and as of yesterday only a dozen students had registered. Seeing almost every seat filled tonight after all, she reveled in pleasure over how it exceeded her wildest dreams.

What she did not know was that once Victoria Hull's attendance had been confirmed, the professor had taken steps to ensure a full auditorium— she put out the word that any student enrolled in any course in the School of Service would receive a certificate to replace one examination grade with a perfect score for attending. Dr. Stumpf's position as chair of the department allowed her this discretion over the other professors; those who had found out about the offer disapproved impotently.

Gwendolyn, Dr. Hull and Cecilia were seated at one side of the stage, and the other side held a table and three empty chairs. Dr. Stumpf began the meeting by welcoming the audience to the panel discussion on careers in charity, and she thanked Gwendolyn for spearheading the event. She alluded to her not by name and not as a Stambridge student—she identified her as the daughter of the Executive Director of the American Worldwide Foundation, Un-Limited, incidentally mentioning that the name had been changed to the 'Worldwide Transformative Foundation.' Gwendolyn was surprised that the professor even knew about the name change. She herself had never heard the new moniker.

The professor asked Gwendolyn to come up and say her few words. She approached the podium with great aplomb, introduced herself by name, and cited the logistics of the evening. First the two leaders would give histories including overviews of their organizations and how they came to be the leaders. This would be followed by a panel discussion where chosen students could ask questions; there would also be time for some questions from the audience. Gwendolyn encouraged the students to be as excited as she was herself, and to contemplate what they hear here tonight and its relevance to their future choices. Despite all her nervousness she was well spoken and performed beyond her years. Dr. Stumpf approached the podium, thanking her for the introductory remarks.

As of that instant Gwendolyn's contribution to the evening's activity was finished.

Professor Stumpf requested applause for the guests, "Please give a warm welcome to our two guests tonight." She motioned for Victoria Hull to stand. "We are honored to host Dr. Victoria Hull, Executive Director of the International Glowing Circle. You may recognize her from her earlier accomplishments in the field of government, as she has held many posts at the national level. You may also recognize her name due to the recent press coverage for her bold action in disestablishing the American Glowing Circle and absorbing its assets into a new International Glowing Circle based in Paris, France, a brilliant insight focusing the organization tightly and unambiguously on the entire world." A publicly smiling Dr. Hull waved and sat back down. Dr. Stumpf stood waiting, and as they caught on to the expectation, the audience clapped sedately. "Also here tonight is Cecilia Strong, of the Saving Arms, another worldwide endeavor. Please, Cecilia, tell us how you came to be where you are." She turned and held out her arm toward Cecilia.

Cecilia, caught by surprise, approached the microphone and lowered it eight inches as Professor Stumpf returned to her chair behind the lectern. Cecilia stood, diminutive and perhaps unimpressive to the students in her green-dun-grey uniform with the sword on one side, a miniature sword scaled to her stature. Normally her dress uniform had a large flat fabric cross hanging around her neck in front of the sash, but she left that off tonight out of deference to Dr. Stumpf. Her shoes looked uncomfortable, but one must realize most women's shoes are such.

"Good evening and thank you for coming. I am Cecilia Strong, and I am the Supreme International Commander of The Saving Arms. I hope to be instructive to you tonight." By nature she was awkward talking about herself. But she choked out a few sentences, "I was born here. I was a schoolteacher for fifteen years. I had a turning point in the immediate aftermath of an earthquake."

Gwendolyn was transfixed. She somehow had no idea that Cecilia had ever made the actual decision to join the Saving Arms. She simply *was* the Saving Arms, probably always had been.

"That evening I had just finished volunteer work at an urban garden a few miles from my home. The quake happened while I was walking home, and as I approached this coffeehouse I saw that the building had partially collapsed. I joined with the impromptu rescue effort, and at one point I was helping carry a woman whose leg had been crushed by falling bricks. Grasping my neck, she looked into my eyes and said, 'You are my saving arms.' Somehow I never got that phrase out of my mind. That next summer I left my teaching job and took a full-time job with the organization we now call the Saving Arms." She turned and walked back to her seat so abruptly that Dr. Stumpf was caught off guard. Gwendolyn watched open-mouthed, nodding with a big smile and wide eyes as the woman returned and sat next to her.

Dr. Stumpf jumped to her feet, went to the podium and invited Dr. Hull forward. Dr. Hull strutted up, dressed in a colorful and businesslike, multi-layered suit with a string of pearls around her neck. She had one of those newly fashionable slanted triangle-mushroom shaped hats, maroon, on her head. She took center stage and stood for the crowd. Gleaming blonde hair streamed from beneath the stylish cap. She looked the very picture of a governor's wife (which, by the way, she was) with her broad smile and bright lipstick. She started a folksy outline of her distinguished history.

"Boy, how did I get here? What a long story. I've been in public service since I left school right here at Stambridge, since before y'all were born." She exchanged an agreeable nod with Dr. Stumpf, turned and stood smiling to silence. She continued. "I've spent over sixty percent of my life—all my adult life—serving others. My first job out of school was as an elementary school principal, a job I sometimes wish I still had." She smiled as the audience politely laughed. "I love the children. Really, everything I do is for children. Anyway, I hate to bore you with all this about me."

In fact she loved talking about herself.

"Next I worked for the mayor of a small town in southern California, then for some state legislators. I took a position for a large hospital system in Arizona, and worked my way up to Vice President for Community Projects and Government Interface. Eventually I ran for Congress and served six terms. During that time, federal grants to my district increased over eighteen hundred percent. Needing to serve people more directly, I left Congress..."

She had left out a few details here. Her move to the public relations office in the hospital system was accompanied by a tripling of her salary. The job was created specifically for her—her promotion happened one month before her husband was sworn in as the new United States Senator from Arizona; this was six days after he was certified to have won his election, and she was now the director of the hospital's governmental interface efforts. During his first term in the Senate, her husband requested seven separate awards, each in the millions of dollars, for her hospital. This activity raised distant eyebrows, but concerns were largely muted based on the result of an investigation by a local Arizona news agency that had endorsed the man as a candidate. The senator's actions within the government and his wife's efforts in advocating for the funds were declared, and generally accepted to be, coincidental and unrelated.

And oh, yeah: when she left that Vice President position it was eliminated.

And there was more unspoken in Victoria Hull's recitation, reflecting the merry-go-round that can be public life. She had left Congress only when she was defeated by a razor-thin margin in a contentious election followed by a legal battle. Her opponent had changed her own name from Sheffield to Martinez in anticipation of her campaign for Congress, a successful attempt to capitalize on changing demographics of the region. The adversary was fluent in Spanish and spearheaded an effort to obtain the votes of many people ineligible to vote, as they were in the country illegally from Mexico.

Dr. Hull fought to overturn the election results, relying on two components in her arguments. First, everyone stipulated that there were more votes counted than voters who cast votes. Second, she proved, by hunting down individual cases, that at least two-thirds of the margin of victory was attained through non-citizens voting illegally. The judge in the case ruled that while it was probable that at least twelve thousand illegal votes were cast and fourteen thousand counted, nobody could say the votes were cast against Dr. Hull; he further decided that affidavits from individuals illegally in the country could not be entered into evidence, due to the illegal status of those swearing out the documents. And since the affidavits were necessarily written in Spanish and unintelligible to him, they were also inadmissible on that basis; any translation would automatically be hearsay.

Victoria Hull appealed the ruling, claiming that all elections fall into one of two classes: fraudulent or legitimate. She argued that those in the former category should not be considered valid exercises in democracy. The appeals court agreed with her reasoning but also ruled that due to the difficulties cited by the judge, only the votes and not the sworn statements of the illegal voters could be considered in America. The appeal went nowhere. Dr. Hull petitioned to her former colleagues in Congress, who had the power to reject the crooked election. Their general feeling was that the fraudulent contest caught her in an unfortunate circumstance, but ruling for her would be akin to poking a sleeping giant surely destined for imminent dominance in American politics. She was ignored in ceremonious silence.

As of tonight several of Martinez's siblings served in Congress alongside the woman herself, though nobody had expended effort trying to reverse any fraudulent elections since Dr. Hull's debacle.

"...I held a number of positions in government including First Assistant Sub-Deputy Lieutenant Vice Liaison of Public Affairs for the Vice President. I have been Ombudsman for Demographic Balance and Allocation for California, and for two years I was Chief Administrator of the U.S. Bureau of Governmental Organization."

Gwendolyn knew nothing of this history and found the woman's path interesting. She liked stories, liked connecting the dots. The names of the offices all sounded similar to her, and this sort of sound traveled a pleasant, unhurried and unhindered path through her brain, entering and egressing her ears in balanced symmetry.

"When I heard that Dr. Bernadette Q. Streak, head of the Glowing Circle, was about to retire, I was worried from afar about the organization. Everyone knows the wonderful work the institution does and how important its mission is. The organization annually collects and allocates billions of dollars. Though I had never been directly involved, I had been a member of the board of directors for years. I felt the organization would need strong leadership in these ever-unique times. Contemporaneously I was approached by a number of concerned civic and governmental leaders who asked me to take the position. They convinced me it was my duty. I did so, and I must say it's been quite a journey. I hope you will join me in helping make the future of the world, and the entire universe itself, brighter and brighter!"

Dr. Hull stood for a moment to savor the silence, which she accepted as testimony to the importance and relevance of her speech. Then she nodded and returned to her seat. Dr. Stumpf approached the microphone and thanked both women for sharing their histories. She invited Cecilia Strong to give an overview of the Saving Arms. Cecilia again came to the microphone and lowered it nine inches.

"The Saving Arms is a worldwide organization run on a shoestring. We have over a million volunteers in more than one hundred twenty countries, and we try to help wherever we can find need. We do hard and unglamorous work, always in local communities. We travel around the world for disaster fighting, but the farthest most of us ever go is one or two cities away from home. Of course you all know us for the little teapots and miniature trumpets outside the stores at holiday time. Please feel free to drop in your extra money if you want to help. Here's what I want to say: don't wait until you can easily donate a million dollars or buy an airplane for a charity. Live now. Drop five dollars, or twenty-five cents, into a teapot. Give an extra large tip to a waitress who did a great job, or to the maid if she made up your hotel room quite well. Send it to us. Or drop it in your church basket. Come on out some evening and help wheel patients around the hospital. Go to the library and set up Saturday sessions to help children learn to read. I've done all those things and never regretted any of them." She paused with a sly smile. "Well, I haven't dropped a million dollars into someone's teapot." The audience loved it.

Gwendolyn sat transfixed; she was thoroughly enjoying hearing her friend speak.

"As for careers in charity, it's a tough road with us. We're happy when somebody wants to commit to the long hours and difficult work, but be aware: we have few resources, we pay little, and we are a very flat organization. I told you we run on a shoestring." Cecilia believed it possible that the only soul in the entire audience interested in work such as hers was Gwendolyn.

"We can accurately be called niggards, but only toward our own soldiers, never to the needy." The audience giggled with a 'she said niggard!' ripple. "I repeat: to our employees we are the cheapest of niggards. We pay very little. Our work is hard and ceaseless, and we demand an almost military level of commitment."

Again Cecilia abruptly walked back and sat down. Professor Stumpf once more scrambled in the dead air. She recovered and quickly walked to the podium, clapping. She glanced uncertainly at the silent audience and back to Cecilia and said, "Thank you, Commander Strong... Please hold your applause till later." She extended her arm toward Dr. Victoria Hull who rose and walked toward the lectern. She stood smiling, comfortably overlooking the crowd and saying nothing for a full quarter of a minute. Professor Stumpf, now back in her seat, nodded to a student volunteer.

The lights dimmed slowly. Decreasingly quiet orchestral music surrounded the audience, its intensity exactly mirroring the decrescendo of the lights. The music exploded in a brass fusillade as a huge screen lit up with the emblem of the Glowing Circle.

"The Glowing Circle's goal is to surround those who are suffering with a protective circle of love," a professional baritone intoned. A female voice intoned "Wherever there is need, there is the Glowing Circle. Who among us can stand aloof when others need help?"

Dr. Victoria Hull's voice emerged from the dark, "That last quote is from our founder, Henrik Brownbee, spoken over one hundred twenty years ago at the exact moment he dedicated his life to launching the Glowing Circle." Still pictures of needy children, hopelessly barren lands and occasional oppressed baby mammals hopped into and out of visibility and danced about the screen. All was accompanied by verbal counterpoint between Dr. Hull and the pre-recorded baritone, skillfully attuned to the individual pictures on the screen. Tailored background music integrated the entire presentation.

This audience found the show dull for six or seven minutes, then the drifting students perked up as the presentation illuminated activities here in the United States—the organization had invested millions of dollars to place its name on professional sports stadiums in a few dozen cities. The screen came alive with aerial views of the Glowing Circle parks in Pittsburgh, Detroit, Raleigh, Millcreek, San Francisco, Buffalo, Ithaca, Boston and Seattle. Images of star players happily posing in the well-marked arenas flashed by, and students shouted in excitement as they spotted some of their heroes. The show then reverted to a slower, quieter pace for a few minutes, and the audience's focus flagged again.

The students' attention was suddenly grabbed again as the time-worn face of one of their idols filled the screen. They all knew Wilbur Buffaloon as one of the richest men in the country, a true role model. The luminous head talked. "I am Dr. Wilbur Q. Buffaloon. When I die, I will be leaving assets worth more than fifty thousand of you to the Glowing Circle and similar organizations." Everyone broke out in raucous laughter at the phrasing delivered by the unsmiling talking head. Buffaloon continued, "Why are they so worthy…."

Gwendolyn was surprised to see Wilbur Buffaloon onscreen. What a small world it is! Nonprofit organizations and famous industrialists all together.

Buffaloon's head talked for only a moment or two, building the case for the Glowing Circle as the best of the best. He ended with a puzzling aside, saying, "Now I have a serious note." He briefly pleaded that the viewers understand that people like him were not paying their fair share of taxes and must be compelled to pay more. He mentioned some numbers: his taxable income was hundreds of millions of dollars, but he paid a lower tax rate than whoever would clean the restrooms where the audience was sitting right now. Sometimes he paid zero, and he was outraged by it; he entreated the audience to share his indignation at a system so unjust.

The presentation ended with a view from a slowly moving camera over a single photograph. The final scene featured the passively distressed face of a beautiful, clean, but raggedly dressed little boy, presumably from Africa. The background was filled with almost-imperceptible music. The camera angle forced viewers to his huge, sad eyes. He was about to break into yet another submissive whimper for lack of food and adequate money. The boy was sitting on dirt on the ground, and as the show ended, his image was artfully moved and rotated in a simple curve, then resized in such a way that he seemed almost to come right toward the viewer. There was no narration until the very end of this scene. The narrator spoke up over the background music and said, "And sad to say, this boy died shortly after this picture was taken. We did not have the resources to keep him fed. And if not us, who? And if us… YOU!" The last word reverberated as the music ended with a matching chord strike.

Just then the lights came back on slowly. Gwendolyn was fighting tears, a battle she had sporadically lost during the presentation. As she dabbed her eyes she could not help noticing that Cecilia seemed to be motionless, maybe even unaffected by the film.

Professor Stumpf joined Dr. Hull at the podium, clapping in exaggerated gestures as she walked. The audience, slow to pick up, responded. Some fraction provided a polite seated ovation. Victoria Hull remained still, hands clasped, mechanically smiling at the students for a few seconds. Her face got serious and she said, "I want to talk to you. Isn't there so very much misery in the world? I hope you all will do what you can."

Now she looked like she was about to break into tears. "That little boy at the end—did you see his eyes? He passed away during that first year I ran the Glowing Circle. They had just shot the film, and I was so very attached to that last scene with him. So sad, so sad. I cried as I approved the final cut of the film. So sad, and so very many are like him." She looked at her shoes for a spell.

All at once she reared her face up and said, "Well, all I can say is that I firmly believe we are the most efficient, well-run charity organization in the world, and we're working hard every day to alleviate misery around the globe in myriad ways. Thank you." She smiled, walked back to her seat, smoothed her dress and sat down.

Dr. Stumpf asked for volunteers for the panel discussion. At first there was no activity, but with continued encouragement, a few students held up their hands. She proceeded to choose three students for the panel. They came up and sat in the chairs on stage left. When things were settled she began the panel discussion. "Now are there questions for the guests regarding their organizations or career choices?"

There were two females and one male on the committee. A young woman seated in the middle said, "My name is Elizabeth Jordan and my major is history. Dr. Strong, the woman that you helped after the earth-quake—does she know the influence she had on you? Are you still in contact with her?"

Cecilia answered from her seat. "First, I mean no offense, but please do not call me 'Doctor.' The title is inappropriate. Now, as for the question, no. We never talked after that time. She was part of a swirl of activity back then. We worked very hard for a few days and pulled many from the wreckage, but so much happened, so much. I don't know who she is, though I can see her face perfectly in my mind. Actually I like to keep it that way; she became abstract to me in a way, the symbol of my work. Kind of a guiding beacon. It would seem difficult to imagine talking to her and finding that she is just a regular person, which she undoubtedly is. Like you are, like I am." Cecilia's face displayed a puckering smile with her bittersweet memory. The young woman thanked her, and Cecilia bowed her head gracefully. Gwendolyn was happy to have learned a tidbit of Cecilia's personal history.

The other girl on the panel had a few questions for Dr. Hull. "Hello, Dr. Hull. My name is Jane Seiden. I am majoring in communications. How much of your time is spent traveling internationally? Have you met the United States President? And do you get any time for yourself, or are you always working?"

Worldwide Executive Director Dr. Victoria Q. Hull stood up and moved to the lectern as Hilda Stumpf walked over to the side of the stage. Dr. Hull answered, smiling like a friendly uncle, "Of course I have met the President and several of his predecessors many times; in fact I was at a meeting last month discussing the country's vision for disaster relief and he stopped in. As for my time—well, you know, I'm on call all day every day. Seven days a week. There is not a minute I have to myself, and that is likely what will eventually make me retire.

"But I should say this: it is important to be willing to sacrifice for the good of others. I see it in our donors, and I expect it in our staff, starting with myself. Every meal I have is a working meal. Every trip I take is part of my work. And my family suffers so much. Jet lag. Foreign food. Distant hotel suites. It seems worst during holiday seasons. Sometimes it seems that is when we are busiest."

She perked up her serious puss. "Now, lots of you here at Stambridge may understand one of the great loves of my life... golf!" She paused and a low good natured rustle went through the crowd—most in the crowd at Stambridge were golfers. In fact, the campus itself somehow reminded everyone who saw it of a golf course. "Every game of golf I have played in years is a business conference, including the few holes I shot today. Yes I travel internationally. I do it all for the children and the needy. Everything. I travel worldwide all the time, and let me tell you it is exhausting work." She smiled and stood comfortably.

Gwendolyn was reminded of her father. *She sounds just like Daddy speaking to the crowd. It's amazing he ever had time to take me to the zoo.*

Dr. Hull's next question was from the young man on the panel. He identified himself, saying, "I'm Joey Mulligan. I'm an engineering major and I am from Boston and I love the weather here." The students were amused. Dr. Hull smiled warmly and patiently at the boy. Joey asked Dr. Hull if she was paid a salary and if so, how much and what it means that the charity gives money to its officers.

"Of course I am paid a salary. Our people cannot work for free."

In fact, by any rational economic standard Victoria Hull did not have to work at all, free or paid. And many Glowing Circle volunteers in hospitals, soup kitchens and disaster relief efforts indeed did work their hours without pay. Those individuals labored for free in company with employees of Glowing Circle or the institutions themselves.

She continued, "As for what it means, it means that we exist within a larger economic system that cannot be denied if we want to feed hungry children, bandage wounds and house the needy. Because our people have to survive in that environment, we must pay them. They must have a place to live, food to eat. Otherwise they cannot care for those less fortunate than themselves. I'm sure you understand." The woman was calm; she was talking to a small child about things he was not equipped to fully understand. She looked out over the crowd, encouraging the next question to come from the audience and not the panel.

Joey tugged her attention back onstage. "Do you mind telling us how your compensation compares to the income of, say, the bottom ninety percent of people who donate money to the Glowing Circle? Those from whom you request funds for the less fortunate?"

Dr. Hull was marginally distressed as she considered the seemingly unfriendly question. She looked at him. She glanced over to Professor Stumpf then turned back and transmitted a careful mien of confusion. "I don't know what you mean, percent. We believe everybody should give to others but we don't ask anybody to donate more than a little bit of their money to us." As she spoke, she became certain that the question was a sarcastically wrapped hostile barb. She decided to assert herself, knowing the direction the boy was taking. "Regarding the statistics, I don't memorize histograms of our donors, but that would really not help you understand our organization anyway. My compensation and that of all our officers is directly in line with current compensation in large national organizations comparable in importance. CEOs of profit-seekers often take more, am I right, Professor Stumpf?" That last clause was delivered as a rapid follow-on to the beginning of the sentence, more in the form of a statement than a question. She glanced in the direction of Professor Stumpf, who gently nodded in support, then back.

"And I should mention that we participate in an industry consortium that collects information on nonprofit organizations and distributes the information to members. Charity Coxswain collates officer compensation in groups like ours. All the biggest charities participate. We use this data to monitor ourselves, to make sure none of us is falling out of line with the others with regard to the trajectory of compensation growth. It's all quite sophisticated, and it makes things predictable in these uncertain times. It helps us keep our top performers. I'm sure you understand." She was not attempting to stimulate understanding with her words; in fact due to the structure of the system, the data never induced an organization to slow its growth curve of officer salaries; these curves had raced ahead of inflation for as long as Charity Coxswain had been in existence.

Dr. Hull looked to the others on the panel in the hope that one of them would be the source of the next question. Joey paused, giving the other girls a chance to speak, but both sat slack-jawed. Then he said, "I see. Let me ask you a question I think I know the answer to: Would you like me to tell you how the compensation of your group has diverged from that of the common people over the past twenty, fifty and one hundred years? The top officers of your comparison organizations, I mean. And do you think that a circular justification of a radically increasing basis of comparison is a valid reason to raise your own salary? Do other people in your industry?"

Victoria Hull decided she was facing a direct assault in which Joey was trying to accuse her of impure motives. This symposium was a bad place to get lost in details, and she did her best to avoid getting dragged down. "Of course I don't have that information. I would happily supply it if I carried it around in my head." She said with a smile and tapped the side of her head. The audience chuckled quietly.

Joey's face was jovial. "I have it in right here in my own head since it's my roommate's thesis topic. He's in Economics, not the School of Service, though, and so he was really surprised when he found it." He turned his head with a grin to the crowd. Many smiled, a few giggled. "By the way I hope nobody here at Stambridge minds me referencing the common people for what they are. I'm probably the exception here—I'm one of them. Don't ask me how I got to Stambridge. Probably an oversight." The audience burst into laughter. "Anyway, I'll spare you the statistics unless you really want them." Dr. Hull flushed but did not speak; her smile had remained, but something in it communicated emotions not normally associated with genuine smiles.

Dr. Stumpf approached center stage, but Joey spoke before she could bring the hammer down on him for his disrespectful words. "You mentioned that charity should be a sacrifice for donors, did you not?"

Donors? Victoria Hull was happy to have the focus moved from her salary, and she gestured for Dr. Stumpf to stand down. "Surely. That is the whole point. We should sacrifice to help others. What do you others on the panel think?" Dr. Hull asked the girls. They nodded. The older woman scanned then the audience slowly. Many were nodding agreement.

Joey Mulligan continued, "Sacrifice is the point. Say somebody is rich and they arrange for their fortune to transfer to the Glowing Circle on their death, has that ever happened? Like Mr. Buffaloon will do in lieu of fifty thousand of us?"

The audience again laughed uproariously, and the girls on the panel chuckled as well. Joey smirked. Cecilia sat on the sidelines in her chair and listened politely, stone-faced with an unnatural, unsmiling expression, a linear combination of a pout and the face of gambler with cards. Gwendolyn disliked tension and sat nervously. *Always money. Maybe Mother is right about that sort of thing, she's always detecting that fixation. This guy is fixated.* Dr. Hull answered after a pause, "Of course, it's one of our most important sources of funds."

"Should you accept that money?"

"I don't understand. Of course we take that money. We do good things with it. That's what the donor intended. It helps us with our mission."

"Is it a sacrifice? Is it really a donation from the corpse? Or is it just a decision by a donor about other people's money?"

"Other people's…." Dr. Hull was not following this complicated turn. Gwendolyn was confused as well. They were talking about the donors' own money. In fact, everybody listening was having trouble.

Professor Stumpf, who had paused halfway offstage, spoke up. "I think we're getting bogged down. Would anyone—" but Dr. Hull gained her footing and broke in, hushing Dr. Stumpf.

"No, wait," she said, gently waving her hand in the air. The professor yielded, and Victoria Hull continued, "I must say I have never thought of it that way. My inclination is to say, yes, it's his donation because he could have left the money to someone else or let taxes eat it up. A sacrifice? I think so, but you may be right. What is your concern?"

"I was just wondering why people give to charity, what they sacrifice for. And why you two are dressed so formally, and in your case, so elegantly, as you come to talk to students. Look at us." He swept his hand toward the girls at his side, down his front, to highlight extremely casual attire.

Gwendolyn did not care particularly about most of what Joey Mulligan said, but she was riled by the implicit reference to Cecilia's uniform as ostentation. *Cecilia?! Nothing could be further from the truth.* She was happy to see Cecilia enter the conversation once it was apparent that Dr. Hull was temporarily speechless. Cecilia spoke up in a commander's voice many times her size, "Young man, Lord knows I have my disagreements with most of the Charity Industry on many things. I refuse to get drawn into a philosophical debate about the proper role of money as siphoned off by administrators. I will state no position on whether sacrifice is required with a charitable donation or whether your hypothetical scenario satisfies some definition of a sacrifice. You have heard what I said about donations and you young people can make your own decisions."

Her eyes swept over the audience, then she continued, "But I cannot let pass your insinuation about our dress, an insinuation which is 180 degrees wrong in the case of your Saving Arms representative. Let me tell you why I am dressed like this. I speak only for myself and the Saving Arms, nobody else. You may think: she wears all this to impress us. She wants us to think she is important. Look at those emblems sewn on that sash! See what she has earned! The woman wants to show us every single battle decoration from her imaginary army! She is the Grand Poobah and she wants us to know it. Let me tell you, here is what *I* know. I have to strain to bring my voice down to alto." She was speaking loudly in something way below alto. "I do not prepare my speeches. I may dominate the stage when nobody else is there, but I am five feet and one inch tall." She paused, her trademark twinkle peeking from her eyes. The audience laughed. "I am not here to impress anyone. I am here because I was asked to say a bit about my organization, in case some of you may consider the information helpful as you decide what to do with your lives. Helpful to you, not me. I wear this uniform because I am here representing my organization and I am the Supreme International Commander; that's my title. I wear it out of respect for my organization and its long history. I put forth the effort to dress this way for my audience here tonight. I believe you deserve to have me dressed in my official uniform, the symbol of the Saving Arms and a representation of our commitment. I put this on no more than a few times each year, and I think very hard about whether an occasion warrants it.

"This clothing is extremely uncomfortable. You can imagine, perhaps, walking in a stiff skirt and jacket…" The audience again chuckled as she spoke to the boy, and Cecilia's face returned to its natural slight smile. Joey played along and smiled, shrugging. Cecilia continued, "…constrained by a wide sash and carrying a sword, of all things. I can tell you I don't wear any of it for comfort."

She transitioned to a ferocious silence and folded her hands. She was finished speaking.

For all the imputed majesty, her uniform was mostly dark green and brown, and it had a little bit of grey. True, there were some patches with tiny points featuring colors as ostentatious as orange, electric blue and yellow on the black sash, but they were too weak to influence the overall impression.

A young woman from the audience had walked up to the edge of the stage during Cecilia's tirade. After a respectful silence but without waiting to be recognized, she said, "Dr. Hull, my parents are very active in fund raising. They coordinate groups who seek donations from regular people, contributions my parents say they never would have made themselves before they had a lot of money. Of course they also gather their friends for fund raisers—"

"Do you have a question for our guest?" Professor Stumpf interrupted.

"Yes I do. I'm sorry. I am Maddy Welden." She smiled at Joey, "Joey, I'm also from Boston." She looked back at Dr. Hull. "My family has means. Joey is getting at a question very interesting to me personally. My question is this: if my parents died and left a will giving all their money to the Glowing Circle instead of me, would they be sacrificing? Would I be sacrificing, since otherwise I would be the beneficiary? I'm not saying I have the answers, just the questions."

Maddy continued, "I've seen my parents attend fundraising balls and contribute massive amounts to charities, including yours. They do it in sort of a ritual up onstage, and it becomes like a game with the audience. Whoever gives more generously is queen for a day. And it works. But I never once heard them talk about their own donations as sacrifices. I will say sometimes they call it 'giving back.' When I ask what the loan was, they say they never gave to charity when they themselves needed money, when they were struggling. I guess all the time they were building their careers they were 'taking' and now they have to 'give back' what they took from… whoever. My father sometimes chuckles and says they are donating 'spare money' and that the government will take it if he doesn't give it away. He explicitly says he does not sacrifice to give money away and never did. But he's a hero to the recipients. He has plaques and a few trophies from you in his office. Anyway it got me wondering if sacrifice is important, and if so, what exactly are donors sacrificing for? To allow, no offense please, bureaucrats to live as well as my parents? To build schoolhouses in a place where a concrete floor is a luxury? To set broken bones or repair cleft palates?"

Maddy glanced at Cecilia then back to Dr. Hull, who said briskly, "It is important for wealthy people to give back. Your parents are sacrificing though they deny it to you. They are doing an important service and I commend them for it. Perhaps you will understand some day." She was angry and her voice rose. "As for the other part of your question: you are all young. Maybe you think somehow you could just throw money into the air and have it come down as food landing in the mouths of hungry children half a world away, but that's not how it works in the real world. Money controls things." She looked up, addressing the whole audience. "Believe that we deliver as much money and support to the final recipient as possible. We are not trying to raise the living standards of, as you call us, the bureaucrats. We could not do our work without supplying a living to those bureaucrats, as I explained to... what's his name..." She looked over at Joey and back. "Joey." She stood seeming perplexed for just a moment, as though trying to remember something Joey's visage had wiped from her mind. She gave up and turned back to Maddy. "No offense taken, of course." She stood, glaring immoderately at the girl.

Maddy blushed at her own careless choice of words. She nodded demurely and quietly faded into the audience as she sought her seat.

Joey picked up the ball and his voice arose, welcome as a fart in church. "Dr. Hull, before we got onto this sacrifice business I asked a question that didn't get answered. Would you like to specify the amount by which your officers' compensation exceeds the income of those you ask to sacrifice to keep you in business? Those who believe that the dollars they cut from their families will improve the life of some unfortunate person elsewhere. People that probably don't think it goes into the pocket of people much richer than themselves. Those people. I'm wondering about the morality of those people, your small donors. Are they doing evil, those benefactors, those regular people, continuing to support the bad apples within a system that seems designed to serve its masters as much as its advertised beneficiaries? Are they blameless if they keep themselves unaware of the problems with the integrity of the industry? Are they committing a sin if they simply check a box at work and let others decide whether their automatic donations feed the needy or fatten the greedy?"

Joey's eyes went momentarily to Cecilia. Dr. Hull's, and Dr. Stumpf's eyes followed and then so did the audience's. There was a pause. Cecilia sat calmly, motionless and emotionless, neither endorsing nor dismissing Joey's overt attacks; she did not speak. Everyone's attention went to a visibly agitated Victoria Hull.

The woman struggled to keep her tone aloof and instructive rather than severe as she answered, "Integrity? Evil? Young man, we are at a fine university having a serious discussion, and I will not engage in this sort of talk. I do not talk about evil. As for the rest of it, we ask nobody to hurt his family to keep us in business. I don't know the national average income per household, but of course charities, like everyone else, must pay a competitive salary in order to keep high performance leaders—"

Joey interrupted, "Like yourself. Why?" and waited. Executive Director Hull was caught off guard. She had finessed the compensation question many times but had never, ever had anyone ask this question, 'Why?' Joey took advantage of the pause to resume his disruption of her speech. "Isn't the entire premise of the organization caring, meaning and sacrifice? Don't you ask your donors to sacrifice in the service of helping others? Are they sacrificing for those less fortunate? Or are they denying their families' own desires and needs in service to members of a superior class whose members can laugh at them for taking bread from their babies to pass up the food chain? Isn't it true that not one, but two groups benefit from that sacrifice? That it isn't only the targets, the ones who need the resources, but also the mercenary middlemen who simply want their cut of things, the executives who run the charities? And do you believe the average individual donor understands and approves of this?"

Dr. Stumpf stayed away; she did not offer to come to the rescue this time. And Dr. Hull had had enough. "Young man, you are out of line. You need to understand that these executive officers at the top of these charities, they can easily walk away and take a larger salary from almost any large public profit-seeking company. They sacrifice by virtue of existing in their jobs. Their sacrifice is different and mostly personal and invisible—they sacrifice by what they *don't* do rather than what they do. And, ..." she seemed uncertain for a moment. "I'm quite sure they quietly give their money..." she slowed down and seemed to be thinking, "...not just all their time and hard work, to the less fortunate anyway." As she tailed off she looked uncomfortable.

She recovered her focus. "And I told you that all of our compensation is exactly in line with our direct peers. You should be ashamed of yourself. Asking questions like that. Disrespectful questions. As a gesture to Stambridge University and to the audience I will pretend you did not hijack this symposium this way." Dr. Stumpf stood frozen in the wing—she knew the students better than Dr. Hull.

Joey smiled maddeningly and said, "So, that's the answer? The question is out of line? Would you like to expound a bit on that? Or how about this question. I mean, let's say some charity executive is paid millions of dollars from donations intended for the poor and he is generous. He drops a thousand dollars into one of Saving Arms' teapots each year. What is his bigger sacrifice, accepting the million dollars or contributing the thousand dollars? I'm wondering what you are saying."

Joey's insubordination fostered a stressful atmosphere across the whole stage; simultaneously it provoked cheerful interest in the audience. The young women on the panel were visibly nervous. Gwendolyn was frozenly apoplectic as the strife paralyzed her. Dr. Stumpf remained motionless.

Joey seemed totally calm, having fun. He broke the silence. "What you said about jobs in industry—if that's true I have two questions. First, who is the last such leader you know of who left to take a top position at a higher salary in what you call a profit-seeker? Second, how much are the top folks in Big Charity sacrificing? I mean, are you bringing home twice the national average income? Four times? And by the way, a third question comes to mind. Can't I just go look up your salary if I want to, isn't that still part of the bargain in being tax exempt?"

Joey was way off in his numbers. It was on purpose.

Dr. Hull saw that her gambit to shut Joey down had not worked. She was in unfamiliar territory. She wondered why Professor Stumpf did not step in, and she realized she had to engage by herself. She spoke up, unprepared and concocting the words as she went. "You could look up my salary. But be careful with your interpretation of numbers. For instance, Commander Strong here runs an organization that is in some ways quite comparable in number of volunteers and so forth. It is also tax exempt, but technically they claim religious status, so I imagine their numbers can be shrouded in Byzantine layers of obscurity. And generally, simple 100-page forms give an incomplete picture. Mrs. Strong here may be compensated by a number of different tax-free organizations simultaneously; there can be many other complicating factors as well. Your search for any of this will give you only a partial picture."

The woman paused for only a few seconds before summarizing. "Understand that making your own conclusions can be dangerous, young man. Whatever numbers you see, they are likely not comparable to dollars in the pocket of those putting forth their energy for the benefit of others. Accounting is complicated. Federal forms are misleading. It's best to leave it to accountants." She was telling truths in the pursuit of deception; the numbers do not represent simple reality. But they are not biased to make those filing the forms look as rich as possible.

Dr. Hull immediately regretted her extemporaneous revelations. "No, even better: forget the numbers. It's really best to trust us professionals who have dedicated ourselves to serving others."

Gwendolyn felt a headache coming on. She looked down at her lap. Suddenly her attention was grabbed by Cecilia rising to her feet to speak. The woman faced the audience and ignored Victoria Hull. "We are not 'technically' a religious organization. Because of academic sensibilities I have avoided spiritual references. But we are… make no mistake, we serve the Lord Jesus Christ. And I have no problem with disclosing our compensation structure. We ask people to drop money in teapots to help people, and I am happy to let them know where all of it goes. We show it in the simplest and most transparent way we can figure out, and any of you can see it easily. Yes, we also publish the complicated government tax forms. But on every single public notice or advertisement we have, you will see three things: the compensation of our top people, our taxpayer identification number, and a location where you can easily get more information."

She continued and specified her total compensation in simple detail. "… no gimmicks, no tricks. No convoluted network of hidden accounts. No multiple interconnected charity organizations shifting costs between accounts. And I feel rich with it yet never have a pang of guilt when I think how many are starving in this world." She sat again, abruptly enough to make Gwendolyn wonder if it sent pain through her bony bottom.

The audience was stunned. A year at Stambridge cost more than Cecilia's salary. Many members of the audience anticipated earning that much money shortly after graduation. For those who expected to earn less at the start of their careers, some were rich children with no interest in making money, and some were bent on obtaining a rarefied government position with luxurious lifetime benefits which would stay relatively opaque to outsiders. These latter students were well trained by Stambridge; their audible proclamations stated that they were entering a life of near-poverty, but all understood that once accepted into the guild, they would be protected and well provided for at the expense of the common population. Stambridge was a feeder school for the government systems at this level.

Not one person in the audience tonight was headed for being as poor as Cecilia Strong.

Professor Stumpf and Gwendolyn were both mortified in ways that shared nothing in common. Eyes went to Victoria Hull who stood like a life-size cardboard advertisement someone had forgotten to remove after the sale was over. Suddenly a girl in the back of the audience looked up from her GVCD and said, "Here it is!" The curious crowd turned to her, and she shouted out the executive director's basic salary as posted last year in government forms. The number was well over a dozen times that of Cecilia's. Incorporating a reasonable interpretation of Dr. Hull's caution regarding accounting tricks, a savvy listener may conclude she was getting a total financial benefit quite larger than that.

Dr. Hull clumsily came back to life. She tried to lighten things up and said, "Is that what it is now? I think it was more the year before," and she coerced herself to an unconvincing giggle. Despite its awkwardness, the move did seem to have the desired effect. The audience went along with a laugh, and Dr. Hull perceived an easing of the atmosphere.

Joey visibly blushed as his question was laughed at. He asked, "What percentage of your salary do you donate to charity?"

Dr. Victoria Hull displayed a surprised look. But she had thought long and hard about this exact question many times privately. She kept her off-balance mien as though the words were forming on the way out of her mouth. "Give to charity? All of my work *is* charity. I give to charity every day when I come to work. It would make no sense for a charitable organization to have to pay its employees and have them pour their money back into it. That becomes a game, no? Think of, think of... let's say someone works on a fishing boat. He catches fish for a living. And he gets paid by being allowed to take a few fish home for his family to eat. Does it make sense for his employer to give him an extra fish every day that he does not need, a fish explicitly given so he can give it back to his boss?" She paused, then continued. "But having said that, even I have heartstrings; logic and economics can never overcome psychology. You see, I worked for absolutely nothing my first year. Nothing at all. Well, one dollar. The accountants insisted."

Nobody in the audience quite understood the woman's explanation. Joey, who found himself surprised to feel that there may actually be a glimmer of a reasonable concept there, nonetheless smiled as a sarcastic rejoinder popped into his mind. "Well, maybe that one dollar could have made up for the retirement package given to Dr. Streak, if it had stayed in place for a few centuries. My roommate noticed that she pocketed over one hundred fifty times the median household income in her retirement package. That's how economists always talk—median household income." Dr. Hull's lips started to move, and Joey silenced himself. But she said nothing, and he went on. "Despite what you said a few minutes ago, I think maybe I do see your point about donating your own salary. You are saying that your money comes out of the money given by people for use in charity, and it only would raise operating expenses to increase your pay so you yourself can donate the increase to charity. Hmmm. I don't know. It may make sense." He was genuinely perplexed by this for the moment. Dr. Hull smiled quietly. Joey went on, "I will grant that is not something I've thought about; most people don't think of contributions to charity as a complex and reentrant mathematical computation."

Dr. Hull smiled understandingly. She realized this was a subtle point and hoped that the youngsters in the room were learning something tonight. Even this smart aleck Joey.

But Joey asked, "One dollar. I guess they didn't have to pay competitively to get you! Did something change after that year, did you need money more?"

Something seemed incongruous to everyone present. Here was an invited speaker and she was being grilled by a teenage prosecutor. It was absurd; really there was no reason she should be letting this young man decide what she must talk about here. But still… it was difficult for her to steer the conversation. Dr. Stumpf was being no help at the moment. A murmur went through the audience, and Dr. Hull smiled nervously. She answered, ignoring the meat of the question. "It's low. But when I came in I wanted to set a good example. I wanted to give back. Giving back is a habit I have had, as you can see from the jobs I've taken all my career. And frankly it felt very good to give back, to work for free that year."

Gwendolyn was somewhat cheered up. She liked Dr. Hull. The woman was clearly a nice lady. And she seemed to be stable, if not comfortable, out there with this jerk hounding her.

Joey said, "So, what is that, since that first year you've had about a 100 million percent raise in salary? How did you plan for that fluctuation? Did it complicate your personal taxes?"

Victoria Hull glanced to Professor Stumpf who timidly and silently made a fake offer to take center stage. Dr. Hull looked back at the boy and listened as he continued. "Should you be sacrificing in that position? Shouldn't you take the maximum salary and benefits you can? I mean, why not just help yourself to as much as you want? Shouldn't you just threaten to jump to another group that carefully keeps its compensation up to snuff if someone on your board objects?" He was having fun trying to keep the important dignitary off balance.

Dr. Hull stayed upright, though, and said, "That's absurd. I am not some profiteer, peddling clean water or medicine at the highest profit to the neediest unfortunates, nor any other sort of robber baron. And I am finished talking about my compensation. We are here to discuss careers. I caution you, however. You know nothing, young man, of what I do with my money. For all you know I donate my entire salary to charities. *That* sort of thing doesn't show up on the Glowing Circle's forms." She looked over the crowd for the next question. But Joey was the master of ceremonies for the moment, and everyone's eyes were on him.

Joey spoke up again. "I don't know, of course, some would say it's none of my business. But I doubt that's what you do, based on what I heard from you a few minutes ago about the logic of feeding fish back to the boat owner. I suppose I could believe it's possible, maybe—if some charity were set up specifically to receive those donations, perhaps one run by your brother or something." There was another quiet flash of laughing in the audience. "But I really don't think so because… think about it. If you run the best charity in the world, that's the one you would be inclined to give the money to. And the most efficient way for you to do that would be to just directly forgo some fraction of your salary. Like you instinctively did that first year."

Victoria Hull understood she had to move the conversation elsewhere. She said, "We will never be able to get to the nuances of these questions in a setting like this."

Joey feigned satisfaction and said, "I think you're right about the nuances. Perhaps it's important for the leader to be far more wealthy than those he asks to donate to his organization. Let's leave the compensation question. I believe you've essentially illustrated the position that 'I can get it so I should take it,' like the leader of any profit-seeker, as you call them. So I can conclude that whatever moral code requires that we contribute to others' well-being is silent on whether the first claim on that donation goes to the intended beneficiaries or to someone who can intercept the donation, someone trusted to make sure the contribution gets to the intended beneficiaries. I would assume you would not dispute that the first few million dollars donated to your charity each year go into the pockets of a half dozen or so deeply embedded individuals including yourself. Fair enough. Let's talk about something else." He gave opportunity for response by pausing. Dr. Hull considered engaging again, but instead chose to fume rather than prolong her time on this road to nowhere.

Gwendolyn was disturbed, and she saw that Dr. Stumpf was also upset. This obnoxious boy was making it sound like the dedicated woman always had her hand in the cookie jar like a common businessman. She glanced at Cecilia for a reference point but discerned nothing there. Joey's grating voice continued like fingernails on an old-fashioned chalkboard.

"So let me repeat the other question. Do you know of anyone who has recently moved from being a top leader of a large nonprofit to being in the leadership of a competitive, for-profit company? Somebody who can lose his job if he does not make his numbers?"

She had fielded this question before, and she had her answer ready. "I can tell you this. I can name two large international charities who have recently gotten new top executives, both of whom came from such companies in the last two years." She named the easily recognized charities and felt the question was settled.

Even Gwendolyn, who hated to argue and could not stand this annoying student, took notice of the trick of using words to miscommunicate, rather than engage in actual communication. She sat in her chair, angry at Joey. But she was bothered by Dr. Hull's argument here, which she decided to ignore.

Joey was not willing to give up the fun. "Isn't that more likely to damage your argument, rather than support it? You claim to believe any leader would be snapped up by industry, yet you give examples of the exact reverse process! I mean, let's say one day they call everyone in town together and fling open the doors to the prison. And you've been telling everyone that it is wonderful in there, easy, cushy. Well, when the doors open, you see people going away from the nice attractive prison cells and out to the world, and you don't see any rushing from outside to get inside and slam the cell door and demand their three squares a day. Would someone see that as evidence that you were giving a correct picture, or would it make them think maybe your words were tricks?" He smiled broadly, as did many of the intelligent young people in the audience.

Just then, well before Dr. Hull moved to speak, the resourceful girl in the back yelled out something again. Glancing down through her thick glasses at her GVCD, she said, "I found some information. Jack Melton became worldwide managing director of the charity organization Relief for Suffering Children (RSC), moving from the a position of head of Lesterton Corporation, where he was retiring. For the past five years Lesterton was the largest single donor to RSC."

Joey nodded and nonverbally made it clear he was finished for the evening. Gwendolyn was relieved, as she was tired of the twists and turns of the conversation. And all this talk about money and musical chairs. *What does money have to do with anything? Yes, they need money to operate, but money is not what they are about.* She herself had never worried about money. She had only seen Cecilia talk philosophically about it. And that was just because the woman was the leader and had to think about it. Gwendolyn's parents never seemed to worry about it at all. Her mother, in particular, always had scorn for people who talked about it. She watched from her seat, glad that she was just a spectator and happy for the expected silence from Joey.

Professor Stumpf took the microphone to get the crowd's attention. "Are there any questions about career prospects?"

Just then the persistent young woman with the GVCD shouted, "I found the other one. Virginia Pippolini has stepped down from Financial Transport Coverage, Inc. The chief executive officer's early retirement was prompted, she says, by the need to do more than make money. She has stepped into the chairmanship of the non-profit foundation originally launched by Financial Transport Coverage's founder and funded largely by the company..." A wave of quiet laughter swept the audience.

Professor Stumpf's voice thundered across the room. "This is enough. These guests are not here for amusement and rhetorical tricks. I will not stand for you to show disrespect. The panel discussion is over." She motioned for the panelists to depart, which they did. The young women left quickly, and Joey danced slowly off the stage, walking backwards and doing a full 360 degree twirl on the way off.

As Joey drifted off the stage Dr. Stumpf continued. "We have time for more questions, but you must accept an answer without contradiction. You are here to hear what these people know and to learn, not vice versa. Does anybody in the audience have a proper question for our guests? I want to warn you..."

Gwendolyn watched the activity with a sense of disquiet. She was uncomfortable and disliked this boy Joey. More disturbing, she felt doubts about her new friend Dr. Hull. She detected a smile in Cecilia, and indeed it was not due to any movement on Cecilia's face or posture; it was only detectable because of Gwendolyn's fine understanding of the woman, perhaps ESP. Cecilia somehow had kept an irreverent sense of fun through all her decades, and Gwendolyn relaxed a bit as the droning wordless sounds of the professor drifted by. *Maybe it's not all so serious. Cecilia seems okay with things.* She relaxed in her chair.

Now Professor Stumpf was surveying the offering of raised hands, an offering quite small, probably in protest of her outburst. Four or five young men and women had their hands in the air. In each corner of the back of the audience a hand from an unidentifiable individual was aloft. The professor selected someone from one far corner, and a young man walked halfway down the aisle and smiled as he spoke up.

"Hello. My name is Paul Killen. I'm majoring in chemistry, and I'm from San Diego and I don't think the weather here is so great." The audience burst out laughing, and Dr. Hull smiled. The atmosphere had relaxed quite a bit since Joey had left the stage. "This is a question for both of you. After the earthquake in Memphis the summer before last I sent donations you may consider small to four different charities. Two of them were yours. As I said, you may consider them tiny contributions, but in total they amounted to almost half the amount I earned that summer. My family is definitely struggling. I'm not well off. I don't have means." He paused with a smile. "Another of the commoners, I guess." He grinned like a movie star and the audience of his peers loved it.

"Thank you so much for your sacrifice and your concern," Dr. Hull interrupted his enjoyment of the group's admiration.

"Well, heh, you shouldn't thank me because as it turned out, since that money did not show up on my proctological financial forms, Stambridge ended up getting the government or whoever to just about make it up to me. In fact I probably almost turned a profit." He smiled and the audience rustled happily.

Now, Dr. Hull was of course childless, and she had been out of touch with the administrivia of how the universities exercise their power over the unwashed by first making it impossibly expensive for most people to dream of attending, then selectively removing the problem for preferred types of individuals. This is done by directing money from government, captive richer students and other sources to the chosen. Confused by Paul's reference, Dr. Hull stayed silent.

"But I do have a question for you both. I sent the donations, four equal things, to the four charities. I mailed them along with identical letters. The donations were paper drafts like you see in the old movies. In the letter I was very clear that this was to be used specifically and directly to help people around Memphis whose homes were damaged in that earthquake. If this agreement was unacceptable, I asked for the donations back. Three of the organizations accepted the money from me.

"So my question for you, Commander, is this: why did you send my contribution back to me instead of using it for the specified efforts? Your organization was certainly claiming to be heavily involved in the relief efforts."

Cecilia stood up, came to the front of the stage and spoke immediately. "I am not familiar with your individual case, your donation. However, our accounting systems are not designed to be able to track donations to that level. In fact, I doubt any similar organization is capable of this." She unintentionally started to follow the audience's eyes to Dr. Hull but quashed the impulse in its infancy.

"We exist to serve needy people. We were indeed working very hard there, and I can say this: I slept in tents for over thirty days. As for our policy on donations, you may or may not know that we only accept donations from individuals. That is, if a corporation wants to donate money, we will accept it only if the corporation certifies that every individual stockholder has agreed to make the donation; by this we mean people, not mutual funds and so forth. In practice this forbids corporate donations. Neither do we accept contributions from government, though there are times when we have done specific work for the government and been paid for it. We accept donations with simple conditions all the time. But as a matter of our standard protocol, we will not accept a donation if it has conditions we cannot fulfill, and tracking of a donation of that size in that environment would have easily been identifiable as a fool's errand. You have mayhap heard your grandparents talk about hospital stays where a tube of toothpaste was billed at five hundred times what it is worth. We will not be installing that sort of accounting system, and we will not break the conditions of acceptance for a donation. I am happy to hear that the system worked and your donation was returned. The only better thing, from my point of view, would be for you to make the donation unrestricted and trust us to use the money well." She walked back to her seat.

"I understand. Thank you, Commander Strong. Dr. Hull, in light of the Glowing Circle's subsequent difficulties regarding the fundraising for that disaster I'm not sure my donation was used properly by your organization. So I have two questions: first, did the organization agree to my conditions by cashing the check and second, if so, did you meet your commitment to me?"

Paul was referring to a scandal that hit the news almost a year after the Memphis earthquake. At the time of the catastrophe the Glowing Circle launched a massive relief effort accompanied by a wide-ranging public relations campaign to stimulate donations. It was actually a risky enterprise: the Glowing Circle committed millions of dollars to advertising, and they did not wait for the first contributions before starting to spend money on the actual relief work. All was soon well, though; the public response was generous, and money quickly started flowing in. The drive for donations was so successful that the Glowing Circle overshot their stated target in less than two weeks, and they quietly lifted the goal. The spending on Memphis tapered off, and eventually the rate of donations dropped. Once the fund raising campaign failed to support its advertising costs, it was closed down. When the dust settled it became clear that they had a massive surplus in the account. Making the best of things, they unobtrusively transferred the cash into their general fund.

The top officers, in recognition of their excellent and extremely hard work that stressful year, a year in which the Glowing Circle had brought comfort to an inordinate number of disaster victims, all received bonuses more than doubling their base pay.

Nobody is quite sure how it happened, but the shenanigans were publicized. The Glowing Circle was deeply embarrassed, and the organization suffered a black eye, at least temporarily. The public, those who paid attention, never understood the actions of the Glowing Circle—to the naked eye the whole affair looked quite unseemly. But accounting is tricky, and the institution's defenders pointed this out. Most people eventually accepted the idea that there were complicated accounting matters involved—that the logic with which they had been trained since childhood was of no use in these situations; the accounting complexities were beyond the comprehension of ordinary citizen donors, citizens trusted to competently manage writing their checks to the Glowing Circle.

This bemusement of the public at large, along with the Glowing Circle's excellent reputation, mitigated most of the long-term damage: the institution had built over a century's worth of goodwill and trust. That such esteem has a life of its own comforted the organization's executive officers as they cashed their bonus checks.

Tonight at Stambridge Dr. Hull's loins were girded for battle after all the talk with Joey. "You are referring to the sensational news exposes bordering on claims that we committed fraud in raising and disbursing funds." Her temper was rising.

Paul was silent for a spell, then he spoke up, "I did hear something about that. I'm wondering if you're running afoul of the rules by taking in more than you spent on the intended targets. I mean, I thought you couldn't make a profit."

"I have heard enough on that subject. I have explained it many times, but the press is simply not interested in the facts, just the misleading headlines. I will answer you, but first I must clarify one technicality for everybody in the room." Her voice slowed down and some of the harshness left it as she spoke instructively. "Everyone is under the impression that nonprofit organizations 'cannot make a profit.' This is a simplification of a complex accounting environment, but a misleading one. We raise revenues, we have expenses. The difference varies from year to year. We hope for revenue to cover expenses. Now, unlike profit-seekers, we don't distribute our extra funds to a bunch of outsiders. There is another year coming, and we keep what we can of that money, that 'profit,' so we can be well-positioned for the next disaster. In fact our top executives suffer personally in years when revenues and expenses compare unfavorably—to mitigate running at a loss, if we don't generate excess cash for the year their compensation is curtailed somewhat, in order to help make up the shortfall." She paused and swept her eyes across the auditorium. "But basically, it's best to banish the troublesome oversimplification that nonprofit organizations cannot make a profit, though I do detest that term." She did not bring up the fact that the mirror image of this executive compensation curtailment was illustrated last year, the year of the Memphis controversy.

Paul was stroking his chin as he listened. "I see," though something in his demeanor gave everyone to clearly see that he was unsatisfied.

At this, Victoria Hull's anger returned after the dispassionate technical elucidation. Her voice changed, dropped. "We exist for a reason, and to fulfill our mission we must act. We may not sit idly by. In a quickly changing emergency situation with people dying underneath collapsed and burning buildings, with polluted water, with sanitation shut down, we move very fast. I would think the news media and the public at large would appreciate that this is what we do. And in pursuing the necessary haste—and yes, I mean necessary—we ramp up our fund raising and relief efforts instantaneously. If after the fact someone finds that a bit of the rubble settled a little outside the dotted lines, well, that's better than slowing down and letting the accountants run the emergency relief efforts while babies die under piles of bricks and pipes." She was hitting her stride. "We too had people camping in tents at that site. I do not apologize for mobilizing the average comfortable American to help, and 'parachuting in' with emergency relief. Not at all." She was upbeat. The effect of hearing her own words was felicitous.

Gwendolyn agreed with Dr. Hull and felt better. Now her new doubts about the woman were subsiding. Things were getting back to normal.

Professor Stumpf moved aggressively to a position beside the rejuvenated Dr. Hull, but she did not speak. The room was silent as Paul stood motionless. Then he asked, "Do you not employ accountants?"

Dr. Hull did not answer. Nobody understood the question.

That energetic and diligent girl in the back of the crowd again cried out, looking at her GVCD. "I thought I had heard something like this. This story is from June. 'Congress voted, ninety-two to nothing, that the Glowing Circle has not broken the laws of any controlling legal authority and is innocent of chicanery in relation to the recent Memphis earthquake relief effort. The vote also specifies that the Glowing Circle has never in its history participated in any sort of fraudulent activity.' The story goes on to say 'the President of the United States spoke as he signed the document...' Remember?" She looked up. Heads nodded as the members of the audience recalled the odd story from the prior summer. Those who had taken classes in government were confused; the rest of the students were simply bemused. That latter group included Gwendolyn, who was glad that the Glowing Circle had been acquitted legally. She was sure that Victoria Hull would not misappropriate anybody's donations.

Paul asked Dr. Hull, "Do you agree with Congress?"

Dr. Hull looked confused, then nodded. "Of course. They make the laws of the country." Her voice became determined. "I am finished with your question and so are you, young man. You may sit down."

Paul felt a surge of anger, to which he responded by doing a little dance. He swept his hand in the air and flounced through half a pirouette and a sort of bow to the audience, "Well, okay then! If you're finished, I guess you're finished!" Many in the audience laughed. He turned, walked to his seat and sat down as the giggling traversed the crowd.

The noise died down as Professor Stumpf pronounced the meeting finished and thanked the guests through a shroud of anger. She admonished the students that certificates of attendance would only be available for the next five minutes outside the rear center doors. The students in the audience talked and joked as they stood up and filtered toward the exits. Most collected the test grade certificates as they left the building.

Afterward, behind the building, Hilda Stumpf and Victoria Hull stood talking agitatedly. They turned and put on cordial smiles as Gwendolyn and Cecilia walked up. Everybody shook hands and exchanged pleasantries. Gwendolyn said, "I am so proud you came, and I was so happy to meet you today, Dr. Hull."

Dr. Hull smiled and put her arm on the girl's shoulder and said, "Please say hello to your father for me. I will say, though, that I should never have let him talk me into this."

"But why not? He did it for me."

Dr. Hull and Professor Stumpf exchanged a glance, Dr. Hull's meaning being, 'Is she for real? Is she putting me on?' Dr. Stumpf's silent reply verified: 'Yes. No.'

Dr. Hull said, "Honey, I stay away from these big public interchanges because they become a circus like that in there." Then she lied, "I'm not a debater. I'm a manager. I am a good steward of things but not especially gifted at showing off. There will always be grandstanders who can twist things and make anyone's efforts look absurd. I'm looking forward to a nice warm bath and a quiet hotel suite."

"Oh. Well, we do have some rude students here. But I thought you looked great! I think people were so lucky to have you here. And thank you again for coming. Thank you for all the work you do every day. Everybody is grateful. We're all grateful. And thank you." Dr. Hull accepted the verbose compliment with silent aplomb.

The two groups bid good night, and Gwendolyn walked away with Cecilia. They stood at the elder's car. "Thank you so much, Cecilia. I know they all enjoyed and got a lot out of it."

Cecilia nodded politely. She said, "Well, I hope I was of some service. There certainly were some contentious moments there. I don't know, Gwendolyn. Nothing really new came up, but I suppose some of it was new to the young students." She looked down and then back up. "Anyway, always remember sunlight is the best disinfectant."

Gwendolyn did not catch the reference to germicides and said, "Some of them talked so fast that I had a hard time following them. Some of the students seemed a little bit... obnoxious. That boy Joey. Some of the others. For a while I thought they were saying Dr. Hull was some sort of charlatan, or even a criminal."

Cecilia reached up and she patted the taller girl on the top of the head. She said, "Never change, Gwendolyn."

Blinking puzzledly, Gwendolyn answered, "Okay," as Cecilia brought her hand back home. Cecilia got into her car and picked up a fabric cross on a string from the seat next to her. As she donned it and smoothed the cross in place, Gwendolyn said, "Isn't that man Buffaloon a saint? I mean, did you hear him talk about how we should make him pay more taxes? And Dr. Hull! She works dawn till dusk and never takes a minute for herself. And still she made time to come here tonight. Just like you. Thank you so much."

Cecilia was tired, and much as she wanted to go home, she could not leave Gwendolyn in this condition. She had ever been concerned about the youngster, and watching the girl's simultaneous worship of both guests had bothered her tonight. And now this. She felt pity for the poor soul standing right next to her, who was verging on brainwashed.

"Get in," she said.

Franco, Giovanni, & Lorenzo Too

Under what conditions does two plus two equal four?

C ecilia leaned out the window and shouted for Gwendolyn's driver to go home. "Come on, Gwendolyn, climb in. I'll drop you back at your room. We need to get a cup of coffee first."

Coffee with Cecilia! There was no need to offer twice. Gwendolyn tossed a nod and a wave of the wrist over to her limousine driver and ran around the little old car and got in. They chugged down the road until Cecilia parked at 'Franco, Giovanni, & Lorenzo Too,' a popular and lively gathering place not far from campus. They went inside and Gwendolyn was a little disappointed to learn that Cecilia was not planning to sit down with her, but she perked up when Cecilia said with a big smile, "I'll brew us a cup at my place. It's one of my vices. I know I shouldn't buy it, but they always have Mississippi Sun-Grown Dark and I love it so."

Her place! Cecilia's flat! Gwendolyn was invited to Cecilia's apartment! She floated outside behind her friend and boarded the car.

The place was only blocks away. Cecilia parked the car in her carport and gathered her uniform pieces, handing the coffee to Gwendolyn. They walked up an outside stairway to the third floor of the building and went into her apartment, a standard one-bedroom flat with a small kitchen seemingly built around her fancy coffee maker. The kitchen's only furniture was a wooden dining table with a few chairs. Cecilia had hung a few artistic pictures on the walls over the years, and no photographs, plaques or memorabilia. A sofa, coffee table and stuffed chair were in the living room, all piled with papers and folders. Along the wall opposite the entrance, below a long window, sat a bookcase holding books with more papers stashed on top of them.

As Gwendolyn surveyed the apartment Cecilia removed her beret, sash, jacket and cross, and she started the coffee. The brewing process was fast, and soon they both sat snug outside tall mugs of the rich, hot brew. Gwendolyn savored every minute of the special attention from Cecilia as they chatted easily, perhaps like an elder aunt and her niece. Cecilia had a few things she wanted Gwendolyn to think about, and eventually she brought the discussion around to them.

"Gwendolyn, you heard Dr. Hull talk about her pay, that she should be paid comparably to executives in a large company. Why do you think Dr. Hull worked for free that first year?"

"?" Gwendolyn shrugged. She sipped her coffee. Cecilia looked at her, letting the girl know an answer was required. "Well, I guess she felt she could get by without it. Maybe she didn't need it."

"So you think she decided she should not receive a paycheck if she does not need it?"

"I don't know. Yes. That makes sense. I guess that's what she did."

"But she needed money the next year? She needed much more than the President of the United States needs?"

"I don't know. I guess."

"But she didn't take it that first year, did she? Was that right?"

"I think so. It sounds… generous."

Cecilia tipped her head down. She looked down at her cup, drew a breath then took a sip of coffee. "I think you should contemplate that. And please promise me something."

"Sure, Cecilia."

"No, listen first. Someday will you tell me if you think the answer is more than 'I guess' or 'it sounds good' please? Promise me you will get in the habit of doing your own thinking, Gwendolyn." She looked back down at her hot coffee and swirled the mug. To the girl the rebuke came across as plenty gentle and not bothersome.

"Okay, I guess." Gwendolyn giggled involuntarily at the slip. Cecilia could not help joining in with a smile. She dabbed at her lips with a napkin.

For a while they sat, wrapping their cups with their hands, occasionally drinking coffee, all the time enjoying each other's presence. In a few minutes Cecilia said, "Gwendolyn, I have met Dr. Buffaloon. I think he comes across as a very nice man."

Gwendolyn nodded. "I've met him too. He really is a nice guy."

"If I told you he is a hero, would you believe me?"

"Yes, of course."

"You would? If I told you he is a scoundrel would you believe me?"

"Um… Yes. I guess so. Maybe." She preemptively wagged her own finger at her use of the word 'guess' with a small smile.

"Do you believe you sound like someone who is in the habit of thinking for herself?" Cecilia was rougher than before but still benign. Gwendolyn did not answer. "Tonight in that little recording, he mentioned that we need to make him pay more taxes. Have you heard his speech about how he makes hundreds of millions of dollars and yet his tax rate is lower than that of his chauffeur, who doesn't make one thousandth as much? How somebody should force people like him to pay more taxes?"

Gwendolyn nodded again facilely and sipped her hot coffee, enjoying it as it rolled across her tongue here in the room with her good friend. Her head cocked up at an angle, she watched the car lights out the window as she listened to her elder. Everybody in the country had heard the man deliver this blurb. He had placed television advertisements and erected old-fashioned billboards with his face on them. Everyone's GVCD occasionally lit up unbidden with the plea from the man whose generosity and thirst for justice was only foiled by the legal strictures of our society, constraints that ostensibly frustrated his quest for that elusive goal, self-sacrifice.

"Did you know his net worth increased by several billion dollars the year he started being so vocal about not paying enough taxes, and that's fairly typical?"

"Nope. Sounds like a lot of money, though." Gwendolyn's mind was on the moving headlights on the street not far away.

"Are you paying attention to me, dear? Are you too tired to show me some respect?"

Gwendolyn was stricken. She blushed and tried to quickly get serious. "I'm not an accountant. Net worth. No, Yes. I don't think I knew but okay if you say so."

The older woman was disappointed. "Listen to me. It's a measure of wealth. The worth of what you own minus what you owe. You know, like the billions of dollars you always hear about when people say Bob Gaines is the richest man in the world. If you own stock and it goes up in price, your net worth increases. Your wealth. There are tax details that mean you have to be careful how you move it around, but tax details are exactly what the man is talking about. So, are you aware his wealth went up a few billion dollars?"

Gwendolyn was paying full attention after the chastisement, though she was exhausted. "No. I thought he said a few hundred million, like you just mentioned."

"He was talking about something else—taxable income. The man uses a variety of techniques to minimize his taxable income and the amount of taxes he pays, not to maximize it. He has sheltered his money from taxes for years. And there are details I won't bore you with. Many rich investors spend a lot of time with companies in different countries, allocating the profits between them to minimize the tax burden. I don't understand much of it myself, but I am subjected to hearing about it all the time because of my position at work. Some of the officers at the Saving Arms deal with these things with big donors every day. Dr. Buffaloon may do some of this, I don't know. It is clear that he keeps much of his money in tax-advantaged foundations."

"I see." Gwendolyn did not see, and it did not bother her. Wealth. Taxable income. They were different, but the subject was boring. How long would this tack of the conversation last? But—she was spending time with Cecilia, and this she loved. She knew that to make this work she had to seem to pay attention, but her tired state did not make the dry subject matter any easier to concentrate on. Her mind wandered as Cecilia's pleasant voice filled the space between them.

"Why would a man so concerned that he should pay more taxes shield all except a few percent of the growth of his wealth from taxes? Or why wouldn't he ask that we demand he pay a tax on wealth itself? Or why wouldn't he just donate whatever he thinks he should be paying?"

Cecilia paused expectantly. Gwendolyn shrugged. What was it Cecilia was talking about? Money? Tax? She did not understand the subtleties of net worth and income accounting, and she was happy enough not understanding them. She pushed a spoon around in her coffee cup.

"I see you are thinking hard about this."

Gwendolyn blushed at this second scolding and replayed some of Cecilia's words back in her mind to find where the conversation had been as her mind wandered. She wracked her brain as though she were in an oral examination, and she actually did pretty well. "I think I heard someone talking about him once. Whoever it was said that he had an obligation to some other people to minimize his taxes. It was not his choice. And I know that when I heard him in an interview he said he will donate his money when he is dead. Almost all of it. Somewhere. I can't remember where. So he does give it away, maybe not to the government though."

Cecilia was familiar with this interpretation of the responsibilities of the corporate executive, and she also knew of the well-publicized intentions of this generous man to give away his money when he made the transition from this world where money is important to the next, where perhaps he believed it was not. In fact, she was well aware that the Saving Arms would be one of a number of organizations reaping a windfall from the man's departure. "When he is dead?"

"Yes."

"When he goes out and broadcasts his plea for us to make him pay more taxes, is he talking about that? About what happens when he dies?"

"I think I did hear him talk about that once, a tax on dying or life insurance or something, too. I don't know. Maybe that's a different thing."

She instantly recognized her own incoherence in the company of this wonderful mentor. Gwendolyn felt like a child caught picking her nose in school instead of paying attention to the teacher. She grasped for diversion in her coffee and took a few gulps, emptying the cup, eyes down. There was a long silence but no escape. As Gwendolyn sat looking at the dry bottom of her mug, her inquisitor took a few very slow drinks of her own coffee. Cecilia's eyes illuminated the girl's discomfort like spotlights. Then she put some more coffee in Gwendolyn's cup. "Gwendolyn, do you hear yourself?"

That was what had triggered her wave of shame—she had indeed heard herself. But she was caught helpless in the machinery of the moving conversation, one in which she fell behind at the initial stage. "Yes. No. Yes... I mean, I'm not an accountant. Other people know a lot more about it. I don't know."

"But is he appealing to you, or just to those other people who truly understand what he says and what he does? Is he just talking about cold hard numbers to those experts? Or does he want to influence people like you to think a certain way, the way he peddles?" The woman beamed intense silence for many seconds, suppressing Gwendolyn's ability to respond. After this she said, "Are you a little girl anymore?" and sat quietly.

This struck Gwendolyn. She had a sudden epiphany. It had never before occurred to her that she could develop her own opinions on such things. All her life, instructions on how to think about matters like this had been supplied from others, be they parents, teachers or groups of friends. These things were served up pre-digested, fully formed and ready for incorporation into her own compatible and unoriginal thoughts—her own rephrasing was all that was suggested.

Gwendolyn did not speak, but a seed had visibly taken root in the girl's—the young woman's—mind. Her discomfort diminished markedly with the perception of her own ability to think, though in truth this relief was also partially a surrender to exhaustion. Couldn't they just sit and visit? She slumped in her seat.

Cecilia sipped her coffee. "Is this an honest man?" Again she received no answer. Again she pushed her friend only with silence. Gwendolyn was quiet and let the pressure to answer roll off her back. She ignored the specific question, did not even think about it. Cecilia saw what was going on, so she dropped some of her own tension and quietly swirled her coffee.

They sat in the pleasant enjoyment of their friendship, tired and contented in the quiet evening. After a few minutes Cecilia went back into motion. "What did he mean when he said people like him should be forced to pay more taxes?"

"I don't know." Gwendolyn's glimmer of composure and self-assurance had dissolved while they sat and sipped. She was back to herself, employing her little-girl reflexes in conversation. But she picked up after a short pause. "He meant that tax rates should change so he can pay more to help society. He's got more than he needs, and he wants to give back."

"Is that so? Were the words crafted to make you think that? Are they true? Is there something else he is not saying, something behind the curtain?"

"Yes. No. Of course. I don't think he is hiding anything. I've met him before. He's a nice man. What else could he mean? What could be behind the curtain?" She had not taken any of Cecilia's implications about the man to heart in a persistent way. She had met the man personally, and he had smiled and been quite friendly to her.

"I am not a teacher anymore and I am tired. But let me play Socrates here. Would you like that?"

Gwendolyn did not know exactly what Cecilia meant. "Yes, it sounds fun!"

"Okay. Is it possible that Dr. Buffaloon was saying he wants to pay more taxes?"

"Yes. That's just what he said."

"Did he say that, really? Or did he say something else and try to get people to hear that in what he said?"

"No. He said it flat out. He said he is not paying his fair share." Gwendolyn was feeling engaged in the game now, energetic and confident. She perked up with the challenge, being pretty sure that Cecilia was playing devil's advocate, and convinced she was up to the task. *Maybe that's what Socrates means.* "Everybody knows he's a good businessman, and he wants to play fair. He wants to live up to his own standards, I guess. I like that."

"I am not sure I've heard him say exactly that, but for now let's assume he did say he wants to pay more taxes, and that the good man would not lie. What stops him now?"

"What?"

"Why does he not just pay more taxes?"

"Cecilia, you're not making sense. Taxes are what they are."

Cecilia was not playing devil's advocate, and her patience was heroic. She took a slow, deep breath and dropped her shoulders, which had begun seeking her ears. "Gwendolyn. Think. You are a young woman now, not a little girl. What stops him now? Does he do what he wants? I mean, can he eat the breakfast food he wants to eat? Does he?"

"Sure he does."

"Does he live in the house he wants to live in? Drive the car he likes?"

"Of course. And it's not a mansion either. He's always telling people he lives in the house he grew up in and drives a car he has had for twelve years. He's a very humble man."

Cecilia paused, perplexed, contemplating whether she had undertaken a task too audacious to carry upon her skinny shoulders. Those shoulders rose and fell again, and Cecilia contemplated what direction to go. For a bit, the two friends just kept each other company and enjoyed their Mississippi Sun-Grown Dark. Cecilia decided not to give up. "So this man, who lets us know how humble he is, this man is powerful enough to do what he wants?"

"Right. Well, he can't break the law. Nobody is allowed to do that."

"I see. Of course. Let's say he would never break a law. He can do what he wants otherwise. Can he pay more taxes if he wants to? Does he have the money? Can he just give the money to the taxing authorities if that would make him happy? Will he break a law?"

Gwendolyn knew nothing about tax laws and authorities. "I don't know," she copped out.

"?"

"Yes, I guess he could. But that's not the rules. He follows the rules. That's what he was saying."

"Okay. Let's summarize. He can pay more if he wants to. He thinks other rich people should also."

"Yes, that's it. That's the exact thing he was saying."

"So he does not pay more than required. He thinks he is not paying his fair share but still does not pay more than the government forces him to."

Gwendolyn was a bit wary. "I guess so."

"He can do what he wants, and he needs no rule change. He has it within his power to pay more. It will not hurt him in the least; he has said so over and over again. He tells us he should do it, and he would do it if we forced him to. But he does not."

"Yes." She answered truthfully and unconvinced of her own answer, but only because she had the feeling of stepping into quicksand that she often got when she engaged in logical arguments with her father.

"He feels others like him should also be willing to pay more. And they are certainly able."

Gwendolyn relaxed a bit. "Yes. Others like him."

"Since he can do whatever he likes with his own money, would it be accurate, would it be fair to say, that the gist of what he says is that others, not he, should be forced to pay more?"

"No, him too." Gwendolyn shook her head in certainty. She was not entering a quicksand swamp after all. She took a sip of her coffee. So did Cecilia, who was again flagging in her optimism regarding the lesson.

"Gwendolyn, listen to yourself. Are you saying he does not have free will? The richest man this side of Dr. Robert Q. Gaines cannot do what he wants to do?"

Maybe this game was not so much fun. Cecilia's question put things pretty clearly. They both drank daintily, as they were both getting sated with the strong late-evening coffee. Gwendolyn wondered how Cecilia had become such a stern taskmaster.

Cecilia was indeed serious. She wanted to impart something to Gwendolyn. The woman was not troubled by ostentatiousness or egotism or ambition. But when she perceived disingenuousness—that she could not abide. It frosted her to believe people deliberately used words to confuse people, along the way making themselves out to be virtuous. She had heard it many times before, and she wanted the few young people she knew to be able to identify it. And she also thought she detected in Buffaloon's words a veiled appeal to a mob mentality that troubled her.

Were the truth to be known, Cecilia would guess that taxes probably should be higher and that they certainly should be loophole-free for everybody, including wealthy individuals. She thought that rich people like Buffaloon probably should pay more in taxes, though she was not really sure. The whole thing was complicated; she had heard some analysts say that since essentially all of the man's gains were taxed once at the corporate level, he should not have to pay any extra tax at all. But all this was a distraction complicating the teaching task she had assigned herself tonight. She refused to think about it now.

Cecilia just looked at Gwendolyn. The girl shrugged. They fidgeted with their cups. Cecilia was indeed willing to play Socrates with one modification—her memory of Plato's dialogs did not include Socrates forbearing speech for long periods. But she was intent on making use of that large, normally underutilized portion of the verbal communication spectrum, silence. And she pressed Gwendolyn quite intensely with it tonight.

"I think you're right," Gwendolyn finally said after a long time.

"Do tell." Cecilia's eyebrows almost met her hairline.

"He's asking for us to force other people to pay more taxes. He's not really asking us to make him pay more, since he can do that himself. He's throwing out a non sequitur."

"But he said he wants to be forced to, Gwendolyn. Didn't he say that?"

Gwendolyn was now resolute. "That has to be some kind of trick. Maybe he wants us to think he is a hero or something. It can't make sense. He is in control of himself. He is asking for us to help him control others." *I can figure these things out for myself. Why didn't I ever think like this before—why don't I do my own thinking?*

"How do you know what he is thinking? How can you say it is a trick?"

Gwendolyn thought for a moment. She was awake, alive, feeling strong now. "I guess I can't say what he is thinking. But he is not stupid; everybody seems to agree that he's a genius. Simple logic tells me that if he understands something and has repeated it and knows it is logically wrong or misleading, then he is perpetrating a trick of some kind. And I'm certain he knows that what he says will be heard as something other than what he is saying—that's why he says it. He knows what he is doing. He knows what he is saying. I claim he is seeking misunderstanding of his words. Seeking to mislead people."

"So now, Gwendolyn, speaking only of the pure logic of his stance, will you restate what you think is his message, the core message, the only purely logical message?" Cecilia asked, sipping almost the last bit of her coffee.

Gwendolyn's eyes went to four o'clock as she thought and formulated his message. "I think he is saying what you said before—what I just said. The pure message is that some other people should be forced to pay more taxes. He is willing to do what is he says is right, but only if we forcefully take money from some other people that, he believes, do not need it. If we do not take money from these other people, he will refuse to do what is right."

"Interesting. Now, that logical message, Gwendolyn—is it the message he wants people to hear? Or is there some other one?"

Gwendolyn smiled and went to drink from her coffee, controlling the pace of the conversation for the first time. "Of course not. I believe he wants people to hear that he is a generous man held back somehow from donating vast amounts of money to their government for their benefit."

"And does the English language have any words for a person who publicly says one thing and does the opposite?"

The girl nodded.

"Well, keep thinking about it, Gwendolyn. I would suggest that you decide what class of man this one is. I will give you a hint: there are two types of people."

Gwendolyn, elated and flush with energy born of her success in fighting through the puzzle, broke into a smile, telling an old joke she knew: "Yes. Those who classify people into two groups and those who don't!"

Crow's feet sprang onto the corners of Cecilia's eyes. The exhilaration of having Gwendolyn reach her lesson, combined with the unexpected joke, took control of her. She burst out in a belly laugh at the silly gag, struggling to put her cup down upright. Gwendolyn tumbled from her own grin into a full guffaw as well. There they hovered, trying to recover from mutually unstable laughter, climbing irregularly toward composure and alternately knocking each other back into a disordered paroxysm. In an episode of what may be telepathy, each independently formed the same image of a toy figure of Wilbur Buffaloon with a broken mechanism, comically oscillating back and forth. First he would start to give money away with one hand and then, just as he delivered it, a spring kicked in and he would grab it back with the other. The toy's tiny voice squeaked with excitement throughout. In a few minutes a sort of exhaustion dampened their convulsions, and they sat quietly, each with water in her eyes.

Cecilia busied herself by splashing the last few ounces of coffee into the two cups. Neither drank any more, though. "Well, dear, I was going to say something different. I was going to say honest and dishonest."

Gwendolyn nodded, still with a smile on her face. She reasoned that whatever else Wilbur Buffaloon was—rich, friendly looking, famous, informal—he had clearly placed himself in one of those categories and not the other.

In the uncharacteristically light moment, Cecilia, still smiling, said, "You know, I always wondered why the 'A' in his name is silent. It makes his name come so close to describing him." Her smile widened. She saw Gwendolyn nod, and decided that everyone must have the same thought upon first hearing the man's name. "Never let other people think for you." Cecilia fidgeted with her coffee. She considered deepening the conversation to see if Gwendolyn understood that thinking along the lines of income tax rates was confining oneself to a tiny realm of imagination in contemplating taxes. But she found it an affront to be required to expend mental effort on the tax system when there were so many more interesting things in the world. Besides, there is only so much one can get across in one sitting. She sat looking at the girl.

Gwendolyn broke the quiet. "But why would he want to trick people? He's got everything. What could it be? It's ridiculous. He's ridiculous." She received no help from Cecilia on this, and the two sat tired and silent. After a while, both at once stood up; it was clearly time for Gwendolyn to go home. Cecilia made a gesture and went into her bedroom. She came back out, and the two headed to the outside stairway without exchanging a word. As they got in the car, Gwendolyn suddenly had a thought. Maybe she had been too constrained in her conversation, what with Cecilia hounding her so closely. She said, "But isn't there another logical situation Dr. Buffaloon could be setting up?"

"Do tell," said the older woman in her trademark scholarly request for elucidation from a student. She started the car and began the drive back to Stambridge.

"I mean, if we cornered him, couldn't he tell us he wants the rules to be a certain way—a way that makes rich people pay more taxes—and that if we're unwilling to put those rules into place, he will not be a sucker? He will not be the only one paying extra taxes? I mean, that he's withholding money as a protest?"

Cecilia was pleased with Gwendolyn's progress in their discussion. She did not want to discourage the girl, but she was a stern taskmaster. "That is a logically sound stance, Gwendolyn. Is it a truly meaningful stance for the man to take? I mean, does it seem like that's what he wants to public to hear in his words? Or does it sound more like a pettifogging, very technical, meaningless escape valve useful in case he is asked about the logical consistency of his words and actions?" Cecilia's questions took the wind out of Gwendolyn's sails. But the luff lasted only a few seconds as Cecilia continued. "Gwendolyn, you are thinking now. I applaud your deduction. I do not disagree with your logic, and I believe not one in a hundred of your colleagues would have come up with it."

Gwendolyn smiled. She blushed. Then she answered Cecilia's question. "Of course this is not what I or anyone else believes Dr. Buffaloon wants us to hear. It is, as you say, a contrived situation where he can claim technical logical consistency if cornered. I'll go further: I'll bet you will never, ever hear him spell it out like I just did." She was feeling confident in her deductions.

Cecilia smiled proudly. She nodded. "So," she asked. "Does it change anything we have talked about? Do you think he wants people to believe that what he is saying is just that he doesn't want to be the only one? That he is worried that people will think he is a sucker, this brilliant man?" Gwendolyn laughed again. Cecilia joined in. They sat quietly as Cecilia took Gwendolyn toward home.

They finished the short drive back to Stambridge, and just after Gwendolyn got out of the car Cecilia called to her. The girl turned and leaned in the window. Cecilia squirmed, plunging her hand into a pocket and wriggling, using her other arm to help free whatever was inside. *It looks like she has a frightened mouse in her pocket.*

Cecilia eventually pulled out a dull, oversized brass coin. "I want you to have this," she said. "But it comes with the condition that you will not accept laziness or the ridicule of others or the rationalization that 'it's obvious' or 'only a jerk doesn't agree' or any variation thereof as a reason to avoid thinking for yourself. If you accept this present you must commit to always do your own thinking. Always."

Gwendolyn nodded and reached for the coin, but Cecilia snatched her hand away, closing it over the medallion. "Always look for the moving parts and try to identify them. Nobody does anything without a reason, and people are not always honest. Not always even aware. Don't be someone who just looks at the surface of that which you are presented with. Treat it as always transparent, never opaque, and look through, look within. Do your own thinking. 'D-Y-O-T' if you will. Think of what it's called when you restrict your calorie intake to try to lose weight. Remember it as expending Calories on brain activity. Diet."

Again, Gwendolyn nodded. Cecilia added, "You must not simply swallow what you are told. Ask 'Why?' Things are not self-evident. Everything has a reason." She held forth the metallic circle. "When you don't understand something, don't just shrug and go on; don't live in a world full of people who do incomprehensible things, a world of events that just seem to happen by themselves." She moved the coin out and opened her hand as though she would give it to the girl but again teased, stopping just as Gwendolyn expected it to drop into her grasp. "Gwendolyn, listen to me. Whenever anybody says, in effect, 'Pay no attention to that man behind the curtain,' what should you think?" She paused. "You initially failed the test with Dr. Buffaloon" she said severely. She dropped the token into the girl's hand without waiting for an answer and repeated, "Do your own thinking." She smiled. "And you came through with flying colors by the time you were doing your own thinking. You can do this."

Gwendolyn felt the pleasingly hefty metal piece. Her eyes averted, she nodded to the older woman, then her eyes bounced back and forth between Cecilia's face and her new possession. They settled on the coin in excitement.

On one side was a raised triangle with the words 'Truth,' 'Persistence,' and 'Integrity' written at its sides. A human brain was engraved within. Around the exterior of the triangle were tiny representations of a microscope, a rocket and a globe. An abstract relief image of a city with the sun rising behind it decorated the obverse. The words 'Build And Trust Your Own Mind' arced over the buildings. Beneath the city, in raised letters, between engravings of a hammer and a tractor, 'TYOM CECILIA 9' was written.

Gwendolyn was elated with the present from her role model. "Thank you so much, Cecilia." She tried to close the distance through the window and execute a hug, but the older woman did not cooperate. "What is it? It's an antique."

"It's just a little something I want you to have. I've had it since well before I was your age. I like the cheerful shining city in the little engraving. And the message. I always remember it by picturing myself tying the sneakers I wore as a child. Tie 'em, Gwendolyn."

"Oh, Cecilia. It's a treasure. I can't take it. It's pure gold and you have to keep it." Gwendolyn could see it was brass, but the dull metal was shining in her view.

"Oh, nonsense. Yes it's a treasure. And I've had it since I was a child. Now it's yours. Meditate on the words. Are they important? Can they help you? Can they help the world?"

Gwendolyn was in tears. "Of course they can help me. Cecilia, nobody has ever given me anything so precious. I'll keep it forever, I vow to you. Oh, thank you. Thank you." Gwendolyn struggled to touch Cecilia's face through the car window.

Cecilia leaned back to stay just out of reach and said, "I'm glad you like it. See you at the Ministry soon." As Gwendolyn retreated, Cecilia straightened up and aligned the mirror, which the girl had bumped. "Maybe now I can get out of this uniform," she said with a smile. She lifted her bottom up and squirmed, tugging at the uncomfortable stiff skirt like a child, then fluffed everything back to smoothness. "Goodbye, Gwendolyn." Almost boring herself with her own repetition she said, "Do your own thinking. D-Y-O-T. Diet."

Gwendolyn waved with one hand as she stood looking at the coin, angling it to catch illumination from a nearby light. Cecilia had turned brass into gold here tonight. The token was actually an antique. As a nine-year-old girl Cecilia had saved cereal box tops for months and sent away for the personalized token. She watched for the mailman every day until it arrived. It immediately became gold to her, but it spent the last five decades or more as a brass artifact rattling around in her underwear drawers before reacquiring its gilded status tonight. Cecilia felt an exhausted and contented smile arise as she drove off among the eucalyptus trees with Gwendolyn standing, hand clasped around the coin, looking after the ridiculous old car admiringly.

Gwendolyn's Dreams

What is within shadows?

That night as Gwendolyn lay in bed she mused on her future. Her thoughts drifted among the many ways she could choose a career helping people. She had been brought up understanding that this is what her family does, and she expected to play her role. She quickly dismissed pictures of herself sitting at a desk filing paperwork for the social-work department of some government agency. Maybe she could be a teacher. She envisioned herself leading a classroom of happy, well-cared-for children. It was a pleasant diversion, but she knew, from a multitude of earlier instances of this exercise, her fulfillment would not last long unless she was working with people who really needed her help, people in some form of trouble. A smile came to her lips as she pictured herself as a fireman carrying a helpless giant man out of the burning building. It wasn't the first time for this scene; like the schoolroom, this whimsical, effortless tableau usually passed through her mind whenever she relaxedly contemplated her destiny.

Gwendolyn's esteem for Cecilia Strong knew few bounds, and she admired how directly Cecilia and all her organization aided those in need. She knew she was no Cecilia, but that woman was the lighthouse, the marker of the direction toward which she would take her life. She played movies in her mind, stories in which she worked in some part of the Saving Arms. One day she was binding wounds after an earthquake, the next she was helping a distressed mother find somewhere to sleep with her five young children. Believing that she did not have the gifts and strength of Cecilia, she pictured herself in a role pursuing goals set from above, unworried about funding, squabbling employees, public relations and so forth.

Perhaps she would set up some small local organization on her own, a place where people needing any kind of help could come. She could feed hungry people and obtain medicine for the sick; surely the companies producing the food and medicine would find a way to get supplies to her without cost, if just for the public relations value of it. She sometimes settled on this script when daydreaming about her future, and tonight she visualized herself in her small, cramped office bustling with needy people and volunteers, navigating between stacks of old-fashioned paperwork and alleviating pain and giving comfort...

THE NEXT MORNING Gwendolyn awoke anxious from a dream, a troubling and confusing tableau. As a rule she did not dream, but she had a quite clear picture of last night's indistinct and gap-filled story. She lay in her bed replaying the dream in her head, confused by the mysterious scenario and her unasked questions.

In her sleep she found herself in a building with an intention to aid some sick children. She wondered what their ailment was, and immediately knew the youngsters had a dangerous disease, and they needed transfusions. A slowly moving, diaphanous veil of mist permeated the whole dream. Grey light beams from unspecifiable sources below and above cast sharp edges through the haze. The dream was eerily silent.

Now she was wearing a hospital gown with long sleeves. It covered her from neck to ankles. The garment, like the room, had no color. Without moving she went to a simple low bed, one among a circle of what she knew to be an uncounted thirty-seven, all spaced around a large round hole in the floor. Each bed held someone who she perceived as her twin, though they varied in age, sex and appearance. Her guide seemed to be a tall, fat, anonymous doctor who transmitted instructions to her in some unknown way. The doctor was wearing a huge, colorless dark robe with an extended, pointed hood, and his face was hidden in shadow. The garment completely concealed his body. Its lower half looked like some sort of hobble skirt that spread on the floor below him. Gwendolyn had the impression that his posture was strained and improbable, perhaps like a dog on its hind legs, or a seal balanced on its tail—but troubling, not friendly or entertaining.

Gwendolyn was lying on the little cot waiting for something to happen. The eerie quietude weighed on her as she lay still. Looking at the others, she saw all were wearing identical gowns. She was granted awareness that they felt relaxed and content, but she felt nervous and frightened in the static silence. She looked down, and a flexible tube protruded from her sleeve. She pulled back the fabric and saw through the transparent hose walls that she was giving blood. She followed the curve of the tube as the blood inside traveled in a motionless flow to a large glass tank that sat on the floor one level below. The huge vessel was almost full with the rich liquid as all thirty-seven volunteers contributed symmetrically to the common pool of life-giving fluid. Yet everything looked frozen still.

For all her life Gwendolyn had been squeamish about blood. In a strange twist of the dream, she was calmed by seeing the blood—she saw it as a symbol of life and health, and she was not reluctant to donate or to look at the tubes and tank. She was proud as she looked at the blood in the curved pipes, and she felt stronger, not weaker, as hers streamed silently out of her arm and down the tube without betraying a hint of movement. She relaxed and lay on her cot, transfixed by the static activity of the tank below.

Now she noticed a half dozen larger hoses that entered the circumference of the container at few inches below the thirty-seven small tubes. Gwendolyn's eyes followed the bigger tubes back to their sources, and the corresponding donors materialized into view, surrounding the tank on large beds. They lay within the same type of robe as the doctor wore. Each was massive and fat; their face-hiding robes were correspondingly huge. Their blood tubes egressed their robes through the hood openings, not the sleeves; in fact she could not make out any sleeves or distinct features in the wrinkled masses of their oversized vestments. These donors seemed formless, almost boneless. Gwendolyn could sense a mild satisfaction from those in the circle around herself, but the donors below basked in a more powerful emotion— they almost glowed with a cold happiness, a lazy contentment, as the blood flowed invisibly through their hoses. Such things are perceivable in a dream. Something about these donors made Gwendolyn uneasy, but she could not identify it.

Now her mind turned to the sick youngsters. As she wondered where they were and how they would get the blood they needed, the answer bloomed. The blood tank sat beside a hole in the floor just like the hole in her own floor. Tiny tubes egressed from near the bottom of the glass vessel and traveled to the arms of the unenumerated fifteen young children lying without cots on the ground below.

Except for herself, nobody moved. In fact she saw no motion in the dream at all. She became uneasy; she had awareness that the children were asleep, and she knew everyone except her was happy, which gave her a disconcerting sense of isolation. She did not understand why she was becoming anxious or why she was the only one. She looked around her circle of unidentified donors and somehow knew that about one-third of them had been substituted while she was looking down below. She looked up to find the doctor, but he had disappeared long ago.

Ambulation, Precipitation, Trepidation

Why not?

G wendolyn completed the fall quarter in good spirits. Her grades were satisfactory and middling. Thinking back on her long seven-quarter career at Stambridge, she was most proud of volunteering at the Helping Ministry of East Altos Flats; an honorable mention went to the career symposium she had recently arranged for the other students. When final exams were over she was happy to travel somewhere nice and cold for the holidays and winter break. As she moved toward Vermont on the airplanes, she looked forward to snow, apple pie and of course, Christmas—the magical holiday where she had received such wonderful presents as a toboggan, ice skates, a pony, and her favorite stuffed animal, one of which presents she owned to this day.

Gwendolyn kept herself busy at home working as a volunteer in her old hospital in downtown Burlington. She spent almost every day reading stories to sick children and wheeling patients between appointments. She often just walked a ward, scanning the rooms for patients in discomfort, doing what she could to help. After work she often met up with her best friend Alitisha, who worked nearby in a fragrance shop for the holiday season. The girls grew up as neighbors and best friends, and they had been inseparable for years until Alitisha went off to college a year before Gwendolyn. Even then, her school was not far away, and they spent a lot of time together. Here in Burlington, Gwendolyn was able to adjust her volunteer schedule to almost match Alitisha's work hours, so they spent many evenings in Burlington's winter-dark, brightly lit downtown.

One night they walked in the falling flakes, sipping fancy coffee drinks, Gwendolyn still in her uniform and Alitisha smartly dressed as always. The two young women ambled for blocks in the crisp cold of the downtown evening. The streets and stores were festively decorated with wreaths and lights, creating an enjoyable holiday backdrop as the girls strolled and chatted and enjoyed each other's company. Gwendolyn loved seeing the points of light in the darkness, and she also enjoyed playing games with the dance of her breath as it encountered the steam from her hot mocha. To her, even the red and green streetlights looked like Christmas decorations. Alitisha was less partial to the season; she schooled at Bornington College, close by in New York. But she was a good sport and accommodated Gwendolyn's desire to bathe in the wintry season, if with a bit less joie de vivre traceable to the weather.

Suddenly they were walking through a flurry of snow. A fresh blanket quickly covered the ground, and Gwendolyn enjoyed looking back at her footprints in the crystal cold night. Burlington is, by city standards, not a dirty town, but Gwendolyn could not help thinking the snow had cleansed the city as though coating it with a layer of fresh, sterilized paint. Even the tracks from automobile tires were bright white in the glare of the streetlights. They formed abrupt valleys in the white powder with wriggling white worms filling the negative space of the treads. Everyone drove slowly, and as the snow accumulated there was a dull quiet underlying the muffled city sounds. Gwendolyn watched the large white flakes halfheartedly seeking the frozen ground as they passed through the beams of the lights. She enjoyed the feeling of her boots on the accumulating snow as they walked. That telltale squeak of her boots on the ground, the familiar scent of air during a snowfall—these told her Christmas was near. As they walked by a uniformed man blowing a toy trumpet on the sidewalk next to a bus stop, Gwendolyn dropped a few dollars into his teapot and got a smile through his snowy grizzle in return.

She had been to cities all over the world, but somehow they were not comparable to her hometown. It was not as though she was unable to enjoy a nice city any time she desired; for goodness' sake, she lived in a massive metropolitan area, schooling at Stambridge, lodged between San Francisco and San Jose, either of which cities is many times as large as Burlington. But Gwendolyn stayed in her own little world close to campus. The only times she had gone to San Francisco were the instances when her family traveled there and she went up to meet them. Here, Burlington was the big jewel-like city, and Gwendolyn knew it as home.

Out of the blue, as much a surprise to herself as to Alitisha, she asked her friend, "Why don't you come with me?"

The question was outlandish. She had launched the query impulsively, but after the words had taken flight they reached her own ears and began working their way into her thoughts. It would do Alitisha some good to volunteer, and she was unlikely to be entangled in anything she could not put on hold whenever the trip finally came up, except possibly a boyfriend. It occurred to Gwendolyn that she herself could be lonely when she went to Africa. She had never before thought of that, but it surfaced in the silence. Who knows what support she would need? Alitisha had hinted that she might take some time off of school. And heavens, what a purpose! If a girl had to mark time, why not do it in a way that contributes? Why spend the time inhaling aromatherapy paraphernalia?

"You're kidding, right?" Alitisha said without a hint of uncertainty, somehow instantly knowing the context of the question. She sipped some of her hot beverage, looking askance at her friend.

"I mean it," Gwendolyn said, realizing it was true. "I'm going. I'm going to save some starving people. It would do you some good too. This is the real thing. They really need help over there."

"Me? To Africa? Really? Helping starving people? Sure I'd go, I really would but... I can't even stick to a diet, let alone live on what they'd feed us over there. I don't deal with starvation very well. I don't know how to spoon-feed sick children. Actually I don't like kids, you know that. And you know getting the low-cal dressing on a salad is the closest I come to starving." She had been smirking at the suggestion, but as her words took flight, a somber feeling overtook her and her expression dropped. Gwendolyn noticed the downturn.

"Salad!" Gwendolyn said, pointing to the restaurant they were just walking past. She was troubled by Alitisha making light of the subject, and even more by Alitisha's mood darkening. Alitisha nodded and they guzzled the remains of their lukewarm drinks, then went inside and sat down. Each ordered a salad, then the conversation continued.

Gwendolyn said, "Come on. This is real. Yes you could come with me. And remember all the fun we had that summer we went to help at the old folks' home near the lake? Didn't that feel good? We'll have fun and do good and feel good."

"Yeah, it felt great, maybe a little creepy being around all those wrinkled old people who smelled funny. I did feel like I did something good. But it was a summer at the lake, skinny dipping and hiking around and not working all that hard, remember? Messing around with boys in the woods. That's a bit different from months in the dust with people dying all around you. Remember we thought we would encounter people dying up there that summer? I'm glad we didn't." She managed a thin smiled as she recollected.

Actually Alitisha and Gwendolyn had not noticed, but three inmates had indeed died during their summer of volunteering; the girls had limited ability to resolve the individuals in the dining halls and recreation sessions, and they certainly never kept an overall count of any of the groups they dealt with, so they did not miss the departed.

"They're not dying. They're being saved from starving. They're *keeping* them from dying all around. I'm going to help them. We'll be helping people, and we could keep each other company. I'm going to be pretty lonely there. You and I, we've had it pretty easy in the world and I don't think it would hurt to see the other side of things. Everybody should sacrifice some."

"Speak for yourself," Alitisha chewed some chicken and croutons. "I wouldn't say I've had it easy." Immediately she felt she should not have snapped. "What I mean is, you don't know what it's like to have it bad—to be the only Dark in your classes. To have the guys always wondering what it's like to be with a Dark. To always have people ask what you think whenever there is a news story with a racial angle. I want to scream *I don't know him!* My father tried to prepare me, and you remember I had a little of it in high school, but everyone was from Vermont. They were mostly all classy. Now, I really get sick of it at Bornington."

Alitisha was of mixed race. Her father had been a successful entrepreneur with a well documented, well exploited African-American genealogy. He had moved his company from Vermont to Boston several years ago, and subsequently the State of Massachusetts purchased the organization, a specialist in diversity and sensitivity management. After about a year he started working to spin the company off, and he succeeded, forming a hybrid enterprise with himself at the helm. Almost immediately he was the victim of a fluke—the perennially-out-of-power party won the government in the state at just the wrong time for him. A new president was installed, and he was pushed into a peripheral role. The company was an unusual, public-private entity, and he now had a staff position in charge of only one program, a big step down from running the whole operation. He commuted home to Vermont on most weekends.

Alitisha's mother was a white university professor. Alitisha's father's coloring dominated her complexion, and her features combined the best from each parent; she was universally recognized as quite attractive. She had embraced her father's heritage, and there was no mistake that a stranger would classify her as 'Dark,' a word she had coined and insisted on using to denote her own African heritage. She hated the various and ephemeral fashionable words people used to describe her father's race. She preferred her own word and felt entitled to give it to the world.

Gwendolyn did not believe for a second that Alitisha felt deprived, or that she was on edge because of her race. She decided not to probe Alitisha's sensitivities at the moment. "C'mon, Alitisha. You know what I mean. We haven't really suffered, not like those people. Don't you want to do something on your own, something important? I'm sure Daddy's foundation would sponsor you. He's not happy about me going, but I know he's resigned and they'll sponsor me. I told you I'm going over for a visit with him to see the place and meet the people running it."

"What does that mean? Can't anyone go and volunteer? What does sponsorship do? Does it cost money to go, is that it?"

"I'm not sure of everything, but I know the Wholesome Globe Project doesn't have the money to pay for volunteers to travel there. It costs them enough to feed and house them. Sponsorship gets us there and makes things easier for them. I think it means that the Foundation donates some money beyond covering our costs. Daddy looked into it and said it would be much better if the Foundation sponsored me. You could come too. I know I could convince him." She had been looking down at her plate as she spoke, and she looked up and saw Alitisha checking her GVCD below the table level. She waited silently.

"Sorry. It was my dad, bitching about something. He's been on edge for a few months. He's let me know that if he loses his job, he won't let me go back to New York because his company won't be paying for me. I'd have to switch to UV and my mom's free-ride-for-children benefits would have to kick in. He says I should have packed more classes in and gotten on a program to get done in four years." She sighed. She took a forkful of salad and ate it as Gwendolyn sat surprised, empathetic. "He's always been one to point out what I've done wrong. Anyway he won't spend the money for even another year. And I've got a lot more than that left to go."

Gwendolyn said, "I had no idea. Sounds bad. He wouldn't really let you go to a state school, would he? He's probably just saying things like that to scare you onto the straight and narrow." She ate a clump of plant matter. "You know, I never knew what he did for work," she said, her mouth full of food. She sipped her water, the salad still inside her mouth.

"Neither did I, till pretty recently when I asked him about it. I knew he worked for the state down there, that's all. He said that's only partly true anymore. He used to have a company that ran training programs for Massachusetts and some other states. Then Massachusetts bought it from him, and he worked directly for the state. He hated it. Bureaucracy, you know, all that. Pretty recently he wangled some kind of private-public deal, where he actually works for this new company but gets retirement and other benefits from Massachusetts, and he said that's what is important. Right now he runs a program that decides, believe it or not, how much money to give to regular non-state-employee families for college aid! What a laugh!"

"Why does he think he may lose his job?"

Alitisha shrugged. "Well, he said that the investors put in a new president, moved him to another position. You know, infighting, budget cuts, new blood. I don't really know. Now he suspects that's why the state was willing to let him spin off. He can be fired and save them some money, which couldn't happen when he worked directly for the government. I don't know. He just can't tell what will happen, and he worries."

"It's going to be a bitch to have to transfer if he loses his job, eh?"

"Tell me about it. But it's not really that bad. It's more just the insult of the thing and the hassle of the change. Bornington isn't that great. It's not that much fun. Remember, I wanted to go to UV originally anyway. And I'm not in too much of a hurry, so it won't be that bad. My mother can't lose her job, and there's no time limit or maximum benefit, so I could take five years off and still re-enroll and go through." She smiled. "And then do seven years of college!" They both laughed.

"I guess I do remember about UV. Hmm. I'm curious. Why did you decide to go to Bornington then, especially since you really wanted UV?"

"He wanted me to go to one of the most expensive schools. I didn't get into Halford or any of the Emerald Vines I applied to, but Bornington is just as expensive.

Gwendolyn was eating as she sat listening.

"Anyway, you remember how serious I was as a student in high school, don't you?" She smiled with a huge eye roll and Gwendolyn broke into a quiet giggle, which jumped back to Alitisha. She said, "Yeah. I know. Still am. Anyway, I guess when I was looking to go to college, my demographics didn't save me; heck my father's may not even save him, now that he's not a state employee and not president of the company." She smiled, "He's not as connected as your father."

Gwendolyn was puzzled, but quiet. *Connected? To whom?*

Alitisha continued, "Anyway he says since Bornington charges so much tuition, we're getting that much more benefit by going there. It's like a pay raise for him. He says he should have stayed with the state, says he's kicking himself now."

"I guess."

Alitisha weakly smiled and said, "It won't be that bad. Maybe I'll take a year and ski."

"Well, your folks must be pretty well off. I mean, your house, the cars. The summer place is pretty nice too. The boats. Wouldn't he just use some of his own money and get you through? Or would he really make you go to UV?"

"I asked him about that. He said no, my college is not going to be paid out of his and my mom's money. It's going to be paid for as part of his job or my mother's. They didn't work all those years to just spend their money on something that their employers are supposed to pay for. Bornington is fine if it's free to us. Otherwise it's UV, which will be. Actually my father said they don't really have any money lying around in savings anyway, because government people are not supposed to save like everyone else—it's not necessary. So all his money is spent. Well, he said 'tied up.' Amazing, given how he and my mother always made me put most of my gift money in the bank rather than spend it on candy or skateboards."

The waitress came by and interrupted, "Do you need anything?" The girls declined simultaneously and she left.

Gwendolyn thought about her own similar little bank account, the one she believed was meaningful until recently when her father outlined the family's financial setting to her. It was a situation she still did not understand, but she knew it meant her piggy bank was not a big part of her own financial picture. "Not supposed to save?"

"He said the things profit-seekers save for are part of his 'background pay.' Same for my mother. I asked what a profit-seeker is and he said basically it's someone who doesn't work for the government or something. Funny. He was a 'profit-seeker' till just a few years ago, but you'd never know it from listening to him. I don't know what he did with the money he got for selling his business to the state. Maybe it wasn't really anything. Do you know what that 'background pay' is?" She paused.

"I didn't, either," Alitisha said as Gwendolyn, who was engaged in a friendly tussle with a slice of pepper, shook her head. "He's still in the state system, and he said that was a real important part of things when he structured the deal to spin off his firm. Background pay is things like what I just talked about, paying for college. And retirement, well he said it's the value of the part of retirement pay he locks in every year. It's complicated but pretty important to him. He knows money. He says he plans to stick it out in his job till Riordan is through school, so we get the full benefit. And he'll be actually getting a raise in pay when he retires too. And if he stays anywhere in New England it's tax-free. That's background pay.

"But now it seems like he may lose quite a bit of it. If they throw him out now he can't draw any of the retirement stuff till he gets almost as old as a profit-seeker would have to, and the college stuff just goes away completely. So it's all pretty painful for him to think about. He's not in the mood to spend all that money to send me to Bornington." She was stressed but somehow smiled as she finished the sentence. She looked down at her plate.

Gwendolyn realized she did not have the grasp of economic issues that Alitisha had developed, and she was impressed with how sophisticated and knowledgeable her friend had become. She seemed like an economic expert, not the doll-playing girlfriend at the slumber parties. Gwendolyn said, "You know, sort of speaking of that, I know Daddy has always asked why people who work for charity or for the government have to pay taxes just like profit-seekers. It does seem a little unfair, and in the case of government workers, just silly since the money is just coming from one pocket to go to another. I will never really understand economics."

Alitisha shrugged and played with her fork distractedly. They had coffee brought over and sat together quietly. Eventually Gwendolyn's mind came around to Swazizibia, which brought her to visions of Alitisha and herself on a months-long adventure. "So, what about it? How about volunteering with me?"

"You're crazy. I told you, Africa's not for me, and I'd think you'd know that living in the desert is not for me. Send me some old fashioned postcards, and keep in touch while you're over there. Let me know how much fun I'm missing."

"So, what will you do if your father is fired? Will you go to UV?"

"Like I said, maybe I'll ski. I haven't really thought about it. Go to UV I guess. Probably. My father said he'll tell me for sure within the next few weeks. If he gets through that, he's locked in for another year's benefit, so it will be next year's problem."

"Well, the Wholesome Globe Project thing is not going to happen right away. Think about it, and I'll soften up Daddy in the meantime about sponsorship. But I know I can get him to sponsor you. And you know, they say it's really warm there. And no, it's not desert and you know it. How many times have you complained to me about Vermont's cold?"

They dawdled awhile over their coffee; eventually Gwendolyn picked up the check and left a generous tip. Over the course of the evening, as the girls spent time at Alitisha's house, Gwendolyn pushed a few more times. She saw it not as meddling in someone's life but rather as advocating for a wise use of time for her friend Alitisha.

None of it surfaced that night, but over the next weeks, at least partly powered by Gwendolyn's incessant encouragement, Alitisha oscillated between yearning for some adventure and wanting to stay home.

The Pursuit of Projection

Is this the place?

"**Y**ou know what, Daddy? Africa doesn't look any different than anywhere else." Gwendolyn's low energy utterance was slow and even as she shifted uncomfortably and continued looking out the window.

Dr. Kingman Q. Dressel-Meier was amused at his daughter's epiphany. She had been all over the world, and maybe now she was realizing that faraway places, mysterious in the mind, are ruled by the familiar laws: the sun rises every day, water flows downhill, the sky is blue.

They had been in the car for five hours, driving over almost flat terrain covered by scrubby vegetation. The only motion they saw outside the vehicle was an occasional dust cloud in the distance and the sudden scampering of nervous lizards closer to the car. The majority of the motion inside the car was just the bouncing ebullience of their native driver.

It occurred to Kingman that in her twenty years Gwendolyn had probably never been in a car for five hours straight. Certainly not in an uncomfortable, springless, hot car. "Well, it's bigger than other places isn't it? And what about all the missing neon signs? How about the dirt ruts they call roads? And don't other places have air conditioning?" he smiled at his daughter.

"C'mon Daddy. You know what I mean. We've been everywhere and it looks like a lot of places." The driver, a cheerful, tooth-challenged fellow threw his nose and chin back over his shoulder and nodded, laughing robustly, face to the ceiling, eyes squeezed almost closed.

"What did you expect, sweetie?"

"I don't know. Maybe desert like up in Egypt. Or something different, something like I never saw before. There's no scenery here."

Kingman smiled. They were nearing the mission in a seventeen-year-old Land Crawler, a car older than any vehicle Gwendolyn had ever ridden in. The car was spare and worn, barely serviceable. The driver was entertaining—mostly entertaining himself—with his sporadic anecdotes. His stories were punctuated with almost spastic issues of his own amusement at, and sometimes before, the punch lines. When he broke up before the end, his jokes were irretrievable, but really any loss on that score was minimal.

Gwendolyn was not precisely correct in saying there was no scenery, though the bumpy flat ground flowing by the vehicle supported only sparse grasses and an occasional bush, and a picture taken from any point on the trip would be identical to one taken from any other spot along the way. There was lots of scenery—but it was all exactly the same.

Gwendolyn and her father had left California yesterday and embarked on their visit to Dr. Florian Bok's Wholesome Globe Project mission in the outlands of Swazizibia. After three airplane hops terminating in the capital city they undertook the last leg of the voyage in this beat-up old car. Everything after their initial trip in the Foundation's jet had been arranged ahead of time by their hosts: the commercial flight from Cairo to the capital, the prior night's accommodations in the capital, and this, the final leg of the trip.

Whenever the driver was so pleased with one of his own jokes that he convulsed in laughter, control of the steering was relegated to the irregular ruts of the dirt path. The guidance of the grooves in the road made this occasional lapse in attention less hazardous than a westerner might think, however. The limit to the car's achievable speed also contributed a safety margin, even though the driver's feet often danced on the accelerator during these interludes. The final increment in their security from the driver's negligence was supplied by the fact that they had seen zero other cars in five hours and seemed unlikely to see much of a larger number.

The driver was a friendly man named John, cheerful and extraverted. He had lived in the capital his entire thirty or so years, and this trip afforded him the opportunity to share episodes from each of them with Gwendolyn and her father. Kingman had repeatedly used his executive skills in an attempt to get the man to quiet down, and sometimes it worked, but only temporarily; the man's personality did not lend itself to long silences. Gwendolyn's general politeness and interest in people, enhanced by the boredom of the ride, compelled her to engage in conversation with the man, so they learned a bit about his life in a dozen or more installments. He owned this car and he owned a very fancy satellite telephone. He was a rich man in Swazizibia.

Both the phone and the automobile were given to him some years ago by the man, a doctor, who runs the mission they were approaching. John told the captives that he had met the man in the capital five or six years prior. He was hired to carry the doctor's bags and be his guide in the city and surrounding countryside. The doctor, apparently a very rich man, had taken a liking to John, and he returned a few months later wanting to visit many places in the region. The doctor purchased the Crawler in the capital and added the large extra fuel tank the visitors had not noticed in the back of the vehicle. John acted as his servant for a month. John remembered it was the rainiest part of the year, and many times he got stuck in mud; he recalled that the doctor always wore white and never got a stain on his clothing.

When the doctor departed he gave both the telephone and the car to John, who was free to use the car to make money but required to be available if the doctor called. Now, years later, the doctor occasionally asked him to transport someone in the car, a request John happily obliged. He found this arrangement to his liking, especially since the doctor paid to keep the phone alive and deposited money in a bank account every month, money which more than covered all the driving John did in the little taxi business he had developed in the capital. John had evolved into a well-off resident of Swazizibia's urban center, admired for his business acumen. He concluded his little story by observing that the doctor was a generous man.

"Do you see him much?" Gwendolyn asked. Her father was listening along with her, as the toll for his boredom.

"No. He never call. I never see him. But I talk to his assistant sometime. He told me to bring you." John laughed for no apparent reason.

Gwendolyn was listlessly looking out the window. "Do you go down here often?"

"Not very much. Not very much. Maybe a few times a year I go down there and pick someone up. Sometimes I bring ladies down there. Nice ladies. American. Young. Good." He smiled. "I bring four ladies down there just about six months ago, I did." He smiled with the memory of the pleasant young passengers. "They are much better than the children, crying and scared of the dark."

Kingman and Gwendolyn looked at each other. "Children?" Gwendolyn excitedly asked, "What about the children?" but John changed character; he was inexplicably nervous, agitated, and he left their interest unanswered by mixing doubletalk, nervous laughter and feigned misunderstanding. After a few minutes of incessant conversation on the subject without any information exchange, the visitors gave up. Gwendolyn thought that John was simply unable to communicate his thoughts well enough in English; Kingman knew better but was not really concerned.

Over the hours the discomfort of the trip had been unremarkable—all heat and boredom. Gwendolyn and her father sometimes exchanged talk of an inconsequential nature. Mostly their minds were dormant on the long, dusty voyage. Kingman worked a little bit locally on his GVCD and even did some paperwork, but he spent more of his time looking out the window and cultivating his melancholy over the idea of his daughter leaving for this godforsaken place. Gwendolyn, though bored, did not distract herself with music or any other electronic diversion. She focused her attention on getting to know Swazizibia, becoming one with the dusty, quiet, desolate country.

Finally, the driver pointed out their destination in the distance. A group of small hills stood in silhouette above the plain two or three miles away. Outlined against the grey haze of the sky, one tall building with two towers astride a large peaked roof was visible. Gwendolyn immediately recognized that it must be the old cathedral that the mission showed in all their publications. The only other outlines visible were two smokestacks, one larger than the other.

The car hobbled across the closing stretch of their journey, and as they drew close to the mission the driver announced their approach by beeping the dilapidated car's tired old horn. When they stopped at the entrance John bounded out, walked open the forlorn wooden gate, and then jumped back in the car and brought his passengers into the compound. Gwendolyn's eyes were busy scanning the scene, a few people among mostly low nondescript buildings. Both Gwendolyn and Kingman were struck by the huge, incongruous cathedral dominating the scatter of buildings in the mission. Its dusty red brick contrasted appealingly with its dirty light green roofing and window trim. John had wordlessly disappeared when they looked back down. As she picked up her pack from the back of the Crawler, Gwendolyn was glad for her father's prior admonition that they pack minimally. She shifted her heavy backpack onto her shoulders.

The visible portion of the mission's perimeter was surrounded by loosely tangled and violently menacing barbed wire; Kingman estimated that there must be twenty miles of the twisted filaments surrounding the mission, whose perimeter could not be more than a few miles. In front of the visitors stood a gentle arc of small wooden buildings reminiscent of a series of little schoolhouses—not the solid, multistorey schools in Vermont, but the single storey wooden ones Gwendolyn sometimes volunteered within back in California. The structures appeared connected, and as they curved to the left, beyond was a more modern looking, taller building. If the small structures were little schoolrooms, the larger structure looked like a university administration building. Off to the left side, unconnected to the end of the arc, they saw another multistorey edifice. They were later told it was where the director lived when he was onsite. Some others lived there as well.

Far to the left, between the residence and the wire fence, there was an airfield: one long runway. A relatively small airplane sat at the close end. Gwendolyn and Kingman could see a few small buildings and some storage tanks across the runway at its far end, and a few small trucks of various types along its length. There was a hangar maybe three quarters of a mile away.

To the right, behind all the buildings in the compound, stood a long row of bare dirt hills running the length of the mission. The hills looked almost as tall as the administrative building, but well shorter than the cathedral.

At the far end of the compound, partly out of sight behind the dirt hills, was a building Kingman took to be a power plant: a big brick building with a tall tapered chimney wafting grey smoke. A thinner column of thick black smoke billowed from a smaller adjacent chimney mostly hidden by the dirt hills.

Gwendolyn was thrilled. This was exactly as she had imagined it. Well, not really imagined—she had seen many pictures of the place, and she had enhanced them with daydreams. Everything was like the picture in her mind, if perhaps a bit more dusty. And maybe the colors were muted here; for example, the cathedral was certainly not as brilliantly red and green as in the pictures. She noticed that the scraggly vegetation did not hide the ground. All the people that needed her help! She could not see them, but they were here. She was sure of it.

Gwendolyn had often done volunteer work at home in America, but teaching children to tie their shoes and picking up trash in the parks paled in comparison to what she was destined to do when she returned to this place. This, right here, was the epicenter of the fight against real suffering, real starvation. This, right here, this mission was changing the world. It was real. It was crucial. And she was finally standing amidst the action!

Kingman noticed that he did not see any starving people from where he stood.

A slender woman dressed in a faint and generically colored, knee length flowered dress and flat sandals egressed the door of the closest of the schoolhouse-like building and approached smoothly. As she got close she developed a medium complexion, perhaps a bit darkened by the sun. Her face was friendly and a tad bony. The woman was probably in her upper thirties, and the dim-hued colors of her hair, dress, skin and her pale eyes contrasted little enough that it is unnecessary to itemize them to paint her picture. All in all, she seemed emotionally relaxed and physically featureless.

The woman stopped, and Kingman and Gwendolyn walked to meet her. She shook hands with them. "Hello, Dr. Dressel-Meier," she said in a friendly tone. "And you must be Gwendolyn. Welcome to the mission. We've been looking forward to your visit. I'm Sarah Greenwater, and I'll be taking care of you today and tonight. You can let me know if there's anything you need." Kingman held the door, and they entered the building. They found themselves in a large lobby that opened to several rooms on the side, with two doors at the far wall. Sarah continued, "Dr. Bok will—oh, here he is now," and she hushed.

A neatly dressed Dr. Florian Q. Bok, the director of the mission, was entering from the one of two doorways at the far side of the room. This was a very well fed man with a cheerful round face surrounded with thinning, slicked white hair and a matching close-cropped beard; the pink of his scalp and cheek were visible through the fibers. He wore oversized, old-fashioned tortoise shell spectacles and smiled with disarmingly crooked, rounded and variegated tan colored teeth. Gwendolyn assessed him as 'old.' He was in fact sixty-two years old and in robustly good health with the exception of his body's overall geometrical shape; his athletic decades were in the distant past. From his demeanor it already seemed unlikely this man ever put himself into a hurry. He moved leisurely, advancing with an expensive carved cane he did not need. Dr. Bok was dressed in a very light colored suit with a plain bowtie and white shoes. His relaxed walk, along with a projected impression of being about to speak, dominated the onlookers' attention and kept them comfortably off balance; Kingman and Gwendolyn both had a feeling that breaking the silence would be somehow an interruption, an affront to their host. For lack of alternative, everyone's eyes rested on Dr. Bok's forehead. Gwendolyn could not help but notice that he was sweating a bit, and that it must have just started.

The man was not emphasizing the fact that he had just awakened, but it was communicated by his walk, more suited to comfortable slippers in a plush apartment than casual leather shoes on a packed dirt floor. Finally he completed the few dozen steps from the door and introduced himself as the founder of the Wholesome Globe Project, a man quite happy for their visit. He would be their host, and of course if there was anything they needed they should just ask Sarah. He directed Sarah to make the two comfortable, and suggested that they start the tour in an hour or so. Sarah nodded agreement, and they proceeded through a door to the right of Dr. Bok's door as he remained behind and indulged in a slow, quiet yawn, leaning on his beautiful cane.

Sarah took the visitors to the nearby dormitory for the volunteers. The corridor was lined with quite spare rooms on either side; most of doors were open, and it appeared that individuals lived in some rooms, and others were vacant. Bathrooms with running water were spaced along the hall, three bathrooms serving perhaps twenty-five rooms. They stopped in the hallway. "Please be quiet," Sarah almost whispered, a mild rebuke to Gwendolyn's involuntary happy chatter as they walked along. "Some of our volunteers are sleeping now. Here are your rooms," she said as she stopped and pointed to rooms across the hall from each other, "so please feel free to freshen up and then we'll get a bite to eat before we take the tour. I'm sure you're hungry from the long ride. I know that long trip. I've done it a few times." Kingman paused and let Gwendolyn choose one room by entering it. Sarah suggested that she would come by in half an hour so they would have time for lunch. She turned and walked away. Gwendolyn felt too excited to rest, and she wanted to spend the half hour talking, but Kingman had other plans, and he kissed his daughter on the forehead, tossed his pack into his open room, and told her he had some things to do. He turned and went back toward the mission entrance, following Sarah's path.

Gwendolyn entered her room and put down her pack. The room was perhaps three and a half times the size of the bed, which was along the left wall, pushed up against the building's outside perimeter. A shallow doorless closet—really just an alcove with a bar for hanging clothes—extended from the foot of the bed to the hallway wall. On the neatly made bed was a stack comprising a few towels and some soap and other toiletries. A set of shelves was against the wall on the other side of the room. There was a single floor lamp in the center of the room, and a nondescript desk chair beneath the shelves was the only other furniture in the tiny room. The window was an opening without glass. The door opened into the hallway, as there was nowhere for a door to go within the room. Gwendolyn opened her pack just wide enough to pull out her traveling companion.

She was twenty years old and often traveled with her stuffed animal, a furry octopus she had found spilling from her Christmas stocking fifteen or sixteen years ago. Somehow, and nobody knew exactly by what route, the cuddly and warm-blooded critter had acquired the name Pyratticus Julius. It showed not only its age but signs of the battles it had endured during its long stay in her possession—the little beady eyes had been replaced more than once, and not always at the same time or with the same hardware. After some incident that left it half blind, Gwendolyn decided to leave out the missing eye, and she made a black pirate's eye patch for it; now the name seemed more justified, though the foppish grin belied any sinister aspect to this buccaneer. The creature was missing a couple of its legs; after the unfortunate incident in which this happened, details of which were long forgotten now, Gwendolyn's nanny had carefully performed surgery to close up the wounds so well that it could have been born six-legged. Stuffed animals de-fluff with age, and over the course of its life, the wickedly smiling, toothless beast had several times undergone operations to pull out its innards and re-stuff it with whatever makes stuffed animals stuffed. Gwendolyn disentangled Pyratticus Julius's legs gently, smiled and stroked her pet a few times, then lay on the bed for a moment with Pyratticus Julius under her arm. Accidentally and immediately she fell asleep.

It seemed just then that Sarah poked her head in through the open door and sweetly reminded Gwendolyn it was time for lunch and the tour. The girl woke up with a pleasant groggy feeling, sweating in the sun that was streaming through the window. She sat up, lifted Pyratticus Julius to her lap and rubbed her hair as her understanding of where she was materialized. She stood up, leaving the imaginary companion behind, and nodded silently. Sarah waited as Gwendolyn walked to the bathroom and splashed some water on her face. When she came out Sarah said, "Let's get some lunch. You must be hungry," and they started walking down the hall. Suddenly Gwendolyn turned back and went to her room. She picked up a disheveled Pyratticus Julius and carefully folded the struggling beast into her pack on the chair. Achieving victory over the last couple of tentacles, she closed the pack and stashed it under her bed.

Sarah and Gwendolyn walked outside and went into the adjacent schoolhouse-like building, finding a small cafeteria with food service on the side and some tables with stackable chairs in the center. As in her room, the windows had no glass. Two native women, one plump and one very lean, stood behind the food counters, watching them. A few people, foreigners mostly, were eating at the tables. One very thin and dark-skinned woman, a nun, was sitting in a chair in the corner with a rosary, eyes closed, lips fluttering as she said her prayers. She had an empty plate in front of her and a glass half filled with water.

Sarah and Gwendolyn chose their food as though they were voting in Moscow in the 1980s. The selection available was some sort of unidentifiable hot soup and bread; they both just selected bread and poured some water for their drinks. At Sarah's suggestion Gwendolyn dropped in the last few limp lemon slices from the nearby tray. They walked to an empty table and sat down.

Sarah paused for a silent prayer, during which Gwendolyn bowed her head and waited. Then Sarah pulled a small clump of pills from her pocket and downed it with a sip of water. Gwendolyn had been trained with a 'speak when you are spoken to' approach to life with her elders, and her education suppressed her desire to ask a zillion questions about the place. They began lunch in silence, but she bubbled with excitement as she ate her bread. Sarah asked her a few perfunctory questions, accidentally hitting on the subject of why Gwendolyn wanted to visit the mission, which ignited the girl.

"Helping people, that's what my whole family is about. That's Daddy's history, the Foundation. But so much of it is… I don't know, so removed, so regular. Office work. When I learned about this place I could tell you're doing the greatest thing anyone can do. I just wanted to, I don't know, see it and touch it. It's hard to explain. I mean, bread and water! I can't believe I'm here!"

Sarah was quietly ruminating a piece of bread, listening. After a little pause she spoke calmly and evenly. "I know what you mean. I felt the same way," she said with a mannerism the exact opposite of the girl's. "It's important to help people. We do a lot here, and it's sometimes difficult, I should tell you. And we're not perfect here…" She paused and looked at the last small piece of bread on her plate. "Sometimes it's just… difficult," Sarah looked down at the table, seemingly visualizing something or staring into a deep nonexistent pit. She snapped out of it and picked up the last piece of her bread.

"Exactly. It's hard. I bet it is. But nobody said it's easy." Gwendolyn was cheerful, excited.

Sarah's eyes went to Gwendolyn's face. They softened to a shallow smile as she reached over and put her hand on the girl's. "Of course, dear. Thank you so much for reminding me."

Just then Kingman came in followed by Dr. Florian Bok. Kingman walked over to a stainless steel refrigerator and noticed how dusty his reflection was, a situation he unobtrusively rectified as Dr. Bok motioned for Sarah to bring Gwendolyn over. Kingman, his eyes freed by the completion of his little task, noticed the praying nun in the chair in the corner as they departed on their tour of the mission. The group could see the administration building and a bit of the executive residence behind them on the left and a number of low buildings all around them. The long dirt hill was visible on the right. Up ahead, next to the hill, was the cathedral, easily the tallest thing in the mission save one smokestack. They saw a few people, mostly natives, moving between the low buildings with air gap windows as they started out.

The tour proceeded along the gently curving path. All the while, Dr. Bok kept up a monologue outlining the mission's mission and its history. He loquaciously previewed what they would see in the tour. "... so very difficult... the sort of suffering we deal with every day... generous people in the advanced world... convinced god has put us here..."

Kingman said, "I meant to ask you earlier. You call this a mission. From our conversation, I imagine you know what I think of religion."

Florian laughed gently as he piloted his cane along. "No, no. We are of course very private in some ways, but I can assure you we don't have a pope back there pulling any strings. There are some religious people here as volunteers, sponsored by their organizations. They're permitted to carry their lucky symbols only in their rooms, though we're certainly happy to have the help. And of course the funding." He turned his head to Kingman and smiled a confidential smile. "But they're strictly forbidden, for a variety of reasons, one of which is that I am largely in agreement with you, to discuss religion with our workers. They're here to help us alleviate suffering, that's all. They can do god's will if they want to, but they can't try to sell god's story. Rest assured our experience has made us careful, and we watch them."

Kingman nodded, but his eyes went to the cathedral. Dr. Florian Bok smiled. "You noticed that, did you? Well, that was here long before the rest of this place. Nobody is sure exactly how old it is or why it was here in the middle of nowhere. It is at least five hundred years old, maybe eight or nine hundred. What is it, my dear?" He was looking over at Gwendolyn.

Gwendolyn had started and stumbled momentarily. She had almost stepped on a lizard that moved just as she went to put her foot down. She was breathless both with fear of the horrible tiny monster and the thought that she had almost killed the innocent thing with her foot. Florian Bok put his arm on her shoulder and resumed their motion.

"Don't worry. They won't hurt you. Usually they stay off the paths anyway. Must be a particularly stupid individual creature." In fact, Dr. Bok was right. There were small lizards and insects around, but people at the mission had amazingly few encounters with them. They were almost unnoticed.

He turned to Kingman and continued, "The church was built by some sect of Irish monks but they're long gone. Hundreds of years. For as long as anyone knows it's housed a small colony of nuns. The locals have some mythology about them and believe them to be magic, and when the government first made this base, they made sure not to bother them. In fact, when we took over and converted the place we had to agree to feed them, get them supplies and so forth. They have free reign, but mostly stay in the cathedral. You'll see some of them walking around occasionally, but they probably won't talk to you.

"How many are there?" Gwendolyn asked.

Dr. Bok said, "We really don't know exactly. They all look the same, pretty much, and they're never all out at the same time. Twenty, maybe. Or perhaps just a half dozen. They're pretty secretive and we think a lot of them never leave the building. The others bring them food and so forth. They just pray all day, I guess."

"What an odd situation," Gwendolyn thought to herself.

"What an odd situation," Kingman said.

"An odd situation." Dr. Bok nodded.

Dr. Bok effused a monologue of meaningless syllables about mission trivia, occasionally pointing to this building or that. Nowhere did he mention any real logistical considerations or anything indicating the scope of the mission. They could see the barbed wire and the sparse, flat land outside the compound; ahead of them on this side of the runway stood a few almost windowless buildings. The cathedral loomed ahead, behind the nearer buildings on the right. They saw some few native workers dressed in faded clothing, moving slowly between buildings. Many were pushing carts stacked with boxes. A larger number of American or European women traversed the complex equally slowly, dressed in colorless undecorated dresses. The group could sometimes hear vehicles and activity on the other side of the buildings but rarely caught a glimpse of it. Sarah walked behind the others and sometimes seemed to be attempting to gesture urgency to passing workers.

Dr. Bok led the party on past the cathedral. More schoolhouse-like buildings slowly approached around the curve on the right. Dr. Bok led them toward a building's entrance, a wide garage type door that was rolled up to an open position. He told them that this was the medical service facility. "We don't really have a hospital here, but we do give a lot of medical attention to these unfortunate people."

They could see inside the building as they approached. The interior was a single large open area, with perhaps ten beds in a row on each side. Windows without panes let in light on the left and right walls, and a door was open on the far wall. There was a caged area with shelves and medicines and what appeared to be several industrial refrigerators and ovens at the far left. A native male worker was making some noise, banging and rearranging something near the far door. The group entered and stepped past some tall stacks of wooden crates on their right.

Gwendolyn's eyes surveyed the room. The beds were tidy and clean, and four or five beds had piteously undernourished native people in them. All were apparently sick, but it was impossible to discern the various afflictions from this distance, with the exception of two that obviously had broken legs. There were three white women and two black women working among the patients; within each of those three classifications the individuals appeared interchangeable. All were slim and dressed in beige shifts. Everything was freshly clean, despite the open doors and windowless windows and the dusty terrain. The white workers seemed not to notice the visitors, and the black ones appeared not to notice them overtly. The patients were oblivious.

The closest bed on the left seemed to be special, with more floor space around it than the others. The bed was unoccupied. It looked like someone had just left it. There were small pieces of aged medical equipment on rolling carts in the space around it. Along the wall behind the bed was a disorganized collection of portable equipment—small ladders, boards, tripods, light fixtures, electronic equipment and what Gwendolyn saw as silver umbrellas.

Dr. Bok, leading them as they entered, swung the group around the crates to their right. Gwendolyn had the feeling of entering a separate room when she came around the obstruction. A boy, a thin but hardly emaciated boy, perhaps five years old, lay in a bed with gleaming white sheets. He was curious and smiled at the attention of the group. At his sides were a white nurse and a black nurse who made way as Dr. Bok and Kingman stepped in near the bed. Dr. Bok walked around to the other side.

Gwendolyn could see that the child had a broken arm in a freshly constructed, old-fashioned plaster cast. She felt a mixture of emotions well up suddenly, and the bundle lodged itself in her throat as she looked at the smiling child. *Something is wrong with a world where a little boy can suffer so.* Dr. Bok stood watching her reaction. After a pause he knelt on one knee so gracefully that one could be forgiven for believing he had practiced it. The white nurse instinctively stepped back to afford Gwendolyn a better view. The boy looked at Gwendolyn, briefly directed his glance over her shoulder to Sarah then back to Gwendolyn. The white nurse reached around Dr. Bok and put an old-fashioned thermometer in the boy's mouth and stood by to catch it when he dropped it, which happened almost instantly.

The director spoke in a way that provoked Gwendolyn to glance over her shoulder to see if there was a crowd behind them all. "This poor boy only wanted to do what boys do. He broke his arm in the camp. And you might think he was doing something nasty boys do. Fighting, or heaven forefend, climbing a tree. No, none of them fight here—the caloric expenditure is too great. And we have no trees to climb. He simply was trying to throw one of these balls…" Dr. Bok, without interrupting his gaze at Gwendolyn's face, pulled a worn rubber ball out of a box next to the boy's bed, "… and his humerus snapped. That's what life is like here. That's what malnutrition will do. On top of the physical indignity—a corroding, rotting body—imagine the psychological pain of these people, especially the children. What child could ever understand his body is too frail to run and play?" He glanced at Kingman then looked directly at Gwendolyn again. "This." He looked at the happy boy then back up at Gwendolyn. "This is what we are here for."

All was still. Gwendolyn looked at the boy's face and the cast on his arm. He was happy, and he smiled to her and Kingman as the nurse whispered something to him in his native language. The thermometer, which had been replaced twice already, would have fallen had the nurse not guided it back in place. The incongruity of the happy suffering boy brought tears to Gwendolyn's eyes. She shuddered as she thought of the thousands of starving people and children at risk of grievous injury just because they were children. Then her mind tried to encompass the magnitude of the suffering here, and she almost collapsed. She quickly scurried out the garage door and squatted in the sun, where the boy was out of sight. From within her emotional cloud she could hear the rumbling of Kingman and Bok's conversation.

After a few minutes the group emerged from behind the crates. Gwendolyn followed along as Dr. Bok walked through the ward holding forth with Kingman, occasionally checking Gwendolyn's face or wafting a hand toward one of the patients. A little way along the walk Gwendolyn glanced back at the injured boy beside the crates. The nurse was starting to give him some ice cream, and he was smiling widely and wiggling in his bed to attain a more comfortable sitting position. Gwendolyn had a pang of distress for his certain but invisible pain as she saw him repeatedly using both arms equally in the squirm. Then she turned her attention to the director's tour. She only heard the more theatrical parts of the narration Dr. Bok was delivering to Kingman as she followed Sarah, who walked behind the men.

They exited the building and continued along the curve of the path. To their left the barbed wire fencing had receded somewhat from the edge of the runway leaving a thin strip of stubby vegetation. They saw some activity between buildings ahead of them as they walked by warehouse-like edifices. Behind and towering over the warehouses was the row of bare dirt hills and of course the cathedral.

They turned and walked toward another building with the standard garage door entrances on the nearest and farthest ends. Gwendolyn could hear some truck engines but saw no vehicles. Inside, there was energetic music playing, and the place was in motion. Rows of steel shelves on the visitors' right and left held a hundred or more boxes and crates, as well as pallets of supplies and equipment. Workers, carts and forklifts went about moving things off the shelves, arranging things, sorting things, placing things on the shelves, transporting things from one shelf to another at a relaxed pace. The far half of the floor was filled with an array of workstations—tables and machines manned by workers mixing foodstuffs. All the workers were thin and dressed in faintly colored shifts or slacks; all were natives save one tall, motionless man with black hair near the middle. He was facing away and talking to one male and one female worker.

On the nearby shelves Gwendolyn noticed packets of canvas and many wood rods. She saw large crates marked as flour and cheese. *Cheese. I wonder how long they can store that in a warehouse.* The building's far left quadrant was enclosed by a link fence with wide open gates. Shelves inside were lined with smaller boxes. There were a number of large industrial refrigerators or freezers in the caged area also. The right side of the building was largely composed of loading docks where maybe a half dozen trucks were parked, either loading or unloading. Gwendolyn noticed that in some cases the same truck was doing both.

They were walking inside and Dr. Bok was shouting his monologue, "...from the advanced world, but that is just a piece of the problem. As far as the physical goods are concerned, they have to get out to every single person who needs them. We serve over four thousand unfortunate individuals..."

Just then a man carrying a container of some kind of foodstuff at the far side of the building dropped his vessel and it broke open. A colorless mass of non-white, semi-solid, semi-liquid substance broke into globs on the floor. The dull thump from the drop reverberated around the room, barely audible above the music and banging and bumping of the activity, but the native workers heard it and many stopped their work, dismounting forklifts and putting down their burdens. They trotted to the scene of the accident and a small mob formed, with individual men competing to get close to the dropped material. Women stayed away. The white man went over, shouting. Sarah broke off from the tour group and also went to the crowd. Dr. Bok slowly glanced over his shoulder and, arms outstretched to catch and spin the shoulders of Gwendolyn and Kingman back toward the entrance, suggested that whatever was going on would be a distraction. "Let's go on out and continue the tour." They walked back outdoors, the director having thrown one hand over each of their far shoulders. Gwendolyn looked back and occasionally glimpsed the donnybrook over her shoulder, but Dr. Bok's face comprised an effective obstruction at this range. Kingman seemed not to care about the melee.

As they walked around rejoining their prior path outside the building, Dr. Bok said in a low voice, "It's a pity. These poor creatures cannot overcome their biological urges. We try to control our foodstuffs and get them to the needy ones, and we feed our workers perfectly adequately, though I wouldn't say it's a luxurious diet. But they just cannot help but fight for food. That broken container was more than they could look at. Human nature, I'm afraid, cannot be overcome by these poor people. To them it's not theft, not disorder, it's just what you do when you are near food."

Gwendolyn said, "But anybody can have an accident. He just dropped a heavy container he was carrying. It just slipped off his shoulder."

Florian Bok's face showed surprise, then that face lost its gravity, and he developed a soft, friendly smile. His voice acquired a low, soothing quality. "Of course, my dear. It was not his fault. I'm sure he was doing his best. Perhaps the fortuitous treat will help alleviate any guilt surely provoked when one's negligence causes such a mishap."

Kingman suddenly flared with potential anger, but he examined Bok's face and relaxed. There was no trace of cynical mockery in this man's face. He was just a man remembering his audience was a young, idealistic girl and adapting accordingly in his words. Kingman listened as he walked along hearing Dr. Bok continuing to gently, perhaps not disingenuously, soothe Gwendolyn's sensibilities. Though Kingman had had many similar interactions with his daughter, it was difficult to listen to someone else do it. Sarah had rejoined the group and occupied herself by alternately looking at the barbed wire and examining her sandals as Dr. Bok held forth.

Dr. Bok stopped walking, but not talking, and wedged his cane against his side with his elbow, the shaft suspended at an angle above the ground. His voice trailed off, and he stood with his hands clasped comfortably shielded from gravity on his convex belly as he silently looked over the top of his glasses at Gwendolyn. It was clear that Gwendolyn was satisfied. She was conversing with a great man. And she, Gwendolyn Dressel-Meier, had helped him understand and forgive a careless accident by one of his workers. Here was a man with huge responsibilities—think of all the starvation he was precluding. Perhaps he was so busy that his patience was inaccessible to him just then. She knew her father had trouble staying in human touch with all the people in his organization too; maybe it was an occupational hazard. Gwendolyn was happy with what she had accomplished here. She had tangibly helped the hungry by helping Dr. Bok assess a difficult situation. This trip had 'paid its freight' as far as she was concerned, even if she were to go home right now.

The group walked along the path within the main complex of buildings. The trail had curved away from the runway, and they were almost even with the hangars. The power plant's chimney loomed, launching grey smoke upwards into a curving filament in the sky, and a smaller plume of black smoke arose from a chimney barely visible past another hill or two. Gwendolyn asked why there were smokestacks. Kingman and Dr. Bok glanced at each other for a second, then Dr. Bok looked back at Gwendolyn and said, "We are not in Europe or America here. Things are different here. We have to make our own power, and any operation of this size has things it must get rid of. That smoke comes from the coal and the incinerator where we burn things that are not useful any more. We wouldn't just abandon things in the land around here. That's unfriendly to the environment of course." Kingman and Gwendolyn were satisfied with the explanation, passively and actively, respectively—and for different reasons.

Director Bok said a few words about the power plant, mentioning that a whole new, smokeless reactor 'which will help us keep the air clean' was almost ready to turn on. He told how they handled water (they had it brought in for the staff to drink, and had some very deep wells for the rest of the mission's needs). He cited some statistics about the four thousand plus inmates and their caloric and medical needs, and mentioned that he could only show them a sampling of the mission in the short time they had. Perhaps it was in fact time to go back and relax until supper time. He would be happy to answer more questions then. As he spoke, his arms again had found their shoulders, and he was turning the guests back away from the smokestacks. Sarah had already walked past the visitors and turned, and she was now ready to bring up the rear.

As the four started back Gwendolyn asked, "Can I see where you prepare the food that the people eat?"

Florian Bok seemed happy for the request. "Oh yes, of course. In fact I am delinquent for missing that on the tour. Here, dear, let's go back." He stepped next to Kingman and walked mildly faster, swinging his cane. Sarah stepped up beside Gwendolyn.

Presently they came back to the building where the brouhaha over the dropped food had happened just a few minutes before. The disruption was over, and the building looked much as it had when they had entered earlier. They followed Dr. Bok to the food preparation area, which was on the far side from where they earlier stood, and saw workers lined up at tables and vats, each putting together a mixture of a doughy material and nutrients of various sorts. Dr. Bok spoke loudly against the music and general noise of the place. "We have a group of scientific nutritionists developing the best possible nutriment for those in our mission. We take our donations from the advanced world, and we buy the ingredients. We bring it to the warehouses, and this room is one of our factories where we mix the balanced meals that our patients need." He was momentarily drowned out by a diesel engine as a full truck started up in the loading docks adjacent to them. A worker closed the truck's back gate, and the truck pulled out, turned to the left and drove away.

The visitors were momentarily thrown off by Dr. Bok's use of the word 'patient,' but they figured out that he meant the inmates at the mission. "Do they eat the same thing every day?" Kingman asked, and Sarah involuntarily nodded in response, though he did not see her.

Bok nodded as well, "Yes, we've found that's best. It keeps the logistics simple. All their meals are the same, and the amount of food served to each person is scientifically designed in light of the patient's size, age and health. Of course we can only apply this in an approximate statistical sense with so many patients flowing through."

Gwendolyn said, "So you keep track of every person's weight and age?" Kingman was doubtful. Gwendolyn thought it was a wonderful system.

"No, dear. I'm sorry if I gave you that impression. We are not a dairy farm where they apportion the food based on the cow's output. What I should have said is that when our people are out in the camps distributing food they allocate an appropriate amount based on the characteristics of the patients."

Gwendolyn understood the portions but was bothered by the monotony of the diet. She could not imagine herself eating the same thing every day. "The same thing for breakfast, lunch and dinner? Don't they ever get any milk or fruit? What about meat? " It seemed odd to her that the mission would not replicate the diet she had back at home in Vermont if they wanted to make the patients healthy. Gwendolyn could not imagine a life without milk, without fruit.

"My sweetness," Dr. Bok gave an understanding cock of the head and a minor smile. He brought his friendly and relaxed face within inches of hers and gazed into her eyes in a friendly meeting. "Most of these people have never tasted meat in their lives, certainly not in the last few years. They come to us weakened from hunger and disease. And finally, think of how you get fresh fruit from your supermarket at home. What happens if you buy two weeks' worth of bananas at once?"

Gwendolyn had not thought of the practicalities. Kingman and Sarah stood silently. "Well,…" Gwendolyn croaked.

"You see one of our problems. Multiply that by a thousand or more, and add all the others. Varying the food requires constant short-term fiddling to keep the nutritional level correct. Variety of diet would assault the systems of these poor unfortunate brothers and sisters of ours. It may sound hard to believe, but if you give a starving person a massive increase in food, if you don't control things, if you try to be too kind, you can kill him. The same is true for the idea of introducing foreign delicacies. It can upset his system. This is science." He paused as though waiting for the wobbling bag of fat under his chin to cease its motion, but went on before it stabilized. "Starvation is a very slow process. Yes, patients must be given Calories and nutrients. But haphazard attempts to do good without the proper scientific grounding is the most cruel sort of exploitation of the sick—exploitation just for the impatient caregiver's own feelings, not the true benefit of the patient. It is a very complicated issue, best left to professionals like us. " Despite his clinical tone, Gwendolyn was pretty sure she could see his eyes watering as he spoke.

Her own eyes welled up with tears as she thought of the starving people in the camp never even tasting ice cream. She buried her face in her father's chest and grasped his waist. Kingman stroked his hair where she had accidentally mussed it, and put the other hand on her back and whispered to her softly, swaying gently left and right as though she were a little girl. Florian Bok looked at Sarah, who returned the glance uneasily and looked back at Gwendolyn.

"Dear, would you please help us mix some of this nutritious food for the hungry children?" Dr. Bok's voice crept around her back and into her consciousness. She looked and saw him standing with an avuncular smile. Gwendolyn nodded, dabbing her eyes. "Come, come," he said, guiding her over to a work area. There were some small portions of unmixed food material in the work bins. The two native workers moved aside and watched as he brought Gwendolyn to take their place. She nodded to them as Dr. Bok spoke and gestured, guiding her as he ad-libbed through the simple activity required. She placed the last helping of a dough-like material into a bowl. Then she scooped several different powders onto it. Dr. Bok picked up a large steel spoon and handed it to her, nodding. She stirred and added some water from a flexible steel hose under his direction. The natives normally used the mechanical mixer and did the work much more efficiently, but the director preferred that Gwendolyn mix things by hand; he was correct in this.

All stood by silently as Gwendolyn mixed, with occasional splashes of water from Dr. Bok as he guessed at the target consistency. It was hard physical work, and she was flushed and sweating before he released her from her exertions, gently tugging her as a signal that she could stop now.

Dr. Bok nodded to the native workers, who stepped in and continued the work with the mixer as Dr. Bok turned Gwendolyn around.

"I think it is getting late," Dr. Bok's voice was gentle. "Let us conclude our tour, and we can get to know each other a bit later over our meal. So, please." His outstretched right arm instructed the guests to come generally toward him, and his straight left arm indicated the way they should walk. They went by, and he joined, bringing up the rear with Sarah.

The four walked back along the path and entered the building with the visitors' rooms. They parted company with the agreement that they would have dinner at seven o'clock. Kingman stood at Gwendolyn's door as she entered her room. She pulled a struggling Pyratticus Julius out of the pack under her bed and curled up with him for a rest, but not before carefully untangling and straightening his legs. Kingman said, "I see you're going to give your hexapod some rest," to which Gwendolyn's response was to roll over in a wiggling motion and face the wall, Pyratticus Julius clasped warmly in the curve of her stomach. She said, "Daddy, you know I hate that name," and rustled, seeking comfort as Kingman turned away from her door.

Florian's Insight

What are the ingredients for alchemy?

"Tell me about Vermont, my dear. I have so very many wonderful memories of New England from my law school days at Yuke University! Beautiful fall scenery, wonderful cruises on the sound, sailing on the lakes. Hiking in the woods. In a way I envy you. It's such a lovely place to call home. Do you go to a quaint little schoolhouse, one with a fireplace like in all the old paintings?" Dr. Florian Q. Bok sipped his drink and tilted his head slightly as he sat back in patient anticipation of the response from the California college girl.

Gwendolyn was mildly embarrassed that the good doctor had broken a silent spell in his conversation with her father and spoken to her. The girl's downward gaze left her empty plate and traveled across the corner of the table to the speaker. Her view lingered on Dr. Bok's hands, which rested in twin satisfaction under his gently curving suspenders, serenely covering the middle north latitudes of the orb that was his belly. She looked up at his face, a study in warmth and welcome. He sat expectantly, arched eyebrows surmounting a wide smile of rounded tobacco-stained teeth, his softly grizzled cheeks nudging his oversized glasses as he smiled. His suspenders and hands rose and fell somnolently, driven by the contented rhythm of his breathing. Gwendolyn noticed that the man's curved shape seemingly took on a more dramatic third 'depth' dimension when he sat. She glanced around the table and saw that her father and Sarah also awaited her answer.

Earlier as they had walked around the mission—the Professor—Dr. Bok liked to be referred to as the Professor—insisted on calling the Swazizibia operation a mission—Gwendolyn had spoken to the man frictionlessly, but her intervening nap and the current formal environment conspired to push her into her little-girl cocoon. The four dinner partners made an intimate group, but her congenital shyness with her elders ruled her actions. She was reticent as they sat in the beautifully appointed, windowless dining room with the fine furniture and elegant tableware.

The girl shyly delivered a diminished nod of her head, "Of course I do, we all do." She quickly looked at Professor Bok then at one and the other of the native servants standing in the corners behind him. The women were trying to avoid staring at the food on the dinner plates of Kingman and Dr. Bok. Gwendolyn looked back down at her place setting, then looked over at Sarah's platter; both were empty.

Sarah and Kingman were quiet now. Kingman gracefully took in a bit of soup. Dr. Bok replied, grinning, "You don't fool me. By now it's probably all been paved over. Replaced with the same stuff that covers the rest of America. Malls, rectanguhedular stores and office buildings. Stoplights. Gas stations. Worthless youngsters." He winked at the girl. "But some things never change, do they? I'll bet it's still cold in the winter. Ah, for the old days... but I suppose there's no return to the old time storybook New England, not even in Vermont, USA." His head shook, and his attention returned to his food. If it can be said that one with that shape can become straight, he straightened up in his chair and lazily considered in what sequence to resume his work on the pasta and steak. His hands were rousted from their comfort, and he launched an unhurried offensive on the carbohydrates.

Kingman lit his old-fashioned pipe. "Well, we've managed to find a few acres for the Foundation's farmhouse between all the schoolhouses and stoplights. Gwendolyn likes it just fine. I wish I could spend more time in front of the fireplace there myself. I'm sure she does too now that she spends all her time in California." He looked at her. "I'll bet you've missed your horses these last couple of years, honey." She nodded. "I knew it," he said.

Kingman puffed on the pipe and directed his gaze at Dr. Bok's eyes. The man should remember she was in college out west. Was he treating her as a little girl or just being the absent-minded, genial host he seemed? Kingman had not noticed it before, but Dr. Bok was wearing a gold 'IDIC' pin in his lapel. The pin and the smoke worked their influence, and Kingman dropped his hackles. He smiled at the completeness of the man's preparations—down to the level of quietly highlighting his endorsement of the "I'm Different—I Care" campaign. Just then Kingman noticed his own reflection in the gleaming silver coffee pot near his plate. He did a quick survey and smoothed his unruffled beard.

Dr. Bok, who was well beyond his respite from eating, nodded, and a stubborn flap of pasta disappeared into the corner of the man's mouth in a swimming motion as his head bobbed. He swallowed vigorously, and his nod grew more civilized with the freedom afforded by his victory over the troublesome edible.

Kingman spoke again, still directing his words to Dr. Bok but including Sarah as well, "Well, maybe we'll be able to host you there one day, maple syrup and all." His overt attention was not on his conversation but on his pipe, and he had the corner of his eye on the coffee pot.

Gwendolyn was oblivious to the fact, but it was a meaningless platitude in the conversation. In fact, her father knew that for Director Professor Dr. Florian Q. Bok there would be no visiting America anytime soon. That afternoon Dr. Bok had told Kingman why he refused even to travel on airplanes that could be diverted to United States soil for emergency landings.

Dr. Bok was born an American. He grew up and spent the first part of his adulthood in the states. After law school he had worked in a number of socially well regarded positions, shunning law practice and instead climbing the ranks in charitable organizations. During that time he had been awarded honorary doctorates from a number of universities, each of which was in commerce with his employer. Eventually he started his own charity, the Wholesome Globe Project, which had grown to a respectable size. About eight years ago the man left the United States and moved the Wholesome Globe Project's base to Brussels, and shortly thereafter to Zurich.

Since just prior to his departure he had been at risk of arrest in the United States. It would be preposterous to think that this cheerful man was evil—he was no criminal, certainly not by his own or Kingman's standards. And while Gwendolyn was unaware of his troubles, she would also find the idea of Dr. Bok as outlaw outlandish. The transgressions, which Dr. Bok outlined only sketchily and did not deny, were things he characterized a bit differently than his American tormentors did. All were related to the tax code, nonprofit organizations, accounting procedures and bank transfers; Dr. Bok termed them simply a cascaded sequence of misunderstandings. When he spoke of the subject with Kingman earlier today, he had added a few cordial epithets directed at the imagination-starved bureaucrats in the United States tax service. The problems were simply technical issues; Dr. Bok had no animosity for America; indeed he would enjoy traveling there if he were not at risk of being stuck in a federal prison. In a way he even understood the position of those who dogged him, prisoners of the letter-of-the-law that they were.

Here at the fancy dinner table Gwendolyn was uneasy. She was energized by being in Swazizibia where everyone was working so hard to alleviate others' suffering, but troubled to be sitting in a beautiful paneled dining area eating dinner in the elegant setting. She preferred to think about the mission outside, not the banquet in the room. Anything good she had ever done was only a warm-up, a rehearsal. The mission's purpose was to alleviate the misery here, and she could think of no worthier work on the planet. This afternoon's tour had engaged her imagination. She had no reason to understand that this happened by careful design, that Florian Bok had carefully managed and tuned it to his continuing estimation of her psyche, adapting in real time as they walked along. She recalled with satisfaction that she had helped prepare food today and how she had calmed the director when he was stressed.

Then she thought of the meal she had just eaten and felt queasy. Her throat tightened. She had been ravenous, but still... *They should have just given us crackers and water, or maybe some of that paste they give the Africans. I shouldn't have eaten the steak. I don't care how hungry I was.* This discomfort was a return of distress she had had earlier, while she was eating the meal. Her only method of dealing with her discomfort had been to eat quickly and avoid wasting any food, and so she had figuratively licked her plate clean.

As he calibrated Florian Bok, Kingman was cautious in his thinking. Though he had heard of the man, he just met Florian Bok today. He had already determined there were good reasons to guard himself in dealings with him. From their brief contact, Kingman could see that Bok was a sophisticated and energetic thinker. He saw the very prototype of an intelligent and skilled interpersonal operator willing to use fact, deception and any other available tools in the service of his goals; Kingman knew that any dealings with this sort of man must be structured to proceed independently of trust.

It bothered him to see his daughter being manipulated, and he was still unsure whether he liked Bok, but his nature impelled him to seek utility in every situation. He knew the man's approach to things differed from his own: Florian Bok was much more brazen and faster moving, while Kingman made his moves only after careful and sometimes very conservative consideration of others' reactions. For their livelihood, both relied on projecting the image of self-denial and magnanimous dedication to the good of the world, but they pursued their common task with very different styles.

Thinking about Bok, Kingman's mind turned over gently, almost automatically. He could not help but play some sort of one-sided mental chess game in situations like this. He puffed on his old-fashioned pipe intermittently as he mused. When one of the serving women finished refilling coffee cups, she conveniently put the pot in exactly the same spot and orientation as before. He indulged in a quick glance at his reflection; it did not occur to him to wonder if her positioning of the pot was in surreptitious recognition of his unconscious desires or just dumb luck.

What should Kingman make of Director Professor Dr. Florian Q. Bok of the Swazizibia mission of the Wholesome Globe Project? Sometimes in such situations he sought some sort of joint venture. That strategy had worked well enough over the years, often yielding a productive arrangement incrementing the Foundation's reach. Would it benefit the Foundation if the Wholesome Globe Project were brought into the fold of the organization's affiliates? Could Bok afford the levies? Could the two organizations capitalize on marketing synergies and increase their overall cash intake? What about risk? How would the public in America and Europe react, were the Swazizibia mission's inner workings, which he could sense clearly enough, though he had been careful not to ask inconvenient questions, surface? Could Bok be trusted to make sure they would not surface?

Much to think about. Kingman puffed his pipe in the room's quietude. The only sounds were those minor signals of Florian Bok eating with his calm composure and impeccable manners.

And what about Gwendolyn? What about his little princess? She had grown to be a prolific generator of simplistic and stubborn thoughts. She had an irrational attachment to this place, an attachment that developed over a year ago when she visited a friend's house and found a nicely produced, old-fashioned brochure describing the mission. Today's carefully crafted tour and her immediate affinity to Florian Bok had done nothing to cool her ardor for the place "well, at least for the facade of the place," Kingman thought as he drew some smoke into his lungs.

The dinner table was quiet; Sarah was placid by nature, Gwendolyn was shy, Kingman was pensive, and Florian Bok was feeding himself. As Dr. Bok neared the milestone of contemplating dessert he looked up and around the table. Gwendolyn and Sarah had cleaned their plates long ago;

Kingman's silver placement on top of the food on his plate indicated he was also finished. Dr. Bok took one last forkful of pasta from the mound still spilling onto the uneaten portion of his steak. His mouth masticating the payload, he lazily circled a finger in the air just above his plate and spiraled it out. This signaled for the two dinner servants to emerge from the corners and clear the dishes. He dabbed at his mouth with his napkin, and everyone sat quietly as the serving women cleared the table and brought around dessert and liqueurs. All the time she served, one of the two kept glancing over toward Dr. Bok's discarded plate, heaped with uneaten food on the dirty dish cart. The other eyed the smaller pile of food on Kingman's. Secret claims were being staked.

Throughout dinner Gwendolyn had tried not to look at the serving women, but now she was struck by their calm, dignified deportment. She watched the dark-skinned, tall, extremely thin and somehow serious looking workers bringing around the delicacies. Their motions and gait were distractingly slow but smoothly efficient. The corners of their mouths drooped. Gwendolyn could not help thinking they were twins, dressed in almost invisible grey print dresses. *Actually, all the native women dress the same. They all could be twins.* Silence, stillness in the corners and gentle bows of the head served as the women's tools for their one-way communication with Dr. Bok.

Gwendolyn had mixed feelings as she sat. This was her first trip abroad without her whole family. It was a product of her own initiative, and she was proud of that fact. The family often traveled to Europe, Mexico, Canada and the Caribbean on vacation, but except for a few long past trips to visit the Pyramids, she had never been to Africa. She was breaking new ground, and it was because of her own drive and commitment. But she was troubled by the reality of sitting so close to myriad people with malnutrition. When the four sat down for dinner, she had been surprised and dismayed at the luxurious food, and Dr. Bok quickly sensed her trepidation. He smoothly interceded and disrupted her attention by feinting a few unconvincing and effective words of thanksgiving to a god he had no other use for, skillfully injecting some reference to 'keeping up our strength that we may help others in crisis.' She was ravenous, and in her hunger this allowed her to suppress her concerns through most of the dinner, though she kept her portions small against the urgings of Dr. Bok. But without the distraction of her nagging hunger, she felt her discomfort welling up again.

Gwendolyn's conscious mind was unaware that she had seen only a façade of suffering on the tour that afternoon. She faced no acres of refugees, no death, no serious medical problems. Neither had she seen, nor missed seeing, happy departures of healthy healed individuals going abroad to resettle in their new homes.

She became aware of the mellifluous voice drifting from the Professor as he held forth for her father. "...and personally I loathe economics as it is normally understood. I feel it is, by definition, the study of exploitation. None of it does justice to the reality of actual economics. Now, we are a very poor country on a desolate and drained continent. Our history has been one of misery. I can tell you that whenever I leave here I have always figuratively been in tears for days. Nonetheless here we are. And here are these pitiful people...." Gwendolyn could not help but let her eyes dart up to the two servant women standing quietly here in the room. They betrayed no reaction; they may as well have been statues. "...situation. It will not disappear if the world looks away; it is real. And if you believe in any sort of benign deity you have no choice but to conclude his plan must contain some sort of significance, some kernel of meaning. He must intend that we do something. It is inconceivable to stand by uninvolved...." Gwendolyn's mind had been wandering, and his voice varied between background sound and meaningful monologue. There seemed to be some gist of goodness in his words. Still, they did not get her to relax so close to these miserable people.

Kingman was listening, perusing his old-fashioned pipe. He had been glancing at his daughter as Bok spoke and was concerned for her reaction to the rest of the discussion. The dessert carts came rolling around, one pushed by each servant, and Gwendolyn was grateful for the distraction from Dr. Bok's ongoing talk.

Now, dessert was one of Gwendolyn's favorite things in the world, and the Professor had made sure the staff concocted attractive, world class treats. She eyed the cakes and puddings rolling forth on the cart with firm resolve, her eyes moistened with salivation but her stomach knotted painfully at the extravagance. Four were at dinner; there were perhaps a dozen fancy dessert choices available. Gwendolyn found it inconceivable to indulge, and she meekly declined when offered her choice.

In fact, only the Professor accepted dessert. Kingman's pipe was sufficient after-dinner vice, especially when accompanied by the fine cognac he had silently selected as Dr. Bok expatiated. As for Sarah, it was hard to picture this thin woman considering dessert; in fact she had barely eaten any dinner at all and only cleaned her plate because the servants knew to give her very little.

Dr. Bok continued his speech, and too tired to de-embed his increasingly philosophical discourse, Gwendolyn became restless. The girl's discomfort was not lost on her father, and he understood that a detailed explanation of the sausage-making of the place would weigh heavily on her. "Sweetie, why don't you go and get ready for bed? We'll be leaving in the morning." She gratefully nodded and excused herself, picturing a quiet end to the evening with Pyratticus Julius. Dr. Bok made a complex wrist-and-finger motion, a command for the closest servant to escort her, but Sarah stood and spoke of her own need to get to bed early as well. She offered to guide Gwendolyn, and the servant bowed her head and stepped back to her corner as the two disappeared from the room.

Recovering from the cruel interruption to his rhythm, Bok resumed his lecture. "Every country must find its place in the world economy. We can pretend we are separate in this failing country, but it's an illusion. We have a position, either a status we construct or one that is assigned. China has spent many years participating in the world economy by exporting the fruits of slave labor. Arabia achieved its recent apogee with well-timed production of petroleum of course. Colombia supplies cocaine and coffee.

"One must be careful. A niche in the world's economy is powerful, and sometimes a trap. You see, when a country has found its groove it's difficult or impossible to shift focus and concentrate on other things, perhaps greater future industry. Colombia is an example, as coffee and drugs have cramped her ability to diversify into modern industries. Every country, even impoverished ones, has a habitat in the world economy."

Kingman played along, but did so with his usual tough skepticism. "So tell me, Dr. Bok, back to Swazizibia. How did Swazizibia gain entry to this world economy you refer to? If it participates, what does it supply? I mean no disrespect for all your work here, but I see nothing but a drag on the rest of the world as people disburse their treasures to you, resulting in no effect on the world except time moving forward." Kingman was no stranger to many features of the upcoming argument he envisioned hearing; in fact his own job often demanded he employ similar tools in talking to clientele.

Dr. Bok was happy with the turn of the conversation, believing he had precipitated the question. His face was becoming, if such a thing was possible, more pink and more round as he contemplated his answer. He was going from one of his home fields (dinner) to another (public relations), and his body was warming to the task, bathing itself in satisfied, fat-and-alcohol-sated blood. He greased his throat with a larger-than-normal sip of his cognac. His voice intensified. "Let me tell you, if they look back and judge that I've done only one thing for the world in this lifetime, discovering the answer to that exact question is my contribution." He paused and took another slow draft of brandy.

Like Florian Bok, Kingman thought he was controlling the conversation, and he was enjoying himself. Before Dr. Bok resumed, he said, "Please tell. And what is this great advance of yours? And to what do you attribute your insight, my friend?" He took a drink.

Dr. Bok sat unaware of the question; his brain was in serious transmit-only mode now. His jowls' oscillations damped at the departure of his animated motions as he focused. "In Swazizibia, before I ever even heard of the place, we used to mine quite a few minerals including gold. We were legitimate members of the world economy, poor as the peasants were. Well, that portion of this country was broken away, puppeteered by western governments and the industries it fed. The gerrymandered remnant we have left comprises all the parts of the original country that had nothing. Nothing at all. Just utter desolation and relative overpopulation. I say relative only because by any western standard, the population per square what-have-you is quite scant. We have excess people—that's just the way it has to be said. We are simultaneously sparsely populated and overpopulated."

"How could such a place become overpopulated?" Kingman asked. "I would think the population would be, if anything, dropping."

"I won't go into detail. I am not an expert on these things, and in fact am uninterested. But here is what I think happened. I think the hardening of borders and controls on the continent worsened the plight of the people. Life here has undoubtedly had a measure of intermittent starvation for centuries, but suddenly the population was forbidden to use geography as a degree of freedom in alleviating its problems, seasonal and otherwise. Droughts happen with painful and unpredictable frequency. Punctuate this with long periods of sufficient stability and outside food supplies to enable population growth, and it is not hard to imagine the evolution of the current situation."

Kingman stroked his beard. Unconsciously grateful that the lonely coffee pot was still on the table with Bok's dessert and their cognacs, he smoothed his hair also. Dr. Bok seemed to be making some sense.

"Our normal state is 'starving.' If we had a trademark it would be 'human misery,' and it would be a pretty complete description of the place." Dr. Bok paused for a breath, took a small taste of his liqueur and spooned in a mouthful of chocolate mousse, the delicacy he had selected from the dessert cart.

Kingman noticed Dr. Bok's unique way of holding the dessert spoon and brandy snifter in one hand, which allowed himself access to either without interfering with the other. No cognac spilled when he spooned, and his sips only occasionally influenced the ever-laden spoon in any disadvantageous way—and never to the extent of losing a gram of the precious, jiggly chocolate. Kingman was reminded of his admiration for a politician he had seen years ago. As a boy, Kingman was modeling an uncomfortable suit for adults at some fancy gathering, and he had entertained himself through his boredom by watching the smooth man, who was able to manage a cigarette and a cocktail with one hand, all the while keeping the other hand available for stroking the silk dresses of the ladies as he strolled through the room in conversation.

Florian Bok waved for the servant woman to refill both drinks. "What can give meaning to all this suffering, this starvation?" Dr. Bok directed his eyes to an elevated plane, suppressing a minor burp. "This is where my personal study of philosophy and ethics has come to fruition. I have synthesized something out of this morass of misery. Something out of nothing." Just then he had to put down his cup for the brandy infusion. Both men had been running low on cognac, and now that was being rectified. "The crystallized insight that there can be some good—some *actual benefit*, not just grudging accommodation—from all this suffering. That insight. *That* is my singular contribution. The world need not waste the pain and misery of those starving here. And this is independent of whether we actually cure the situation." He was emphatic and enthusiastic. The fat-filled wattle beneath his chin underscored his pride with proud resonant vibrations along two oblique axes.

Kingman had started to fall under a spell. This was complicated, but there was something here. He had forgotten to smoke and drink, but he remembered now and did some of each without degrading his full attention on Dr. Bok during the latter's theatrical pause.

"I have instituted a way to transform the raw material of human suffering into good. And I've done more. I've shown how to convert it into actual capital in the world economy. Think Purgatory. Here at the mission, we have given Swazizibia a valuable export for the first time since the gold mines. I have made Swazizibia a full participant in the community of nations, transforming it from a helpless parasite into what can legitimately be called a nation. It now has a valid claim on its economic place in the world hierarchy. The country's balance in trade, by any rational mathematical standard, is highly positive; more wealth enters our possession each year than leaves.

"You may ask, how could the country export anything real when it has nothing, when it cannot feed its own people? In fact the computation is simple: Swazizibia exports nothing tangible. Zero. Yet every year we get hundreds of millions in income from the rest of the world, much of which is safely stored in Swiss banks. I am responsible for all this."

Now he paused, one suspects, for dramatic effect. Dr. Bok always loved an audience and especially enjoyed performing for a high level visitor like Kingman. He quietly ingested another, the last, spoonful of mousse. The cognac swirled briskly but maintained its respect for the snifter's orifice as it traveled with the spoon. After savoring the entirety of the moment and allowing the mousse to melt on his tongue, Dr. Bok chased the delicacy with a warm and sweet sip of his drink.

Kingman would have asked, "What is this valuable export?" several times by now, but he was enjoying the theater and knew an answer would come only in Dr. Bok's own good time. Throughout, he sat puffing on the pipe, arranging the tobacco and fire in it. Occasionally he sipped cognac, which never again verged on bottoming out, as it was carefully attended by the servants.

"My great contribution, then, is this: we can export a massive supply of valuable intangibles. They are no less real than all the intangibles the advanced world argues over: patent rights, workforce skill, films, ladies' fashions and so forth. ..."

Kingman sat against the back of his chair. Despite the minor distraction of a dab of chocolate on one of Florian Bok's cheeks, he was captivated. He was about to grasp Bok's line of thought, and he was developing a genuine admiration for the creativity of his new acquaintance. His mind came alive and oscillated between following Bok and forming proto-thoughts about practical matters regarding ways to harness the man's creativity for the Foundation. Mayhap they could indeed do something together, their organizations.

"... in fact, our output, impalpable as it is, is certainly more important than whatever is judged to be in fashion for abstract economic output in the west. They need us." Dr. Bok abruptly froze, silently looking at Kingman. Dr. Bok's spoon and snifter stilled; the brandy within obeyed as well.

Kingman was enthralled, but his mind was not quite apprehending the concealed concept yet. He could sense something coming. It was something beautiful or powerful, but the dots were not quite connecting. He did not answer the silence; he sat forward with his elbows on the table—a very rare posture for this man—as he tried to conceive the missing component in his understanding. But he said nothing.

Dr. Bok continued with the crux of it all. "We have identified a need and a product that fills the need. It's that simple. I have a commodity that is more valuable per ounce than gold, a commodity that, by definition, cannot be supplied by the advanced world. Only by us or a similar country. Even if the United States had no iron mines and had to buy iron, there is always the possibility that some of the element would be discovered domestically, and you could stop importing it. But this product to which I refer, this thing that Swazizibia can supply, cannot ever be produced domestically in any of the advanced countries of the world, at least not so long as they need it. And there is a universal need, universal not in the sense that every individual person requires it but in the sense that every large group, every country in the advanced world, contains many who need it."

Kingman's excitement and anticipation showed uncharacteristically. Florian Bok had been enjoying the situation, delaying his unveiling to savor it, but he finally lifted the veil.

"In the comfortable countries people go through their lives knowing that others are starving and falling to diseases that should be part of the past. It eats at the heart and soul of any normal human to enjoy security and comfort while cognizant of the fact that others are sick and suffering, afflicted by maladies and economic problems long ago conquered.

"To capture the essence of my concept, were I to discuss this with a large potential donor I would ask this: Would your god impose all this suffering without reason? I think not. I believe the misery here is meant to alleviate your torment—that pain you undoubtedly feel every time you think about these poor people while you are so comfortable."

Kingman felt a glimmer of the idea, but it was as yet indistinct, somehow a foggy, unconnected argument. Dr. Bok obliged. "So for Swazizibia, to put it succinctly: what we have is suffering people; what we export is peace of mind. And we get paid for it. Donations. Since I have run this mission we've exported an awful lot of it. We give people in the advanced world an opportunity for respite from the nihilist depression so common in successful nations." He raised his glass and sipped, and Kingman lifted his own snifter thoughtfully.

If Dr. Bok's story was the pieces of a jigsaw puzzle juggling in the air, they abruptly dropped down fully assembled on the tabletop as Kingman swallowed. He suddenly grokked the idea of what Swazizibia sells, though he did not understand the theological portion of Bok's argument. "Indulgences. You sell indulgences."

"Not exactly. A cynic may think it an indulgence, just like the old kings got from the pope for their transgressions. Lord knows the people in the advanced world feel they daily commit crimes against the planet, against the other people—it's almost a definition of what the advanced world is. But no, it is not an indulgence we supply. We are in no position to forgive sins, nor to send people to heaven. We rely on their own consciences for all that. We simply make available an avenue for self-improvement to those who need it. People in the advanced countries feel they must 'do their part' for others; they are sure they are failing in this. We help them fill a need they have, a need generated only because we exist as we do. A need for which we can export the cure only because they exist as they do.

"An economist who is also an expert psychologist could undoubtedly tell you that this allows the gross domestic product of the advanced country to increase; its wealth will grow due to the psychic power of the healthier human mind and its effect on a nation's economy. Therefore I claim our product grows the global economy, not just our own. And as a citizen of Swazizibia, I think I speak for our patients in saying that we should be happy to know our suffering helps people on the other side of the world, just as those in the advanced part of the world are undoubtedly happy to think their donations are helping us here."

Kingman, enthralled, said admiringly, "Okay. Not indulgences. Interesting. If what you say is true, you've identified a real need, a need born of the differential levels of success across the world. A need born exactly of your ability to address it, a need resident only in those who have the ability to pay for your product. Perfect symmetry. Perfectly efficient design. Arbitrage between cash and misery in far-flung corners of the globe. A win-win!"

Dr. Florian Q. Bok smiled, basking in his visitor's esteem. His face beamed with roundness in a silent boast of his personal creativity and effectiveness.

Dr. Bok's controlled passivity made Kingman aware of his own undisciplined state. He replayed his words mentally and realized this sort of talk was beneath his dignity; the man never engaged in spontaneous conversation outside his own family—no, more specifically, outside his conversations with Gwendolyn. He took a breath, dropped his shoulders, knocked his pipe against the table and slowly fiddled with reigniting some tobacco. Leaning back in his chair, placing his pipe in his mouth he pronounced in a lowered voice, "And of course you are compensated for your valuable service." Dr. Bok could not help layering a thin, sly smile over his existing radiant expression. Kingman questioned in mock interview tones, "So tell me, Florian, how did the idea come to you?"

Florian Bok cleared his throat and scratched distractingly close to the chocolate smudge on his cheek. "For decades due to my line of work I traveled and observed an impoverished world with numerous quasi-static crises. They never ended; in any case if one did end by some miracle, another just popped up somewhere else. Famines, war between struggling tribes, tsunamis, droughts. Everything. Volcanoes. And when you see the people who have dedicated their lives to helping the victims, well… you just have to wonder who could give themselves to such a thankless and endless job. They're like suckers. And don't get me wrong, most of those suckers, especially the ones far from home, you have to take your hat off to them." He smiled as cleverness surfaced within. "And then you have to scratch your head. They don't get it. It will never end. Even if they get enough food supply somewhere and manage to stabilize a whole country, which they won't, there will be an earthquake somewhere else. Then a war. That's the world, and none of them know it."

Kingman nodded understandingly, and Florian continued. "And the other side, the bigger part of my job, was fund raising. Something rattled around in my mind for quite a while before it crystallized. The world has complementary needs in search of each other. Reciprocals, two sides of a single coin, as it were. In search of each other but out of sight of one another. Yes, a coin, a single golden coin.

"Suffering impoverished people with simple needs—like enough food to get through the day. Suffering rich people with complex needs—like the desire to feel clean in their privilege. Exact inverses. Yin and yang. If I could construct an interface between the two, a transfer layer that mates each side properly with the other, I could be in a wonderful position. I suppose I'd heard of Swazizibia, but it was just another anonymous famine-stricken war zone to me.

"When I started the Wholesome Globe Project the idea was already resident in the back of my mind. It took several years of back-burner scheming as I grew the organization, but I was intent on somehow engineering this transfer layer machinery and making it part of the Wholesome Globe Project. When I got a good vision of the details of how it could be done I looked all over the world and found a number of candidate locations. Thinking about the reality of spending quite a bit of time somewhere clears the mind wonderfully when it's half a world away and always raining. Or when it's lodged between cannibal tribes. Or in the middle of a desert. I decided Swazizibia is the best compromise, and the intervening few years have proven I was right. It's relatively convenient to my home base in Switzerland. Starvation, the most intense form of suffering, is well established here. We have a great climate. Other African candidates would be intolerable with desert or monsoons. The demography in this part of Africa is right for accessing the heartstrings of the average person in the advanced world. There was already an old military base here with an airstrip. And that oddball cathedral lends some mystery and is great in all the marketing materials. It's perfect here.

"If I had one complaint, this place is a pain in the neck to travel to. Well, and there is always the instability that comes from the fact that the country is in incessant war. You are actually in a war zone right now, but it's mostly in other parts of the country at the moment. Just as a diamond mine would be at risk, we are aware that we attract attention, and we are always at some risk of being overrun by shortsighted Neanderthals. On the other hand, the bad guys can take over a diamond mine and still have the diamonds, so the government, at least, has some interest in keeping us going. Golden geese are valuable but fragile, something well worth considering.

"I've transformed the Wholesome Globe Project into that transfer layer I mentioned. We have streamlined things, and this is almost our whole operation now, other than some administrative activities, banking and the like. I have closed down many smaller projects, and the organization is much simpler to run." He stuck his thumbs under his suspenders in pronounced satisfaction and overt comfort.

Kingman said, "I see. But if life has taught me anything it is this: an idea is nothing. And is it an idea at all? How is it really different from what we already do? My foundation does the same thing in lots of places. We work on eliminating poverty, suffering. And we're set up to pump money through our machinery, and we don't answer to anyone. We make our donors feel good. People are well disposed to the whole thing; we exist in a taxation system so tailored to our needs that it allows donors to deduct appreciation they never even realized when they contribute to us. I know this. I make my pretty good living at it, just as I am sure you do. I mean, you put the bargain quite clearly, but in fact aren't there already hundreds of organizations doing the same thing, more or less unwittingly or even deceptively? What's new about any of this?"

Bok paused in silence for many seconds then answered, ignoring the reference to his personal financial situation. "You've asked a lot here. I'll try to answer. Firstly, as to why this is not just 'more of the same' as other charitable work: there is no charity in the world advertising what I have just described. And of course I don't either. But I know it and they don't.

"There are surface similarities. Yes, sometimes you promote your haphazard set of disjointed efforts, and everyone claims to work to end suffering. Yes, you all extract money from, thereby stimulating satisfaction in, your donors. The big charities run the gamut, but we're not like any of them. You, for instance—we're much more than a clearing house like you. We don't just farm out our delivery to missionaries or do-gooder volunteers or traveling bands of doctors and such.

"And those do-gooders. Those volunteers. What a life they have in the business! They leave their homes and in many cases, their families. I've seen them all over the world. They come to Africa and sleep in huts and try to change the very geography of the place, try to help the native population become something it cannot be. They work themselves to the bone. They cry themselves to sleep. And when they finally give up, someone else comes to take their place. Places like America and Europe have an inexhaustible supply of these people. They come to Africa or wherever, thinking they're going to eliminate misery. I've met some who have been around here for decades. It's been their life's work. Can you imagine? Them—they're the ones who do nothing but slide time forward, not me. No. We're different. We don't put people through all that."

For an instant Florian Bok looked almost empathetic with those he described. But he recovered. He took a breath and said, "A lot of our volunteers are like that when they arrive. We try to make it easy on them, try not to push the hopelessness in their faces. If they've already been on a tour of duty somewhere else we simply don't accept them here. They should go back and work again at a place where people are killing themselves to accomplish the impossible. Or better yet, stay home and do something with their lives. We can't take them. It just wouldn't work out for them or especially for the others who have to be around them.

"So we're different from the other organizations. If you look carefully at what we say, technically we never, ever claim that we are eliminating poverty or suffering. You and I know it absolutely cannot be done. And my lord, if we succeeded at it, we would all have to find something else to do to earn that nice lifestyle you just referenced. We don't perform magic, but we can legitimately say that we feed people. We have a well designed machine in place, all the way from ground zero here to the internet to the bank."

Kingman was listening patiently, though the explanation seemed little more than an advertisement for the Wholesome Globe Project.

"Secondly, we have tackled the worst problem in its real form. None of the other charitable organizations in the world has an understanding of the steady state nature of the misery in places like this. Therefore none has optimized its structure to be efficient in the light of it. No, existing charities have all sprung from the old ad hoc 'intention to do good' model of asking people to drop money into a hat. They act as though they believe that if they just feed people every day, then one day something will change, and hungry people will stop arriving. As if Sisyphus were only some sort of mythological construct, not a high fidelity representation of reality."

Kingman's face betrayed a vague unfamiliarity with the legend of Sisyphus, so Dr. Bok digressed for a minute and told the story of the man condemned for eternity to roll a boulder up a slope, almost reaching the top before it breaks free and rolls back down. "And it's all because the guy thought he could outsmart the gods themselves. It's reality. We don't fight against the gods' designs.

"I looked at Swazizibia. Yes, there are too many here. Yes, people are starving. And there are impediments to our efforts. Our work is burdened and attenuated by corruption and losses at every step of the distribution chain. But I have my own business model, and it accepts these realities as part of the system, while keeping the public trust by keeping the public thrust of ostensibly doing good."

Kingman could not help but think that little things like the adverb 'ostensibly' spoken out loud were figments of the cognac and Florian Bok's relaxed stance at the end of the day, symbols that Bok was unguarded in Kingman's presence. Indications that Bok trusted Kingman.

Dr. Bok continued, "Thirdly, I have discerned the true moral justification for transfer of resources from the comfortable western societies. I claim to increase the world's economy. Ask any other charity if they make that claim. I've clarified a reality: the engine of the charitable act is the need of the donor, not that of the recipient." He took a sip of his drink.

Kingman asked, "What are you talking about? If someone didn't need help you wouldn't have donors."

"Yes, there must be a correlation of the two needs; the donor must perceive that it is of value to him to address some need of the recipient. And once in a while the world encounters some happy coincidence where both needs are met and everyone goes home happy—think of a bone marrow transplant. But the recipient's need is the catalyst, not the actual cause of the action. The impetus for the transaction resides entirely in the donor. This is unrecognized, at least publicly, by every other organization in our field. Of course I'm discreet about how we handle this knowledge. But our awareness has allowed us to design a system optimized for reality. We perform our duty without the distortions inherent in a system designed by those with a more wishful view of the way the world is. We're more efficient at what we actually do.

"So you see, I've provided a marketplace without the overt pretense that cripples everyone else. I developed the economic formulation of the basis for steady state operation of an organization like mine. Unlike others, we recognize that we will continue to exist where the population is distressed, and no pretending will change that. Could the world's resources fix tiny Swazizibia's hunger problems? Certainly. Will they? Certainly not. We exist in this reality. Others do not."

Dr. Bok sipped some brandy. Kingman sat quietly, ignoring the other as he rolled the man's revelations around in his head again and again. After a bit he asked, "So, you plan for no improvement in the situation. Won't that bother your donors?"

Dr. Bok said, "I don't think so, not if they don't think about it. And our history bears me out. They're dispersed individuals, corporations and government offices. They have a need to contribute to us, and lord knows I don't try to put a damper on anyone's motivations. Our private understanding of steady state is just that: our own confidential assessment. I think your question shows just how revolutionary this whole idea is. You have not understood. I'm filling their need to perceive themselves as helping, not their need to end starvation. The latter need does not exist, but they don't know it. They still feel its effects—the human mind is an incredible thing."

Kingman sat, skeptical but curious. He took a few puffs on his pipe.

"Why won't they be upset by steady state? Think of it this way. When a young child could first discover there is no Santa Claus—let's say the parents inadvertently left some presents somewhere in view a few days early—why does he not immediately jump to the conclusion that Santa Claus is a horrible lie perpetrated on him for years by his supposedly loving parents?" He paused and let Kingman think. But between the alcohol, creeping exhaustion and the sheer speed and sophistry of intellectual exchange, Kingman's brain could not follow in real time. Dr. Bok answered, "The reason is this: he's not looking to debunk a familiar and comfortable concept. He will accept any cockamamie answer with only the slightest plausibility. 'Santa wanted to make sure not to forget our house this year, so he sent an elf to deliver this stuff early, just in case. But it's a secret. Don't tell your father.' Or, 'He knew he couldn't fit this into the chimney because he isn't magic enough for this year's stuff. So he came by early and left it in our garage.' That's good enough. Santa Claus has been spared the gallows by the flimsiest possible explanation! People are not looking to find out that they're helpless to help, that they've been throwing their donations away all this time." He smiled shrewdly. "Of course, I'd beg to differ as to whether the contributions have been wasted."

Kingman lightly nodded; though he would need more thought to grasp everything the man had said tonight, it sounded believable. And perceptive. "Bok is good," he thought.

"So it's a conceptual problem, our inability to change the situation, but it's not a real one in the sense of something that will impact our cash flow. But I'm glad you asked about it. It comes down to something very, very basic. Reality is not the building block for understanding. In the world there are two separate things that most people don't distinguish: perception and reality. Only one of these is real, and that is perception. I live in the real world—that of perception."

"Hmm," Kingman rubbed his eyes. He was tired now. He rearranged the tobacco in his old-fashioned pipe and quietly took a few drags on the instrument. Fatigued as Kingman was, he put forth effort toward understanding what Bok was telling him. The reality that perception surmounts reality captured something Kingman had never consciously perceived, though in reality it had long been a guiding principle of his life. He struggled with bringing it forward in his mind.

Dr. Bok continued, "Individuals, communities, and even nations can act only in accord with what they perceive, not in some scientifically-derived fashion of following supposed physical laws. A few minutes ago I mentioned that I hate the classical understanding of economics. But experience in the world has shown me that economics, more than any other discipline, is reality, it defines what actually happens. Collective perception and the consequent actions are, actually, 'economics.' Economics, not physics, is thus the true basis of scientific study. 'Perception as the determinant of what happens,' you could say. Reality."

Kingman crumpled into a confused mental exhaustion. He was only catching a portion of Dr. Bok's speeches now.

Florian Bok drained his cordial glass with enthusiasm. As the servant approached to refill it he continued, "Countries can try to mask it with collective action or with praise for the greedy. But the one reality in a world of men is economics, and that is driven exclusively by perception. In fact, economics defines the real world in the sense that every human interaction, from the most personal decision to international declarations of war, are driven by it. At a more easily perceived level, mass shortages, economic bubbles and booms, such things are economic realities that everyone understands are figments of perception. Not physics encompassed in Newton's laws or Maxwell's equations." He had been taking ever larger drags from the bottomless cognac snifter. He did so again now; the servant stood at the ready.

Florian Bok surfaced from his brandy glass. "And so let's understand perception and economics. Swazizibia has thousands who die each year from starvation, and many more die of preventable disease. The population replaces these people. In fact, one effect of my mission here is likely an increase in the country's population by the exact number in my camp, if you think about it. There's an inexhaustible supply of raw material for my operation. But consider this: I don't need a huge supply. The donor in the advanced world strongly believes that one death to starvation is too many.

"While our communications show blurry masses of people in the background to elicit donations, the simple fact is that the human mind cannot perceive a large number. Psychologists will tell you that numbers become abstract after a very small level, maybe three. Maybe five. Certainly a marketing display of one or a few carefully chosen unfortunates is at least as powerful as one showing a thousand from a larger distance. Or a million. Perception is reality."

Kingman was intensely interested, despite the weight of his eyelids, a purely physical reaction to the reality of the exhausting trip and the things he had ingested. All this dulled his perception.

It was a lot to take in. Dr. Kingman Q. Dressel-Meier was a man clever by any standard, and he had demonstrated so in wide-ranging societal contexts from scoring well on tests to supercilious suppression of suspicion by skeptics to extraction of donations from the most unlikely sources. But the late hour, the speed of Dr. Bok's animated delivery, his recasting of the foundation of professional charity—a foundation Kingman believed he understood for all these years—these were conspiring to leave Kingman behind. And his current bodily state militated toward a limit on the effectiveness of his mental processes. He puffed on his pipe, unable to speak meaningfully on the subject.

Florian Bok had abruptly stopped talking, and now he emptied his glass again. He put down the snifter, exhaled, and waved away the servant woman as she approached with more. Then he sat, hands folded gently at their home latitude. Director Professor Dr. Florian Q. Bok was satiated with his dessert and after-dinner drink. Dr. Bok's revelations echoed around in Kingman's exhausted mind like the disobedient balls in some silly child's maze game; he was not capturing the gist of all that Dr. Bok said. But at some level he was energized, and he wanted to get the most out of the meeting. He shook himself, sat up and summoned his focus. "Interesting. Tell me again how this allows Swazizibia to participate in the macroscopic context of world economics."

Dr. Bok was patient and comfortable. One could develop the impression that he would happily talk for hours. "Let me summarize. Now, for the first time since its partitioning, I have allowed Swazizibia to participate as a respected, contributing member in the world economy. It is not a standard textbook case based on crop production or mineral exploitation. It is not founded upon some slave driver with a whip beating factory production out of his workers.

"Think about how the understanding of the reality that perception is central and reality is peripheral relates to our country's economic state. Our single exportable product relies on the very fact that reality is simply whatever perception makes it into. We ship something that can only be perceived. Well, we don't actually ship it; if it were a reality-based product we would ship it. We supply it, we make it bloom in the minds of those in our market. We make them perceive it. And pay for it. For both our benefit.

"Based simply on perception and feelings we have created Swazizibia's first export since the mining days, and the world's first explicit, if quiet, instance of optimized capture of economic value from unavoidable large-scale suffering. I have been able to develop an actual economy here. There are dollars circulating in this country buying gasoline, providing food and entertainment for the rich, doing everything real money does. It is real money. And as I told you before, the increased satisfaction in the developed world increases their economic output as well. That's real money too."

Kingman nodded. He had learned a lot over this dinner table tonight. He felt he understood as much as he could for now; clearly he would need some more time to cogitate and mine the finer points. He exaggerated, "I think I see it all. Seems like you've really built something here. I have found this trip educational, and I wish you the best. Gwendolyn thanks you too."

He stood up with a yawn and glanced at the servants, then stretched his arms. Bok hesitated in his comfortable chair, then stood and agreed with Kingman's yawn and movement. He made a final spiral gesture to the expressionless servants, then he picked up his cane and directed Kingman out the door, following behind. Their parting impended, as Dr. Bok would be asleep when Kingman and his daughter left at the crack of noon tomorrow.

The servants gingerly approached to clean up the napkins and remaining dinner detritus, their eyes glancing to the doorway and back. The women slowly orbited the table, and each lifted one of the empty brandy snifters, not yet daring to touch any leftover food. Then the woman at Dr. Bok's place lifted the little mousse bowl and quickly licked it clean. As the voice of the men in the hallway faded with distance "… and maybe we can do some work together…" both women moved toward the beckoning dinner plates piled on the cart.

Cocktails and Camaraderie

Will we have order or chaos?

D r. Kingman Q. Dressel-Meier stood quietly by the door and surveyed the activity. Though he hated the stuff, he accepted a glass of champagne from a passing tuxedo-clad waiter. Right now this ballroom here at the Abraham Cornwallis Hotel in New York City held the robber barons leading the better part of a dozen of the most respected universities in America, along with their chief financial officers. Kingman had selected the group for prestige and its raw form: wealth. The universities' assets dwarfed those of the richest men in the world. He smiled as he mulled how he could command attendance so reliably every year. He watched the interactions of the guests and spouses here at the pre-dinner reception, and he could not help feeling that these tycoons of the intellectual world were his lieges, even as he bordered on wondering if that would change after this year's meeting. "No, they'll stay with me," he thought with genuinely cordial contempt. He sipped the expensive sour liquid in his hand.

The hotel was owned by Cornwallis University, and it was Kingman's favorite gathering place in all New York. The service was the best in the world, and sections of the large complex were remodeled every few years. The upgrades usually pushed the decor farther into the past, as some region of the hotel was reconstructed to mimic James Clerk Maxwell's estate in Scotland or the Mediterranean palace retreat of the famous queen from the middle ages—upgraded, of course, with twenty-first century plumbing.

Most of the Emerald Vine universities were represented here. Halford, Yuke, Quinston and Pennumbria formed the core of that elite group, and Kingman spotted an irregular circle of jovial conversation containing their presidents and their spouses. Cornwallis University was included by courtesy—the annual event was always hosted at the fine Cornwallis Hotel, and besides, the university was technically an Emerald Vine member. Darthmoor, also in attendance, accompanied Cornwallis in the peripheral reaches of the Vines present.

For most of its history the Emerald Vines had contained the country's richest and most prestigious schools. However, a number of other universities had amassed large endowments and the concomitant scholarly prestige to be recognized as members of the academic elite. Some of these schools were naturally included here in Kingman's group. Stambridge, the University of Cathargo, Embry and Rose were present today.

One outsider seemed an awkward fit when its history was compared with the others: Massasoit Technology Institution was located only a mile from Halford, and its past had centered on science and technology before it evolved into the top tier of prestigious universities. For the first century and a quarter of its life, Massasoit had had a difficult time compiling enough esteem—psychic oxygen—to nurture its reputation in the higher level academic circles, a predicament exacerbated by the fact that the school was not founded until the latter half of the nineteenth century. But then a few presidents ago, the school settled on the strategy of building up its cash position and deemphasizing its focus on science.

The institution redirected its resources and fought hard, eventually graduating from the leader in the 'man discovering and harnessing nature' arena to one leader among many in the 'man harnessing man' disciplines. Its transition away from technology was incomplete, but sufficiently advanced that the school had become recognized as a top tier educational organization. It now concentrated on the most highly evolved human disciplines: film, oppression studies, law, 'social justice,' mass media, practical economics and politics. A number of famous faculty members kept the school's name in front of the public, holding forth on issues prognostication and contemporary gossip.

Meanwhile other less renowned universities had happily moved into the vacuum created by Massasoit's withdrawal from technical leadership, in accordance with the natural laws governing human pecking orders.

Every university president here understood his exact numerical rank in the prestige hierarchy, though of course all but one were compelled to dispute this fact and argue the point good-naturedly. Certainly if any of the male presidents misstated his school's rank to his disadvantage, his wife had the correct number at the ready with decimal precision.

Kingman knew the sequence as well; in fact he tailored the Worldwide Transformative Foundation's annual donations according to the list. The next couple of days were this year's instance of an annual tradition Kingman started almost a dozen years ago. Looking toward the long-term future, he had judged it important to get his foundation involved with the elite educational establishment. He started by contributing a token amount of money to each selected university, then he ramped up the amounts and broke it into installments. After the amounts became significant to the recipients he started summoning the leaders to this meeting every February.

The presidents had gotten to enjoy the whole process, and now the ritual was affectionately called 'Homecoming.' The Foundation closed the hotel for three evenings and two days as the presidents of the universities mingled, engaged in social dominance rituals, and generally clawed for attention from their peers. Kingman always used Homecoming as a unique opportunity for training his sons. Marshall and Hunter would practice their skills in working the room by engaging in clever superficial repartee. This year, to Kingman's consternation, Marshall had decided not to attend because there was a heavy snowstorm in Vermont. It had been a bad year for winter sports, and Marshall refused to pass up an opportunity to go skiing. "Well, Hunter is the important one for this year anyway," Kingman comforted himself through his angry thoughts.

Kingman had cultivated personal relationships with most of the 'Vine Plus' presidents, as he called his group. The educators viewed Homecoming as you or I view a visit with Santa Claus. Kingman's donations were substantial and currently constituted an injection of a few percent of the annual budget for most of the schools. Each year's Homecoming festival culminated with randomly ordered personal visits as every university president was summoned to Kingman's suite on the last day. During these visits Kingman announced the year's commitment, reified by an ornately designed, old-fashioned paper check.

Today was Thursday, and all the presidents had arrived the prior night. No business was formally discussed on Thursday of Homecoming; it was a relaxing day of intellectual stimulation. The spouses had been sent on day trips to interesting parts of New York City as guests of the Foundation. All the daytime activities were complete, and now everyone was here having cocktails before the dinner meeting.

The university officers loved spending time with their carefully filtered peers. It was like a tiny vacation, with well-known speakers brought in to hold forth on subjects chosen by Kingman, subjects that were always interesting to the elite audience.

Now, a university president rarely has an opportunity to relax in a peer group. In fact by definition and self-perception he has few peers. His job is an endless battle on many fronts; these leaders all share the relentless burden of the daily assaults from competing interests. And the buffeting is not just from within the university halls; plenty of pressure and stress arrives from the outside world every day. A few years back one of the presidents had drawn friendly chuckles at Homecoming by quipping that at home they all feel drawn-and-quartered each day—if 'four' means 'one hundred!' Today and tomorrow they were in the company of others with common pressures, the same shared encumbrances. Most knew each other fairly well, and overall they formed a cordial, stimulating group of elite colleagues. Thursday at Homecoming was enjoyed by all.

This morning had been filled with coffee and cocktails, free-form camaraderie around breakfast tables and cheerful visitation in comfortable lounge chairs. In the afternoon the financial officers were separated from the presidents, and they met with representatives of the most prosperous, most ethical accounting firms. The outsiders informed them of the latest developments in taxation and investment, not incidentally mentioning their firms' dedication to education and the ways they could help these universities manage their stupendous endowments. Kingman did not broker sales here at Homecoming, but the firms had contacts who did. His quiet commissions on deals made here sweetened the Foundation's life; in more than one instance he profited from one of these transactions enough to offset that year's donation to the participating university.

This evening was predestined as follows. Supper would follow cocktails and conversation. At the dinner meeting Kingman would give his annual speech on the Foundation and its support of education. As they listened, each bureaucrat would show the exact amount of interest Kingman showed as a boy while reading the poetry on a birthday card from his grandmother— a card surrounding a small sealed envelope enclosing a bill of unknown denomination.

During the afternoon, while the financial officers had met with the financial corporations, the presidents were relaxing and attending lectures. Today there were four presentations. Two were given by the CEOs of large government contractors, another was by one of the presidents here today, and the fourth was to be a lively talk by Dr. Finbarr O'Mulligan, the Distinguished Professor of Thought at Ollscoil College in Ireland.

One guest speaker canceled at the last minute. The head of the world's highest visibility cancer-fighting cheerleader, the organization that had made it so nobody could see the color turquoise without wanting to send them money, would not be speaking. The CEO of Cancer, Inc. was detained at a resort in Mexico and missed the meeting.

Most of the university presidents were familiar with the CEOs who spoke today. These corporate leaders often steered some of their stockholders' money to the more well-endowed universities. They occasionally attended charity balls and played golf with some of the presidents here today. And these two CEOs had committed their companies to large and increasing multi-year donations to Emerald Vine Plus universities—legally binding donations that ran far past their upcoming retirement dates. The Worldwide Transformative Foundation had acted as an intermediary in the formation of the deals, and all the donations were to be processed through the Foundation, which would divide the funds as it saw fit between the universities after subtracting its own fees. As of now, the plan was for a relatively uniform distribution among the universities here tonight with the exception of Pennumbria—Alison Higgenbottom, the wife of the president of Pennumbria, had affronted Winifred Dressel-Meier with Winifred's table placement at a charity ball a few years ago here in New York. Kingman knew it would be easier to blackball Pennumbria than to convince his wife such a move was unjustified.

Under these Foundation-brokered corporate funding arrangements, each CEO was slated to begin a consulting relationship with the Foundation upon retiring. He would have an advisory role helping the Foundation determine proper allocation of the money arriving from his prior employer. Each CEO's compensation would be computed as a top-line cost of a few percent of the cash flow from his prior company, and it would be paid out over time through escrow arrangements minimizing taxes, facilitating estate planning and so forth.

For today's talks Kingman had worked with the industry speakers to craft their presentations. They touched on something increasingly nettlesome to Kingman, a matter especially troubling in America: it seemed the general population was becoming accustomed to questioning everything. People had come to consider themselves wise enough, educated enough to weigh in on matters better left to experts. Average citizens felt the need to promulgate opinions on everything—ideas ranging from which schools should educate their children to whether mankind's activity was disturbing the earth's orbit around the sun. The resulting vagaries of popular emotion often favored policy positions more conducive to chaos than reasoned progress. Further, many popularly held viewpoints negatively impacted Kingman's line of work—his funding, his future.

The common man had been getting 'too big for his britches.'

This afternoon the first CEO to speak was Dr. Manfred Q. Michaels. He was the man at the helm of Media Channels Unlimited, Ltd. Though based in East Anglia, the company was the largest United States governmental contractor in the business of processing transfer payments from the U. S. government; it also held a dominant position in personal communications and data control. The company controlled a similar market share in Europe, and it was now largely owned by Dr. Wilbur Buffaloon, whose stake had increased markedly over the past several years as the company came to dominate the United States market.

Dr. Michaels centered his talk on the misuse of science in the public sphere. He gave examples of how some maverick scientists had recently been presenting their methodologies and raw data to the public as though the populace were qualified to interpret such things. Along with measurements and context, these scientists not-so-helpfully promoted their own conclusions, judgments independent of the settled scientific agreement on the issues involved. He made the point that this led to pressure for changes in funding priorities; as the public became engaged, nonscientists were advocating things that would disrupt the orderly flow of research funding to established universities and their partners. He did not mention impact on the flow of money to and through his company.

The speaker emphasized that the troublesome actions of the renegade scientists were in opposition to the well-formed accord of scientists funded to work in these disciplines. "Consensus is the cornerstone of scientific progress; factors that weaken agreement between the population and the established professionals are unambiguously malevolent," he intoned in a way that made Kingman admire the man's self-interested projection of certainty.

The university presidents could be seen nodding and elbowing each other in agreement with Dr. Michaels; they were familiar with the issue because most of the schools had at least one safely tenured high profile dissenter they would like to get rid of. Dr. Napoleon Burnside Turnbull of

Quinston University turned from a group of gabbling presidents to ask, "Dr. Michaels, I've heard that the National Science Funding Board is cracking down on these grandstanding so-called scientists. Can you update us on this?"

Dr. Michaels said, "A timely question. I was indeed about to say that the National Science Funding Board is working on such situations. I wish we could call it cracking down, but it's really just damage control; the renegades are untethered by any of it. The Board has held inquisitions into a number of cases of scientific fraud that have been in the news because of charges from some of these apostate lone scientists. Unfortunately in this case, where there is smoke we must admit there is fire.

"In these cases the mavericks called attention to the fact that large groups of collaborating scientists at universities and government organizations have, we cannot varnish it now, crossed a line. They cooperatively cheated on experiments, though no sinister motive was behind it. I must emphasize that the tampering was well-intentioned, and it was not done in a way that should weaken scientific consensus in important areas. In fact the tainted results were uniformly in favor of established scientific knowledge."

Several presidents looked at Dr. W. Spencer Beaverbrook and Dr. Napoleon Burnside Turnbull, as their universities housed the most prominent recent examples of the bad science. Neither president betrayed a blush; theirs were the latest instances, but most of the universities represented here were in on the game over the past decades, and none knew to what extent.

"Since the fraud in these situations was undeniable, the whole thing became a mess. The cowboy scientists attacked the scientific accord supported by the questionable analyses, ignoring the other mountains of published research. All this other work, never proven fraudulent, has been incorporated over the years to develop the current scientific consensus, and they gave this no credence during their grandstanding.

"Fortunately, in every case that has surfaced publicly, the National Science Funding Board's review has found the result of the false experiments to be 'Fake But Accurate.' The Board created this classification as a category for experimental results that were fraudulently obtained but nonetheless correct. They have stated that they use this term only in cases where the results agreed with what an honest experiment would have shown, had one been run. The Board made a recommendation that the data from the bad research not be relied on as a basis for future scientific work, pointing out that this should be no handicap since the conclusions of the tainted science duplicated what was already known through other means, or reasonably speculated."

Dr. Michaels continued on, communicating that the scientific community was relieved by the rulings and found it felicitous that in no case did the Board detect that the perpetrators acted against the public interest, an ideal all good scientists held sacred. The doctor said that while the Board acknowledged there were undoubtedly other unknown instances extant right now, there is essentially zero likelihood that any of this would damage the public good. Most of the gathered presidents nodded agreement. "There is no reason to expect curtailed funding for research in any of the areas involved, so long as we put in the requisite effort and maintain vigilance," Dr. Michaels stated to an agreeable reception by the audience.

On another optimistic and favorable note, Dr. Michaels mentioned that the National Science Funding Board had created task forces and public relations campaigns to educate the public. Their message was that unity of opinion is essential to good science, and that pronouncements by sanctimonious lone wolves can only degrade the public trust in those professionals responsible for scientific progress. The Board had commissioned development of uniform instructional materials for science classes in schools. This sort of education is best started young, and the early childhood educational materials were now in place, and teachers had been trained. The curriculum would soon roll out to the higher grades and the university level. National legislation was in the works to compel all schools across the country to incorporate the materials into their teaching plans.

The presidents found the man's talk engaging and stimulating. Kingman was pleased with their reaction; he took it as a vindication of his work with Dr. Michaels in preparing the material.

The second industrial speaker was Dr. Trinquilia Q. Grabber, whose company was formed by the recent merger of three leading companies in the field dealing with government regulations. Kingman had suggested that she start with an overview of her fabulously successful business and then plunge into the substance of her talk. She spent a few minutes talking about the company's history.

Regulation Associates, Ubiquitous Regulation, Inc., and The Compliance Company were combined into General Regulation Unlimited, Ltd. in a merger a few years prior. Dr. Grabber had been the leader of The Compliance Company and became president of General Regulation when the three companies combined.

The company marketed products and services that helped organizations discover applicable government restrictions, hunt for violations, and bring themselves into compliance. Its claim to fame was a powerful piece of software that could detect and flag potential infractions of ordinances. The tool kept records of all the layers of laws in all municipalities in the world's two dozen most regulated countries. General Regulation promoted it as a way to earn a 'clean bill of health' and operate in good conscience. The company's bread and butter was the consulting contract to correct the infractions it found.

"Since we're all friends here, I want to tell you that, as a special favor to Dr. Dressel-Meier," she gestured toward Kingman, who nodded politely, eyes closing. "We will license our machinery to your universities for a period of one year free of charge."

Nobody seemed visibly interested in undertaking a search for their own heretofore invisible legal code violations.

As she described the company's flagship product, she noted that it was powerful enough to find problems practically impossible to find in any other way. Actually the algorithm had become perhaps too effective—it had started reporting cases where there was no mathematical solution, cases where the overlapping laws woven across the situation occluded the possibility of complying with them all.

In fact what she said was true but somewhat misleading. Though the doctor did not highlight this, it would be more ingenuous to point out that these 'null' situations had been unearthed all along. A teenager with a set of rule books and a red crayon could find them in almost any jurisdiction. The real problem was that it was becoming impossible to design the software to automatically ignore such situations, and so they became visible to the customers. This was a result of increasingly powerful mathematical searches and correlations, which detected null results that had escaped detection in the past. Many of these null results could not be predicted and therefore suppressed; they could only be found by the extensive number crunching done when the software was executed. Thus they started surfacing in the reports, which led to headaches.

Dr. Grabber was very forthcoming on her difficulties: the company's clients were usually lukewarm customers at best, and most did business with General Regulation out of fear, rather than as part of a positive strategy for higher profits. This made the marketing of her products a complex and difficult task. Recently customers had started asking, 'If nobody else on the

planet can detect a violation, how important can the infringement really be?'
and 'If there is no way to act legally with all these conflicting laws, why
should I pay good money to craft a mathematically impossible path through
them?' These considerations decreased prospective clients' inclination to
buy General Regulation's products, let alone hire General Regulation to
design a compliance strategy for them. It was General Regulation, Inc.'s
biggest problem right now.

To address the threat of customers ignoring their infractions and
dropping their subscriptions to the product, Dr. Grabber said the company
was pursuing two thrusts. First, they were working with regulators to have
rules written requiring the use of an automated tool such as theirs; with luck
the regulations would call out specific models of her software. Second, they
had started emphasizing to customers that the system is also sold to
regulating agencies at a deep discount; the agencies could use it to examine
the customer's situation directly. "Would it not be best to know exactly what
the regulators will find when they look?" She smiled at the audience.

Dr. W. Spencer Beaverbrook of the University of Cathargo, the richest
and most prestigious university in the middle of the country, interrupted her
talk. "Dr. Grabber, where do you see your growth markets? My university
holds an investment in your new company, and I am curious about your
plans."

"Thank you for the question. I worry I'm spending too much time talking
about my company but I love it so. I'd talk forever if you'd listen.
Regulations. Clarity. Control. Order. It means beauty. To your question: our
largest growth area is one I must humbly say I pioneered personally." She
went on to elaborate. She discovered a few years ago that governmental
regulating authorities were the worst offenders of ordinances and executive
orders from other government departments, and in cases where they had
neglected to exempt themselves, of their own.

She called this a potential gold mine, and said that her exploitation of
this market propelled her career. Her company had achieved a period of
explosive growth in the time prior to absorbing the competition, and its sales
were continuing apace. She emphasized that she was taking advantage of
the natural process for developed countries, in which the central government
consumes a larger and larger portion of the economy as time progresses. As
government staff workers find more areas in which to serve the public good,
there is an almost automatic increase in the number of official agencies. A
creatively staffed, vibrantly growing and increasingly diverse government

sector creates the perfect environment for the company's intra-government business thrusts. Dr. Grabber outlined the obvious mathematics: since regulations must be considered in terms of their mutual interactions, the number of opportunities for violations grows geometrically with the number of different bureaus. She proclaimed that the rapidly expanding government market was mostly untapped despite her success. "If market penetration is a trip from New York to London," Dr. Grabber said, "We are right now passing the Statue of Liberty."

She was an accomplished business leader, and as he listened Kingman was proud that he had identified her promise and built connections to her a few years ago, back when she was just an anonymous manager in her company. In fact, the idea to pursue this government market had originated in him; he fed it to her, and she ran with it. They had been friends ever since.

Kingman had been pacing at the side of the room, and now he drifted to the back and stood next to a fancy array of sconces surrounding a huge antique mirror. As he listened to the doctor, his eyes wandered into a happy coincidence, encountering a matching set from his reflection in the handsome old looking glass. His attention was thus for a time divided between the pleasant tasks of hearing the speaker's enthusiastic words and admiring his own agreeable countenance.

Dr. Grabber's main address proceeded now. She spoke about the cost of nonconformity of thought, and she congratulated the university presidents on their efforts to increase the efficiency of education by promoting intellectual homogeneity. Kingman could see the backs of heads, most of them covered with stately locks, nodding as the audience recalled headaches due to manifestations of strident individuality. All had faced contentious reviews of tenure denials for outlying faculty members, and each had encountered the noisy student who somehow penetrated to him complaining about a low grade that reflected punishment for Thoughtcrime, not work of poor quality.

The speaker skillfully poked fun at the 'cowboy' American to the delight of the assembled crowd. To unanimous understanding and amuse-ment, Dr. Grabber continued, illustrating the folly of surrendering to individuality with wide ranging examples and pointing out how those in charge of any process must seek control and uniformity. Without these, efficiency is impossible. She spoke of farmers growing everything from corn to earthworms. She mentioned factories making simple and complex products: pencils and GVCDs and paper and lasers. Laboratory rats and bacteria figured in her discussion.

The list went on and on. Her last and most picturesque illustration was that of the old men in the Black Forest who have made the world's fanciest string puppets for hundreds of years, a craft passed from generation to generation, and one that would seem inimical to homogeneity of process, considering the variety displayed by the final product. She nonetheless made a convincing case that the men would starve if they had not developed a uniform set of tools and practices for their work. Standard materials and techniques yielded puppets with a manageable range of head size, control bar dimensions, lever design, string length and so forth. This did not preclude the appearance of rich diversity we all treasure: face shapes are fine-tuned, and puppets are dressed in all sorts of different clothing; their countenances are painted to cover the spectrum of colorful emotions. They give the appearance of individuality while actually containing almost no real individual variation.

Dr. Grabber emphasized that all of the processes she mentioned demand control by those in command. She called attention to the fact that this was largely unrecognized in realms where humans are the material to be controlled. Most managers believe that human interactions are different from those of material things and lower forms of life. "We have not yet evolved to where we apply these principles to handling people," the doctor said. "But how arrogant we have been to think that natural laws governing the rest of the universe don't apply to humans! And how much productivity is lost!"

Summarizing her message would go something like this: Who can say commonplace humans should not follow the paths of bacteria, vegetables, worms and puppets?

But Dr. Grabber noted that there were some signs of progress in the modern world. She acknowledged strides in the past half century in the educational establishment. One very concrete example she singled out was a change from decades ago—the re-centering of nationwide standardized test scores for college admissions. Prior to the modification, the scores showed fine-grained resolution in the achievement levels of the highest performers. This had two odious features. First, the 'best of the best' performers could be specifically identified. The second effect was an unfortunate salience of the truth that the highest scores were demographi-cally unfair—for whatever reason, they were mostly achieved by members of disdained demographic groups, groups that were the targets of loathing and self-loathing of people like university presidents.

The recalibration successfully blurred the results on this high performance portion of the scale by lowering the achievement required to attain the highest scores. After the adjustment many more test takers' scores were pinned at the top of the scale, promoting homogeneity by blurring distinctions, therefore affording more opportunity for previously excluded groups to gain the markers of excellence—all without the trouble of having to actually attain excellence.

Dr. Grabber used this particular change as a model of how the transition to increased conformity can be managed without undue public criticism or stress. To the extent that the public noticed and voiced concern, the change was explained away as a method of gaining crucial insight into the gradations of near-average performance; professional statisticians and researchers either remained mum or were quietly dismissed from their positions. Overall, the transition was very smooth. The doctor also took the opportunity presented by this example to emphasize that academics is a rare field where one can increase productivity without any extra effort and, in some cases, no actual content change—just a change of viewing the results. She encouraged the university officers to consider this in their future decision making.

The presidents enjoyed Dr. Grabber's talk as much as they had liked that of Dr. Michaels. All agreed with her overall thesis one hundred percent. While admitting that their campuses had made progress on this score in recent decades, however, they expressed skepticism about ever reaching a satisfactory level of dissent-free thought in the academy, at least in America. As for the country at large, they were very pessimistic about prospects for reasonable advances.

Kingman took the podium and thanked the speakers. The group broke for drinks and free conversation after this second talk. The presenting CEOs shook hands and perhaps pledged a few dollars to their alma maters. Most of the university presidents flash-exchanged their GVCDs with those of the CEOs with settings wide open, thereby transmitting several levels of formal, business and direct personal contact information. All stretched their legs and chatted jovially as the CEOs departed. Kingman was mightily pleased with the atmosphere, and he unconsciously savored the moment by absent-mindedly walking back over near the mirror and checking his profile, which spurred him to tighten his tie ever so slightly.

After the break he called the group to order. "Please, please. I know you will all be interested to hear what Dr. Munghorn has to say. Each of your universities has developed a sophisticated financial system. I think even those of you most proud of your fiscal infrastructure will admit that Stambridge has made a high art out of leveraging the tax advantages you all share. You all know of their forays into life insurance, medical insurance, healthcare delivery, retailing and finance, areas dear to the heart of academia today. Her presentation is about Stambridge's newest endeavors in donation extraction." He paused and looked down in humility. "A wonderful system that I must humbly say we at the Worldwide Transformative Foundation helped design." He looked at Stambridge's president, and she rose and walked to the front, nodding a friendly smile to her peers.

Dr. Athena Sterling Munghorn took center stage, thanking Kingman as he receded. She turned to the group with a serious face and said, "Well, I don't know if I should be sharing these details with all of you." She paused as the audience sat waiting. "You know, we have a heavy overlap in our alumni universes." She smiled genially as she revealed her small joke.

The audience laughed in polite confusion. She went on to outline Stambridge's system, which could be licensed through the Foundation to the other Emerald Vine Plus universities. The school had set up a fee-free estate planning system for high net worth individuals. The service was open to alumni only, and it required that at least fifty percent of the client's wealth be transferred to Stambridge in a living trust. Stambridge had already found the new endeavor to be a symbiotic undertaking. Many wealthy people were in need of tax breaks on appreciated property, and Stambridge always had a need for more funding. The system was only a few years old, and it was not publicized widely, but they had already succeeded in monetizing the deaths of several elderly donors and the demise of a young victim of a terminal disease.

"There are many hurdles. Legal complexities, family challenges, changes of heart and so forth. We have a robust system, with pre-qualified contracts in many jurisdictions. Please contact Kingman if you would like to get involved with a similar plan for your university."

Dr. Clementine Dunster Trafton, president of Halford, asked a question. "Dr. Munghorn, why limit this to your alumni? There are plenty of wealthy individuals outside your umbrella. It would seem an attractive piece of machinery to use in setting up post-mortem donations from forward thinking individuals even outside your alumni universe."

Dr. Munghorn smiled. "Well, before I answer I should admit something to you. Our two schools have many alumni in common; in fact we sometimes call you the 'Stambridge of the East,' you know." The room chuckled lightly. "The first alumni we have pursued were those that also count themselves among your alumni. You're welcome to what's left."

The room burst into laughter. Dr. Trafton flushed but smiled a tight-lipped smile.

"But to answer your question: The same insight occurred to us. But we have been able to obviate the consideration. Yes these individuals are out there. But there is a bond, a friendship, a family feeling when you are an alumnus. We don't want to lose that, and we have developed a way to bridge things, to get the best of all worlds. As part of our program we have instituted an 'instant' master's degree for individuals with sufficient means.

"We've found that every high net worth candidate is qualified for the new Stambridge degree we offer: a Master of Science in the Human Situation. All have sufficient life experience to warrant this diploma and become instant alumni upon irrevocable transfer of a sufficiently meaningful financial instrument. We refer to this instrument as 'imputed tuition,' and of course the dollar amount is based on the net worth of the donor. Think about it: for a person to amass enough wealth to be in our estate planning program, it is almost a tautology that he is educated."

W. Spencer Beaverbrook smiled and said, "It's almost a definition of a sophisticated education," garnering sedate laughter from the group.

Dr. Munghorn smiled at the joke and continued, "And the newly graduated individual is now eligible to enter our estate planning program. The problem disappears."

The crowd was quiet. Athena Munghorn watched as they thought about the system, then when the time was right she preempted the obvious thought starting to go through most of the room. "And we've found that inherited wealth, which our research shows is the bulk of the wealth available to tap, is no exception. Again, think about it. Who has a parent of significant means and yet grows up without enough sophistication to call himself a graduate of Stambridge? Even those dismissed as ne'er-do-wells by their parents usually qualify, once you look into their situation carefully. In almost every case they already have graduated from college or are old enough to have accumulated life knowledge worthy of education credit. If there are exceptions, we shall fix the problem without undue effort on the part of the donor."

The audience sat in unanimous admiration of the creative and productive use of the university's good name, the respect the general public felt for it—its brand. Dr. Munghorn said, "Credit has to go to Dr. Dressel-Meier and his Foundation. They conceived and built the whole process for us." Kingman, standing in his favorite spot in the back, hearing his name, turned to see the presidents glancing toward him approvingly. He modestly smiled and bowed his head.

Dr. Munghorn finished up her talk by mentioning several other incipient but related projects. She spoke of a program to award posthumous degrees to ancestors of wealthy donors, and another targeted to a much wider community. The latter was a program for hereditary transfer of Stambridge degrees upon the death of the original degree holder. As the plan now stood, inheritors would have the ability to choose a new academic discipline when the degree was transferred from the deceased. Neither of these new programs was in place yet. There were difficulties in their implementation, especially in the case of the inherited degrees. At this point, that plan had many unresolved logistical issues including pricing, attributed degree award date, and upgrade options. Dr. Munghorn emphasized that neither of these two programs was a guaranteed success. "Indeed they may not even be formally launched."

The day's schedule provided for one more talk, to be followed by a free hour preceding the dinner-preceding reception. Everyone had been seated for quite a while, and Dr. Finbarr O'Mulligan granted a quick break before he spoke. All stood, stretched and picked up a cocktail. After a few minutes O'Mulligan went forward with his discourse, 'The Epistemology of the Nature of Economic Progress and Its Relationship to Individual Freedom and Human Exploitation.' It was the most jovial and interactive of the three talks due to the lighthearted nature of the subject and the joie de vivre of the presenter. His lecture turned out to be the longest one of the day, but the time went quickly for the listeners. Spirits were not at all dissipated by the spirits coursing through the blood of the audience and especially the presenter; there was gaiety and laughter for all.

Not one of the presidents later remembered anything of O'Mulligan's talk except that it seemed informative and addressed fundamental issues.

Now, here at the reception a little over an hour after Dr. Finbarr's presentation, the hall was abuzz with happy friends in cheerful conversation. Kingman stood by the door of the Abraham Cornwallis Room, holding the champagne glass fated to remain mostly full. He spotted Finbarr central to a circle of chattering officers and spouses. It was a violation of the normal Homecoming protocol for a speaker to stay for the reception, but Finbarr had spent the open hour in the hotel bar, and in some mysterious way he caused Kingman to invite him to stick around for a few more drinks. The Irishman held forth joking, telling entertaining anecdotes, amusing himself deeply. He flirted with the females and generously refreshed their drinks from the waiters' passing trays. One of their husbands could perhaps be heard muttering to another that the man's jokes were told in 'An Irish accent—the sound of the English language spoken by an Idiot.' Kingman could not help smiling at the ruffled feathers of the male concubines.

He swept the room with his eyes. The other guests gathered in clumps of mixed good natured and severe-looking people. Kingman had noticed that while university presidents could work a room with seductive grace, they always seemed to choose spouses that are uncomfortable and clumsy. Hobnobbing was a strain for many spouses, but the female ones were typically more alive in the situation; even the introverted women seemed to get some pleasure from dressing up and attending an elegant get-together with peers. Generally the husbands appendaged to the female presidents and financiers were less comfortable, and Kingman observed the standard pattern tonight. As for his own wife, he had long ago stopped insisting Winifred attend such functions. Tonight she would be catching a show on Broadway with friends.

He felt a surge of pride as he spotted Hunter, suave and magnetic, holding court with two presidents and their spouses. He felt a quick pang of worry over whether his son would preview the evening's subject, thereby robbing him of contextual setup. After a second or two he dismissed the concern about Hunter leaking his thunder.

It was time to meander through the crowd, and so he centered himself, breathed for a few seconds and concentrated like an athlete preparing for an important match. He affected his most genuine and cordial smile as he stepped forth into the crowd carrying that modern replacement for the secret handshake, the social drink.

Chitchat and good natured competitive babble about sports, academic pecking order and famous alumni burbled through the room as Kingman circulated with his drink. He engaged in small talk and generally promoted good cheer as he mingled from group to group. He was a man working a room full of masters of working rooms. He was in wonderful form, and his smile beamed quasi-authenticity as he put his hands on men's shoulders or the smalls of women's backs, threw his head back in laughter, and lightheartedly grimaced in friendly interaction with his guests, all without spilling a drop of his drink onto the plush carpet.

Tonight the college presidents were in good cheer after a low-key day with their friends. None showed the gravity that so easily tugs at the corners of one's mouth, dragging the jowls earthward. For now they had no need to listen to tiresome blowhards in the form of potential donors discoursing on philosophy and giving shallow, easily anticipated advice. Tonight the relaxed atmosphere and the concomitant freedom from the forced smile engendered voluntary gravity-defying smiles that were as authentic as these practiced faces could contrive

Even regarding the Foundation and its donation, the pressure was off today and tomorrow. None of the presidents felt he had influence over Kingman's allocations; all knew the die was cast before Homecoming. Each expected something approximating what he felt was his standard allotment. It was like a weekend retreat with the promise of only good news, a well-deserved few days of ease among friends sponsored by one of the more stable benefactors in these uncertain times.

In the run-up to Homecoming, Kingman had structured all communications such that a reasonable president would assume that the annual gift giving would continue largely as in the past. Perhaps a dreamy university leader would hope that the Foundation would step things up, maybe funding a badly needed new athletic building. But such a president understood this as just a pipe dream. Though he took pains to soft-pedal it, Kingman infused this year's outgoing Homecoming messaging with terms like, 'synergy,' 'partnership,' 'common goal,' 'participate' and so forth, and downplayed the traditional 'supporting you', 'donating to you', 'financing your critical mission,' 'helping you' and so forth.

Tonight's dinner meeting was to diverge a tad from past tradition. Kingman had recently named his son Hunter to head a new, legally separate branch of the Foundation called the Lobby For Good. The Lobby's purpose was to intervene in government affairs to fend off threats to the tax-free sections of the economy, and to actively help form the government environment for nonprofits toward the congenial. Prestigious universities were central to his vision of the Lobby's constituency. Tonight's dinner show would start with the normal generic talk about the Foundation, then Kingman would introduce the Lobby For Good. Hunter was to follow up and steer the rest of the evening under Kingman's watchful eye.

Tomorrow was to be a more radical departure from history. Tonight there would be no disclosure of any change in the pecuniary profile of relationships; the presidents would simply think they were being subjected to an opportunistic, captive-audience public relations session for Kingman's new baby. But Kingman wanted the imprimatur of these universities behind his new project, and the plan for tomorrow afternoon was different from prior years. The presidents, but not the financial officers, would all be shuttled to a yacht for a cruise during which they would learn in detail about Kingman's expectations for their participation in the Lobby. The spouses would again be separated, touring museums and restaurants as guests of the Foundation.

On the boat Kingman would present his new vision for monetary flow among the institutions while the presidents sat captive with only their colleagues, not their accountants. This new course was a change from the steady one-way financial currents of the last decade. He knew the initial psychic impact on the presidents would be one of shock, but he had no doubt about the operational outcome of the meeting. He would obtain commitment—willing or more likely grudging—from the presidents.

Each president would be dumbfounded upon becoming aware that he was to supply cash to the Lobby For Good in the short term; Homecoming had always been a time to contemplate income, not outflow. This was a risk, but Kingman believed he could manage the disorientation to his benefit.

He was resolved that charter membership in the Lobby For Good was mandatory for universities expecting to continue their close relationship with the Foundation. He would threaten to let the connections die over it if necessary. He knew most of the presidents well, and he had made careful preparations on a number of levels, planning the day to exploit their personalities. So Kingman was confident that each president could be induced to participate in the new protocol before leaving the boat. He knew that most of these executives held a conviction that they were decisive leaders, and he understood they were maniacally focused on money. He expected a quick dismissal of his proposal as their unanimous opening gambit, but he had no doubt that he was destined to win the day's game.

He would make sure his case would be clear, and the commitments would be public. The first president to declare participation was the most important; each succeeding one would get progressively easier. In a gathering of such egos there is a strong desire to be viewed as the leader and an even stronger need not to be left behind the group. Kingman was certain that once the group started moving, the presidents would herd in a way that makes cattle mindlessly propelling themselves along the ramp to a packing house seem recalcitrant and contentious. It would be like watching one of those children's sets of magnets all jump together in a single line once the first two are snapped together.

Yes, once he wedged that first president to mate with the Lobby For Good, nary a one would fail to proclaim the beauty of the emperor's new clothes. The trick, of course, was to start the cavalcade. Kingman was ready with his attack; he knew whom he was targeting for the position of first off the diving board, and he was confident that the combination of egotistical and tribal impulses would, in the end, push the whole group into unanimous compliance with his desires. Neither would it hurt that they were to be isolated from their financial officers.

But all those machinations were tomorrow's problem.

We're All Friends Here

Don't neophytes say the darndest things?

R eturning his attention to the here and now, Kingman walked over to the room's entrance and made a theatrical show of ringing an old-fashioned set of dinner chimes. The group cheerfully filtered down the hallway and into the dining room, occasionally spilling a splash of liquor onto the fine carpet. They were presented with an irregular array of round tables, each seating six or seven persons. The place settings were beautiful, the linens folded dramatically into origami birds and whales. A waiter and waitress stood by each table, the male grasping a carafe of red wine, the female holding white. The servers intercepted and directed the guests to their chairs (Kingman had arranged seating and trained each server to recognize the faces of those assigned to his table.) This procedure was a departure from the open and casual seating of years past, and led to some confused and good-natured babble as the group bumbled around to get seated. But nobody attached significance to the change.

Each president was seated with his wife or husband and separated from his financial officer. Kingman called dinner to order, standing at the front of the room and imploring the guests to enjoy their meal. He promised an interesting update on the Foundation, then left the microphone and wandered among the tables as all began selecting and enjoying their wines.

This was the Primo Ultimo Room of the Cornwallis Hotel in New York City and so there were, of course, no insects present. However, had there been a tiny housefly flitting around the room, he would have to be forgiven were he to eavesdrop:

"…pushing for him to get another Nobel Prize…"

"…gold mine… admit Americans are too stupid to do the technical work…lazy anyway…"

"…expect us to win another national polo championship…"

"…don't realize we are citizens of the world…"

"…no they won't. We've been doing it for years…"

"…then why do your students always want to come to us for graduate school?…"

Kingman meandered through the room on a path perhaps not unlike a two dimensional projection of our imaginary dipteran trespasser's. He stopped occasionally to praise a woman's appearance or deliver congratulations on some accomplishment of one of the presidents (well, to be precise, on an achievement by someone associated with the president's school). Served false modesty and compliment bait in return, he indulged smoothly. He strolled through the elegant room enjoying the upbeat chatter of the academia's royalty. Wine glasses were already being topped off, and everyone was happy and smiling as Kingman approached his table.

He walked toward the three presidents and their spouses sitting at his assigned table. Dr. Hawkins Q. Higgenbottom, president of Pennumbria, was next to the wife of Dr. W. Spencer Beaverbrook. Adjacent to Alison Higgenbottom sat the interesting husband of Dr. Wanda Worthington, president of Cornwallis. As Kingman walked around toward his seat between Drs. Beaverbrook and Worthington, he was looking forward to getting to know Dr. Worthington's husband, an unpolished fellow who was appointed to a faculty position as Professor of Individualistic Culture at Cornwallis as part of Wanda's employment package. Cornwallis had insisted on awarding him a doctorate which he initially refused, saying he didn't 'need one of them things.' But his wife intervened and he was now Dr. Travis Q. Worthington IV, and Cornwallis's faculty Ph.D. ratio was undiluted. The man was the fabulously wealthy scion of a silver mining family, completely uneducated in the traditional sense but known to be quite a character.

A conversation, or perhaps a monologue, was in play as Kingman approached. "…since they're both overrated and myths have developed to raise them to demigods. They were just men, and flawed ones at that. The common wisdom that Lincoln saved the union and Churchill saved Europe has grated on me since I first heard the stories as a child. And all the other scoundrels as well: Aristotle, Roosevelt, Einstein, whoever." A crotchety and animated, slightly inebriated Dr. Beaverbrook paused and took a drink of wine. He sniffed, "We really must help people to dispense with the hero worship. There are no cherry trees, no eureka moments, no fairy tales. Honest Abe, my arse. People don't step in front of tanks, They don't climb on top of tanks. No one is larger than life." He suppressed a small burp or hiccup just effectively enough that no one can say which it was.

Kingman quietly sat down as Dr. Beaverbrook's conversational partner, Alison Higgenbottom, smiled across the table and said, "Really? Not you, not you and not even you?" looking at each of the presidents in sequence with a mischievous but good-natured smile, finishing with Wanda Worthington. Travis Worthington was chewing a toothpick, drawing eyes to the unkempt and uncomfortable-looking stubble around his mouth as he said, "Well I for one—I'm larger than life." He slurred just a little, probably no more than Dr. Beaverbrook. There were smiles around the table at Alison's question. Dr. Beaverbrook's forefinger gestured 'touché' to the woman, and he smiled warmly and took another drag on his wine.

Betsy Beaverbrook leaned sideways onto her husband's shoulder and said, "It's going to be a wonderful biography. And two subjects, not one. Pretty innovative, honey. Huh?" She smiled and distributed her happy glances at each in the audience.

Dr. Beaverbrook's quiet interlude was disturbed, and his blood temperature rose. He shook his head impatiently, "Ah, my dear, that's where you are wrong as usual. I tell you once again I am not writing a biography." Betsy drew back, frowning. Her husband paused, his face flushed and his gaze down, then relaxed a bit and broke a smile. "Actually, at the rate I am going I'm not writing anything." Amiable chuckles rang from the others. "Drat this administrative burden of running a university!" He smiled. The others, including spouses, all nodded or rolled their eyes indicating familiarity with the situation.

"I will not attempt to trace their lives. I will use facts from their lives to demonstrate that these were men who, largely through bumbling visionless actions, presided over inevitable events and got the credit for successful outcomes. I am, or was," he chuckled, "a sociology professor, and I know from years of study that one man cannot make a difference. It would be irresponsible for me to go to the grave without sharing that information, knowledge it took decades to confirm. Nobody lives outside the system. We are all participants in a random social soup, playing our parts in an accidental and chaotic script. There are no individual heroes, nobody who makes a real difference."

Dr. Alison Q. Higgenbottom was an historian, a professor of history at Pennumbria. She said, "I don't necessarily buy it, but let's say there's no Isaac Newton, no James Clerk Maxwell. Perhaps science is too fundamental. Let's pretend somebody would have made their contributions anyway; they're not inventions but just discoveries. But really, in human events? Are you saying Benjamin Franklin, George Washington—they didn't make a difference to history?"

Dr. Beaverbrook scowled, pausing to beam the expression's intensity into Alison Higgenbottom's face. "Don't start me on the so-called American Founding Fathers, those loquacious bickering buffoons who benefitted perhaps more than anyone in history, save Jesus himself, from retroactive reinterpretations of the facts." The good doctor's blood pressure had risen again. His face flushed, and that vein near the middle of his forehead bulged.

Hawkins Higgenbottom was tired of listening to this conversation. He felt that maybe Spencer Beaverbrook should stick to sociology and leave history, mythology and motivational speaking aside. He turned to Wanda Worthington and said, "So I guess you had a bit of an initial rough ride in the press, no? So much for that veil of anonymity you probably wore out west."

Dr. Worthington said, "You can say that again. In my last position I had all the control of a tennis ball in a championship match. After that job—returning phone calls, making command performances, performing dog-and-pony shows—I thought this would be one position where I could focus. Focus on whatever Cornwallis needs, focus on how to get us ready for our third century. Ha! A university president, focus! We're veritable laser beams!" She sipped her wine. Dr. Higgenbottom smiled thinly. Most around the table smiled equally strongly at the reminder of their day-to-day lives. Dr. Beaverbrook was now breathing normally, and he seemed tired and happy enough to listen for a bit.

Betsy Beaverbrook asked her, "Dr. Worthington, what was the most difficult part of the whole process of getting the job at Cornwallis? From afar it seemed so… public and so contentious."

Wanda thought for a moment then answered, "You know, it went on for the better part of a year. They never explained why they were considering me—I never asked for the job. That whole year was difficult. They did a great job of keeping a lot of the details secret, for which I would praise a god." The table smiled at the embedded implied truism. "They asked me to articulate my vision for Cornwallis, and that was difficult, since I didn't know or care about the place. The worst though? A simple thing. Silly, really. I'm afraid of needles. When they drew that vial of blood in front of that whole committee..." her head trilled, eyes closed momentarily. "It should have been degrading, submitting to all that in front of them, but I was so terrified it never crossed my mind."

Some background on Dr. Worthington's selection as head of Cornwallis is in order here. Without noticing, Wanda Worthington had become quite a topic of conversation in the education world over the course of a few years. She worked as director of development at a small and famous liberal arts school in the west for ten years, and she had the magic touch with donors. The school had raised more money during her last year than half of the Emerald Vine schools, an amazing feat for a school of that size, and for a woman in her lower thirties.

When Cornwallis launched a search for a new president three years ago, the university's trustees had the normal qualifications in mind. The official pronouncement sought candidates fulfilling four requirements: ability to raise funding, transnational orientation, respect for academic and Emerald Vine traditions, and adding balance to the cumulative historical gender inequity of the preceding list of male presidents.

Unlike every other school here today, Cornwallis had not cycled through any female presidents. Most had also gone through a minority president or two; in all such cases the school deserved credit for hitting both the gender and race birds with a single stone. Due to an accidental error in document editing when the qualifications for the job were being promulgated, no specific requirement was included to redress the racial injustices committed by the university for centuries.

The four requirements, when made public, had caused an uproar due to the missing racial component. In response to the outrage, the search committee put effort into identifying candidates of African heritage, though they made it clear that the only hard demographic requirement was gender. They publicly maintained this stance but quietly instituted a blood test whose results would be interpreted by a committee of Anthropology, Grievance Studies, and Biology professors. As it turned out, they learned that four of the five finalists were qualified to be considered African in heritage, though only three could pass for black in normal intercourse. The threshold they eventually set was equivalent to one great-great-great grandparent being fifty percent African in genome.

Wanda Worthington had been judged to meet the four published criteria. She also barely cleared the phantom racial criterion, and it was no coincidence—the level was chosen retroactively after she was selected, set to match the results of her blood test. To the best of her knowledge, and certainly to the best of her husband's and his family's, she was pure white. This lasted until the press release disclosing her appointment as Cornwallis's first African president, an announcement that surprised Wanda and her family as much as it did anyone.

Betsy Beaverbrook and Alison Higgenbottom exchanged confused looks. Alison looked at the others around the table and asked, "Blood? Whatever for? Were they worried you had cancer or something?"

Travis Worthington had been silent beyond his normal tolerance of a few minutes. He downed his drink and circled his finger, notifying the waiter to of his desire for a few more jiggers of Kentucky bourbon. He broke into the conversation with a silent gesture, moving the signal finger to a stationary upright position to silence his audience as he savored the burn in his throat. "They should of taken my blood, not hers. I've got something of everyone. Sasquatch. Every known disease too." He guffawed before turning his attention to his line of shot glasses on the table.

Wanda smiled at him patiently and turned to Alison, "No, nothing like that. It was completely voluntary, but they asked me for it. They wanted to do a genetic analysis to see my ethnic background, and that's all I knew. I thought it probably wouldn't add points to my score—I didn't know I had any African blood. But they told me I do. Who knew? I'm kind of glad, and I've been reading about my people whenever I get an extra few minutes.

"So the needle and the blood were awful, and you know what? I've started requiring a similar test anyway for professors we hire. Actually most of them say they don't think the needle stick is a big deal, and for the others, well, it's a single moment of terror for a much, much greater good. We get some flak for the effort, mostly from outside the university, usually politicians charging us with 'unfairness' and that sort of thing; they're really talking to others while pretending to protest to us. Fortunately the tenured faculty is backing me on this, though they're refusing to let their own blood be analyzed to form a baseline benchmark. We really should have that, but what can you do?

"Of course I'm always expanding the list of advantaged ethnicities, and I've raised the blood threshold for most of them. I want everyone to be able to look at our faculty members and instantly identify their racial heritage with just a quick glance. We'll get there eventually. I've also gotten the faculty to back a resolution that whenever I leave, the next president must not be white, and I don't mean it can be someone 'not white' like me. The faculty feels the same way about their own positions as I do about mine—historical wrongs must be addressed. And there is no better time than when each of us retires."

She smiled and sipped her wine. Her husband nodded and drank a fresh shot of his whiskey. Betsy Beaverbrook asked, "Well, the needle was the worst part. What was the most surprising part?"

Wanda Worthington thought for a moment, rolling the wine in her mouth. "The biggest surprise actually is also probably the best part. I learned that they used a secret system for the final selection. They chose me randomly!" She smiled as the confusion invisibly rumbled around the table. Then she elaborated. "Well, partly. It turns out that capping a social process with a random component can lead to beneficial, even optimal results. If I may modestly say so, I'm living proof." Most around the table smiled quizzically save Kingman, who just listened.

What Wanda referred to was an innovation Cornwallis used during the selection process. The trustees had received a challenge from a famous thirtysomething quasi-alumnus that cried out for them to engage. Conner Fitzgibbon had studied engineering at the school and dropped out in the middle of his second year due to boredom. He went on to become very wealthy by producing processes and machines that incorporate randomness as part of their central design. He made some hardware in a company of his own, and he licensed other parts of his technology ubiquitously. His devices were used in financial, gambling, medical, communications and research settings, and they facilitated performance impossible without their unique statistical character. Having observed the common haphazard application of quantitative measures in social systems, he had become a public advocate for introducing stochasticity into their management. The man licensed his technology free of charge to governments and organizations committed to public good. He offered Cornwallis a staggeringly large donation—the largest in the university's history. But there was a condition attached.

The trustees had gone public with the names of five finalists for the position of president. They had called an old-fashioned press conference and proclaimed that all five were fully qualified; they would be happy with any of these candidates, but the decision was not finalized. Then Fitzgibbon made the offer for his massive donation. The contribution was contingent on changing the selection process for the new president. Fitzgibbon believed strongly that we overestimate what we know, and that adding a random component to a controlled process could be beneficial. He proposed that a machine make the final selection randomly using one of his algorithms. The trustees were uncomfortable with what they perceived as a runaway process, but intrigued due to the weightiness of the donation. Further, Fitzgibbon had them trapped in a sense—they had no leg to stand on if they claimed to worry that the wrong candidate may be chosen after they had so publicly endorsed all five finalists.

The university trustees had a dilemma. The twin considerations—having five publicly acceptable finalists and having a record-breaking donation in the balance—animated a drive in the trustees to let go of their psychological need to control the selection process, but they still could not accept what they perceived as the gambling aspect of Fitzgibbon's game. They were, as they reminded each other, trustees who were obliged to think of nothing but the good of the great institution, and they themselves were the only ones qualified to make the decision. After a short deliberation they reluctantly decided against Fitzgibbon's proposition. On principle they absolutely refused to allow the choice to be made using a random process. At the last minute one creative trustee proposed a solution that all accepted, and they were sure they had salvaged the deal: they offered Fitzgibbon the right to choose the president himself, extending an invitation for him to temporarily join the board of trustees as part of the arrangement.

Fitzgibbon refused the offer, and he tried to communicate that they were missing the point—he did not believe his own selection would be better than theirs. Conner Fitzgibbon realized he could surreptitiously use a random machine, and he understood that the trustees were not blind either. But he never considered the approach. He felt that it would demonstrate nothing. He added a face-saving clause that the university could choose from several of his random algorithms and repeated his offer.

The proposal still seemed wrongheaded to the trustees. The traditional approach is to reconcile the competing considerations in favor of the various candidates through a procedure that varies from 'wow, what a great candidate X is!' to 'we have a mathematical number (six decimal digits) for each candidate's quality, and so we can see who is best.' At the moment of decision, each voting member typically felt he fully apprehended the factors in the decision.

That was the traditional approach, and it relied on committee members fooling themselves.

Uncomfortable as some trustees were, it was hard to reject the deal, considering the money and all the good it would lead to. They agreed to Fitzgibbon's terms after the severe and tortured process of modifying a few commas in his proposal.

So the process was carried out, and Dr. Wanda Worthington was the choice. She was much younger than any other candidate, and the selection surprised the outside world—the betting had been that she was not really in the running. Wanda Worthington took over the university just before graduation last year, and this was her first Homecoming.

Alison Higgenbottom searched her memory, "But the blood thing and the selection, they're not what's been in the news lately, right?" She looked around the table. "It's something else, no?"

Hawkins Higgenbottom answered his wife, "Yes, dear. The biggest thing is her proposal to introduce the use of randomness into her university's admissions process. I think the crux of the problem is the weakening of the image of pure excellence." He turned sternly to Wanda. "Publicly highlighting anything about admissions was surely a faux pas." He paused with a severe expression. "And there is no way to promulgate this randomness gimmick without people jumping to the conclusion that you're suggesting we go from a meritocracy to a lottery. That's exactly what they're saying ever since the first gossip site got ahold of your proposal."

Wanda looked at Dr. Higgenbottom and said, "Let's forget the lightweight commentators. They'll never be any help to us anyway. But isn't the whole process just so... dishonest the way we do it, the way we talk about it? I would think my method would at least give it a bit more integrity. I'm just saying we don't know everything, and let's select that last fifteen percent of our students randomly from the pool of thousands of qualified applicants. And we've sort of publicly admitted we don't do it on pure merit."

"Wanda, dear, we have never admitted such a thing. What are you thinking?" Hawkins Higgenbottom's mood was shifting from one of censure to a patient mien of correcting a misguided soul.

"How many times have we said something like, 'We choose those who will get the most out of the experience of being here?' or something that means, 'If you share biological classification with historically disadvantaged people, don't let your low scores and lack of accomplishment dissuade you from applying?' Please."

Drs. Higgenbottom and Beaverbrook looked at each other, then turned to Dr. Worthington with the composure of club members patiently initiating a greenhorn. She did not yet grasp that fifteen percent was essentially the whole non-protected portion of the admitted class—at most of these schools that was the entire portion into which all the 'pure merit' students were selected. The other eighty-five percent was determined by demographics, connections, wealth or family political power.

Dr. Higgenbottom said, "Wanda. You're new to all this, and you're looking at it all wrong. You have to remember what we're trying to do here. Dishonest. Don't think of it that way." Dr. Beaverbrook nodded and took a drink of his wine.

Wanda said a confused nothing. She just looked at the man demandingly. Hawkins Higgenbottom eventually yielded and came close to answering her question. "All right. Let's suppose you're correct in the most technical sense. When you just look at it in full isolation, you could say we have to send our people out to make pronouncements one could call 'False but True.' That is, if you parse our words and look at all the numbers, it's possible to say the statements are technically false. But we're trying to do much more than generate batches of numbers. And, remember, only we have the data. Outsiders won't see them. Nobody can prove anything's false. Even inside our administrations, we restrict access to this sensitive data. Better than Top Secret." He displayed a proud and friendly, confidential smile.

W. Spencer Beaverbrook burped. He spoke, grumbling. "People of my stock have raped this country, and I'm ashamed." He tugged at his collar and wiggled his neck. "You should be too. You share ninety-eight percent of all of it but gender, it seems."

This was news to Wanda; she had always known white males were designated oppressors by many, and she did not disagree. But never had she considered white females complicit. After only a second or two, she realized he was right—she was one of them. Dr. Beaverbrook went on. "My shame for my fellows is exceeded only by my clear vision that it is up to those of us who transcend our genetic heritage to act. Someday this will all be corrected. After we're gone. After I retire. It is such a slow process." He hiccupped.

"But back to the outside assaults on our admissions. Remember this: when they attack us, they're guessing. Like Higgenbottom says, our numbers are secret; we may say how many category X students we have, how good they are, how they are better than people like me, like you. But we're going to keep the objective measures, the standardized test scores, and even the grades, to ourselves. We're not going to give our enemies a stick to hit us over the head with."

The four others around the table, save Kingman and Wanda, nodded in agreement. Kingman had no opinion on these matters, and Wanda was contemplating the man's use of the word 'enemies.'

Just then Travis Worthington again exceeded the amount of time he was able to sit in a group without speaking. He dropped a shot of whiskey down his throat and broke in, smiling, waving his finger. "I heard one lady, a judge somewhere, in an interview the other day. She said it was more likely that lightning would hit the tip of her dog's nose on the same day that she won the TeraLottery than that some kind of students at one of your schools were more qualified than her son. She was pretty much just plain vanilla." Then he hooted, "And then she goes and says she doesn't play the lottery!" He guffawed and faded away, laughing heartily and reaching for another shot.

Hawkins Higgenbottom's thick and powerful eyebrows chided Travis, then he turned to Wanda and nodded. "And draw strength from one more thing: most people are docile about this. They've been trained since childhood that it's churlish, unseemly, selfish to ask for details, data. To think for themselves. It's mean-spirited. Discriminatory. We believe that only the ones with an ax to grind are out there complaining like that woman your esteemed husband mentions. What fraction of the population is facing this issue at any given moment?" He bristled with indignation and said with a shudder, "It's absurd. We shouldn't be put in the situation where we have to answer questions that force us to foist lies on the public anyway. We're university leaders, and I'm getting more than tired with the disrespect, the lack of trust we're getting lately. I say ignore them all." He sipped his wine and became calmer. "It's worked for years; it will work again. Our assignment as universities is to improve the world. Lead. Do some overdue social engineering." He smiled genially at the younger woman. "We're being true to our mission. True. So, use the word 'true' when you describe these things. Not 'false,' do you understand, dear? And my lord, banish the word 'dishonest' from your vocabulary." His patience showed as he took on the manner of long-past instances when he would teach a naive student about some nuanced subject; right now he faced a young university president.

Wanda Worthington was new to this. She was unconvinced but careful to try to glean whatever information was present in the men's' words. If she were not part of the inner circle she would have been affronted by his twisting of language, but in reality she was willing to suspend final judgment for now. But not to surrender. "And we have to say false things... why?"

W. Spencer Beaverbrook took up the thread. "Don't dwell on it. Don't use that word 'false.' Let's grant that you're correct. Forget about it. Here's what happened when you surfaced with your new proposal for freshmen admissions. You rocked the boat and called public attention to the arithmetic of the whole admissions process. That opens up discussion of all the—let's grant—mathematically ridiculous public positions we take in the process. You've complicated all our lives, not just yours." He let out an exasperated sigh.

"Ridiculous. False, you mean?" She was not trying to needle the men; she was trying to figure out exactly what they were saying and how it relates to real things. And maybe to get them to stop dancing around and say what they meant. She was not being fully successful at this last effort.

"I don't think you are hearing us. There's that word again. We are working in the service of the greater good. Higgenbottom told you. Truth. And everyone thinks they like truth. Well, little children like sugar. Candy. Chocolate. Do good stewards surrender to every impulse of those in their charge? It's maddening. However good our intentions, we get a lot of criticism. The last thing we need is for someone to call attention to all this admissions stuff, to constantly reignite the bickering."

Wanda sat, pondering whether fraud cannot be used, by definition, in the service of truth... maybe with some weird definition of truth. This was not something she had ever considered, nor thought worthy of reflection before. She was skeptical of everything she was hearing.

Beaverbrook continued, "We've always been able to deflect the questions. But somehow these 'coin flip' and 'roll the dice' stories about you have attracted people's attention. The demagogues are having a field day. I hear people in coffee shops passing judgment on standard deviations, confidentiality of our databases, demographics, oppression—all of it. What are we hiding? They're all experts. The guys plugging holes in the road. Ladies at their hairdressers. Everybody. These kids pouring our wine." He gestured at the waiter refilling his wine glass. The young man smiled nicely at him, and they exchanged ostensibly pleasant nods. He turned back and shuddered. "What a mess." He paused, then shook his head, and Dr. Higgenbottom confirmed things with a genteel side to side head motion of his own.

Dr. Beaverbrook was frustrated by the outside interference, the need to generate the absurd rationalizations about how candidates are selected for admission to his university—justifications only a dishonest cynic would produce, justifications only an idiot would believe. He said, "What a waste to be forced to contrive defenses from the outside world as a cover for the privilege of helping the benighted ingrates evolve." He settled his temper and said, "So, Wanda, that's just where we are. That's what you've ignited, bless your heart. But even without your idea, it's been getting harder and harder to do what's right. Between court orders and outside complaints, threading the needle is getting to be quite a fight. Our legal folks are stretching more and more in coming up with plausible-sounding arguments that we're technically clean." He smiled wryly and sipped his wine.

Dr. Higgenbottom broke in, "Yes, well, as you often say, let's don't dwell on it." He took a drink of wine.

Dr. Beaverbrook's momentum carried him despite the request from his friend. "So we go through the process with our legacy admits and the political connections. We add the checkbox categories. We account for the children of the super-rich as automatic admits—"

Dr. Worthington interrupted him. "I don't buy that. This is my first cycle, but I'm sure Cornwallis won't admit people just because they're rich or because they have connections. I guess I've asked a lot of questions but not that one. It never even occurred to me. You're wrong, at least there." Wanda Worthington, regardless of her own family's wealth and despite the fact that it was the subject of her attention almost every waking hour, felt money was dirty. She could not conceive a great university mixing it into the admissions process. She took a drink of her too-long-neglected wine.

Dr. Higgenbottom smiled and glanced at Dr. Beaverbrook before breaking in again. "Wanda, dear, do you believe that your admissions committee wouldn't notice if Bob Gaines's child applied to your school but only had average grades? How about the daughter of the United States President? Are you pretty sure the committee would reject these kids? Let's say they do, and you get an angry phone call about it. Would you go and talk to the admissions folks? I know what I'd do. I know what I *did* do when my school made that exact mistake a few years ago." He smiled and drank. "Would you talk to Dr. Gaines differently from how I talked to the President? Tell me what field you think your successors will farm for donations ten, twenty years from now if you reject today's children of the super-rich. For that matter, would you call one of them for money a week after rejecting his niece? Please, I'd like to hear your thoughts on this."

Wanda looked away and stroked her chin as she thought about it. She realized that there was no merit to the position represented by her instinctive exclamation. The men were right, and her school was certainly engaging in the practice. Dr. Beaverbrook continued his earlier thread. "Let's continue with checkboxes: sports, race—oops I didn't say that—gender, redlines and so on." He saw that Wanda Worthington was distracted, thinking. He quietened in response. She thought about her prior discussions with the admissions folks, and they started making sense. Since taking the reins at Cornwallis she had begun to notice how the people in that department seemed to speak in doubletalk, or at least in some sort of code she could not understand. She was formed in the same environment as them; she shared essentially all their beliefs and even biases. There was nothing for her to hide. But they would not engage her in actual conversation.

Wanda Worthington had never felt there was any sort of moral uncertainty in the typical university's stance of singling out individuals and handicapping them for the offense of sharing ancestors with the privileged few. After all, it was intended to make up for the exact reverse process perpetrated by their great-great grandparents, and it seemed appealingly symmetrical on that basis. And she did not balk at excepting those who actually *were* privileged from this sort of discrimination—for the good of the university. The process all but blackballed the individuals in the out-of-favor class who were unfortunate enough to not actually *be* privileged, since slots were reserved for allocation to those who actually *were* privileged. This had been of no interest to her in the past. But now that she was at the top of a university, she was examining it for the first time and questioning things. The admissions people were always dodging around some 'truth that cannot be spoken,' averting their eyes and giving her slick answers that did not really satisfy her but served their purpose—delaying things until she had no more time for the conversation and had to give up.

She completed her reverie, and Dr. Beaverbrook, who had paused while she considered, continued, "For the rest, we do a crap shoot, let's all admit it. We're aiming to compute an estimate of which students represent the highest net present cash value for the university. But we know we're not going to bring in some anonymous but brilliant piece of white male trash from a mining town in Kansas or a fishing village in West Virginia. Let 'em stay in their trailers. I'll take the risk.

"The fiction, half bolstered by the contradictory public factors they make us put out there, is that we always select the best candidates for admission. And my dear, you have brought all our processes into the limelight. That kid in the mining town is not stupid. But we're forced to say things that like this: we give preference to our favored groups without discriminating against you. Your competitors don't need to measure up to the same standard as you, but we assure you that they do anyway. We will hint at it with certain portions of our data, commingled test scores and such, the ones that support our public position against you. You cannot see the gestalt of the information we possess. And these things cannot be quantified anyway so you don't need to." He stopped for a drink and a pause. His countenance growled, "And listen, kid. What you must understand is: shut up—you have no business questioning these things. Just close your eyes, pay your taxes and leave decisions to us." He smiled in a confusingly placid fashion, lightly lifted his shoulders and dropped them.

By now Dr. Higgenbottom was feeling his wine. He threw his arm around his wife's shoulders and leaned across the table toward Kingman. He said genially, "Dressel-Meier my friend, what do you think?" as he flipped the index finger from his dangling hand toward Dr. Beaverbrook. "I can't tell what side this fellow is on. Do you think he's with the bad guys?" W. Spencer denied it with a simple smile and a shake of the head.

"Isn't that a little harsh?" Kingman turned and asked Dr. Beaverbrook. "Is that what you think?"

Dr. Beaverbrook wet his palate with wine. He swallowed leisurely. "That's what *they* think they see. I hope you know what I think. I'm one of the good guys." He was shaking his head as he turned back to Wanda. "Anyway, that's what got you into the crosshairs. There's been real anger out there from people who have felt insulted, disrespected. It's not your random cap at the end of the process, though that certainly makes it harder to explain to the average Joe. It's the whole procedure. I can't say why, but they just don't trust us any more, people don't. And they think we should be required to satisfy their curiosity. They just don't seem to want to leave it to us professionals anymore."

Wanda mused, "So it's like he said in that first talk this afternoon." She absorbed Dr. Beaverbrook's words quietly for a moment. "But then why should I take fire from *inside* the universities? I'm not changing the game. I'm not even changing the demographic categories. All the randomness would be done at the very last step. I'm just directing that Cornwallis, when down to those supposedly qualified unfortunates who aren't on what you called the 'checkbox' list, choose fifteen percent—*fifteen percent*—randomly! I have proof—I am proof—it works. Listen, there is no doubt in my mind that society will be better served." She looked at Dr. Higgenbottom, then at Dr. Beaverbrook. "The mission you talk about. Everyone will be better served by throwing in a bit of unpredictability. I'm not even proposing that we put new clothes on the emperor here. We're not talking about substance here. It's not a change, really."

Dr. Beaverbrook briefly considered whether to be affronted by Wanda's bringing in the fable about the exploitation of groupthink, but he put it aside and asked, "Did you hear what I just said? It's not your randomness. To stretch your own metaphor, your random component—that's the little boy calling attention to things, crying out loud that the emperor has no clothes. We're not stupid. We know you're not attempting to reform anything, to drape the emperor in different robes. But now everybody is starting to feel they can comment on the quality of the emperor's... er... tan." The whole table chuckled except Wanda and Kingman. All but Travis Worthington understood the issues, and they knew that Wanda's proposed change was purely one of form, not substance. None thought Wanda was wise to have opened Pandora's Box.

Alison Higgenbottom was tired of the subject of admissions. She remembered the story she had tried to bring up earlier, before the discussion turned to admissions. "Tell me, Dr. Worthington, how did that whole tax thing come up? What was all that sniping about?"

Travis Worthington was agitated and butted in. "That's just an attack by the bastards, those bastards. It's stoked by her enemies, because she's trying to fix things up. It's got nothing to do with nothing. Just one more way to throw dirt at her. Tax attacks." He nodded at what he perceived as a pun when he heard himself, then surprise and alarm flashed through his face as he saw only empty shot glasses in front of him. He settled for picking up a toothpick and starting to chew it for the time being, but looked around nervously for a waiter.

Wanda answered Alison. "You know what? I don't even know why any of us in this room, excepting, of course the help...," She glanced slyly at one waitress two tables over, then another, "have to file tax returns at all. For goodness' sake, I'm the president of a university. My mission is to improve the world, not go out and grab as much money and profit as I can for myself like the speakers this afternoon." Most around the table nodded.

"The system is schizophrenic. Either as universities we're doing good or we're not. It makes no sense to have this halfway status, where other people give us money to save their own taxes, where we don't pay tax on our property like they do, where our funding is largely from taxes, but yet as individuals we're treated like crass opportunists for income tax purposes. Our purpose is worthy enough that even when people buy our product, education, they get to write down their taxes. Why am I even paying income taxes, let alone being ridiculed for them?"

"So then, how did the whole thing happen, anyway? I mean, how did they get ahold of the returns?" asked Betsy Beaverbrook, who had been listening raptly.

"I'm an idiot," Wanda glanced at her husband. He nodded agreement. She continued, "Completely my fault. For whatever reason, I still like to have a paper copy of all my records. Call me a dinosaur. Well, when the accounting people got me the tax forms I tried to print them. But somehow I got something wrong; they didn't come out on my printer. I sent them somewhere else, and I had no idea where. Somebody got the papers, I guess."

"I see," said Betsy. "But why did it cause such an uproar, getting national attention and all?"

"We really don't know. Of course, some of my current compensation is public knowledge, just like your husband's. So all we got on that was just some carping about how the university should not be grossing up my salary to compensate for taxes, how I should be volunteering to work for free, that sort of thing. No, the real silly thing was the inane pickiness over the tax schedules. That's what got us on the late night comedy shows."

"We all saw some of the routines," said Alison Higgenbottom. "How they twisted that. I tell you, facts mean nothing anymore." She was lying, as she knew nothing about the level of truth in the jokes. She tried not to respond to her memory of some pretty amusing takes on the subject. She did not smile.

Kingman vaguely remembered a flurry of bad publicity for Cornwallis months ago. He busied himself trying to remember details. He twirled his wine glass. Betsy waited while her salad was served and then asked, "What exactly was the scandal?"

"They picked apart my tax schedules, complaining that I don't donate enough to charity. People believe I should be giving it away to everyone else, I guess. I refuse to discuss it; I will never satisfy my critics. We're trying to shape the future. It's a distraction, that's all."

Travis smiled and said, "Nah. They're bastards, that's all. We're already rich, baby." He leaned his face toward hers, and she dodged gracefully.

Now Kingman remembered the scandal, and he was silent, observing the couple, especially Travis, with interest. They all started on their salad as Wanda continued between bites. "At first I was caught off guard by all this. Back home my university was never the target of such bile. People behaved. So I'm here at Cornwallis trying to do something for people, and everyone, these outsiders, they're criticizing me. I'm working dawn till dusk every day. They're complaining that I send out letters asking people to give us their money. I won't engage them. Anyway, I think the whole thing has blown over now; it was right before that singer Zululu was murdered by his girlfriend."

Travis feigned patience, "There you go again, dear." He turned to look at Betsy, then Kingman and Dr. Beaverbrook. "What she didn't say—I had to go out and make the case myself since she thought it was all below her. I told the world that we drop giant donations to charity every year. We just don't care to claim credit for it. Why should we? We pay enough taxes." The toothpick rolling around his mouth, and his logic, distracted the listeners.

Kingman thought about what he remembered. In fact, the woman had been harshly attacked, and her youth had come back to haunt her some. She grew up poor. Her doctoral dissertation, written before she had met Travis, severely criticized Americans for their individualism, greed and drive for personal gain. Once she moved to Cornwallis, somebody dug up her thesis, and it got a whole lot of attention. The juxtaposition of the document with the reports on her taxes made for lively entertainment, and her old dissertation had been translated into French, German, British, Chinese, and a few other languages.

Scanning his memory in search of the bad publicity, Kingman felt Dr. Wanda Worthington had maintained her dignity through all the attacks only to be clumsily torpedoed by her husband's public proclamations and appearances. Travis had appeared in interviews, sitting on his motorcycles and snowmobiles, attacking those who questioned his wife's values. Tonight Kingman surmised that it happened in defiance of Wanda's instructions.

One particular detail weakened Travis's vitriolic case about their huge, secret charitable contributions. The man had not considered the embarrassing implications of the very tax schedule at the heart of the controversy. It showed that the couple took a charitable deduction for donation of their used underwear to a local charity's second hand shop. Kingman recalled classifying the man an idiot from afar, a decision he heartily endorsed tonight. He gathered that Wanda and Travis Worthington do not try to get a tax write-off from their worn undergarments anymore.

Yes, Travis was a moron and a clown. Kingman metallically bonded another piece of information along with this into his memory: the man was staggeringly wealthy. In fact, Kingman found himself chastised by himself. "I'm surprised I didn't know how stupid the man really is. What kind of a job am I doing?" As leader of the Worldwide Transformative Foundation, Kingman made it his business to know something about everyone with this level of wealth in the country. Here, he had failed.

After the Zulolu story helped dampen the criticism, Wanda had performed a stroke of good strategy. She committed to a substantial, very public, personal donation every year to a cocktail of charities. The amount exactly matched the bump in salary the trustees much more quietly awarded her for this selfsame purpose. The university's tuition and their overhead recovery charge to the government edged up approximately one zillionth of a percent as a result.

The conversation meandered, diffusing through the whole table through much of the meal, lightly tethered to tax problems and traps. After a while, Kingman mentioned, "I guess I won't be having any tax hassles. I have no taxes, so I need no deductions. Nobody can pick apart my tax forms."

The group quieted down. Kingman consumed a leisurely forkful of dinner. Answering the quizzical silence he said, "I have no taxes because I have no salary. Well, for legal reasons they have me taking a symbolic salary. It's well within the zero tax bracket." He smiled with his control of everyone's attention.

All stopped eating their fine meals. Kingman took a sip of wine. Dr. Beaverbrook said, "Surely you have some income in your personal accounts. You run the most successful meta-charity on the planet. I understand your decision to reject a salary. Nonetheless…" his wife was listening intently and looking at Kingman, as were all the others.

Kingman enjoyed the disbelief all around the table. "I assure you, we at the Foundation know these areas very well. You are thinking that I must have some income from my personal wealth after all these years at the helm of such an organization. But I am actually a pauper. My net worth is far less than the value of the car any of you drive every day. When you look at me you see a man with essentially no possessions, one with almost exactly zero income and no income taxes. It's been over a dozen years since I paid a cent of income tax."

They were interested. Dr. Travis Q. Worthington IV grumbled under his breath, "Sleaze."

Kingman smiled as he glanced at Travis, then around the table. "Our lawyers have set things up so I have no need of wealth, almost no need of money at all. The Foundation takes care of my expenses. I am on call 168 hours per week. We're intertwined perfectly. My family will carry on when I am gone. The transition will be seamless—certainly much smoother than that of any other organization with a budget of tens of billions." He took another bite of dinner and chewed patiently as the audience waited for more. "And oh, yes. I don't plan to go anytime soon." They all chuckled jovially, led by the man himself.

He dabbed at his mouth with a napkin and continued. "We are experts in this sort of thing, and you should all remember it. Now, you all are not in the same situation as I. We'd all like to think of you as the cornerstones of your respective universities, but in fact you're just holding a position for some tenure. Here's to a long healthy one for all of you." He raised his glass. The others followed with hesitation, confused glances exchanged. Everyone took a sip. Where was this going?

"Now, your situations are not altogether without advantages. You work in nonprofit institutions and have an extraordinary amount of control compared to your equals, say in industry. Obviously at your level any of you have the intellect and ability to run a corporation with a comparable number, say 30,000, of employees. But there would be some complications and a loss of much of your freedom if you took that hypothetical job. Certainly your interaction with the taxing authorities would be more complicated."

Kingman paused for a few bites of dinner, enjoying and extending his time onstage. "My main point is that others compensated at your level have fewer options for shielding themselves, individually, from taxes. You should all be taking advantage of the sorts of mechanisms the Foundation has developed. Think about it. Dr. Worthington was correct. What sense does it make to have your own personal salaries and other compensation come through the system just to be taxed like the salary of the leader of a company that makes toilet paper? We at the Foundation can help structure things to your advantage. And it is not a selfish advantage—any dollars that don't go to taxes can go to directly doing good. Remember, all of us have that as our mission. Or the savings can go toward keeping it for the equally important good of providing for your offspring. Society needs leaders in every generation, and without proper financial provisions your children and grandchildren would be left to fend for themselves among the general population. We could be denied an entire generation of our future leaders."

The audience was rapt and silent as Kingman went on, taking advantage of their attention to try to heighten their interest in his new project. "Oh, and pay attention to my son Hunter's talk later. He will tell you about our newest initiative, into which you are all invited as charter members. The Lobby For Good is poised to make sure the legal system evolves logically and begins to recognize the unique plight of the nonprofit institution. And, of course, those dedicated individuals at its helm."

Kingman turned his visible attention back to his dinner plate. "Whew, I've said enough. I suppose you can see I'm quite passionate about the goals to which we have all dedicated our careers." Around the table, many wondered if they had been availing themselves of the proper tax strategies; several made mental notes to fillet, or at least flay, their financial officers if not.

Dinner progressed, and dessert was served along with coffee, tea and cordials. Toward the end of the dinner hour Dr. Kingman Dressel-Meier approached the podium according to the normal Homecoming protocol. He gave a shortened version of his annual talk, perhaps sprinkled with some hints about a surprise in tomorrow's unusual session on a yacht in the sound. Then he turned the floor over to his son, Dr. Hunter Q. Dressel-Meier, who gave a cheerleading overview of the Lobby For Good, the new wing of the Worldwide Transformative Foundation.

Hunter's style was not as dramatic as that of his father. He was hesitant and stultified. The presidents, spouses and financial officers from the universities were polite and mostly inattentive to his preview of the Lobby For Good. They could be seen in side conversations and making small jokes over their desserts and after-dinner cordials. Hunter's goal was to communicate the importance of the hands-dirty job of architecting new laws to the health of the nonprofit world. But the detached self-identified intellectuals comprising the top tier of the audience were not captivated enough to grasp his message, though there was a glimmer of hope that the financial officers would accept the planted seeds and nourish them to fruition. Still, Hunter did not stimulate nearly enough enthusiasm for the Lobby to give the desired boost to its prospects.

Trimming the Vines

Does this maze have an exit?

"Magnificent, isn't it? I think it's more beautiful than the widest valley, the tallest waterfall." Dr. Kingman Q. Dressel-Meier stood at the railing of the Foundation's yacht amid the Emerald Vine Plus university presidents, admiring the Manhattan skyline. All chatted over coffee or cocktails, and hors d'oeuvres as they watched the inspiring man-made horizon drift slowly by the boat. Kingman walked around and placed gold "IDIC" stick pins on the lapels of those who had forgotten to wear their own; it was a tradition for everyone to make sure they don these ornaments on Friday of Homecoming. This year the gathering was unusually intimate—the financial officers were elsewhere today, and it was just Kingman, Hunter and the presidents on the boat.

The craft drifted along lazily and soon made its way to open water. Kingman gathered everyone inside to hear Hunter's presentation on the Lobby For Good—its inception, vision and the coming formal public launch. Kingman initiated the session, and after a buildup he turned over the floor to his son. Hunter's talk offering charter membership to the universities was not well polished. It presented facts but did not score as many emotional points as Kingman had hoped. The crowd was less than enthusiastic.

The audience did perk up a bit when Hunter mentioned the progress of the current legal action claiming that their admissions processes were illegal. The suit asserted that universities should adhere to equal opportunity laws applicable to the rest of society, challenging the varying collection of exceptions granted to them by judges over time. It also characterized their sharing of applicants' personal and financial data as somehow wrong and illegal. Neither of these subjects were novel; for decades there had been nagging suits and back-and-forth rulings allowing and prohibiting the practices in question. But legal observers felt this was a more serious challenge that could lead to a more permanent set of rules, and it was gathering more than passing attention for that reason.

Hunter took no advantage of the audience's interest in the suit, however, and their attention loosened as he wended along in wordy blather on other aspects of the Lobby For Good. His own resolve flagged in the face of everyone's disinterest as the talk progressed. He failed to mention the Lobby's financial demands on the universities, due to a faint heart resulting from the bad energy in the room. The presentation tapered down into a subdued and vague exhortation to join as a charter member.

Kingman thought, "What a disaster! This thing, especially the ending, was flawed. He didn't request anything specific, and the promised benefits seemed far off. The mission itself seemed non-urgent. A throwaway, if I ever saw one." He cursed himself for overconfidence in Hunter. He had left most of the preparations to his son. He had not drilled Hunter and forced him to rehearse the key points and style. The omission was perhaps understandable; these things were second nature to Kingman and, not being a natural teacher, he forgot that the necessary skills were not inborn for everyone. This was the first time he had trusted one of his deputy sons with such an important pitch. He decided to jump in at the end and revive the circulatory systems of the presidents.

"Gentleman," Kingman interrupted Hunter amidst his dwindling sentences, "and of course Ladies!" He nodded to the females clustered at the edge of the group. "Let me connect the dots on some of this for you. I am sure you are aware of the pressure in the United States Congress led by our friend Senator Lover of Illinois. He is attempting to punish universities, and doubly so large-endowment universities, for the crime of being universities." He looked at Dr. W. Spencer Beaverbrook who, as head of the University of Cathargo, knew exactly what Kingman was talking about.

Senator Fredrick Q. Lover was a crackpot politician who had gotten on the United States Senate's Education Oversight committee. The man was born poor and grew into a successful businessman and wealthy property owner living not far from the University of Cathargo. He was a popular man known universally by his childhood nickname, Frog; nobody called him Fredrick or Fred or Mr. Lover.

Nine years ago Lover suddenly came into conflict with the university— by pursuing his daily business life exactly as he had always done. The university needed space to accommodate its expanding foreign student population, a group that was becoming more critical to the financial growth of the school due to intense public pressure to limit costs for domestic students. As United States citizens' slots were reallocated to foreign students, more physical space was needed to accommodate the incoming pupils, since by definition the foreigners who came were wealthy and expected comfortable amenities.

The school filed the necessary paperwork, and working with the government, efficiently took all of Frog's real estate from him, including the building he lived in. He fought the takeover, and he also contested the terms of 'sale.' For purposes of this transaction, the property was valued using the university's own innovative statistical sociologic-economic models. In both efforts he failed to gain the ear of the executive and judicial government officials; contacting his Congressional representation was of no avail.

In addition to the indignity of having his home and property transferred to others, Frog was disadvantaged in losing his life savings. You see, he always loathed debt and had been quite conservative in his monetary dealings. Based on actual market values he had millions of dollars of equity in the properties, equity which somehow became not negative and not positive, but exactly zero when the purchase price was computed by its buyer, the university. He walked away not owing a cent on the properties' mortgages but sucked dry of his wealth. By the time he was forcibly evicted from his home he had few friends in government, and (if zero is not the smallest countable number) fewer in the university.

Near the end of that year the unpopular man's tax assessment for the portion of the year that the buildings had been on the tax rolls quadrupled retroactively, a move intended to help the local government ease the transition to the new tax-free status the land had acquired. This left the penniless man millions of dollars in debt. Mr. Lover fought the bill and made no new friends in government in the process; his language was immoderate, and some bureaucrats and magistrates characterized him as verbally abusive. Shortly thereafter, a penalty was unveiled for the now-demolished real estate: Lover was fined for asserted code violations in a number of buildings, violations he denied. The amercement was assessed at the union labor cost of construction to rectify the problems in the phantom buildings plus a punitive component. Lover contested all these heretofore-concealed findings but was unable to prove to the judge's satisfaction that the now-nonexistent buildings were indeed up to code when they were taken from him. He failed to meet the burden of proof, and the assessments stood.

Proving that government is not heartless, once it was clear that the man would never be able to pay the assessments, the authorities granted a continuing series of annual interest free delays contingent on his good behavior. Frog never acknowledged any of these maneuvers and for some reason he never appealed his fines further. They are still on the books.

Incidentally, in a true demonstration of the synergy within the American economic system, once ownership of the property transferred to the university, its computed valuation (as determined by the university's innovative model) was much higher due to the changed circumstances and forgiven tax burden. This bonus expedited demolition and construction financing, and the land soon hosted a series of beautiful and luxurious apartments and shops for the alien elite. Local residents could be seen admiring the splendid architecture of the fenced complexes, and the press widely applauded the award winning designs. No True Scotsman could possibly doubt that the properties had now been put to 'highest and best use.' This group, of course, excluded Lover's former customers and employees.

In a turn of events illustrating the resilience of the American entrepreneur, a few years after the confiscation Lover's eldest son Douglas, who was universally known as 'Dog,' built a viable business there. He leased a fine car and ferried the buildings' inhabitants to and from the airport, downtown and the center of the university at all hours of the day and night. As of the time of this Homecoming meeting, he was boldly contemplating expanding his business by installing a shoe shine station within the complex.

Dr. W. Spencer Beaverbrook was a gifted and impressive wordmonger. During the noisy takeover battle he made public statements on behalf of the university and its allied public servants in the three government branches, statements the public received well enough. He criticized Lover's intransigence as well as the man's nickname; he especially denounced the man's lack of foresight. You see, Lover owned property only in that single neighborhood—the area where Frog grew up and raised his family. Every university president knows that an investor must diversify his portfolio or risk this exact sort of personal catastrophe. To the public at large, Dr. Beaverbrook made the case that the university had no choice in its actions; regardless of whether there were some trifling imperfections in the takeover paperwork, it was no more guilty of malice or misbehavior than a hawk is guilty of following the natural law dictating that it must dismember and eat small mammals. He pointed to the unanimous alignment of the government at all levels with the university's actions. Dr. Beaverbrook also highlighted that society must not tolerate one greedy man standing in the way of a great university, a point few outside Lover's circle of unemployed employees, evicted tenants and abandoned customers disputed.

To make a long story a bit shorter, throughout the battle Lover developed an unpleasant relationship with the university. Frog accused the university and the local government of dishonesty and malicious corruption. He was a changed man, and he developed a grudge that impelled him to look at universities and government bureaus with extreme skepticism. He became a crusader for what he called the 'common man,' and somehow over time he captured the imagination of the wider public by railing against the whole government establishment in sort of a David-and-Goliath, American myth fashion. He twice ran as a demagogue for U.S. Senate with the slogan, "If they can do it to Frogs they can do it to chickens. Don't be a chicken, Vote Frog!" and he accidentally won that second election. Pundits conferred with each other, but never could explain this result. Since then, all polls showed him quite popular despite universally scathing news coverage.

Until recently Lover could safely be ignored; his ignorability was now in question given his Senate office and his noise in the Education Oversight committee. He was dangerous. The presidents here today, though largely ignorant of Senator Lover's history, were all aware that there were unwelcome myopic rumblings about fantastically punitive measures in Congress. The whole scenario the senator advocated seemed surreal to them, but Kingman had gotten them to take notice, and their attention was now available as it had not been for Hunter.

He said, "Hunter has been monitoring the situation." All glanced at Hunter, and he nodded timidly. Kingman continued, "The Lobby For Good has not made any contacts or taken actions to influence this process because we have not gotten launched yet. You should be the charter members. Make no mistake here. If Lover's proposals somehow get traction and start wending their way through Congress, it will be like a nest of snake eggs hatching pregnant snakes. Remember my words here: this process never ends. Snakes breed like rabbits once they see the light of day. And snake pits don't disappear by themselves."

He paused, looked at three or four presidents and then said, "I am not talking about the ongoing carping about good governance, oversight, self-serving decisions and so forth. We have lived with these for years. I am talking about new and very specific threats." Kingman had a cup of coffee nearby, and he took a few sips of lukewarm java.

"The sections most anathema to you, I would have to believe, are an item imposing the annual mandatory spending fraction for your endowments and the meddling section levying a punitive tax ensuring you cannot profit from enrolling a foreign student. And, of course, the provision making you retroactively liable for loans defaulted on by your students, even with its limitation to money you actually received.

"Senator Lover and his supporters are trying to equate universities with other tax-exempt organizations. They are required to dispense money from their endowments annually in order to maintain their tax advantages. This demonstrates a basic misunderstanding of your mission. The same error underlies their charges that you have unjustly increased your prices—the accusation that you have monetized the dreams of your students and pocketed the current cash value of those dreams, leaving a trail of suckers with crushing debt. As for the proposal for the foreign tuition tax, that's nothing more than bigotry. This whole situation is a mess." Heads nodded.

"Listen to us. You must retain access to your lifeline of government loans. You have to keep your ability to grant visas to foreigners without real government interference and profit from it. You can't afford to lose your foreign sources. We all know the triple benefit of bringing in the children of the world's rich—the money, the prestige boost of rejecting Americans, and, outside the technical fields, the pre-established international connections as the next generation of rulers takes over back home.

"We cannot allow this single disgruntled lime biter to design national educational and immigration policy. The proposed legislation is full of such nightmares. Imagine regulators, or worse, groups of your local neighbors deciding the year's valuation of your assets, or how many foreigners you will bring in to bid up their rent. It may not be an exaggeration to say Lover's initiatives could spell the death of your universities as we know them."

He stopped for a long interval, looking each president in the eye. "You, right here on this yacht, you are the leaders with the most to lose. Lover & Company perceive some attractive targets here; he is always mentioning your huge trove of defaulted student loans while he points out your salaries and the size of your endowments. He asks his crowds if the universities thought nobody would notice decades of their prices climbing at many times the rate of inflation. Once he gets the crowds really worked up, he asks if anyone has a son or daughter whose place went to a foreigner. And guess what! He always finds some. Everybody's kid is qualified to go to Halford, everyone's seat was taken by an outsider. Your foreign cash intake is at risk. You live in a highly tax-advantaged world. Huge portions of your budget are sourced through taxes, one way or another, and Lover and his ilk are whipping up those who somehow feel they fund you just because they have to pay taxes. He is barking about congressional subpoenas to identify whether any of your foreign tuition money originates as American foreign aid."

There was a gasp in the room.

"Between us girls, you have all enrolled the royal families of third world countries, and you can imagine how tracing the source of *that* money will play in Pretoria! This must be stopped in its larval stage, before it sprouts wings, if you will." Kingman normally did not sling metaphors so colorfully, but he was enjoying the zany twists in his diatribes today. All of the presidents save Wanda Worthington shifted uncomfortably; with a year or two of experience in her, her bottom would be wiggling in the seat like the others.'

Kingman went on. "You must engage the threat in a carefully coordinated fashion. The Lobby For Good is your horse to ride. Your vehicle. Your weapon. We will take this fight to every level of public relations, and I plan to identify and exploit every conceivable fear or insecurity that legislators have. We are forward-looking: we will put in place similar research on judges as well.

Dr. Wanda Worthington spoke as Kingman accessed his coffee again. She asked him, "Do you really believe this can get through? It seems so almost other-worldly. And what would be some of the detailed effects if these things pass?"

Kingman answered, "Probably not right now, but who knows? I agree it seems like a bad dystopian story line from an old television movie. It's hard to fathom. Nonetheless, we need to be prepared in case it gathers momentum. Else in a few years we could be wondering what swamped us, what destroyed such things of beauty. I give the endowment valuation tax about a one in ten chance of becoming law in the next two or three years. The foreign student thing—I think that's too complicated for people to get behind. Especially if we're all out there directing the discussion away from money and pushing the idea that it is meanspirited and selfish for Americans to rail against reserving seats for foreigners; the wonderful moniker of the

Know-Nothings has given us a great tool. Americans will do almost anything to avoid that tag.

"As for the defaulting loans, that may be a little more of a threat. On this score, all of you have, let's admit, converted your students' enthusiasm to ready cash, propping up your immediate top-line revenue and spreading the students' problems over decades. Your increased access to money from loans has given you the opportunity, which you have not wasted, to steeply increase your prices, and that has pressured many people. They are starting to band together, and there are increasingly coherent-sounding calls for those who actually ended up with all this money to be responsible for repaying bad loans." There was some shifting in the seats, and some of the executives flushed; Kingman was not normally one to speak so bluntly among his compatriots, but he was being quite severe today because he wanted to keep up the tension.

"Since this problem is so widespread, Lover has a bigger constituency for this piece of his agenda. It just hits home with too many people. Everybody has a relative who claims he should not have to pay off his student loans. Unfair as it is to blame you for the problems these people chose to encumber themselves with, we do have to worry about this one." Kingman slowly looked at each president in turn. "It hurts because we know all of us here are committed to fairness." He softened his expression and lifted his voice. "Still, I don't give it anything near an even chance to pass in the immediate future. So the odds are low, but think: on the endowment thing you have that ten percent chance of losing billions of dollars each year."

Wanda Worthington asked another question, "Dr. Dressel-Meier, why would people fall for this? I can understand political pandering and circus acts, but do you really think the public would accept such a ridiculous, and even draconian, system?" She and the others listened for Kingman's thoughts.

Kingman took a sip of cold coffee before answering. "Senator Lover has characterized his actions as remedial measures. His position is that you have built up a sort of nobility free of the restraints and reporting requirements imposed on other institutions, and that you have abused the power granted you by the country's trust. Lover's ilk speaks colorfully. They say that in the face of your ability to help yourself to increased treasure, you have behaved with the self-control of pigs smelling slop, not that of storybook royalty looking out for the good of the people." He paused, looking from Wanda to one or two others. "No, I don't believe they would be supported by most people. But here is the danger: many unpopular things become law. If this weren't true nobody would need to hire lobbyists; it would be a waste of money.

"The hell of it is this: inherent asymmetry is working against you: it took centuries to build your schools, but they can be crushed in a few years. A tsunami or earthquake does not respect a thousand years of construction. It destroys in seconds. Have you ever been careless and broken something beautiful that was made of glass? Even if you're remorseful afterward, the damage is done. That, *that* is the biggest threat from the public—a transient but destructive wave of emotion or even disinterest, whether later regretted or not." He was looking at Wanda throughout. She nodded silently.

"This fight will not be inexpensive. We expect your assessments from the Lobby For Good ..."

Bang! The group was instantly stunned. Presidents looked at each other. They lost track of Kingman's continuing speech. Seeing puzzlement on each other's faces they turned back to him. "...a sacrifice taken in service to your universities. Charity begins at home, and this is the greatest form of charity—generosity that redounds to the benefit of your own great universities. Your organizations are intended to be permanent institutions. Let's protect them. Confront the future. Engage this effort. This is an investment well worth making." He paused and wet his palate again with coffee.

The presidents were uneasy. Kingman's emotional address was setting some of the officers on edge, if alcohol and lukewarm caffeine consumption rate is any indicator. Especially nerve-racking was that hint of assessments and sacrifice after all the talk about threats to their way of life. And of course, that word 'investments.' This particular word was one they all used every single day in the course of separating people from their money or from other people's money put in their charge. They knew the code, knew what it meant.

"I should not allow it to escape mention that just as we have worked with legislative and executive branch officials and candidates, the Foundation has historically engaged the judiciary, both the federal system and that in many states. We have filed countless briefs combatting some of the more egregious and opportunistic 'common man' lawsuits, a nuisance that has been growing in popularity recently. This important work will also be carried forward by the Lobby For Good."

Kingman finished his awful, cold coffee as his eyes asked if anyone had questions. Then he continued briskly. "It's not all beating back the forces of darkness though. There are positive benefits to belonging. On a more cheerful note, you are undoubtedly aware of the movement in the U.S.

Congress to assess a flat five percent fee on personal income on the entire population, a fee which will be directed by the government to nonprofit organizations."

He was referring to the 'American Generosity Enforcement' law which would create a tax on the first few hundred thousand dollars of annual personal income and direct the money to worthy causes. The act was at an early stage of drafting. A murmur broke out as presidents looked at each other quizzically and exchanged partial queries. None was aware of this proposal. Dr. Napoleon Burnside Turnbull, in particular, was nonplussed. He shook his head and said to his neighbor, "What do I pay my people in Washington for anyway?" as he put his finger into his ear and scratched heartily and deeply through the nest of hairs within.

Kingman pointed out that the Foundation expected to be a preferred beneficiary if the proposal became law, and that the universities should work with the Lobby For Good to advocate similar status for themselves; to the presidents it sounded well-reasoned that their universities should be given preferred status.

Kingman shifted gears to bring up a source of income he had identified for the universities. "Now I want to identify for you an untapped reservoir of funding, one that has been building up over the years and is ripe for the picking." With the signal of more positive discussions, the presidents started loosening, relaxing. A few partook of their drinks as they all sat patiently through his dramatic pause.

"Our universities in this country have long supported the tax-advantaged pension status of government employees, the largest group of which is your little brethren—the public school teachers in each state. These government employees number well into the millions. You have supported union protection and annuity-based retirement plans for them by supplying carefully designed academic studies and research proving their worth in the face of public skepticism and contrary evidence; you've been stalwart in helping them resist erosion or taxation. It has been a demonstration of unity in the face of the nemesis, the common and uneducated man, and it is laudable. But in doing so you have cost yourselves billions of dollars."

A wave of surprise went through the gathered intelligentsia. Glances were exchanged up and down the row.

"This has been going on for decades, as has the growth of your own claim on the national wealth. There is a huge, as yet untapped reservoir of money out there in the form of future guaranteed cash flows for retired government employees, wealth to which you are blind in your student financial award decisions. You have done admirably in making sure you access the savings and retirement assets of those in the private sector, and it has served you well. It is now time to put all that government money on the table, time to make it available for your consumption. You must start incorporating the present value of these benefits in your computations, just as you do for the private sector.

"Of course, on another subject, you grant free and reduced-cost education to preferred types of students. From others you demand money to cover not only the cost of their own education, but that of these preferred students. Please understand that I am not suggesting that you change this." All the presidents were following, paying close attention.

"Now, you make some financial aid decisions based on ability to pay; some of you publicly state that you make all of your awards that way. In many cases it could be considered true if we ignore the powerful incentives you give to your clients to lie about their assets to whatever extent they are able. So far as you can, you audit the family history and assets of applicants and judge how much of their wealth you are entitled to. And it is admirable that, up to this point, you have exempted the value of future public pension payouts; it has allowed you to subsidize the good work done in government. For your purposes, privileged government employees claim poverty while in fact they often have a present-value net worth of millions, and comprise a very rich demographic group. Now that this potential wealth has accumulated so staggeringly, it is time to tap it. You could ignore it when your claim was smaller and when it was not so dominant, but you must change your process now and get to this money."

Dr. W. Spencer Beaverbrook broke in, "Dr. Dressel-Meier, surely you do not ask us to demand sacrifice from schoolteachers! Why, they are our comrades, a veritable army aligned with us against the mobs, the uneducated, the unappreciative, the outsiders. They have been some of our best friends. I won't countenance odious attacks against the dedicated schoolmarm."

Kingman smiled as the picture of the friendly, dedicated and dignified schoolmarm of yesteryear came to his mind, supplanting today's image of the overfed and grotesquely grimacing union member hurling bile from the picket line, bile proclaiming solidarity against the general public. "You will be convinced. It's not schoolteachers. I'm talking about the professional employees of government at all levels. Many government professionals retire with annuities worth millions of dollars. You are leaving this money on the table, don't you see?"

Seeing the confusion of several presidents, he elaborated. "What I am saying is this: cash flows have a specific dollar value. They are bought and sold all the time. And the dollar amount it would take to buy out the pension of many government employees is millions. That means this: A person with such a pension could, in principle, sell it for a lump sum of cash. Of course he would not sell it for one dollar, and he would not get a billion dollars for it. But there is a market price, and a person with the pension would be unwise to part with it for less than that. Of course, determining it is somewhat complex; there are assumptions and interest rates and timing and so forth. But try it. Ask some retired government worker in his forties or early fifties whether he would give away his pension for a half a million dollars on the spot. It matters not how mathematically illiterate he is. His union has likely made sure he knows to laugh at you." Some of the presidents understood, once the example was baked for them.

"You must access that goldmine just like the wealth of individuals who have saved their own personal money in the hopes of giving themselves an annuity when they retire. You are entitled to it. There is no difference other than its visibility on the books. But as you do things now, you remain blind to all that money. And remember, I am not talking about waiting around till these people retire and their children have already gone through your schools, largely on your money. I am talking about assessing the present, not future value of the cash flows. Today's value."

There was still doubt around the room; by and large the leaders were trained in sociology or communications or political science, not finance or mathematics. Kingman realized he had probably made a mistake in citing by name the largest class of government employees, schoolteachers, who had a fraternal bond with the listeners. This, combined with the audience's genuine lack of understanding of money beyond its magical ability to generate power, stimulate admiration and distribute favors, formed a barrier to communication. One of the presidents, nonetheless, was curious and asked, "How much money are we talking about?"

Kingman threw out a few quick numbers. "There are millions of these people with vesting in invisible guaranteed pensions. You all should know the word for 'millions times millions.' I am talking about trillions of dollars of deferred cash that you do not officially perceive, you do not access." The number was too big and too general for mental access by the elite. Kingman got their attention by pointing out Cornwallis and mentioning the number just for New York. He said that the universities should be able to consider well over one hundred billion dollars in assets they were now overlooking due to vested pension benefits of New York state employees. "Imagine the decreased financial aid requirement." The inquirer's eyebrows rose at the number. Around the room, there were mental efforts to understand what this meant, as translated to each university. One could almost feel everyone's fraternal bond with the schoolteachers weakening.

Kingman finished, "Imagine all the good you can do with that money. It's not like you are taking it to gorge yourselves on it, buy yourselves nice diamond rings. And remember, at least so far as the teachers go, these are people who are committed to higher education. Their children absolutely will go to college, whatever the cost. For years these people have made the same arguments as you have as to why the education establishment should be entitled to an increasing share of society's wealth. And what universities do they hope and dream their children will attend? Yours, of course. Our estimates are that, with current student demographics, you will be entitled to collect, as pure profit, a few percent of your annual budget."

The eyebrows of all the presidents jumped almost simultaneously; it would have been difficult to judge whether those of the furry bushes of the males or the delicate lines of the females were more animated. All the officers were able to reckon the number at the end of the computation of a few percent times a few billion dollars of budget. The only remark was from Dr. Napoleon Burnside Turnbull, "Please, we prefer not to use that word." Kingman nodded.

Kingman mentioned a few other things the Lobby For Good would pursue. He spoke of eliminating the need for students' families to file financial disclosures by granting the universities access to all financial accounts for the population, with some exceptions, of course. He mentioned his early career, during which he was instrumental in getting tax preference for public and university pensions for New Yorkers; he picked up on Dr. Worthington's thread from last night, highlighting the need for tax-exempt organizations to be truly tax exempt: their employees should not pay income tax.

Kingman sipped some water from a cup on the nearby table, as all the talking had dried his throat. "None of our battles can be won by a haphazard group of individual Emerald Vine Plus lobbyists in a disordered contest with thousands of other interest groups. We need a carefully orchestrated symphony, not a cacophony. Centralize your governmental relations. Cancel all your lobbying contracts, terminate your employees in Washington, and place your bets on the Lobby For Good. This will defray a significant portion of your assessment from our revolutionary new charity."

Most of the presidents were pensive. Dr. Clementine Dunster Trafton spoke up, "It sounds like you want to control a pretty important part of our work, basically taking over our governmental relations." She glanced along the row of presidents. "I don't think we could just hand over the keys like that. And this expectation of funding from us... From us?"

Kingman answered, "The world is moving along. You need to get more effectively embroiled in down-to-earth, dirty politics, and the best way is to avoid appearing to be involved in down-to-earth, dirty politics. Make a meaningful commitment to the Lobby For Good. It will be expensive, but you know the old saying about that.

"I hope you all do coordinate with us for the overall good. But I understand it may not suit some of you. We all have to make decisions best for the institutions entrusted to us. As for the Foundation: I assure you that any efforts we undertake are with the intention of helping the finest universities in our great country. However, we are bound and determined to be a pilot and not a passenger; you may stay behind, but we will not be left ashore as the ship sails away. We hope the great universities represented here today join us. Work with us. Let's shape the future to your advantage."

The presidents had been patient, speaking little, occasionally sipping coffee or cocktails. They were accustomed to politely letting others have their say, no matter how long-winded. By now, of course nothing Hunter had said was resident in their minds; Kingman's artful delivery of information and his borderline threats had gotten notice, but no deal was in the offing. This increasingly bald reference to money flowing from the universities to the Foundation was bothersome.

The most distinguished-looking of the presidents, Dr. Napoleon Burnside Turnbull of Quinston University, was also the elder statesman. He was not the oldest, but he had been president of his university for over a decade and a half; in fact he had been around when the predecessors of all the other presidents were installed. To the consternation of the two female presidents to his right, he had been puffing on his old-fashioned pipe the whole time Kingman and Hunter talked.

Dr. Turnbull stood up, uncurling his rigid body very slowly, displaying his starkly chiseled profile to the group's view, pipe in hand. The man was the picture of a university president from the nineteen-forties. The wavy-grey-haired statesman was bony, tall, relaxed and severe in his tweed jacket. The down-forward tip of his head, the flip of his wrist—these things indicated a man accustomed to sitting in judgment.

He inserted his pipe and lingered for all to admire, then let out a lazy puff of smoke. He flipped his pipe toward Kingman in his hand. "Dr. Dressel-Meier, every university in this room, even including Cornwallis," he turned stiffly and gave a playful smile and wink to Dr. Worthington, "has been through many cycles of legislative danger. Each of us has developed a toughness that has served, and will continue to serve, our schools well. We are not easily intimidated by threats." His speech was wrapped in an accent vaguely British, though he was born and raised in North Carolina.

He looked side to side, his body pivoting so his neck did not have to move much. Half of the others were nodding and half were still. He looked directly at Kingman and repeated, "Threats." He continued, "In my case, I suppose I had a head start over most of my colleagues in dealing with bullying. Growing up I regularly had to face oppression and torment from my elder brothers Luke, Joe, Jerry and Lou down on the farm. But I think I can say the others join me in having the strength to fight off these annoyances." He scanned his fellows again, in a motion reminiscent, perhaps consciously, of old movies about Abraham Lincoln.

"We appreciate your concern for our future and will assume it is born of the best of intentions. I am sure we all fear it is an overreaction, however. Thank you, young man." He replaced the pipe in his mouth, waiting to see if Kingman had a response. The other presidents found his statements approximately correct for the occasion; some were perhaps a little less assured than he. Kingman, standing, was the most relaxed person in the room.

Seeing no comment forthcoming from Kingman, he went on after a few puffs, "Leaving that aside for a moment, I have a mathematical question, if you will. We hear your suggestions, but for the life of me I cannot understand how this fits into our universe, our ecosystem as it were. Many of us have known you for years. We all admire your creativity, your energy, and of course your generosity. However, you are laboring under a fundamental misunderstanding, young man."

Though this was the second time he was so designated, Kingman was hardly young. In fact he was only a few years younger than this elderly looking gentleman. But the statesman's characterization did not seem misplaced in the relative sense—Kingman was an excellent physical specimen, and he certainly seemed more exuberantly vibrant than most in the room, certainly less wizened and grizzled.

Dr. Turnbull continued, "You need to understand this: our universities don't *give* to charity. We *are* charity. You yourself know that our task is to make sure that whatever profits are harvested from the private sector and allocated to our universities are well spent. That's what we do, how we work. Your proposal runs afoul of logic, of nature, of mathematics. To help you to grasp my point, let me make a simple analogy I think you will understand."

Kingman sat down and smiled, cordially bowing his head. He was within reach of a coffee pot, and he poured a cup as Napoleon Burnside Turnbull spoke.

"A university, let's say, is an organism, some living animal committed to growth and to doing only good for mankind, citizens, the world. Let's say you are that huge and complex beast. Imagine yourself going about your business, Dr. Kingman Dressel-Meier, the encapsulation of an elite university. You burn oxygen with every breath. All of a sudden, I demand that you start to exhale oxygen and breathe in carbon dioxide. Surely your days at East Overshoe State, or wherever you got your doctorate, supplied you with enough basic chemistry knowledge to see that this is meaningless. Yet this is what you seem to be asking of us, correct me if I am wrong."

The last clause was one of attempted intimidation, clothed as faux courtesy, not communication. He stood silent.

The other presidents nodded agreement; the case was proven to their intellectual satisfaction and emotional relief. None could have expressed the incongruity, nay the silliness, of Kingman's reverse cash flow proposition better than this distinguished man did. Surely a chastened Kingman would understand.

Kingman was quiet, listening and contemplating politely over his coffee, its saucer balanced on his knee, steady as a rock. But he did not respond. Mayhap he did not comprehend.

Dr. Turnbull resumed, "My friend, you need to understand our mission and our position in the world. The funds we have at our disposal are not ours. Any financial assets we control have been entrusted to us only in order to enable us to further our unique and inviolable educational and social-change mission. It's clear that the Foundation is a grand partner, but I would have to say that this idea of reversing a portion of the natural cash flow, violating the very architecture of the elite university system, is an abomination. Clearly untenable.

"Lord, how I hate that word, 'cash.' It almost rhymes with 'crass.' But there is no avoiding it. The crux of the thing is this: the cash must flow inward, toward our universities, to be employed in our good works. The laws of nature dictate we cannot reverse its direction. In any case, even if we were individually convinced of its propriety, dispensing money in the fashion you propose is certain to subject us to blistering resistance from within our university communities. And violent criticism from outside as well.

"In summary," Dr. Napoleon Burnside Turnbull prepared to deliver a conclusion, with the others in tentative silent assent, "We cannot help you here. We live in a very real world of constraints, and our budgets have been stretched to the limit. We find it preposterous that after all these years together you should understand us so little as to think we could accommodate your request for us to fund your new adventure in legislative tampering." He straightened his curled frame a bit against internal elastic forces that typically had him leaning over his prey in conversations. "And frankly, it's a bit of an affront. And as for you personally, we find your obsession with the pecuniary a tad base, beneath your normal dignity. Of course we all must deal with the financial but it seems it is becoming an obsession with you, and I think we all worry about you. We encourage you to return your attention to the natural and historically validated work of the foundation you created."

These last few sentences he delivered with apparent indignation, and as the upbraiding concluded, the man turned stiffly to the motionless ladies to his right, then to the equally still gentlemen on his left. "Am I mistaken?" He reinserted his pipe without awaiting an answer, and sat down with the slow movements of one fifteen years older. Then he turned to the task of fiddling with his tobacco. He was a patient man, willing to sit quietly through the rest of the discussion, especially since he was quite sure it was over. The other presidents telegraphed nervous relief that Dr. Turnbull had so eloquently identified and outlined the absurdity of Kingman's proposal. Surely the man would drop his campaign now. Wouldn't he?

Hunter trembled under the attack on his father, an assault that would have had himself in its crosshairs, had he not failed in his job today. He seemed to be taken by surprise, and was alarmed by the portions of the speech he apprehended. Kingman's steady, thin smile betrayed no surprise, worry or doubt. He had listened, holding his coffee, and now he sat in exaggerated motionlessness. He and Dr. Turnbull let the silence cascade into a tense acoustical vacuum among the presidents. One can imagine that everyone could hear the waves quietly lapping the boat below. At his chosen moment Kingman stirred, smiled and answered Dr. Turnbull.

"Dr. Turnbull, thank you for the clear exposition of your thoughts. Mistaken? Don't be preposterous. To this day I have never seen you mistaken, and I'm sure you've had the same experience." Dr. Turnbull ignored Kingman's smile and the older man smoked patiently, not biting at the bait, not showing his cards. Kingman continued, "Now, what is the Foundation? I submit that it is indeed a charitable organization quite similar to all of your universities, and equally elite in its own ecosystem. All of our organizations move billions of dollars around every year. In the case of mine it's often in the form of cash, while in your organizations it's sometimes cash and sometimes some other form of value. If you penetrate to the underlying realities, the underlying basis of our organizations is money, albeit sometimes wrapped thinly by many layers of high-sounding regalia."

Kingman noticed involuntary signals of disbelief from most in the assembled group; they could not accept that their mission started and ended with money. He feigned surprise, eyebrows arched, eyes wide, corners of his mouth pulled down. "If you doubt me, please, please... will one of you identify the last three large projects you authorized in isolation, projects which required a substantial cash investment? Cash that came from your own endowment or operating budget. Please."

Two or three presidents stirred, seemingly in preparation to speak, but Kingman spoke again, "I want to hear about projects not designed to increase your fundraising ability in the future. This rules out projects suggested by the need to spend in order to keep your standing in the eyes of the world, projects that enhance your own university's brand. Pure altruism. No monetary value, present or future. Are there any takers?"

Examples started to form within a few of the leaders' minds, but all were silent like schoolchildren in the principal's office. As the seconds wore on it became clear to each person with an idea that the projects moved other peoples' money around or resulted from pressure to preserve or build prestige. Many were concocted by the schools' expensive branding consultants.

If there were grass outside instead of water, if the windows of the yacht were not essentially soundproof, the assembled group would have heard crickets.

Kingman paused again for a sip of coffee, enjoying the silent symphony of the nonexistent crickets. He resumed. "Don't get me wrong—you are all doing good; that's what defines you. I'm just saying that money is your fundamental value, your motivating force, and that is natural. Now, getting back to our subject, thank you, Dr. Turnbull, for the biological metaphor. And I hope you will appreciate its elasticity. Elasticity. I love that word!" He smiled. "I will merely point out that a small fraction of what you breathe into your lungs *actually is* carbon dioxide; and an even larger portion of what you exhale is oxygen. What Hunter is proposing for a charter membership is a tiny piece of your budget, not that much bigger than what the Foundation has been providing you recently. Think of it as the oxygen you exhale, all the while understanding that some of the oxygen you originally inhaled was sourced by the Foundation in the first place. Consider it just a round trip! I believe all future oxygen sources are critical to you. We hope and expect to be one of those sources.

"We all like to think universities are above economics, but let's face it: each of you identifies your primary job as fund raising." He was channeling Florian Bok now. "Economics is the heart of any social system—the most fundamental of, shall we say, sciences. Money is an abstraction that underpins every flow in a social system. This is true regardless of how far removed an activity seems from fiscal considerations. Nothing moves without value transfer—i.e. money. Nothing. Do not fool yourselves into thinking you take in money and convert it to goodness or education or some other high-minded thing. They are mathematically bound, identified with each other. They are all representations of value. Without value, something that can be represented by the abstraction of money, there would be no motion at all, no society, no university even. Value is the defining kernel of any transaction. Money is the unit in which we encapsulate value."

He waited for an answer from Dr. Turnbull or another, but all were too cautious in the face of his unfolding argument. Then he went on. "Now, having dispatched with all that, all I can say in reference to the criticism you will receive from those who see a few visible percent of the iceberg that is your university is this: you have all been selected for your elite positions due to your extraordinary skill and communication ability. I think you will not be overmatched by your enemies who mount assaults, most of which fail to exceed the level of the intellectual adolescent in quality. I have confidence in you, as I know you yourselves do. I should mention the package in front of you." The presidents all looked down. During Kingman's beguilement a gilded envelope had appeared on the table in front of each. Hunter's talent for being unnoticed, a liability in normal situations, had some advantages too.

"Inside that beautiful envelope you will find the history of our interactions. In this confidential information you can examine the Foundation's annual one-way contributions of cash in both discounted and non-discounted forms, along with the total income and budget each of you has reported publicly. You will all realize the Foundation is generous to a fault."

Anxious, they unfolded their parcels. Each saw a colorfully personalized and cleverly unbalanced set of numbers and flowing graphical representations. The folding design facilitated privacy, and the careful illustrations guaranteed quick understanding of the data by the least mathematically inclined of the group. The design was splendid; even an unassisted university president, far separated from his chief financial officer, could autonomously absorb the message in seconds. Each spent a few heartbeats surveying the attractive overall vista, crafted for the aesthetically tuned portions of the brain. There was a split instant of pure enjoyment, appreciation of a work of art, while the form was grasped but the substance undeciphered.

Then the messages traveled to the brain's cortex and were interpreted. Numbers seemed to gel on the page in sequence—first, the pleasant numbers on the upper portion reinforced the feeling of bliss and enjoyment. Teamwork. Friends. Donations. History of success.

Then the carefully wrapped threatening numbers, designed to take a few seconds longer to perceive, unfolded.

These envelopes contained a clear, static communication of the historical asymmetry of cash flows between the Foundation and each university. In fact, were the presidents less dumbfounded, perhaps they would have believed Kingman had anticipated Dr. Turnbull's oxygen metaphor—the financial transfers in the graphics somehow had the quality of life-giving (and life-threatening) flows of fluids. Oxygen, maybe blood. Size, rate and direction of each event was instantly perceivable through the use of cleverly crafted icons, curving arrows, colored pathways, subtle shading and such devices.

The executives quickly started to treat the parcels like poker hands. None could suppress a glance among his colleagues, poker cards closely held, as the numbers on the charts seemingly enlarged and throbbed and hardened in their visual fields.

One number designed to emerge exactly in the middle of the process was the contribution expected for the Lobby For Good.

The portion of the page designed to sink in penultimately, but most deeply, was a particular graphic that showed the Foundation's marginal contribution during the reader's presidency and how it bent the curves for his predecessors. It was brilliantly designed and accomplished no small task in giving the same impression to every one of the dozen or so presidents, each of whom had differing financial circumstances in his university. Using only absolutely true numbers, each diagram implied or hinted that its reader exceeded the cash raising productivity of his predecessors. Also clear was the suggestion that the Foundation was responsible for most or all of his excess productivity; in most cases this chart showed that without the Foundation's donations the current president was behind most of his forerunners.

The last chart represented possible future curves labeled cryptically as "Legal Scenario 1," "Legal Scenario 2" and so forth. The graphs diverged widely, and there was a hint at the date of each president's retirement, a date that varied between the different future curves. As the curves were examined, each president could understand what the titles symbolized on the personalized scenarios.

Kingman's concentration was seemingly engaged in refilling and sipping his coffee during the silence. Eventually the presidents' eyes started to rise. He waited for the last to finish studying the charts, then he spoke to the shell-shocked audience. "Let me conclude by saying that I think those reports clarify our position. Now let us talk a bit more about the mission of the Lobby For Good …"

The recitation carried on for only a few minutes, with Kingman cheerfully recounting the key points of Hunter's initial discussion. The overall energy level among the presidents was deadened after the golden envelope presentation, and they listened slack-jawed. The idea of becoming charter members of the Lobby For Good looked less outlandish to the officers now, and soon it even seemed reasonable—reasonable in the same way that it is reasonable for a train to follow a curve in its track, or for a ball to roll down a hill once released.

Kingman's next order of business was to give a crutch, a face-saving device to each of his prey. Everyone went out on deck, and he cycled through in small private conversations. His words managed to instill in each of the intellectual giants a belief that his own university was benefitting from a favorable agreement while the others were being marginally disadvantaged. Once Kingman was certain that this secluded universal theme was secure, he took Hunter and left the deck to allow the presidents to confer among themselves. As they discussed the situation constrained only by their asymmetrical mental images and their own ego needs, a smoldering ember of camouflaged groupthink in favor of the obvious choice took hold of the presidents and ignited. In fact, the first to commit, and the largest cheerleader turned out to be none other than the illustrious Dr. Napoleon Burnside Turnbull. As the wave of certainty crested, each president filled out the forms that had been conveniently placed in the golden envelope, forms pledging the universities' assessments along with nondisclosure agreements.

In a little while Kingman and Hunter stood at the top of the gangway. Kingman saw his reflection in the window and noticed his hair had been blown out of place by a gust of wind, an indignity he corrected quickly. Just then the group of university leaders walked up. Kingman greeted each president, and Hunter silently collected their paperwork.

The guests walked on toward the gangway. As they progressed a seed of worry gently emerged and asserted itself in each president's gut—each secretly felt the same unspecified unease as he walked the ramp. Every step down seemed to add an increment of burden to his shoulders as he started to break in his new, custom-fitted yoke.

Kingman, document folio in hand, looked down the ramp with a teeth-hiding smile. He waved cordially as each of the presidents sequentially glanced over his shoulder. The executives proceeded to their waiting limousines, and as each grasped the door and leaned down to board the vehicle, Kingman thought he could almost perceive a shrug.

Induction

Why am I surprised?

T here were seven passengers on the flight from the capital to the Wholesome Globe Project's Swazizibia Mission. Gwendolyn and Alitisha were accompanied by five other young women (well, one was perhaps in her thirties) coming to volunteer as workers. The airplane seemed bigger than what Gwendolyn remembered seeing on the runway during her prior visit, and most of the space in the vehicle was dedicated to cargo. It carried several tons of food, medicine and other supplies along with the passengers. Overall there was seating for about twenty riders up front; the freight was visible as a haphazard collection of strapped boxes, behind a half curtain in the back. Far in the rear were several large tanks, presumably filled with liquids, though nobody heard anything sloshing around in them. Gwendolyn and Alitisha sat in the front seats, separated from the other passengers by unused seats stacked with boxes. The flight was comfortable, especially as Gwendolyn compared it to her memory of the long, bumpy, boring ride on her first visit. She sat behind the lone pilot, a young man of perhaps thirty. Alitisha sat across the aisle. Gwendolyn's ebullience kept her on edge, and she alternated between talking with Alitisha and the pilot, and looking at the African savannah through her window.

Alitisha expended most of her attention on chitchat with the pilot. On occasion the man used the airplane as an extension of the conversation: to make a point or just to break the flow of chatter, he sometimes took the passengers on a sudden thrill ride, unexpectedly banking and swooping the airplane dramatically. The first time or two he did this Alitisha was alarmed like the other passengers, then she was delighted by this sort of attention from the man in control of the powerful machine. The two laughed and talked like chatty friends on a trip to the beach.

Alitisha had been reluctant to come here, and for months Gwendolyn had pestered her friend to come along. Gwendolyn's father had weighed in with Alitisha's school and the mission to ease things, helping make the decision easier for her. With his smooth attention to the financial accounts and some intercession from the Foundation, the girl was able to get academic credit for this fall while at the mission. Along the way she got a few extra credits that made up for classes she failed to complete the prior year.

The pilot suddenly pulled the aircraft into a tight 360 degree turn and allowed a giggling Alitisha to help control the yoke. The other passengers were confused, and some were upset when the circle was complete. Gwendolyn was happy to have Alitisha for company, but moments like this reminded her that Alitisha did not think of their mission as a sacred quest; for her the trip was just a diversion.

The pilot's name was Aidan something, and he was from the United Kingdom, though he was born somewhere in the United States. Alitisha asked him where he would fly next. "Nowhere. Don't have to. Can't," he told her.

"What do you mean? Aren't you going somewhere else? Or back to the capital?"

"Nope. The director of the place makes us keep a fueled plane and a pilot on standby all the time when he's there. It'll be my turn to be onsite for a while. There is another pilot there now. His plane will take off pretty soon, probably later today or tomorrow. He brought the director to the mission a few days ago, and he'll probably carry out some volunteers since they have a fairly constant number at the mission. It seems like whenever some come, some go."

Gwendolyn broke into the conversation, "Do you fly out refugees when they're healthy enough for relocation?"

The pilot glanced at her and back to the front, seeming confused by the question, and it took him a few seconds to answer. "Just volunteers and visitors and supplies. And of course, the director and his things."

Gwendolyn was about to ask another question, but just then Alitisha asked, "How long will you stay, then?" Aidan indicated he didn't know. "Why the extra airplane?"

The plane bumped along in some choppy air as the pilot answered. "Safety, I suppose. The orders are, if a quick evacuation is needed, we are to get the director and anyone he designates onto the plane first, then the other staff and volunteers. We can take twenty-one, and maybe a few more in a pinch, in the passenger area. In a real emergency we could take another thirty or so rattling around in the cargo area, but I don't think there are that many foreigners in the whole mission."

Gwendolyn was confused. "Evacuation?" she asked. "Whatever for?"

Aidan shrugged. He picked up his beer, which had been hanging in a sling from the dashboard. So far, over the two hours of the trip he had consumed quite a few cans, and the empties were distributed on the floor. All the beer was warm, a fact that made good use of his British adaptation. He did not seem curious. "You know, things, I guess." he said meaninglessly.

"I thought there were thousands of people in the mission. What good is removing thirty of us?" Gwendolyn was perplexed.

"Well, you're right, the mission's huge. But most of the workers are locals, and of course I'm pretty sure all the people inside the camp are Africans. For evacuations we're mostly focused on the foreigners."

"But what would happen? Hurricanes?"

"I don't know. No. Not hurricanes. I don't think so, anyway. I don't know. Never thought too much about it. Maybe an earthquake or something. Yeah, maybe a hurricane. And the whole area is powered by a little nuclear plant now. Those things can blow up. But that's pretty new and we've had the same orders for years, so it's not just that."

Gwendolyn was surprised and alarmed to hear that the mission had a nuclear reactor making its electricity. It seemed like a disaster on the brink of happening. She had some doubt about Aidan's understanding of the things; she was uncertain, after many science classes since middle school, whether nuclear reactors explode if something goes wrong, creating a catastrophe like Hiroshima. But she was certain that if something small fails, they will spring leaks like Chernobyl and poison the neighborhood for thousands of years. She also knew that even with the best of intentions, people always make mistakes.

The pilot noticed her concern as he took another drink of his beer. "They say it's buried under the ground. Anyway an explosion is too sudden to gather the important people and fly away." Then he thought a minute. "Unless they get some kind of warning. Maybe they have a dial, like the one on a boiler that shows the pressure climbing before it blows up." He shrugged and looked out the window, thinking. "Yeah, that has to be it. Hope it works better than this one." He flicked his finger twice at a dial on the dashboard, and the needle, nominally stuck past 'H' at the end of the red zone, shuddered and settled at about the middle of the scale. He seemed to have gone through a round trip from comfort to comfort, with a nuclear explosion right in the middle. He sipped his beer. "Who knows? Maybe the landlord will catch up and Dr. Director will have to get back to Switzerland in a hurry!"

Again he shrugged his shoulders, threw a smile back over his shoulder at Alitisha and Gwendolyn, and took another sip of his beer. "They pay me, I hang out, usually for a few days or even a couple weeks, and I go on. I'm on the clock for twenty-four hours a day, and it's boring, but it's a great gig. The money's good. I'm so bored when I'm resting that I've even gone so far as to start reading some of the books they have laying around for the volunteers. Never could get into the things, though. Books. I mostly just hang around. You know." Aidan considered making a crack about how friendly some of the native women were, but thought the better of it. He sipped again. "I have to keep the keys to the plane on me, and the plane is always supposed to be fueled up. I'm supposed to stay close to it, whatever that means. But really how far can I go?"

Aidan remembered another potential reason. "The surrounding country is pretty violent when the other armed gangs come through. For the past couple of years one of them—I forget which—has claimed the province where the mission is. The director seems to have them figured out, and they get along well enough. He works well with the government too. I guess you could say he has both sides covered. You'll see lots of guns around, but I don't think I've ever heard any gunshots that didn't just turn out to be someone firing aimlessly, either drunk or emphasizing how funny a joke is. They all seem to get along with the director, I guess. They seem pretty good-natured, but I know they've run off other thugs who have come by."

Alitisha was not as relaxed about all this as Aidan. Gwendolyn was also troubled, and she was unsatisfied by the answer. She did not remember seeing any guns on her prior visit, and she was about to ask more when Alitisha broke in and changed the subject, "What do you have here today?" She was pointing her thumb over her shoulder toward the cargo. "I see some food. But there's lots of other stuff too."

"We're always packed to the rafters on the way in. In fact, we've got dozens of pallets of stuff back at the capital still waiting for transport. I never seem to catch up, even when they're bitching that they ran out of one medicine or another. I can only carry so much, and I have to take it in the order I'm told. Anyway, always the largest single supply by weight is water, then fuel. Each trip in carries a tank with more than enough extra jet fuel to fill one of these planes. When we land, we immediately fuel up and put our extra jet fuel into the storage tanks. We bring in food, both in powdered form and high calorie gel/goo concentrate. The ghosts love it I guess. That's some behind you on the next seats."

His reference to the supernatural caused a hitch in the girls' minds, but he continued without slowing down. This simple-seeming pilot was transformed into an expert on transport and logistics now, with a memory like a steel trap. "Logistical supplies are next. Tents, stretchers, spare parts, computer and communication equipment, flexi-coffins, tools, hypodermic needles, plastic bags, dog food, pumps, gas cylinders. And of course, each trip we bring a few hundred pounds of miscellaneous stuff people have ordered for themselves. Toiletries, regular old books, liquor, electronics, requests from home, that sort of thing. Special foods requested by the director. Oh yeah. Lots of rectangular unbreakable windows this trip too. And then we carry regular old food for the foreigners working there too: cryogenically frozen meats, usually, and a lot of the stuff you eat at home. Lots of canned goods and dry groceries. Cereal. Powdered eggs. Lots of pasta."

Alitisha and Gwendolyn both were a bit bemused by the list and its rapid-fire delivery from such a relaxed man. Who knew he could remember a list of three items, let alone more than a dozen? There were some very strange things on that list, but they were hard to remember in the long recitation. They looked at the boxes on the row of seats behind them. Alitisha made a sour face. The boxes were starkly marked:

One daily serving*
Average human 1000 Calories
Mix with 200ml water

There was a list of nutrition information that did little to stimulate a westerner's appetite. Alitisha pointed to another seat, and Gwendolyn looked over. One of the boxes was split along an edge, and a cloudy plastic bag holding a sand-colored liquid or paste was visible inside. The bag had a white label proclaiming the same information as the outside of the boxes. Alitisha wrinkled her nose and shook her head back and forth slightly. Gwendolyn agreed.

A speaker crackled with two quick blips, and Aidan's attention went back to piloting after another quick swig of his beer. They were approaching the mission. He straightened himself up and soon started his landing maneuver, a large clockwise circle around the mission. As the plane approached the camp, Alitisha and Gwendolyn saw dozens of small sideless tents in haphazard grids, with a few larger versions interspersed occasionally. There were hundreds of people on mats, and hundreds more standing or walking on the barren ground. Gwendolyn could see people gathered in the sun in open areas near the tents. Some were in lines. *There are so many of them! People look so much like ants from above.* On the west side was a large group of totally bare hills. The complex of buildings comprising the mission's operational organization was beyond the dirt hills. Gwendolyn had visited these building earlier in the year with her father. She pointed out the top of the cathedral as they circled, and Alitisha strained to see out Gwendolyn's window.

The runway was beyond the buildings, and the smokestacks were near the end of the runway. Gwendolyn could see the barbed wire periphery, wider and denser than she remembered. She also noticed from above that some barbed wire separated the camp proper from the hills of dirt.

Regardless of Aidan's illuminating discourse, Gwendolyn was stunned by something she saw as the airplane dropped low and flew parallel to the runway: a group of four jeeps manned by soldiers with automatic weapons sat astride the entrance gate at the edge of the mission. The airplane passengers were low enough to see the men's eyes as they watched the plane go by. Gwendolyn and Alitisha knew guns are evil, and what did that say about these men in possession of so many of them? The girls exchanged glances, each correctly identifying the queasy feeling in the other's stomach. Gwendolyn's mind, after a bit, surfaced the fact that the pilot told her this was a war zone. There were undoubtedly bloodthirsty pirates in this region of Swazizibia. She found herself thinking that perhaps it was good to have armed guards protecting the mission, whether or not guns are bad things.

Gwendolyn was surprised that she was surprised by the violence in Swazizibia. She had been in quite frequent contact with Dr. Bok since her prior trip here, and she did not remember him mentioning anything. But maybe it should have been expected; politics bored her, and she realized that she had not sought out news of any political nature. Sitting at Stambridge, busy with her studies, she did not search for news of violence in some insurgency on a continent halfway around the world. She did not even keep abreast of American or European news; whenever she had the choice, she tuned it out. Why should she not expect violence in Swazizibia?

The plane flew past the power plant, turned around and set its glide path for the runway. As they landed the plane almost touched wings with an identical counter-traveling plane taking off from the narrow runway. Their own vehicle came to a stop by a small wooden building near the gate. There was a group of people outside the building, and a jeep was parked quite nearby, its guards loitering within.

As the passengers carried their things off the plane, the pilot led them into the small schoolhouse-like building Gwendolyn remembered as the main reception area for the mission. Behind them another jeep entered the compound and drove up to the plane. Several armed guards dismounted the vehicle, walked to the plane and went inside.

Gwendolyn and Alitisha entered the building with the other new arrivals. The pilot directed them into an alcove on the left, a room with a few sofas and some folding chairs that Gwendolyn did not remember from her prior visit. The wall facing the runway comprised mostly windows; none of the windows had panes. The newcomers took seats, Gwendolyn and Alitisha on a sofa against the inside wall with one of the volunteers, and the other women on the other sofas. Everyone watched a disorganized commotion around the plane. The armed men were scurrying around under the direction of first one, then another, of their leaders. Stacks of boxes and crates were accumulating on the ground around the vehicle as workers bumbled about, carrying things in haphazard disorder and dropping them onto the earth. Several men, apparently mission representatives, were present but kept their distance from the activity. One tall white man stood with his back to the building.

Gwendolyn recognized Sarah Greenwater as she emerged from one of the two doors away from the runway. Shortly after, two native women came in and stood by the other door. Sarah was exactly as Gwendolyn remembered her. *She might even be wearing the same dress. Doesn't her hair grow?* Gwendolyn also mused how the woman exuded quiet and, though below middle age, seemed almost part of a faded painting. Gwendolyn, herself no glamour hound, found herself giving mental advice to Sarah: some makeup with color would give a refreshing jolt to her appearance.

The pilot walked over to the native women, and the three left the building. Sarah spoke up, scanning the group of seven new arrivals. "Thank you all for volunteering. We know this is a great sacrifice, and we assure you that you are making a difference in the world." She walked over to Gwendolyn and took her hand. "We are especially happy to welcome back our return visitor, Gwendolyn Dressel-Meier." She looked down at the girl, who blushed. "I'm so happy to see you. And this must be Alitisha." She walked over to Alitisha and put her hand on the shoulder of the girl, who involuntarily flinched and hunched a bit.

Just then Dr. Florian Q. Bok came into the room, ambling through the door Sarah had entered. His walk was unhurried, an effect enhanced by the fancy cane he used. He smiled and winked at Gwendolyn as Sarah continued, "Everyone, we welcome you. If you are wondering, I know Gwendolyn because she has already visited once. She and Alitisha have come sponsored by the Worldwide Transformative Foundation." She looked at Gwendolyn. "And I must say we're thrilled to have you." The others sat in their seats, neglected.

Florian Bok walked up next to Sarah, who noticed him and stepped back a bit. "As Sarah says, welcome. We are happy for your assistance in this crucial mission. Before we put you to work helping the sick and starving, I have a few words concerning rules and regulations. Be aware that these are for your safety, and they are not optional. Safety is paramount.

"I'm Florian Bok and I am the founder and director of this place. I am happy to be here to greet you; often I don't see some of the new arrivals for months, due to my travel schedule and the fact that you will go immediately to work and spread out in your assignments. But be assured I know every one of you. I have seen your paperwork, and on behalf of our thousands of troubled patients I thank you for your sacrifice and dedication." The group rustled a bit. Dr. Bok continued, "Soon you will be hard at work helping these pitiful people. Be aware that you will experience a sudden psychological shock. You are around suffering that could not be forced to fit into the limited confines of a nightmare back home." From the hands of a tall, black-haired man now standing beside him, Dr. Bok accepted the striker to a heretofore unseen ancient Chinese gong Sarah was holding.

Suddenly Dr. Bok struck the gong, provoking a deafening ring and startling the volunteers. Even the armed men outside paused in their haphazard inventory of the plane. It was an incongruous experience—the gong's sound reverberating and volunteers shaking while the avuncular, white-appareled, barrel-shaped man and two others stood calmly as though deaf. Gwendolyn and Alitisha clapped their hands over their ears and doubled over.

The sound died down. Gwendolyn looked out a back window and noticed that the pilot and the native women were approaching a building a few hundred yards away, laughing as they walked, his arm around the waist of each female. Dr. Bok's voice arose, and Gwendolyn turned back to face him. "Hear me. I am not being overly dramatic. Paint yourself a picture and be warned. Be ready to see a mother who looks eighty though she is not yet twenty-five, nor perhaps will she be. Though starving, she is trying to secretly direct her food ration to her wispy sketch-like child. Are you painting the picture? She is emaciated and hungry. Flies and perhaps their larvae crawl unmolested on her, especially content in the large open sores in her skin. The woman has some dried feces about her thighs and rear. She is covered with dust. Her flat leather breasts can deliver no milk; she is barely able to move and has a clubfoot and cleft palate. Her maw surrounds teeth so sporadic and brown that you are horrified to see inside as her chin quivers in a begging motion. Her spine is bent and weak; she will tear the heart out of your chest. I won't even mention what the sight of her baby will do to you. If you come near, the woman will try to kiss your hand. The next time you see her, she has a broken leg, but everything else is the same. Despite her predicament she expends all her energy trying to obtain and direct food to her baby. This, this is what we face here."

There were only six dry eyes in the place. The volunteers were all stunned and overcome. These pictures had not made it into any of the mission's literature that they had seen.

"Do I have your attention? This is not our median patient, but she is not an outlier either, and certainly far from the most heart-wrenching case. Be strong. You are here because you realize that if nobody faces the pain of looking on these poor people, then no good can come of this place. We will help you deal with the grief, the shock. We are committed to getting you through this difficult trial. Stay capable. Maintain your balance."

He unexpectedly struck the gong again. Gwendolyn had fillings in two of her back teeth, and the gong made them hurt. Her head throbbed. Alitisha and several of the other girls covered their ears and ducked their heads into their laps.

"We want to get you to work. There are good things to do. But first I must drive home our rules for safety. You are to follow the instructions of your supervisors at all times. Insubordination will not be tolerated. Think of this as a ship in the middle of an ocean of earth and dry grass. Your captain has full responsibility for your security and for execution of the mission.

My deputy, Aloysius Fink here, has full authority when I am not here."
Everyone noticed the tall, pock-marked, dark-haired and bearded man
standing in front of Sarah, who must have stepped back a few more steps.
Fink nodded imperceptibly.

Dr. Bok continued, "My absence is regrettably frequent due to my
commitment to keeping these people helped. The travel and effort required
in the public relations realm to keep funds coming in for these people is
enormous. We don't just drop a bill into a beggar's hat here. I am committed
to putting forth the requisite energy for these unfortunate people, no matter
how exhausting. And you are proving you are too."

Gwendolyn examined the deputy as Dr. Bok spoke. Aloysius Fink
stood as still as a crocodile but not as handsome, though there was something
kindred in his mien. His skin appeared rough and mottled, perhaps due to
irregular coloring, maybe due to texture variation—the concept of determining
which source caused the blotchy appearance did not warmly beckon. The
man's forehead, nose, cheeks and jaw were the shape of any tall, dark
athlete's, but his coal-black eyes were odd somehow. As he stood quietly
he appeared slightly walleyed, and occasionally just barely cross-eyed.
Somehow it became clear that this impression was in part due to the fact
that the man was standing completely still. And one never caught his eyes
in motion, but somehow they were in different positions whenever one
looked at them.

Dr. Bok was speaking still. "Now, on the subject of safety: I will spare
you the gong, but internalize this: you are not at home here with all the
security and conveniences you take for granted. This planet is a harsh world,
and you are much closer to danger here than in Europe or America. We have
had no mishaps with foreigners like yourselves so far. But think on this: we
are at the intersection of a harsh natural habitat and a horrific man-made
terror campaign. We have been transported into a war zone—we traveled
into it by staying right where we always were."

Gwendolyn shuddered as the doctor's words penetrated and the
perception of real danger started to form; the others were also dealing with
an uneasiness that was blooming at an alarming rate.

"You do not have freedom here. Understanding this may mean the
difference between life and death. Firstly, if you were to strike out in this
environment alone you would be dead within days at most, just from natural
causes. Secondly, as I said, we are in a war zone. You would never get the
luxury of dying of natural causes. Since this current phase of the war started,

which was just about a year back, everything has gotten worse." He paused dynamically then said, "Are there any questions about your safety here in Swazizibia?"

There were none. He scanned the volunteers' eyes sternly, and after a wait he said, "Are there any other questions?"

After an anxious silence a volunteer woman asked, "What is the history of this mission? I am amazed to find something so large in the middle of nowhere like this. I did my research, but there was not much mentioned about how the mission actually came to be here. Did you build it? And what's the story with the huge church?"

Dr. Bok started to speak, then thought the better of it. He should let Aloysius Fink step up and start to interact with the volunteers. The man needed practice dealing with people. With some active effort Dr. Bok silenced himself, nodding for Fink to step forward and answer. Fink opened his mouth. "It was a military base built a while ago." He looked at Dr. Bok for confirmation of the number. "Umm, a forward outpost... between the capital and the mines..." He coughed, then stumbled to silence as he tried to remember the official account of the place.

Dr. Bok took over, "And it was built around the existing cathedral. The military forces occupied the bottom of the cathedral while they built the buildings here." He smiled and said, "That didn't make them all too popular with the good sisters living in the building, who had to retreat to the upper levels. But we've made amends in the intervening time. This region was always contested, but no powerful tribe or group has been particularly interested in it, certainly not to the level of mounting a force to drive others out just for this specific piece of land. It was not among the operating mines, after all. The military eventually got tired of manning a base way out here, and the place was abandoned except for the nuns in the cathedral. They've been there for centuries. Nobody really knows how they subsisted or even what they do; we still don't know much about them, really. They're not very talkative.

"My organization needed a place to pursue its purpose, and I was searching for a site five years ago. The government basically gave the place to us, and it's worked out famously since. We came in and rehabilitated the physical plant and started to bring in help for the indigenous population. We got to know the nuns a little when we arrived. They had a feeble effort in place to help people in the region with medical needs; they were sharing food and water with them. I never really did figure out where they got it all, but it wasn't much—the food looked like things you dig up from the ground with garnishes of lizards and squashed bugs. That's the past. Now the nuns are welcome to our food. Other than that, we leave them alone, and they leave us alone."

The volunteer enhanced her query about the cathedral, asking about its history, where it came from. Dr. Bok answered, "Before all that, for hundreds of years, this place was a monastery. An oddball outpost with some sort of Celtic roots. Everyone seems to think that some monks from Ireland took it upon themselves to withdraw from the world, and they ended up here. It was hundreds of years ago, and nobody knows how they chose this spot. It was probably before gold was discovered in this part of Africa, and it seems pretty far from the mines anyway. The area looked just like it does now: scrubby grass, dirt, nothing. Certainly nobody understands how they got bricks and then made a huge cathedral instead of simple, small huts built from local materials. Actually it was quite an engineering feat, given what they had. We've had historians here tell us that the building must have taken a hundred years to build, probably more. It's all a real mystery, but from local lore and so forth it seems it's been continuously occupied. Local legends have the place full of magic and spooks, not just monks and nuns.

"Another mystery is where the monks went, and why it's all nuns now. They look like they're converted local natives. And we don't even know for sure how many there are, because most of them stay inside. I would guess a dozen, but perhaps there are many more; it seems each one eats very little, and they seem to carry a lot of our food into the place. By that measure there could be a hundred. Anyway we got up and running with a bit of funding from the Swedish, European and Swiss governments and the United Nations. And a little tiny bit from the Irish. This cathedral is considered an international historical treasure; it garnered attention when the military took it over while they built this base. One of our requirements in being here is that we agree to give food and supplies to the nuns and cannot interfere with them. The military brought utilities into the cathedral when they were living there, and we keep it up. They have more electricity than they need. Actually I'm not sure they use any of it.

"Mr. Fink here has been with me since the beginning. He was the superintendent during our construction, and he is really the only person who has had any meaningful contact with the nuns, though that was years ago." He glanced at Fink, who nodded slowly, his motion rigidly confined to a single sagittal plane. "Right now, I have…"

As Dr. Bok droned on, Gwendolyn had been watching the activity outside the window vacantly, and she noticed several more jeeps with armed men coming inside the fence now. As the director talked she watched the newcomers bossing the others around. They were transferring some of the cargo from the ground to the jeeps at the direction of one large man who had two guns on his shoulders and wore expensive sunglasses. As he paced around the ground pointing and barking orders, his minions scurried about obeying, moving boxes around and loading the jeeps. It looked like they had accumulated quite a bit of food and some other items. Gwendolyn noticed that the crates of food gel from the plane remained on the ground, but many other cartons that seemed to be regular American foodstuffs were taken to the jeeps. There were several pallets holding bundles of black plastic or canvas. She saw other pallets of stacked boxes of various sizes, many undisturbed by the outsiders. There was a separate pile of cartons, some of which appeared to be smoking mildly, marked with large red stickers that read 'Director.' These were arranged haphazardly on the ground away from all the vehicles.

After some interchange between the armed men and those from the mission, followed by minor back and forth motion of the boxes between piles on the ground and in the jeeps, the outsiders turned their attention to the non-food items in the cargo. They broke apart pallets and examined individual boxes. Most items got tossed into sloppy piles on the ground; they took possession of only a few. The mission's men stood by and watched silently, occasionally straightening up stacks on the ground. Gwendolyn noticed that the armed group did not seem to concern themselves with water, fuel or windowpanes.

"…grown to be internationally known for our humanitarian work, as all of you know…" The voice in the background traveled between the girl's ears as Gwendolyn watched one of the men outside break open a box and demonstrate disinterest in the contents, then she turned her attention to the director. "…but enough. Our senior staff will work closely with each of you as you get acclimated; eventually you will feel you know the ropes and can pitch in with unmitigated energy."

Florian Bok then outlined the organization. "I am the director, and as I mentioned Aloysius Fink is my deputy. You have all met Sarah Greenwater, our operations supervisor. We have over eighty native employees here and about thirty-five volunteers. We run this place for the benefit of the patients and not ourselves—not even for the benefit of our native workers, really, though we certainly provide more than the legal minimum."

One woman asked, "Are the workers volunteers too? What do you mean, 'legal minimum'?"

Dr. Bok smiled. "Well, of course they're volunteers in the sense that we would not keep them imprisoned here if they prefer to quit and go back to dodging criminals and scratching the ground for food. They want to work here. And we pay them."

"I would hope so. People are not slaves."

"Well, we do pay them. They are happy working here, given their choices."

"Of course you pay them. They're working for you."

"Well, that's a little simplistic. But let's not get bogged down in trivia here. Let's move on," Dr. Bok said, trying to steer the conversation back to the orientation by force after his gaffe. But he had piqued the interest of the crowd, who all thought the issue actually was pretty simple. The volunteers glanced at each other; Gwendolyn and Alitisha exchanged looks. Everyone looked at Dr. Bok.

He sighed patiently and increased his lean on his beautiful cane, "All right, then. Fair enough. Let's talk about it. Are you here to work for us?"

The woman said, "Of course. We're volunteers." She looked uncertain.

"All I am saying is that work does not always require payment. You will undoubtedly be surprised that, though we don't take advantage of it, there is no local law against slavery here; in fact the government has offered many times to supply us with slaves. I reject the offers. I find the idea distasteful. I insist on allowing the workers freedom to choose to work for us and I choose to pay them for their work."

"That's absurd," the nameless woman said. "Slavery is against international law."

"It's a moot point," Dr. Bok answered. "Yes, there are resolutions condemning slavery, and there are theorists who claim international law has teeth. Others disagree. In any case I can assure you that if it has force, it is a toothless law indeed. Slavery is alive and well in portions of the world, regardless of what the Europeans and Americans and other insulated societies may wish to believe. I've looked into the matter and as I say, I don't consider it a valid option, not for an organization like ours. I don't really like it. I think it's wrong." He looked over his glasses at the group.

The woman shook her head and stood, speechless and somewhat disgusted. Nobody else spoke. Gwendolyn thought Dr. Bok was making a simple subject sound complex, but she was inclined to interpret his words as he would prefer—articulation of the ethical stance of a strong man in the face of a world with lower standards than his.

Dr. Bok went back to his main thrust on safety. "Getting on with our orientation, I repeat my caution: this is not familiar territory for any of you. Do not go outside the prescribed limits, and I must emphasize that if you come in contact with the patients from the native population, except under direct supervision of our senior workers, you must not engage them in any way. You are not a medical expert, and this realm of medicine is mysterious and counterintuitive. You must resist the temptation to smooth feathers that you believe are ruffled. You will not cure that woman's cleft palate by giving her a chocolate bar. If we are to function as a humanitarian organization, then it is imperative that you turn your back on her pleas unless specifically instructed otherwise. I know this is troubling. I know this... because I have had to learn to do it myself and it grieves my heart. This, reigning in your instinct to give superficial help, will be the most difficult lesson here, more difficult even than knowing death is ever stalking these poor unfortunates. You must trust me on this."

By nodding in his direction, Dr. Bok gave the floor over to Aloysius Fink, who spoke up, "You'll get your tour after you eat. Don't access any outdoor areas except for the region near the dormitory and the cafeteria. When you get your work assignments you'll go to other places. For now stay where you have permission." He stood stone-faced.

All of these restrictions surprised a thirtysomething woman on the couch next to Gwendolyn and Alitisha. She asked a question that was going through Gwendolyn's mind also. "But I volunteered to help the starving children here and their mothers. Are you telling me I won't be able to go to them?" She looked at Aloysius Fink, though the question was really for Dr. Bok.

Aloysius Fink made uncomfortable signs that he was going to answer; he seemed to be thinking, and his jaw quivered as though he would form syllables. But Dr. Bok interrupted and asked her name. She told him she was Sandy Crittenden. Dr. Bok said, "Ah, yes. Our new psychological expert." Sandy was surprised that he knew so much about her, and she internally recoiled at the 'expert' tag but sat motionless. "You can't know how glad we are to have you here, it's such an honor to have someone with your skills. We'll talk together, but in the meantime understand that your skills will best be put to use by dealing with our volunteers and staff as they grapple with the pain of being in proximity to such suffering and sickness. You can rest assured that you'll indeed be helping the children, albeit perhaps a bit indirectly. The problems these people have are more physical than psychological; as you will find out, the problems our volunteers from the advanced world have here are essentially all psychological."

Sandy looked confused and dissatisfied; she had thought she was volunteering for general labor here as well, not just psychological counseling. This answer was not exactly what Gwendolyn needed to hear either. She had no identifiable skills, just a general desire to help, but she craved direct hands-on contact. She considered asking about her assignment but decided now was not the time.

Sandy's eyes darted among the volunteers. She was the oldest in the group. She looked up and asked, "Dr. Bok, how does the government guarantee the mission's safety? I notice the military men at the gate, and just now they were unloading the plane. They don't look very organized, to tell the truth." Everyone looked out the window just in time to see an armed man drop a box. Another came over to him and slapped him multiple times, cursing and gesticulating wildly. As the first man bent down to pick up the box his rifle slipped off his shoulder. He somehow bumbled upright, juggling the position of the box and his weapon.

Everyone's attention came back to the room as Sandy continued, "Are there enough soldiers assigned to protect us from the warlords? I have to say it's a bit scary here. I hate to see all those heavy guns around." She glanced out at a man with two guns over his shoulders and two pistols around his waist. Other volunteers were nodding in agreement and looking at Aloysius Fink and Dr. Bok. Outside, the armed men just now started mounting their jeeps, and the mission workers were getting ready to handle the cargo that remained behind.

Dr. Bok stepped in front of Aloysius Fink and for a moment looked like he had two heads, as Fink's head towered above his own. Fink stepped away, and the odd creature dematerialized. Dr. Bok said, "That's a good question, and it helps me get to my next point. As I mention, we've been here for years, and I can tell you we have had no injuries and heaven forfend, no deaths due to lawlessness or mayhem. But understand that the government is *not* able to guarantee our safety. Those armed men around the mission are not government soldiers assigned to protect us. They are local tribe militia who have been stationed here by their chieftain to watch us, keep us within our pale, and to, shall we say, tax us." Several women glanced around the room as though to see if anyone else had heard the same bombshell they had.

Dr. Bok continued, "The government of this country is not too different from them. There are no good guys except us. Remember that. We are the only good guys." The volunteers fidgeted. Dr. Bok noticed. "You wonder if I should say that out loud. Believe me I know these people. In their minds I have given them a compliment, praise from a clueless outsider, a sucker who supplies them with food, whiskey and other things. No, don't worry about the militia or even the government being angry with me for calling them evil. More likely they would laugh, slap me on the back and demand a drink from me if they heard about it.

"Things are different here. You all are accustomed to a form of rule of law, you think extortion and bribes are sources of shame. Life is sacred where you come from. But you will learn the customs of reality. You will learn what life is worth in this part of the world, and it ain't much." Dr. Florian Bok paused, both hands on his elegant cane, so the listeners could process the incongruity of this dignified looking man's vulgar colloquialism.

The group sat in stunned silence, still mentally processing the fact that the armed guards protecting the place were in actuality armed criminals imprisoning them. And possibly, just possibly, their own leader Dr. Bok was some sort of schizophrenic, a masochist with a streak of sadism that drove him to bring unsuspecting innocents here. The man seemed to be driven to exacerbate their fears, alarm them to the maximum possible extent. This was not the Dr. Bok Gwendolyn remembered, and she gulped a tortured swallow; Alitisha and most of the other volunteers had tears welling in their eyes.

"You should know that bribes and protection money are the only way of surviving here. I'm sorry if this rough introduction stresses you, but you are not at home now, and I am responsible for your very survival. That world your parents told you existed… that world the teacher on the playground concocted when there was a conflict—that world is an artifice, and we have not the means to support it here. You have chosen to enter this world and must obey the local laws of human nature to survive. These laws can be deadly. And understand that 'deadly' does not mean only deadly to you, but that you can place all of us working here and the patients in our care at risk as well. How long do you think it would take a tribal leader on a rampage to devastate this place?"

He paused to silence. "All I am saying is this: stay in line here."

The volunteers were all visibly alarmed now. Aloysius Fink stood expressionless and immobile behind Dr. Bok. The women looked at Dr. Bok. He answered their gazes, "You are not in danger here if you follow our instructions, which are designed to keep you safe. I know these people well. The government is more or less indifferent to our existence. The different sets of rebels are also mostly neutral about us. Both sides—that is the government and whatever rebel band controls this region at any moment—get some benefit from our being here. First, the government: you noticed that you came through the capital city. All of our supplies, including fuel for our two airplanes, come by air, and all of our aircraft travel is restricted to directly flying between the capital and our site.

"The government inspects all cargo and exacts a heavy, situation dependent, let's say, 'duty,' on everything we bring in. Out of courtesy for your American and European sensitivities I won't comment at this time on whether there is an informal exchange of cash with certain officials as well. You are not to speak of this; disclosure of anything resembling bribes made in this way would upset the Americans or Europeans, who, as you must learn, are not living in the same world as you now. And let's face it—the Americans and Europeans don't want to hear this sort of thing. It complicates their consciences. It would threaten our funding, our existence.

"Nobody here in Swazizibia would feel the slightest bit shamed or angered by such disclosure. In fact, Swazizibia is not the exception. Your home countries are. I hope you understand why I had to allow you to be surprised upon your arrival here. It would be impossible to communicate through our normal public relations and marketing channels that you are actually safe while simultaneously describing the situation on the ground here. In the context of a westerner in his air conditioned living room, the facts on the ground here would sound, well, like they probably did to you just now. I was not happy when the rebels came and disrupted my peaceable mission here. But I adapted, I assure you, and things are stable enough if you follow the rules.

"I should add that there is another reason the government should want us to be safe and protected, though they cannot supply that security. They get some acclaim worldwide for allowing efforts such as this to proceed. And we have been very proactive in garnering attention for the mission, as you all know. With us working here, the government has the opportunity to publicly align with somebody who is trying to help their poor people. Admittedly, this public acclaim is not their biggest concern—surviving and staying in power is, but the effect is beneficial so long as the government is stable.

"As for the rebels, there are several factions, and they murder each other quite as ruthlessly as they would kill government soldiers or step on ants. As it happens, this area has been stably under the control of a single rebel faction—those heavily armed gentlemen you see around our periphery—since the first rebels presented themselves over two years ago. Before that we had a few blissful years with no interference beyond the simple governmental arrangements I just mentioned."

Gwendolyn could not help wondering why she had not noticed any militia on her earlier visit, much as she wracked her brain.

Dr. Bok could see that the volunteers were still terrified. He attempted to use logic to calm them. "Put yourself in the position of the rebels. You live a dirt poor existence in a squalid land. You can grow nothing and cannot even manage to steal cattle. There is one source of outside food and comforts, and all you have to do is help yourself to what they bring in. Some of you just noticed the tax collectors outside our window as they simultaneously set and collected their levies. We have developed a situation that the rebels do not want to disrupt; in fact I have spoken to their commander many times, and they have accommodated my modest requests for changes in their behavior. For instance, all women on the base are off limits, even the natives. I have been able, on occasion, to have them withdraw from sight when important people visit." The group was surprised and pleased with these last pieces of information. Maybe Dr. Bok had things under control here.

"I have more orientation to give you, but right now I'm sure you're hungry. Let us have a modest lunch and continue afterward. I should mention this: what and how you eat is up to you. My suggestion is to try to keep close to your normal diet. To the extent possible, keep a routine as similar to that at home as you can. You will need to make accommodations for dearth of fresh produce, but do your best. We have found this is the healthiest approach. For some of you this may be the last of what you consider normal meals. That is up to you. We take great care to make sure to have food and common medicines similar to what you had at home, but some volunteers have a difficult time continuing a normal existence. We suggest working toward it. Now, before we break are there any questions?"

Gwendolyn had about a hundred fragments of questions in her mind, churning in rapid motion and far from articulable status. Alitisha was consumed wondering what she had gotten into and whether she would make it. Sandy Crittenden seemed to have questions, but her lips were pursed. Nobody asked anything.

Dr. Bok said, "Well, then." He started to turn, then stopped. "One last thing. We expect that you will focus your attention on your work here. You cannot engage in idle electronic diversions or communications with the outside world. We have not connections onsite, and your volunteer agreement affirms your cooperation in this area; specifically, satellite access is forbidden. Please send your communications through us. We like to think we have helped our volunteers develop their writing skills as they revive the old-fashioned custom of letter writing. Perhaps you will be pioneers in the archeological reconstruction of that old-fashioned method of communication, cursive writing." He smiled. "If you think you will be bored, fear not. We have many books available, as you will see in the shelves in the halls and around the rooms. They are the works of great literature. Enjoy them. As for loneliness: write letters."

Dr. Bok nodded, continued his turn, his cane swinging, and walked out through his door. Sarah Greenwater gathered Sandy, Alitisha and Gwendolyn and led them through the same door a few minutes later. The native woman who had somehow appeared led the other young women through the door to the dorm rooms. Aloysius Fink stood alone.

Sarah led her charges to a neighboring building where they climbed up to the second floor. She walked with concise efficiency and engaged in some small talk with Sandy as the others followed. They learned that Sandy was from Indiana, USA. She had grown up on a farm and gone to the university there. She had taught school in Indianapolis and became interested in psychology, returning to school to become a psychologist so she could help people. Alitisha and Gwendolyn gathered that Sandy and Sarah had had some prior contact, and they were correct; Sarah was also from a small town in Indiana originally, and when Sandy appeared on the mission's radar screen as a potential volunteer, Sarah had been put in contact with her. They communicated for over a year before they offered Sandy what they called a 'scholarship.' She did not have to pay money like almost all of the others to be a volunteer here.

They entered a room that looked like a casual dining restaurant back home in America. The room had glass windows most of the way around, and they could see many of the mission's buildings. Sarah led them to a table, and they all sat down. Indeed, with the exception of bills and tips, it seemed to be a normal restaurant; a white woman, a mission volunteer, came out and gave them menus that could have been from Burlington or Indianapolis. They ate their light lunch over casual conversation. Sarah and Sandy had salads, and the girls had soup and bread. Both older women said they had always wanted to visit Vermont, and they engaged in lively talk about the state, its cosmopolitan people and its colorful and exciting history. Sandy said she envied the girls—so young and so adventurous. Sarah participated in the conversation, but whatever she said, the friendly woman never seemed carefree. Her smiles seemed strained today. Maybe she had a background level of stress that kept her from fully relaxing even at lunch. Gwendolyn figured this was just the weight of being a supervisor here.

They loitered over the last of their lunch, progressing toward the undisclosed time when Sarah would lead them back to orientation. At one point Sandy asked the girls out of the blue, "How did you feel about that speech down there?" She glanced at Sarah. Sarah's eyes went to Alitisha and Gwendolyn, who glanced at each other, not knowing what to say. Sarah's mouthful of salad seemed to demand her total concentration; these particular lettuce leaves apparently had to be processed with extra care. Gwendolyn spoke up, "It was pretty scary." Alitisha nodded, mouth slack.

Sandy said, "Well, I was pretty shocked. I'll tell you, frankly it scares me too. And something else bothers me. I knew I was volunteering to help people who are helping people, because I can imagine how difficult it is to be around such suffering. But I thought I'd be directly working with the locals too, which sounds unlikely. In any case nobody told me I may be dodging bullets and running from rapists." It seemed she was talking toward the girls but intending to communicate with Sarah. Sarah was calm and did not answer. She continued her own efforts with the salad.

Alitisha became visibly alarmed. The older woman was distressed, and that could not be a good sign. Gwendolyn was also uneasy, and the younger girls stopped eating. After a bit Sandy and Sarah finished lunch, and all four sipped from their cups of tea. Nobody said anything more till, after a long interval with guns and bad men swirling in the girls' heads, Sarah looked at her old-fashioned watch and said, "We'd better get back down there."

They walked back and joined the group as it formed again. Florian Bok stood patiently in front of them all as they gathered, and Aloysius Fink was nowhere to be seen. Dr. Bok started right into his speech. "Now I want to continue to orient you to this place which will be your home for the near future. There is a lot to know. We were talking about government protection and the rebel tribes before lunch. We are all quite safe here, but remember that could be lost by any of you. These people are acclimated to seeing and even dealing out death. They carry lethal weapons everywhere they go, and they are used to being in charge. If things go well you will have no dealings with the militia members. However, if for some reason you meet up with one of them, here are your instructions. You will treat every native with a gun as your superior. You will look down when speaking to him, which you will do only to answer questions he has asked. The word, "sir" should end every sentence. But remember, you speak only when spoken to. When in his presence, you will speak only to him, not to mission personnel or your friends or coworkers. These are important customs and expectations, violation of which may cause temper problems, problems which are inconvenient when experienced in the presence of such firepower."

The volunteers stood still, the blood gone from their faces, unable to move. After a pause, Florian Bok asked, "Are there any questions before we start our walk-through?" Nobody was eager to think about the subject, let alone prolong things by asking about it. Their silence answered his question. "We will proceed," he said. He lifted his chin and turned to walk down the hall, an imperious bow-shaped curve to his back, redundant cane pacing the way, looking for all the world like the little tycoon on the Monopoly game cards.

As they emerged outside and began the tour, Sarah spoke. "We have our own vocabulary here. Dr. Bok, our director, is identified as the Professor." Without breaking his stride at the front of the group Dr. Bok turned his head and bowed it, eyes held closed in a prolonged blink, mouth pinched downward at the corners. Sarah continued, "As you know by now, we call those people we are helping 'patients.' And this place is of course the mission."

One of the girls in the group asked Sarah why they used the monikers for the Professor and the clients. Dr. Bok took up the task of answering "I think of myself as teaching the world the proper way to help the disadvantaged, and 'Professor' seems to describe my view of what I do. As for the mission itself, we could call it a refugee camp or an emergency center or such, but I think the word 'mission,' despite its sometimes religious connotation, brings forth a better picture of what we are trying to do. These people are not inmates, not numbers. I call this a mission to remind us that we are serving them, to remind us that we are caring for the underprivileged. I have found that this naming convention helps our staff feel they are doing good under a strong leader, not just babysitting or marking time. They can truly feel they have done a service, almost and in some ways precisely a medical service at the end of each day."

The tour geography was mostly the same as the one Gwendolyn remembered, with excitement replaced by an underlying uneasiness as militia members, saliently invisible during the prior visit, lurked in her mind. Gwendolyn's impression was that maybe there was some newer equipment and some of the service areas were rearranged. The power plant was visible far ahead, but it was not billowing smoke, and the smokeless smokestack looked somehow incongruous and absurd. The other barely visible, smaller chimney still spewed unctuous black smoke. They went into a number of buildings with bustling activity; they saw food being prepared, and they walked through a clinic where it appeared that sick native workers were being cared for. There were very, very few patients visible. Actually, none. This made a confusing impression on Gwendolyn.

When they got to a point on the curving path near the power plant, Dr. Bok pointed at the building with his cane and noted its dormant smokestack. He told them the place was now powered by some kind of new device that could power a whole city. The compact, silent device was many times more powerful than the coal burning machines it replaced. It resided here in the ground below the power plant building, and they could think of it as a giant battery that would not run out in their lifetime. The group could see the in-place carcasses of a number of furnaces, boilers, conveyors and the like through the mostly open wall. Outside, behind the building, a new cooling tower accompanied the original old-looking tower, both in front of a massive pile of black coal. The huge smokestack was merely a decoration now. The newcomers could not see it, but there were acres of ash piles beyond the mountain of unburnt coal.

The compact power plant was built free of charge by Thorius Energy, a Russian company. It was a fission power plant, the first of its kind in actual operation; most of the rich countries had laws against advocacy of nuclear power, and the countries clamoring for energy were too poor to pay for the devices. As of this time, Russia had freed itself from the ubiquitous worldwide anti-nuclear groupthink, and Thorius had installed the generator just for the opportunity to demonstrate the simplicity and efficiency of this type of reactor; as a bonus the company got good press for being aligned with such an esteemed charity. The machine was heavily instrumented, and it reported its operational parameters by satellite. The plant was mostly stocked with dummy fuel; fully loaded it could produce over one thousand times the amount of power the mission needed. The company's goal was to demonstrate a plant that could power a city. Though it produced only a tiny fraction of its rated power, it exceeded what the mission could use, and most of the energy was dumped into the new cooling towers.

Thus the power was supplied free to Dr. Bok. He mentioned to the group that the power plant was fully automated and only needed a visit from a company employee occasionally for a quick spot check. His logistical burden had fallen considerably. There was no need to truck in coal, no ashes to move around. In several decades, producing Terawatt-hours of power, the total amount of waste generated would not fill one of the executive residence's large freezers—machines, incidentally, that run on the electricity the plant produced.

Through the open front of the power plant building, Gwendolyn could see Aloysius Fink and some native men working at the old coal plant's far end, where the building joined the next one.

"And so we can air condition our complex for free once we close up the buildings, which we have been doing for a while. You will notice more and more buildings that are not the 'open Hawaiian schoolhouse' design. That is, the design with no windows and flimsy doors. All this is so we can serve the patients in the camp more effectively. We can purify water. We can, over time, flood the camp area with light at night if we desire. Power is free for at least the next thirty years, and we can get plenty more with one visit from a technician. In fact, Thorius would like us to."

Everyone knew the dangers of nuclear power plants; they had all been raised in Europe or America. One of the volunteers spoke up. "It's a nuclear plant, isn't it? What if it blows up?"

Dr. Bok, to the best of his knowledge, lied. "My child, don't worry about that. It's called a thorium plant. It is literally more than perfectly safe, this kind." All looked unconvinced, and Dr. Bok had to continue. "Yes, you could call it a nuclear plant, but I assure you it's safer than the generators at home. I'm sure you have never heard of thorium. Well, this is the first large-scale thorium generator in the world. It's far safer than the reactors in your home countries."

Whatever the difference was between this machine and the plain old nuclear plants in America, Bok did not know it. His words were meant to alleviate fears, but in light of the group's ubiquitous, nonspecific certainty about nuclear energy's danger, the words did not land as intended. Everyone's alarm level increased as they considered living next to such a thing—a machine whose safety was reasonable to compare to the disasters-waiting-to-happen that were the few still-operating nuclear plants at home.

"The ones in Japan? Or Chernobyl? Or Three Mile Island?" asked a wisecracking girl standing near the back.

Dr. Bok suppressed his full agreement with the sentiment and answered the group with words the Russians had supplied him in perfect English. "There was a time when man was afraid of fire. We have to understand that nothing is completely risk free. You can be assured that any danger assigned with the energy source is far smaller than that associated with the fire it replaces." He continued, "If what I am told by experts is wrong, and this reactor blows up... well, we'll all be incinerated, and the world will have learned something. There are not many of us foreigners here, just a few dozen. But let me assure you this reactor cannot blow up. Experts have no inclination to mislead us. In fact, that is one true feature of the geek, the dedication to strict technical truth. And I have met these Russians. They are geeks in the truest sense of the word." He smiled a friendly smile and continued leading the tour, ignoring the continuing murmurs.

None of this calmed the almost atavistic terror of nuclear power in every single volunteer, a fear which had been cultivated and nourished by years of dedicated educational messaging. These were well educated people; all were in college or graduates. Gwendolyn was a typical example. Of course she had not studied any sort of science at Stambridge, but she remembered that most years in middle school and high school she was taught about nuclear power—by teachers who had never studied the science themselves. One theme stood out from the years of instruction: many countries were duped into accepting the transitory comfort of electricity on demand at a horrible risk of wiping out their populations in a conflagration or at least experiencing a cloud of radioactive poison destined to create deformities in succeeding generations.

Gwendolyn figured that this power plant here in a remote part of the globe was probably just a temporary hitch along the way to safe, clean and most importantly, risk free energy from the sun or ocean or mountains or clouds or somewhere. For instance, she remembered Mr. Blound, an authoritative teacher in high school who let the class know that the ocean has lots of energy—if it did not, it would be frozen solid. His opinion was that man should pull out a tiny fraction of that energy and change it into electricity. Gwendolyn knew that engineers had been assigned to develop a trouble free energy source years ago. Knowing that men first walked on the moon many decades in the past, she was mystified regarding the delay in delivery of the clean energy plants. The only explanation she could imagine was that those technicians working the problem had lost sight of its urgency, but she did not doubt they would complete their task someday. Anyway, regardless of how this plant fit into the scheme of energy evolution, it was disquieting to think about living so close to what was likely a very powerful bomb.

Sarah shared everyone's fear below her brave face, and the switch away from simple, understandable coal to this nuclear power plant frightened her. Not just nuclear power, but some new type of nuclear power. She did not believe Dr. Bok's assurances. But this was not the only psychological tormentor she had at the place, and it didn't dominate her attention. As for many volunteers, Dr. Bok's soothing and assured manner, if not his words, helped at least a little.

In fact, Director Professor Dr. Florian Q. Bok did not believe any of the words he said on this subject, and he was anxious about the power plant exploding too. However, he saw no reason to propagate or even display this fear. The convenience of practically unlimited hassle-free power, along with his small personal duty cycle onsite here, had combined to convince him to accept the plant when offered, and he was perfectly willing to give the reassuring speeches in absolute certitude, employing his trademark melliflu-ous charm. Dr. Bok and Sarah turned the group to start walking back. Gwendolyn remembered vaguely that they had turned around at this same spot when she took the tour before.

A nameless volunteer girl asked, "How many patients are here?"

"We've been quite stable at four thousand to forty-five hundred patients for the past two or three years. The camp was limited in its early days, but today we are comfortable operating at this level. We have had as many as six thousand, but that was a real strain on everyone, including the patients. Since then we've been able to upgrade, and it would not be impossible to go to even maybe seven thousand now, speaking strictly of mechanics."

"But if the camp can handle seven thousand then why not keep seven thousand here? Isn't the famine getting worse all the time? Why don't you save them all? That's what I want to do," the girl said. Gwendolyn agreed wholeheartedly. Alitisha and the others listened silently and looked at Dr. Bok.

"Well, there are degrees of need. What did you say your name is?"

"Tammy Van de Bunt. I'm from Chicago." Tammy appeared to be among the youngest of the young group.

"Tammy, this area of the world is very poor," Dr. Bok displayed a friendly smile. He dropped back as the group continued and threw his arm around her shoulder as they all walked back. "We're doing what we can. While it is true that we have been quite successful in fund raising in Europe and America, there are limits to what we can do. We have to turn away all but the worst cases. It vexes me deeply. These are my countrymen, you know. I have dual Swiss and Swazizibian citizenship. So I feel it intensely. You can't know." He slowed down, still walking, chin on his chest. "You can't know."

Sandy Crittenden was near him at the back of the group, and she asked, "Where do the patients go from the mission? Do you resettle them in other countries?" Gwendolyn and the others now wondered as well. They looked at Dr. Bok.

He continued walking and took a long, slow breath as he dropped away from Tammy. "At the practical level our donors, without really meaning to, set our level of funding more or less directly proportionally to our headcount. But when the government and the militia see more goods coming in they both become greedier with their demands. Negotiations with them become more and more difficult. I think I've found the balance, though it's dynamic. I've found I cannot justify the extra effort needed to push the number of patients up beyond where it is. The pressure manifests itself in two places. First, it shows directly in the stresses on the staff due to their increased workload. Second, it becomes very difficult to handle the worsened corruption in the supply lines as the parasites demand their take. I wish I could serve more sufferers, but in the current political situation we will be bled to death. And for what?"

For what? Gwendolyn was confused by the question. So were most of the others.

"No, four thousand is just about right. We are helping many people without killing ourselves. As for funding, in the past several years we have worked with our sponsors to shift their thinking from an implicit 'per head' basis to a larger camp wide basis. Ironical, isn't it? Only a few years ago we worked hard to get the 'per head' thinking in place with them; we were working hard to keep the number up. And we have had better luck in increasing the 'per head' allocation than in getting them to think of us more holistically. So, that's where we are now." He looked up, his forehead wrinkled, mouth hanging open in a friendly grin as his eyes went out over the top of his spectacles, checking from face to face.

The group walked on. Most had never thought through the practicalities of executing any real task with a tangible end product—they were young, and they had never been required to accomplish anything beyond taking tests, following instructions and filling out forms. Actual achievement was always done by others. And of course, the processes supporting a huge, ongoing, life-or-death endeavor in a remote corner of the world are extremely complex.

All of the volunteers had contemplated their desire to help the suffering; few had done more than donate time or money to that cause. Those that had donated sweat had done so in the context of seeing tangible success—that is, building schools and latrines in Central America, accompanying doctors on an assignment inoculating children in the Caribbean, traveling with dentists who move their family to coastal towns in Costa Rica for a few weeks. Things like that. Some of these youngsters had spent their school holidays onsite at these projects. None had thought about how to ensure they run effectively. All were thus satisfied, bamboozled, or both by Dr. Bok's numbers.

Sandy repeated her question in almost the same words as before. Dr. Bok said, "Oh, yes. What is the question? I am a bit hard of hearing in the one ear." He gestured for all to continue walking and moved along, his walk decorated by the tap and swing of his beautiful cane.

Sandy asked, "Where do the patients go when they are better?"

Dr. Bok stopped, put both hands on his cane and looked down, then he scanned the air above the group as though he did not know which member had asked the question. Sarah's attention was gripped by some mineral on the ground beside the path. The crowd paused, and as he spoke Dr. Bok lowered his eyes to each individual in turn. "Our patients come to us in very bad shape. We are able to feed and provide medical treatment for many patients, but unfortunately far more come to our gates than we have the ability to serve, as I just mentioned. We have ongoing relationships with a multitude of countries and with the government here as well. We have made many of these people more healthy and certainly more comfortable. I have been working internationally on behalf of our patients, even to the point where I believe I will be allowed to address a committee on starvation and refugees next year at the United Nations. If you are interested I can supply you with a copy of my talk. It is essentially finished already. We are always progressing in our efforts to secure these people from their suffering." He knew the questioner was Sandy, and he stood momentarily staring into her face through the large, heavy lenses of his spectacles.

Sarah had actually stooped to pick up the rock. The others were silent.

Something made Sandy understand that any elaboration would only be amplified noise and chatter, not more signal. Dr. Bok nodded, straightened and started walking again, his cane joining in the motion. "So as I said we have found that four thousand is our best size. Of course there is an unbounded need; as I said we can't help them all. We cannot eliminate the causes of the starvation and the sickness, but we can alleviate some of the suffering."

Everyone was quiet; everyone was nervous and confused. They were, consciously for some and unconsciously for most, developing an understanding that in hoping to query Director Professor Dr. Florian Bok, silence on their part was often no less productive than asking the questions.

They walked back to the dormitory area without any conversation; apparently the elucidated portion of the tour had concluded. Dr. Bok paused as they approached the door of the schoolhouse-like building at the edge of the mission. He said his goodbyes and walked off toward the administration building where Gwendolyn had eaten lunch, his cane happily dancing at his side. Sarah took over and handed off the newcomers, excepting Gwendolyn, to the two women who had materialized in the doorway. Gwendolyn and Alitisha were alarmed at being separated, but Sarah assured them it was all right. She explained to the group that Gwendolyn was a sponsored volunteer, not a regular volunteer, and her room was in a separate area. It was perhaps a formality to have Gwendolyn live away from the rest of them, but even so, it must be observed.

Sarah split Gwendolyn from the main group and took her to a stairway inside the nearby building where she was to live. She gave Gwendolyn a cardboard card with a room number on it and said that as a sponsored volunteer she was in no need of supervision. Gwendolyn was puzzled that anyone needed oversight; they were mostly college students. She asked about it, and Sarah said the supervision of the others was really just to help them feel at home and stay safe, and it would last only a few days. She said she had to run, and as she left she suggested Gwendolyn go to meet the other sponsored ladies; her belongings would already be up in her room.

Gwendolyn glanced at the door as Sarah held it open for her. The others had disappeared around the cafeteria building. She started up the stairs to her new home away from home.

Gasping for Traction

What am I willing to do?

G wendolyn's first moments alone at her new African home found her walking up the steps to the second and top floor of the building where the sponsored volunteers live. She emerged from the stairway and found herself in a large, carpeted lounge with windows all along the right wall and multiple small bedrooms along the left. Several white women were reading in cushioned chairs scattered about the room, and a few more were standing, smoking. All noticed her entrance. None said anything.

Most of the dormitory-like rooms along the left wall were open. All were empty, but it appeared that the majority of the rooms were lived in; the beds she could see had linens, and there were possessions in the rooms. Along the far wall were three clean, reasonably well appointed bathrooms with their doors open. She saw towel racks in two of them and could see part of a sink in the other. There was another she did not notice on the wall next to the stairway entrance behind her. The bathrooms were marked with stylized international 'female' icons.

Gwendolyn walked to the windows. Outside she saw the taller administration and executive residence buildings and a long section of the runway. Across the runway, beyond the barbed wire at the mission's periphery, sparse grassland extended to the horizon. With a little neck-stretching effort, she could look to the left and see the entrance gate where she entered the mission. Outside the gate there was a single truck holding four militia members sleeping with their guns on their laps. All four automatic weapons had their barrels outside the windows; one was pointed right at Gwendolyn, which made her recoil.

She turned her attention back into the room and noticed the ugly bright turquoise carpet. This well-lit room had panes in the windows. Other than the offensive color of the carpet the room seemed remarkably comfortable, and quite a contrast to the other places. This room was clean, full of nice chairs and air conditioned. A few tables held lamps and old-fashioned magazines. Some old books were scattered about on the tables, and more were on a shelf next to the entrance stairway.

In the center of the room, smoking a cigarette on the most comfortable chair, sat a pasty and flaccid, middle-aged white man. Gwendolyn noticed him abruptly. He was looking at her. *I must have walked right by him. Yikes, look at the curve of that spine, that head hanging forward—like some kind of Dick Deadeye, Ichabod Crane sitting there. He sure looks out of place.* One could conclude that the man was not able to control the ceiling fan directly above him, as it was lazily dispersing his treasured smoke into the room's atmosphere for all to share. The man was dressed in grey shorts and a white shirt, and he had an old-fashioned watch on his right wrist. His shoes were black wingtips, and his presentation was completed by the thin and translucent black socks reaching almost to his unfortunately projecting kneecaps. *He must be quite tall. Or maybe it's an optical illusion due to his skinny legs.* He was holding a book and had probably been reading it before he started looking at Gwendolyn, an activity that consumed all the attention he had left over from enjoying his cigarette. He moved; the man put down his book and raised his flabby thin body from the plush chair with a hint of a struggle as the deeply curved cushion seemed to hold on to that last portion of his body as though he had to break a vacuum to escape. He approached Gwendolyn so closely that his nose seemed to project over her. "If I were a betting man, and thank the Lord I'm not ma'am, I'd bet you're Gwendolyn Dressel-Meier of America." He yielded to a goofy smile and extended his right hand for a handshake, putting his left hand on her shoulder.

Gwendolyn heard nothing but her name in that greeting—her attention was elsewhere. She did not even notice the physical contact from this tall and curved man. Somehow her focus was transfixed by his face. The widely stretched expanse of crooked beige and grey teeth limned by the thin smile, the wrinkled contortion of his forehead—these caught her notice. But her attention was captured by his nose. The long, thin, detailed nose. She had to look almost straight up to see it, but she could not help being fascinated by the way the end of it dithered as he spoke; of course she tried not to look at the root end from this angle. As his words impinged on her ears she wondered if a scientist could decipher his speech simply by tracking the motion of the end of this bony and animated nose, perhaps by using some apparatus constructed from mirrors and laser beams.

"… name is … close-knit group of us…" the nose flexed cheerfully and its tip traversed a complicated curve in space.

"…looking forward to your arrival." The man stood smiling, still holding her shoulder. The nose-bob had stopped for a full two or three seconds before Gwendolyn was freed. Released from the tip of his nose, she looked at the man's face.

"I'm sorry. I didn't catch your name."

His smile stretched a bit wider, more whacky, and he bobbed his head in a happy nod. "Yes, yes. So sorry. I am the reverend Dr. Phineas Q. Boseau. I'm the chaplain on duty here for the volunteers… Yes, you heard it's a soft 's,' a 'z' really, if you know what I mean." He leaned down momentarily with a wink. The nose started to control her focus again, but she fought it off, and the tip blurred and never got a lock on her fovea. She shook his hand and nodded. She instinctively turned to her left, dropping his other hand more or less harmlessly from her shoulder. Then she broke his lingering grip on her hand and stepped back sharply.

Gwendolyn's quick judgment of Dr. Boseau: the name fit this man just fine.

Two white women had come to the doors of rooms and were watching. Phineas Boseau introduced Gwendolyn to most of the women present in the area now, speaking in an annoying stentorian tenor. He led her around the room, and she exchanged greetings with the other sponsored volunteers who happened to be there. Again and again Gwendolyn had to force her attention not to converge on the reverend's nose each time he spoke, and she remembered no names.

Dr. Boseau said he had to go home, touched Gwendolyn's shoulder and hand, and left. Gwendolyn went to the room nearest the bathroom wall, the one containing her things. It was a decent room, a larger version of the room she slept in when she visited before, with a bed on the left beyond a small alcove serving as a closet near the doorway. This room had a desk with a light and desk chair on the far wall, facing out the window. A small set of shelves on the right side held some old worn paperback books, mostly classics, and a Bible. A comfortable chair with a floor lamp stood at the center of the right wall between a chest of drawers and the little bookcase. It seemed a pleasant enough setup.

Gwendolyn busied herself in putting her things into the dresser and conversing with a few of her new neighbors as they came by for small talk. Many were from America, and one was from California, but she did not know her. She hung a few things on the rod in the closet, then she put her backpack in the closet and sat on the comfortable chair, but not before pulling out her stuffed amputee octopod Pyratticus Julius. She found that the chair was a recliner, so she lay back and sat stroking the stuffed animal's surviving tentacles, looking out her door at the common area where several women were sitting and reading. Then she turned the chair and looked out her window. She saw only sky and the barren dirt hills a few hundred yards away as she sat in quiet relaxation.

She noticed the Bible passively at first. Then it slowly robbed her of her repose. She straightened the chair, stood and picked up the book. Gwendolyn had never felt at ease with the Bible; in all her family's conversations it had been understood that people who read that book are insecure and intellectually weak. They are bitterly afraid of the world, and sense that they are unable to comprehend and deal with it; they cling to the book hoping it contains some sort of magic that will help them navigate their lives through this mysterious world. She also had been taught that the Bible is responsible for a huge amount of the suffering in mankind's history, and she could never forgive the tome for that. She buried it below some old classics on the shelf. Then she sat back down on her chair and relaxed with Pyratticus Julius.

But somehow the Bible was there, dominating the atmosphere of the room from just out of her view. After a few minutes of trying to relax she got up and dug it out. She slid it under the bed, figuring it was the best she could do, then again sat back on the chair and reclined with her stuffed companion. Perhaps assisted by her tiredness after all her activity, the book lost its menacing influence over her. She looked at the sedentary activity of the women in the common area and drifted off into a doze.

Gwendolyn was awakened by a gentle knock, and she saw Sarah Greenwater at her open door, knuckles at the ready for an enhanced knock. Sarah looked tired but in good spirits as always. "I thought I would fill you in on our schedule for meals and so forth. Would you like to take a little walk?" Gwendolyn had woken without grogginess; she must not have been asleep long. She got up and nodded as they left her room with the door standing open. They walked through the lounge, nodded to a few other women and went downstairs and outside. Sarah said, "I was hoping to get up there with you sooner but so many things. So many. With the new volunteers and all."

Gwendolyn noticed militia men playing some kind of card game near a vehicle outside the barbed wire as they walked. Sarah gave her instructions, "You should have no worries as a sponsored volunteer here. In the morning and early evening food is served up in your lodging area, and there are always snacks there. You are, of course, free to go and eat with the regulars in the cafeteria any time." She flipped her wrist as they walked, indicating the building they were nearing. "It's a little less elegant in both the food and the appointments, but it can be good to mingle with them too." Answering Gwendolyn's forming question she said, "We usually call the unsponsored volunteers 'regular volunteers' or 'regulars.' Like your friend Alitisha."

Gwendolyn asked Sarah, "What will my job be? Should I report to work somewhere in the morning?"

Sarah smiled, "I know you are a bit younger than the other sponsored volunteers. It's quite expensive to be here as a sponsored volunteer. The mission benefits both from the work you do and from the sponsorship dollars as well. Most of the sponsored volunteers are seeking some kind of personal growth. We look forward for you to see how you can fit in and contribute. And you will let us know, I'm sure."

Let her know? Gwendolyn was surprised, perplexed. She had expected an exhausting, sweaty, underfed stint in Africa, and she had only the most vague idea of the difference between a sponsored volunteer and a regular. "The only thing I want is to do is help people. I don't want any personal growth. And Alitisha—she's the same way."

"Well, maybe you do and maybe you don't. Sponsored volunteers have the chance to deepen their understanding of themselves while they're here. Being away from your day-to-day life gives you a chance to contemplate things, and you should take advantage of it. And we have quite a range of sponsored volunteers. Many are donating their talents and skills to helping other volunteers here cope with the difficult conditions and even learn new things while they are away from home. Be open to it. Look around." The woman smiled warmly at the younger girl. Gwendolyn looked at the ground, pensive, still confused. She was not here to find herself, and she suspected she was not qualified to assess the needs of this complex mission and pronounce judgment on where she would best help. That should be Sarah or Dr. Bok.

They continued their walk, and Gwendolyn kept pushing for a work assignment. Sarah gave no substantive answers, but based on the mostly repetitive conversation, eventually Gwendolyn formed the perhaps unjustified opinion that Sarah would make sure she got a specific job tomorrow morning. As they continued to walk Sarah diverted the conversation, pointing out many of the buildings dedicated to one form of logistics or another—storage, loading areas, water pumps and so forth. Gwendolyn told Sarah she wanted to visit Alitisha, so as they finished their discussion Sarah looped them back to the entrance to the regulars' living quarters.

The two parted company, and Gwendolyn went inside. She found herself in a hallway with rooms on both sides. She remembered that she had slept there when she visited the mission before. There was no lounge area like the one in the sponsored volunteer area; it was just a hallway with rooms and some bathrooms. Also unlike the sponsored volunteers' area, the windows had no panes. As she walked down the hall glancing through the open doors she noticed the younger age of the volunteers. None of the girls were more than a few years older than Gwendolyn. She walked along, passing doorways and exchanging pleasant nods with the rooms' occupants. She found what must be Alitisha's room. The door was open, and Alitisha's things were recognizable, but she was not there. Gwendolyn was basically shy and did not ask anyone about her friend; anyway they probably didn't know her yet. She went over to the cafeteria to see if she could spot Alitisha, but she was not visible in the groups sitting at tables or with the people selecting their food. She left. Just then, Alitisha and two other girls came into the far side of the room and started foraging among the offerings to pick out their dinner.

Gwendolyn had hoped to be with Alitisha, and now she was lonely. She went back to up her room, picked up Pyratticus Julius and said, "Well, it's just you and me. At least I have you, hexapod," using the formerly disdained nickname her father had for the stuffed beast. She lay down on the bed, and the debt she had acquired from the long journey and the stress of acclimatizing to the new surroundings came due. She fell quickly to sleep. Pyratticus Julius slept too, comfortably cradled against her breast.

Gwendolyn slept the night through and was awake the next day before any of the others in the sponsored volunteers' suite. She lay quietly, looking out the window at the dirt hills. She was afraid that she would wake someone if she started moving; she still felt like a guest. Eventually there was someone stirring, banging doors, taking a shower. Gwendolyn gathered her toiletries and walked over to a bathroom and did her morning cleanup. The shower supplied a luxurious stream of hot water which felt very good after her long journey. For a few moments she had no troubles, but standing in the pleasant stream in the impoverished and semiarid country, she became conscious of a need to conserve; she felt decadent indulging herself in the hot water. She resolved that from that point forward she would take only quick, lukewarm showers in recognition of the difficulties inflicted on those in the mission.

She dressed in her room, fluffed her hair a bit with her hands and went out into the lounge area with a randomly chosen book and started reading, not knowing what her assignment would be. The woman from the other bathroom emerged after a while and walked back to her room, launching a noncommittal nod as she went by. Gwendolyn had met several residents but at this point, owing to wet hair and similar builds, she could not tell if she had been introduced to her earlier. *Anyway, I've always been bad with names.*

Gwendolyn had not noticed the collapsible partition that comprised half of the wall beside the stairway to the room. But there it was, and there was motion behind it. Presently the wall opened into another small room. One thin black woman was retracting the wall, and another was standing behind a serving counter containing various breakfast items, hot and cold. The two women looked to be about the age of her mother, and they beckoned her. She put down her book and walked into the room. The ladies both spoke a bit of English and used it in conjunction with animated gestures to insist she take a plate and eat a hearty breakfast. Gwendolyn was excited and not very hungry but nonetheless wound up with a plateful of food and a glass of juice. She sat at a table near the window for a long time and thought about eating.

The showered woman came out into the room, and the two workers attended to her wishes as she chose items, giving her a plate similar to Gwendolyn's but much lighter on portions. The woman was lean, probably about forty years old and, as it seemed with most there, physically nondescript. She came over and sat across the table from Gwendolyn, lit an old-fashioned cigarette without saying anything and took a drag, all the while looking at Gwendolyn. Then she exhaled and took another.

Eventually she started speaking. Her name was Sonja; she did not ask Gwendolyn's name. Sonja was from Switzerland. Her English was flawless, if a bit slowly delivered. She opened up far too much for Gwendolyn's comfort after her almost arrogant introduction. Sonja had just gone through a divorce, and she came here to get away from the stress; she said she had some lingering guilt over her dealings with her husband and knew she could not enjoy a getaway to Greece or Italy. She had considered going to Morocco but finally settled on coming to the mission in order to be around people doing something positive. All this she said between puffs on her cigarette. Sonja had been here for almost four weeks and was planning to stay for three months. It was expensive to come as a sponsored volunteer, and she was sponsoring herself; since the final financial result of the divorce was not yet known she was somewhat concerned about her ability to afford her stay, but was pretty sure that it would not be a problem for her. Florian Bok had made inquiries back home, and he was satisfied; this probably meant things would be okay on the financial front. She shrugged, lit a second cigarette and started her breakfast after a few more puffs. "What is your name?" she asked.

"Gwendolyn."

"Oh, I thought so. You are the golden girl." Sonja smoked on her cigarette and smiled.

Gwendolyn hesitated, not knowing whether to take offense, and decided not to. She told Sonja about herself—her schooling, how she was stopping out after planning it for a year. Sonja expressed surprise at the planning cycle, saying her own visit was almost unplanned; once Dr. Bok was satisfied with her finances, she came just as quickly as she could arrange to get transportation here. She smiled and added that just before leaving she had to scramble to find someone to care for her cats during her absence.

Gwendolyn spoke of how she loved animals and bored the woman with a few stories of her pets back home. Then she said "I learned about the mission back home. I got my mother to donate a few dollars a month, and I've felt so good about it ever since. I even came and visited. Once I saw the place I knew that whatever my future held, it included some kind of volunteer work here, at least for a while. I knew it instantly. I've worked on my father for a long time to get him to allow me to come here, to sponsor me. His foundation is my sponsor."

"Yes, well, we all knew you were coming. There is not too much news to talk about around here. And that foolish director mentions you and his 'partnership' with that foundation every time he gets a chance." She gave a disparaging exaggerated grimace with the word 'partnership,' and her eyes bounced up to the buildings outside the window and back. "So, what is your claim to fame, child?" She was almost finished with her third cigarette by now. She speared some food with her fork.

"I don't know what I'm going to do, exactly. In fact, I was kind of wondering where I'm supposed to be. Sarah didn't give me any instructions. I know I want to be working with children." She poked her fork at some eggs and took her first few bites of the morning.

Sonja ate a little as well and drank some coffee. She told Gwendolyn, "You know, they really do not push the sponsored volunteers much. Unless you are different from the rest of the girls, you will be able to go help when you want and come back here when you want. For the regulars it is like a job. They have set hours and tasks. We mostly stick around here anyway." Her eyes wandered out the window.

Gwendolyn noticed a few other women sitting down with their breakfast at another table. She asked Sonja, "That weird minister guy— what's his story? Is he for real or was he putting me on?"

Sonja laughed, involuntarily exhaling unprocessed smoke she had just sucked in. Her face down, she said, "Bozo? He is from Sweden. He will talk your ear off. Mostly when we see him he is just flitting around. I think he is the mission chaplain and he is on call for something else too, but… whatever. He was hanging around here yesterday doing nothing really. Just drinking with a few of us."

"I met him yesterday," Gwendolyn said.

"He is harmless, except if you do not like smoke." She smiled cruelly in recognition of the fact that she herself was pushing smoke into Gwendolyn's face. "But he does sometimes have good Scotch. Yesterday afternoon he had some great stuff, we mixed some drinks. He told us he steals it all from the director, but I doubt that. He is not exactly a gangster." She smiled.

"Which room is his?" asked Gwendolyn as her eyes darted over her shoulder a bit tensely, looking at the doors opening to the lounge.

Sonja laughed again. "He does not live here with us regular old sponsored volunteer girls. He lives in the executive residence building, over there." She pointed out the window, and Gwendolyn could see a little portion of the building, beyond what she knew was the administration building.

By now perhaps a half dozen women were eating breakfast or sitting in the lounge. The closest were at the far end of the same table as Gwendolyn and Sonja. Most were silent or in quiet conversation.

Gwendolyn asked Sonja, "What do you do here?"

"I have not decided yet." She had been here a month.

"?"

"As I said, they do not push you too much. I have been walking around trying to figure out what I want to do. At home I was especially good with decorated desserts. I made them for family occasions and even for friends. I even made a really opulent wedding cake for some ambassador that my husband had business with. Maybe I will give some classes on how to make the different frostings and decorate cakes and so forth."

At first Gwendolyn thought Sonja was joking. As the woman continued without pause, Gwendolyn caught herself before forcing herself to smile at the nonexistent, horrible-taste joke. The woman was serious.

Sonja continued, "I should bet most of these ladies would enjoy that. Anyway I cannot teach meditation or painting like some of them." She pointed the glowing end of her cigarette at women chatting and eating at a nearby table as she exhaled a puff of smoke.

Gwendolyn's mode relaxed to minor incredulousness. The two women at the end of the table were participating in the conversation passively. One looked along the table to Sonja and spoke up, "That sounds like fun. I hope you do it. I'm in." The other nodded agreeably.

Sonja puffed on her cigarette, then said, "At least that will not get me in trouble with the director."

Gwendolyn was again surprised. "Dr. Bok? Why would you get in trouble? He really only seems worried about us hurting the patients or maybe fouling up his arrangements with those thugs outside. Why would he bother you?"

Sonja and the women at the end of the table laughed. Sonja said, "It is pretty easy here. We can go anywhere on this side of the mission when we want. But do not get out to the actual camps. That is for the locals, the employees only. I do not think they want us seeing the ghosts. That brings out the crazy in old Bok. They tell me that some regular sneaked out there about three months ago. She was not part of a working crew. The director was so angry he cut off their desserts over in the cafeteria for a week. And he was not even here at the time!"

One of the women at the end of the table spoke up, "I wonder about that guy. It's almost like he wants us to think he is just about to go insane; that way we'll follow his rules so he doesn't go nonlinear on us or something."

The woman across from her, who by looks could have been her sister, added, "Yeah. Maybe he'll blow up the nuclear plant by remote control next time someone peeks at the ghosts." Sonja nodded, chuckling. Sonja was finished eating and lit another cigarette.

Gwendolyn sat bemused by it all; Dr. Bok seemed kind and quite reasonable to her. These women were all well older than her, and yet they were acting like high school girls. She was also confused by the strange word spoken in reference to the patients here. She asked, "Why do you call them ghosts?"

Sonja exhaled. Her shoulders shrugged, and she looked at the women at the end of the table. "That is what they are called. I do not know. But make sure that nobody in administration hears you. They go crazy if they hear that, too." The other women were nodding. She continued, "We are all theoretically one big happy group helping the 'patients' here at the mission. It is kind of two-faced."

"What do you mean, two-faced?"

"Well come on. Nobody thinks we can really end the starvation here or that we are really even trying very hard."

Gwendolyn was stunned. The other women were listening, one expressionless, the other eating some of her breakfast; neither seemed to be hearing anything surprising. "But to hear the Doctor talk you would think we were going to feed thousands with a couple of fish and everybody will go home happy after dinner. Change the world." She returned her attention to her smoke.

One of the nameless women at the table's end said, "It's really a pretty hopeless situation. I'm not sure why I even came here. I thought I'd be helping people, but what have I done?"

Gwendolyn stuttered out, "What do you mean, can't we do anything? Why are we here? What do you do every day?"

"Well, so far I've taken two yoga classes a day. She teaches them." The woman indicated someone eating breakfast at another table. "I've lost a little weight. I've walked up and down that path outside a zillion times. But I'll bet everyone out in the camp is hungry again this morning." She shrugged.

"Why don't you tell Sarah you want a specific job like the regulars?"

"I may," said Nameless. "But some of those jobs are pure drudgery, so I've been putting it off. I have gone and stopped in to help at the infirmary, but I mostly just stood around. Nobody really needed anything."

Her companion said, "They don't bring the worst cases anywhere near this side of the mission. They stay out over the dirtpile."

Nameless continued, "Anyway when I think of how many are out there it just seems so hopeless... I don't really know where I would start. Or if I will. I may just go home. If I go early I don't care. They can keep the money."

"What do you mean, 'over the dirtpile?' Do you mean the hills?" Gwendolyn looked up at the hills through an open bedroom window on the opposite side of the lounge.

"Where the ghosts are." Nameless put her fist above her shoulder with her thumb extended backwards toward the bare dirt hills. "I don't think any of the volunteers—certainly none of us—have been out there." She looked at her companion and Sonja. Both were nodding agreement and Sonja spoke up.

"A few of the regulars have gone out there," Sonja said.

"Oh. I didn't know. Anyway, that's where the tough stuff is. And the dirty laundry, probably."

Gwendolyn shuddered and changed the subject. She asked Sonja, "How about the others? What do they do?"

"Well they are all different, really. Monica, for instance," she tipped her forehead to the yoga instructor, who was now reading in the lounge, "She is from Boston, America. She gives those yoga classes I mentioned. They are right here at ten thirty in the morning and at three o'clock in the afternoon every day. Most of us go to them."

She indicated another woman at the farthest table, "And Molina helps serve lunch to the people who work here and the regulars. I forget her name," she indicated a woman who was selecting breakfast items. "She sometimes works with the native men on motors and carpentry and such. But mostly she just walks around. Like all of us."

Gwendolyn was trying to remember the different people and their occupations when Sonja spoke up, pointing to a few more women in turn. "That woman there teaches art to the sponsored and regulars. She gives religious services every morning," she nodded toward a woman who had just come up the stairs. "She never mentions having seen Dr. Boseau there." Sonja smiled. Having filled her lungs with at least five cigarettes, she yawned and abruptly said, "I am going to go out to get some air. It was fine to meet you. Have fun here, sweetie." She crushed out the remnants of her cigarette, then got up and walked to the stairway. She left her dishes in place, with half the food still present.

Gwendolyn had eaten only a few bites. She tried unsuccessfully to force herself to finish the large pile of food on her own plate, pushing well past hunger. As she stood, feeling stuffed, she looked for where to bring the plates. One of the serving women came over gesturing Gwendolyn away and took the plates to the back of the room.

Gwendolyn glanced around, lingering on each visible sponsored volunteer for a second or two. She went to the window and stood looking out, disturbed at the prospect of not working with the starving children, and she shuddered at the threat of boredom in this place. She noticed Sonja lingering on the path just outside the building. *How do these women do this without going crazy?* She resolved to get herself an assignment putting her hands on the suffering children. She hoped Sarah would arrive soon or send someone for her, and felt confident of it after their conversations yesterday. But today's conversations had implanted some doubt. As she tossed a glance around the room she shuddered at the prospect of becoming one of these people.

All morning she waited around in the lounge, trying to kill time by reading a book. She largely avoided conversation with the others there. Nobody came looking for Gwendolyn all morning, and she was crestfallen. Nerves and boredom drove her outside on her own for the first time. She felt like a trespasser, an outsider in a world where everyone else was a bonded insider. She was hesitant to go inside the buildings, but she walked along the walkways looking for Sarah. Sarah would certainly have something for her; in fact Sarah probably had a backlog of work, and she must have forgotten to come for her. Gwendolyn smiled as she thought of Sarah finding her and faux-complaining that Gwendolyn was already behind in her work. She snaked among the buildings, impressed with how many of the essentially identical edifices she had not noticed before. She was happy to be around people as she walked around the mission. It seemed like it could have been a weekday afternoon anywhere in America.

She encountered polite nods as she passed volunteers and native workers. None of the volunteers she accosted knew where Sarah was; some seemed not to remember who Sarah was at all. In her travels that day Gwendolyn found that there were many more African employees than volunteers. Most were female like the volunteers, but there were a significant number of men. The Africans had a native language Gwendolyn did not understand. A small number knew some English, but Gwendolyn learned to do little more than exchange friendly nods with the native workers as she passed, since when they talked it was usually in their own language. It frustrated her to be unable to communicate. *Why don't they learn English? What's the matter with them?* In her conversations with volunteers, she learned that the regulars always wore simple beige shifts, and the sponsored volunteers wore anything they chose. The local women all wore dresses of an identical undescribed color; the men wore shorts and shirts of the similar hue. As Gwendolyn walked, she ranged the whole mission complex and went all the way past the power plant, partly out of curiosity. The path turned toward the bare dirt hills that formed the border of her world here and dropped down a small gully. She approached and saw that there was an unlocked gate across the path; curiously the gate was insecure—on one side its fence extended only a little way down a slope, then abruptly ended. It would be easy to walk around even if locked. Beyond the gate the path zigzagged through passes in the dirt hills.

Gwendolyn turned back to continue her search for Sarah. She wended along the buildings, walking around most of them, traveling through some of the more accessible ones. Overall it was a frustrating afternoon, but since she traversed many of the buildings she actually learned quite a bit about the mission, and she may have seen her first patients of the visit—she witnessed some medical attendants apparently serving a few emaciated and sickly individuals in one building. She saw food preparation in another. Some buildings had closed doors and panes in the windows, and she walked around them. She encountered a few mysterious fenced off outdoor areas, but her curiosity was passive and unobtrusive. The only door she actually opened was one that seemed to call to her unconsciously. She walked up to a small building with glass windows through which she could detect activity and opened the door. She was surprised and delighted to encounter a schoolroom of clean and happy-looking African children, all looking directly at her and smiling. She only lingered a minute before an adult volunteer looked over. She quickly ducked out and resumed her search with a bit of a spring in her step.

Having failed to encounter Sarah all day, she went to the regulars' dormitory to find Alitisha in the late afternoon. Nobody was around Alitisha's empty, open room.

Gwendolyn went back home. She sat down in the lounge and thought about her first frustrating day. True, she had seen more of the camp, but she had spent the better part of morning in her dormitory flapping her jaws or waiting for Godot, and she never talked to Sarah, never got put in a job. She had not seen Alitisha in twenty-four hours, and she chose to go down to the regulars' dormitory looking for her again, rather than eat dinner with the sponsored volunteers. She went inside and milled around the hallway near Alitisha's still-empty room.

Sandy Crittenden walked into the building. She was cheerful, if a bit tired from the day. She greeted Gwendolyn soothingly and directed the conversation to her day's work. She mentioned that she had found an acceptable location and worked all day to set up a room where she could let individuals come in for counseling. With Sarah's assistance she had obtained some furniture and gotten a few native men to move it into the place. Her little studio now held a desk, a couch and a few tables and chairs. Gwendolyn told her of her own frustrating day and mentioned that she was starting to feel lonely here. She felt tears welling in her eyes. "That's understandable," said Sandy. "Come, sit down in my room for a minute." They entered her bedroom, Gwendolyn sat on the bed, hands on her knees. She looked at her hands as Sandy sat down on the chair in the center of the room and gazed at her silently.

Gwendolyn complained, "I just want to be doing something important, something helping people. Not helping myself, not helping people to help people help people. I know I've just been here a day, but it seems like there's no urgency at all with anyone. I hear we're saving people from a horrible fate, but I'm doing nothing at all, and I may as well be in Iowa." Sandy was silent but moved to the bed. She sat down and cradled Gwendolyn in her arms. Gwendolyn dabbed her eyes. "I mean Indiana," she sniffed, and Sandy broke into a gentle laugh. Gwendolyn smiled weakly as well. They sat together for a few minutes.

The place was largely a mystery to Sandy, at this point probably more so than to Gwendolyn, despite Sandy's long correspondence period with Sarah. Sandy had her own consternation now as she comforted Gwendolyn. She was also in her initial phase of calibrating the mission after yesterday's surprising revelation that she was basically in a lawless land best described as a war zone, possibly just now between battles. Sandy was older than Gwendolyn and more appreciated some of the complexities in running such a mission. Maybe Sarah was just too busy today to accommodate Gwendolyn's needs.

As for her own situation, Sandy was starting to understand that she may not be working with the patients, and maybe that was okay. Dr. Bok might be right—her professional skills would be of little help to those in such a survival predicament. Sandy shared Gwendolyn's drive to help others, though she was probably more willing to be satisfied if she only worked indirectly. She herself had been troubled by the relative comfort of the 'quiet college dorm' atmosphere. But at least the regulars around her had jobs where they labored to keep the place going. She could certainly be of service as they struggled to cope with the stress of living so far from their homes, all the time subjected to the stress of knowing the patients were in a terrible plight just over the hill. Perhaps some of them will actually be ministering to the patients directly, and *that* would certainly take a toll. Sandy could help them. She didn't know much about what the sponsored volunteers did, but she assumed it was more important than the menial tasks the regulars seemed to be doing.

Gwendolyn felt better for the physical contact and the conversation with Sandy. She dabbed her eyes one last time and broke away from Sandy, saying, "I think I'll find Alitisha now and get dinner with her." Gwendolyn was indeed hungry, not having eaten since breakfast. Sandy was happy for the prospect of being alone after a long day and glad to have helped. She nodded quietly and moved back to the chair in the room's center.

Gwendolyn again went to Alitisha's room. Finally she found Alitisha! She was sitting on the bed talking to a girl from a few doors down. She stood up as she saw Gwendolyn.

"Gwendolyn! This is Jane. She's from North Carolina."

Jane smiled and stood. She was dressed in the same simple drab shift as Alitisha. "My pleasure," she said, extending her hand.

Gwendolyn shook her hand. "Gwendolyn's stopping out from Stambridge. She's a sponsored volunteer. She's up there with the shi-shi ladies," Alitisha said playfully.

"Well then I see. Am I allowed to be shaking your hand?" Jane played along with a theatrical flourish. Gwendolyn smiled without understanding the slang.

She looked at Alitisha. "I thought we could get dinner together in the cafeteria." It was agreeable to Alitisha, and Jane seemed amenable, so they went over. There were about fifteen people in the cafeteria when they entered. A few black-robed nuns were along the far wall; it was unclear whether they were eating. The three girls gathered some unremarkable food and sat. Jane was talkative, and her slow speech, delivered in a pleasant Southeastern drawl, had Gwendolyn, a rapid-fire New-Englander, off balance waiting for the end of every clause. Jane was also in college, back in North Carolina, and she had been here since the beginning of summer. She wanted to be a doctor, specifically a psychiatrist. She was unsponsored and was paying the mission for her room and board out of her pocket—well, to be more specific, her father's pocket. She said he was not against it because he planned to take a tax deduction, and Jane thought that meant that it cost him nothing.

Jane's job was in laundry. She worked in the area where they washed the linen and clothes for the volunteers and local employees. "Beige dresses and white sheets." It was terribly boring, and often quite hot, but she viewed it all as a cost of getting a good blurb on her resume—all the volunteers knew Dr. Bok was generous with superlatives in his references. Alitisha and Gwendolyn occasionally chimed in but mostly listened.

Alitisha asked Jane, with a mischievous smile, "So tell us, what are the secrets? Is there any good gossip around here? Unwritten rules, secret hideaways? Who's doing what with who?"

Jane continued, "Secrets? Well, not really. It gets boring around here. As you know, they don't believe in electronic entertainment. They say it has history going back to native superstitions, but really it's just a control thing. Dr. Bok has forbidden any devices; you probably noticed there are not many things like that here, not even phones." The girls nodded. They had left their GVCDs at home.

"How long do most of the people stay here? Are they all like you?" asked Gwendolyn.

Jane thought about it for a minute as she ate. She took a drink of her water and said, "I'd say the ones that stay remain for a semester. Quite a few don't make it past two weeks or so before they're clamoring for the next airplane out, and some stay for a whole school year but, mostly about one semester."

Gwendolyn and Alitisha looked around. There were some other regulars eating, and they noticed all were somewhere around their own age. They looked at each other, and Gwendolyn asked Jane, "They all look so... regular. Do they all come from America?"

"Lots of them," Jane responded. "There are some from Europe. She is from France," indicating a girl sitting alone a few tables away. "But it's sort of an American thing. Most of us are trying to help people, sure, but almost everyone is either in college or recently finished, and we're all trying to get experience. I want to be more qualified in the eyes of medical school. So... Daddy can cough up a few more bucks and I can live in the dust for a while." She smiled.

Gwendolyn thought about probing, but saw that Alitisha found Jane's comments unremarkable, so she shrugged it off. She asked, "Jane, have you fed anyone hungry? I haven't even seen anyone. I could be in Kansas for all the help it seems like I'll give anyone."

Jane said, "I haven't seen anyone. You probably won't. Thank god. From what I hear you don't want to. They're in pretty bad shape out there."

"That's what I want to see, to help with. That's why I'm here."

"Well, the volunteers usually never go there. But my friend that left a few weeks ago was working in the dustbowl every day for a month or two. She never said anything about it, hardly."

"Dustbowl?" Alitisha asked. The girls exchanged glances.

"That's what we call it. Or just the camp. The director likes to call it the Inner Quad." She smiled in amusement. "It's where the really wretched people are, where the true suffering is performed. We don't get to see it. It's not inner—it's everything over the dirtpile. And it's not a quad. It's more like a tilted, oblong bowl. There aren't any buildings, just tents. Everyone just calls it the dustbowl."

"What did this girl do over there?"

"She was my roommate. Let me tell you, she would never talk about it. She's the one that told me about the shape of it and the tents and everything. Sometimes I tried to find out what it was like. She was normal enough before she took that job, but I don't think she'll ever be the same. She never talked, not willingly. Not about the ghosts." She looked at Alitisha and then back. "You don't want to go out there. We all help well enough by working on tasks that, you're right, people do in Nebraska. You're still helping people. It's still difficult enough. Actually some of your neighbors, sponsored volunteers, run lots of little classes and projects to keep the rest of us from going crazy with the stress of knowing what's right out there over those hills. It's pretty tough, and I think we can be proud of what we do and proud of getting through all of it. And anyway, there is lots to do on this end of the camp. If the food doesn't get loaded onto the trucks, nobody gets to eat out there. Heck, I do laundry. All kinds of things. Medical help. Paperwork. Taking care of the kids."

"Kids?" Alitisha asked. She had been monitoring the conversation, and she and Gwendolyn looked at each other. "What kids?"

"The orphanage, the schoolhouse. I thought they gave newbies tours on the way in. Didn't you see it?"

Gwendolyn's interest was piqued. "I think I saw it today. But no, on our first tour they just walked us around outside buildings and after a while most of the places looked the same." Alitisha nodded agreement.

"Well, they have a little nursery school. They take care of about a dozen kids."

"A dozen? I thought there were thousands of patients. Only twelve kids?" Gwendolyn was confused. She and Alitisha looked at each other, then back to Jane.

"I don't know. Not very many. Maybe twenty. They are all little, I think they move them on when they get to be what we would call school age. But we never really see them. They stay to themselves. Another girl that left used to work in there."

"Where do they move them to?" Alitisha asked Jane.

Jane looked like she had been asked why gravity makes acorns fall. She looked at her fork for a minute, and said, "I don't know, really. I guess they get adopted somewhere. I never wondered." Gwendolyn was amazed and waited to see if more was coming. Jane had no further answer. Then Alitisha said something inconsequential, and the conversation wandered meaninglessly after that. In a few minutes they all got up and walked back to the regulars' lodging, and Jane parted from them. The other two sat on the beds in Alitisha's room.

Alitisha said, "How about all that? Wow, I thought I'd understand this place. Anyway I guess I'd better get ready for work." Gwendolyn was surprised.

"I figured you were at work all day."

"I started to, but they told me I'll be working the late shift for the next couple of weeks, and they let me knock off early. It normally starts before now, but I can go in whenever I want tonight, since I was there a while today. Anyway it's not like I'm being paid or they can fire me or anything, but I want to do the right thing, so I'll go in pretty soon."

Gwendolyn was surprised at the thought of shift work but said, "Well, I suppose the needs are around the clock here. But I came by looking for you."

Alitisha smiled. She said, "Some of the guys here are very nice." Gwendolyn tried to get more details, but in truth there were none to give; Alitisha was an extravert and a pleasant girl, and she had befriended a few of the workers who knew English. For the afternoon she had followed one around in his work. It was a pleasant interlude in the foothills to the mountains of boredom Alitisha felt looming in the near future.

Gwendolyn soon parted company with Alitisha and went back to her own room. She read for a while on her bed with Pyratticus Julius close to her and then fell asleep. Later she woke up, cleaned up and went to bed.

Morning came, signaled by the sunshine penetrating her disheveled hair and illuminating her eyes and face. As the world materialized and her memory banks initialized, Gwendolyn became determined to find herself a meaningful job today. She rushed through a shower. She ate alone and walked the complex again. More assertive today, she went into buildings, and she came upon a regular volunteer supervisor who was assigning a woman to clean floors inside one building. Gwendolyn interjected and asked if she could help. Both volunteers saw from her lack of uniform that she was a sponsored volunteer. The supervisor sent the other volunteer on her way, and turned to Gwendolyn as she rolled one of a pair of pails with mops down the hall. Gwendolyn walked beside her and rolled the other bucket along.

"You don't need to do this kind of work here."

"But I want to."

"Don't you have something else you need to work on? Are you sure you want to clean toilets like a janitor?" She was speaking in metaphor.

Gwendolyn took her words literally. "Cleaning toilets is perfect! I'll empty garbage or scrub floors. Let me help. Please. I can do this." Gwendolyn stepped in front of her, stopping her, and trembled, unblinking. Swallowing. Her eyes burned into the woman.

The woman's face relaxed into a soft smile. She looked down at her tan dress and said, "Okay, then. If you really want to work. You can work with us for a week. Then you'll have to move on. And be quiet about it. I'm just a regular and you're a sponsored volunteer. I don't want to interfere with the way things are here. You say you want to work for me; okay, let's do it. I'm Charlotte Wentworth."

"Thank you, thank you. I'm Gwendolyn Dressel-Meier and I just got here the day before yesterday and I'm ready to help." She hugged Charlotte, knocking her back into the handles of the mops behind her. Charlotte peeled Gwendolyn's arms off, and they started forward.

They conversed lightly as they walked back to the supply area where Charlotte had a sort of a desk. She was from New England as well, being born in Maine and having lived in Massachusetts. She was here for probably a year. Her three daughters were grown, and she had just started a divorce. Charlotte set Gwendolyn up with an assignment for the day before going back out to her own work in the hallway. She took advantage of Gwendolyn's enthusiasm; the morning started with toilets indeed.

Sarah never came by to reassign or even visit with Gwendolyn during the week. Gwendolyn worked hard in three different buildings. Since she did not mind cleaning bathrooms, and most of the regulars hated it, she swapped work and washed toilets and sinks every day. Charlotte did not seem to mind the assignment shenanigans, and Gwendolyn became a popular member of her team. She worked like a dynamo, and all the others were amused by her enthusiasm in a spectating sort of way. Gwendolyn quickly got the bathroom-cleaning process down to a science and progressed at a record pace. Her reward for efficiency was brushes with boredom. These she fended off through activity; she sought out Charlotte and scrubbed doors and walls, pulled weeds, even engaged in the self-assigned project of sweeping loose dirt off the unpaved paths outside on the dusty African plain. Most days, after she finished her chores she hunted down regulars who were not done with their work. She relieved them of some of their unfinished cleaning duties. If she met co-workers in passing as they mopped floors or dusted fixtures, she joined right in with what they were doing. She got to know some of the regulars casually and temporarily. Small gossip ensued; Dr. Bok seemed very fond of Sarah. The militia was unobtrusive. The entrance gate for the incoming patients was at the far side of the camp.

Some few of the regulars she met shared her discomfort in being disconnected from the patients. One named Evelyn who came from Switzerland was especially troubled by it, almost to the extent Gwendolyn was. She was the only one who truly chafed at the waste of her effort; most were satisfied with their work situations, and if Gwendolyn brought up the issue, they were not eager to approach the disconcerting mental imagery attendant to discussions of the patients.

Gwendolyn pried her friends a bit about Dr. Phineas Boseau; he seemed such an oddball feature at the place. All the regulars knew of him, by sight if not by name, but few had talked to him more than a couple of times. The man was gregarious and garrulous, and as he walked along he seemed to follow a gravitational path toward any volunteer he spotted. Human defenses being what they are, most regulars suffered only one encounter with the man; they learned to alter their course and velocity to their advantage when he came in sight. He was not dangerous or menacing, just tiresome and childish. None of the regulars had much of an impression other than that he was gawky and mysterious. Gwendolyn encountered none who had taken advantage of his services as chaplain.

Gwendolyn asked what people thought of Dr. Bok and Aloysius Fink. The read on Dr. Bok varied widely. Some thought he was a grandfatherly teddy bear, and others thought he was a slick operator. All agreed that whenever they had interacted with him, he always had just the right thing to say. As for Fink, he provoked universal shudders. Most regulars had essentially no contact with him, but the man seemed surrounded in a field of something awkward—no, not awkward: cold-blooded. Dark. Some had a physical reaction at a distance from the man; if Aloysious Fink were detected nearby, their spines would tingle and badger them until, through some form of action, they achieved a comfortable distance from him. They described the feeling as something like fingernails on a blackboard. Regardless of the level of autonomous reactions to him, the man seemed crocodilian, bloodless, scary to the regulars without exception.

During that janitorial week Gwendolyn learned quite a bit about herself. She was happiest while working and a bit depressed when she was not. In the evenings she was lonely and did not find much satisfying companionship with her compatriots among the sponsored volunteers. Most mornings she only saw zero or one of them as she got her breakfast before reporting for work, and she got in the habit of choosing something she could eat while walking. After dinner time, there were usually some sponsored volunteers lounging around, but her interactions with them were always superficial. Most were older than her and many, it seemed, did not care whether their work really helped the starving children here much at all. She knew Alitisha was working the late shift, but a couple of times she still went down to Alitisha's hallway after dinner. Sandy was usually in her room at that hour, and she always seemed to have time to talk for a while. Mostly Gwendolyn just read in the evenings. In the one week she read *Moby Dick*, an accomplishment few people have ever matched. She started *Uncle Tom's Cabin* and became quite attached to the story.

On the seventh consecutive morning, as Charlotte gave Gwendolyn her assignments and the others waited outside for theirs, Charlotte reminded her that it was to be her last day. Gwendolyn offered to keep working, but Charlotte would have none of it. She liked the girl but knew she was a destabilizing influence among her workers, and besides, she did not need the attention from Sarah and Dr. Bok that probably followed Gwendolyn around.

Gwendolyn went through the day figuring it was probably for the best; maybe she could find something more directly related to the patients. This work was good work, hard work, and it contributed. But she yearned for more. *One thing is sure: I'm not going to have another day of walking around doing nothing tomorrow.* Three times during the day she ran over to the administration building and tried to find Sarah, but she failed each time. She had not seen Sarah once in the whole week, though Sarah had been watching her.

The next morning Gwendolyn ate breakfast early as she walked to the administration building to find Sarah. She felt there was a chance that Sarah would be there planning her day if she went early. Gwendolyn wanted a specific work detail, something Sarah had never given her. Outside the building she pressed the button, and the door popped unlocked. She found Sarah in her small office. She seemed surprised but happy to see Gwendolyn and said she had seen Sandy Crittenden last night. Sandy had mentioned Gwendolyn.

Unbeknownst to Gwendolyn, at Sandy's suggestion, Sarah decided to give Gwendolyn a rotating series of very specific tasks for individual days. Sandy thought that the unpredictable sequence would occupy Gwendolyn's mind and help distract her from creeping feelings of depression that were a real threat. Sarah told her that she was going to give her assignments each day. Gwendolyn was happy to hear it, though she quietly wondered why she would not be working on a single project for her stay here. She was thrilled to hear that the first day of her surprise tasks was already upon her; Sarah told her that Dr. Bok had a special job for her for today. In three hours Gwendolyn should go to the executive residence and meet Dr. Bok.

Gwendolyn was pleased to have a project assignment and such an important one—she had been assigned to work for the director directly. Having hours to kill, she decided to walk around the complex again like she had done a week ago, with one modification: today she had a mission. She was relaxed, and she would pick a few buildings, go inside and observe some of the activity.

As she walked along away from the building she looked and saw a truck behind her, beyond the barbed wire, with a few militia men sleeping in and around it. She walked over toward the hills where there was some activity and saw trucks being loaded with crates at one of the buildings. Native workers and some volunteers were already at work, leisurely transporting the carton to the vehicles. Upbeat rock 'n' roll music was emanating from the openings of the building. She approached the dock area and looked inside. The place was busy and strangely happy; the workers were not dancing, but Gwendolyn thought she perceived synchronization between their movements and the music. The crates held food product for the patients. Gwendolyn saw tables and vats of doughy batter with water and several types of powder being mixed into it. She felt bold today and entered the building, feeling almost a mission participant now that she had her own job.

She had to step out of the way a few times as workers and volunteers buzzed by, bringing powered carts to the trucks and stacking containers of the mixtures. All work seemed decentralized and relaxed but efficient. It was the kind of operation she would enjoy being involved with. She was pleased to have a chance to participate in this feeding of the needy, however vicariously.

As it turned, she went beyond observation; she contributed a little—at one point a native supervisor overseeing the mixing of a batch of the various powders seemed to detect something wrong in the actions of one of the workers. They exchanged some words, and the worker looked confused, as though he did not understand. The supervisor tried to explain, but the worker could not grok the problem, and he grew exasperated listening to his boss's complaints. He distracted himself by looking over at Gwendolyn as the boss talked, probably wondering why this strange woman was standing there. Eventually he shrugged, took his hands off the equipment, put them on his hips and just stared in Gwendolyn's direction. The supervisor continued his rant, then paused and followed the man's gaze. He looked toward Gwendolyn. His face leapt to a smile, and he nodded as he quickly walked around the work table and started toward her, looking back over his shoulder and bobbing his head agreeably. As the supervisor approached her with increasing speed, Gwendolyn wondered why they were involving her in their dispute. Just as she was about to ask him what he wanted, he swerved around her and took a carton from a stack of boxes behind her. He smiled genially at her as he pivoted and started back to the table, where the contents of the box somehow solved the problem. He happily walked away, the worker seemed content enough, and Gwendolyn was passively proud to have been standing in the right place to help them along.

All the while, trucks were leaving sporadically. Gwendolyn liked it there and spent most of the morning watching the activity. This was critical work; they were preparing and shipping food for starving people. Gwendolyn was wearing her own clothes, and as such, all the workers and volunteers assumed she had free reign to walk around the building, which she took advantage of. Eventually it was time to go and meet Dr. Bok.

She had not seen Dr. Bok since the day she arrived, though their beds were no more than two hundred yards apart. She looked forward to seeing her old friend as she happily walked to the executive residence. Passing some native workers on the path, nodding as she went, she noticed how happy everyone seemed today. The warm sunshine transformed the sparse weeds lining the dusty earth path into voluptuous garden flowers as she walked to the executive residence. She could hardly contain her excitement after days of boredom and mundane tasks only tangentially related to helping the hungry people just over those bare dirt hills. The director was going to give her a special job today. Maybe her efforts would save some little baby's life or at least help stockpile some medicine. And the director himself! It must be important if he was involved. And he chose her!

"Excellent. Wonderful, my dear. You're here!" Gwendolyn was roused from her reverie by Director Professor Dr. Florian Q, Bok's ebullient voice as she lingered outside the executive residence building. She turned and instantly felt the warmth of his friendly face on hers. Then an incongruous scene sprang upon her.

The man was striding toward her, irregularly orbited by two huge, kinetic, irregularly spotted Great Danes: one grey, one beige! Dogs! Here at the mission! Gigantic dogs! Incarnations of the caricatured, muscle-bound animals in animated cartoons from her childhood. She half expected to see them pumping dumbbells or sniffing dynamite. *But in the cartoons they were never so big, so…unmanageable.* Dogs!

As the sudden impact of her shock dissolved she was permeated by mental dizziness. Dogs out here in the African plains. Dogs wearing collars and tags, and well groomed and bouncing and happy.

Dr. Bok deployed an animated and warm smile featuring arched eyebrows, eyes widened by the lenses of his glasses, and a gapingly friendly mouth. She stood looking at the dogs as he approached.

"Gwendolyn, meet my babies Colonel and Bourbon." He bent down and the dogs licked his face, their tongues dancing right through knots with each other. "Colonel, Bourbon, this young lady will be taking care of you today." Gwendolyn was alarmed. "You be good for her, and you will have a treat. You will spend the day outside in this glorious sunshine." The dogs, excited and happy to be outside, listened impatiently until the man stopped talking. He looked up at Gwendolyn. "I am very strict with them. I never let them outside here at the mission except, of course, in the courtyard for necessities. Today will indeed be an exciting one for these little boys." When he had released their attention they had approached Gwendolyn in excited doggy-style friendship and started sniffing her and licking her struggling arms. Dr. Bok stood watching approvingly, nodding as he spoke. One of the dogs placed his front leg on her chest and slapped her cheeks with his swinging tongue. He managed to flap the thin moist thing between her lips before Bok reprimanded him: "Bourbon. Down. NOW." At the last verbal snap the dog dropped to all fours, and Gwendolyn caught her bearings, wiping her arm across her face and lips. The animal started licking her other arm, then switched to her legs, starting at the calves, alternating between them and traveling up into her skirt and back down. Gwendolyn loved dogs, but this was not like playing with puppies in her backyard in Vermont. She had never been overwhelmed quite like this, never had to ward off brutes with tongues like these. She stepped back a few times to little avail, as it was a fraction of a step for each Great Dane to match one of hers.

"I see you will get along famously," Dr. Bok said. "They're angels, they are, angels. And it's such a grand coincidence. I was just feeling for them, cooped up inside all the time. I don't have the time to bring them out, and I can't trust just anybody with them. And well, you know how the natives feel about dogs."

Gwendolyn knew nothing about natives and dogs. She was concerned.

"And I know you love animals, so when Sarah told me you're available," he prevaricated—Sarah had generated the idea, picturing Gwendolyn distracted and kept happy by the company of the animals, expecting the same effect as if they were fuzzy little puppies. "I jumped. I thought I would introduce you to the boys. Bourbon and Colonel just love people, they love 'em. Sometimes I think people are scared by their size, I don't know. Some people just don't take to these magnificent animals for some reason. But I can see you and the boys are getting on fine already."

Gwendolyn was still backing up, bent down with her face up toward Dr. Bok, alternately tugging at her skirt and pushing Bourbon's head away, a gesture he took as friendly petting—which did not simplify her situation.

"I don't know… they're so… big. What do they…" stumbled Gwendolyn as she danced and bent, her voice trailing off.

"You'll be fine, you will. They love you. Look at them, how excited they are. Just remember you're in control, you're the boss, not them. These naughty boys will try to get away with things," he said as he reached down and scratched Bourbon's head and said in a playful, drawn-out voice, "Won't you boys?" The momentary distraction resulted in the dog unwinding his tongue from one of Gwendolyn's thighs and letting it flutter happily in the air as he turned to Dr. Bok, whose other hand was now engaged in patting and lovemaking with Colonel. One of Bourbon's paws pinned Gwendolyn's shoe to the ground as he basked in the scratching Dr. Bok was delivering. Dr. Bok straightened up, his eyes on the dogs, head shaking, corners of his mouth pulled down, "But don't let them do it. No, don't you let them." As he retreated Colonel came to Gwendolyn and pushed her, making her step back. Dr. Bok continued, "I have much to do today, and I am so happy that you're able to spend the day with them." Abruptly, woefully belatedly from Gwendolyn's viewpoint, he barked "Sit!" to the canines. The animals sat looking at him, bobbing expectantly. "What a treat! I so rarely get them outside." He unhooked a heretofore-unnoticed satchel from his cane. "Oh, yes, I have leashes here, not that they will do you any good—your size and all. But the dogs will obey your commands."

"What did you say about how the local people feel about Colonel and Bourbon?" Gwendolyn awaited an answer she considered important.

"Oh, I see. You should know that the locals don't like dogs, any dogs, and they're a bit fearful of them. It's silly, especially with these two little boys. In some ways, even in this day and age, people in some parts of the world are savages." He bent toward the dogs, whose tails thumped as both licked his face and glasses. "I think it is not purely physical; I mean the men in the militia have guns after all. But they are just as reluctant to come near the dogs as an old woman is. There is some supernatural mythology that they attach to dogs. All of them believe it, but I've never dug into exactly what their fables are. I keep the dogs inside. It's just some idiotic superstition. Savages, as I say."

Gwendolyn glanced past the barbed wire perimeter. Several of the local militia were there near a truck. They seemed to be gesturing and talking about the dogs.

"But pay no attention. They will not bother you or the dogs. They like to keep their distance. For whatever reason, they just stay away. Part of the belief system may even include not harming the beautiful creatures. Maybe they will be haunted if they kill one, I don't know. I'm sure even if they are deathly afraid of them, they surely see their beauty. Anybody would. Uncivilized, really.

"Goodbye Gwendolyn. Bring my boys back safely. Now, they eat dinner precisely at three o'clock so be back here with them." He handed her the leashes and turned and walked back toward his building. The canines watched Bok disappear, then Bourbon turned his head to Gwendolyn, and his tail started thumping again. He stood and resumed licking her legs. Colonel observed patiently.

Gwendolyn stood frozen. Bourbon, apparently less interested without her struggling, turned away and started sniffing the ground. Gwendolyn started walking away from the executive residence without destination. The canines traveled with her, running back and forth around her, sniffing things, watching people from afar as the three meandered along.

Gwendolyn did not know where to go, so she walked more or less along an outer path in the complex, closest to the runway and barbed wire. The dogs were incredibly responsive, normally staying within about twenty feet of her, and the average of their motion matched hers perfectly. As she came upon an open patch of sparsely covered ground between buildings, the dogs started running away into it. She was instinctively afraid they would escape from her. She shouted, "Stop. Sit." Both dogs instantly braked and sat looking at her. Comforted by their acceptance of her as commander, she relaxed a bit and called the dogs over, petting them and generally giving them attention, which they lapped up. It is indeed fortunate that people have two arms, for the animals' heads bobbed and shoved each other in competition for her stroking hands. To her satisfaction, while they did not keep their tongues retracted into their mouths, they kept the wobbly appendages out of hers.

Gwendolyn started forgetting her troubles and played with the dogs, trying out commands to see what they knew. Each knew how to 'speak' and 'shake hands' and 'play dead' and 'beg.' Each knew its own name and ignored the other's name completely. She had fun getting the dogs to jump up and down and roll over.

Inside the satchel she found hard rubber toys for the dogs, one blue and one yellow. She found that Colonel fixated on the yellow toy, and Bourbon watched the blue one. For a while she threw the toys and the dogs fetched, each taking his turn and paying attention only to his own property. Gwendolyn lost herself in play. Then she stood and let the dogs run around by themselves.

Eventually she was tired out from watching all the exercise the dogs did. She walked to a bench on the edge of the field and sat down. The panting carnivores sniffed around in her vicinity then wandered back into the field. She lay down on the bench and relaxed on her side, head on her arm, watching the dogs. They seemed to entertain themselves, chasing dust specs in the dry grassy field, rooting in the ground with their noses and scratching with their paws, freezing completely in the face of noises inaudible to humans. They frolicked with each other occasionally. Bourbon seemed to give chase to some sort of ground animal several times, ending up scratching at the dirt with his paws and looking around with the confused expression dogs so easily fall into in such situations. Colonel had a few less intense interactions of the same kind. A smile formed on Gwendolyn's face as she watched the dogs' antics. She passed the time lazily watching.

Bourbon trapped something with his paw. He squealed with delight and lifted his foot, grabbing whatever was below in his jaw. He brought it back to Gwendolyn, the poor thing's drooping appendages and head flopping with the motion of his trot. Gwendolyn sat up transfixed in minor horror as the conqueror grew closer and closer. Then Bourbon dropped the fatally injured animal in front of her. It was a lizard of some sort, or perhaps a squid, and that was the entire level of detail Gwendolyn's senses discriminated. The quarry could not move, yet it refused to lie still. Bourbon stood proudly triumphant waiting for some sort of congratulations. In this he was disappointed.

The intensity of Gwendolyn's devotion to nature's creatures varied. For instance, she loved her pets most of all, and this is right and good. But though she could never justify the discrimination, her love was also apportioned by species. Of the small mammals her life had given her reason to contemplate, she liked rats the least, but cats finished in an honorable mention for last place. It was not because cats are not cute or even loving; for instance kittens ranked near the top. But they turn into cats. Her dislike had a specific source. Early on her family had a cat, and she came to realize that they are almost perfect killing machines that prey on, and torture, much smaller animals. Her bloodthirsty cat would often bring a maimed victim back to the house and graze on parts of it as its life leaked into the ether.

So Gwendolyn was here, half a world away from home, and a seemingly friendly dog had broken a small animal and dropped the struggling-to-die thing at her feet. She jumped to erectness, stepping back and shouting, "Bourbon! Bad dog!" The giant was caught completely by surprise. His mood fell, as clearly indicated by his tail and his general droop. He glanced down at the writhing mass on the ground then back up, confused.

Meanwhile Colonel had trotted over, and he sat down. He was watching the scene sans understanding; one of Colonel's enduring features was a sort of baseline bemusement that underpinned most of his life.

Gwendolyn was crushed, thinking about the dying reptile. She looked at it, then quickly away, tears forming in her eyes. She jogged aimlessly down the path in their original direction of motion without picking up the satchel. Colonel and Bourbon happily scampered along with her, crossing in front and behind, playing with each other as always. She soon slowed to a walk and the dogs matched her progress. She was simply putting distance between herself and that poor lizard.

Just then as the path crossed between a couple of buildings, Sandy Crittenden came out of one of them. First she noticed the dogs and was shocked enough to stop in her tracks. She saw Gwendolyn and smiled as the girl approached. The dogs were excited to see her, and suddenly she was absorbed in parrying off the advances of the animals and making sure she could remain standing. Eventually she petted them firmly in turn, and they settled down.

"Where did these guys come from?" she asked

"They belong to Dr. Bok," Gwendolyn answered. Sandy seemed unbelieving, her head waved back and forth, but she did not protest verbally. She noticed Gwendolyn's distress and queried her about it. Gwendolyn nervously described her traumatic experience. Sandy sized up the situation and said she would take care of things. Gwendolyn asked what Sandy had in mind, but Sandy just said, "You go back there and find the poor dead animal. Wait there. I'll be along and we can fix this up."

"But it's not dead. We have to help it," Gwendolyn protested.

"We will take care of it together. Go." Sandy disappeared into a building.

Gwendolyn was initially doubtful that anything could be done to deal with such a crisis, but she reluctantly turned back, leading the dogs toward the scene of the violence. As they walked back, they approached a native woman who was carrying a jug of water. The dogs recognized the jug and must have been thirsty. They ran toward the woman, startling her, and she dropped the jug. It lay on its side pouring out water; the woman was out of sight in an instant. The dogs busied themselves licking the little pools of muddy water then discovered the stream from the jug and competed for it till it stopped. Gwendolyn scolded the beasts, but they ignored her and kept drinking. Finally they retracted their muddy tongues, and sat lickingly looking at her from a safe distance. They followed her as she walked along.

The three continued on their way back to the open field where Bourbon had caught the lizard. The animal was there where the dog dropped it; it was lifeless and somehow seemed more shrunken and desiccated than just a few minutes before. Gwendolyn stopped a distance away and sat down on the ground to wait for Sandy. The dogs busied themselves rooting around in the ground, playing with each other and occasionally pursuing some small insect or animal. Gwendolyn watched the activity, and whenever it seemed they were molesting anything bigger than an insect she broke up the game with verbal admonishments and nasty gestures, communications that the dogs seemed to understand and remember for seconds at a stretch.

Gwendolyn was exhausted from her guard duty when Sandy approached. She was followed by... Alitisha! They were each carrying a shovel. Gwendolyn had not seen Alitisha in a week and was happy for the friendly face. She ran to her and they hugged, Alitisha dropping the shovel. Sandy said, "I thought the two of you could give that poor critter a decent burial. What do you think?" Gwendolyn let go of Alitisha, dabbed at her eyes and nodded, accepting the shovel from Sandy. Sandy then said, "Listen, Gwendolyn. You have to realize they were just being dogs."

Gwendolyn nodded, and Sandy walked away. Alitisha and Gwendolyn approached the scene of the dead animal. "That's the dead animal we're going to bury?" she was amazed. It seemed perfectly natural to see such a dusty dry corpse on the dusty dry ground; it did not seem worth burying. Not two shovels' worth. Not like a pet rabbit or something.

Gwendolyn nodded, "Yes. What?"

"That thing? Who cares about that? Leave it there, and something will eat it." She shrugged her shoulders.

Gwendolyn was flummoxed. It was true that she had never thought of anything except small furry animals as worthy of any real attention, and this was no baby seal clubbed to death by barbaric Newfies. But it was wrong—just wrong—to kill anything, even for a dog. She remembered many times when she tricked a spider or insect onto a piece of paper so she could carry it outside, delivering it from her mother's wrath. She had never been partial to scaly or slimy things and in fact had never willingly approached one. But Alitisha! Her best friend—acting as careless as any slob on the street. It's just wrong to leave something dead right there on top of the ground. Alitisha must know that. She looked at the carcass at her feet. "Come on. Let's bury it. That's what Sandy wants us to do. Sandy wants it covered up."

The dogs were sniffing in the field. Colonel came by asking for attention, and Gwendolyn mindlessly petted his head. Alitisha shrugged. She probably did not fall for the white lie but went along. She picked up her shovel and scooped up the dead body of what could now, at close range, be verified to be an unfortunate quadruped. In doing so she stepped back onto the path and crushed the front portion of a huge centipede or such. It made a combination of a crunch or snap and a squishy sound, then it looked like a clump of wriggling hairs emerging from a blob of jelly. She looked down at it, paused, glanced at Gwendolyn, then turned and walked a few steps off the path, putting down the lizard carcass as the dogs showed interest in her actions. Alitisha started digging a hole in the hard dirt. Meanwhile Gwendolyn took her shovel and made sure the syrupy crustacean was dead, then brought it over and put its body on the lizard carcass. She and Alitisha dug a shallow hole in silence, placed the dead creatures inside and filled the hole.

Gwendolyn and Alitisha sat reclining on the ground, visiting and giggling as the dogs frolicked in the field. They threw the toys for the dogs. Gwendolyn showed Alitisha the tricks the dogs knew, and they played like silly schoolgirls, which the dogs loved. They stayed there together for a long, pleasant time. The day's tragedy receded into the depths of memory.

After a while Dr. Phineas Boseau came bobbing along. He saw the girls and followed the point of his nose over to them. "Hello, Gwendolyn. Wonderful to see you out here. I see you have met the director's excellent animals. They are quite famous, you know."

Gwendolyn was uninterested in the origin of the dogs, but was again almost hypnotized with the motion of the man's nose tip as he talked. She said, "This is my friend Alitisha. She's from Vermont. We came here together." Alitisha and the man named for the clown shook hands as he bowed his head.

"I am delighted to meet you. I'm Dr. Phineas Boseau." Alitisha glanced over to Gwendolyn in amusement. "Yes, it's a soft 'S.' I know. I'm the chaplain here." He smiled in a foolish grin.

Alitisha smiled almost uncontrollably. "You just missed our funeral, chaplain. How unfortunate you weren't here in time."

Dr. Boseau showed interest. "A pet?" he said. "I understand, but that's why you're not supposed to have them here. Here, here girl," he gathered Alitisha to him, her head squeezed against his neck, his arms around her head and back as he pressed her against him. "It's in a better place. I understand what you are going through."

Alitisha broke free, laughing, and said, "Not my pet. Hers," pointing to Gwendolyn. Boseau started approaching Gwendolyn with open arms, but she shifted and leaned on the shovel, placing it between the two of them at a passively threatening angle.

Alitisha was giggling behind Boseau as his concerned face hovered in Gwendolyn's view, his head almost below shoulder level, his hands clasped lightly. "What can I do?" he said.

Gwendolyn answered, "Nothing, thank you. It's not really my pet. One of the dogs found a little lizard and played too rough with him, I guess. That's all. We just buried it."

Boseau nodded, "I see." He would have been happy to stay there and console the girls; he seemed to have nowhere in particular he had to be on any close schedule right now. He stood, hunched, hands folded in front of his chest, head cantilevered on an incredibly long, drooping neck, nose directed forward, looking into Gwendolyn's eyes. He had a warm, if silly, smile on his face.

After an awkward pause Gwendolyn talked around the man and told Alitisha that she must soon bring the dogs back to the executive residence so they could be fed. They took leave of Dr. Phineas Boseau, Reverend, who suggested he could help them bring the dogs, but they politely refused his offer. He went on his way cheerfully enough, and the girls proceeded to walk away. The dogs scampered before, between and behind them. Alitisha laughed for a long time and then asked, "Wow! What's his story?" but Gwendolyn ignored her.

"Are you working at the same place tonight still?" Gwendolyn asked as they neared the executive residence.

Alitisha answered a different concern, "You know you're going to have a real problem here if you don't get a thicker skin. I know you've always been a softie about animals. But come on! Lizards? They're filthy. When we have people dying just over the hill?"

"What, dying? What, the patients?"

"Gwendolyn, bless your heart. Don't you get it? Don't you know where we are? Whatever they tell us officially, people are starving and dying around here. It has to be happening. And they don't really seem to want us to get it. It's like a feel-good make-believe game. I'm not sure I can take it. But I know you're going to have to toughen up if you're going to make it. That's for sure."

Maybe she's right. Of course people are dying here. People die everywhere, and there are four thousand people in an extremely dire situation here. That's why we came here. But Alitisha sounds like she thinks it's worse than that—people are dying all the time, what we're doing is not helping. Or something like that. But that can't be right. Dr. Bok is obviously in charge. Looking around this place you just can't say it is run by a bunch of incompetents. Alitisha is wrong, and it's not good for her... I worry about her.

Just then the dogs got excited. They looked into the sky and scurried back and forth, barking. Their frenzy seemed to catch the attention of the militia men in a truck outside the fence some distance away. They were starting their engines. Then the girls heard the quiet hum of an airplane and saw it approaching from quite a ways off. They could see activity at the far end of the runway around the other plane that had been dormant for days. They continued toward the executive residence, and as they approached it they saw Sarah come out holding a covered pewter serving platter. The dogs lost interest in the vehicle and excitedly sprinted the last forty yards to Sarah, surrounding her in counter-traveling ellipses. She walked a few steps more, the ellipses moving like a protective bubble, then she told the animals to sit. They obeyed, Bourbon's flat tongue tracing an arc of over two hundred degrees as the flapping appendage swept from one corner of his mouth to the other twice. Colonel bobbed nervously from side to side, licking his lips and teeth. To the dogs' excitement, Sarah put the platter cover on the ground as the girls drew near. Sarah greeted them saying, "Perfect timing. Dr. Bok was sure you would be back just at dinner time for his pups." Gwendolyn nodded, accepting the compliment. Alitisha looked on.

Gwendolyn saw two separate wooden plates on the platter; the dogs certainly saw them too but remained still a few feet away. A huge steak, cooked rare, bone running along one side, was on each plate. The dogs sniffed the heat from the plates as it drifted to them with its luscious hints.

Sarah looked back at the door, then she placed one wooden plate on the ground in front of each dog. Neither animal moved, unless one counts as motion excited wiggling, weight shifting and the flapping of tongues now incessant on both the canine faces. She said to Gwendolyn and Alitisha, "The director hates this, but I think it's important." She commanded the animals, "Give Thanks. Pray." Each canine came close to making a recognizable sign of the cross—for animals without ball-and-socket joints the gestures were truly remarkable. The dogs' contortions stimulated equally egregious contortions on Gwendolyn and Alitisha's faces as they first looked on in amazement and empathy, then had to look away. They looked back, and the dogs were frozen, paws together in mock praying stance, or whatever approximation of such can be made by cumbersome, graceful, thumbless brutes. After a stationary few seconds the dogs started bobbing and pumping, their hands still folded in prayer as earnestly as the mindless beasts were capable of.

After a dramatic pause Sarah nodded, and each dog dropped from his pose, came forward and greedily took the steak from his plate. They dragged their meals in different directions and settled down to eat the dirt-covered meat without benefit of silverware or napkins, with no fine wine to drink. Sarah gathered up the wooden plates, put them on the platter and covered it. She smiled at the girls, nodded and went inside.

Gwendolyn felt disoriented. The girls could smell the meat, and she found herself hoping that the scent did not drift over the nearby hills into the camp. The girls mounted disgusted looks on their faces as they watched the dogs eat the fine filthy steaks.

Breaking away from her morbid fascination with the bizarre scene, Gwendolyn asked Alitisha how things were going and she answered, "I was pretty happy when Sandy came and told me to come here. I'd be going to work in a while otherwise. It's pretty boring in the box filling business. I've been there every day, and it looks like that's going to be as interesting as any of my work here will be. I don't know how they all do it. It's so boring I can't stand it. I tell you I'm going crazy. This thing about reading a book or painting or whatever in our spare time—I feel like I'm going to explode. What are we doing here anyway? How about you? Have you been as bored as I have?"

The girls were momentarily distracted, as the airplane had landed, and the vehicle full of militia men was inside the fence. Another jeep could be heard outside. The militia men were talking to some natives from within the camp near the parked airplane, always keeping an eye over toward Gwendolyn and Alitisha—really toward the dogs.

"It's been really strange. The sponsored volunteers don't have any exact assignments. So I go around and see if anyone needs help. Most of the sponsored volunteers don't really do any work at all; certainly they seem to do nothing for the patients. You've probably never seen most of them. Lots of them just seem to stay upstairs. We can eat up there. We could stay up there all the time and never come out into the mission.

"Some seem like they cannot be bored by anything. Or nothing at all. As for me, till today I was scrubbing floors and bathrooms, so I haven't been bored, but I wonder when I'll get to do anything more direct. And look at this today! My surprise assignment—I guess that's what I get for asking for more work—I'm babysitting these dogs who are right now eating a month's worth of Calories for the patients."

Alitisha nodded. "Yeah, I've seen some of the sponsored ladies giving art and exercise classes after dinner for us plain old regulars. I notice they don't wear the same uniform every day. You're not wearing one. What's with the uniforms anyway? I hate these things." Alitisha scanned her plain beige dress, put her hands in the sewn pockets and flipped the hem up and down. Gwendolyn smiled and shrugged.

The girls stayed together, walking around the complex and visiting for a long time after taking the sated animals, each carrying his bone, back to the executive residence. Eventually Alitisha said, "I probably should get to work," but Gwendolyn convinced her to stop at the cafeteria and have dinner first, so they got in a little more visiting before parting for the evening. As Gwendolyn walked back to the sponsored volunteer area she heard the hum of an airplane taking off. She looked up just in time to see the plane climb and turn, disappearing as it banked behind the dirtpile.

The Factory is in Good Hands

Who knows what the Fates may bring?

G wendolyn's next five workdays after babysitting the dogs were spent in office work. She reported to the administration building and worked on papers all day. The mission ran its operations, at least the local ones, on old-fashioned paper. There was a seemingly endless stream of the stuff indicating receipt of material, production and allocation of food, medicine tracking, and especially processing of patients. Sarah had assured her that every piece of paper and all the individual lines on each list had important financial meaning. Gwendolyn learned that there were over sixty tons of coal in the pile behind the power plant and various other marginally boring pieces of trivia; she also discovered that over twelve thousand individuals had been given unique identification numbers as patients.

Director Professor Dr. Florian Q. Bok was out of the country now, having left on the airplane that departed shortly after the dogs' feast. This was the most common state of affairs at the camp; He came regularly but spent only a small fraction of his time in Africa. For most of these days Gwendolyn was alone in the small office, a situation she did not prefer, and Sandy had made sure Sarah arranged to break up her days with periodic visits. Sarah came by several times each day and spent a few minutes going over assignments and progress, but mostly she was there just to keep Gwendolyn from getting too lonely. Sometimes Sonja, the first sponsored volunteer Gwendolyn had met, came in and 'worked' for a half hour or so; Gwendolyn had invited her while they were in the lounge on the first night of her assignment. Gwendolyn found the level of isolation in this job burdensome, but she was resolved to absorb her suffering quietly, in light of that of the patients. Occasionally Aloysius Fink popped his head in, smiled and did his best job of exchanging niceties, but he did it so poorly that Gwendolyn thought the dogs making the sign of the cross seemed more natural. Like most people, she did not like the man; his visits were the only thing that made her crave loneliness. Dr. Boseau stopped to visit more than anyone else, and Gwendolyn actually got to look forward to his unpredictably timed visits. They helped break up the days, and she felt relaxed talking to this appropriately named harlequin across the safe personal distance afforded by her desk.

Alitisha was still working the late shift, and Gwendolyn went to eat lunch with her on these days. On the last day of Gwendolyn's assignment. Alitisha had salad and a bowl of soup, and Gwendolyn sat with a cold sandwich. Alitisha dawdled with her spoon in the soup for a span of time, then suddenly spoke up. She was depressed. "I don't know about this whole thing, it's not for me," She took a bite of her salad, chewing listlessly, mouth open, eyes on her plate.

"What do they have you doing?" asked Gwendolyn, misunderstanding.

She had just been reassigned. "Laundry. I guess I'm not packing boxes anymore." She managed a faint smile and a slight shrug. "All evening till the wee hours. Every day it's the same. Maybe it's good to be busy. Lord knows, we're busy with the endless laundry. I don't know what would happen if one day we lost a washing machine. It would be like a train wreck. If something stopped working but things kept coming in… it would pile up, what a mess! Those monster machines are always going. It's a hot, steamy, awful job. And the dryers—talk about hot! But those are taken care of by native workers, not volunteers. It's rough enough working the washers and dirty linens." She sipped her soup, testing, and blew halfheartedly across a spoonful. She watched the dark figures of two nuns at a table against the wall dance through the vapor from the hot soup.

Gwendolyn responded. "Well, my job is air conditioned at least, but I don't think it does any more good for the children than yours. Probably less. I've been shuffling papers. There's a big old backlog of them, and we do everything by hand. It's just like living a Dickens novel, like trying to make progress on a treadmill! I don't even see Sarah add anything to the piles, but each day there they are, seemingly identical to the day before. Did you know that we take in a couple hundred people every month? About once a week they bring in a batch of people." Nobody had told Gwendolyn this. She had gleaned it from the papers.

Alitisha's mind had been wandering, but she had heard. After a pause she said, "Wow. That's a lot. I guess it makes sense. I mean we have thousands here." She took a sip of tea and did not think about the numbers further.

"But Alitisha, doesn't it seem like we should explode with all those people?"

Alitisha shrugged. "I'm sure they know how to handle the numbers. Remember, Dr. Bok told us they turn away people because they only have so much room. Shouldn't you be worried that they don't take in more, not that they take in too many? That is, if you're going to worry about any of it."

"Hmm… Yeah, I know. I guess so. No… Maybe." Perhaps it was not such a crazy set of numbers… but… She started her sandwich. "One good thing about this boring job," she said with a conspiratorial gesture, leaning her head forward. Alitisha listened, not much more interested than before. "I get to see lots of what they're doing. Did you know that the patients have tattoos with letters and numbers on the inside of their wrists?"

Alitisha nodded silently, much to Gwendolyn's surprise. Neither girl had really had contact with patients, but the combination of Alitisha's personality and her status as a regular combined to place her more in the informal gossip flow than Gwendolyn. Alitisha said, "It encodes the village and tribe they came from, their entry date and some future date, and some number that's supposed to represent their name."

"?" This was more than Gwendolyn knew.

"It's pretty boring in the laundry. We spend a lot of time sweating and waiting for batches of garments and linens, so we talk. Garments. What a funny word. I've never used it before coming here. Did you know that they buy expired medicines and vitamins to save money?" She seemed to stare over Gwendolyn's shoulder but didn't really see the nuns her eyes settled on.

Gwendolyn nodded. She did know about the durgs, having seen lots of their paperwork, and she had noticed the dates. Much came from the United States and Europe. It probably made sense to buy technically expired but perfectly good medicines. But she was surprised that Alitisha was so much more a part of the sensory nervous system of the mission than she was. They ate quietly for a while. Gwendolyn wondered how she could get more connected here. She had already been here two weeks, and she felt her bits weren't biting.

"I'm going home." Alitisha spoke out of the blue, ending a quiet interlude.

Gwendolyn's head was a bell and someone had just slammed the clapper into the metal. She was disoriented, deafened; she could not answer because she had not really heard—only her reptilian brain's alarm system had triggered, setting all her nerves to full gain. The words started their slow journey from her senses to her consciousness.

"I'm going to be on the next little plane out of here. I don't belong. I already told Sarah. I'm not helping anyone…"

Gwendolyn's consternation was validated as Alitisha's first announcement emerged into focus. She started hearing Alitisha's elaboration. She gasped as she listened.

" … bored to death. What are they thinking here? Something is just not right. This is a strange place, and I don't just mean unusual. The whole setup… is weird. Something's wrong here."

Gwendolyn stammered, "I can't believe it. We're in this together."

"Are we? This was your little vision, not mine. I live in the real world, and I don't see anyone saving anyone here. I see a lot of activity, lots of nice people with good intentions, and probably there is some comfort to the wounded. But I belong back in New England. And anyway, I'm not a sponsored volunteer like you. I'm grateful to your father and all, and from what I see, I'd have gone crazy by now if I were a sponsored volunteer. At least my work keeps me busy. But I need to go home."

"I'm busy," Gwendolyn was hurt in many ways. She felt the sting of Alitisha's assessment of the mission, her friend's disavowal of full commitment, and most of all she felt the prospect of losing a companion and being alone here. In truth, she was most severely crushed by the fact that Alitisha was right. It was Gwendolyn's crusade, not hers. Alitisha had come along for the ride, and Gwendolyn had never really admitted that to herself; she had created, ingested and digested the fiction that Alitisha was as determined as she herself was. Further, she had a subliminal worry that perhaps her friend was right about the whole mission being ineffective, or worse—a charade.

"Well, you just told me what you're busy with. Listen, are you sure you don't want to come with me? You can volunteer in the soup kitchen in California or wheel kids around in a hospital ward or something."

Gwendolyn shook her head and put down her sandwich. "I've already done that." Alitisha reached over and held her hand. Gwendolyn withdrew hers. Both girls had eyes welling with tears now. Gwendolyn's heart was heavy with the prospective loss. As she sat, she unreasonably hoped Alitisha would spontaneously change her mind, and perhaps more reasonably hoped there would be no airplane for a long time. Gwendolyn said she needed to get back to work, and so she left her sandwich on the table. As she departed she glanced back and saw Alitisha fiddling with her spoon and soup.

She went to the office and pushed work around the windowless room. She processed, marked and sorted stacks of old-fashioned paperwork. She was despondent through the afternoon. She could not help noticing papers with dates for some of the vitamin mixtures; of course the dates verified Alitisha's statement about the expiration times. Finally, just before the end of her day, Sarah stopped by and gave her instructions for the next day: show up at the executive residence in late morning.

Gwendolyn was not hungry and did not eat dinner that night. She sat aloof in the lounge area in her dormitory and started an unconscious anticipatory mourning process for the loss of Alitisha. She protected her personal space with a few unfriendly signals and did not speak to anyone. She picked up the old paperback copy of *Uncle Tom's Cabin*. It was still dog-eared where she had left off; nobody had picked it up in the meantime. Her mind kept drifting, but not to anywhere—perhaps shifting is a better description than drifting. Eventually she realized she was not reading and gave up the effort. She retreated to her room and sat swaying, hugging Pyratticus Julius. They quietly sobbed as she thought about the gap Alitisha would leave if she went, then blubbered on until they fell asleep.

The next morning Alitisha's decision to go home surfaced in Gwendolyn's mind shortly after she awoke, and it asserted control over her mood. She struggled against it through the morning, and when she finally succeeded in pushing it out of her mind, the picture of Colonel and Bourbon rending their sizzling steaks emerged to take its place. She loved dogs, but something bothered her about Colonel and Bourbon's presence here. *How can that be right with so many hungry people here?* She softened a bit. *But I guess, aren't dogs people too?* The question of the dogs seemed a cloudy judgment call, and she put it out of her mind.

Having moped all morning, Gwendolyn walked toward the executive residence to begin her day's assignment. As she walked she saw Evelyn, the regular she knew from her assignment as a janitor. Evelyn was carrying a basket, and she hailed Gwendolyn as they converged. "Don't tell anyone. I'm getting some supplies from the warehouse," she giggled.

"The warehouse? Isn't that down there?" Gwendolyn pointed back over her shoulder.

Evelyn smiling, bobbed her head conspiratorially. The girl was always upbeat. "Just taking a little walk."

Gwendolyn told Evelyn of her ambivalence about the dogs. Evelyn said most of the volunteers who had been around for a long time had seen the dogs and that the animals usually traveled with Dr. Bok, so they were here whenever he was here. At first she thought it was odd too, but she had come to find it invisible now. Everybody did. Today, with Gwendolyn bringing it up, she thought about it for the first time in a long time. Out loud she walked through her thoughts, saying, "Would it really be any different if they were moved somewhere else? Say they stayed in Switzerland where people aren't starving. How does that really change things? The world still has the same dogs, the same hungry people. Or what if they were fed cheap dog food instead of steaks? The dogs would suffer. Dr. Bok would suffer. But would they really give steak to the starving people in the camp? And they're really not around here all that much. It seems like Dr. Bok is usually in Switzerland or traveling somewhere else. We really don't see him here much. Is it really that bad?"

"Hmmm." the logic seemed plausible. Gwendolyn wondered if she was able to think clearly enough about it—she was struggling to keep her preference for dogs over cats from taking a decisive role, but it was probably clouding her judgment here. *She doesn't seem to know what she thinks. Maybe she's right, it's not that absurd after all. I don't know. But... I don't know.*

Evelyn continued, "It does bother me anyway, somehow. But you know, I can't control everything, and I don't know everything. I'm volunteering, trying to make a difference. I just work with what I have. And I won't be here forever." She smiled again.

Gwendolyn indicated a passive lack of disagreement, at least for the moment. They walked on, looping around buildings and exchanging chitchat till Evelyn turned back, saying she'd skipped out long enough. Gwendolyn soon approached the executive residence, the door where she had taken custody of the dogs a few days before. Another regular with an average American appearance stood outside the building. She introduced herself as Ashley. She knew Gwendolyn was to work with her today and said they should wait right there. They were meeting Bertha Martha and would go to work in the goo factory together.

"Bertha Martha? What do you mean, 'goo factory'? Does she work at the goo factory too? Who is she?"

"Yes, she's the production manager. And call it the 'factory', not the 'goo factory' with her." Ashley rolled her eyes from ten o'clock to two o'clock and swung her head correspondingly.

"Okay. What is it?"

"That's just what we call it. We mix powder and some doughy stuff with water and load containers of it onto trucks so they can take them over into the dustbowl and feed people. So all day you're covered in some kind of vitamin-infused flour dust and paste. Gooey. The work really should be done by machines. It sure could be. We have some small ones we use, actually, but it's all pretty much done by people. Really mostly native workers, but we'll probably be getting our hands dirty." She smiled. "Dirty with the nice, clean dough."

As Gwendolyn tried to picture the place—it was undoubtedly one of the buildings she had been inside—the door to the executive residence swung open, and an uncharacteristically expressionless, silent Dr. Phineas Boseau appeared. He yawned and seemed tired as he came closer. He was pushing a wheelchair containing an enormously fat woman.

The lady was meticulously groomed and wore elegant makeup. She was dressed in a shiny blue mid-length dress. Her hair was chestnut brown all the way to within a centimeter of her scalp, and it fell in a single orderly curl above her shoulders. Gwendolyn could not help but notice that the woman had no arms or legs; otherwise she impressed one as a financially well off, if perhaps hormonally imbalanced or undisciplined, matron in a sleek, and even attractive, wheelchair.

The woman began to speak out, "—"

In the split instant between when Gwendolyn saw the woman and when she heard her speak, Gwendolyn's mind was absorbing the scene and scanned through a zillion thoughts; not all of them featured penetrating insight. *What happened to her? She's so overweight. Well, maybe she doesn't weigh as much as I think, but if she had arms and legs and especially if they matched her shape she would weigh a metric ton. How did a quadruple amputee get so fat? How does she eat at all? And if she eats and drinks, how does she…? Hmmm.* Gwendolyn pulled herself back down to earth and hoped she had not embarrassed herself with some gaping or surprised expression.

Dr. Boseau was slowly walking back down the hall in the building. Only his back was visible, but he gave the impression of one who was again yawning. He had not said a word.

The static visage the woman had worn since coming into view was severe, though not hostile: brow furrowed, corners of the mouth downturned forming manlike jowls. Gwendolyn heard the woman say, "...oo is this, Ashley?" in a slow, singsong foreign drawl as she looked Gwendolyn up and down.

Ashley smiled as she walked around to the back of the wheelchair and started moving it forward. "This is Gwendolyn Dressel-Meier. She will be the one working with us today. Gwendolyn, this is Dr. Larssson. May she call you Bertha Martha too?" The woman's eyes were fixed on Gwendolyn as she nodded without disturbing her seemingly permanent expression, one of emotionless seriousness, something like a fixed frown.

The motorized wheelchair had a complicated mouth-and-chin-driven control stick. Since that stick would be exhausting to use for any length of time and the battery was limited in capacity, Bertha Martha found it most practical to be escorted by others. When she was being attended by volunteers Bertha Martha asked that they work in pairs. This allowed for contingencies—sometimes the chair got stuck in a rut, a situation not easily rectified by a single woman without upsetting things, especially since Bertha Martha refused to use the safety straps designed to hold her in place. The shape of her body, that of a large pear, generally supplied stability on the chair, but that factor was far from definitive—she probably could be pitched off the platform by serious rocking. The wheelchair was quite heavy, and it was unlikely that a single assistant would be able to maneuver it gracefully in case of any sort of trouble on the road.

The second escort was handy in other respects as well. Bertha Martha was largely helpless on her own. For instance, during the day Gwendolyn would learn that Bertha Martha was usually able to shoo a fly from her face, but sometimes a persistent insect was not scared off by the shaking and the little skin-distorting earthquakes meant to threaten the pest, so of course it was convenient for her to have someone nearby. Bertha Martha felt that having redundant volunteers was felicitous in case one fainted, or fell down dead, or encountered some other exigency resulting in her unavailability.

Gwendolyn smiled and nodded her head, "Pleased to meet you, Bertha Martha." She intercepted her right hand as it moved forward, improvising to continue its motion in a large arc to her hair on the left side of her head, which she fluffed unconvincingly. She felt awkward and could not bring herself to concoct small talk as she walked beside the chair, so they were quiet for a while.

Bertha Martha seemed to be in her mid-fifties, but over her life Gwendolyn had learned that when one estimates another's age, there is a gestalt that includes not just the face but the whole body, trimmings and way of moving, so she had doubt. Nonetheless, Gwendolyn assigned Bertha Martha an age of fifties in own her mind for the time being.

"This is Gwendolyn," Bertha Martha said after a spell. "We all knew you were coming. From America. My parents, especially my mother, were enthralled with America and American history. I have been there many times." Her face kept its standard expression throughout.

Gwendolyn replied, happy for the opportunity for facile conversation, "It's a wonderful place. I live in New England and I go to school all the way across the country in California."

"It is a horrid country," the older woman said with precise Swedish certainty.

Ashley and Gwendolyn exchanged glances as they progressed, Ashley pushing the wheelchair and Gwendolyn walking beside Bertha Martha. After an awkwardness, Gwendolyn said, "That's a beautiful dress," telling the truth, trying to break friendly ice. Except by accent, affectation and affection, Bertha Martha could have passed for an American. "Where are you from?" the girl asked.

"My family is from Stockholm. A wonderful place, and in some ways I would rather be there, truth be told. But we are all called to make sacrifices, and I have chosen to use my talents to help others here. Perhaps I will be going back to Sweden sometime. Meanwhile I must do what I can here."

The girls were silent, nervous. Gwendolyn found herself wondering if the woman's forehead muscles were overdeveloped. *Her eyebrows have been pulled into that frown all this time. How can she do it?* Then she realized she did not really know if people even have muscles in their foreheads. How can they? It's all bone, you can tell by touching. As they walked forward she concluded people must have muscles somewhere in their foreheads. But since she had never studied it specifically she was not really sure, despite her occasional glances at the wheelchair passenger's face. It seemed a puzzle.

Just then Reverend Dr. Phineas Boseau traveled by. Somehow he was walking in the direction toward where they had just seen him minutes before.

He must have been in a strange mood, because he walked as though he could have been anyone in the world—he made a completely nondescript, almost nervous impression as he passed them; he did not seem the foppish and clown-like bouncing Ichabod Crane all knew as Dr. Boseau. He did not greet the women, and he did not slow down. He just passed by. Bertha Martha's face darkened. "Stop," she said, and Ashley brought the chair to an abrupt halt. Bertha Martha drew a few breaths and growled, "That man is dreadful." She contorted her face into a post-growl scowl as the back of the man shrank from the girls' view and disappeared around the corner of a building. Gwendolyn and Ashley again glanced at each other, this time more surreptitiously. Bertha Martha silently nodded, and they continued along, soon approaching the goo factory. It was indeed a place Gwendolyn had been in before. In fact she recognized the supervisor to whom she had given such assistance four days ago by standing in front of a box of powder he needed.

An inexhaustible supply of old British and American rock and roll music was piping through the room and escaping the building through all the openings. A truck laden with crates pulled out of the docks on the right side of the building and drove off along the path to the camp. When the newcomers entered they were presented with a whirlwind of motion seemingly driven by the powerful beat of the music. Twenty or so workers scurried about, moving boxes, mixing food, sweeping the floor and loading trucks. A forklift moving a full pallet of crates crossed so close in front of them that they could smell the ozone from its electric motor in the hot wind it created. Gwendolyn's pulse locked to the upbeat tune of a song she recognized; she thought it was from just after the silent movie era. The rhythmic music of the old rock 'n roll classic 'Video Killed the Radio Star' was filling the place, and she imagined she saw everyone's movements synchronized with the music.

A second truck was half full of crates, and its driver was moving them from a nearby pallet to the truck. The forklift dropped another full pallet of crates nearby. A number of the workers had stopped working and were standing looking at the Bertha Martha and the two girls. As the entrants proceeded to the wall along the left side of the building, Bertha Martha's countenance expressed strong disapproval of something, communicated through the exact same expression fixed on her face since Gwendolyn first saw her. They arrived at their spot, and Ashley turned the wheelchair around to face the production floor. The native man that Gwendolyn had recognized was talking with three regulars, clearly imploring them to do something differently than they had been. They were listening, but Gwendolyn thought she could see that whatever the request was, they had no intention of changing their process to satisfy him.

Bertha Martha closed her eyes momentarily, communicating impatience through her otherwise static face; Ashley flipped a switch and the music stopped so suddenly that Gwendolyn wondered how the fast-moving workers kept their balance through the shock of it. Everyone stopped working and turned to face Bertha Martha and the two girls.

"My spectacles, please." Bertha Martha's eyes were on the production floor as she addressed Ashley. Ashley opened a drawer beside the battery in the wheelchair and pulled out a pair of large, dark-framed glasses. She placed them on Bertha Martha and the woman said, "Please, Ashley."

Ashley smoothly swung the wheelchair platform ninety degrees. It had a wonderful and complicated swivel mechanism beneath the seat. Bertha Martha turned her head through an additional ninety degrees to study a nearby chalkboard containing a grid filled with numbers and colored squares. Stepping up the intensity of her frown, she tipped her head back and examined the board through the spectacles. Gwendolyn had never seen a chalkboard before. She had read many stories about schools and so forth, where in the olden days the rooms had such things, but she had never seen one; she was also not sure she had ever seen chalk. There were fragments of several colors of chalk in a tray on the blackboard.

In front of the board was a table holding a gridded log sheet and a number of colored cardboard rectangles with writing on them. Bertha Martha's voice, powerful enough for an opera singer, rang out. "Jumo. What is your report?" She was still looking at the board as the native worker who had been instructing the volunteers came to attention and trotted over to face the wheelchair. He nervously picked up the cards scattered on the table and started changing markings on the grid cells on the chart, referring to the cards. Then he turned and rattled off numbers in almost perfect English, reading from the grid. He was relating quantities of truckloads and crates sent that morning and how it compared to the number planned for the day.

Bertha Martha sat with her head bowed, looking at him over the top of her spectacles. She asked him if any native workers or volunteers had been late to work. Jumo said no. She emitted silence indicating disbelief. The glasses slipped down her nose in the tense quiet. Then Jumo elaborated. Two of the volunteers had been late to work by perhaps fifteen minutes, but they were on track to get all the food mixed on schedule. Bertha Martha dismissed Jumo, who went off to a work station different from the one whence he came. Bertha Martha said, "Ashley, please." Ashley stepped forward and pushed Bertha Martha's glasses back into place. Gwendolyn had not noticed before but Bertha Martha had a distinctly concave curve to her nose. *It's a miracle those glasses stay up at all.* It struck Gwendolyn that the nose was more like that of a pre-teen, maybe an elf, not a crotchety old upper middle-aged woman.

Gwendolyn's attention came back to the factory as Bertha Martha instructed Ashley to enter Jumo's name and the fact that two were late into the records. Ashley dutifully opened a compartment in the bottom of the wheelchair, pulled out a clipboard, made some notation and stored it away again. Bertha Martha turned to Gwendolyn and said, "I am responsible for the productivity of this factory. Here at the mission we have two similar factories...," and Gwendolyn's attention was suddenly distracted as the spectacles again slid down the tiny ski jump of the woman's nose until the temples caught her ears and restrained them. Ashley quickly interceded and repositioned the glasses as Bertha Martha raised her head upward to capture the correction, all the time without slowing down.

"...approximately eight thousand meals every day for the patients. Keeping half of that supply line alive is a massive burden. These people are undisciplined natives and perhaps more undisciplined American brats." She paused, looking squarely at Gwendolyn. "Jumo, he is quite a good man. But you can see from his answer to me that he lacks respect for the need to maintain order in the service of achieving productivity. It seems inborn with these people. I worry about him. I worry. I will not be here forever."

Ashley found a wooden chair and sat next to the wheelchair. Gwendolyn said, "It must be a huge responsibility. And so difficult for a woman with..." her eyes dropped to Bertha Martha's dress and continued down to the floor before returning; her voice trailed off and she had a sudden pang in her stomach. She stood and flushed as Bertha Martha glared, the message being, "What?" She scrambled toward an acceptably symmetrical magnitude of dissatisfaction, "I mean, in this part of the world. They must have archaic thoughts about women and their place."

The workers had all gone back to their work. Compared to when the newcomers arrived, the pace was less hectic, and there seemed to be lighter activity in direct proportion to the lessened energy expenditure of the workers. The inescapable impression for anyone except Bertha Martha was that productivity dropped with the music cutoff. Ashley turned on the music again, but at a volume level at least twenty decibels lower than before. Though Bertha Martha had authorized the move, she winced upon its startup. Gwendolyn recognized, but did not know the name of, the song that arose, and she could not help feeling the music. She was soon to find out that the older woman was in a talkative mood. Bertha Martha said, "How I hate that music. But the director is insistent that I have to let them listen to this trash; we'd all be better and more productive if they listened to fine art. What do you think is better for them: Tubin, Sixten or Twisted Sister? Be that as it may, we work far harder than the other factory. We keep up our deliveries, four thousand per day. You can see on the board we have already delivered... JUMO! COME HERE NOW!" her voice exploded in mid sentence and her glasses slipped again. This time Gwendolyn felt bold enough to reach over and correct the position of the eyeglasses, an action Bertha Martha accepted without protest.

Jumo stopped whatever he was doing over at a table with four people. Upon his departure the others instantly stopped as well. He dutifully jogged over for the opportunity to have Bertha Martha berate him for a recent incident—a truck had left and yet the numbers on the chalkboard did not reflect it. She added a few more details about his work performance as he picked up the chalk and changed two squares of different colors on the board. Again her glasses slipped. This time she asked Ashley to remove them, and so Ashley put them away.

Gwendolyn asked, "Where should I work today? What would you like me to do?"

Bertha Martha answered by telling Gwendolyn and Ashley about her own life history, a story with which Ashley was triply familiar. Until a few years ago, Bertha Martha was a manager of research at a Swedish medical instrument firm. She mentioned that although she was entitled to it, she did not require, nor even allow, people to address her as 'Dr. Larssson.' Just Bertha Martha was fine. She looked at the distant parts of the factory as she talked. "My husband was a man of music—an opera singer, though never a successful one. But he did not need to be, as I had an extremely good position with the corporation, which was securely connected to our government.

"Seven years ago I was happily riding my new motorcycle in the Swiss Alps on our way back to Sweden from Italy. It was a wonderful machine, one of those massive, underpowered but distinctively under-muffled American brutes, the ones where they offset the phase between the cylinders for the intimidating pounding sound. I can still identify the type from a kilometer away, though I refuse to state its name after the tragedy I suffered on it. We had just bought the motorcycle in Italy with the intention of having a pleasant ride home. We had no children, and perhaps this machine could be our adopted baby.

"We were planning to spend a few days in Lucerne on the way home. I was driving, my husband on the back holding my waist. The weather was beautiful; the air was rushing by, and the sun was shining. The views were spectacular as the sun ignited the beautiful autumn leaves." She paused and looked up and down Gwendolyn, and did the same to Ashley, which required stretching her neck to see the girl to her left. Gwendolyn flinched as the woman's base moved forward incrementally with the stretch, but she was stable enough. "You ladies may have trouble believing this but I was tiny, petite. I weighed less than you do, Gwendolyn." Her face was softening below the harsh eyebrows, which were themselves relaxing into a marginally more gentle shape. Gwendolyn was beginning to feel less tense with the woman as she listened. "They say spring is the season for lovers. You are young, but do not be fooled. Beauty and love and happiness are in the air in the fall; spring is merely a soggy pastel transience. But autumn is the robust, invigorating, sensual time of the year." An uncharacteristic smile asserted itself on her face as she reminisced. The girls stirred awkwardly, very awkwardly, in the pause.

The woman started again, "Only one thing marred the trip. An obviously Italian driver had been harassing us for the better part of an hour, wanting to pass on the winding road on the Alp. But there was nowhere to pull over, as the narrow road was carved into a steep hill, and a cliff hung closely to our right most of the time. I did not want to be teetering on the edge while a wop in a big truck accelerated by us, probably giving a not-too-good-natured Italian swerve on his way by. Also, being new to the huge motorcycle, the last thing I wanted was to stop it on some unlevel nook and have the massive thing topple over, stranding us on a remote mountain."

Somehow Gwendolyn knew a tragedy was coming, that this was related to the woman's current body configuration. She had forgotten the factory. Ashley sat listening without visible reaction, perhaps beyond an involuntary check of details against her memories of the story.

"Finally he nonetheless passed us violently and dangerously. Perhaps in his excitement or hurry, he lost control a few kilometers ahead. He must have swerved into the side of the hill, and his vehicle flipped down on the street, turning over and spinning like a dreidel. It was amazing—twirling there, apparently with all the energy of his travel transferred to the rotation. It was not slowing down, though I could hear the grinding of the cab's roof on the road. At one point in each cycle the back of the truck actually hung out over the edge of the road, which was almost a cliff. We stopped to help. My husband stood aside and tried to contact the authorities, but I felt time was of the essence with this stupid and unfortunate Italian man; as the windows strobed by I could see him crumpled between his seat and the roof. He was bleeding from the face. He was not strapped in, and I thought I could get him out. I approached the vehicle thinking its spin was manageable and I could insert myself in through the window. But I miscalculated. The bed of the truck spun around and knocked me down and dragged me. Quickly there was no ground below me. I was dropping over the cliff. My fall was long and arduous. On the way down, I never lost consciousness and I felt every collision as I tumbled from rock to tree to granite outcropping, my rotation reversing several times. I came to rest on the hillside but had lost the use of both arms and both legs—when I tried to move them, all I could do was twist, and they dragged like boneless sausages attached to my body. After a few minutes, pain flowed in from all my limbs; blood flowed out. First the pain was a throbbing, then it became a crushing ache, and finally it turned to a sharp burning pain and rose to a blinding crescendo. Should I say pain or pains? Each limb and of course my entire midsection was damaged, and they all simultaneously pumped lightning into my nervous system. Finally I lost consciousness, a great mercy I must say. Would that there were a god; I could credit him with this small favor.

"The next thing I experienced was to awaken in a hospital. In the long bouncing fall, many of the bones in my body were broken badly, including my spine." She pulled her lips into an odd and puzzling configuration, forming an expression somewhere between gritting her teeth and a confusing, grim smile.

Gwendolyn, riveted, had tears rolling down her face, and was suppressing convulsive sobbing. Ashley was unhappy and engrossed now, though she had heard all this before.

"It is lucky, or unlucky, depending on one's point of view of life—and mine varies—that I had not the time to take off my helmet; otherwise I would certainly have been killed."

Gwendolyn broke into audible crying. The older woman was impassive.

The factory was chugging along at the sedate, low-music-volume pace. "Well, the long and short of it is this: I had to undergo lots of body-altering surgery. My husband and I have, shall I say, grown apart." Another wry smile. "The whole experience made me think about my life's work, which had always been important and fulfilling. I was recuperating for many months, a time during which my husband did some soul searching and probably body searching. He decided to move to Italy and pursue his opera efforts more strongly, undoubtedly along with some other ulterior, perhaps more biological interests. I don't know. I suppose he heard that they are looking for aging, and to be frank, mediocre, balding, pot-bellied opera singers to herald the next phase in the evolution of the art. Or perhaps the change in me and my newfound dependency signaled to him that he should go forth. I suppose we will have to guess.

"In Sweden one in such a position has an absolute right to return to his work, but he also has the alternative of receiving a pension, which in my case would be far above the standard wages in the country. First I elected to return to work, but there were many obstacles. The organization made the required adjustments, and I had four women assigned by the government to my twenty-four hour care. But it seems that after the accident and my long absence, people somehow did not feel I belonged. None said so, but it became clear that most thought that somebody in my situation should stay home. I have mentioned the level of my government pension would be more than adequate for a comfortable life. As for the team I led, they were able to cope adequately with my return, and I started working. We quickly hit a productive stride. While we had never had warm relationships, we had been an effective team since long ago when I had assumed the leadership, and we did well enough after I came back.

"But in the hallways people were uneasy with me. In the toilet and in the cafeterias they were uncomfortable suffering the indignity of seeing my helpers attending to my needs. I had never had friends at work, but now that fact was somehow painful. In short, things had changed, and I was unhappy. I guess I had never been happy, but until I experienced unhappiness I suppose I did not know that emotions really existed; to me they were relevant simply as something you read about in stories. I don't come from a society where people wear their hearts on their sleeves.

"I decided to withdraw from my position and went home with my caretakers to contemplate. I remained at home for several years. I became an outspoken public citizen. I led some public efforts. For instance I have been credited with influencing the riksdag to increase the leverage on the index for pensions of disabled individuals. There were many instances such as mine, though few so severe, and I helped all those people. The many acts of selflessness I performed during these few years gave me satisfaction, but I decided I needed a change; I wanted to directly apply my expertise in management for others again, but never for my old company."

Ashley was watching the factory, which seemed to be humming along nicely without Bertha Martha's intervention or the need for any elbow grease from the girls. Gwendolyn, through her discomfort, asked, "Is that when you came here?"

"Yes. I found this mission as I thought about where I could make a difference to others, in payment perhaps for the good life I had made for myself in the past. I contacted Dr. Florian Bok, and he was initially thrilled with the concept of a sponsored volunteer of my experience and stature from Sweden. I tried hard to learn more about the mission; our Dr. Bok is a gifted wordsmith, and I never got an accurate picture of the place, but our discussions progressed and we made the decision that I would come here. I was excited. Bok balked, though, when I revealed my physical condition to him." A thin smile displayed Bertha Martha's amusement with her unintended pun, then evaporated. "He pointed out that it would not be feasible to have me as a sponsored volunteer. However, we had sporadic, short discussions on the subject whenever I could get ahold of him, usually when he accidentally failed to avoid my calls.

"One day Dr. Bok came to Sweden to accept an award from the government for his humanitarian service, and I was able to have one of my acquaintances in the riksdag schedule a meeting with him. We kept it unclear to him with whom he would be meeting. I surprised Dr. Bok and was able to plead my case. As the details of his reluctance became apparent, my confidant excused himself while Dr. Bok and I continued our discussion. The riksdag member consulted a few colleagues and came back with the assurance of funding for the mission so long as they would allow me to be here. Dr. Bok drove a difficult bargain and achieved a very lucrative subsidy for the mission as part of the deal. I am not a sponsored volunteer, but as you know I live in the executive residence. Bok's organization receives monthly deposits to accounts in its Swiss banks, and I receive my own much smaller pension as well, though there is nowhere to spend it. I have considered going back to Sweden; however logic tells me I must stay here right now, for the factory has not been well enough developed."

Tracks of tears streamed down Gwendolyn's face.

"Staying is good for everybody. Those learning how factories should run are educated by me. Dr. Bok gets a substantial amount of funding. The only downside is that I am not in Sweden and so cannot visit the riksdag members regularly and keep them apprised of the needs of the populace; however I am hopeful, if not confident, that others can do that to a satisfactory degree."

Gwendolyn was barely able to speak. She wiped her face with her arms in turn and said through stifled sobs, "Bertha Martha, what a wonderful sacrifice you are making! Such an inspiring story. You've turned tragedy into triumph. I hope to make a difference someday too." She glanced at Ashley, who was tapping her foot to the current rock song in the air and watching the factory workers.

Bertha Martha bowed her head modestly and said, "Thank you, dear." She looked pensive for a few seconds, then stiffened abruptly. "Now we should get back to work." She looked up at the factory. "We have much JUMO COME OVER HERE." The abrupt and powerful verbal explosion startled Ashley, and she sat bolt upright; Gwendolyn jumped as well. *Well, her lungs are certainly fine.* She looked at Bertha Martha then followed the woman's fixed gaze.

Bertha Martha had noticed that a native woman in the nearest team of laborers was accomplishing a task by filling and closing containers of food individually, rather than filling a whole group then closing the whole group. As she awaited Jumo's arrival, Bertha Martha communicated the problem to Gwendolyn and Ashley, who did not understand the trouble—given the geometric constraints of the factory floor and tables, the worker's approach seemed most efficient, and probably safest from the sanitation point of view. Both girls were surprised it would catch negative attention. But it was a deviation from Bertha Martha's established factory process.

Jumo had been aligning a machine that extruded some almost-finished paste into vats while adding some liquid medicine or vitamin substance. It was nearly the last step of preparation of one of the forms of finished foodstuffs, and there was a backlog of incoming batter beside the stopped machine. He heard Bertha Martha's voice and flinched suddenly, knocking his head on the underside of a flange. He arose and put on a friendly smile as he trotted over to Bertha Martha, all the time rubbing his head. Bertha Martha tipped her head to Ashley, who turned off the background music. The whole building stopped working and looked over toward Bertha Martha.

"What is that woman doing?" Bertha Martha asked, pointing as best she could, given her bodily constraints, indicating the work team containing the transgressor.

Jumo looked over to the table. Nobody was moving, just like in the rest of the factory. "I don't understand, ma'am," he said, switching hands with which he rubbed his head, now slowing down the rubbing.

"Is she following procedure? Why do we have procedures?"

Jumo was genuinely confused. He looked back at the close-by table and saw nothing awry. He walked over. The innovative native worker, who understood her offense by now, explained quietly, nervously, eyes darting between Jumo and Bertha Martha. Jumo came back to Bertha Martha.

"I see," Jumo said.

Bertha Martha glowered severely. "Why do we have processes and procedures?"

After a few seconds, Jumo recited chapter and verse. "Yes ma'am. We use our procedures to run an efficient operation to supply the patients in our mission with the best possible care and sustenance in this difficult situation."

"You are dismissed."

Ashley switched on the music again. The idle workers went back to work. Jumo trotted over and picked up his repair task, and the native woman resumed her job according to established procedure. Bertha Martha turned her attention back to the girls, soon after which the worker reverted to her preferred method of work. Bertha Martha's head quavered momentarily, and she told Gwendolyn, "We have two identically equipped factories here. My workers work much harder than those in the other factory. I am proud of them, but it takes much effort from me to maintain discipline. We work several hours per day more." She paused, a disgusted look on her face.

"This factory is an island of excellence in this godforsaken place. My people get here before dawn and work long and hard producing the food. You saw that when we arrived they were already well into the day's work, albeit without any sort of self-control. The other factory may as well be unmanaged. They have a native manager, and he has no discipline at all; all day long his building looks just like what you saw here in my absence. His workers come in, it seems, almost whenever they want to. They are always gone by early afternoon. And the place is a disaster—disorganized, cluttered, crowded, noisy. Before their daily cleanup upon closing it looks like a tornado went through a cotton mill. I am amazed that the native workers don't just return to their emaciated villages rather than spend time in that place." She paused reflectively. Then she said, "You may go to work, girls."

Ashley quickly turned and signaled Gwendolyn with a "Let's go while we can!" nod of the head, then she repositioned the mouth-driven stick on Bertha Martha's wheelchair. Gwendolyn gave a quizzical glance to Ashley, but decided Ashley knew enough that she should follow her. Just before they departed, Bertha Martha detained Ashley to have her log another demerit against Jumo for some transgression; in truth his history was full of demerits; every day he got a dozen or so.

The young women briskly walked side by side, with Ashley leading, not looking back for worry of catching Bertha Martha's eye and being called back for some piece of trivial business. They went to the farthest part of the bustling factory. In the middle they passed Jumo. He nodded and smiled amiably as he pushed the first squirt of goop through the machine he had just fixed.

With Gwendolyn following Ashley's lead, they started staging boxes of powder on tables, making cuts in the outer layers of the containers and aligning them for further work. They went about chatting as they gathered small packages of nutrients to add into the mix. Ashley smiled as she mentioned that the other factory prepares exactly the same amount of food as this one. Gwendolyn said, "That's not what Bertha Martha said, though. Why would she lie?"

"She was not really lying. She didn't say anything she didn't feel was true."

"But she said that this factory is better."

"Well, she talked about discipline and the number of hours her people work each day. By the time she gets here every day, both groups have been working for hours. I was happy when I got the temporary assignment to be her chair driver. It lets me lollygag most of the morning while she is gotten ready, and it's not too bad at the other end of the day either. But when I'm working on something else, it's always a ten- or twelve-hour day." Gwendolyn was following Ashley in the factory operations as a chorus dancer follows a lead dancer. The two girls were using some of the equipment to mix a number of the variously colored powders into the flour mixture now.

Gwendolyn was confused. "Well, the other factory can't be keeping up then. ...?"

Ashley knew nothing about calculus. Nonetheless, she felt like she was explaining calculus to a cat. That, or perhaps the opposite—defending the bold statement that two plus two equals four. "Gwendolyn. They work three or four hours less each day and put out the same thing using the same equipment and about the same number of people. Actually I think they have fewer workers. Certainly fewer volunteers anyway. I only know one who has worked there."

"So you're saying Bertha Martha was lying."

"I'm saying she's nuts, that's all. She doesn't get it. She thinks she runs the place from the top down like some famous Swedish watch factory. Listen, it's not rocket science. It's a goo factory. We mix flour and dough and vitamins and whatever powders together, and we put in water. It gets stirred and pushed through a hole. We fluff it up and put it on trucks in portions serving forty people, along with some water containers. Then we go back and do it again."

Ashley's characterization of Bertha Martha helped Gwendolyn understand. A story forced itself into her consciousness, rising from her deep memory. She remembered Mr. Bluen, a high school mathematics teacher in Vermont who had tried to explain something to his students. The story was just the key needed for her to grasp Bertha Martha's position on the factory.

Mr. Bluen had run the Boston Marathon the year before he was Gwendolyn's teacher. The man seemingly believed he had done a more impressive job than the race's winner, because the winner only ran for about two hours—but Mr. Bluen had run for well over four hours! Much verbal exchange and interactive discussion had convinced the students that this man was trying to teach them something, but whatever it was, it never reached their minds. Looking back at the incident, she now grokked Bertha Martha's position without endorsing it in the least.

"You're right," she said with an insuppressible waxing smile. It was involuntary. She was facing away from Bertha Martha. Ashley, suppressing laughter, walked around beside her to turn away from Bertha Martha, as she was also giggling. The girls broke into full laughter and masked their mild convulsions with rapid work-like actions of moving and mixing the batters. Eventually they settled down to work steadily, and Ashley moved back around the table to her original position facing Bertha Martha.

Over the course of their stay in the factory that day, the music stopped another half dozen times. Each time, Jumo's name rang out from Bertha Martha's powerful lungs. For the first several instances, Gwendolyn looked back and saw Jumo approach the wheelchair, listen for an interval and go off to one of the groups of workers who had paused working to watch the conversation. Ashley rarely glanced over. She and Gwendolyn worked well as a team; now that Gwendolyn knew the process, they flexed back and forth to cover variations in each other's ability or motivation toward the boring set of tasks.

A little while into their work the music quietened, and the other workers went off to eat lunch. Jumo came over and introduced himself to Gwendolyn. The three chatted meaninglessly for a few minutes, then Jumo made a mild joke about jumping up and down to Bertha Martha and ran after the others.

The three latecomers were not hungry. *Maybe Bertha Martha doesn't even eat every day, who knows?* Ashley and Gwendolyn came over to Bertha Martha, and Ashley disconnected the mouth-stick on the chair. Bertha Martha instructed Ashley to upgrade the number of nasty notices regarding Jumo in the daily log. She dutifully did so under the older woman's dictation, dictation comprising a remarkable display of her capacity to remember the minutest detail. Ashley then took care of some other administrative details under Bertha Martha's instruction. This took up most of the lunchtime. Gwendolyn walked around looking at all the stations.

The workers started arriving back from lunch, and as they approached their work stations, Bertha Martha rolled her eyes, shrugged and said, "Let 'em rip," to which Ashley's response was to turn the music back on and reconnect the stick. The girls returned to their own station and resumed work. They managed to get focused during the boring tasks, somehow treating the work as a puzzle or game. The two hardly noticed the sporadic production stoppages attending Jumo's upbraidings after the lunch break, though they occurred with the same predictable irregularity as before.

In a little while, Gwendolyn and Ashley had produced a backlog of mixed material for the next processing station, and Ashley told Gwendolyn it was time to get Bertha Martha home. They went back to Bertha Martha, who nodded to Ashley in answer to a silent lack of question. Ashley unplugged Bertha Martha's control stick and queried Bertha Martha for the number of black marks needed to bring Jumo up to date for his accumulated transgressions. They updated the log much more quickly than at lunchtime.

As they turned to go, Ashley flipped the music back to full acoustic power, prompting a tolerant grimace from Bertha Martha. Coincidentally, 'Video Killed the Radio Star' was playing again, and the room's energy level seemed to rise in response to the beat and the higher volume. Jumo looked over and waved with a friendly smile, which the girls returned, and Bertha Martha and her entourage left the goo factory with Gwendolyn pushing the wheelchair. Outside she proceeded with caution, carefully watching for ruts and holes that could tip the seat and allow the precious cargo to slip off.

They approached the executive residence, and Gwendolyn rolled the wheelchair to a stop. Bertha Martha told Ashley that she was dismissed. Ashley said her goodbyes, then skipped off. Gwendolyn started to reach for the bell to notify the executive residence's occupants that she needed entrance, but Bertha Martha's voice stopped her, and she froze.

A much lower than normal voice intoned, "My dear, you will do well to find another place to work if you want to help people." Gwendolyn looked down at the woman and saw her eyebrows arched, almost touching each other over her frown as she looked up, her expression frozen. Gwendolyn was taken off guard.

"?"

"I can tell you are a good girl. You have drive, and I admire it. It reminds me of myself. But this place is not breaking any new ground in helping people. I know. I started more than a year ago with high hopes. I wish I could even say that we are harmlessly marking time here. In fact it is much worse. I know it is hard to understand, and I will not subject you to the details. But you will find it is true. The sooner you do, the better your chance of leaving undamaged. Take no notice of the fact that I am staying here."

Stunned, Gwendolyn said, "You? But you're in charge of feeding the patients every single day. How can you say that? And why would you stay if all you say is true?"

"Where would I go? Would Sweden be any better for me really? Gwendolyn, think of it this way. Yes, I go in there every day, with a couple of volunteers. Yes, we provide food for people who would otherwise starve, if you pick any single day and examine it. But life is part of a continuum. Pretend this is a movie. Now, fast forward this one year, or two or five years. Allow the movie to resume playing. What do you see?" She was frowning a severe, standard Swedish expression.

Gwendolyn could not answer, and the older woman refused to elaborate. She parried each attempt by the girl to transfer the problem solving back to her. All Gwendolyn could see in her imaginary theater was a replay of the today, over and over, whether one year, two years or five years. Clearly that could not be what Bertha Martha meant. What was she saying?

She puzzled as Bertha Martha waited patiently without communication. Finally, Gwendolyn shrugged and started to press the bell button on the executive residence, but she hesitated. "Bertha Martha, can I ask you a question?" she asked.

"Perhaps, dear." She had already become fond of the girl, by Swedish standards.

"Why do you stay here really? And who takes care of you? I don't mean who makes decisions for you. But who tends to your ... needs. You know..."

Bertha Martha was not offended. This was an analytical woman, and she saw a young girl in an unfamiliar setting ingesting a massive amount of new data and trying to put the pieces of the puzzle together. "I make my own decisions, I have since I was a tiny girl. As for why I stay—the answer is simple inertia amidst my options. I have had a long and productive life in Sweden, but that is gone. When I go back there I will become another anonymous citizen dependent on the government; perhaps I can gather a following in some political discourse, as I dabbled in before, but my heart was never in that. The problem is, my heart is not in anything anymore, it seems. But I will undoubtedly go back."

Gwendolyn stood listening.

"You ask about my needs. Very well, though I blanch at the thought of the details." She pursed her lips. "In Sweden there was a set of four people who attended to me on a rotating basis every day; the four actually were a cycling set of seven or eight women over the course of any few weeks, working in six hour shifts. I was very fortunate to be a Swedish citizen, rather than living in another part of the world—this is an expensive setup, and in most countries I would have been warehoused to slowly die, or neglected to die more quickly. When Sweden sent me here at great expense, it was because I chose to pursue it. I was tired of activism, and I wanted to be of some kind of direct service rather than staying at home where nobody really needed me. Well, there is still a rotating assignment of attendants. But it is now one at a time, twenty-four hours a day, for a year at a time. For now my needs are seen to by the Reverend Dr. Phineas Boseau." Her face winced in displeasure.

Bozo? Gwendolyn was dumbstruck. She had expected to hear that a group of nurses had traveled with Bertha Martha. The thought of this man, so appropriately named, with the serious assignment of feeding and caring for an invalid seemed incongruous. And an invalid with this sort of intellectual capacity and wont.

"…," was all Gwendolyn could muster.

"I see from your face that you have formed an opinion of the man. You are correct. The arrangement is, to say the least, not to my liking. But the Swedish government is in control of this, and they have made their arrangements, financial and otherwise, with Dr. Bok without my input. For the first cycle I was fully involved and could choose my caretaker; I chose one of the women who came to my house every day in Sweden. But I have not been consulted or involved in the decision on the second caretaker. Phineas had his own reasons for wanting to be here and was able to get himself assigned to the job.

"Of course I find it both humiliating and offensive to be dependent on the court jester. Not just dependent. To be regularly manhandled by him. Have you ever had anyone bathe you or dress you, place you on a toilet? I am guessing no, not since you were a baby. Well, imagine having these things done by one who finds a self-amusing anecdote in everything he does, a man who believes the world is full of playthings." She trilled, and the waves rolled laterally across her face and neck, below her chin, into her dress and to regions found there. Her face stretched itself with disgust.

Gwendolyn was horrified, quiet. She wanted to be empathetic, but felt nausea when empathy for this particular situation approached. She stood still, trying to make her mind blank.

"I am tired," Bertha Martha continued. Please ring the bell for me, and let us hope I am met by the brute Aloysius Fink, rather than Phineas Boseau." Gwendolyn, in paralyzing silence because of Bertha Martha's revelations and the pictures they generated, nervously pressed the button, ringing the bell inside. She could never have predicted someone preferring interaction with Fink to dealing with anybody else. *It makes sense for her, I guess, though.*

"Gwendolyn, child. Think about what I have told you here. Think about where you should be." Gwendolyn nodded, though she did not believe the content of Bertha Martha's admonition. She tried, unsuccessfully, to classify it as a warning not to get into an accident resulting in amputations.

The door opened, and the women were exposed to only mild, rather than severe, disgust, to see the homely, crusty and humorless face of Aloysius Fink. He emerged and silently walked around the wheelchair to take custody of Bertha Martha as Gwendolyn stepped out of his way. She saw the two disappear into the relative darkness of the hallway as Bertha Martha's voice trailed off, "Remember it, Gwendolyn."

The Girl is Broken

Why can't you know?

A s she left Bertha Martha, Gwendolyn realized it was early enough in the afternoon that she could find Alitisha before she went to work for the evening. She walked over to Alitisha's room, but it was empty, and nobody seemed to be around the area. She wandered around a few buildings looking for her friend, aloofly nodding as workers or volunteers passed. She looked inside the cafeteria and saw only a few people scattered around the room. An old nun was silently praying at a table in the corner of the room, with a few others following her lead. No Alitisha. Gwendolyn walked the length of the mission, meandering aimlessly. She smiled as she went by her own factory, seeing the workers moving in time to the blasting music as they worked toward completion of the day's production. Eventually she found herself back at the cafeteria and looked in again. The tableau was identical to before but excepting the nuns, the faces were swapped with new ones.

She went back to her room, and as she crossed her open doorway she found a note from Sarah instructing her that tomorrow would be spent in the nursery school at the mission! She was to go early in the morning and stay all day. Her mood had sagged as she unsuccessfully sought her only friend, but this note thrilled her to her toes! A chance to work with the children here at the mission! She forgot her worries, not needing to forget the already-disremembered warning from Bertha Martha. She grabbed Pyratticus Julius and did a little dance around the room, bubbling happily to the stuffed animal as one can only talk to an intimate. She responded to his yen to have every single tentacle stretched and massaged and tickled as they gamboled about. Finally she put her pet on the window sill, so he could watch the thin grass through his unpatched eye. All was well.

Gwendolyn settled down to read before dinner. She would go to the cafeteria and eat. She always ate breakfast from the sponsored volunteer lounge, but she never ate dinner there. Today had started with a real shock, but the day had ended well. Thinking about it, she realized she had perhaps made some level of connection with a new friend—Bertha Martha. The woman's exhortation started to approach her consciousness; she quickly distracted herself with her book.

Tonight she arrived at a point in *Uncle Tom's Cabin* where the character's prospects seemed dimmed. Saddened enough that she had to break away, she gathered Pyratticus Julius to her and sank down on the bed before she continued reading. She bathed in the melancholy of the story, holding her pet close to her and sympathizing with the distressed character, who was descending into increasing trouble. Her mind came back to the mission, to the hungry people here, and everything seemed to weigh on her. She wished that she had a psychic talisman as effective as the Bible that Tom always carried in the story. She remembered she had a Bible here in the room. But her father had inculcated in her the understanding that that book was tonic for simpletons and weaklings. *Well, much as it's a comfort to him, it's not doing old Tom too much good right now.* She slowly read on in quiet sadness.

Gwendolyn did not know it as she sat with Pyratticus Julius and her book, but today a manpower problem had arisen in the mission. A crew of a half dozen native men who worked over in the camp had been frightened by a sudden and inexplicable event—one of their number dropped dead right in their midst as the group waited for their morning transportation. The workers ascribed a supernatural source; they panicked and were inconsolable. The men could not be coaxed to go to work today.

Later Gwendolyn would learn from Dr. Phineas Boseau that it was simply a rare but natural occurrence. A man of perhaps thirty years old, malnourished for his entire life, fell victim to a heart attack and died instantly. The conversation between Gwendolyn and Dr. Boseau would start with her struggle to control her urge to fixate on the wobbling of the end of his long, skinny nose even on such a doleful occasion, and it would end with this sequence:

Gwendolyn: Oh, I see. Sad, though. I feel for the poor man's family.

Dr. Boseau: Yes, of course. But you must realize that most of these men have not seen their families for years. Tribes expel many of the boys as they reach manhood. There have been famines that wipe out entire regions, so his family may not even exist. But you are right, nonetheless. If there is a family I hope this weakness to heart disease does not run in the family.

Gwendolyn: (Trying not to be distracted by the seemingly choreographed motion of the end of the man's nose): He just dropped and died? Do you know what killed him?

Dr. Boseau: Of course we will never have absolute certainty. But I think the circumstances and the condition of the man's body, the coloring of his palms, these things all indicate a heart attack. I was close by, though I did not see the actual event. I ran over when I heard the commotion. He was dead when I got there, and the others had formed a wide circle around him. This was a heart attack.

Gwendolyn: Poor man. Have you had to examine many dead people? That must be a horrible part of the job.

Dr. Boseau: I am a man of god, and I can deal with such things; I see the way before us. But really, no, this is the first time I have touched a dead person.

Gwendolyn: "?"

Dr. Boseau: (Nods)

Gwendolyn: Didn't you have to, I don't know, dissect dead people in school?

Dr. Boseau: (Confused, then recovering, blinking rapidly as he speaks): Oh, no my dear. I fear you are misled by my honorific. I am not a medical doctor. I have a doctorate in Theological Interpretations from Bridgeford University in England. My undergraduate studies in Stockholm concerned the history of medieval Europe. I don't know a lung from a liver. (Chuckles at his own wit)

Gwendolyn: (With a stunned expression): "!"

Dr. Boseau: (Stands, fingers intertwined, silently looking at Gwendolyn with a cocked head)

Gwendolyn: But I thought you were here with Bertha Martha Larssson, taking care of her medical needs.

Dr. Boseau: I am trying to take care of her needs, and lord knows a part of that is attending to her physical needs, but I am not a medical doctor. I am an itinerant preacher from Sweden. If you know anything about that country, you will know that such an occupation is a recipe for starvation. And Dr. Larssson has certainly not required any of my counseling or spiritual guidance. No, I am here because the woman needed somebody with two arms to accompany her, take care of her, and the government found me at the right time. That's all.

Gwendolyn: (Absolutely flummoxed; looks at Dr. Boseau speechlessly)

All of that was a conversation soon to happen; as of now Gwendolyn knew nothing of the incident. But one of the consequences of the sudden death was that the native men were too distraught to go over to the camp and do their jobs. It was an emergency, and Sarah had gathered all willing regulars for emergency duty helping with the feeding today. When she came by early in the day, Alitisha saw the opportunity to do something different, and knowing she was soon leaving, she volunteered to go. She worked into the evening feeding many hungry patients their tardy rations.

Gwendolyn went to eat a light dinner in the cafeteria and returned to the sponsored volunteer lounge. Later she took a walk around the mission. She was sitting in her room reading before retiring when she heard a commotion near the lounge entrance. She walked to her door and looked over in time to see Alitisha burst in, dusty, disheveled, agitated. There was a sponsored volunteer behind her. Others were stunned to see a straight volunteer in her plain shift, a black westerner, here in their lounge. Alitisha was oblivious to them.

Sonja was walking through the lounge on the way to the pantry area, and Alitisha almost bumped into her. She stopped and told Alitisha, "You cannot be in here. Only sponsored volunteers may be here."

One thousand years ago there was an old Japanese jujitsu master who had refused to fight for a warlord, refused to do violence of any kind. For this he was imprisoned in a cage with little food or water for many days. The warlord eventually decided he would never break this man's spirit, and so he decided to dispose of him in a spectacular piece of entertainment. He scheduled a feast and invited all the powerful nobility in the region. The jujitsu master was brought to an arena for all to see. He stood at peace, not knowing, not anxious over what was in store for him. A door opened, and a huge tiger which the warlord had kept unfed for days entered. The monster immediately started moving toward the jujitsu master. The sensei was neither angry at being the entertainment, nor afraid of the tiger, for anger and fear were emotions with which he had no direct experience. He had no grudge against the animal, and he stood still as the tiger circled. The cat snarled and made repeated tentative lunges toward the jujitsu master, but the man remained motionless, even as he was scratched and his clothing torn. Finally at the instant the beast made its decisive pounce, the jujitsu master assaulted the hungry tiger with a single weapon: he unleashed his furious glare, an assault originating in the depths and darkness of his soul and harnessing the energy of the universe. The power encapsulated in the master's glower struck the monster in mid leap. The animal dropped dead in the air and crumpled straight to the ground. The jujitsu master bowed lightly, slowly turned, and walked away in freedom, unchallenged by the thunderstruck warlord.

Alitisha gave that sort of reception to Sonja's interference. Sonja fared better than the tiger; she was able to shrink from Alitisha's view and simply avoid further interference as the newcomer approached Gwendolyn.

Gwendolyn dropped her book when she saw all this. Alitisha approached her, grabbed her arm and turned, tugging Gwendolyn toward the door. It was a command, not a request. An alarmed and compliant Gwendolyn went down the stairs and outside, dragged by her friend.

"Gwendolyn you have to come home with me."

"What? Calm down, Alitisha. What are you talking about?"

"I saw the ghosts. They really are ghosts. They just don't know it yet. Gwendolyn, you don't want to be here." She was shuddering, still compressing Gwendolyn's arm with her hand.

Gwendolyn touched Alitisha's other arm. The girl recoiled and dropped contact, then stepped back, looked earnestly into Gwendolyn's eyes and said, "They had some kind of emergency, and they took eight of us over to feed people today. We went out to the very far side of the dustbowl. Outside the camp there are hundreds of people hoping to get in. Lord knows why they want to come into this godforsaken place; they must be blind. They just stay out there and wait. All of them look horrible. Lots of them lying on the ground, some moving. The militia guys are outside the gate over there too. I heard they only bring in the worst, the ones with the least chance of pulling through. I don't understand it. Dr. Bok told us the opposite.

"But that's not the worst part, those outside. We were feeding people. They were in awful shape. Just awful. Near the beginning I saw a few children moving around, some even playing, but almost nobody else does anything more than stand if they can; a lot just sit—lie down, really." She stopped and started to blubber. Gwendolyn broke down too. Alitisha parried off Gwendolyn's proffer of physical contact. "And—and it got worse as we went along. It was like walking down a path to hell. We came by and handed out this pasty stuff. They were so happy to get it. They were desperate. But do you remember Dr. Bok's description when we got here? It is so much worse, so much worse."

Gwendolyn did not remember any more than that Dr. Bok had said people were in very bad shape and the volunteers should stay away from them.

Alitisha continued, "I didn't see anybody with clubfoot. But I wish I had seen people whose worst problem was clubfoot." Now she clutched Gwendolyn's arms, buried her face in her shoulder and whimpered. Without letting go of her arms, she put her face in front of Gwendolyn's and said, "I am telling you, you don't want to be here. I can't imagine we're making it better. In fact the people outside the fence looked better off, ours looked worse off." She burrowed back into Gwendolyn's shoulder, rubbed her eyes against Gwendolyn's blouse and looked up again. "This place is a nightmare. A nightmare. I'm so glad I'm leaving. I wish the next plane were tomorrow. You have to come with me." She broke down and cried, returning to the shoulder.

Gwendolyn was stunned, silent. She did not really understand what Alitisha was saying, nor how much of it was literally true and how much was created in the girl's distressed imagination. She stood, whimpering, supporting Alitisha. She reached around Alitisha's back and locked her hands as her friend sobbed and sobbed. She did not know what to think. *Alitisha must be exaggerating; she never was really ready for any of this.* "You said they take only the worst?" she sniffed.

Alitisha nodded, without robbing any engagement from her crying activity.

"Well that's why they look worse inside." Gwendolyn was talking to herself more than to Alitisha. "Listen, the mission is doing the right thing. We need to keep at it. Stay here with me."

"No! You didn't see it. Nobody's doing anything for those poor people. You're not helping them. You're not. Come home with me. This is no place to be, I tell you. Come home."

Gwendolyn realized she had been given this advice twice from completely different directions today.

Sonja and a few others had followed the girls down the stairs and were eavesdropping. Others people were gathering together to look on. Sonja walked up to the girls, pulled her cigarette from her mouth and said, "Honey, you had to know it's bad here." She shrugged, replaced her cigarette, and went back to the door. The others followed her back inside. While this was not the farthest Sonja had been from her own bedroom here at the mission, it was a finalist for the distinction, and it was probably as distant as Gwendolyn had ever seen her.

Both girls were silent. They stood, arms clasped around each other's backs, eyes closed now. Sandy Crittenden was in the gaggle that had collected, and she heard most of the girls' exchange. She stepped forward as most of the crowd dissolved.

Sandy said, "Some things can't be changed. Life is like a river. We can make our best efforts to dam it or send it somewhere, but the water gets to where it wants to go. For all man's efforts, for all the marvelous dams in the world, there has never been a river whose water does not get to the sea. We can only do so much, but that doesn't mean we shouldn't try."

To the extent that the girls were listening, they were not following. Sandy put her hand on Gwendolyn's shoulder as she continued, "I don't know. Maybe it's hopeless. But maybe this place is like a dam in China. Built to hold the water back so thirty million people would not be flooded. Well, the water gets to the ocean eventually. They have to let it trickle through. And maybe the dam even fails catastrophically some day and they get flooded. But in the meantime they are better off. For hundreds of years, maybe forever. Should we never build the dams? Never work on keeping them up?"

The combination of Gwendolyn's hug, a few minutes' time, and sounds from Sandy's sweet voice reciting the unintelligible fable helped Alitisha. The piercing spike of her emotions diffused into a simple mountain of indistinct sadness. Some of the broadening, less focused gloom seemed to be conducted to Gwendolyn in the hug. Her feelings changed from alarm and empathy for her friend to a mixture of self-doubt and a gnawing anguish as she contemplated the people in the camp, even at the abstract level at which she conceived things.

Sandy put her hand on Alitisha's back for a moment, then turned and went back toward her room, leaving Gwendolyn and Alitisha in the dark night air. Gwendolyn guided Alitisha, whose welling eyes were closed, to a nearby bench, and the girls sat down, still clasping each other. Nestled together in the warm night air, they remained without speaking and drifted off to sleep.

When Gwendolyn woke up, the girls were still clutching each other in the darkness. The stars were manifold, and the night was silent. The moon was not full, but it was shining down along the path to the power plant. All was silent, and the only motion was the waving of some smoke from the smokestack against the dark sky. Gwendolyn thought about the thousands of patients in the camp just over the hills and how there was not a sound. She tried to look and see the militia outside the gate but could not turn her head far enough to see the truck's usual position without disturbing Alitisha. She pondered the community at the mission. There were a few dozen volunteers, ten or twelve sponsored volunteers. Maybe a pilot, and the few people in the executive residence, not more than five or six. That was the entire list of foreigners here. All in all, not very many.

Her eyes went toward the dormitory where perhaps a hundred local workers were sleeping. All so quiet. She pictured the barracks and the other residences, with walls, floors and furniture invisible—people suspended in all orientations in the air, sleeping on the different levels, silently posed in different forms, feet pointing in every direction, nightgowns drooping. These people all had enough to eat. They were resting comfortably. The workers' diet was not opulent, but it was far from starving. Could that itself justify the mission's existence? The care of the native workers?

Gwendolyn was surprised by the sound of an approaching truck. It came from the direction of the power plant and chugged along, bumping over the rough path. Gwendolyn watched as it closed and passed. She could see the driver. It was Aloysius Fink. He was wearing a baseball cap, and his face, beard and clothing were dusty and smudged with dark patches. He did not see the girls, though he passed only a few dozen yards away. The truck drove to the side of the executive residence, and Gwendolyn could see Fink dismount, take off his hat and beat it against his overalls, then beat the dust out of his clothes before entering the building.

She looked at Alitisha's sleeping face for a long interval. It was as sweet as an angel's with her placid eyes, smooth cheeks, relaxed lips glistening grey in the moonlight; her eyelashes were tufts of silver thread. Gwendolyn found herself unable to sit still right now. Restless and prospectively lonely, she slowly extricated herself from Alitisha's arms, leaving the girl comfortably asleep in an awkward, relaxed pose on the bench. Gwendolyn stood and stretched in the moonbeams. She savored the silent darkness and felt the emptiness of Alitisha's coming departure. Just then, as she happened to glance far down the path, she saw three black-clad nuns scurrying through the darkness carrying a large, oblong bundle through a gap between buildings, hustling their burden in the direction of the cathedral. All this happened in absolute silence.

It was a strange thing to see. She had only witnessed nuns in silent prayer, eating or walking slowly in a procession to their church, and she certainly never thought they would be out at night. Without knowing why, she ran toward them. They took no notice. Regardless of the fact that it was a losing effort, she increased her speed, trying to intercept them before they got to their destination. They winked out of sight behind an intervening building as she ran, and when they came back into view they were not far from the wide open doors of the cathedral. They struggled along clumsily with their heavy payload, entering the building before Gwendolyn was anywhere close. The doors shut. She stopped running.

Gwendolyn felt a stab of loneliness in the dark, hundreds of yards from Alitisha, abandoned by the black robes, soon to be deserted by her best friend. She walked slowly back and took her place with Alitisha, wrapping the girl's arms around her shoulders again, and sat comfortably in profound pain. Nobody understood why she was here, and soon she would be completely alone. She amplified her loneliness by imagining the lurking buildings empty, the mission deserted, the two girls alone under the moon in the darkness. Somehow, in consideration of Alitisha, she was able to suppress a shudder as she looked at the colorless frozen silver glare of the deserted path shining in the moonlight. Her mind centered on Alitisha's imminent departure, and tears welled up in her eyes. She closed them for a few minutes, then gently woke Alitisha and suggested that they go to bed. Alitisha blinked, nodded and ran her hand through her hair as they stood up, still in each other's grasp.

The two walked to Alitisha's building together, then they briefly engaged in a less passive hug and parted. Gwendolyn slowly transited the quietude and went back to her room. She was exhausted, and her mind was blank. She took Pyratticus Julius from his perch at the window and dropped into bed with him held close for warmth. She fell immediately back to sleep, a sleep that had never fully departed since she had slumbered on the bench outside in Alitisha's arms.

Dignitaries Using Diapers

Are they not interchangeable?

I t was early morning, and Gwendolyn found the door to Alitisha's room closed. Torn between waking Alitisha up and just letting her sleep, she decided she could not wake her today. She went back to the sponsored volunteer lounge and had breakfast inside, keeping to herself and contemplating Alitisha's decision. She chose eggs and pancakes, but she had a difficult time eating; her stomach was bothering her. She dawdled over her plate, her chin on her fist, pushing the eggs around. Suddenly she remembered her job—she was working with the children today. She bounced up and started moving toward the door but quickly turned around and sat down to eat. It would be best for her not to get too hungry during the day, so she gobbled up food just in case she did not get a convenient chance to eat later. She smiled as she thought about the children; she had peeked inside their building and seen them a few times, and they were all well dressed and happy. Her mind went to Alitisha's mention of children over in the camp, and she wondered why they would be in two different places at the mission. She put it out of her mind, but not before committing herself to going out to the camp and working there at her first opportunity, sanctioned or not. But for now, she would be attending the happy youngsters. She finished her meal in an upbeat mood.

Gwendolyn walked quickly to the two storey building housing the children's nursery school. She had noticed before that this building was one of the few, along with the executive residence and administration building, that had panes in the windows. She entered, and her eyes were drawn to the happy scene centering on the youngsters. There were fifteen or more young kids in a carpeted and colorful room full of small tables and chairs, books, toys and art supplies. It could have been in Vermont. The children ranged from infants to six or seven years old, the older ages represented in small numbers. There were about twice as many girls as boys. One boy was circling the room with a toy airplane, making sounds impressively varied for a simple airplane engine. The others were playing or creating pictures as they sat at low tables, or sat or lay on the floor. All activity stopped as she came in, and all the little ones looked at her.

Gwendolyn had entered at the long side of the building. A little to her left was a movable partition closing off something like thirty percent of the building. The children and their supervisors were in the open area in front of her and to her right. She could see a split door with the top half hanging open on the far wall. Inside she saw a bathroom with three small toilets in a row. There were two other doors in the right wall; one had a window leading into an office area with a desk, and one was closed.

She surveyed the happy children as they gradually resumed their activities. She smiled and watched the boy zigzagging along contentedly with the airplane, varying his altitude, yaw, pitch and roll to suit the topographical features of the room: chairs, children, walls and so forth. As the plane buzzed a woman's head, Gwendolyn detected the adults in the room. A sponsored volunteer Gwendolyn knew casually was reading a book out loud, holding up each page for viewing by kids in a semi-ellipse at the foot of her chair. Another familiar sponsored volunteer was in the room, arranging some things in the far left corner. Each volunteer acknowledged Gwendolyn with a bow of the head. The names of these two similar looking neighbors escaped Gwendolyn at the moment. There were two other adults in the room: a regular and a native worker who would later be introduced as Julia.

The room was permeated with the chatter and bustle of the happy children. Gwendolyn flushed with satisfaction as she stood at the entrance. It seemed like a respite from the troubles of the world, this nursery area with its colorful painted decor and cheerfully disordered art supplies.

The regular volunteer had been arranging a stack of folded sheets and towels in the corner. She turned and walked over toward Gwendolyn, smiling. She was probably the oldest regular Gwendolyn encountered here; she seemed to be in her forties, even older than many of the sponsored volunteers. Gwendolyn had seen her around the mission before but did not know her. She went forward and met her in the middle of the room. The regular introduced herself as Dorothy.

"I'm Gwendolyn." She was eager to get to work.

"Yes, I know. Sarah told me you would be with us today. I hear you're from Vermont! I'm from right across the lake. I teach school in Plattsburg. Listen, today should be an exciting day. We're going to have visitors. For now, why don't you go over and see if those children need help with their art?"

Visitors? Who visits here? Gwendolyn put the surprising information out of her mind and walked through the area, looking at each child individually as she passed by. All met her glance except two babies who seemed to be uninterested. She was absolutely struck by the eyes of the youngsters. She was sure that every one of these children had the largest and happiest, most luminous, shiny brown eyes she had ever seen. The children were beautiful, and she loved the way they smiled back at her as she passed.

Gwendolyn contentedly approached a table where three youngsters were coloring and knelt next to them. The children started chattering to her while they worked merrily away at their tasks. As she visited each one she tilted her head and asked what the picture was. Each cheerful response, usually in quite good baby English, was an elixir to her soul. She loved the way the youngsters' eyes jumped between hers and the page as each explained his artwork. The first piece of work she examined was by a girl of about four years age.

"Oh, how pretty. Is that a bug?"

"No, it's the sun."

"Oh, how pretty and bright. A nice bright brown sun."

The others gave similar elucidations. Gwendolyn had not had such wonderful human contact since coming to Africa. She felt the comfort of an inner warmth welling up, a feeling reminiscent of what she sometimes felt in California during a pause in her work as she talked with Cecilia.

The boy with the airplane ran by, threw it down in front of Gwendolyn and pretended to run away. The vehicle passed her and made an abrupt, unassisted landing on the table, sliding onto a little girl's drawing at the far end. She was startled and upset. She pushed the plane off her paper and started to cry. Gwendolyn walked to the distraught girl and asked what was in the picture. The girl calmed down and explained that she had drawn a tree with a monkey in it. Gwendolyn commented on how nice it was that she drew a monkey with so many tails touching all the branches. The girl smiled, and Gwendolyn's heart melted. Meanwhile the pilot saw the attention he was passing up and came back over. The girl squealed in laughter as the boy swooped in to get the airplane, guided it through a looping and improbable takeoff, and disappeared into the open spaces of the room—but not before looking over his shoulder to make sure Gwendolyn was watching. All the kids at the table were now laughing. Gwendolyn, laughing along, lost awareness that she was not one of the children.

The morning progressed much like that. Gwendolyn forgot where she was and happily carried out whatever tasks Dorothy suggested. In late morning, as most of the older children were looking at books and the younger ones were engaged with toys, Gwendolyn asked Julia if the kids would be going outside to play. Julia smiled and shrugged; Gwendolyn could not tell if she did not understand or did not know the answer. Gwendolyn asked a sponsored volunteer the same question. The volunteer looked at Dorothy, who noticed and approached. Gwendolyn repeated her question, to which Dorothy answered that it was not safe for them to go outside, so they remained indoors.

"Never?" Gwendolyn was shocked. She realized she had not once seen the youngsters outside playing in the dirt.

"Sarah doesn't want them outside today," was Dorothy's cryptic non-answer. Gwendolyn saw from the woman's vacant standard-issue pale blue eyes and relaxed expression that no further answer would forthcome.

Gwendolyn was puzzled. *Why? What is so unsafe?* She walked outside and around to the back edge of the building, the side nearest the dirtpile. There was room to run and play in the dirt and sparse vegetation there. She walked back to the front, the side facing the main path. Standing looking at this more familiar side of the building, she looked left and right. Just a little way down the mission's major pathway was a sizeable field where Bourbon had killed the lizard a few days ago. The memory made Gwendolyn realize she was looking at a graveyard and coated her mood with a brief twinge of sadness for the dead creature.

Maybe it had something to do with the militia men. She looked over to the fence. It was true that the militia men would usually be visible from here, but today she saw none. She remembered that oddly enough, she did not see them as she walked over this morning either. They could be the problem Dorothy had in mind—the armed men could easily enter through the gate or come straight through the mission fence with a pair of wire cutters if they were dedicated to hurting or kidnapping the children. Gwendolyn understood they had guns and they could be dangerous; in fact she was terrified of them. But she had a hard time believing that they did not know the kids were in this schoolhouse; that was preposterous. Even more outlandish was the idea that these men would make a priority of noticing, let alone hurting, the children. Like so many things in the world and especially here, it did not add up. She shrugged mentally and went back inside to be with the youngsters.

After helping with lunch, she played some games with the older children. In the early afternoon a circle of children and two adults was clapping and laughing after a chase during the game 'duck-duck-goose' when Dorothy opened the building's door. A commotion arose outside and penetrated into the room. Everyone looked toward the door. Aloysius Fink and a tall, handsome and impeccably dressed man crossed the threshold into the building. Three of the older children ran to the farthest corner of the building and cowered.

The man accompanying Aloysius Fink had a surreal quality: perfectly groomed, not a jet-black hair out of place, rugged jaw. He seemed to be illuminated by an invisible diffuse spotlight, and he ambulated smoothly, with none of the normal speed variations or bobbing and twisting one never notices in a regular person's walk.

It was hard for Gwendolyn not to imagine a camera crew filming him and simultaneously projecting a perfectly edited version to replace the subject. Yes, a lurking camera crew would explain the man's deportment. As he entered, his face was turned to Fink, and over the general hubbub of the place Gwendolyn could hear Fink say, "…medical needs as well. We're sorry Dr. Bok isn't here."

The visitor spoke, "Don't worry about it. He can just buy me a drink or a steak next time I see him. I'm just glad to be here, glad to help." He smiled, glanced at someone yet outside, then looked back to Fink and said, "And I'll get something out of all this too." He chuckled. The children's noise happened to drop into a bubble of silence just as two more people walked through the door. Gwendolyn was thunderstruck when she immediately recognized Clif Rockington—the activist Hollywood star almost as well known for his political activity as his wealth, playboy lifestyle and action movies!

The room disappeared for her, and she could not take her eyes off the man. Only a few hours ago she was anticipating a wonderful but uneventful day with the children. Of course she had met famous stars before, but Clif Rockington was a personal favorite of hers, and she had never met him. She was breathless. Gwendolyn was attracted to him—all females were—but it was not completely physical for her. This man's dedication to making the world a better place stood out in Hollywood. Hardly a month passed during which he was not in the national spotlight decrying the plight of some unfortunate people, pleading for compassion, for money. The man's jaw alone, his shoulders alone, his magnetic smile alone—any one of these justified the world's adoration, but Gwendolyn knew he had a higher calling than being admired for his beauty. He felt exactly as she did about helping people. Vice versa. She knew it. She knew it.

At his elbow walked Sarah Greenwater. They came in without conversation, so far as Gwendolyn could tell. Trailing behind were a few young men and women, all dressed as though they were going to a business lunch at the top of a tower in downtown Manhattan, perhaps a bit more dusty.

Aloysius Fink was in mid sentence beside the first visitor. Gwendolyn's ears resumed working. "...the kids he was talking about. We're always ready. Again, Dr. Bok really apologizes for the delay but the authorities, they're inflexible..." He was grinning with his all-purpose, reptilian smile, the only smile he possessed.

Fink walked to the partition that Gwendolyn had noticed when she came in and slid it open. She left the children and went over to watch the delegation. The little room was packed with cameras, light diffusers, electronic meters. Her instinctive feeling that the visitor belonged near cameras was vindicated. Dorothy whispered to her ear, telling her the unknown man was a United States senator, mentioning his party. Gwendolyn was impressed with the man's station. As for the party, she had been told repeatedly since babyhood that one party loved and fought for the regular people and the other party hated them and wanted only to exploit them on behalf of the powerful. She herself had never noticed either side acting interested in people at all, outside the habit of tricking them. *But you know, I've paid very little attention to politics.* She always forgot which party was which. And it did not matter, as her father had always told her it was important to treat them equally—except while in a group of one or the other.

The newly visible room was a studio. On a far wall were racks and shelves of children's clothing ranging from little formal dresses to rags. There were tripods and several complicated-looking cameras set up facing two different stage sets. One stage was empty with a backdrop that had a window and an almost bare bookcase painted on it. The other had a simple chair and an old-fashioned incandescent light, with a plain off-black screen as a background.

The motion around the entrance damped; the visitors were all inside by now. Many eyes were on the senator and Clif Rockington. The movie star stepped back and settled into a silent background position. The man looked perfect—exactly as he did in the movies—but Gwendolyn was surprised by both his diminutive stature and his apparent shyness in real life. The man was a dynamo in theaters and an absolute Greek god when he pleaded his case for compassion. Today he seemed to play the wallflower.

Aloysius Fink barked some order to Dorothy, who turned and went to get something from the nursery as the senator inspected the photography set. Dorothy soon came back with a glass of water and tried to hand it to the senator, who declined it but smiled magnetically and thanked her cordially. Clif Rockington stood silently all this time. The two female newcomers had taken up positions beside him.

Gwendolyn forgot about the children in the nursery and milled about with the crowd now inside the studio. The young assistants were fidgeting and walking around chattering impatiently at each other without saying anything. Gwendolyn sidled over to the clothing racks. She picked up some outfits, and as she perused them she noticed the clothes were all quite rugged. Some were cleverly designed little formal outfits that looked as though they were made of the most delicate lace and taffeta, but they were almost indestructible. There were also suits that were apparently rags, but upon close inspection she saw that they were carefully patterned costumes made to look soiled and ragged. The colors had gradations giving a splotchy appearance. Jagged holes and 'broken' edges were designed into the garments, carefully engineered to preclude the normal progression that actual rips follow. It was puzzling. *Well, they are costumes after all. They probably have to be pretty tough if they're going to be used in a stage set.* She was also baffled by the existence of the photography studio here in the plains of Africa.

"Is this one okay?" It was Sarah Greenwater holding one of the boys, a happy-looking tot. His big eyes were looking all around the studio, lingering on the shiny cameras and racks of clothes and most of all, the group of adult faces that had taken a cue to evaluate his appearance. He jostled with excitement at the faces stretched in his direction. The child reveled in the attention and danced, almost becoming unmanageable for Sarah.

The senator and Aloysius Fink frowned and shook their heads almost concurrently as though they were appendages of the same two-headed beast, with Fink just slightly more distal from the organism's motor control center; the men's heads moved in slightly phase-offset unison. Sarah transported the boy back and picked up a younger girl. She carried her over to the group, and this time it was a closer call, but this child also failed to make the cut for whatever awaited. Sarah approached Gwendolyn and handed her the girl she was holding, a burden Gwendolyn happily accepted.

Aloysius Fink tipped off the world that he was impatient by brushing past Sarah and Gwendolyn, almost making the baby drop, and briskly walking over to the nursery. He looked into some of the cradles and seemed bored by what he saw. He walked among the children as they sat on the floor ignoring their toys and looking up at him. Fink orbited for a bit and noticed the three children still cowering in the farthest corner. He paused, looking at them; this action seemed to pump energy into their fear, and they all started visibly shaking as one started bawling out loud. Fink turned back to the other kids on the floor with all the youngsters' eyes following him. He spotted one girl of about three years who had wild hair and a pouting demeanor. He hovered for a few seconds, then started walking away. Quickly he turned back, bent down and swooped up the child with one hand, holding her by a strap in her outfit. The surprised toddler screamed as she swung into the air. She struggled against the ether, but Fink effortlessly bested her. He walked calmly back to the senator with the dangling, flailing, crying girl. He raised her to eye level and said to the senator, "I think this is the one." The senator moved his head back away from the screaming tot, nodding. Sarah took her from Aloysius Fink's dangling grasp, and the baby calmed down a bit at the feeling of human contact.

Now the group of young visitors got to work. They turned on bright lights and moved reflective shades around. The senator sat in the chair in front of the featureless backdrop, and several of the helpers made sure his hair and clothing were in order. He sat erect and stone still amidst the flurry of activity. Clif Rockington quietly stepped forward into place a few feet to the right of the senator. Sarah was still holding the toddler girl with the distinctive luck. The girl happily played with a small toy car Gwendolyn had given her, running it around on Sarah's arms and shoulder. Two men readied two cameras as Fink handed Sarah a costume for the little actress.

Gwendolyn noticed something waving around at the rear of the crowd, slowly bobbing along and sometimes protruding between heads or over shoulders. Her eyes automatically followed the oblong and tapered object's motion as it winked in and out of view through the crowd. Finally its position and orientation stabilized, projecting in a lazy cantilever between the tops of two people's heads. She traced it to its root: Dr. Phineas Boseau had apparently followed his nose into the schoolhouse and was observing the excitement around the senator's photo session. His eyebrows jumped in astonishment as he surveyed the scene and saw Clif Rockington. Gwendolyn was surprised that she had never noticed his goofy eyebrows before, but then excused herself: his nose left little attention unconsumed whenever she saw him.

All was quiet, including the tot. The senator nodded to Aloysius Fink, and in a sudden move, Fink swept his face toward the girl in Sarah's arms, startling her. The baby, now dressed in one of the ragged outfits and still holding the toy car, froze, her eyes and mouth wide, looking across the few millimeters separating her from Fink's face. She pushed her face into Sarah's neck and began to cry again. Just as Sarah recovered from her own appalled surprise, Fink snatched the car from the girl's grasp. The girl burrowed into Sarah, crying more vocally. Sarah broke her free and held her out cantilevered at arm's length, scaring her further. The girl grasped wildly at the air, bawling louder than ever. After letting her steep a few minutes, Sarah brought her in and held her as a mother holds a baby. The girl quieted and sucked her thumb. Gwendolyn's eyes welled up in sympathy with the little girl.

Fink motioned with his head, and Sarah walked past him with the child, who buried her face again in Sarah's neck as they passed the menacing man. Sarah handed the nervous but quiet toddler to the senator and arranged her rags so they flowed nicely onto his lap. The curious little girl sat looking up at the senator's face. He sat upright, ignoring her and looking at the camera. The man maintained a satisfied and disciplined pose as he sat completely still with the baby on his lap. Most people sitting straight like that would look like they are waiting for something, but somehow he looked natural.

The tot looked at the lights and at the cameras. She was the picture of a perfectly clean and well fed baby clothed in filthy-looking, ragged, rural African garb. Her upturned face confined pools of tears at her eyes, and they sparkled in the light. She had streaks of tears on her cheeks.

One of the men behind the camera motioned, and a tightly dressed woman signaled the senator. He stretched his neck through his collar and tightly knotted tie, his head struggling as it rose, and cleared his throat. The senator barked and hummed out a few syllables as he tuned the pitch of his voice. He turned his face into final position facing one of the cameras, and his features settled to their appointed positions. The man paused, appearing totally at ease. The camera operator fiddled with the lights and settings, and filled the frame with the little girl for a few seconds, then gave the senator a signal and moved the camera to capture the overall scene.

In unhurried and friendly prose the senator began a one-sided conversation with the camera. "Why does it matter? Do I need to ask after you see their faces?" He slowly looked down, then back up and paused. "Why should we support the Wholesome Globe Project?" Again, in slow motion he turned his head down and gazed with apparent benevolence at the tiny girl on his lap. This time she looked up at him and came to the brink of a smile, some of the teary fluid from one of her eyes leaking into a rivulet on her cheek. The senator lingered then looked back at the camera. The little girl directed her view toward the camera as well. Gwendolyn looked over and saw a woman from the senator's entourage waving her hands back and forth to capture the child's attention.

The camera panned up to the quiet, erstwhile off-camera movie star. He stood, apparently isolated on the set in front of the bland background and spoke mellifluously, "Hello. I think you know I'm Clif Rockington." He stopped for a few seconds, eyes to the elevated distance, jaw set tight. With a slight repositioning of the head he continued, "The senator and I have come here to assess the work the Wholesome Globe Project's Swazizibia mission is doing, and let me tell you, they are making a difference. Saving lives. But the task is huge." He gave a smile. The camera zoomed slightly. He turned his head to the other camera.

"I am a wealthy man, and for that I am thankful every day to that powerful entity who brings me my abundance: the American public! But even my wealth is a drop in the bucket compared to what is needed to end suffering in the world. We need your help. I want to tell you today that I am pledging a personal match for all the American donations to this worthy effort, and another match for Senator Kimball Brewsterford's campaign. The senator is doing so much at the government level for this and so many other projects. We need men like him for the fight to keep your government's money flowing to those doing good.

"My promise is this: In the next year, I will personally donate an amount equal to the per capita donation America makes to the Wholesome Globe Project. So the more you donate, the more I match. I am John Doe!" He paused, for though he had practiced this speech many times, he did not understand the John Doe reference, and it always caused a hitch as he traveled through it. "I will do the same thing for contributions to Senator Brewsterford's reelection campaign. Remember, the cause is worthy but these people cannot do it by themselves. So long, and see me at the movies," he smiled slyly as he waited for the frame to fade out, then stepped away as the camera faded back in for the senator to continue.

We take a quick peek into the future now and find that the American population as a whole donated hundreds of millions of dollars to the mission in the next year, as well as a few million to the senator's campaign. When it would come time for Clif Rockington to write his own check at the end of the year, he would round upwards. He more than quadrupled the amount he had pledged and donated exactly ten dollars to the mission. He was also destined to round up for matching funds to the senator's campaign and write a check for one dollar. Florian Bok and the senator were to be quite happy with this; they were far more interested in the effect of the perception of the celebrity's words than in his own donation, and all turned out wholly to their satisfaction. The movie star would meet the letter of his commitment. Donors had helped the needy. Everyone was happy.

Clif Rockington was finished with his portion of the filming, and he quietly went outside the building. The two overdressed female visitors went with him, and the camera returned to the senator. As he finished his session, he delivered every movement and sound in slightly slow motion. Pauses were liberally interspersed; his certain face and creased forehead, his talented and cultured eyebrows, delivered a message of seriousness and ostensibly genuine concern. Gwendolyn's mind drifted off with the soothing cadence of his voice, then she reminded herself he was speaking and listened to the words, not the sound. "…because we are some of the luckiest people in the world, living in Vermont."

Vermont! Gwendolyn was not much interested in politics, but this must be her senator. Her mind wandered to the many times she had heard her father tell the family that someday Marshall, or perhaps even Hunter, would be a senator. That was the moment she noticed his hugely obtrusive two lapel pins: an American flag on one side, and the familiar gold 'IDIC' logo on the other.

"… campaign will donate five percent of every campaign contribution…countenance starving like I see right here, right now… the world is not all like Vermont. We all need to share the world." Gwendolyn recovered her attention and listened closely.

"Look at Jumaya's eyes." The senator sat silently looking down at the toddler on his lap for perhaps four seconds, then looked up at the camera and continued, "The mission has cared for her for almost two years now. Her mother and father are gone..." The baby was perfect for the part. She was shy and glossy-eyed. She pouted and played her part exactly on script—she kept looking right where they wanted her to, and she alternated looking happy and crestfallen. She rubbed her eyes in the light. Those big round shiny eyes penetrated to Gwendolyn's heart, something Gwendolyn was certain she would do across the airwaves as she entered the comfortable homes in Vermont. "... will continue my effort in Congress to keep up our government's donations and to encourage corporations to donate a responsible portion of their profits... many more like her... and the mission needs your contributions now..."

Just then the senator's body jerked and he let out a sudden yelp. He swung up the arm that supported the child and slapped at the back of his neck as his body twitched violently. The little girl grasped the air as he twisted, then slowly tumbled off his lap in an improbable somersault powered by gravity and boosted by his moving thigh. She landed on her bottom, unharmed, then toppled over onto her back. As soon as she had obtained enough composure, she clenched her fists and kicked her feet and screamed in terror. Gwendolyn was the first to reach the baby; she had started pushing through the crowd, crying out "Kaliki," the child's name, at the instant the man let go of the baby. She got to her just after she started crying.

At this point in time nobody else had moved; their contribution to the rescue was one of contorting facial muscles and gasping audibly. Like many in the crowd, Dr. Phineas Boseau was pained at having to witness the cruel turn of events. His face twisted in reflexive sympathy so severely as to curl the very end of his nose. But Gwendolyn saw none of this.

Now the senator was looking at one hand and scratching the back of his neck with the other. "Damn bugs," he scowled in a voice so ugly that Gwendolyn could scarcely believe it was real. She stood with the baby in her arms, comforting her, kissing and hugging and gently bouncing her. Some of the children in the other room had come to investigate, but Dorothy, Julia and the others rounded them up and took them back.

The senator looked around the group with awkwardly veiled embarrassment. He was rescued by the cameraman. "This is good. This is good. Her

eyes were starting to look a little dry anyway. Let's get this going again."
Everyone seemed in agreement with the exception of Gwendolyn. Sarah
walked to a reluctant and clinging Gwendolyn and gently, without help from
her, freed the little girl from her grasp. As Sarah walked back to the senator
she smoothed the girl's hair and clothes.

Once the toddler understood her destination she communicated her
preference to decline the invitation. As Sarah leaned down the girl clutched
at her hair and clothing, her legs pumping, bare feet pounding the senator's
thighs. He clamped her with his hands on the sides of her thorax. She struck
his thighs simultaneously with both heels in a jumping motion and screamed
bloody murder, but the man was tough enough to enforce his will against
this determined, tiny combatant.

Senator Kimball Brewsterford of the Great State of Vermont was
frustrated. This simple African girl refused to cooperate; he was more
accustomed to dealing with people who could be influenced by innuendos
and smooth conversation. The man who had been a picture of composure a
few minutes prior had become helpless, sitting there clasping the baby's ribs.
The energetic child continued her exertions; they took a step up in amplitude
as the little girl spied Aloysius Fink's face hovering near the front of the
group. Gwendolyn's eyes had teared up, and as she wiped them with her
finger she wondered if she or the baby was generating more tears.

Fink was a man of few words but a man of action in a crisis of this
magnitude. He walked to the nursery to procure another child. He was less
choosy this time and made a quick choice: a boy, slightly older and bigger
than Kaliki, but one with an appealing face. The boy seemed overtly cheerful,
and that gave Fink momentary pause, but that consideration was overpow-
ered by his certain knowledge, anchored somewhere in the brainstem, that
any child's eyes can be wetted with a little effort. There was no strap to lift
the boy by, so Fink bent down and scooped him up in both hands. The boy
giggled.

Fink returned with the curious little boy, and the cameraman said,
"Senator, you can just go on to the wrap up now. You were almost done, and
we can cut the scene. In fact, using more than one kid probably makes it a
more powerful commercial. It'll give folks less reason to think you just
dressed up some brat in Vermont and faked the whole thing." The senator,
agreeing, held the little girl out to the air. Gwendolyn fought her way forward
and took her up. Senator Brewsterford rubbed his thigh through his fine
wool slacks. He and the cameraman nodded in unison. Fink signaled to Sarah

with his head, and she followed his instruction by approaching Gwendolyn and trying to take the young girl. The toddler had taken a liking to Gwendolyn and resisted, burying her face in Gwendolyn's breast and clutching her. Gwendolyn came to understand that they really only wanted the tattered dress, so she gently guided Sarah's hand off the girl, then equally carefully untangled the girl from her wrap, leaving her in underpants. She handed the garment to Sarah.

Aloysius Fink found that the boy was still in his arms as Sarah came over and started to undress him. A squirming confusion with six writhing wrists and two lashing legs, with giggles and muttered curses ensued. Fink's shoulders alternated elevation randomly throughout the initial struggle. Finally, having made little progress, he just put the boy on the floor, and Sarah succeeded in changing the laughing baby's clothes. The boy had enjoyed the struggle, thinking it a game. Watching the battle, Gwendolyn thought they must have tickled him through most of it. Overall, emotional anti-symmetry was attained, as Fink was mentally madded and physically flummoxed, while the boy was wholly happy.

It was time to get ready to shoot. The senator repeated his earlier meditation, creating his confident and apparently confiding, friendly and focused countenance for the camera. He again became the picture of eloquence. Sarah carried the boy to him and handed him over. The senator awaited the signals and started to perform the wrap up, looking at one of the cameras, "Look at the information below and contact us now. Remember…"

One of the idle assistants interrupted the session. "Wait. He isn't crying." All looked at the little boy. He was enjoying the whole process, especially the lights. This was not good. There was some discussion among the senator's entourage and Sarah on how to get the toddler boy to improve his acting ability, to get him to follow their implicit script—to be miserable. The discussion cycled without noticeable progress. As the controversy raged, Fink, the man of action that he was, approached the boy, and swung his bearded, pock-marked face right up to the child in a scowl, his smoke-stained teeth visible between the black bristles of his whiskers.

It was a brilliant strategy, one that would work on most of the world's billions, child and adult alike. A far milder version had already worked once today. But this boy thought Fink was playing. Perhaps he had seen uglier men. Or maybe Fink was some kind of make believe creature, clearly uglier than anything real could be. The baby bounced on the same thigh that Kaliki had so recently bounced on. He pumped his arms in glee, and smiled widely, laughing raucously. Fink could hear the conversation still orbiting the idea of destroying the boy's composure, but it was not converging to any strategy. He slowly turned away from the boy then in a furiously sudden snap, whirled his face back into the boy's and thundered, "Cry. Damn you. Cry."

The little boy was about two years old, and he did not understand too much English, but he validated Fink's communication channel. He froze for a second or two, terrified, then his face exploded, launching an ear piercing howl directly into Fink's ear. Fink flinched with pain. As he withdrew, he mentally congratulated and cursed himself—for solving the problem at hand, and for leaving his face so close to the boy, respectively.

But the situation was not quite corrected. To rectify the happiness surfeit was to solve only part of the problem of setting the boy's mood right. The screaming boy was no use for the shooting session, so close to being completed. The senator sat, face turned away, uncomfortably holding the wailing boy as he pounded and jumped on the man's lap. The boy screamed and battled, not knowing what he wanted, beyond simple sweet distance from everybody. Gwendolyn, still holding Kaliki, came and knelt close to him and cooed his name, which she knew, softly. All through this the little girl was complacent, clutching her. The boy looked at Gwendolyn, and his screams trailed off to sniffles as he calmed down. Gwendolyn kissed his forehead and wiped his cheeks and eyes with her blouse.

There were plenty of tears still welling up in the boy, so as it turned out Gwendolyn's little act of kindness did not set the efforts back; in fact, in about half a minute it was judged that the boy had just enough tears showing. They were ready to complete the shoot.

Quietly humming, Gwendolyn walked away into the other room with Kaliki, placing her lips on the top of the tot's forehead and giving her a kiss. She partially heard the senator's voice as he completed the advertisement, "… it takes the world to make a world for our children and children all over the world."

Gwendolyn found some clothing for her little girl Kaliki. She dressed her and sat down to read a book to a group of children as the senator's entourage finished in the background. When the work was done Sarah and the visitors, and to some extent Fink, proceeded in the normal manner of groups of mingling businesspeople—standing around blocking the doorway, consuming oxygen, congratulating each other on accomplishments, promising great future cooperation, complimenting the surroundings. One could be forgiven for suspecting that this last part—complimenting the surroundings—was less than sincere on the part of the senator and especially the young visitors.

Just then Alitisha burst into the building. She ruffled and fractured the cloud of loiterers in inelastic collisions as she spotted Gwendolyn and trotted right through it. Gwendolyn stood as she saw her friend run over.

"I'm going tonight," she gasped.

Gwendolyn, caught by surprise stuttered, "Going? What?"

"Home. I'll be home the day after tomorrow. I can't wait to see Fred again." Fred was her dog, a smooth, nondescript dachshund.

Gwendolyn was stunned. She processed the words then spoke, "So soon? How?" She ached at the reminder and proximity of losing her best friend.

"They have a plane leaving in a few hours, and I'm going to be able to go on it. It's going right to Cairo, so it's going to be a quick trip. Sarah will make arrangements for my travel back from Cairo tomorrow. I'm going home." She smiled broadly and tears welled in her eyes. She leaned over and hugged Gwendolyn, who dropped the book. "I'll miss you. Some VIP visitor has to be flown out. I'm going on that plane." Gwendolyn's eyes lifted, and she looked over Alitisha's shoulder at the satisfied mob now leaving the building as Sarah Greenwater closed the partition to the stage set.

She closed her eyes, and they held each other quietly for a few seconds. She wished Alitisha would stay, but by now she understood her friend's situation. "I hope you have a good trip. Tell your mother and father hello for me." They continued their hug for a bit, then Alitisha broke off, wiped her eyes and left. Gwendolyn dabbed her eyes as she looked after Alitisha.

She turned back to the children and the book. Kaliki had picked up the book and was tapping her finger on a picture of a turtle and babbling happily, occasionally looking up to Gwendolyn's face, a face of mixed emotions—smiling and genuinely loving the time with the little girl while still emitting tears over her best friend. Alitisha's adventure was over. Gwendolyn would not have a chance to see her again until she herself went home to the United States. Somehow, however impossibly, she had an uneasy feeling that by then they would be starting to grow apart. Or maybe they would not meet again. She dismissed the thought, but it recurred occasionally as time progressed.

The rest of the day was uneventful, but in some ways it the most pleasant time that Gwendolyn had spent at the mission. She lost herself in drawing and practicing letters and numbers with the young children in the schoolhouse. The senator's bizarre visit quickly dropped from her mind as she laughed and played with the kids. Even Alitisha's ghost left her after a little while. She was starting to bond with the children, each and every one; she was disposed in such a way that they were each headed toward being her favorite.

She especially enjoyed the afternoon snack time. They passed out treats to the children and watched as the kids ate slowly with playful abandon and sipped drinks from tiny cups. Most were horsing around with each other and didn't focus on eating. They were in no hurry to finish, and indeed, few of them actually ate their entire cookies or emptied their cups of sweetly colored water. It was hard to imagine she was in Swazizibia, and in fact it was a blessing for Gwendolyn to forget where she was. The children, dressed in colorful clothes and playing with their toys and art supplies, could have been home in Burlington.

Toward evening Tammy Van de Bunt, a regular volunteer, came in with another regular, Gloria. Gwendolyn had met Tammy when they both arrived here, and she had seen her briefly a few times. Gloria was in charge of the overnight shift. Julia was scheduled to work through the dinner hour before she left, and Gwendolyn insisted on remaining to help. Both newcomers had little overnight bags with them.

The dinner did not compare favorably to that of a fine Italian restaurant in Vermont. But it was pasta; children around the world love any food that can make a mess. They played with the noodles, sliding them in the sauce, sometimes with their fingers and sometimes with their spoons. The younger children had less freedom, as they were strapped into their chairs; nonetheless they participated fully in the joviality, sometimes swinging a noodle or tossing a chunk of something. The adults kept the food throwing to a minimum, but they allowed all sorts of dawdling and finger painting and so forth. They made sure that each child finished a vitamin-infused drink but let the children decide how much pasta to eat. The youngsters, though not in a hurry, eventually bored of suppertime, and one by one they walked away from their little tables. After being intercepted and wiped off, the kids began playing with toys or each other. The younger ones, imprisoned in their chairs, signaled their completion through fidgeting and gesturing toward the play areas. As they played after dinner, Gwendolyn mused that dinner tonight was a perfect mix of finger painting and nutrition delivery. The volunteers cleaned up the dinner wreckage as the youngsters played.

They herded the children in several groups for small-group baths. The tots were separated by age but not by sex, and they were supplied with bath toys, which prolonged the wait for the kids behind them. The bath capacity was two tubs, or six at a time. The splashing and playing exacerbated the stress of those waiting, but it made their turn in the shared water all the more sweet. Gwendolyn, who jumped right into her adoptive job, kneeling and armed with rags coated with shampoo and soap, was lost in wantonness as much as any of the toddlers; her clothes were quickly soaked as she captured, soaped and scrubbed the slippery bodies. She enjoyed helping with all the ages, but she was especially partial to the older boys, and they seemed to like her as well.

The evening was darkling, and Gwendolyn was plenty tired from all her exertions and excitement. She was happy to hear Gloria tell the young ones it was time for a story before bed. They gathered the children in a circle on the floor, and Gloria picked up a picture book and showed the cover to the children. Gwendolyn could see it was an old beaten-up copy of *Make Way For Ducklings*, a book that was one of her own favorites when she was little. It brought back memories of sitting on the floor at the feet of her first grade teacher and hearing about the plight of the tiny hatchlings in the big city.

Tammy quietly went upstairs, and Gloria read the book, pausing at each page to show the engravings of an absurd procession of ducks meandering through big city traffic to the children, who delighted, though none had ever seen a city. Or a duck. One of the children, Lamaya, asked Gloria to, "Wead it in Fwench," and it caused a short argument among the children, most of whom knew English but not French. They all settled down in favor of French when little diplomat Lamaya, who could be no more than four years out, pointed out that the pictures were the real story. Gwendolyn later learned that Lamaya did not know French but liked the sounds resulting from Gloria's attempt to speak the lusty language. As Gloria read the story, translating to French, the little ones betrayed no less understanding than if it were read in English; the visuals were indeed the key to the evening's entertainment.

As Tammy came down dressed for bed and went into the little multi-bathroom to brush her teeth, Gwendolyn realized that she had never thought about how children need twenty-four hour supervision. She knew there were jobs that required night work—for instance, Alitisha's—to keep the mission operating. But she had always thought of child care as a day job.

In fact, she had never considered where they slept; now it seemed pretty clear that the beds and cribs were upstairs. She slipped away from the storytelling, went up the stairway and found herself in a single large room. Most of the second floor was dedicated to this room, with two doors on one wall leading to other smaller rooms. Two rows of beds and cribs lined the long walls. At the far end was a large window with panes. There were light switches at the top of the stairway and spaced at several locations along the long wall. The room was illuminated by three old-fashioned hanging light fixtures. Each was presumably controlled by one or more of the switches. The two beds nearest the stairway had night stands with lamps beside them. A few books and an empty pitcher were on the closest night stand.

So the children lived here! It made sense to Gwendolyn, but like so many of the peripheral details of the mission, it had never occurred to her to wonder about it. *How many other things do I forget to think about?*

She went back downstairs just as Tammy and Gloria were preparing to herd the children upstairs to bed. The kids took the opportunity to delay, dancing around Gwendolyn's legs, pulling her hands and clothes, and asking her to stay overnight with them. She was on to them, however. She good-naturedly declined and told them she would see them tomorrow. The cloud of kids, under gentle pressure from the volunteers, drifted to the stairs, their motion mostly random but with enough of a coherent component to produce slow progress. Gwendolyn was in no hurry to go to her lonely sponsored volunteer dorm, and she would have lollygagged, but she could see Gloria and Tammy's job would be easier if she left. So she said goodnight to the children, a several minute process as hugs were exchanged—not just between Gwendolyn and each child, but between many pairs of the children in that less-than-hurried way children sometimes have at bedtime.

Walking along in the early dark, Gwendolyn had a shifting mosaic of feelings as she recounted the day in her mind. She was thrilled by spending the day with the children. Despondent that Alitisha left. Excited by proximity to her hero Clif Rockington. Perplexed and troubled by the spectacle of the senator and Fink, and Sarah too, in the strange photo session. And how could somebody like Clif Rockington stand by so callously? *Wait. I think he went outside before they started filming with the babies. That's it. He didn't know. He would have put an end to all that.* Gwendolyn had never warmed up to Fink, but she thought he seemed unusually cold today with the babies, almost inhuman. Maybe it was the stress of hosting the important visitors; anyone could see that was more of a burden for Fink than it would be for Dr. Bok—he lived for that sort of thing, whereas interacting with people was something Fink probably detested.

As she put distance between herself and the schoolhouse, between herself and the day's events, one emotion dominated: Alitisha's departure depressed her. While she recognized a quarantine gladness for Alitisha's relief from what the girl must have perceived as a shrinking prison, that was an intellectual phenomenon; it did nothing to help Gwendolyn cope with the pain of losing her best friend. She went back to the sponsored volunteers' area sullenly. She had eaten only a few scraps with the children, but she was not hungry. She talked to nobody, an activity that was developing into a habit, and she read more of *Uncle Tom's Cabin*, which left her mood low and her psyche exhausted.

Gwendolyn slept with Pyratticus Julius that night in a fitful slumber. Her subconscious discarded the salutary psychic effects of working with the happy children. Her dreams turned dark, unleashing the crushing force of losing Alitisha's companionship. She woke up several times through the long night, thinking of Alitisha or, implausible as it was, she believed she had heard some of the children crying and screaming in terror. Eventually she slept undisturbed until a time before the sun rose over the dirtpile and attained her window. She woke up with a drained and neutral mind, not happy, not sad. She was very hungry. She cleaned up for the day and stowed Pyratticus Julius, who had culminated the night on the floor beside her bed. As it became light, she had a quick breakfast in the lounge. The other sponsored volunteers were sleeping, and she was glad to avoid exchanging trivial niceties. Finishing her breakfast, she remembered she had not really been directed to go back to the nursery; she had no job assignment. She resolved to find Sarah Greenwater and demand at least a quasi-permanent place with the children.

She went to the administration building. She got inside and did not find Sarah there; in fact she did not see anybody. She walked around the mission, stopping in the buildings and quietly looking for Sarah. Though it was early, many buildings in the place were alive with activity; trucks were pulling out from the factories, and people were walking along the paths.

Gwendolyn did not ask anyone where Sarah was. She walked along the whole mission, forcing herself not to approach the door of the nursery schoolhouse; she did not want appear there uninvited, and she was quite sure she would be able to wangle an assignment there as soon as she could find Sarah. After walking most of the way to the power plant, winding around, peeking in buildings and looking down paths without success, she doubled back along a slight variation of the same itinerary. By the time she came even with the nursery, she had lost her prior resolve to stay out. She was drawn to the place like everyone is drawn to chocolate. She entered and found the children already at work practicing writing letters with crayons. Her entrance sparked an uproar as three or four of the older boys and girls ran to her and grabbed her around the legs; the others giggled in place. Dorothy invited Gwendolyn to stay all morning and help with the lunchtime activities, which she did. She enjoyed the long morning with the children, participated in lunch, then excused herself to find Sarah.

She went back to Sarah's office and found the woman talking to Sandy. Sarah was at her paper-covered desk, and Sandy was sitting on its edge, legs crossed. They looked like sisters relaxing cozily, having a cup of coffee together. The ladies noticed the newcomer and almost simultaneously smiled at her. Gwendolyn sat down in the unused chair against the wall. Sandy stood up and walked over and dropped into the adjoining chair. She put her elbow on her leg and her chin on her fist, and looked at Gwendolyn with streaming patience.

Sarah said, "Hello, Gwendolyn. Did you enjoy working with the kids yesterday?" Gwendolyn, distracted by Sandy, blinked, looked over to Sarah and answered after a bit of a pause, "I loved it. They're wonderful. Kind of a weird day over there, I guess, yesterday." Sandy looked confused, and Sarah smiled thinly. "I want to go back. I want to be staying with them overnight. I can help those kids."

Sandy listened quietly, turned her slow eyes to Sarah, screwed her lips slightly, and moved her eyebrows as though to say, 'you see?' Sarah nodded surreptitiously and took a sip of her coffee. She was not surprised by the request. In fact, she and Sandy had just been talking about it, predicting it. Sandy looked back at Gwendolyn. All was silent as the girl looked back and forth between the sisters.

Sandy said, "You feel it would realize what you came here for." Gwendolyn nodded. "You want to help people," Sandy's eyes and her own nod captured Gwendolyn, who continued moving her head in phase with Sandy's, looking attentively at her eyes. "Yesterday was the first time you really believed that you were helping."

"Yes. Yes," Gwendolyn said, eyebrows raising. She broke her gaze and looked at Sarah, her head bobbing more emphatically.

Silence.

Sarah stood and came around her desk. She put her arm around Gwendolyn's shoulders and said, "Of course. You've seen other positions, you've scrubbed floors. This is what you want, and this can be your position here." She smiled an understanding and genuinely friendly smile.

Gwendolyn said through her watery eyes, "Little Jojo is such a darling. He is so big, and still so patient, helping us with the little ones." She laughed, "For five minutes at a time. And that biggest, fattest boy! While we were all over watching the senator, he built a tower of blocks with a procession of dinosaurs climbing it." She dabbed her eyes, grinning as she remembered. "And Kaliki, with those huge eyes! Well, you saw her when they were taking pictures. Hey, what was all that about? That was horrible. How did Clif Rockington get here?"

The boundary around Sarah's eyes bounced like a cat hit with a flash of light. Her expression dropped slightly, but she kept her genial smile frozen in place. She glanced quickly at Sandy. Sandy had heard a movie star was there yesterday, but did not know any more details.

Sarah blinked once or twice and looked down. She guided Gwendolyn toward the office door and said, "Oh, that? Just some international relations Dr. Bok arranged. He usually hosts those things himself but got held up getting here. It all went very well and should help us quite a bit with the American and European donations."

Gwendolyn was confused. She was being led down the hall now. "It sounded like the senator mostly just pitched things for his Vermont election. And all that crying and resistance from the babies? What was that?"

"Oh, he did that too. But they can rearrange and edit it. Those writers wrote it very carefully. It will be sliced and diced and that senator will not just be a politician running for reelection but also an important United States government representative presenting our project to the public on two or three continents. This sort of thing can work wonders." The two progressed down the hall toward the exit.

Gwendolyn supposed it was true; it made sense. She had heard the words about the man donating some of his campaign funds to the mission. "But why did…"

Now they were at the building's door. Sarah interrupted, "As for your work assignment, we'll arrange the ongoing details later. For now, go there today after dinner time and you plan to stay overnight with the children. We'll fix up a real schedule later. I'll work it all out with Dorothy and Gloria."

She opened the door, and the hand on the small of Gwendolyn's back urged her forward.

Gwendolyn dabbed at her eyes again as she stopped, turned and hugged Sarah, then departed. Sarah watched after Gwendolyn and turned back after a long delay, walking with her eyes on the ground. Sandy, who had been watching from the office door, looked at Sarah questioningly as she passed by and entered the office. Sarah shook her head, "Nothing. Nothing at all, really. I should get back to work, though." She sat down at her deskful of papers. Her eyes darted up to Sandy and then back down. Sandy finished her tea in a gulp.

The sun warmed a happy face as Gwendolyn ambled through the compound in sweet anticipation of her new job, with no hurry to use up the day. She had no particular goal, so she walked along the main path; by the time she got close to the power plant and turned around she was almost skipping.

Small Good Things Must End

Must I leave these hugs?

H er relaxed timetable did not last very long. Thoughts of Alitisha moving away from her on the airplane crept into Gwendolyn's mind, and no matter how she tried to banish them, they kept returning. She could not wait till after dinner; she delayed as long as she was able—which was not very long. She came back to the schoolhouse, her toothbrush and things in a little tote bag just like Tammy had done the day before. She had only been gone for two hours. The children were playing, most on the floor, a few running around. Jojo, the little boy who was piloting the airplane yesterday when Gwendolyn arrived, was at the helm of a ship sailing across the carpet. The ship's engine pumped out chugging sounds through his mouth as the vehicle wove between all sorts of feet: adults, children in chairs, tables. The ship approached, passed and sometimes circled other children's toys on the rug, annoying their proprietors as Gwendolyn watched. She observed a girl as she slithered a long toy snake along the wall. Gwendolyn nodded to Dorothy and dropped her overnight bag in the little office. Dorothy suggested to the other two sponsored volunteers that they could leave if they wanted to, which they did. Julia remained.

As dinner approached, Tammy and Gloria arrived for the evening shift. Tammy helped Julia prepare the food while Gloria and Gwendolyn took care of the children, and Dorothy left quietly before the meal. Dinner went much as last night, with the distinction that instead of pasta they ate some kind of processed cheesy food. Gwendolyn ate the food and found it bland and unobjectionable. After dinner Julia left, the children tugging her hands and clothing, begging her to stay. She was laughing when she went out the door.

The little tribe immediately recovered from any trauma instilled by Julia's departure, and they turned back to Tammy and Gwendolyn.

Everyone settled down to some storytelling and other quiet after-dinner activities. There were no baths scheduled for today, so Gwendolyn had extra time to enjoy playing with the children before they had to go to bed. The evening passed pleasantly. Bedtime cleanup went easily; the children cooperated as everybody's teeth were brushed and their fingers lathered with soap. While Tammy and Gloria gave the smallest babies their bottles, Gwendolyn led the others upstairs in a happy gaggle. She tucked each one into bed, starting with the youngest, all the while followed by those yet free. It was still daylight, and the room was not really dark, so the process was a bit like putting a bunch of frogs on individual lily pads with the intent of instituting order. At the end of the task, each youngster was sitting up in bed to watch Gwendolyn. There was conversation and laughing as the kids tested the new supervisor, asking for delays, requesting stories and so forth. They achieved a victory of sorts—eventually Gwendolyn agreed to tell a story.

Like children everywhere, these youngsters were less than fully honest about their intentions, and they engaged in deception and gambits causing various delays, with complexity correlated with the age of the perpetrator. There were wrinkles in sheets. Children were too hot. Too cold. Some were thirsty. Some had a pain or a worry. A few just said they didn't want Gwendolyn to leave. She did not really mind, and at some level the children knew it, despite her seemingly harsh admonitions. In truth she was having as much fun as the children, forgetting the godforsaken place called Swazizibia. And forgetting bedtime deadlines.

Gloria came into the dormitory entrance with the first of the infants, intending to put him down for the night. She was surprised and cross that Gwendolyn had not settled the older children. She chastised her strongly for the delays, and Gwendolyn had no choice but to break her promise of reading the story. Several of the most spirited leaders of the delaying efforts ended the day feeling genuinely cheated on that score, but with Gloria's strong insistence and watchful eye, Gwendolyn got them all settled quickly, at least nominally.

The women took the baby back downstairs and killed time with Tammy for a little while as the older children quieted down. After a while the three took the babies up into their beds. As she left the dormitory, Gwendolyn could see that the infants, who were so carefully placed down for the night, had stood up in their cribs. The older children were in their beds, at least in a transitory, perhaps only statistical sense.

The three workers spent a little time downstairs with mild cleanup and organizational chores, exchanging small talk as they worked. Gloria left, and Gwendolyn got to know Tammy a bit that evening. The girl was from Chicago, and she was here after finishing a two-year degree in child development. She planned to go back home and become a teacher. Tammy and Gwendolyn played a few games of checkers before retiring. During their games they heard an occasional set of feet running around upstairs, and they heard tiny voices a few times. But they did not intercede, and things settled down on their own.

When Gwendolyn was tired, she and Tammy formalized the sleeping arrangements. Gwendolyn would sleep upstairs with the children, and Tammy would unfold the cot stored in the office and sleep on it. Gwendolyn got herself ready and went upstairs to go to bed, and she found most of the children still awake, though everyone was in a bed and all footsteps had ceased as she climbed the stairs. She enforced quiet in the room, and over time the giggles and horsing around died down; the littlest ones had nothing to watch, so they lay down in their cribs and almost immediately fell asleep. Like water slowly rising and irregularly submerging things in a rocky pool, sleep slowly covered the dormitory as one child, then another winked off to slumber; there was no reason to believe Gwendolyn was the last to succumb.

Tammy was to sleep downstairs. The cot was supposed to be placed blocking the door to the dormitory's stairway, but it was more comfortable to set the bed up in the office. Whoever had that sleeping duty just slept there, making sure to awaken early enough to be up and about when Dorothy came in. Over the next few weeks Tammy and Gwendolyn would work almost identical schedules, and in the evenings they often passed the time playing checkers or another board game stored in the office. They adhered to the same sleeping arrangements, with Gwendolyn upstairs and Tammy downstairs.

These weeks were perfect from Gwendolyn's point of view. She worked at the schoolhouse every day during the day; often she was on an overnight shift as well. Dorothy worked every day, as did Julia, and there were always one or two other volunteers sharing the duties.

On some nights the older children were uneasy at bedtime, and Gwendolyn's heart reached out to them. They were afraid of some sort of unpredictable but ever-lurking ghost, which they said was coming to get them in the dark and take them back to its lair. Gwendolyn heard fragments of rumors about absent predecessors who fell victim to the spook. She reassured the youngsters that there was no monster; nothing was coming to hurt them. Sometimes she went through a ritual of looking under their beds and down the stairs to verify absence of the menace; on difficult nights she spent extra time settling the kids down with an impromptu story, and it usually worked. The boys and girls listened quietly as she made up tales of happy adventure, or stories about her pets in Vermont, or sometimes just almost-random sets of sentences. The children particularly liked anything with mice, Gwendolyn found. They had never seen a mouse and were delighted when she first randomly brought them into her performances; she assured the kids that they look exactly like those in all the storybooks downstairs. The babies would invariably begin these sessions standing in their cribs and end up asleep before the other children.

Gwendolyn spent almost all of her time at the schoolhouse. She went there every morning, whether she was scheduled to work the day shift or both shifts. On the days she was staying overnight, she usually took a little time off in the morning or the afternoon. She finished *Uncle Tom's Cabin* and spent many of her off-hours sitting in the outside air reading the old books from the sponsored volunteer lounge. She made no new friends in Alitisha's wake, though she nodded in a friendly way to lots of increasingly familiar faces.

She often walked by the cathedral and sometimes saw nuns, usually in pairs or larger groups, going through the front doors. They were a strange group, those nuns, similar in appearance, each dressed in black, their hair and bodies covered. They walked slowly, always with their hands clasped in prayer under their habits, almost giving the impression of extreme pregnancy. Whenever Gwendolyn passed one, the nun's dark face and eyes were down, and often her lips seemed to be mouthing prayers. She saw nuns only in the region of the cathedral and the cafeteria.

Sarah asked that Gwendolyn stop by her office every other day, and Gwendolyn complied. She came in the early afternoons, and whenever she visited they would have a low-key talk, with the girl updating the manager on her feelings and making myriad suggestions. Several times when Gwendolyn came by, Sandy Crittenden was visiting with Sarah and the three of them had a friendly conversation.

Sarah often, and perhaps increasingly over this time period, suggested Gwendolyn try other assignments. She tried several gentle tacks in this effort.

She pointed out that one can stagnate in one's own development by finding a niche, and reminded her that there was much valuable effort needed each day in simply doing laundry or preparing the rations of the nutritional concoction the patients eat. Gwendolyn did not disagree with any of this, but she did not see personal relevance, now that she was happy at her work.

Gwendolyn did not encounter Dr. Bok during these few weeks. A few times, in the hallway of Sarah's administration building or out among the grounds she espied Aloysius Fink or Dr. Phineas Boseau, but they were just peripheral presences in her world. Occasionally when she wandered in her off hours, if it was around midday, she would see Bertha Martha at her factory. She sometimes entered the building and said hello to the woman in the wheelchair. But Gwendolyn was actually relieved that Bertha Martha always seemed too busy to engage in extended conversation; she only approached the woman out of a strange mixture of feelings including pity and obligation, remembering that Bertha Martha had confided in her and tried to give her unsolicited, if probably flawed, advice. It was uncomfortable for Gwendolyn to be around the imperious invalid, and she generally enjoyed staying away from the Swede. *Why would the mission let someone like that come here?* The question was one she could not conceive an answer to.

Overall, on the time scale of days, Gwendolyn was basically happy. Alitisha receded into the distance, and Gwendolyn seemed to be healed from her friend's departure. After a week of working with the children, on a lark Gwendolyn even took advantage of some of the leisure activities offered by sponsored volunteers. She stopped by a yoga class once, but neither the physical effort nor the mental focus came easily, and she never went to another session. She went to a few art classes and engaged in pleasant diversion, painting flowers and trees and forests from memory or from the sample pictures.

Gwendolyn had hit her stride. She was farther from home than she had ever been on her own. She was doing something important for others. She was not communicating with her family except by way of old-fashioned handwritten letters, and those letters were never even launched from the mission until an airplane left. She received a couple of letters from her mother; the usual fond references one finds in such messages were present in each, accompanied by several forms of Winifred's opinion that Gwendolyn was wasting time.

One evening after work Gwendolyn found a note from Sarah at her room. It instructed her to come to her office the next day before going to work. She was scheduled to work overnight that next day, so she was not planning to go to the schoolhouse early, and the office visit would not be difficult to accommodate. So Gwendolyn skipped breakfast and went to Sarah's office early the next morning. The woman was already working, with several stacks of old-fashioned paper forms on her desk. She greeted Gwendolyn, gestured to a chair and offered her coffee, which Gwendolyn politely declined. Sarah said, "Well, let's get down to business. We've been thrilled with your work at the schoolhouse, but I need you to work at the clinic for a while. They're swamped. I'd like you to start today."

Gwendolyn felt as though she was struck in the solar plexus. She was caught off guard; somehow she had come to assume her entire tour of duty would be working with the children in the schoolhouse; she had even forgotten her commitment to go out into the camp and feed the patients soon. She said, "Why? Can't someone else do it? I've been doing so well with the children. Little Kaliki has learned so many songs. Nundo and even Jojo can bang out the alphabet backwards! They can write so many letters. You should see them. Please. What?"

Sarah told Gwendolyn a technical truth summing to half-truth, which, in plain English, was an untruth. "I understand your frustration. But right now we have a crush of patients in the clinic." She added a blatant falsehood, "And no, nobody else can do it. We need you there." The part she did not say was that they had artificially gone out to the camp, selected patients and transported them to the clinic—all to create the illusion of a crisis for Gwendolyn. It was Dr. Bok's idea.

Director Professor Dr. Florian Q. Bok had a busy fundraising and management schedule. He ran a famous charity organization. He visited five or six continents every year. He carefully planned and executed the most complicated financial transactions. The man attended countless receptions, often in his own honor, and received awards for his sacrifices and commitment to humanitarian good. He was no less busy than the head of a tiny country or a large international company. But from afar, the busy man kept himself apprised of one young girl's work situation and, to the extent possible, her mental state. The mission was an isolated place. Nobody in the mission had electronic contact with the outside world, with an exception. Florian Bok was in regular communication with Sarah and Aloysius Fink over a satellite connection that followed him wherever he traveled. The young and fragile relationship between his Wholesome Globe Project and the much larger Worldwide Transformative Foundation was too valuable for him to allow himself to be caught blindsided by some calamity with Gwendolyn's psyche, and so he exercised his satellite link to obtain regular updates on her situation.

Dr. Bok proposed the charade at the clinic in an effort to alleviate a problem Sarah had identified in conversations with an innocent Sandy Crittenden: as Gwendolyn worked at the schoolhouse, it became clear that she was becoming attached to the children, especially the older ones, as individual people. When Dr. Bok heard about this unexpected turn of events, it triggered a series of alarms in him.

There was a reason for the existence of this incongruous little nursery at the mission. Dr. Bok maintained a collection of attractive, healthy children at the ready for use in photo sessions and marketing promotions. His research had proven that many adults in the western world, on whose donations the mission relied, did not respond optimally to appeals picturing truly emaciated and sick-looking patients; Americans and Europeans often employ some psychological mechanism that attenuates impact of such images. Therefore it was untenable to staff photo shoots solely with inmates chosen on the fly from the camp proper. This process must be planned and kept under steady management. Dr. Bok typically ran two parallel fund raising campaigns: one with actually distressed children and adults, and the other with children that were not so disturbing to the audience.

From experiments, Dr. Bok knew that the ideal child for this latter campaign was between one and about six years old, and dressed in ragged native garb. It must be a beautiful specimen, captured in an unhappy but not really distressed state. The process he instituted—the schoolhouse with the crop of youngsters—was quite successful for its purpose.

Dr. Bok had found that as children grow older they consume too much attention and staff effort. Their natural curiosity and adventurous spirit, implicitly cultivated by the fine care they received as they grew through the nursery, became a liability that he was not willing to put up with; in discussions he often invoked the picture of teenagers running wild throughout the mission. Since their usefulness in their assigned occupation dropped off with age also, children were 'graduated' and moved out of the nursery between the ages of six and seven.

The problem Dr. Bok needed to solve right now was this: there was no doubt that Gwendolyn would be distraught over the graduations, which shared little with the connotation of the word in the western world. Graduation was one of Aloysius Fink's responsibilities. Though Fink appeared awkward and even clumsy, he was gifted and remarkably agile at working in the dark. Graduation happened in the nighttime, so quietly that even the volunteers sleeping adjacent to the distinguished child did not wake up. In the morning, the graduate was simply nowhere to be found. Graduation was complete.

Nobody talked much about it, but the impression encouraged in the volunteers was this: as children graduated, they were sent abroad to welcoming and prosperous homes. The fact that it was all done as nighttime deviltry was explained away by a gentle and friendly Dr. Bok as an act of compassion: the graduates were spared the anguish of saying goodbye to their friends and vice versa. Despite Dr. Bok's gifts and flair, this rationalization was never fully accepted by the volunteers and native workers. But they all found ways to put it out of their minds.

Due to Fink's slack attention to detail in the year before Gwendolyn came, the oldest children, Jojo and Nundo, were well over seven years old. Another little girl was now six and a half years old. Bok angrily pointed out that this situation should never have arisen; Fink should have taken care of things long before Gwendolyn even arrived at the mission. He growled, "If we had just pursued a paltry piece of proper prior planning, this pathetic prospect would have been prevented." Aloysius Fink was not an imaginative man, but even Fink could see Bok closing his eyes and squeezing the bridge of his nose under his glasses in frustration when they discussed this subject over their voice-only satellite link.

Gwendolyn could be expected to ask many troubling questions. Sarah felt that the best solution was to send the girl home, somehow declaring her work complete. Alternatively, she suggested stopping graduations during the girl's sojourn. Dr. Bok rejected both courses of action. Stopping graduations would not stop Gwendolyn from feeling a kinship with her little friends; she would certainly want to become pen pals with children she had come to love, even if they moved to comfortable beach houses in France. Sending her home early was unacceptable for the same reason, and also due to the importance of the Wholesome Globe Project's nascent relationship with the Worldwide Transformative Foundation.

Dr. Bok insisted that she had to be removed from personal contact with the youngsters. He decided to take a calculated risk. They would put distance between Gwendolyn and the children, in an attempt to weaken her bonds with them. With any luck, in a little time she would forget the individual youngsters; the whole situation would simplify. In the meantime there would be enforced separation.

He created a pretext to move Gwendolyn away: Fink would grab some number of patients from the camp and bring them into the clinic. Sarah would then claim that the staff there needed extra help. Gwendolyn would be put to work in the medical facility, safely away from the schoolhouse. This would provide a receptacle into which she could plug her need to contribute and exercise compassion; she could also share vicariously in the patients' suffering.

Now, anyone chosen at random from the camp, a place Gwendolyn had never seen though it was just over the dirtpile, would spark sympathy in Gwendolyn. In principle any patient would be able to get her attention. However, Dr. Bok instructed Fink and Sarah to be cautious. They should choose patients from among those closest to the camp's entrance gate. All must be adults whose conditions were not too very shocking.

Each nominee must be selected with an eye toward survivability, at least for a while. The intention was to gently transfer Gwendolyn away from babysitting, not to shock her sensibilities. It would not help the cause if patients started dropping dead in front of her. Also, Dr. Bok considered the extra effort Fink would have to exert in the event of patients dying on the mission side of the complex. Everything was set up to deal far more efficiently with the demise of patients out in the camp than with deaths back in the mission proper; Fink would have to work doubly hard transporting corpses and retrieving new patients to keep the clinic looking full. All in all, it was best to choose patients who would stay alive. Dr. Bok suggested that the bulk of them could be those with broken bones, which was a common affliction. Alternatively they could work with intact bones, dressing them as though they were broken; Gwendolyn would not know the difference.

Here in Sarah's office, as she faced the prospect of being separated from her children, Gwendolyn sat silently. She processed her shock. Sarah was saying that right now the clinic was brimming. "...every cot is full, and so many are on mats on the floor, Gwendolyn. The staff is working their fingers to the bone. We need you."

Once Gwendolyn began digesting the information, she saw that these people needed help and that the children could do without one volunteer for a while. *It would be selfish for me to turn away from them if they need help, just because I like working with the children. I came here to help people. And there is nothing—nothing worse than being selfish.* Her evaluation of the idea started thawing, prompting a melancholy warmth as she contemplated the new assignment in the medical facility. She acquiesced and asked Sarah for details: when to go, who to ask for, and so forth. Sarah supplied the information, and Gwendolyn left in an unidentifiable and shifting mood.

She returned to her room and sat with Pyratticus Julius for a few moments. In conversation with the fuzzy invertebrate she alternated between lamenting the loss of her old job and being positive about her new assignment. In a little while she got up and went out to her lounge. She ate a late breakfast alone, bringing Pyratticus Julius along as protection from the other sponsored volunteers. They all left her alone, her only obligations being polite nods and exchanges of 'good morning.'

At the appointed time Gwendolyn approached the clinic. She entered and stood by the door in the corner. She saw three regulars and a similar number of native women attending at least twenty suffering people in the beds. True to Sarah's word, there were another six or seven patients on the floor on mats. There was a line of large roll-up doors in the wall at the far end of the building. Outside was a loading dock like many of the buildings had. Two native men were standing and talking there, smoking old-fashioned cigarettes.

Just after Gwendolyn entered, one of the white women nodded to her without diverting her own activities. Nobody else seemed to notice her entrance. Gwendolyn was shocked at the condition of the patients—she had never seen anyone in such bad shape as any one of these emaciated people. Along with their horrible general condition, many of them had identifiable physical injuries. She quickly saw people with broken legs and several with broken arms. Two had bandages around their heads. Many patients were almost completely covered with sheets, so this initial inventory was tentative.

All the patients seemed ancient, though she knew that she could not judge their ages by appearance. They were all gaunt, with dry and wispy hair; gaping shadows served as eye sockets and cheek hollows. Their limbs were like sticks wrapped in leather—long, very long, and not tapered at all. From what she could see of their bodies, each was also shapeless. Most were wrapped in clean cloth. She saw no blood, which she counted as a blessing.

The white women were all straight volunteers she had seen before. They were among the older volunteers; all appeared to be around or above thirty. The volunteers and natives seemed busy working among the patients, checking things, assisting them to drink water and so forth.

"Looks like they need a lot of help." The soft voice from behind coincided with a hand placed gently on her shoulder. Startled, Gwendolyn turned and saw Sandy Crittenden's calm, lukewarm face. Gwendolyn looked over Sandy's shoulder and scanned the region outside, *Where did she come from? Who else is here?* then looked back at Sandy and nodded. Sandy said, "Quite a change from the little schoolhouse, no? Well, these people really need help too. I guess that's why we came to the mission." She gently stood, patting Gwendolyn's shoulder. Gwendolyn was confused. Sandy was a psychologist. Was Sandy pitching in, helping at the clinic in this current crush? "Sarah asked me to help here because they're overwhelmed. Just like you," Sandy's even voice answered Gwendolyn's unasked question. "So I guess today we'll be—"

Gwendolyn saw that Sandy sensed some disturbance in the clinic's atmosphere. Sandy's eyes sought the two native men at the far side. Gwendolyn's eyes followed. The men were completely still except for the minor activity of handling their cigarettes. As Sandy and Gwendolyn stood and watched, the men threw down their cigarettes and started walking along between the two rows of beds. Gwendolyn noticed that one was carrying something like a black blanket, rolled up or folded under one arm. The native women stopped their activity and watched silently as the men approached a cot along the wall across from Gwendolyn and Sandy. Nobody else in the building seemed to even notice the men's mission; one of the volunteers had swerved to avoid colliding with them without even breaking stride.

The men stopped at the cot. The one carrying the bundle dropped it and began to unfold it on the ground. Suddenly Sandy brushed by Gwendolyn and hustled over to the men. She talked and gestured to them in a blur of excitement. All the workers, white and black, save the woman who had nodded to Gwendolyn, stopped working to observe the activity. That volunteer woman quickly came over and joined in discussion with the others, alternately nodding and shaking her head. She glanced over to Gwendolyn a few times during the commotion. The patient in the cot was not disturbed by any of this; in fact, few patients paid any attention. Soon the discussion adjourned. The men folded up the blanket and took it back outside.

Sandy came back to Gwendolyn with the regular volunteer, introducing her as Sissy. Sissy said that she would be supervising the two of them on most of their shifts for the next few days. She said she would like to get to know Gwendolyn and hoped to have a less busy time to do so. She excused herself without giving any assignments to the newcomers, leaving Gwendolyn standing confusedly with Sandy.

Sandy suggested that they go to her office in the other building and talk for a few minutes, but Gwendolyn wanted to stay and help out. Sandy persisted, telling her that Sissy was not ready to give them assignments yet. She put her hand on the girl's shoulder again and gently guided her to turn around. Gwendolyn went along, and they started walking the path.

"We're going to be busy for a while," Sandy said. Gwendolyn did not answer. "They're so overwhelmed right now. She doesn't even have the time to tell us what to do."

Gwendolyn, after a pause, said, "What happened?"

"What happened?" Sandy looked a tad nervously at one of Gwendolyn's eyes, then the other. She repeated the motion in silence.

"Yes. Why do they have so many sick people right now? What happened?"

Sandy shrugged and raised her arms palm-up, then threw her arm back around Gwendolyn's shoulders as they walked.

"What are we going to do at your office?"

"Well, let's visit. We haven't seen each other much recently. Let's catch up."

Catch up? Gwendolyn wondered what world Sandy was living in. She stopped and looked at Sandy, who returned the stare with relaxed and actively vacant grey eyes. "I'm going back," she said as she spun Sandy's arm off her shoulder and launched herself back toward the clinic. Sandy was taken by surprise and had to run to catch up with her. She trotted alongside Gwendolyn, saying "She needs more time to figure out where to assign us. Relax. Let's go sit for a few minutes." She stumbled over a bump in the ground but recovered as they walked along briskly.

Gwendolyn was resolute. "Then I'll find someone who needs water, or a bandage that needs changed. I'm not going to talk, not going to sit around here. I've done that enough."

Sandy was flummoxed. She sprinted ahead and planted herself in front of Gwendolyn. "No," she said sharply, almost a shout. Gwendolyn stopped abruptly to avoid bumping her. She stepped back. "Sissy said we should go away and let them work. She'll tell us when she can give us our assignments."

Gwendolyn was confused, not having heard Sissy say that. What was going on here? "How will she know where to find us?" Sandy was caught off guard, and Gwendolyn decided to ignore her. She stepped around Sandy and continued on. "I'm going. You can come or not. Everything you just said means they need the help." Sandy followed behind, hopping and skipping to keep up.

They entered the building and reoccupied their positions from just a few minutes earlier. Gwendolyn noticed that the two native men must have had time to smoke another cigarette, as they were just approaching the same bed with the bundle. Sandy stood watching as well. She glanced over at Gwendolyn momentarily. The other workers including Sissy went about their work, dispersed among the patients, paying no attention to the men.

The men put down the black bundle and unfurled it on the floor by the patient's cot. They separated, and each took hold of one end of the patient's body, picking her up and placing her on the fabric. Her midsection settled first as the men lowered her. She offered no assistance or resistance. They arranged her legs together and folded her arms over her flat chest. Gwendolyn watched, too stunned to see what she was seeing. She gasped as they brought up flaps from the side and fastened them over the patient's entire body including her face. Nobody else seemed to take notice, but Gwendolyn and Sandy watched as the men, each holding one end, took the drooping black container away, leaving through the door where they did their smoking, and turned out of sight.

The men returned and resumed their loitering by the far door, lighting cigarettes and leaning against the wall. Gwendolyn noticed that Sandy's arm was slowly rubbing her back. "Let's go sit down," Sandy said, putting her arm around Gwendolyn's shoulders and again turning the girl around gently. Gwendolyn was shaken and stunned. She did not resist.

Silently, slowly, the two walked over to Sandy's office. They went into the office and sat down, Gwendolyn on a small sofa and Sandy in a chair.

Silence.

More silence. Sandy looked at Gwendolyn expectantly.

"Do you know what happened back there?" Sandy white-lied in an attempt to get Gwendolyn talking. Gwendolyn shrugged but nodded. Her eyes teared up. Sandy said, "How do you feel about that?" Gwendolyn's eyes flashed, then subsided. They glistened.

Silence.

Sandy sat looking at Gwendolyn. After a pause, Gwendolyn said, "I know people can die here. I know the mission can't save everyone." She cried. Sandy made no motion. Time went on. Between sobs Gwendolyn said,

"I just never saw it. I never really saw the patients, not really. The whole building. They're in such bad shape."

Silence. Quiet crying by Gwendolyn.

"Why did I never notice before? I've looked into buildings, that medical building, lots of times before. Whenever I've walked by and looked in I didn't notice it very full. I hardly even noticed the patients. I guess I never went inside, but the ones I saw didn't look that bad, not like today. I guess I thought that not very many people were sick here. I've been so blind. I was even inside there when I visited the mission with my father. It was pretty full then, but I just don't remember them looking so terrible. My memory is of a group of sick people, somehow basically happy and cared for. And not so horribly thin. Today they looked like ghosts just waiting to be rid of their dried leather carcasses—they look like they're dead but just don't know it yet… and now I find some are already!

"Omigod, omigod. Listen to me feeling sorry for myself." She put her head down, shaking, hand to her forehead. Suddenly she shuddered and her sobs escalated as she recalled the pejorative term so many volunteers privately used for the patients. It had flowed so smoothly from her own mind as a simple and obvious description. Sandy came over and sat with her, arm around her shoulder again, and remained speechless.

"What did I think?" Gwendolyn sniffed as she picked up her head. She wiped her eyes. "People are starving here. Did I really think I could come and draw pictures with little children and it would stop? Who am I? I can't do anything here. I'm not a doctor. Jesus Christ, I'm not Jesus, the guy the nuns think is able to feed the world with a couple loaves of bread. I'm nobody. Lady Gwendolyn Dressel-Meier from Vermont. From Stambridge. From thousands of miles away. From halfway around the world. I skip meals. I take cool showers. I try to go hungry, but I don't. I've never been hungry in my life. Not actually hungry. None of us have." She looked at Sandy, then down again.

Sandy looked out the door and thought for a moment. She had experienced the discomfort about eating well, just like everyone who arrives at the mission from the west. All, including Sandy, managed to put it out of their minds within days of arriving. The obvious surface-deep rationale each concocted individually was sufficient for most of them: in an airplane emergency situation, the mother is told to put on her own oxygen mask before helping her baby with his. Yes, the justification was practical. And for many it was enough, but it was not the most complete philosophical analysis of a genuinely difficult and complex problem, a problem to which there may be no truly satisfactory answer. Sandy, herself a psychological professional, was careful not to ponder the question too much. She tried to help Gwendolyn.

"Why do you think that is?" Sandy asked, moving closer to Gwendolyn.

"Because we have plenty to eat, while they're starving. Most of the sponsored volunteers walk away from way more Calories than our patients eat," came the pained, smart-alecky response.

"No. You know what I mean. I mean why do we have plenty to eat?"

Gwendolyn was in thrall to a twisted knot of emotions including guilt, anger at the world, loneliness and frustration. And in this conversation she felt a bit like she did whenever her father was trying to manipulate her words with the goal of controlling her thoughts.

"So we won't be jealous of Dr. Bok's dogs." Gwendolyn regretted the caustic outburst instantly.

Sandy showed no sign of being troubled by it. "Why do they give us enough food, Gwendolyn?" she repeated. Gwendolyn had never fully accepted the idea that she should be well fed while others were given measured dribbles of food paste and drops of vitamin-infused water. It cropped up in her mind occasionally and bothered her. The question is objectively very complex and difficult for anyone to resolve. However, Gwendolyn's mental discomfort over it had been far from alleviated by exposure to things like dogs eating steak at the mission.

"Alitisha was right. I'm going home. This is crazy. I'm not doing anything here." She wiped her eyes and folded her arms.

Sarah had appeared at the open door unseen by Gwendolyn. The last thing she wanted was for Gwendolyn to go home just after receiving a traumatic psychological injury. She came into the room and sat quietly in Sandy's original seat. She was starting to doubt Dr. Bok's gambit. He had apparently underestimated the risk of exposing Gwendolyn to actual death when she moved to the clinic.

Gwendolyn's eyes darted to Sarah and back to the floor as the older woman sat. Sandy said, "Do you really believe that? Think back a few days. Helping those children. Were you not doing anything? Really?"

"Nothing I couldn't do at home."

"Are these children in Vermont? Are children there hungry? Would it be the same?"

"Nobody's hungry in Vermont. Don't twist my words. I'm even not saying I would work in a preschool in Vermont. I'm saying..." Gwendolyn exhaled. "You know, I don't know what I'm saying. I don't know." She buried her face in Sandy's shoulder and sobbed.

Sarah was nervous. Had they taken the wrong approach with Gwendolyn? Shouldn't Dr. Bok have just delayed moving children out of the school while Gwendolyn was here—let her finish a few months in happiness and send her on her way with good memories? The girl's face ranged Sandy's upper torso as she continued to weep. After she stilled Sarah spoke. "I knew this would be difficult. Gwendolyn, honey, this is what we face. How many times have you thought how much you want to help people? This is what they need right now."

'This' was not what the patients needed right now. 'This' was what the mission administration needed right now. It was important that Gwendolyn return home with a good feeling about her stint at the mission. Dr. Bok had not been alarmed when Alitisha decided to go home; she was of no consequence. Right now, though, Dr. Bok, Sarah and Fink were united in their intention to make sure Gwendolyn was a happy participant here. Sandy was not in the inner circle; she was not playing mind games. Sarah had been watching Sandy talk to Gwendolyn with the feeling she was watching someone walk across a tightrope without knowing it.

Gwendolyn straightened up and dabbed at her eyes again. She folded her arms across her chest and threw one leg over the other. She asked Sarah, "How do I really help over there with my training? And anyway, what if someone else dies while I'm there?"

Sarah drew a breath and sat, worried. Sandy put one hand on each of Gwendolyn's shoulders, aligning the girl to face her, saying, "Yes. Some-body else may die while you're there. These people are in a very difficult situation. Some will if you stick around for any significant amount of time. Do you think you're helping them by running away? We know people are in trouble here. That's why we're all here. But is perfection too high a standard? Should we do nothing unless we're guaranteed things will come out perfectly? What if nobody made any effort, took chances? Would anyone be helped? Ever? Would this mission even be here?"

Sandy's efforts were genuine, not manipulative, and they were having some effect. Gwendolyn softened from the arms-folded fortress her body had become, and it was clear some trace of guilt was percolating through her subconscious. Sarah sensed how to use this guilt and broke in. "How can you leave those people in the clinic?" She looked down at the floor, shaking her head as one disgusted would do. Sandy was stunned. She looked up at her and back to Gwendolyn with wide eyes.

Gwendolyn precipitously stood up and said, "You're right. You gave me a job to do and I need to do it." She dabbed each eye. The older women were taken by surprise. Sandy and Sarah looked at each other and back. "I shouldn't let them down. I'm going to work now." Gwendolyn started toward the door.

"I won't make you do anything, Gwendolyn. You can go back to the schoolhouse if you really want to," Sarah said, gambling gratuitously as the girl was already leaving.

Sarah's manipulative words penetrated into Gwendolyn's conscience, but they did not seal the deal as intended. They ricocheted through the girl's psyche releasing pain and guilt everywhere. Gwendolyn suddenly exploded. She turned to face Sarah. "I'm going," she almost screamed. Sarah and Sandy felt the impact of the blast without having anticipated the sudden transformation in the girl. Alarmed, they sat leaning away from her as Gwendolyn's new presence asserted itself in the room. "I will go finish my work assignment," she told Sarah as she approached and leaned over the sitting woman. "You didn't say how long I am to work at the clinic, so let's make it a week. But after the next week I will be out in the camp itself. I'm going to distribute food and help people." She glanced to Sandy and back. "I'll still bandage broken bones if I find them, but I'll do it out there. I'm tired of nibbling around the edges here. I've heard too much about the camps." She paused, then with a dropped voice she said, "I'm not the one suffering. Do you understand?"

Sarah, flummoxed, looked at Sandy, who was equally nonplussed. "Oh, no, honey. You can't go out there. And you don't want to," she said, head turned toward Gwendolyn and eyes looking at Sandy, whose confused silence reflected no assistance back to her. Sandy had never been out to the camps; she had no personal drive to go there anymore. She had settled into seeing her purpose as helping the volunteers themselves. She had heard some pretty troubling descriptions of the camp and its inmates, but she could not instantaneously form an opinion regarding what she was witnessing right now. This was manifest in her lack of participation in the conversation.

"Then I'll go home. When is the next plane going to the capital? Alitisha was right. We can't really help here. And if we could, you don't want us to. My father was more right than he knew. He hates this place," she lied; all she knew was that her parents preferred she stay in America; in fact Kingman had come to believe Dr. Bok was a genius. "He was right. I shouldn't have come. But in all our conversations he never, ever conveyed to me that he understands anything at all about what this place is really like. He couldn't know. He hasn't been here, really. He only came here that once, and now I realize we never saw anything. I'm going out to the camps in a week or I am going home now."

Her resolution stunned Sarah and Sandy both. Sarah had an infinitesimal flash of wishing Aloysius Fink were here to back her up, but it passed quickly; the absurdity of Fink's particular set of interpersonal skills being helpful here was self-evident. But if Dr. Bok were here... that would be different. She wished he could be standing here employing his silver tongue and genial seduction to reorient the girl. She sat mute.

Sandy suggested, with real-time, unspoken consent from Sarah, that Gwendolyn not go back to work today. Rather, she should go to her room and think about things. She said Gwendolyn could come see her tomorrow in the morning after some reflection, and they would figure out the right thing together.

Gwendolyn wanted to help, she wanted to matter. But at this moment she had a hard time seeing how much help she would be in the clinic, assisting the half dozen people superintending the twenty-five patients. The eruption was sudden and, while based on her true feelings, it had blown off some steam and given her some relief. She assented to Sandy's suggestion. Gwendolyn committed herself to thinking about things in the meantime but warned Sarah that she meant what she said about going out into the camp. She departed, leaving Sarah and Sandy together.

The next day Gwendolyn came to see Sandy at the appointed time in the morning, and Sarah was there also. The more they talked about the prior day, the more Gwendolyn realized she may actually be helpful to the patients in the clinic. Maybe she was needed there; Sarah certainly seemed to think so.

Nobody mentioned it, and Gwendolyn was fully unaware of it, but the camp supplied plenty of opportunity to see death—in fact it was an unavoidable consequence of the confluence of the Swazizibian human circumstances, Dr. Florian Bok's insights, the advanced world's frame of mind, and the resultant careful design of the camp. Sarah knew it was best if that door never got opened by Gwendolyn, and so any delay was good. Almost all of the work in the actual camps was done by native workers; only a very few seasoned and trusted volunteers were ever sent there, excepting the single case of the emergency that had sent Alitisha and a few others out there for one day.

They conversed about Gwendolyn and the mission and the patients. Sarah and Sandy mostly facilitated Gwendolyn's stream of thought, occasionally attempting to block some alley they considered blind; each had reasons to classify some of these avenues as such—Sandy out of concern for Gwendolyn, and Sarah out of concern for the mission's relationship with the Worldwide Transformative Foundation. Gwendolyn was less emotional than yesterday, and her hard-edged commitment to dominate her destiny did not surface so belligerently as they talked. Gwendolyn and the two older women eventually agreed to focus on the next week. She would indeed work in the clinic all week. This matched her resolution from the prior day so far as it went but left unspecified where she would be after the week, as she did resist anything that pushed the one week limit. The meeting was not very confrontational overall.

Gwendolyn went to the clinic. She did not notice a minor difference in the patients: while she had spent time during the prior day alone in contemplation of her future, Aloysius Fink and Sarah had made an adjustment to the roster of patients in the clinic. They had 'kicked the tires' on the inmates with an eye to identifying the weakest. Then they gathered them for transport back to the camp, and Fink went out to the dustbowl with some workers. They placed the outgoing patients where they found room and chose replacements that Fink felt were stronger. They selected for an approximate statistical gender match to the abandoned patients, but other than that the only requirement was relative robustness.

In the clinic Gwendolyn found it difficult to be near patients in their distress, but she carried out her duties responsibly. Sissy made sure to keep her overtly busy. Gwendolyn helped feed patients; she cleaned them up and changed their bedding; other chores cropped up. She was not allowed to touch any of the temporary casts on patients' limbs.

Over the course of the entire week Gwendolyn saw nobody else die, but the number of patients dwindled to about half as individuals were discharged, being carried on stretchers and put on trucks. It was puzzling. It seemed the ones being discharged were not in better health than those remaining. Gwendolyn was aware that small numbers can make for misleading statistics, but it certainly seemed to her that those discharged were, if anything, in worse shape than the ones who were kept.

Gwendolyn asked if there was a more intensive-care clinic section, but Sissy told her they were being discharged when they were ready to be sent back to their places in the camp. It did not make obvious sense—some had broken bones and all were weak and sick, but Sissy assured Gwendolyn that looks can be deceiving, and these patients should go back; Aloysius Fink and Sarah Greenwater designated each one as they did their daily review of the status of each patient. Every time she saw someone loaded onto the truck, Gwendolyn was puzzled and subconsciously troubled, although her struggling conscious mind accepted that the decisions were made correctly. On one occasion she saw two patients loaded onto the bed of the truck; the second was placed with her body overlapping the first in a way that must have been painful, but the offended party continued sleeping through it all. Had Gwendolyn not just seen and interacted with that bottom patient three hours prior, she would have sworn he was dead on the truck.

By late in the week the number of patients was down to around ten—under half of what the week started with. Most of the patients seemed fairly stable, if still in bad shape. They had been eating their rations with minimal assistance, and Gwendolyn had been giving most of them a mixture she had made under instructions from Sissy and the others. It contained vitamins and some medicines; she did not know the details of its exact function, beyond knowing that vitamins are important and medicine is good. By late in the week she had gotten to know the names of some patients, and while none knew any English, she often communicated, even provoking smiles from some of them.

Sarah, and through her, Aloysius Fink and Dr. Bok, kept tabs on Gwendolyn's mood. They crossed their fingers regarding her intentions for the future and hoped for the best.

Whirlwind in Europe

How can I hope to understand this world?

N ear the end of the week she worked at the clinic, Gwendolyn was feeling like she was doing some good, and this pleased her. Sarah asked her to stay there and work for another week, saying the crisis would be under control by then. Gwendolyn was fairly comfortable in her work assignment and felt that if they were that close to victory she should stay. She agreed.

As she looked up while cleaning a bedpan for a patient in the early afternoon on the penultimate day of that next week, she was surprised to see Aloysius Fink and Sarah Greenwater standing there. Sarah had stopped in a few times, seemingly alternating with Sandy, but Fink had kept his distance. Each time Sarah came they exchanged pleasantries; with Sandy things usually evolved into an easy conversation of about fifteen minutes. Right now Fink dominated her field of view, lurking behind Sarah's shoulders. After a tip of her head to the visitors, Gwendolyn proceeded with the cleanup job, always a minor task due to the limited flow through the patients.

"I have some good news for you, Gwendolyn," Sarah smiled broadly. Gwendolyn was near to the end of assignment here, and she figured the news probably had something to do with talking her into another mission-side work detail—keeping her away from the dustbowl. Sarah turned to Fink and pointed to some old medical equipment in the corner, and he departed after exchanging a few syllables with her. Gwendolyn quietly finished her task then washed her hands. She ran one hand over her forehead pushing back her hair, glanced at Fink and stood looking expectantly at Sarah, with wet streaks showing up dark in her hair.

"You're going to Switzerland! You're going to see your family for a few days!" Sarah bounced onto her tiptoes like a schoolgirl. She seemed elated by this news for some reason. Gwendolyn was surprised, bemused. Gwendolyn's expression signaled a request for details, and her gaze lingered, frozen on Sarah. She was already unconsciously building reluctance to taking time away from her mission work for some kind of vacation. As she considered this incongruous piece of strange information, this trip, she thought about how she belonged here, and she reminded herself, for the first time in days, that she was very close to the time when she would be doing the real thing—working in the camp. Sarah's news puzzled her. *How in the world would Sarah know anything about my family?*

Across the room, she saw Aloysius Fink poke at the pile of old machinery and shake his head. He walked back as Sarah continued. "Your family will all be there. It's starting the day after tomorrow."

"?"

"Dr. Bok will be there too. Your father requested that we send you." Sarah was about two inches taller than Gwendolyn and eighteen inches away. She stood smiling hugely, head drooping over hands clasped in front of her chest, eyebrows at full mast, well clear of her vaporous grey eyes. Fink lurked off to the side. Gwendolyn stood confused, waiting. Sarah started to turn. "We should go call him now. He's waiting."

This was a bolt from the blue to Gwendolyn, on yet another level. Since arriving she had not so much as touched anything that served as a telephone. *They have phones here?*

"Let's go back to my office and call," Sarah said. Gwendolyn shook her hands, shedding the last few water drops. She looked over to her sans-bedpan patient, then picked up the container and brought it back to her. Sarah had started toward the door, followed by Aloysius Fink. She made hand signals to Gwendolyn's supervisor Sissy, pantomiming that she was taking Gwendolyn. Sissy responded with a "whatever" shrug, and Gwendolyn walked out after Sarah.

They went to Sarah's office, and Fink continued down the hall as the females turned in. Sarah opened a drawer and took out a satellite telephone, an odd thing that looked like a something out of an old movie: large and clunky, nowhere for images of any sort. Gwendolyn was amused as she watched Sarah manipulate the controls to place the call to Kingman in Switzerland. In a moment, he came on the line and said something Gwendolyn did not hear; she was busy being thrilled to hear the unconvincing electronic representation of her father's voice, a voice she had not heard for weeks. Sarah started the conversation with a few niceties, then progressed to, "Well, Dr. Dressel-Meier, you must talk to Gwendolyn. She's right here now."

"Daddy!" Gwendolyn excitedly spoke up.

"I'm here too, baby," her mother's tinny vocal representation joined the conversation. "We miss you so much. Are you ready to come home?" This led to a disputation between Kingman and Winifred, with some muffling-over of the remote microphone. The controversy settled down.

"She's just kidding, princess. How's things?"

Gwendolyn was flushed with emotions, her mind running a mile a minute. "I'm so busy here. They're worse than you think, the patients."

They were not worse than Kingman thought; Winifred had no opinion on the subject.

"We have a little schoolhouse for the young ones and I've been working in the clinic and I've scrubbed floors and worked in the food factory and…"

"Well, well, well," her father interrupted. "You can tell us all about it when you're up here in Switzerland. We should have plenty of time at the conference before the awards ceremony."

In her excitement over talking to her parents Gwendolyn had forgotten about the proposed trip. "What is all this about? What are you saying?"

"We want you to come to Zurich tomorrow, princess." She heard both parents' voices at the start of the sentence, and her father's at the end. "We're here right now," her mother's voice picked up the thread.

"Zurich? Why? What are you doing? What are you talking about? Daddy?"

"Well it's a few things. For one, and it's probably overdue, you've been elected to the Worldwide Transformative Foundation's board of directors. You're joining the rest of the family. And we're all in Zurich to participate in an important conference and accept an award for the Foundation, jointly with the Wholesome Globe Project—your mission! Florian Bok is here. He lives here in Zurich, you know. We're going to have our entire board of directors at the award ceremony. You'll fit right in."

"Board of directors? But I don't know anything. I never did anything. Weren't Hunter and Marshall older when they went on the board? Wait. And what is this award?"

"Honey," her mother's voice broke in. "You can't do anything about it. The whole board voted unanimously, and you're elected already. It's done. But you have to come here for the award presentation. Be happy, sweetie."

Kingman picked up. "You aren't going to start missing board meetings already are you, princess? But seriously, it's time for you to be with us. Someday you'll graduate, you know. You have to be ready to get on with things. Right now you're funded as a dependent. The thing to do is to get you on the board now and have you there for a few years before you finish school. It will let you build up a little nest egg." Sarah showed visible surprise that Kingman had simply stepped right into family financial business in her presence. She looked at Gwendolyn, who was listening, oblivious to any breach of propriety. Kingman continued "Besides, I need your input on the board. Time to shuck that security blanket of 'junior observer' at the meetings."

Kingman realized Gwendolyn was not of a mind to absorb adminis-trivia right now. He knew she had no idea why she could not just get some anonymous job like all the other sociology graduates and make her own way in the world. She did not see herself as different, did not think of herself as really affiliated with the Foundation. It was a problem he wanted to solve gradually, hence the promotion to board member. He was in new territory here; he never had this sort of trouble with Marshall and Hunter. They just glided through graduate school until they were tired of it, then sidled smoothly into their jobs at the Foundation. Neither of the boys ever gave a thought to building aqueducts or curing cancer or wiping runny noses. Gwendolyn was different.

Kingman shifted, "The award—it's the Sacrifice Against Poverty Award, from the organization Charity Coalescence of the World. It recog-nizes the Foundation and your mission down there as the most effective team fighting for the disadvantaged. In the world! The whole world! The Foundation is recognized as the senior partner, but we nominated ourselves in conjunction with the Wholesome Globe Project this year. I've been pursuing this award for years now, but your little mission down there is the game changer—we've been working on our angle together since I met Professor Bok." He next made an uncharacteristically stark admission—his own daughter Gwendolyn had never conceived that he could need anyone's help. "Without his creativity I would never have been so bold as we were in this year's application. We're redefining the concept of charity. You know, I don't think we could ever have won this alone, regardless of how much support we've sent to Charity Coalescence over the years. I should compliment you on fixating on that place." Kingman beamed through the phone.

The trip sounds like a big deal to him, important that I go. Gwendolyn was almost between assignments here. Maybe she should go. She missed her family. She had some consternation over walking away from the mission's patients, though. But wait. Why now, when she was working here? "Daddy, is this the Zurich thing you do every year? Why couldn't you take it next year instead?"

She heard a quiet chuckle at the other end of the phone. "Sweetie, it's not that simple. Yes. This is the Zurich meeting that I put together every year. People from all over the world come for it. But it's not a Foundation event really, it's a Charity Coalescence event. They're the sponsors, they're the ones who get the profits, they choose the winners. I'm on their board, but that's the extent of my influence on it. One vote. No, this is the year for me."

Winifred broke in. "I've picked out a few beautiful dresses for you to wear in the evenings, dear. And suits for the daytime conferences. The prime ministers of Sweden and Belgium will be here. And France, I think. And some more politicians, am I right? Oh yes—the UN Secretary General and quite a few famous people too. It will be a grand time."

Kingman broke in. "Influential people. From Hollywood, too. They're always here. We're getting more universities involved each year too. Athena Sterling Munghorn is coming." Gwendolyn did not place the name; it was the president of Stambridge, her own school. "And probably a few of the other presidents. Maybe you'll go to graduate school after all if one of them twists your arm. Anyway, sweetie, it'll be a good break for you. And like I said before, you're a board member. Your presence is required."

Gwendolyn felt dizzy. "But..." She looked at Sarah. Sarah was quietly nodding with a facile smile on her face.

"Florian Bok wants you here too. They can manage down there for a few days. Sarah's made all the arrangements. Besides, Marshall says he owes you a dutch-rub or something." Gwendolyn heard a chuckle in the background.

" " was all Gwendolyn could muster.

Sarah respected the pause, then spoke up. "I think you can count on her. We'll be there, won't we Gwendolyn?" Gwendolyn received the new surprise while still dizzily balanced on the pedestal of astonishment built over the past fifteen minutes: Sarah would be going along too?! She pulled her head back a bit and nodded, not sure of anything.

Kingman's voice spoke up and answered the silence, "It's done then. We'll see you tomorrow at the airport. Sarah's fixing thing up down there. Love you, sweetie."

"Love you, honey," Winifred added.

"Me too, Daddy. Mother." Her face was confused as she said, looking at Sarah, "I guess we go tomorrow?"

Sarah smiled understandingly in light of the girl's confusion. Gwendolyn was still drifting in bewildered contemplation when she heard Sarah say they must leave today. "We take off in about an hour." Before Gwendolyn could even speak, Sarah told her that Mr. Fink and the others would arrange to take care of all their work assignments here at the mission. The pilot had been notified, and Sarah said he was undoubtedly preparing and fueling the airplane; what she did not add, and did not know, was that he was also sobering up. Aloysius Fink had found him in the company of some off-duty native workers, and they had been having a sort of afternoon party. Sarah said she needed to go get herself ready, and she told Gwendolyn to meet her at the front building in sixty minutes.

Gwendolyn walked quickly but light-headedly back to her room. Luckily most of her clothes were clean. She gripped herself and quickly showered, then put a few handfuls of clothes in her bag. She pulled out a box she kept under the bed with her small personal things, grabbed an item or two and replaced the box. She put her toiletries in her bag and then, not believing she needed it, she nonetheless went and picked up a tattered paperback book of mystery stories from the lounge and stuck it in her luggage. She patted Pyratticus Julius on the head and placed him on the shelf where he could look out the window and watch the door to the room for a few days. She offered him some words of consolation over their parting, then scampered over to meet Sarah for the airplane ride.

Their pilot was Gwendolyn's friend Aidan. Today he was not very chatty. The trip to the capital went uneventfully, and the women arrived in the capital in the late evening. Tonight they were staying in the busiest hotel in town; it was probably the city's only hotel, in the western understanding of the word. Gwendolyn and Sarah stayed together in an uninspiring room of minimal cleanliness and old plumbing. Their shared bed was not nearly as comfortable as those at the mission, and sleep quality was not enhanced by both women's unconscious suspicion that it may be unsanitary. Though small, the hotel was a center of commerce in town and apparently the focus of nightlife. Their room was on the ground floor, as the building had no second or third storey. The women were disturbed by people and traffic on the street outside, as well as people and traffic in the bar down the hall. Well into the night they heard raucous laughter, seemingly including that of their pilot. All night long they were sporadically woken by cheerful noises from other rooms in all directions.

They managed to get a sampling of sleep in patches throughout the night. As it turned out, they could have taken turns with the bed without losing sleep, since their periods of slumber followed the phase of their tossing and turning, activities in which they seemed to alternate. The next morning, when the hotel staff woke them before dawn, was the first time they noticed silence from the pilot's room next door. Gwendolyn sat up sleepily and rubbed her eyes. *I'm glad he won't be flying us today.* They went to the airport for their early flight. They flew to Cairo, boarded the Foundation's jet and flew to Zurich, arriving in the afternoon, exhausted.

Kingman met them as they cleared customs in Switzerland. They boarded his limousine, and as they waited for their luggage to be loaded, he told Gwendolyn of the evening's plans: the family was to have a nice dinner in a tiny town in the Alsatian region of France. They would visit and conduct a bit of Foundation business over dinner, then return to Zurich late that night, or more likely, in the wee hours.

"But I'm exhausted, Daddy," Gwendolyn protested.

"Sweetie, I understand. But your mother misses you so much. She wants to have a nice family evening. If you're really tired you can sleep on the drive over."

Gwendolyn calculated the likelihood of that, with the five of them in the limo, but she resigned herself to an exhausting evening after a tiring trip in the car following a wearying plane ride subsequent to a semi-sleepless night. Awkwardly, since it was not her own party, she turned to Sarah and asked if she would like to come along. Sarah declined, saying she, too, was tired and would rather have dinner at the hotel and go to bed early.

When they got to the hotel, Kingman gave Gwendolyn notice that they would be leaving in an hour. He gave her a key, and she went up to her suite for a quick shower. She dressed and sat down to relax on her balcony overlooking the attractive town with half an hour to spare. The next thing she knew, there was a knock at her door followed immediately by a noise at the lock. Winifred rushed into the room, arms spread as Gwendolyn's eyes opened from a very deep sleep. The girl groggily turned toward the sound and struggled to remember where she was as the oncoming form enlarged in her field of view. She recognized her mother just as they made contact. "Gwendolyn, honey. I've missed you so, so much. You look terrible. Here, take some of this." She sprayed some perfume on Gwendolyn's cheeks as she hugged them with her own cheeks, her lips making kissy noises into the atmosphere.

Gwendolyn coughed. She coughed again over her mother's other shoulder and turned her head back just in time to have another spray of perfume hit her nose and mouth. She struggled free, sputtering, and ran to the bathroom to get a glass of water. Hacking and coughing, she rinsed her mouth repeatedly. As her breathing stabilized she dabbed at her watering eyes with a towel. She composed herself and stepped back out to see her mother gaping. Winifred uttered a lie and a truth, "I'm sorry honey. I just wanted to help you freshen up."

They hugged. Gwendolyn was not in a condition to talk yet. They went downstairs, the mother chatting and the daughter occasionally choking ostensible agreement. Gwendolyn was fully recovered by the time they emerged from the building and found the men waiting at the limousine. Kingman nodded to the chauffeur, and they all climbed into the vehicle. Marshall and Hunter engaged Gwendolyn in friendly, meaningless teasing as they pulled away. Drinks were poured, and the jovial group headed for France. Gwendolyn was happy to be with her family but felt like an outsider somehow—disconnected, unanchored, less gleeful than the rest of them. Only when talking to Kingman about the Foundation's impending award did she find herself engaged, but even then every mention of Dr. Bok inexplicably seemed to weaken her focus, to incrementally distance her from the conversation.

About an hour into the trip Kingman forbade the boys to mix any more drinks, and with good reason. Both Hunter and Marshall soon drifted down into sleep as the limousine continued on its short international voyage.

It was dark when they arrived at the tiny town in France. The cozy tableau was striking in the moonlight—narrow streets bordered by brick buildings with dark sloped roofs. The scene was a study in absolute silvery stillness. The buildings in the village were attractively colored shades of tan, white and beige, though there was no way to know it at this hour. Gentle off-amber light wafted smoothly out into the silence through small, thick-glazed windows in walls abutting the street. This glow was the only sign of electricity, the only indication of life in the dark and silent village. The hazy spots of illumination gave a warm feel to the scene, signaling safety and contentment within the abodes and permeating the air outside. As for architecture, every building in the place could have been a domicile. Most were in fact homes placed complacently along the promenade with larger buildings, or situated on the small alleys feeding the avenue. The street itself, about five blocks' worth, was cobblestone and gravel. Gwendolyn noticed there was not a sign in the whole village. Not an advertisement, not a street name, not a name over a doorway. Even the picturesque little mailboxes gave the postman no hint as to their owners' names or coordinates.

The chauffeur maneuvered along the main street, avoiding resting carts, bicycles and a few cars. He parked the limousine in front of the largest, though not very large, building; it had several windows sharing the place's light with the night outside. Gwendolyn's attention returned to the vehicle as she heard Kingman and Winifred wake her brothers. The boys sat up instantly as though they had been listening for the notice while they slept. They straightened hair and clothing with their fingers and seamlessly exited the vehicle; this seemed a familiar ritual. By the time they were standing waiting for their mother's emergence they looked perfectly groomed and composed. Gwendolyn climbed onto the street as the driver helped Winifred out. Soon the whole family stood beside the fine restaurant. Kingman nodded to the chauffeur who melted away as the family entered the establishment.

At the start of pre-dinner drinks Kingman made sure to propose some trivial Foundation business, thus satisfying a requirement in the organization's by-laws for board of directors meetings. It was Gwendolyn's first voting presence, and she abstained on all the items despite pressure from her parents for the usual unanimity. In fact, her behavior threw a hitch into the cadence of Kingman's familiar and integral 'All in favor, all opposed, the motion is carried' pronouncements on the agenda items. She was not opposed to any of the measures, but she found them so trivial she just couldn't weigh in on them—she could not believe that they were sitting in a dinner meeting in France, voting on the color (white, as always) of the limousines being leased next year. Ratifying another year's extension of the contract with the company that cleans the New York offices. Agreeing to continue with the landscapers that trim the lawn in Vermont. *Six months ago I would have thought nothing of going along with all this. Have I never noticed the types of things they vote on?* There was some discussion of the next board meeting's location; Marshall proposed Bermuda again, but Hunter advocated Hawaii. The board, without Gwendolyn's vote, decided to place the matter under Kingman's sole discretion. This was the usual decision whenever there was dissent, an occasion that only occurred between the brothers, and one that never happened over anything objectively important.

After the formal portion of the meeting, the family enjoyed their appetizers and soup together with wine pre-arranged by Kingman. Gwendolyn had not realized how hungry she was before she smelled the stuffed mushrooms. She paced herself for the evening, however, eating only one. Then the soup came out, and Gwendolyn reveled slowly in the hot, nutritious liquid. As she approached the achievement of an empty soup bowl she heard her mother's voice die down and pause. Then came the rebuke, "Gwendolyn, have you heard a word I've been saying?"

She realized she had been treating the family conversation as a comfortable background decoration like the curtains and chandeliers, like the pleasant incomprehensible hum of the French clientele enjoying their meals. "Deer in the headlights, eh?" Hunter said. The three men laughed, visibly annoying Winifred and alarming Gwendolyn. She flushed, but then relaxed and joined in the laughter. Winifred's stone face broke, and she showed some softness too, reaching over and touching the girl's wrist, so happy was she to have the family together. Marshall proposed a toast to the family, and they all joined in, Gwendolyn bypassing her untouched wine and raising her bubbling water. The meal continued with a serving of fish, a fresh, long lost delicacy that thrilled Gwendolyn's palate. She was careful to engage in conversation during the new course and that of the sorbet that followed. Finishing the cold treat, she had an odd mixture of feelings; she felt sated with the dinner, and she reveled in the family's loving atmosphere. Nonetheless, she could not help thinking how many meals tonight's meeting would represent back in Swazizibia, a thought from which she had somehow been spared so far.

Soon the entrée came: huge, sizzling plates of filet smothered in mushrooms and some sort of French sauce were placed in front of each family member as the wine was removed and replaced with another variety. Gwendolyn, being full already, felt uneasy and a bit queasy. Then the aroma of the fine meal triggered memory of the last time she had seen a steak of such quality—Colonel and Bourbon were pawing it, dragging it through the dust at the mission and ripping it off the bone. She looked at the beautiful pewter serving dishes and thought of the beautiful pewter serving dish in Sarah's hand, still sizzling with juices as the brutes followed their atavistic programming in the presence of the meat. Suddenly she was overcome as metallic ringing waves seized her mouth, ears and throat. Her stomach gulped and heaved, and her mouth watered profusely. She fought quietly as her carnivorous brothers and Kingman leisurely began to engage their steaks. She glanced at Winifred, who was stopped, holding her knife and fork, looking at her quizzically.

Gwendolyn burst to her feet and ran from the table. She went to the toilet and threw up a few times. Winifred followed, arriving during an active phase of her vomiting. As Gwendolyn obeyed the demands of her own situation, Winifred peppered her with questions and offers of help. Gwendolyn completed her involuntary chores, then stood up and rinsed her mouth with water. In answer to whatever her mother had asked and offered, Gwendolyn said, "Mother, I just ate too much too fast."

"Are you sick, honey?"

"Not really, just tired. And definitely not hungry anymore."

Her mother hugged her. They walked back to the dining room. The men, engaged in conversation and possibly not having noticed the ladies' absence, paused and looked at them as they occupied their seats. Kingman's expression seemed to ask if everything was all right. Winifred nodded and made some gesture with her hand instructing him to continue, so he glanced at Gwendolyn, then turned back to the boys. They continued discussing the world's best male tennis players.

Gwendolyn sat as aloof as possible for the rest of the meal, trying not to look at the food. She counted courses, hoping that the seventh would be the last, but not really sure of it. Finally the dishes were cleared and she could relax. As he drank his fourth or fifth glass of wine, Kingman dropped his normal controlled façade. He boasted that he would be giving a blockbuster speech to the assembly in a few days. None at the table doubted it. Winifred lifted her Drambuie in salute.

To Gwendolyn's chagrin, they were just in a pause before dessert, which arrived well after midnight, and which the rest of the family dispatched with varying degrees of enthusiasm. Kingman and the boys bit in heartily, and Winifred nibbled at hers. Finally, after dinner, after after-dinner drinks, the meeting adjourned, and the family boarded the limousine for the drive back to Switzerland. Gwendolyn verged on sleep a few times during the trip, but Winifred somehow brought her into conversation every time she started to nod off. The males slept contentedly in their seats.

They arrived at the hotel in Zurich before three o'clock. Outside the elevator on the top floor, they stood talking about nothing before retiring to their suites. Gwendolyn, caught passively in the polite conversation, could not help noticing the fine sconces and light fixtures along the halls, the velvet wall coverings and the plush carpets—all this had escaped her perception earlier. Kingman had unconsciously positioned himself in profile to an ornately framed mirror that subsequently distracted him; he could not help admiring his view of the patriarch of the fine family out of the corner of his eye. Objectively, even in the middle of the night the man did look striking in his tailored suit and neatly groomed beard, everything capped off with his expensive IDIC tie tack, his watch glistening below the chandeliers.

As the family stood they heard a disturbance in the hallway. It startled them and surprised Gwendolyn since Kingman had reserved the entire top floor and, forgetting about Sarah, she thought they were all accounted for in the standing group. The commotion grew louder, and everyone in the family looked in its direction, though the view was blocked from where they stood. The banging continued, and loud panting breaths came forth from the hallway. *Panting!?*

All at once in a cacophony of ten pounding feet, Bourbon and Colonel nosed around the corner excitedly, dragging Dr. Florian Q. Bok, dressed in a warm-up suit, behind at an awkward trot! Here in the middle of the night the animals looked as fit and sleek as ever; ignoring their undisciplined demeanor, it almost seemed appropriate that the majestic beasts were in the penthouse in the most expensive hotel in Switzerland. Dr. Bok was his normal cheerful self; he seemed more lively than any flabby old athlete embarking on a middle-of-the-night jog could possibly be. As he spotted the group he let out a raucous laugh, greeting Kingman with, "Congratulations, laureate! Are you ready for the big speech? It's almost time, you know." He smiled jovially before he remembered to tighten the leashes on the excited animals, who had almost arrived at the shiny and expensive dress of a horrified Winifred. "Sarah pleaded with me to get them out for just a little while, so I thought I'd show them downtown Zurich at nighttime. Care to join me, anyone?"

Bok's suggestion provoked most of the group to break for their suites. Kingman grabbed Colonel's leash and, apparently forgetting it was going on three o'clock in the morning, dropped to talk to the massive animal, saying, "Of course I'll come. We have a few things to talk about, don't we, pup?" The family dispersed as an energetic Kingman and an indefatigable Dr. Florian Bok disappeared into the elevator.

As they walked in opposite directions, Winifred turned to Gwendolyn and shouted, "I've set us up for a Swedish massage. We'll go to the spa straight after breakfast tomorrow."

"Mother, please. I don't need a massage." An exhausted Gwendolyn mumbled as she continued walking, shoulders curled forward in a slump. "I'm going to the work sessions tomorrow."

Winifred reacted suddenly. She turned around and walked speedily toward her daughter, saying, "Oh nonsense." Hearing the determined footsteps and voice, Gwendolyn turned to face her oncoming mother. Winifred asserted herself, nervously fingering her gold engraved 'IDIC' necklace as she arrived. "I told you, you look horrible. Look at what happened at dinner. I knew we shouldn't have allowed you to go to Africa. You need to relax and get away from some of this stress. You're skinny as a rail, and I knew you would be. I've cried for you in Africa all this time, knowing you're not eating right, wondering if you can sleep. Tonight I saw that my worst fears have come true. You are destroying yourself, and you won't let me stop it." Tears were starting to distort the expensive makeup around her eyes. "Do this for me if you won't do it for yourself. I can't stand the thought of you out there. Let me see you relaxing for once. Acting like a lady. Being my daughter."

There was little chance of convincing Gwendolyn that it was the right thing to do, the morally correct way to spend her time, but if anything had a chance of changing her decision, that thing was appealing to her sense of pity. Gwendolyn regretted stressing her mother so, and she changed her mind. "Okay mother. I'll try it. It'll be fun. I've never had a massage."

"I'll see you at breakfast. You're doing the right thing." They kissed the air over each other's shoulder and exchanged a quick hug.

The next morning, Kingman and Florian Bok were long gone—off to work sessions, or networking, or whatever they do at these conferences— before the ladies and the younger men awoke. At breakfast Winifred was happy to play the hostess to her daughter in this foreign setting. She quietly pointed out a prime minister breakfasting in the room. Gwendolyn glanced at the anonymous-looking bald man dutifully but did not register any real impressions.

A few moments after they sat down, Victoria Hull appeared at the doorway. She walked across the room, waving greetings to several tables, including that of the aforementioned prime minister. Gwendolyn recognized her as familiar but could not place her face. She watched as Victoria approached her table and was shocked to see the woman pull out a chair and sit down. Winifred said, "Gwendolyn, I know you remember Dr. Hull of the Glowing Circle. She has some time today, and she's coming along for the massage with us."

Gwendolyn's memory of meeting Dr. Hull back at Stambridge revived, and she nodded. The three chatted, sipped coffee and started a leisurely and relaxing breakfast in preparation for their appointment. The ladies' circle was broken up after a while—Marshall and Hunter came in and invited themselves to join the females. The five engaged in small talk over breakfast, enjoying the fine food, coffee and, of course, Bloody Marys for the older women and screwdrivers for the boys. Gwendolyn did far more listening than speaking throughout this effervescent interlude.

At a lull in the conversation, Marshall dabbed at his mouth with his napkin and turned to Gwendolyn, "Well, I guess your old friend is busy over in the United Kingdom, eh?"

"What are you talking about?" Gwendolyn asked, smiling quizzically, accustomed to being teased by her brothers.

"The riots. Cecilia Strong, she's your hero, right?"

"Cecilia? Yes. No. What?"

"Didn't you know she's over in Wales right now? I guess she thinks she can make things better in that whole mess. You have to admire her gumption, but she's gotta be the exact wrong person to try to broker any kind of peace."

"?"

Getting no answer, Gwendolyn looked at her mother whose eyebrows and shoulders transmitted ignorance, whose wrinkling brow conveyed concern, concern for her daughter's distress. Gwendolyn glanced at Hunter who seemed to know nothing, apparently cared nothing and said nothing. Finally she turned to Dr. Hull.

Victoria Hull spoke, "Oh, my dear. I guess you really have been incommunicado… it started months ago. There were terrible riots in Wales. Hundreds of people have been killed. It's been quite bloody. It's died down, but what a horror! All hand-to-hand, farm implements, axes, fire, explosives and weapons like that. I don't know if they're using guns. They're against the law there. It's pretty quiet right now though." She looked over to Marshall.

Gwendolyn was stunned into a depth of silence. *What does this have to do with Cecilia?* She looked and saw Winifred's empathetic and grave face. She turned over to Marshall to see him fighting with a particularly truculent piece of crisp bacon that kept fracturing and jumping off his fork. Hunter sipped his screwdriver. Gwendolyn searched her brain trying to think if she had ever heard news about the Wales situation—maybe she heard something before she went to Swazizibia. She squeezed and pounded, but nothing percolated up out of her mind. *Oh, why did I move back to Vermont for the summer? I could have been with her on those Thursdays. I may never see her again. Will she be all right? Why is she over there in such a mess? When did she go over there?*

Victoria Hull saw Gwendolyn's distress and understood Marshall would be no help—he was clearly clueless about the effect their words were having on Gwendolyn. "All the charities have stepped in to help. We had a few dozen people there ourselves, but the upheavals reared up again. There were attacks on our workers, and one of them was hurt badly. We pulled our people out, but we're sending money and supplies. Actually we've seen a spike in our donations. Money is coming in faster than we can spend it on helping those people."

"What about Cecilia? Is she all right?" Gwendolyn was less than interested in financial accounting. Tears were welling in her eyes.

"She's fine." Dr. Hull's voice was steady as a military commander supervising his battlefield from an electronic surveillance post. "She was arriving there just as we were pulling our last people out two months ago. She took over our materials and is running one of the sites we set up, so I've talked to her directly a few times. The last time was the day before yesterday. She is tough, just like her name. She's working very hard, and she thinks the violence may be almost over. There hasn't been much bloodshed for a couple of weeks. I have to say, though, that woman is not afraid of death. She told me about some of the thugs she has had to face down without any sort of weapons or militia backing her..." Her lips pursed, her eyes slitted and her head twitched sideways in an involuntary spasm.

"But why... what is she doing there? How is she going to help things?" Gwendolyn glanced at her mother then back to Dr. Hull.

Dr. Hull answered, "She's just helping people who are victims of all this. Last she told me, she had gathered a whole group of orphans. Some are injured. All are scared to death. Some may not turn out to be orphans; it's pretty chaotic. She has them living in our old warehouse, and so far she's been able to get and keep most of the food and medical supplies that we've sent her. She has other people, mostly locals I think, manning makeshift hospitals in a few places too. It's pretty difficult there. She's the only person from an outside group I know of, though the United Nations is about to deliberate whether this qualifies as genocide, so maybe she will get help in a while."

Gwendolyn's surprise and alarm were elevated to yet another stratum. "Genocide? What? In Wales? The UN?" She dabbed at her eye.

Victoria Hull nodded, "Yes. It's on their schedule for debate next month. If it's judged genocide, they will schedule another discussion regarding whether to organize an effort that will prepare to gather resources in anticipation of mobilizing to get ready to begin combatting the xenophobes."

United Nations? Xenophobes? Off balance from the surreal conversation, Gwendolyn was alarmed and in pain from the picture of Cecilia in such a dangerous place. Recovering her footing, she turned to her mother angrily and said, "Why didn't you and Daddy tell me about this?" She looked at Marshall and Hunter. The boys looked at their mother.

Winifred stammered, "Oh, honey, I had no idea. And I'm not sure I know who this Cecilia is." Her face was instinctively contorted in the canonical representation of the emotion 'concern.'

Marshall said, "Ginny, nobody thought it would make any sense. You're in Africa. But don't kid yourself. This stuff was brewing for a time; you just weren't watching it. We know you're friends with Cecilia; we know she's special to you. But what would you do anyway from Swazizibia? You can't send her an old-fashioned postcard to cheer her up. Anyway, it looks like it's cooled down now. Still, nobody knows who to bet on."

"But how can this happen? And how can Cecilia think she has to go to places like that? She's almost seventy years old, for Pete's sake. How can she think she can stop a war? Is it a war?"

Hunter broke through his bored indifference. "Well, I can't say how the old lady decided she had to go herself. It's a waste of time. Nobody was really getting traction helping over there, though some groups were already working even during some pretty nasty parts of the uprising, like Dr. Hull says. But it's useless. Your friend won't get anywhere, and she may get herself killed."

The last clause, emanating from a clod, changed nothing in reality, but it sent Gwendolyn's alarm mechanism into high gear. She felt her heart banging as though it would burst from the confines of her ribs. She went woozy and started to faint, but caught herself. *I'm not a little girl. I'm not the one in danger. I'm not swooning.* She reasserted control and groped with the senselessness of it all—the meaningless killing, the danger for Cecilia. And all this—not out in some cave dwelling prehistoric society. This was Europe, Britain.

She cried, "But Wales! Hasn't Wales been around forever? What do you mean, xenophobes?" Perplexity aggravated Gwendolyn's anxiety cruelly. It made no sense, and anyway why should something halfway around the world have to put Cecilia in danger?

Dr. Hull explained, "It seems the violence came from new immigrants who have been pushed to their limit by the locals. These people are lashing out to defend themselves from the indigenous population who have been tormenting them for months. A few years, really. The relocation program has been going on that long, though the problems were not getting much international attention.

"Cecilia is sort of a special case, bless her heart. She thinks 'violence is violence' and anyone who needs help should be assisted. I guess I can't really say she's wrong. We're helping her, and she doesn't care who is who. But these locals have steadily resisted accommodating the newcomers. The last eruption was almost a real war."

Hunter said, "My bet, from what I've heard, is that she thought that if she went in and led an effort herself it may have a better chance to succeed than if she just sent workers. Or maybe she thought it was dangerous, and she wouldn't send volunteers anywhere she wouldn't go herself, so she had to go. But Marshall has to be right about her being an unlikely leader there. I hope she isn't wearing any crosses or rosaries."

"She doesn't wear rosaries. Get your religions straight. But what in the world happened over there? And why is Cecilia such a wrong person to try to fix it?"

Marshall picked up. "There was a lot of animosity in three or four towns over there. Wales has been mining and shipping out coal for a long time—ever since the UK declared nuclear power to be, what did they say, 'Antithetical to Human Flourishing.' Actually, they were mining coal there even one, two hundred years ago. It's like its own little world, away from everything. I never knew anything about it, but at the Foundation we get a lot of questions about the situation, and Father appointed me to be the expert, so I've learned a lot about it."

Marshall transitioned into a mode reminding Gwendolyn of a history professor talking about his area of career expertise casually over breakfast, albeit sans tweed jacket. He leaned back in his chair and as he spoke, the only motion was the occasional flipping of his gold-wristwatched hand as it projected out of his fine silk jacket. She had never seen him as anything but a big brother—part hero, part clown, with increasing motion toward the latter as she grew more mature. But she listened carefully as he continued. "Anyway, the UK government has been encouraging migration from poorer areas. Many have attacked the nation as being too much a 'White Northern European Christian' nation in a multicolored world. The government has decided that the country must accelerate acceptance of immigrants of another demographic profile, so they've been relocating people from abroad in pursuit of the goal.

"People in the places where these immigrants have been planted have quickly rejected them, shunning the whole process. The larger English cities were off limits for political reasons in the first place. Efforts in Northern Ireland didn't hardly last months before they were dropped. People in Scotland reacted the same way as the Irish, a bit more slowly. The immigrants did not stay in any of these places; the government was judged to be failing miserably.

"The newcomers have gravitated to this region in Wales, and they have essentially declared that it will belong to them. It's the only area still in play, and the government is adamant that the immigration project will succeed. And in order to keep the total national intake up to a level that the national social engineering central authority has calculated as required to meet demographic goals, the number coming to Wales from outside the United Kingdom had to go up. They're making up for the rest of the UK. So over the past two years —"

"Two years?" Gwendolyn broke in, stunned. She had noticed nothing of this even before she left for Swazizibia.

Marshal nodded. "With both the ones trickling down from the other places in Britain and the outsiders, the rate of resettlement there has been accelerating. The guests have been uncomfortable with some of the British culture they found as they arrived. Anyway, discontent started manifesting itself as mayhem. There is the struggle one would expect in the situation, and there are two sets of nucleation sites where the violence condenses: churches and pubs."

Victoria Hull took over, "There's been increasing pressure to dismantle Christian churches there for the last year, and finally it started yielding fruit a few months ago. There was lots of arguing back and forth about it. Some saw the churches as an affront to the newcomers and others belligerently felt they should let the newcomers just swallow their pride and leave the churches in their new homeland alone." Hunter yawned as he fiddled with his GVCD across the table. This distracted Dr. Hull and the others momentarily.

She continued, "I think a lot of all this has been disingenuous. Wales may have lots of churches, but I've been there in normal times, and they're always empty except for a few old women. I think the locals are bitterly clinging to them as a symbol of the past, a past that is gone. But they pretend to be believers. The churches are a tool to use against their new neighbors, a symbol of defiance. A Confederate flag, if you will. When I was last there some of the natives were being shipped out to their newly assigned home regions. I saw them on the buses. I can tell you, these are intolerant, bigoted, ignorant people and any region is better off without them. In fact I don't envy the receiving locales. If that's what supposed churchgoers are like, the area will be better off with their replacements."

Gwendolyn was confused. *Natives being shipped out?*

Marshall nodded his head again and picked up. "There was lots of name calling and noise. The locals started planning their political strategy, meeting in the Christian churches, and I'm quite sure that a lot of rabble rousing against the immigrants was going on there. So, the newcomers naturally eventually started to attack the Christian churches, at first just breaking windows and statues and things with rocks and clubs, and then later attacking with fire and some home-made explosives. The natives, who for all their Christian religion have never willingly extended the hand of friendship to the immigrants, cry like innocents that they are being persecuted in their own land. Well, whoever is right on that, the churches are an 'attractive target' situation. The pubs also draw the ire of many immigrants who believe they're signs of Welsh decadence and must be closed or destroyed.

"Anyway, there are all sorts of arguments about who is to blame when immigrant mobs assault the churches, but one member of Parliament captured a simple definitional truth: The fact is that if there are no Christian churches there will be no violence at Christian churches, and Parliament has acted to calm the situation by creating just that situation. The UK central government ruled that these old churches are an egregious violation of the freedom of the new population and has ordered a number of them destroyed. You can imagine that doesn't sit well with the natives. The rule passed in Parliament requires that all Christian churches more than ten years old in certain counties in Wales must be torn down by the middle of next year. They've been wrecking them for months."

There were no Christian churches built in the past thirty years within many miles of the districts in question; there were dozens of Christian churches in the region.

Gwendolyn was rapt as she absorbed the crucial information, struggling to process it all. She glanced around the table. Victoria Hull had an air of polite attention to someone promulgating old news. Winifred was expressionless as she listened to her son.

Marshall went on. "And the drinking places. There's been a lot of violence there. You know Wales. The men there have always spent their leisure hours exploring the stages of drunkenness with their mates, and I don't mean their wives. For centuries. Anyway, the central authorities in London ruled that the pubs there must be closed, because they attract attacks by immigrants who believe drinking is sinful. In Wales! There are no open pubs now, at least aboveboard. So there is no violence at open pubs. There is lots of violence. Tons of violence. Members of Parliament are pretty indignant about that, and they're considering drastic action—passing a law that states unequivocally that violence in Wales is a crime." This last was delivered without the least hint of sarcasm, and the reason is that this was exactly the solution being seriously processed in Parliament.

"This has been going on for years?" Gwendolyn looked around the table in amazement. Dr. Hull and Hunter were nodding. "How can they try to push their own citizens around like this, and what did they expect? How can I never have heard about it? I pay attention. Wouldn't even not-yet-violent wholesale citizen replacement in some remote Welsh towns have caught my attention in California?" Gwendolyn suddenly realized how much her thinking process had changed since even a few months ago. In the past she would only have seen the violence and never wondered if anything precipitated it. Actually, she would not have noticed activity across the world at all. She was not sure why, but she seemed to be paying more attention to things now.

Victoria Hull answered. "It hasn't been bad till the last half year. Locals grumbled whenever a church was attacked, but the explosive uptick in violence started when some Welsh men seized bulldozers in two cities, moved them from their worksites at the Christian churches, and started knocking down the places of worship of the newcomers. It was a well-coordinated, conspiratorial effort, and they were accompanied by drunken crowds of unemployed native miners and men who used to work in the shipping yards. Well, it's naïve to expect it to go easily if you attack those buildings in an area whose population is now over half immigrant, and whose adults have known nothing but war as a way of life in their homelands. Basically it erupted in riots across the whole region. Bloody, slow fighting. Stonings, hands cut off, that sort of thing. A real mess. I mean, as I understand it, maybe a quarter of the buildings in several towns are completely leveled by fire and hundreds, maybe thousands, are dead. Lord knows how many people are maimed for life, how many broken bones, smashed teeth, blinded by…"

"All right all right." Gwendolyn's lips were pursed, eyes closed as she grabbed and pushed Dr. Hull's arm. "So, Cecilia…" Gwendolyn said.

"All the big charities and lots of local British ones tried to help. We had some people helping, you know, with food distribution, medical supplies. Tents. But like I said, we had to pull them out. The Saving Arms had a different approach. They hid for a few days, then resurfaced. But Cecilia sent all her workers home when it got really bad. She came over herself." She closed her eyes and paused, shaking her head.

Gwendolyn looked nervously around the table at her family members, then back to Dr. Hull.

Dr. Hull continued, "She appears to be okay for now. Nobody seems to be molesting them, at least not systematically. We're helping get food and supplies to them. Our planes have been able to land, and we have ground transportation which is reliable at the moment."

"How do you know so much about this woman?" Winifred asked Victoria Hull. Gwendolyn was curious as well.

"We all work together as a team when there's a disaster. We share communications, transport routes, everything really."

"Except cash," Hunter said, grinning the biggest smile of the morning, proving that he could monitor a conversation even while gaming on his GVCD.

"Except cash," Dr. Hull agreed gravely. "That steps on too many toes, especially in cross-border activity." Her eyes swept over Winifred and Gwendolyn.

The table fell silent. The others took the opportunity to sip their coffee or drinks, and Gwendolyn focused on her own thoughts. She was unconsciously impregnating the conversational pause. She gestated things in internal indecision, then finally she brought the process to parturition: "I'm going to see her!" erupted forth from her mouth and dropped like an anchor onto the dull quietude of the table.

Winifred looked at her as though her daughter had stricken her in the head with a hammer. All around the table were dumbfounded. Dr. Hull recovered first. "That's not possible," she said.

Winifred balanced herself and said, "You will do nothing of the kind. It's a war zone."

Behind Gwendolyn there arose a commotion in the room, a disturbance she completely missed. A famous couple from Hollywood had entered to the subdued gasps and the overt gawking of all in the room; the prime minister seemed as engaged as anyone. Dr. Hull and Winifred were momentarily distracted by all the activity and looked over at the handsome pair, and they surveyed the attendant wave of activity traversing the tables. Hunter and Marshall exchanged some private joke and chuckled quietly.

Gwendolyn was resolute, but then even as she sat, her conviction started corroding. She felt nascent doubt; would the trip indeed be impossible? Her worry disregarded physical danger; it focused only on logistics. Her resolution never flagged, but her thoughts fluctuated radically. She ached to see Cecilia. *It must be possible, it must. No it's not. What if Cecilia is killed? But... There's no way I could pull this off... I have to, though. I must go to Wales. How would I get back to the mission? It won't work.*

No. She would go. But how?

She instinctively understood that a time when she was assaulted by her own dizzying hodgepodge of competing thoughts was not a good time to convince her mother of anything, not a good time for arguing. She retreated and lied. "Mother, let's worry about it later. I don't know if I should go." Winifred's eyebrows were grateful as she nodded and reached across the table to touch her daughter's hand.

"Come, dear. You're here for a vacation." This was not Gwendolyn's understanding of her trip here, but she let it slide. "You've been working too hard and it shows. Finish your coffee and let's go. It's almost time for our appointment."

Soon the boys departed together, and the ladies went down to the spa. They undressed, wrapped themselves in luxurious plush towels, and emerged into a warm, dimly lit studio with three massage tables. Along one wall was an immensely long fireplace; gentle orange flames lapped at artificial logs. The room was suffused with flower-blossom incense and a faint synthetic hickory smoke scent, and permeated by soft music.

As the three walked to the fireplace the older women shed their towels. Winifred and Victoria Hull turned and stood nudely facing the fire, talking casually. Gwendolyn clutched her wrap, bemused and uncomfortable at being forced to witness the relaxed immodesty of her elders. *Look at them. They may as well be two mothers talking about their children's schoolroom activities!* Her mother and Victoria cajoled her to join them. She resisted; she was starting to learn that she had some old-fashioned American hang-ups about displaying her body, limitations foreign to a spa in this part of Europe. And apparently foreign to her own mother.

Two athletic and attractive young men clothed in white, who pretended to know no English, entered the room bantering gaily in some Swiss dialect of German. Gwendolyn noticed that they entered from the same locker room the women had just undressed within. The smiling pair pantomimically instructed the women to lie down on their backs. The obedient ladies moved toward the tables as Gwendolyn tried to avert her eyes in a crescendo of distress.

As she and Dr. Hull stepped toward the tables, Winifred said over her shoulder, "We thought you would be more comfortable." The answer to Gwendolyn's question came seconds later as the unseen young woman who had quietly walked up behind her reached between her breasts and disentangled the ends of the towel. It fell to the floor before she knew what was happening, and she flushed in embarrassment. She looked over and saw the masseurs manhandling the bodies of the other woman.

Though naked herself, she could not help staring at the older women. She followed the smooth motions of the masseurs' hands artistically manipulating the lubricated bodies. She watched as those hands roved the regions of the ladies' personal topography, expertly adapting to the texture and give of the regions under them. She saw transient elastic sculptures created and subsiding as fingers and palms chased bulges of flesh in slow and graceful dances.

It all momentarily captivated Gwendolyn, but she returned to her own situation, distressed over her nakedness. She reluctantly obeyed her masseuse's guidance as the woman took her arm and conducted her to a supine position on her own table. She initially gulped and gasped as the masseuse started to knead her shoulders and their surroundings, but soon she started to melt into a calm and almost somnolent daze.

The massage was a new and wonderful experience for Gwendolyn. She swooned among varied states of relaxed semi-consciousness. When certain spots on the soles of her feet were manipulated she went into sudden dreamlike patches of clouds. She forgot all concern about her nakedness and the larger problems of human suffering that so often monopolized her conscious thoughts. Nary an appearance of so much as a homeless puppy made its way into her mind during this time.

The other ladies were enjoying their massages, perhaps even more than Gwendolyn. The stronger and larger hands of the masseurs petrissaged their oiled skin, kneading their muscles and leaving utter relaxation in their wakes. Body parts were traced and chased symmetrically round and round. Fingers explored and tucked under ribs; thighs that never knew they cried out for attention were melted into pliant doughy masses of flaccid muscle and fat. The attendants delivered long strokes to shoulders and necks. The men lifted heads and massaged the junctions between muscle and bone. Clamping their subjects' hands with their own arms, they explored and manipulated forearms and upper arms. Fingers, toes, ears, scalp—all were attended with lingering care. Even the eye sockets were not missed as the trained experts deftly probed the recesses and traced the nerve notches at their edges. Faces and cheeks they carefully pampered, and the other body parts received similar expert attention. The heat from the fire and the warmth of the massage merged into a continuum as time and care dissolved away, transforming the subjects into a serene gel of pleasant repose and sensual enjoyment.

When the time came for the women to flip, the attendants gently summoned their presence for the turnover. Each rolled over, eyes closed, pausing halfway like a sleeping baby before being coaxed onto her stomach. Had they been more alert, they would have noticed the skill of the masseurs in steering them to the comfortable depressions accommodating faces and other body parts. In fact, the two older women's massage tables were covered with a custom-cut mat for this purpose; Gwendolyn's was a standard mat chosen in the absence of specific measurements, but it served its purpose well enough.

All the sensuous relaxation of the first part of the massage faded to nothing as the masseuse began stroking Gwendolyn's back. The woman delivered expertly long strokes from Gwendolyn's neck and shoulders all the way to her feet, varying the pressure and speed as she passed over the warmly prepared skin of each body part. For her too, time became a meaningless concept as Gwendolyn slipped to a meditative state disconnected in every way, save tactile feeling, from her own body, absolutely passive in her surrender to the woman. Though totally tranquilized, she put forth effort to enjoy the petrissage on her back, the focused pressure on points in her buttocks, the wrapping strokes on the back of her thighs, the kneading of her feet...

Gwendolyn opened her eyes and saw her mother standing at the side of her table wrapped in her thick robe. She was talking to Gwendolyn's masseuse in some form of German. The masseuse left, and Winifred handed Gwendolyn a robe. She groggily got up and followed Dr. Hull and Winifred to a small sauna, wondering how much time had elapsed. Outside the sauna entrance the older women casually clothed themselves in full nudity again and entered. Gwendolyn hesitated, less than she would have before this morning, but followed suit. Victoria Hull dropped water on the rocks, and they sat in the heat. Gwendolyn's mind was dull as she listened to the banter between the two older women. After a while Victoria Hull poured another helping of water on the rocks. The puff of steam rose, and eventually the clouds cleared and Gwendolyn remembered Cecilia's predicament. But she did not disturb her mother's relaxation, and their spa visit finished pleasantly enough.

Gwendolyn kept quiet until after lunchtime, then launched her broadside to Winifred. She insisted that she was going to Wales to see Cecilia, by whatever means she could find. Then afternoon was spent squabbling with Winifred, who occasionally contacted Kingman for support which he did not give; Kingman's feeling was that Gwendolyn was growing up, and she was pretty headstrong; maybe she had to go see things for herself. In truth, while she was away in Africa he had gotten more comfortable with her travels than had Winifred.

"But it's a war zone," Winifred protested to no avail. Kingman did not judge the Wales situation particularly dangerous right now. In the end, Winifred relented but insisted that she was coming along to help protect her daughter. Victoria Hull had been present with Winifred through most of the skirmishes throughout the afternoon. Once the battle was over she quietly extended to Winifred a surprise piece of assistance—she graciously offered her organization's jet as the quickest, most efficient way to travel. Apparently Gwendolyn had not thought about demanding use of the Foundation's jet, something Kingman would almost certainly have acceded to. Having a borrowed jet would allow Winifred to claim they had a time limit, hopefully discouraging Gwendolyn from a temptation to stay for days. So the decision was made, the constraint of time secretly imposed. Dr. Hull pulled some strings, setting up logistics on the other side for them as well.

Finally Gwendolyn and Winifred made their preparations and set off for Wales in the jet. It was well into the night when the airplane landed at the little airstrip outside the mining and fishing village. A small van was waiting to meet them. They had loaded some hastily gathered supplies in Switzerland, and the pilot helped them transfer the boxes to the vehicle, then returned to his airplane as the van drove off. The driver was terse and difficult to understand. Through fumbling exchanges in their nominally common language they learned that it would be about a half-hour ride to Cecilia's operation, and Gwendolyn fell asleep in the van. Winifred nervously looked out the windows at the nondescript countryside as they drove over rolling hills in the dark. She saw no signs of destruction or controversy.

Gwendolyn was awakened by her mother shaking her as the van slowed on a dark street lined with industrial buildings. The driver rolled to a stop by a large cargo door and honked the horn. The door started to rise, and the driver nodded to the passengers, who climbed out of the vehicle. When the door was open fully they saw a cluttered office area to the left and a large open area with various crates and machines straight ahead of them. A tiny woman walked out the edge of the door—Cecilia Strong! Gwendolyn ran to her and threw her arms around her, almost knocking her down. Cecilia motioned for Winifred to come inside quickly and closed the door behind them once they were within. She opened a smaller door leading outside from the office and signaled the driver to bring in the boxes from the van through that door, then turned to her visitors.

Gwendolyn looked around the building. Off to the right in rows near the far wall were ten or more small cots with children on them. They spanned a range of size, color and health status. Most were sleeping. Some had bandages on them, and one or two had casts. The building had been some sort of factory or work area. The lighting and plumbing were spare and uncovered; only a few of the lights were on. The floor was long-ago-polished concrete. There were large oblong pieces of industrial equipment taking up the center of the room between the visitors and the children. Along the front wall, to the right and behind Gwendolyn's back were stacks of supply boxes: dried food, linens, bandages, paper, portable lights, cooking fuel, tents, blankets, pots, small stoves, medicine and so forth, all piled to the ceiling. *This must be a storage area for more than just this little group of children.*

Gwendolyn's eyes cycled around to where Cecilia stood. Even here at night halfway around the world in the midst of an exhausting stint, the corners of her mouth were curled up, and her crow's feet were setting as she began to speak to her friend. "Gwendolyn Dressel-Meier. You made good time... but what on earth are you thinking? And, Winifred, I presume." Cecilia Strong wore blue jeans and a beige smock. She looked smaller, older than Gwendolyn remembered from just last spring in California. In the harsh factory light her skin appeared as grey as her hair. The woman seemed weary and would have appeared stooped except for her military-straight back. Gwendolyn could see her moving with the stiff gait of one with incipient arthritis. Nothing, however, contradicted her name; Gwendolyn saw a woman destined for decades more work in the battle for goodness.

"I have your coin!" Gwendolyn almost shouted, pulling a string from within her blouse. She wore the medallion that Cecilia gave her last year. It was in a holder suspended around her neck by a knotted leather cord. "I tell myself I'll always wear it when I travel anywhere." She kept it in a box at the mission and had instinctively grabbed it as she readied for her trip.

Winifred reached out and grabbed the pendant from her daughter's hand, struggling to read it in the light: 'Trust Your Mind. Well. Truth. Persistence. Very nice.' As she dropped the medallion, she was glad that her daughter chose to wear the trinket inside her blouse instead of outside.

The driver closed the door as he exited. He had finished moving supplies and went back to the van to await instructions.

Gwendolyn excitedly said, "I had to see you when I heard you're in Europe too. Cecilia, everyone thinks you're crazy to be here."

Cecilia pointed to the mostly sleeping children. Winifred nodded understandingly, wondering what Cecilia meant. Gwendolyn also nodded. Cecilia explained, "Every one of them would probably be dead by now. We found them all inside damaged buildings or wandering the streets. We've seen quite a few that didn't make it, ones we could not save."

"But what about you? The rioting, the war? You're all alone!" Gwendolyn started to cry.

"I'm not alone. I have two men helping me." She pointed to the rear corner nearest the office area where two men were sleeping on cots; Gwendolyn could only see the bottoms of their boots and a few empty liquor bottles around their beds. "As for the violence, it's been a bit of a hiatus, thank God. But they all know we're here, and they sometimes come by with their guns and ask for food, which we refuse. Once or twice they've threatened to take it. But they never did." She paused and pointed toward where the wall meets the ceiling over the little office area. Both were riddled with bullet holes and broken material where an angry man from one side or the other, Cecilia didn't remember which, had shot a few dozen rounds in a useless attempt to intimidate her when she refused him. "Mostly they don't bother us anymore. Sometimes we have people who come looking for their missing children, but it's been in vain so far. Now you should go back."

Gwendolyn was perplexed; she had been taught that guns were against the law in the United Kingdom. *Shows what I know about the law. Maybe not in Wales.* She was worried about Cecilia in such a terrible area. She glanced at the children's' cots. Two youngsters were sitting up, and two or three more were awake. All of these were watching the adults. She looked back to Cecilia. "But what's going to happen? What about you?"

"I won't stay here forever. Pretty soon I will go home. I actually am very tired, and things will probably change in the near future. It looks like the government is coming in soon with the military. They've started with their final solution to the problem. If there's a burst of violence again, there will be soldiers here when it flares up, so it won't be the same next time."

Winifred spoke up. "How is the government going to solve things?" She sat on a stack of crates wide enough to be a sofa.

Cecilia looked grave, "The British have a habit for use in such situations. They call it 'partitioning,' and they're doing it here. In this case it means moving the original population from this area to small towns in England and leaving these towns to the immigrants."

"Forced relocation?" Winfred said.

Cecilia nodded, "Actually the British don't think of it as a big deal. They did somewhat similar things all around their old empire. They've already quietly started, and quite a few people have been shipped out. The other approach in Britain, and it is much less popular, is to declare that Wales, or this part of it, is not part of the United Kingdom anymore. But they have economic reservations about that because of all the coal mines and fishing and shipping and so forth. And you can imagine for yourself whether it quells the violence or just gives it a new nickname."

Winifred said, "In that case no soldiers would come here to put down the fighting?"

Cecilia nodded.

"It would be a bloodbath!" Gwendolyn exclaimed.

Cecilia nodded. "Maybe. But that whole scenario is very unlikely. It won't happen. They're going to continue with the partitioning."

"What about you?"

Cecilia shrugged and said, "We'll see. I'm not committing suicide here. That wouldn't help anyone. I think within a few weeks the military will arrive, and they'll step up the pace of forcibly shipping people out. Once that starts, I think my presence here won't be a thing that makes any difference. I will be useless. There will be others, organized efforts, running things."

Gwendolyn had been thinking about the resettlement. "Won't the partition just move the same problem somewhere else?"

Cecilia said, "If you think it's an absurd strategy you will get no argument from me. I can't say Britain's history with partitioning has been a pinnacle of success in delivering peace to any of the places I can think of. These people know nothing about farming, about sheep. They're miners and fishermen, some workers and roughnecks. And liquor-hounds! Well, I suppose I can't say the average Brit has anything against drink, that's for sure. You can imagine whether the agricultural towns in pastoral portions of England will be happy to see thousands of what they consider filthy uneducated foreigners with a strange dialect—really another language— coming to their area, people whose only discernable skill is getting drunk. The small towns are already up in arms about it. The heck of it is this: these folks actually have been hard-working sorts, accustomed to being stepped on by their masters in the unions and corporations that control things in partnership with the government here. So they know how to obey. It's just that they won't have anything to do when they're dispersed except drink and complain. They'll make trouble."

"Shouldn't they just send them to the big cities where they can find work, any sort of work?"

"But the larger cities—London, Birmingham, Glasgow, Edinburgh— they're afraid these drunkards would be harder to control there, since they would inevitably coalesce. Besides, the decision-makers are largely from those areas. I'm glad you're thinking, Gwendolyn. It makes me believe you remember what we talked about that night I gave you that coin you just showed me. I hope you continue to. The world needs more young people who do. And Lord, I worry about young people and thinking."

"You bet I remember. Do my own thinking. I try, but… there is so much I can't understand, so I have to take steps on faith sometimes. Every day at the mission. Here in Europe… Well anyway, this sort of situation—this is why I want to be like you, Cecilia. You know everything. You see everything. We have to change the world and stop these incidents from happening. I should stay here with you." Gwendolyn had tears in her eyes.

Winifred was horrified to hear this, and Cecilia was not pleased either. Cecilia put her arm up on the girl's shoulder. She glanced at Winifred, then nodding to Gwendolyn and speaking in contradiction to the gesture she said, "No, Gwendolyn. Listen to me. You are growing up now. If you see a person in a whirlpool can you help them?" Her voice was gruff, serious.

Gwendolyn nodded. Cecilia agreed. "You can knock down a tree and break off a branch. You can get a rope, or throw a life preserver." She looked sternly at the girl. "Can you help them by jumping in with them? If you see a whole crowd in a whirlpool can you help them all by jumping in?" She guided Gwendolyn over to the crate and had her sit next to her mother.

Gwendolyn wanted to split the two situations, but she realized Cecilia had a reason for commingling them. She shook her head. Cecilia nodded again. There was a pause. "But you jumped into the whirlpool! You broke your own rule. And I shouldn't jump in after you did it yourself?"

Cecilia shook her head. "No, Gwendolyn. I'm the one *not* jumping into the whirlpool. I am doing what is possible, what I can. Soon there will be nothing for me to do. Everything I have done has been undertaken after a lot of cold, analytical thought by this cold, analytical old lady soldier. I am staying outside the whirlpool, and these people here, they're in it. You can't come here just because it feels like you want to help somebody somewhere. You would be slipping into the whirlpool. Think about it. If you come, what milestone would convince you it is time to go home?"

"Well, when it's over." She dabbed at her eyes.

"Listen to yourself, Gwendolyn. Whatever happens, I will be leaving soon. I won't be here to work with you." Winifred was pleased with this turn of the conversation, and she involuntarily smiled. Her head bobbed up and down. Cecilia continued, "You need to keep doing what you are already doing in Africa. You thought about that, analyzed that, and made a decision. Are you denying this now?"

Gwendolyn shook her head.

"So, is it right to just hop from one unfinished thing to another?"

The girl shook her head. "You may not stay with me. I promise you I will make it back home, and I will do it in the not-too-distant future." Cecilia planned to go home soon, but she did not really rate her chances of accomplishing it. The young woman sobbed. Cecilia sat on the crate next to her, and Gwendolyn buried her head in the loving comfort of the old lady's bony shoulder.

Cecilia continued, "And don't kid yourself, young lady. I am detecting hero worship. Be careful with that—it is antithetical to real thought, real understanding. I don't see everything, know everything. I'm not changing the world from this old factory building. I am helping some individuals, mostly children, avoid getting killed. Maybe I'm just delaying it, I don't know. I'm not going to single-handedly stop the violence here, and I'm certainly not going to be able to derail any population relocation scheme. Go ahead." She put her hand on the back of Gwendolyn's head. "Crying is all right. Do you think I don't cry every time I learn of another church demolished, another child maimed?"

Winifred's vision blurred, and a few blobs of tear dropped down to her cheek. Gwendolyn pulled her face from Cecilia's body and dabbed at her own eyes, still sniffling. Cecilia guided her to a standing position. Somehow there was something uplifting in Cecilia, something that palliated the serious warning she delivered, something like an invisible smile. "Yes, help people in need. That's a worthy goal. Yes, you can make it better. But only incrementally. As you go forward and find your way in life, understand this: You will not reverse the direction the globe is spinning. That way madness lies, as the saying goes. There are some rules of human nature, and there will be no utopias. You need to return with your mother." She signaled for Winifred to get up and move toward the door and started following with Gwendolyn.

Gwendolyn took another look at the children on the cots, and her heart melted. One of the little boys was happily strumming his lips with his fingers as he watched the conversation. She broke away, tiptoed over to the boy, finger upright across her lips, and rubbed his head. Then she did the same to the other three or four children who were awake, all the while hushing them. Cecilia and Winifred saw Gwendolyn straighten up, turn and stand still for a moment. Her face dropped to neutral expressionlessness. She walked back to Cecilia and gave her a protracted, wordless hug. She broke off and said, "Mother, I think it's time to go. Thank you, Cecilia. And I hope you succeed here."

Winifred nodded, touched Cecilia's shoulder with a nod and turned to go toward the small door. She exited with Gwendolyn following her. At the last instant Cecilia grasped Gwendolyn's shoulder and stopped her. She made a conciliatory motion to Winifred, who was outside, and closed the door. Winifred seemed alarmed, but Cecilia made another calming gesture through the window, and Winifred leaned against the van to wait.

"Gwendolyn, I hope you know there are thousands of people working very hard to alleviate suffering in the world. And they are having an effect, even if they cannot eliminate the problems they are fighting. They are giving up their comfort, and in many cases giving up their ability to live a normal, happy life with a family. They are doing this for others. From what I know about you, I think you aspire to be one of them." Gwendolyn nodded. Cecilia continued, "And starvation in Africa is one of the most difficult of the things to deal with." Gwendolyn gestured agreement again, confused. "Think hard about things. Then trust your own mind, dear. I am telling you there are dozens of organizations working themselves to the bone in Africa, people sacrificing their own future, their own health, to bring relief to helpless populations. Getting them food, medicine. Working with the governments to change things. "

I know all this. I'm working at one of those places. Gwendolyn was loosening up. She blinked confusedly and nodded again, starting to smile. She began an answer. "Yes…"

"No. Gwendolyn. Do your own thinking. Understand the massive effort that people, people like you or me, put into restoring health to the suffering. To find places for them to live. To give them hope, to educate the children. And this is a long, long process." Winifred was getting impatient, and Cecilia waved to her through the window again. "It has been going on for a long time. Understand that there are thousands of good-hearted and strong-armed people who have elected to give up what they have and come to Africa and live in squalid conditions in the hope of doing God's work for these people. And thousands of others who support them as they stay behind. And the same is true for many other places in the world."

The girl looked at her in full agreement. It was all obvious stuff.

"Gwendolyn, listen to me carefully. You are young. You have seen none of it. When you go back home, to California I mean, you must think about whether you have been part of that. You must come to your own conclusions about it."

Gwendolyn started to open her mouth, but Cecilia hushed her. "I am not here to debate you or to hear what you think right now. I know what you think. I want you to understand that there are many groups with which you are unfamiliar. Why? Why am I so hell-bent on repeating myself so many times? This is a serious thing, and I want you to be quiet and to promise me you will do your own thinking after your tour of duty in Africa. Promise me. Do the work."

Gwendolyn easily nodded. If Cecilia wanted it, sure. She would do it. No problem.

"No." Cecilia slapped the young girl smartly across the face. "Listen to me, Gwendolyn." She grabbed both of the girl's wrists in a stiff grip. She was looking deep into the girl's eyes. Outside, Winifred rushed to the door, and Cecilia lodged her foot against it as she fought to enter. The tiny woman stood, one ankle calmly holding off the wild woman outside as she pounded against the door and called after her daughter. Cecilia exhorted Gwendolyn, "Do your own thinking. Trust your own mind. How can I say it so you hear me? Hear me. Think about the things you think you know. Think about why you believe them. Things you don't even question, things you have always known. Don't just swallow everything. Do this thing."

Gwendolyn was stunned. She stood, mouth agape, looking back at Cecilia. The older woman was standing looking up at her, lips pursed, brow furrowed. A minor whimper crawled up inside Gwendolyn. As she stood crying, eyes closed, the burning sting of the serious blow transformed into the psychic pain of her upbraiding. Cecilia released her wrists, which dropped limply. The older woman reached up and pulled the girl's head forward and down. She placed a kiss on her forehead and said, "Now it's time to go." She unblocked the door, and Winifred's next impact opened it with a crash. The woman rushed to her daughter, who pushed her away. Gwendolyn turned and walked briskly out the door, looking at the ground. Winifred followed, glaring over her shoulder at Cecilia. Gwendolyn and Winifred climbed into the van and rode away.

After a half hour they approached the parked airplane at the little airfield. They saw the pilot leaning against a fuel truck, and upon seeing the van he threw down his old-fashioned cigarette, crushed it out and started toward the plane. Moments later they were flying back to Zurich. They slept fitfully on the airplane and arrived near dawn. Gwendolyn slept curled up in her suite until almost two o'clock the next afternoon.

The Sermon From the Fount

Why don't I feel what they feel?

W hen Gwendolyn awoke, the whole trip to Wales was as if a bad dream. She had awakened just in time to get to Hunter's presentation at the convention, so she pushed the memory out of her mind and quickly readied herself. She went to hear Hunter's talk, arriving just as he started speaking. She quietly took a chair in the back of the room as he got going. He introduced the Lobby For Good and focused on one of its early efforts as he encouraged the listeners to join the confederation. The Lobby For Good had been contracted by the largest drug company in the world for a project. The corporation was owned by Wilbur Buffaloon, and the Lobby's task was to advocate in Congress for a floor to the price of proprietary drugs in the United States market. The intention was to compensate for the fact that other countries imposed a ceiling. Hunter expected success in the effort, and he believed this was a good example for use in convincing an unsure audience of the organization's efficacy.

He explained that in most countries the price of a proprietary drug is set by a government committee, a group that negotiates extensively with itself over price in order to determine a level fair to the producer and simultaneously acceptable for the buyer—the government is essentially the whole market. Prior efforts by Dr. Buffaloon's companies to combat governmental price-fixing had been met with counterproposals to eliminate intellectual property protection for the drugs completely; the new initiative with the Lobby For Good was Buffaloon's attempt to avoid discussion of such things. The Lobby's proposal was popular in most countries; all wanted advances in medical technology; most considered it worth the investment so long as the cost of the underlying patent protection was isolated to the United States and a few other countries.

There was some resistance within the United States, and success was far from guaranteed. Buffaloon had delayed action due to his insurance interests, which opposed the idea of a floor price. But his economists had worked with the federal government to develop sophisticated financial models, and he now believed that once the limit was in place he would benefit; the models showed that he should be able to capture an increasing fraction of the United States gross domestic product for his companies considered in toto after the change, provided that he drastically cut back research on new drugs. One wildcard they had not been able to fully evaluate was the well-developed arbitrage industry fueled by cross-border price variations; the effect of the floor price on this activity was hard to quantify, but analysts deemed it unlikely to be large enough to influence conclusions. To spearhead the domestic effort for changes to the law, Dr. Buffaloon had tapped the Worldwide Transformative Foundation's new Lobby For Good. His goal, of course, was to have the American people transfer a larger portion of their treasure to his corporations.

Hunter's talk was politely received, and the audience was almost unanimously supportive of the American minimum prices. During the question-and-answer session many thinkers brought up sublime insights like the idea that the floor price could be considered a gift from the people of the United States to the world. Gwendolyn judged the Lobby's project to be praiseworthy. The American people certainly were rich enough to participate in this generous undertaking in the service of the greater world, and she was proud to be affiliated with the Foundation's efforts, however indirectly.

There were many small workshops that afternoon, and Gwendolyn went to a few presentations. Having always liked dogs, she chose a session called 'Borderless Lawyers for Dogs.' She listened as the group's director discussed some of the cases he had handled, situations where the dignity of domestic canines had been affronted. The group traveled the world and filed lawsuits on behalf of aggrieved hounds in cosmopolitan European and American cities, as well as tropical vacation areas. Their funding was evenly split between individual donors and grants from governments. Most of the information feeding the legal actions came from neighbors and other observers who suspected or had actually detected disrespect of the animals. The group was a spinoff from another organization that claimed credit for closing off public access to the zoos in Europe. By the end of the talk

Gwendolyn was ambivalent. She wholeheartedly endorsed their mission; she herself had seen the furry creatures treated inconsiderately many times. But she was far from convinced that they were an up-and-coming force in what Cecilia Strong called the Charity Industry.

She had time for two more sessions. Titles piqued her curiosity about many of the presentations, but she had no trouble passing over things like, 'Streamlining Governmental Funding Access' and 'Tax Strategies for Enhanced Charitable Giving and Living.' She considered attending 'On the Way to Imposing Uniform and Shared Values and Funding: Art as a Part of Community Life.' and 'Harnessing the Power of the Mind and Beyond: Employing Psychics and Visualization to Help the Forgotten.' Only having time for the two visits, she settled on attending 'Defending Children Against Their Parents' and one last one entitled 'Art, Morals and Obligations.'

Despite their tantalizing names neither session was as interesting as the dog talk. The former session was presented by a group in the United States that intervened in the face of unreasonable parental restrictions on their offspring. The premise was that society granted these parents the privilege of supporting and raising their children—the global village's most crucial task—and therefore the parents owed obeisance to current theories of child-rearing. The man presenting the session decried the unfair situation children live in, with adults using their superior position to take advantage of their innocent offspring; in most cases the youngsters did not even know they had rights that were being violated until the organization got access to them. He gave heart-wrenching stories of legal battles over oppression of children by their own parents, examples of corporal punishment, withholding of privileges, and tyrannical supervision of youngsters in the company of their friends. Of particular note was the all-too-common occurrence of forced religious indoctrination, and he reserved a special vocal viciousness for when he spoke of this cardinal offense.

The session leader related that the group's efforts had failed to reach their full potential due to the maddeningly slow process of societal evolution. Some teachers, doctors and caretakers refused to cooperate with the group in gathering data on prospects. When they did find a potential vehicle for one of their lawsuits, private access to the minor was usually difficult to arrange, and even when the group could isolate the child, he was often too distraught to provide meaningful help. To this day many children are fond of their parents, and the stories had to be puzzled out in that context. Most of the time the child could not be convinced that the problem existed, and often the youngster recanted later. If a case did made it to trial, parents dragged out the legal fight until they had spent their last penny, making victories slow and expensive. He said that the organization needed to find more funding since their normal source of financial support, earmarks in public budgets, was being attacked by increasingly vocal and effective enemies of children.

The presentation was skillful, and Gwendolyn's impulse was to sympathize with the children who were held up as the victims of their despotic parents. But she hesitated, on the fence in her thinking about the organization, as the creepiness of its underlying premise irritated her psyche and kept her from full endorsement. Finally she walked away hoping they dropped out of existence in the near future.

The last talk, the one on morals and art, was given by another United States group. All Gwendolyn remembered was that the group was a nascent organization formed by sculptors in New York, and they were in Switzerland raising funds for a lobbying effort to get a law in place sequestering a few percent of New York state's budget for the support of artists—sculptors in particular.

Gwendolyn retained no strong impression from the talks of the day, though she did remember some of the nicer images of puppies from the first talk and a few beautiful centuries-old statues in the background of pictures of current sculptures displayed during the last presentation.

She was tired by evening, and she was quiet all through her dinner with her family and the heads of three international charities in the banquet hall. She excused herself immediately after the meal, saying she wanted to be rested and ready for the big day at the conference tomorrow. The sessions were scheduled to start early, and the activity would continue till late in the evening. She pled the need to compile extra sleep tonight after her exhausting trip. The rest of the family attended festivities hosted in hotel suites by various conference participants while she returned to her suite and went to bed.

The next morning Gwendolyn went down to breakfast early. She sat alone and watched well-bred people from all over the world as they dined and discussed important things. Sarah came by and joined her, and Gwendolyn was happy for the company; with a few reservations she liked Sarah and felt they were basically friends. Sarah told her she had not been going to many conference sessions, and today she was going to be a tourist around Zurich again. Sarah opined that Kingman's talk, the meeting's keynote address, was going to be dazzling, and she mentioned that she would definitely be back for that. A few minutes after she finished her meal they went their separate ways.

Walking around that morning, Gwendolyn was impressed with the size of the annual gathering. In fact there were over two thousand attendees at the conference. Though the attendance was large, this was an exclusive conference; Kingman had, over the years, created a sort of bidding war among charities and service providers for invitations to give presentations and set up booths at the meeting. Large international charities and friendly corporations were automatically invited; they were the most able to pay the hefty fee assessed on them for participation. A Charity Coalescence committee kept the convention interesting by choosing sixty or so small charities and granting them a marketing platform for a much smaller fee. These they selected in much the same way as Winifred Dressel-Meier chose spices for a recipe. As for the general attendees, the convention was open to all who paid the general registration fee, which was comparable to that of any normal industrial get-together. The organizing committee kept an eye on attendance numbers and made sure the conference was always well-attended; they engaged in outreach and offered discounted or free registration if necessary to fill the place.

Again, the day offered many sessions. Gwendolyn wandered alone among the presentation rooms. The main event was scheduled to be anchored by Kingman's late afternoon keynote address in the largest and most ornate meeting room in this, the largest and most ornate hotel in Zurich, the largest city in Switzerland. She walked by the empty room and looked in. It held hundreds and hundreds of chairs. *They're expecting a crowd for Daddy today.* During the morning, she listened to a few short talks but found none very interesting. The presentations all seemed to be related to accounting, taxation, monetary transfers and so forth, and all were subjects that bored her wickedly. She was apparently in the minority; most sessions were standing-room-only. Due to her exhausting travel and irregular sleep schedule, she found her mind wandering, and by late morning she was having trouble staying awake in some of the workshops.

Gwendolyn decided to play hooky. She did not want to encounter her family at lunch or sit in boring workshops before her father's speech that afternoon. She went outside to the busy streets of Zurich and felt her energy level rise as she sampled the bright sunshine of the fall day, but she felt a pang of guilt at the idea of pleasantly strolling while she should be with the people so painstakingly gathered from around the world. She decided to assuage her conscience by first taking a quick stroll through the building where the various organizations had set up their tables and displays.

She went inside and was assaulted with banners, video screens, expensive curtains and noisy crowds among the booths of dozens of charitable organizations and service providers. People were plying their wares, capturing passersby, trying to set up organizational connections, making deals. She walked, ignoring those in the booths tugging at her attention, and her glance bounced from banner to screen to animated face. In the middle of one of the rows of booths her attention was captured by an organization called 'Plaintive Eyes.' She approached the table which was attended by a smoothly professional man who stood motionless as she walked up. Her eyes darted between the large video screens above, beside and in front of his table. She glanced at his stacks of literature as he greeted her and introduced himself as the founder of the organization.

"What do you think of them?" he asked, smiling like a proud parent.

"They're amazing. The eyes! They almost jump off the screens, out of the pictures at you."

"That's the idea."

Gwendolyn was looking at videos and pictures of dogs, cats and even a few rabbits, all seemingly about to burst into tears. It was like the standard scenes she had seen many times, tugging at donors' heartstrings, but somehow much more powerful; it encapsulated a mysterious and troubling dimension of enchantment. "How do you get them to look so sad, almost like they're crying? You don't scare them do you?" She asked, knowing the animals did not look frightened but having no other words to represent the incongruous appearance of the creatures.

The man laughed, "No, no, no. We don't even make the pictures. We just retouch the eyes in other peoples' pictures. We have technology that can take a video or picture of any animal and give it eyes that would make your grandmother turn over her pension check." He stood proudly displaying a sleazy smile, and advertising his conviction that his presumed co-conspirator would find such phrasing admirable or at least amusing.

Gwendolyn was disgusted and broke into a frown. But she was curious, and she asked, "How do you do it?"

"Well, it's our secret sauce, and it's all very complicated." He handed her one of the old-fashioned, glossy fold-out brochures on the table, the back page of which was covered with stridently meaningless graphs and mathematical symbols. He elaborated in kind, "When we started making materials for our clients we simply played the numbers game. You know, stepping on tails, taking a hundred pictures to get just the right expression. We've evolved quite a ways in a short time, and nobody can touch our technology now. We use a physics-based set of two-and-a-half dimensional models for optical refraction, reflection and even dispersion, employing spatially varying dielectric and conductivity values for the lachrymal fluid in the eyes. We do multi-step filtered ray tracing and have developed a few other things like a finely tuned ellipsoidal model of the oculi in situ, with a complicated three-dimensional elasticity tensor representation of the surrounding tissues. We generate and solve the equations, and we tune things parametrically. This lets us match the visually perceivable boundary conditions of the oculi and the palpebrae, fur and so forth. I'll let you in on a secret: gravity. Nobody else uses it in their computations because it's so difficult to account for its effect on viscous liquids. But that is part of our secret sauce. It's why we don't have to do the obvious retouching the other guys do, in order to have the tears welling most thickly at the bottom. The final step is the actual rendering of the result right into the digitized original picture. Presto! Crying Eyes!"

Gwendolyn did not follow it all, but she got the message that he wanted her to believe the result was the product of a complicated process. She lodged a suspicion that his secret may not be so very confidential, given how publicly he detailed it. Cognizant of the small crowd that had gathered behind her to hear his theatrical voice, the man said to her, "Here, let me show you." He brought up a garden-variety advertisement requesting donations for an animal shelter. It featured a sad-looking dog and a confused-looking kitten facing the camera. The man slowly showed steps in the development of the Plaintive Eyes process, flipping screens back and forth to the gasps of the people standing behind Gwendolyn. He let each stage run for a few seconds of video as the dog and cat sat motionlessly, eyes directed to the camera. The audience saw the animals' eyes seemingly elongate and reach forward out of the screen. The pupils and irises morphed into a symphony of heart-rending melancholy. Gwendolyn heard sighs from the crowd as the fur in the animals' faces adapted to the eye transformations, becoming ever-so-slightly wet and stretching imperceptibly. The reflections from the pitiful mammals' increasingly teary eyes subtly modified the colors and darkened the mood. The effect was enhanced by slight changes to the overall background and texture of the video as the steps progressed, accompanied by increasingly lugubrious music.

Gwendolyn was transfixed, and the video had its intended effect. It weighed on her. The man stood beaming with pride. She was brought back to earth by a someone calling out, "Can you do this with children?" as Gwendolyn dabbed at her eyes with a handkerchief. Then suddenly, *I have to get out of here for a while.* She turned and fought her way through the growing crush as she heard the proprietor's voice beginning to answer; it sounded like a complicated version of 'not yet, but we're working on it.' She emerged from the outer layer of the herd and headed for the door. Bursting out into the sunshine, she stopped and leaned against the building wall for a long time, looking at her shoes. She calmed down and eventually turned her attention to the city around her. She was somewhat cheered by the happily busy population going about their daily business.

Gwendolyn lost herself in the glitter and activity of the big city for hours. She ambled in careless abandon, turning down interesting streets and window shopping for jewelry, trinkets and clothing. She spied on well-behaved diners at their window tables as she strolled by cafes. She traveled busy streets and narrow alleys, took detours through some big stores, and she forgot completely about Swazizibia and simply enjoyed walking in the pinnacle of civilization. She lunched alone at a little hofbrau, sitting on the balcony above the street, watching the traffic below. After her meal she drifted indirectly toward the conference center, allowing plenty of time and stopping whenever the inclination struck her.

She bought a cup of cocoa and some roasted chestnuts from a street vendor at a plaza, and she stopped where two craggy-faced old men were playing chess on a huge outdoor chessboard. The pieces were each the size of a small child, and the old men strained to lift them. Gwendolyn did not understand the rules of that game, but she had always admired the artistic design of the tokens and enjoyed seeing people playing it. She joined the small group of people watching the men. She had never seen combatants in a chess game joking and laughing as they played, but these old men seemed as cheerful as if they were swapping lies over their beer, which stood in fancy steins on the nearby table. The chess pieces seemed to be moving randomly, not collecting around any goal or coalescing in kindred groups. Of course the score was not posted on a scoreboard, and Gwendolyn could not tell who was winning; neither team seemed to be dominating the playing field. She stood in the sunshine inhaling the aroma of the nuts and sipping her pleasant warm drink as she watched the good-natured camaraderie of the old men at their game. Eventually she drifted away and continued her trek through the town.

When the convention center arrived she turned inside. Kingman's keynote speech was scheduled to start within the half-hour, so she went to the Helvetica Room and found a seat early. She had her choice of places and took one in the exact center of the audience. She was glad to get off her feet after walking quite a few miles outside, and she found the chairs surprisingly comfortable. The room filled, gradually at first and then in a more hectic fashion. She found herself among a happy crowd of mostly similar white middle-aged men and women eager to gather pearls of wisdom from her famous father. About ten minutes before the presentation start time, large screens above and on both sides of the podium lit up. The coming talk's provocative title was revealed: "Why Your Charitable Donations Are Immoral."

At the appointed time the lights dimmed, and the audience quieted down. Gwendolyn was surprised, and she smiled as she recognized the man who took to the microphone. He introduced himself to the crowd as Director Professor Dr. Florian Q. Bok, founder of the Wholesome Globe Project, and the co-winner of this year's award. He gave a sentence or two about the Wholesome Globe Project's Swazizibia Mission, then said, "I want to welcome you all to what promises to be today's most exciting talk, and I see you prospectively agree, at least those of you standing several deep in the back." There was a rustling as audience members turned to see the crowds along the walls at the back of the room.

Gwendolyn could not help wondering why there were so many standing; certainly the room could have held several hundred more chairs—easily enough to seat all the standing people—if the seventy or eighty huge potted plants that had appeared since the morning had not been brought in, replacing many of the chairs she saw here earlier.

Dr. Bok continued, "I must say I'm proud to be part of the team receiving the cooperation award today. I flatter myself to think that my little mission has contributed in some modest way to the betterment of the world. Our work with the Worldwide Transformative Foundation has led to benefits beyond productive synergy in delivering care. We've expanded the boundaries of the concept of charity itself. Carefully cultivated, our insights should lead to growth in every single one of your organizations, and I know Dr.

Dressel-Meier's Foundation is set up to give you all great assistance in that regard.

"And we're hoping to work with the major players in international governance. We believe one day soon we'll see worldwide law superseding the parochial restrictions that weaken you, harass you in your work. We have a vision of the final defeat of those who would treat your organizations like common profit-seekers, corporations, rapists. I digress here. You will be as inspired as I am when you hear Dr. Dressel-Meier share, to the greatest extent possible within the cruel constraints of time, a few small slices of the wisdom he has garnered over decades in the business."

The curious souls in the audience were interested in learning about Kingman and his innovative approaches to his vocation; he had developed a world-class talent for promotion and showmanship in the furtherance of his good work. He was a charter member of the steering committee of Charity Coalescence of the World, the organization sponsoring this annual gathering, and many listeners were considering affiliating with the Foundation's network. The cost of this decision was far from trivial, and so they were all the more determined to size up the man.

Dr. Bok continued, stretching the truth. "I have gotten to know Dr. Dressel-Meier well over the past few years, and my mission is fortunate to have him on our board of directors. For those of you who don't exist… " He paused as the confused audience quietly supplied a few laughs audible here and there. "And by that I mean those in the improbable state of not knowing who he is, here are a few facts. Dr. Dressel-Meier founded the Worldwide Transformative Foundation thirty-two years ago and has directed it himself all this time. In that time this unique organization has cumulatively raised or directed more funding to charities and governments than any other institution in the world, all the while without an endowment of its own. It builds no general-purpose cash fund, but it relies on recurring donations from individuals, corporations and government entities to keep doing its good work. Charity Coalescence, the Glowing Circle, the Wholesome Globe Project, everyone—everyone works through the Worldwide Transformative Foundation these days. Here is the man himself now." Dr. Bok stepped aside and applauded, looking to stage left as strong music filled the air.

The audience clapped rhythmically as Kingman approached the microphone, his modest walk and gestures communicating an incongruous 'aw shucks' with every leisurely step. When he arrived at the podium the music was cut and his demeanor transmogrified. He struck an exaggerated leaning pose, hovered pregnantly for a few seconds, and then his voice boomed, "Did I get your attention with the title?" There was laughter in the crowd, and nobody noticed Dr. Bok's exit. "Incidentally, I refuse to use the word 'ethical' in the title of this speech. That word has been hijacked by the various professional guilds to such an extent that it has lost its meaning, unless that meaning be 'Let's don't compete with each other for our captive customers' or some other such convenience." The audience murmured in understanding. "When I say 'moral' I mean 'moral' in the dictionary sense of the word. Good.

"Now, I want to talk to you about the most common blockages individuals, corporations and especially governments have that interfere with the funding of charitable groups like your own. Organizations taking care of needs that the rest of society turns a blind eye to. You've all run into good people, moral people, who want to make donations, to contribute their resources or those of the organization they represent, but who have reservations. There are some natural laws in play here. Even, and maybe I should say especially, some of the most able to invest large sums fall victim to a common small set of questions and doubts. You will recognize them, and I will tell you how to deal with them." The screens above and beside the central stage simultaneously lit up with the same objection:

- But you spend my money on overhead.

Each screen displayed the statement in a different color. Kingman continued, "When some people want to do good, they need to jump right to the solution. They want to get their hands dirty and participate in the results. These are universal and understandable human impulses. But somehow we must grapple with the fact that though a donor has become, say, a sophisti-cated billionaire contemplating his legacy, or a high-level government official considering the best place to put his constituents' spare funds, he is still subject to these normal human needs. And worse, this sort of donor, the accomplished person, is difficult because he is thinking of himself as a proven problem-solver entering the situation.

"Indeed the cynicism I have encountered in these individuals—and I would include the high-level corporate executive in search of a home for some of his stockholders' money—this trustlessness is a real problem. It combines with the arrogance so often developed along the way to worldly success, and it confronts you with a problem. That problem sits across the table from you: a donor who believes he knows how to do your job better than you do. A person who assumes he needn't go through the proven, established channels for realizing and distributing the benefits his donation should make possible. A donor who believes that he should somehow act in a direct fashion. Cut out the middleman, so to speak. And he sees you as nothing but that middleman." Three hundred or more of the thousand or so heads in the crowd—males grey and most balding to one extent or another, females carefully coiffed—nodded in recognition.

"But in what other complex human endeavor can a neophyte—let's even stipulate it is a highly intelligent man or woman, accomplished in an unrelated field but a greenhorn in ours—in what other discipline can such a person instantly deliver high performance results all alone without tapping the existing infrastructure to support his efforts? That infrastructure is the thing that facilitates our productivity; it is also the thing he so disparagingly calls 'overhead.'

"In the United States, in the century before last, they built a railroad across the whole continent. It was a massive undertaking with a huge cost in time, money and even lives. It was so expensive that to encourage the development, the government gave away grants changing the ownership landscape of the entire western part of that country, changes which persist today. Once the railroad was completed it revolutionized the entire continent. And now of course, anybody could walk up and ship a package a thousand miles. It's pretty simple: just put it on the train.

"Let's compare some charitable work, say feeding the hungry, to shipping something across a continent. Nobody says, 'I have a package, and I think I'll get on a bicycle and take it across myself,' do they?" The audience laughed. "They understand that the way to get a package across the continent is to use the existing systems. Railroads. Airplanes, Trucks, whatever. Overhead. Well, we, all of us in this room, we are that railroad infrastructure. That's overhead."

Gwendolyn's mind started to drift as she found her father's subject less than compelling. She remarked to herself how soft the chairs were in this room, how much more comfortable they were than the ones she filled for the other sessions she had attended. The rest of the audience seemed to be eating up Kingman's speech as Gwendolyn sank down in her seat.

"Most large charities lose millions of income every year to this false impression, the idea that, 'since I am a highly accomplished individual, I can go it alone,' or at least, 'You waste too much of my money.' You are perfectly justified in telling your benefactors that donations circumventing the existing charitable systems are not just misguided—they're destructive to those who need help. They are nothing short of immoral. We must all unite behind this position to open our donors' eyes and close our deals.

"When pressed for details the donor invariably starts with, 'You put too much money into administration and not enough is left to buy food for the needy.' Insert your own charity's end effect here, of course. If you are a charity that helps in the Central American wilderness, say, not enough money goes to paving the floors of the mud huts in the woods.

"Most of you answer by falling into the trap of quoting third-party auditing organizations who certify that you are operating within acceptable limits. This coaxes some donors into the fold, especially those in a corporate or government setting whose only reason for the protest is fear of criticism. Those folks can use your documentation for defense if they're later attacked for their decisions. But this approach makes others yawn; it misses the point and does not address the emotion at the heart of the complaint. We at the Worldwide Transformative Foundation never employ this argument. We never go into a defensive posture. Ever."

Through her drowsiness, Gwendolyn noticed that the audience was rapt. Something about Kingman's delivery or content was mesmerizing them. He continued. "It is true that one of my organization's services is, as many of you know, to compute these comparative overhead numbers. Indeed when we direct funds to our affiliated charities, we require that they contract us to determine those levels first. We do this not because we endorse it, but in order to function in a world we don't control. Everyone wants to see those numbers. When pressed for such overhead numbers for the Worldwide Transformative Foundation itself we never argue, we supply them. But we treat them as auxiliary information.

"I recommend you resist getting caught in the spiraling chase of debating whether some other charity has a percent less overhead. The number is meaningless. For instance, though we at the Worldwide Transformative Foundation do not focus on such ratios, our overhead level could be computed to be very high; we are a meta-charity and do very little work directly with the suffering. It all comes down to definitions. In fact in our case we take pains to calculate the number in the most punishing way, making sure it appears so high that observers cannot consider it to be computed on an apples-to-apples basis with the numbers from other organizations. They must enter into discussions with us to understand things."

Kingman was still rolling and the audience still enthralled. "Let me add, if you insist on being judged by this number, funding that comes to you through our organization can be accounted for in a way that cuts the overhead measured at your organization. In the limit, you could essentially 'outsource' most of your expenses; you could transfer your directors' compensation to our organization's books and have a very lean reporting number. There are also tradeoffs between expensing deferred compensation for your officers and handling it other ways. We can help you dress up your numbers for proper impressions. And we have expert partners within helpful international banks in many locations including here in Switzerland, the Cayman Islands, Hong Kong, and the Bahamas, just to mention a few."

Despite the mention of the exotic travel destinations, Gwendolyn was starting to feel sleepy in her soft chair. She looked around and saw many others with covered cups of wonderfully warm, caffeine-infused coffee and wished she had had the foresight to bring some in with her. Through her heavy eyelids she did not notice anyone looking bored or tired in the wide-eyed audience around her. She was alone in the crowded room.

"Fundamentally, the right answer to the overhead question is to fight fire with fire. The best defense is a good offense. Our real answer proactively promulgates the fact that it does cost money to grow, gather and transport food, fuel airplanes, and pay the hardworking people at each step of the way. We cannot give people a full education in economics, but we absolutely must convey that these things are not free. And the artificial classification of something as 'overhead' does not make this easier. There is no such thing. This is not a separable part of the process, not something that can be made to magically disappear."

Gwendolyn kept pricking herself up whenever she started to slump down during the prolonged monologue. She dealt with her boredom by looking around and marveling at this master, her own familiar father, holding the audience rapt with this arcane accounting jargon—one could hear a pin drop. She realized with some pride that her father was amazing right now. He was in his element, and he was delivering what the audience needed. This helped perk her up, and she renewed her attention on him.

"...we turn the discussion to our Foundation's food efforts when we discuss overhead. Always food. If we have to go elsewhere, we go to our medical efforts, but this is more complicated—people get confused when they think of costs allocated to paying for doctors traveling with their families to tropical locations with beaches during their children's school breaks; they don't perceive the inoculations, the risks, the surgeries. Just the beaches. The average American or European slob cannot comprehend the situation—the idiot wishes he could have a job where someone pays him to travel the world for a few weeks a year. He thinks he would happily bandage some sore feet in the bargain. And I emphasize I'm talking about not just Joe Six-Pack. I'm talking about heads of corporations, foundations. People with stressful jobs. Stick to food or something like it if you can."

Something in the atmosphere changed. Something silent. Gwendolyn had never heard her father talk like this. It was strange, as though he was a wind-up toy or something. She looked around and thought she saw others noticing the difference as well.

"...teach you many ways to respond and direct these conversations, none of which include calling our prospective donors idiotic slobs to their faces." He paused, and some in the audience expressed amusement. "I am getting a little silly here, but the point is that you can pick some single area for your own response. Just do it carefully. You need to counter all the objections people will use in their perhaps greedy, perhaps simplistic quest to avoid allocating their rightful donation to your charity. You need to be at least as convincing as the next guy on their list.

"When talking about overhead, we stay away from discussions of long-term investments, financing, salaries, leases and so forth. We concentrate on what a potential donor can grasp easily. So, concerning food: we emphasize that we cannot grow the food ourselves in New York City. We cannot get it for free. The man who pays out money for fertilizer, seed and equipment, and then breaks his back on the farm to produce wheat would himself starve if we could not direct money to him for his these things.

"And donors respond well to this line of reasoning. Seeds—that's overhead! It's not something we feed to the hungry, it's something we require along the way to produce the food we do feed them. Hmmm. Maybe overhead is necessary, maybe the distinction is artificial. And somebody has to arrange to purchase the seeds, store and transport the grain, all the while making sure it doesn't spoil and that too much won't be diverted to pirates outside or within governments. So the prospective donor sees that there are other higher-level people too, not just the farmer. We make the argument for truck drivers, airplanes and fuel, and so forth. It all comes down to this: if we tried to get food for free, with no overhead, no seeds, then how would we feed the starving? If you, Mr. or Ms. Donor, need to personally hand porridge to the mouth of a hungry child, what are the exact steps you have to take, and do they cost money? That's our overhead.

"As you see the donor soften, you may be inclined to lift your skirt a hitch or two. Let me give you a warning here. Stop right where you are. Never, ever discuss administrative workers. Nor facilities. Never mention anybody's tax situation except the donor's. And for goodness' sake do not allow the discussion to turn to your salary. Ever. All of us, all of you here today, work in nonprofit positions. You're in charities, universities, non-governmental organizations and government bureaus. You know there are too many people asking the question of how someone can go into a career serving others and become so wealthy. Don't provoke the query; it cannot be answered to the satisfaction of most of your contributors, not with the time you have, not with the educational level he has.

"As a side note, our organization has tools you can use. Of course we can work the compensation issues for you, but on the general overhead question, think about it: if you become a member of our network, then whatever your end focus is, you can steer this discussion through our food relief efforts with good conscience—we're involved in scads of food efforts, and you would now be affiliated with them. In fact, if you're working a particularly large donor, I suggest you enter our network, and we can send some of our folks to help talk him off the diving board. We are experts in this. We know how to close deals. My message to you is this: we are professionals. This is what we do. Your organization is almost certainly uncomfortable with this psychological science, and you hide from it. You face it only when you can't avoid it. Then you treat it on an ad-hoc basis, a stepchild if you will. This is understandable, as you must concentrate on what you are good at, but it's a mistake that is costing you dearly, especially with the large donors. And by extension that means it increases suffering in the world. You exist to alleviate that suffering. It's nothing short of immoral for you to fail to get better at this."

The last few sentences were delivered in a tone presaging a pause for applause. The audience complied mildly. Given his harsh language, Gwendolyn could not help wondering ironically if their approbation was in recognition of Kingman shutting up for a minute. As the clapping subsided he said, "I look forward to hearing from any of you who wish to explore our prospecting and closing services. We can talk at any of the receptions this week, or just make an appointment and we can visit another time."

One distinguished, European-looking man stood and spoke with a northern accent, "Will you be in the Alps with us next week, Dr. Dressel-Meier?" He sat down.

"Oh, yes." Kingman answered. "I almost forgot. For those of you staying for Charity Coalescence of the World's ski holiday, I will be there as well. I never did get the hang of skiing, and don't like the cold either." He smiled genially, and the audience chuckled. "But I will be going along, making myself available to all of you, working from my suite. Please come and share a drink. Thank you, Lars, for the reminder."

The audience was rustling, preparing for the close of the session, which was scheduled for five minutes prior. But Kingman was far from finished with his talk. The redundant screens darkened and then simultaneously shouted:

- I should just give this money to my church

There was confused movement as everyone realized the talk was continuing. Those who had risen sat back down. Good-natured nods from many in the audience who had remained seated indicated that they knew Kingman and had faced this challenge before; the nod from Gwendolyn indicated she was teetering on the edge of falling asleep. Kingman stood silently surveying the audience for a bit then said, "This is a common one for smaller donors, but it also arises with some large ones, and it's a dangerous thing.

"Here is the answer for the smaller donors: 'Look, I am all for churches. They do gods' work. When it comes to getting down on the streets and finding and helping the needy, these devoted individuals must be supported and admired. You should drop some money in the collection basket. And many churches send people overseas to serve the poor. This too requires support if it is to continue. Feel free to drop in a few extra bills.

"But understand this. Churches are, by their nature, one of two things. On the one hand, a church is usually just a small group of individuals. They may go so far as to sponsor a member to travel far away and do missionary work, someone to help with health needs of the unfortunate. But just as a farmer can only do so much with some horses and a plow, churches are limited in what they can do with the tools they have. We need to use a more powerful system to perform at a higher scale.

"I think you will agree that these smaller churches are not too much of a threat; any donor with enough money to be truly interesting will instinctively avoid dumping too much in the lap of some local pastor. That brings me to the opposite type of church: a huge organization. A megachurch or a denomination, which can be seductive and is able to absorb a large contribution from a benefactor. Now, in most of your countries this only threatens your money from a few individual donors—civil society proscribes the involvement of corporate or government donors, and an adult outlook stops most individuals from donating too much to churches.

"But sometimes a church can have a pull on a contributor. He feels it is close to his heart; maybe his daughter got married there. Opportunistic ministers will happily produce charts that show their church has a very low overhead as measured by accounting rules. You must make your prospects understand that this is smoke and mirrors; it is supported by untaxed property and invisible deferred moral obligations to the ministry and other employees. Religion is a problem in most of your countries.

"And if we're talking about a large giver—if someone is on the brink of funding construction of an entire church wing, we at the Worldwide Transformative Foundation have tools to walk the potential donor through the decision process. We can help him discover why it is more efficient and more morally correct to donate the money to your organization, whatever it may be, than to the religious one. If he still insists on building the wing, our sophisticated analysis can prove it's more effective for the church to contract you to build it with his money. We outline the advantages—professional management and the corresponding increased efficiency, the checks and balances that come with having a third party involved. In fact, we have managed the building of several entire churches and in each case we've obtained at least twenty percent more from the donor than the amount he promised originally. None of projects came in over budget either; the increases were voluntary enhancements the donor was moved to make as we progressed, which means we did what the people in industry call turning a profit." There was a quiet, amused and satisfied current of smug laughter in the crowd.

"I should add here that I just use the example of churches because that is what comes up the most often, and it's one of the most difficult ones. But be aware there are many small charities, founded by well-intentioned individuals, usually people who are not notably rich. Each tries to address a specific niche directly. These may be substituted for the church in the example. The group helping disfigured soldiers adjust to life back home. The local food drive for the needy. The person who funds a summer recreational program for young children who are otherwise trapped in a desert of cement. The veterinarian who treats animals for free. Groups of people visiting the sick in their homes. This list goes on and on. The principles are the same. Use us."

Kingman took a drink from the glass of water in front of him and stood quietly in a deliberate and calm pose. Gwendolyn had been daydreaming, and she was jarred to awareness by his sudden silence. After a pause Kingman's screens put up big red letters. They said starkly:

- It is immoral to give charitable help to one with whom you have direct contact

He stood, extending his calm through the small murmur of confusion that ran through the crowd. He said, "Think about it. Why do people give money to help other people? Is it really to help the other people, or is it some selfish action to gratify their own need to feel good about themselves? It is incumbent upon us to force the public to face this question, so listen closely: if an act of charity is to be valid, its function cannot be to simply alleviate some mote of misery resident in the eye of the giver. The act of giving to charity is not the act of scratching an itch or lancing a boil. In fact, I claim *that* is the exact opposite of charity. Selfishness." He paused to let the gathered crowd think. There was quiet shock and a few whispers rumbled around.

"Many people understand, at least on some level, that handing money to the local beggar is wrong, because he will just buy rum with it. And they are correct. But these very people would be surprised to know it's equally wrong to buy him a nutritious supper!" The audience whispered in captivated confusion.

"Let me explain. First, something on this scale is not charity in any worthy sense of the word—it's not a sacrifice. And if the situation of the giver is such that it could be considered a sacrifice it's perhaps even more wrong—because it is just the expression of the inborn human quasi-masochistic impulse to hurt oneself and feel good about it. Hurting yourself is never good. But the biggest consideration is the fact that this sort of giving does more harm than good. Sporadic and temporary measures to alleviate ongoing problems are a mathematical mismatch guaranteed to be ineffective. Think about all the warnings you have seen, 'Do not feed the animals.' Those signs are there because feeding the creatures is ill-advised; it can harm them, lead to their starvation.

There was a noisy ruckus several rows ahead of Gwendolyn and about twenty seats over. Six or seven people sitting in the audience started an excited discussion among themselves, rudely interrupting everyone around them. Kingman took no real notice from his distance; he went on with his talk in the background of Gwendolyn's awareness. But over the next few minutes much of the audience's attention was drawn to the commotion, and it seemed to be replicated in a half dozen spots in the room.

Kingman ignored what became a growing annoyance of fluctuating noise at dispersed points in the large crowd. "...work with us. These are subtle arguments that you are most likely to get right by using our materials. You cannot win over a donor by using the words I just used here; your quarry will perceive you treating people like nothing more than animals; he will think you are discounting the noble human impulse to help others. The sort of words I use is just between us girls, just to make you clearly comprehend what I am saying. But when this is expressed delicately, a thing we can help you do, your charity should be able to convince potential donors of the wrongheaded and counterproductive nature of this sort of contribution. Their money will end up in your pocket, not the local soup kitchen or liquor store."

Gwendolyn's thoughts were circling Kingman's treatment of people and animals when one of the audience members, a heavy-set woman sitting near the front, spoke out loudly, "What about the individual approach to stimulating donations? Not the individual donor, but the individual charity target? You know, the picture of the little starving girl we offer to our prospects for metaphorical adoption? We use that all the time. Are you saying this is wrong?"

Kingman's answer surprised many after his prior words. "Thank you for the question. I fear I would have left a wrong impression without it. This is quite a different thing. This avenue is a morally valid choice. It's part of a professional, ongoing effort by an established charity, not a one-time offer from a dilettante to essentially buy a bum a drink. Now, one may ask if the process allows the individual to trick himself into pretending to believe he is gruntling one heart-wrenching case. Well, yes. That's the gambit, let's be clear. But it's used in an organized way, within the established professional infrastructure. And if there's trickery, it's not you who is launching it. Overt deception is wrong, and we must not engage in it. In this situation it is the prospect who feels the need to trick himself in order to satisfy an impulse to feel he is doing good. You can be assured the approach is good, moral. And I think you all know that this method, tying an individual face to funding appeals, has been shown to be effective in increasing and stabilizing cash flow. We at the Foundation have products all of you can use for this." He stood overlooking the audience as though waiting for another question; perhaps he was waiting for the now almost-contiguous shuffling and controversy in various places in the crowd to settle. Gwendolyn ruminated what her father said, and she was uncomfortable with this subject, especially after watching that senator at the mission. She was starting to think her father may have a hidden side she had never seen. The thought was uncomfortable.

Just then a group that had been making a disturbance not far from Gwendolyn stopped chattering among themselves. They arose in unison, shaking their heads as if in disgust. Without regard for disruption they were causing others, they fumbled their way to the aisle, bothering everyone they passed. Kingman stood patiently. The entire room watched as the disruptors proceeded on down the aisle, shaking their heads and emitting throaty noises. Gwendolyn looked around and saw that in at least ten more places in the audience, similar groups followed their lead. Not a word was spoken, but the whole room sat and waited as fifty or more apparently disgusted or angry people slowly and theatrically harrumphed out of the room. *They all look the same. Even the men and the women, they seem counterparts of each other. Actually, so does the whole audience.* Gwendolyn wanted to be angry with them for disturbing her father's speech, but she could not; her own trepidation with what she was hearing gave her some empathy with them. Just then the overfed and well-dressed man to her left elbowed her in the ribs and smirked, "Rookies." She looked at his smiling face and almost shared in the revulsion of the protesters.

"I would be remiss if I failed to mention one more logistical matter here." Kingman resumed his speech with nary an acknowledgement as the last of the protesters approached the back of the room. "And remember this is, as I said before, just between us girls. This is shop talk. Unrestricted donations, of course, are the preferred type of contribution we all seek. But the Foundation's materials can also be employed with more emotional leverage to reach people who would never donate into some kind of pool.

"Of course, you can arrange your pitch such that a donor would form the opinion that his money is channeled to a certain piteous individual whose plight is used to pry the donations from his reluctant fingers. Let's call her Sally. Let's say she is suffering from cancer in Southeast Asia. But there absolutely must be fine print specifying that the final destination of the funds is up to you, not the donor. If you fail in this, you are not meeting your ethical obligations, let me assure you. You must keep your noses clean here.

"I encourage you to have letters and pictures and videos made on behalf of, or even personally by, Sally and sent through you to prospective benefactors. This perceived human touch is the icing on the cake that can enhance donor commitment and really lock in your cash flow. But somewhere in whatever agreement the prospect signs there must be content which you can use to claim that he should have understood he was donating to your general fund, not directly to Sally. Personally I think it's optimal if you can arguably direct a portion of his donation to that individual, though. It's pretty easy, and we can help here. All it takes is some amount of cash flow to something serving Sally, however indirectly.

"And one more thing. As a practical matter it is essential that the same individual case is not recycled to different donors likely to compare notes. This puts any pleasant fiction generated by the donors—the illusion on which some depend—in the worst sort of jeopardy. Imagine Aunt Betty visiting Cousin Jane and seeing a framed picture of her own adopted refugee on the coffee table! Pay close attention to the postal codes of your donors or risk this disaster!" The now-distilled audience laughed, and Kingman paused as they elbowed each other in jest, amused at the scenario of the unsuspecting donors colliding.

Gwendolyn was nonplussed. Kingman's speech and his answer to the fat woman disturbed her increasingly. *It's just… dishonest. That's not like Daddy.* With the crowd's laughter she felt as though she had been psychologically ejected like an unwelcome virus from the collective body in the room. *But he wouldn't play people. Maybe it's actually impossible to track thousands of individual monthly cash donations to thousands of victims. Hmm. It can't be how it sounds.* She made a mental note that she had to talk to her father about it later. She instantly forgot.

"…track the history of all efforts using the same database of needy faces. Be careful with pictures, and even scripts for appeals. You can probably guess by now that the Worldwide Transformative Foundation has significant apparatus to streamline all this for our partners. We have several non-overlapping databases indexed by distress type and all the tools and scripts for dealing with donors. And I should mention that the Foundation has much more sophisticated ways to warn of probable collisions than just postal codes. Methods based on social networks and relationships. Work with us"

Gwendolyn was partially listening, but by now she was spending some of her time bewildered. Unable to figure things out, her mind wandered as though she were reading an inconsequential, peripheral passage in a novel. She was not an inhabitant of the world of this audience, she was an alien; she was that virus. There was a shared set of assumptions and understandings among the people in the room, and she could not grasp it. Her own father was included in that group. She started to feel stupid, or at least guilty for not concentrating enough to understand. Then she snapped out of it. *But wait a minute. I'm not so bad. Imagine someone who has never been on a boat coming onto our sailboat. He would need time to understand the words and all the rules and assumptions about how the wind and water affect the different sails, and the lingo. The keel. Gunwales. Starboard. Jibe. Tack. Learning anything takes time. I'm new to this.*

"... remember time is part of the equation. Aunt Betty can't see her little Velma remain four years old for all the years she is funding you..." More knowing chuckles circulated in the audience. More discomfort grew in Gwendolyn. "...want to return to the overall subject of direct individual action. Let me summarize by saying we need to tactfully make the donors understand that the act of doing a direct donation to someone seemingly in need is morally indefensible and that while such acts may make the giver feel better, real charity must be left to those professionals who are dedicated to its permanent pursuit, those who have created the machinery to make it efficient."

Next, Kingman's screen posted summary points. "I want you to walk away with these points firmly lodged in your psyche. They will help our industry and therefore not just the world but the entire universe." He stood uncharacteristically silent as he let the audience read:

- The goal of charity is to help others
- It is immoral for individuals to seek to feel better by helping others directly
- For an act of charity to be valid it must be executed by established professionals
- Large operational scale is important for proper delivery of humanitarian aid

The screen darkened and changed to a dancing pattern of geometrical squiggles. Kingman took a sip of water, then motioned to stage left and a reluctant-looking Dr. Florian Q. Bok was coaxed onstage. Energetic and subdued music rose in the hall as Kingman said, "Thank you all, and I hope to see you all working with the Worldwide Transformative Foundation! I am so proud of my organization and of Dr. Bok and the Wholesome Globe Project!"

Simultaneously the GVCD of everyone registered at the conference received an incoming notice. The auditorium's music piped from every device and simple contact information was embedded into the GVCDs.

Gwendolyn slipped out during Kingman's first standing ovation and went back to her room for a nap. She ignored the stacked messages from her mother on the GVCD that Winifred had insisted on loaning her. The woman had sent most of the messages to Gwendolyn during Kingman's speech, a speech she did not attend. Gwendolyn shrugged as she saw the device sitting on the shelf with its urgent notices flashing anxiously, and fell comfortably asleep on the soft bed.

Gwendolyn woke with help from her mother bursting noisily into her room. "I've been so worried about you, dear. I've been trying to find you all day," Winifred said as she pocketed her quasi-illicit copy of Gwendolyn's room key. She rushed over as Gwendolyn sat up and gave her daughter a hug. Gwendolyn reassured her that she would be at the dinner table with the family at the awards ceremony, and a mollified Winifred left to get herself ready.

The dinner and the evening ceremony were tolerable; there were no long-winded speeches. Kingman and Dr. Bok accepted the award with the briefest of addresses, and most of the evening was spent in facile conversation at the table. Gwendolyn enjoyed watching people whirl to the wonderful Viennese orchestra on the flourishing dance floor. She blushingly accepted dance invitations from several of her father's business partners, but mostly she sat and visited with her mother and Sarah as Kingman and his sons worked the room with Dr. Bok. The only tarnish on the evening was her mother's fusillade of nettlesome pleas for her to leave the mission and come back home.

Finally, late in the evening, Gwendolyn sat relaxing in the luxurious accommodations of her suite, almost disappearing into the pillow-like sweetness of a cushioned chair. She thought about turning on the television or connecting but decided against expending the energy. She sat mindlessly for a while, then had a sudden thought. She impatiently wiggled free of the body-hugging cushions and rushed over to pick up the GVCD. She would talk to Alitisha! But the device was paralyzed, frozen in a state flashing notices about calls from her mother. She fumbled with the small, sleek European device, searching for the magic combination of manipulations to bring it to attention. It had no moving parts, but she poked and stroked with increasing frustration. The machine never changed state; it just kept blinking its varying-color message at her. She replaced the device on the table and turned her thoughts to getting some sleep. Some of those thoughts must have happened out loud, as the GVCD heard something she must have said, and immediately turned itself off.

The result of this act of insubordination was a burst of energy as Gwendolyn tried all sorts of likely phrases in the only language she knew, in the hope that the intransigent machine would hear a command forcing it to wake itself. Five full minutes went by this way.

The hotel was opulent and historic, and one of its claims to fame was its old-time decor. The beds and the fancy bathroom fixtures in Gwendolyn's suite were crafted to represent the nineteenth century. The hotel rooms had actual working telephones from the late twentieth century, devices that transmitted only voice without any images. She had an idea. She picked up the old-fashioned telephone and felt like she was in a black-and-white movie. Soon she had the woman downstairs summoning Alitisha's GVCD. She held her breath as she waited for her friend.

"Hello?" the tinny electronic voice in the massive earpiece was a bath of warm brandy and honey to Gwendolyn' spirit, despite the fact that Alitisha sounded like she was sitting in a garbage can and pinching her nose.

Gwendolyn spoke, "It's me!" The phone only produced silence. Alitisha was confused—rarely did she get a call from an unknown source during her dinner; perhaps never had she gotten a call without being able to see the caller. And who knows what Gwendolyn's voice sounded like on the other end? Gwendolyn tried again, with more identifying information: her name.

"What? Who?" It seems that even the name could not get Alitisha's mind to wrap around the odd call with the blank screen.

Gwendolyn started blubbering, a signature instantly recognizable to Alitisha even with the decreased bandwidth of the old equipment. Not only could Alitisha tell it was Gwendolyn, she decoded information embedded in the sobs—it was not a cry of distress or angst, fear or pain or anger. This cry communicated love. She replied, approximately word for word, in exactly the same language.

After this initial phase of their communication the girls both sat silent, magically exchanging deep emotional content over the narrow communication channel. Then they simultaneously transitioned into a more sedate continuation of the initial sobbing communication. This went on for a few minutes, alternating crying with silence. A few of the quiet spells on each side were consumed not with communication, but with attempts to gather composure and form words.

Eventually the girls switched to spoken English as their communication protocol and began a traditional conversation. Gwendolyn talked little at first. She learned that Alitisha had a new kitten whose name at the moment was Kitty. She kidded Alitisha about Kitty's name, about how temporary pet names are never temporary. They laughed. Alitisha confessed that she had developed a crush on a guy she hardly knew, a man who worked downtown. As for Gwendolyn's contribution to the conversation, her emotions flew high as she described working with the children, then low as she described that day when the patient died in the clinic. Alitisha listened well, but asked for no elaboration about anything at the mission. She was generally supportive regarding Gwendolyn's work there but as could be expected, she thought Gwendolyn could come home now and told her so. Gwendolyn was in a good enough mood to say, "Have you been talking to my parents?" to which they both had a good laugh.

Finally, Alitisha indicated that she really, really had to go; she was destined to be late for work. She worked at an eating and drinking establishment in Burlington. Not coincidentally, it was a place frequented by the unnamed but handsome figure currently animating her dreams, and she expected he would stop by there tonight.

The next morning the family said a leisurely goodbye over coffee and breakfast. Winifred was emotional but held back her tears and did not suggest Gwendolyn come home. Around midday Gwendolyn and her mother met the limousine; Sarah, Bok and his two canines were already inside. Gwendolyn gave one last hug to Winifred. They exchanged their contact-free kisses, then she turned and climbed into the vehicle. She maneuvered into the only available seat in the plush automobile, resigning herself to enthusiastic tongue-wielding greetings as she lodged herself into the place Dr. Bok had saved for her, knowing how she loved animals. She settled between Colonel and Bourbon, both of whom were happy to have her company. Gwendolyn sullenly envisioned eighteen or twenty hours in the company of the cheery animals with the nasty breath as they traveled through the several hops from Zurich to the mission. As the limousine pulled away she glanced out the rear window and saw her mother motionlessly biting her nails and watching the vehicle shrink in the distance.

A Yield of Darkness

Can I just go back in time?

T he sun winked above the horizon, and its heated deep-orange beam brushed Gwendolyn's face, piercing her stiff and comfortless sleep. The airplane was approaching the mission. She broke the seal between her eyelids, and she was looking at Sarah, who was sleeping awkwardly in the row ahead of her, across the aisle. Gwendolyn's muscles were still asleep, and without moving her head she looked at the pilot. He was happily tapping his foot to music presumably coming through the electronics in his earpiece. A half dozen empty beer cans littered the floor under and around the instrument panel, occasionally jumping as his foot squeezed the end of one of them. Gwendolyn's eyes swept back and alighted on Dr. Bok, directly across the aisle. He interrupted his work to smile in her direction and launch a friendly wink through his thick glasses, then turned back to his reading. As she approached wakefulness, she perceived the cabin's permeating canine aroma, and she heard the dogs rustling, shaking off their own slumber. Early in the flight Dr. Bok had drugged them and led them to their cages in the cargo area, cages which were perhaps better described as little dog castles—carpeted, doorless things with little curtained windows on the side walls.

Gwendolyn looked at the animals. Bourbon was leisurely licking his genitals, one leg in the air. Colonel was observing, seemingly indecisive about whether to mimic his brother or help him or do nothing. Default, Colonel's main guiding principle, ensured that he selected the latter choice. He commenced shaking his head in the air and swinging his flapping tongue around the edges of his mouth.

As Gwendolyn turned back, the glimmer of a dream washed partly into her mind and drained away. She sat still, instinctively reaching for the disappearing tendrils of the story before they were gone, but they slipped into the void, and her effort came up empty. The more she forced things, the clearer her failure became. She gave up and flipped her head toward the sun and closed her eyes tightly. As she relaxed, verging on sleep, she caught a glimpse of the dream, but again it dropped slowly away from her helpless grasp as though taunting her. She was still tired, and she surrendered herself within the shrinking confines of an increasingly somnolent shroud. After a timeless period she noticed the dream showed itself to her from the periphery of her mind. She turned toward it, and as she barely touched the ephemeral thing, she had a glimmer of a feeling that it was a recurring story. She pursued it. Just then she dropped off to sleep, and her quarry turned, spread out and enveloped her.

She was participating in some strange ritual of giving blood to sickly children who needed transfusions badly; the scene was indistinct and mysterious and strangely static. Blood traveled through a complicated apparatus of transparent hoses that seemed to motionlessly mix the fluid of thirty-seven people with that of a group of six other strange donors, huge and mysterious individuals situated one level downstairs from her. The blood went into a huge tank near the six strangers. Gwendolyn was one of the thirty-seven, and her precise knowledge of the exact numbers was an incongruous part of the background, as though it had been set up in some nonexistent introductory chapter. The pipes entered the glass tank and then the liquid flowed statically through tiny tubes to a group of sleeping children lying on the ground yet another floor down. All was visible because everyone was situated around large openings in the floors, and the hoses ran through these holes. Gwendolyn and her counterparts wore long hospital gowns that hid everything but their heads. The donors below were somehow foreign, ominous. Dark, hooded robes completely hid them. She could not identify the color of the robes; in fact the only color in the dream was the subdued dark red of the blood. The children slept innocently in normal clothing as they received their life-giving infusions.

The hoses from those around Gwendolyn were thin and egressed the gowns of the motionless donors through the sleeves. The robed individuals downstairs were attached to much larger tubes that emerged from the darkness of their draping hoods. Blood was visible through the tank and pipe walls; Gwendolyn could see no motion anywhere in the dream but knew the blood was moving within the tubes.

As she was looking at the mysterious donors on the level below her, she saw her father standing among their beds, entreating her and motioning to her. His arms swept over the five beds of the donors around him, and he stood in his heavy, shiny shoes on a robe, impeccably dressed as always. He repeated his silent calls and gestures. Symbolizing something she did not understand, he swept his two arms in a circular motion, one up and one down, as though he were turning a ship's helm.

There was other motion in the dream now. Gwendolyn noticed a barely perceptible change in the big donors around her father. First she noticed the one next to him. His robe was moving, ever so slightly. Closely examining the other four she was presented with the same thing: the impression of balloons being slowly inflated under the cloaks. She paused to look at her own arm and saw that her tube had disappeared; looking at her colleagues, she saw that the other thirty-six donors were still giving blood through their tubes. Just as she looked back downstairs, the robe of one of those next to her father fell open, dragged apart by the expanding girth of the donor and exposing its occupant—a huge, reddish-brown worm of some sort. The pipe entered the maw of the faceless beast whose other end drooped over the edge of the table, a slimy boneless appendage hanging lazily in the air. She lay horrified, looking as though at a monstrous, discolored turnip, a snake that swallowed some huge prey, a bladder about to burst. She noticed the other still-covered donors had similar tails hanging off their tables, protruding from their robes. Now several other robes were coming open.

She watched for a long time, paralyzed, as the invertebrate hulk adjacent to Kingman lay, its only motion being a gradual expansion of its circumference, which was soon accompanied by a gentle sweeping of its tail, which shortened as the creature's girth expanded. It was a disgusting sight, but she was somehow compelled to stare at the slimy monster. After a little while she looked back to her father. He stood smiling and nodding to her, answering a question she could not fathom.

Just then there was a flash of light and a wave of heat as though all the walls had burst into flames. The fire was over in an instant. A distant, dull hammering sound rose in the background.

Gwendolyn was back in the airplane's cabin. The plane was banking, and she could see the outlines of the windows carved by the rising sun as they moved forward along the wall. She realized she had seen this dream before, and she sat wondering what could it mean that the weird and formerly forgotten dream was now a repetitive occurrence, and it featured her father.

These things troubled her, and she found no interpretation. She sat looking out the window, occasionally glancing back at the dogs.

The plane eventually made its wide banking turn to approach the landing strip, and Gwendolyn could see the refugee camp itself directly below her window. The dustbowl seemed much larger than she had been envisioning it. She could not help turning to glance at the satisfied Dr. Bok sitting quietly across the aisle as she thought of his incongruous title for the amorphously designed camp: the Inner Quad, an expression she had never heard really used.

The trip had been long; they left the prior morning and had taken two other airplanes, the last of which made many stops before arriving at the capital. And then there was their pilot—he was not exactly sober when they met him at this plane. At Sarah's insistence Dr. Bok had forbidden takeoff until the man ingested multiple servings of coffee. Everybody had waited a long hour, sleepless for all, to make sure his body tissues were suffused with the caffeine. It was a most unscientific approach to physiological engineering but one that Sarah demanded. Interestingly, though Sarah protested during the flight, Dr. Bok refused to forbid the man's ingestion of beer while they were in the air.

The airplane made its run around the camp and approached the runway. Gwendolyn saw a truck and a group of local militia outside the perimeter. The men were stirring in preparation for the arrival ritual. She thought about the cargo. Today they may not be happy, as there was nothing to plunder. Dr. Bok must have been reading her mind, as he again winked at her with a smile and indicated the last row of seats with a tip of his head. She saw a few previously unnoticed stacks of small boxes marked 'Chocolate' in several languages.

The plane touched down with Gwendolyn listlessly looking out the window. The militia men were climbing into the trucks, several holding weapons, as the plane passed. Just a few seconds later something bright flashed by. It passed quickly, but she thought it looked like a colorful flag entangled in the barbed wire at the mission's perimeter. Sarah was starting to stir, but waking very slowly, some of her honey-colored hair flowing over her similarly complected face. Dr. Bok had put away his work by now.

The plane slowed. Gwendolyn could see another airplane at the end of the runway when her own pilot turned his vehicle around to taxi back. As they traveled along, Dr. Bok looked out the window aimlessly. Gwendolyn tried to see out the windows on his side, but Sarah in the seat ahead obscured most of the window, and Dr. Bok blocked her line of sight to all but a few slivers of the window directly across.

As they taxied Gwendolyn saw the brief surge of color scan by the interstices between Dr. Bok and his seat. Dr. Bok twitched suddenly, craning his neck to lock the mystery object in his sight. But Gwendolyn could not see anything. The plane lumbered along the runway, and she turned to look out her own window. The top of the dirtpile created a jagged silhouette dancing against the brightening pink-orange sky.

When the doors were opened, the pilot picked up his duffel bag and disembarked immediately, trotting off toward the buildings. Dr. Bok deplaned next and approached the waiting militia truck where he started a conversation with the leader; he had picked up one of the boxes of chocolate with which to launch the discussion, and he presented it forthwith. Sarah and Gwendolyn came out next. Gwendolyn noticed that she never got used to being close to men so casually carrying automatic weapons.

Bourbon and Colonel sat outside their houses within the airplane, agitated. They whined loudly, but they had been trained not to leave the cargo area in such situations. Dr. Bok soon interrupted his conversation and sent Sarah and Gwendolyn in for the rest of the chocolate, which they got, disappointing the dogs in the process, and egressed. They emerged barely able to carry all of Dr. Bok's gifts to the armed leader.

Sarah opened the hatch to the luggage area. She brought out all the pieces, placed them on the ground, picked up her own and headed back toward the executive residence. Dr. Bok called the dogs, and as they disembarked the militia men gave them a wide berth; upon seeing Bourbon and Colonel they became wary but not panicked. Guns casually swung forward and trigger fingers quietly lodged on triggers as the leader continued to talk to Dr. Bok, albeit from a few steps back. Dr. Bok commanded the dogs to sit, and Bourbon began walking in a circle with a diameter a fraction of his body length; Colonel sat sniffing the air as Bourbon revolved, then both dogs looked down the runway. The militia leader sent two men into the airplane and they returned quickly, apparently verifying the dearth of cargo. The leader nodded to Dr. Bok, and the men returned to their truck carrying guns and chocolate.

While Dr. Bok was distracted with the militia leader, the dogs had started trotting down the runway with Bourbon's nutating nose preceding them, held high in the air. Colonel followed the lead dog, settling for Bourbon's decisions on such things as where, why, and how fast to run.

Gwendolyn remembered the brightly colored flag and wondered if that was what the dogs were after. She started walking after the animals. After a time the beasts sped up, then suddenly they veered toward the mission periphery. Gwendolyn saw their target a half-mile from where she was, and she started jogging along the animals' trail. When the dogs reached their goal they danced excitedly, hopping in tight ovals. Bourbon barked. Colonel howled. Gwendolyn inexplicably descended into bewildered alarm and accelerated into a full run. The colors on the splotch started to become distinct as she approached.

Long before her brain identified what she was seeing, her unconscious mind told her that she was facing a terrifying tragedy. Without willing it she broke into a frantic sprint, hoping against hope that the unfathomable and nightmarish, though yet indistinct, horror would not be real. Her heart pounded. She found herself panicking. She marinated in the purest form of dread—fear of the past—as she rocketed with all her might toward the frightening mystery.

Now, Gwendolyn had been carefully raised from babyhood with no inclination to believe in any universal power greater than man. Nonetheless she possessed the shared atavistic impulses of the human race, and she hammered out frenzied, unformed prayers and promises to God in senseless, oxygen-starved desperation, hoping hopelessly to bribe Him to alter this grisly unseen prior event before it reified for her.

As she got close a ghastly scene came into focus. A small, brightly colored blanket flapped in the wind, caught on the fencing. Gwendolyn stopped, gasping as she took in the rest of a shocking and gruesome tableau. Adjacent to the rippling blanket, a motionless Jojo was suspended upside down, ferociously entangled with barbed wire. The filaments and blades of the ruthless steel clasped him from myriad angles, tearing into his body and holding him almost upside-down. Rivulets of blood had flowed up his to his head and spiraled along his arms, leaving viscous tacky trails and culminating in simple desiccated stains on the dry dirt beneath stalactites projecting from his inverted body. Bourbon sat near the little boy, tentatively probing with his paw and whining. Colonel observed, also whining.

Gwendolyn looked at the wires around his waist, leg and neck. At least five razor edges were embedded in his torso and neck; numerous barbs penetrated his skin from head to feet as well. He had a gash in the side of his abdomen the size of a small cucumber. It was clear that the boy had struggled mightily, all the while becoming more entangled as the cold metal spikes and razor edges combined the strategies of the boa constrictor and the knife fighter to extinguish his life in a death of a thousand cuts. The boy's eyes were closed, and his mouth was open. His only motion was a lifeless springing response to the jostling of Bourbon's prying nose and paw.

Standing still on the motionless ground, Gwendolyn fell. She crumpled to the earth, eyes on Jojo all the way down. Her head slammed into the hard dirt, and somehow that seemed proper. Vaguely she heard a motor; the militia truck trundled up slowly. The machine looped in a circle, almost stopping as the men gaped to see the boy. Gwendolyn, her cheek in lifeless contact with the ground, blinked motionlessly as the truck accelerated away, kicking dirt in her face. Observing as a dead person would, she saw the vehicle shrink in the distance as it drove directly away from her on its way back.

She turned her face into the dry ground, lingered, then struggled to her feet. She became aware of footsteps. Without taking her eyes off Jojo, she saw Dr. Bok saunter up behind her, cane in hand. His brow was furrowed and his pace steady, controlled. He walked around her and went right up to the boy and stood stroking his beard. He alternated looking at Gwendolyn and Jojo. "Oh, my goodness. Oh my goodness," he said in a raised pitch. He shooed Bourbon away and got down on one knee, his white trouser leg lowered into the dirt. He theatrically steadied himself with one hand on his cane and superfluously felt for signs of life in the cold lifeless child with the other. He touched a few clean spots along the boy's body, brushing his skin, palpating, probing. Still kneeling, his head turned to face Gwendolyn atop his plump neck and traced a single slow round trip of an arc to one side. He stood up and looked down.

Gwendolyn burst into tears, and Dr. Bok came over, taking her shoulders in his arms. She felt the head of the cane on her arm as Bourbon started whining.

"That boy is gone. Such a terrible accident," Dr. Bok said gently, placing one hand on the back of Gwendolyn's head as he buried her dirty and streaming face in the warmth of his corpulent chest, likely staining his clothing.

She started, lifting her head to look at his eyes in sequence. "Jojo. It's Jojo." There was fire in her soaking wet eyes.

"Of course. Oh, my dear. You know the boy?" Dr. Bok thought he was comforting her.

Gwendolyn was incredulous. She pulled back in a violent heave, pushing Bok away. She glared into his face and pounded her fists on his shoulders and chest. He took the punishment without yielding, without complaint. She said, "Of course I know him. Don't you know him? What are you ..."

He was looking at her gently, expectantly, with questioning eyebrows. There had been unperceived mystery surrounding Dr. Bok, and it captivated her for the first time. Looking into his eyes in her distress, she suddenly understood that she did not know the man. She became certain she had seen only a mask, a facade. Perhaps the trip to Europe had set the stage for her deepened perception; maybe it was simply the integrated amount of clock-time in his presence that gave her to see a glimpse inside. Whatever caused her to discern, she saw that there was something hidden and dark about this man—Bok was not easy and friendly behind that easy and friendly visage. She recoiled with an instinctive sting of horror, focusing on Bok's neutral and vague eyes as she backed away. Just then a glint of reflected light from the rising sun caught her eye and drew it down to his cane. She had never noticed before, but the head of the cane terminated in an ornate, golden 'IDIC' logo. She stepped back another step.

Just then she heard heavy, slow footsteps far behind her, and she turned around to look. She saw a tall, disturbing man approaching. He looked like some kind of old-time pirate emerging into proximity. The bearded man wore a black eye patch on his left eye as he dragged his heavy boots along the ground. He closed in, his form integrating increasing detail, and she recognized a blissfully forgotten Aloysius Fink, eye patch or no. His face was freshly scratched, and his skin seemed more pallor-infused than normal. The black eye patch and band added to the chilling effect of the man's hair and beard as it highlighted the lifeless blotchy skin on his face. As he approached, he was looking over Gwendolyn's head at Bok, his lone eye darting like a hypertensive raven between Bok's face and the boy.

Bok seemed to understand Fink. He stepped over to Gwendolyn and threw his arm around her shoulder, turning her toward the residences. Surprised and confused by the whole scenario, she complied. "You must get Dr. Boseau to take care of it," he said to Fink as they started to walk away.

Gwendolyn asserted control of herself and jerked free, almost falling over Bourbon. "Take care of it? Jojo?" Bourbon was snaking among and in front of her legs, blocking her and making her stumble. She kicked the monstrous dog, who howled in crestfallen surprise and ran a few steps away. "What is Dr. Boseau going to do for Jojo? He's not even a real doctor."

Bok made an attempt, violently rejected, to gather her shoulders back into his arm. He gave up and looked at Gwendolyn as he uttered, "Poor child." He repeated, shaking his head, "Poor child." He turned slowly and walked sluggishly toward home, shoulders drooping, looking at the ground, head still shaking. "There's nothing to do for him now, poor child." His words, drifting feebly over his shoulder, dissipated in the air as he walked at a pace so slow as to almost convey motionlessness. Gwendolyn was still furious with him, and her anxiety was exacerbated by proximity to Fink. She turned to the work of surveying the boy.

Aloysius Fink, having seen her first-in-her-life mistreatment of an animal, cautiously kept his distance from the young woman. He made the most of his unpatched eye; it traveled the region as he scanned the scenario. He watched carefully as Gwendolyn started to extricate the boy's upended body from the wires and blades. Bourbon repeatedly tried to participate, but Gwendolyn fended him off repeatedly, twice landing kicks to his ribs and once hitting his head. The dog eventually contented himself with snuffling along the ground, being careful to avoid entangling himself in the wires or approaching Gwendolyn's shoes. Meanwhile Fink seemed to be doing the same from a distance, his available eye serving as his search tool. Colonel had long since lay down about twenty feet from all the activity and was watching without interest.

Gwendolyn, having refused canine assistance and without human assistance, had difficulty unraveling the boy. Her strategy was to methodically move Jojo toward her from amidst the tangle of wires, all the while working from head to feet—from bottom to top. He was about four feet tall, and she was not accustomed to manipulating such an unwieldy fifty or sixty pounds. Her vision was repeatedly blurred by fresh tears, further impeding the delicate extrication process.

Wherever the coating of dust on the dried blood was broken, the blood was the consistency of glue or thick syrup, and though it did not flow, it spread to all it touched. She carefully freed his arms first with some success. They had been resting against some of the wires, pinned into place by spikes; they could move once the piercing spears were dislodged. Next she tried to move his head free, but first she had to dislodge the beveled edge of a razor flange from deep in his neck. As she cleared it, the springy wire bounced forward, the razor almost hitting her face as it jumped free, and a surge of blood flowed down the side of the boy's head. The razor hung shaking on the stiff metal two inches from her eye. She noticed that in the process, one of Jojo's arms had been pierced by an unseen spike, and she dislodged it. Soon Jojo's head and arms were free and hanging in front of the wires. Gwendolyn wet the bottom of her blouse by brushing it across her eyes and cheek, and she delicately cleaned the sticky, dust-infused blood from Jojo's face. She licked her hand repeatedly and wet the particularly offensive, tacky new streamlet from that last razor, scrubbing away all traces of it with the cloth. His countenance was now that of an inverted sleeping angel marked by bloody gashes.

The others—Colonel, Aloysius Fink and Bourbon—watched quietly. The dogs' tails wagged occasionally, and Fink's eye sometimes broke away to scan along the wire and the ground. At intervals he turned around a full circle, looking toward the schoolhouse and the clinic and even the dirtpile. Then from far away Gwendolyn faintly heard Bok whistle, a dramatically plaintive shriek from the better part of a mile away. The sound was so quiet and dispersed that it seemed optional and even irrelevant, but Colonel and Bourbon immediately jumped up and started slowly trotting toward Bok, who was finally arriving at the executive residence.

Now that Jojo's head and arms sections were out, the wire had tightened around his chest and stomach. His left leg was twisted in a convoluted mess of wires and his right leg had single wires running in front and behind. She lifted his torso, struggling for the strength, attempting to free two razors that penetrated from the lower side. Instead the wires just moved along with the body as the razors held firm where they bit the boy's flesh. She thought about asking Fink for help, but the idea extinguished itself with a quick look over her shoulder.

Gwendolyn crouched, holding onto the child's hips, carefully lifted her foot and brought her shoe down across the relevant wires and, with a massive effort, arched her back and lifted the boy's body up. The razor elements dislodged from his chest and abdomen. Mustering all her might she stood straight up and stepped back, bringing the body with her. Two wires jumped irregularly, but the rest of the motion was predictable. The wires tangling the legs were strained, but the child's body was otherwise free. Gwendolyn started to drop down for a rest, but just before letting Jojo go she saw he was headed for having a razor flange on the ground pierce his shoulder. She tensed her muscles and, with a strong effort, froze the boy's upper body momentarily in mid-air and moved away the offending blade with one foot. She let Jojo down, the body unfolding to the ground, and exhaled exhaustedly.

Now Jojo's weight was transferred to the ground through his back, and only his legs were still snarled in the wires. Gwendolyn let go of him carefully, making sure Jojo would not collapse catastrophically, and sat down. There was activity at the building beyond the power plant, and by now workers were getting ready for food preparation at the processing factories. But Gwendolyn was unaware of anything; all this activity was distant and outside the focus of her perception.

Gwendolyn had minor cuts on her arms and some rips in her clothes, none of which she noticed as she sat resting. She resumed her task, going to work untangling first the easier leg, then the other. Finally it was done, and the boy lay supine. Gwendolyn collapsed over him, sobbing, resting her face in his bloody stomach for a long time. She stood up and looked down, brushing dirt off his face. *At least his face is clean.* Unsuccessfully suppressing a whimper, she lingered a minute then, after a struggle, picked him up in a tremendous effort. She stood and held Jojo fast, her arms pressing him to her, his head over her shoulder. The boy's arms and legs flopped and bounced, and his feet dragged as she maneuvered him away from the scene.

Aloysius Fink did not think to make an effort to move out of Gwendolyn's way, just as it had not occurred to him to help her free the boy's body or pick him up. She bumbled clumsily around the enormous man, carrying the boy's body back toward the schoolhouse. As she walked around him Fink scanned over her head, looking at the barbed wire region where Jojo had been killed, and then he looked at the ground behind her, at the trail in the dirt. She stumbled along, and Fink remained behind, seemingly fascinated by the blanket, the fragments of cloth on the jagged wire, and the ground around the scene. After a few moments Fink's lonesome and darting eye must have tired of traveling the circuit of the tableau; he turned and walked toward the executive residence. He quickly passed Gwendolyn and her burden, sweeping them with one last stroke of his eye.

Gwendolyn staggered along carrying Jojo's body all the way to the schoolhouse. She put the boy down outside, not wanting to wake the children. She did not know why she brought it here; she simply had no other ideas, and neither Bok nor Fink had been of any help in the matter. In any case it was a good, if temporary, decision—she could go inside and find some things she needed for him. She brought out a blanket and some damp rags, then cleaned up Jojo's skin as best she could. She looked at the boy in the tattered, blood-stained clothes and spent a short interval sobbing. Not knowing what to do with, him she wrapped him completely in the blanket. She picked him up and looked around, turning a full circle with her mind idling and her back aching.

She found she had trudged back to her building in a single hop, with the incredibly difficult burden of the heavy child wrapped so as to afford no gripping point. She carried him up the stairs and through the lounge area, clumsily stumbling with his legs dragging between hers, as the other sponsored volunteers slept. She gently lay the bundle on the floor in her room, ineptly knocking Pyratticus Julius from his perch. She experienced the springy lightness of her own body without the burden of the dead boy as she stood up straight and stretched her aching back and arms. Her arms, especially, hurt and felt like they were made of rubber. She took a hot shower, her first in a long time, alleviating some physical pain. But she did not relax in the steam after the surreal adventure. Back in her room she picked up Pyratticus Julius, collapsed on her bed and fell into a forceful sleep.

Until early afternoon when something woke her up, Gwendolyn engaged in a somnolent frenzy of disturbing dreams. As she lay on the floor where she awakened, she recalled impressions of indistinct, frightful supernatural nemeses, ghostlike menaces approaching and encircling her and children from the schoolhouse, trying to tug the children away from her. Next her mind called forth other participants in her dreams: horribly detailed and bizarre apparitions including luminous skeletons with skin melting off their faces. She had the feeling that some of the monstrous ghouls were animated as representations of unidentified yet somehow known people, the sort of entities that can only exist in dreams. She lay still in an attempt to gather detail from her unconscious, to decipher the identities of her tormentors, all to no avail. Eventually she shook off all thoughts of the hallucinations.

Gwendolyn lay achingly on her side in the bright room, anchored down by the grogginess one gets from sleeping during a warm day. Pyratticus Julius was on the floor with her, four of his six tentacles bent under him. She sat up, warm and woozy, and wiped sweat from her cheek. She picked up her friend and held him to her, confused without knowing why.

She slowly remembered her father's triumphant speech in Zurich. Then she recollected the whole European trip, seeing her mother and brothers, the fine dinners, the incongruous sight of Colonel and Bourbon in the luxury hotel. She smiled warmly at the image of the dogs, seemingly never with more than one-quarter of their paws on the ground. Her massage had been wonderful. Then she shuddered as she saw Cecilia in Wales. Bok entered her mind. First he was jovially managing the bounding canines in the velvet halls of the hotel, then he delivered his enthusiastic warm-up routine for her father's speech. Gwendolyn's mind continued to awaken and storm clouds gathered within her. Suddenly the lightning struck, and she saw Bok standing over Jojo's body, fully composed, trying to wrap a core of nihilism with soft words that may as well have been copied from a cheap greeting card. Aloysius Fink's outline stood menacingly behind him in the greyish morning light.

This could not be Director Professor Dr. Florian Q. Bok. Or could it? Bok had tried to give Gwendolyn the impression that he felt Jojo's death was more consequential than getting his clothing dirty. She stood up and sat down on the edge of her bed. She thought about her disgust with Bok. In fairness, she knew only a small portion of Bok's world, and one of the things he dealt with regularly was the death of those under his care. But this morning she seemed to have some sort of x-ray vision; she saw something in him, something far more callous than a man forced to deal with mortality. Despite his forlorn demeanor, this was not a medical surgeon who must take calculated risks and lose patients, not a firefighter sorrowfully encountering a victim he is too late to save. This was a man who had no emotional connection to his patients at all. *And what right does he have to call them patients anyway?*

Gwendolyn, now having seen two dead people within two weeks, and exactly two dead people in one lifetime, one of whom she had come to love, had a difficult time trying to fathom how anybody could feel justified in continuing to draw breath in the face of such a tragedy. *How do people go on with their lives? Why?* She sat rocking back and forth, hugging Pyratticus Julius, staring vacuously at the floor.

An invisible smudge in the center of that floor triggered something in her mind. What was it? Something distressful. Jojo was here. *Jojo is gone. I put him on the floor before going to sleep. Didn't I? Yes, I did. But that was just...* she checked the time... *about six hours ago. Jojo vanished. But that's impossible. He is dead... He was dead... Maybe he is alive after all... Oh No! He needed medical help and I wrapped him and dropped him on the floor here and he got up and struggled out...*

No. Jojo was dead.

She bounded off the bed. She looked over the whole room, but nothing was out of place. She rushed to the door and opened it in a frantic panic. Heads of several of the sponsored volunteers turned at the sudden disturbance as though they had felt the wind from the door. The other room doors were mostly open. It was an average day. Nothing was out of place. She closed the door quickly, turning back into her room, hands on the sides of her disheveled, downcast head as she scanned her mind for clues to what was real.

It was all real. Jojo was dead, and he was not here where she laid him this morning.

A sudden revulsion flourished and gripped her from deep within. When it reached her skin she felt a flush of heat and a wave of goose-bumps from her chest out in all directions, reaching her head and extremities before it transformed to a cold wave and reflected back to her viscera, forcing a massive shudder. *Somebody came into my room and took him.* The reality of someone entering her unlocked room in the post-dawn hours, just inches from where she slept, was troubling enough. That this person would steal a corpse, the body of her beloved friend, toppled her into disequilibrium. She clasped her arms, curled up in a ball on the bed and shivered, rocking slowly on her side. An observer would see her as the classic maniacally disoriented Hollywood crazy lady, locked in the attic and hidden from the world. She shook back and forth, hair disheveled, imprisoned in an emotion between tears and madness. She settled into a muttering, sobbing ritual for a long time.

Finally, something within Gwendolyn exploded. She burst off the bed. "No!" she screamed loudly enough to again turn the heads of everyone in the lounge outside her closed door. Then she erupted through that doorway. She drove herself across the lounge and down the stairs, seeing nothing and nobody.

Gwendolyn went outside and made a bee-line for the administration building. As she approached the door, Sarah Greenwater was arriving at it from within. Gwendolyn blocked her exit and asked her if she knew about Jojo. Sarah bowed her head slightly and said, "I heard." Gwendolyn asked if she knew where the body was, and Sarah, seemingly knowing nothing beyond the fact of the boy's death, showed surprise. She said, "They've probably cremated him by now. Oh, and you left your luggage—"

"Cremate? Here?" Gwendolyn, who would have told Sarah how she had wrapped the body and taken it back to her room, and how the room was invaded while she slept, was instead caught in urgent shock. Sarah nodded, and her eyes involuntarily went over Gwendolyn's shoulder to the other end of the mission complex. Gwendolyn turned her head, eyes still on Sarah's eyes, which returned to Gwendolyn's face and bounced back to the more distant of the smokestacks, the one that was always active. Gwendolyn followed Sarah's gaze and saw an average amount of filthy black fumes being pumped into the sky. The evil smoke curled lazily, then traveled parallel to the ground as it transformed from unctuous to darkly vaporous, finally dissolving into a widening dirty stream of grey, pale grey and finally invisible grey.

Gwendolyn was thunderstruck. She had seen that smokestack every single day, noticed the black smoke and the contrast to its sibling inactive tower a hundred times—but never wondered what it was. It rose from the building just past the power plant at the far end of the mission, a building partially obscured by the dirtpile as paths curved. Some days it emitted a grey smoke; other days like today it chugged out syrupy black smoke that almost fell to the ground. The building was contiguous with, and maybe part of, the power plant, and she had always considered it just a 'utility building.' She looked at Sarah, who stood looking back at her face with a sympathetic expression.

Gwendolyn shook her head and told Sarah an abbreviated few sentences about the body disappearing from her room. She pushed past Sarah and went into the building. She passed Sarah's office, going deeper inside than she had ever been. Sarah followed her calling, "Wait. Wait, Gwendolyn."

Gwendolyn reached a locked door at the end of the hallway, and Sarah caught up to her, putting her hand on Gwendolyn's shoulder. Gwendolyn spun around before Sarah could speak, and the fury in her eyes convinced Sarah to open the door. Gwendolyn burst through the door, not knowing where she was; she was inside Bok's office suite. Sarah trailed behind. There were several couches and two desks in a common area, and Bok was visible at another desk in an office across the room, reading something. The commotion surprised him, and he quickly stood, came around his desk and met Gwendolyn just outside his inner office. "What is it, dear?" he asked, a concerned look on his face.

"Jojo is gone," Gwendolyn snapped, her anger partly morphing into sorrow when confronted by the friendly façade of the gentle man. She started to sob but caught herself and stiffened. Bok gave an ostensibly puzzled look over Gwendolyn's shoulder to Sarah, who gave no answer, shrugging and looking back at Bok's eyes.

"Yes, dear. He is gone. A tragedy. So young. But even with our best of intentions we cannot save them all. Come, have some tea, and we'll talk." He grabbed her upper arm. Gwendolyn resisted the urge to violently reject his motion.

"Where is he?" she asked as Bok directed her toward a sofa. He walked her into his inner office, went over to a teapot behind his desk and filled two delicate china cups with already-steeped tea. She remained standing.

"One lump or two?" he asked as he brought the saucer to Gwendolyn. She took the tea and put it on the nearby table. Bok sat down at his desk and sipped.

"Where is Jojo's body?"

Bok looked at Sarah, who stood in the doorway blankly. He looked back to Gwendolyn. "I am not at all sure what you mean, my dear. We all saw that he had an accident with the wires. I suppose they have moved him by now."

Gwendolyn became enraged. She wanted to attack him and let him understand that she knew he knew she carried Jojo's body back to her room. Still, something deep within her also wished to believe that Bok was Dr. Bok, a friendly and kind man who started this wonderful mission and knew nothing about this. She stood silently, ignoring her tea. Bok summoned Sarah with his index finger, and she approached around Gwendolyn, leaning her head near his. They whispered for an interval, then she gently nodded and left the office.

"You know where they would move him, right?" Gwendolyn said.

"Gwendolyn, this mission is trying to help in an extremely difficult situation. These people are in desperate shape, and, yes, sometimes they die, and they believe they go off to some wonderful land with succulent fruit and live forever with all their ancestors. But they leave behind the shell we all live in here on earth. When this happens we must deal with that husk in an appropriate way. Leaving them on the ground would do nobody any good. And storing them under your bed wrapped in a blanket is just as bad."

Gwendolyn's fury was ignited by the man's choice of words. And his admission that he was involved with kidnapping Jojo. She controlled herself.

Bok continued, "We have a place where we cremate the remains. And it is unpleasant to think about, but so it must be. There are many logistical tasks in an operation this size. You have seen the power plant of course.

Think for a minute. How much thought have you given to what happens out here in Africa? Have you seen any lakes? What happens when you turn on the water tap in your dormitory bathroom or kitchen? What happens when you throw away things? How do we clean things? Keep the lights on? For that matter, what happens when the toilet flushes?" Gwendolyn's anxiety about the boy's body was not lessened, but her mind was becoming cluttered, less focused on her rage. Bok was influencing her.

"I am not saying these things are all the same in importance or emotional value. But every single day, every single night, this mission has to pursue its purpose. We have not the luxury to slow down and take a break. There are many less-than-pleasant components to our work. But they're critical to keeping it moving. And at all costs it must be kept moving, or we will not be helping anybody. You want to help people, I know."

Sarah reappeared outside the door. Aloysius Fink stood behind her, his eye patch menacing Gwendolyn as she looked at his face. *What is going on behind that patch? Why is he wearing it? Is he hiding something? What is he doing here?* Bok nodded to Gwendolyn as he rose and went outside, turning Fink around and strolling, his hand on the taller man's arm. Bok and Fink walked, looking down at the carpet in the hall, talking quietly. Then Fink left, and Bok came back. His eyes were downcast, sad. He avoided touching Gwendolyn's shoulder as he said, "That poor child's body, what did you plan to do with it?" This caught Gwendolyn unprepared—she had not planned so far ahead.

After a silence she said, "Jojo. Bury him. That's what you do with people. I didn't even know we had a crematorium here anyway."

"Where?"

"?"

"Where were you going to bury it?"

Gwendolyn paused. She was caught off guard again. "I would bury him in the graveyard, I guess." Gwendolyn scanned her mind for the components of the mission. *Where is the graveyard?*

"But we don't have a graveyard here. We can't. The ground is so hard and dry, and the local population does not bury their dead, they burn them as a religious matter." He mixed truth and lies and unknowns; despite his years here, he did not know how the natives dealt with dead bodies. He walked around and sat down in his chair, leaning slightly back. He put his hands together, his two sets of fingers doing a little mirror-dance with each other. He tugged his beard, resumed the hand-dance and emitted silence, which he felt was his strongest communication tool in dealing with Gwendolyn.

She thought about the mission. Everyone had been warned to stay within authorized areas. But there were very few locked areas. She knew she was forbidden to go to the camp, the 'Inner Quad,' but probably nothing would stop her from walking right out there; certainly with determination she could go easily enough. She had traversed the mission area a multitude of times and never thought to go all the way to the power plant and utility infrastructure at the far end. She was never very curious about the smoking tower of what she now knew as the crematorium. And after the first week or so her general curiosity about the different buildings and processes had already dissipated. But she had walked around the grounds for many bored hours and surely would have noticed a cemetery.

Bok sat quietly. One hand moved to his beard again, and he savored a comfortable scratch, after which the hand returned to its interplay with its mirror image. He watched her face.

She said, "I want to see it. I want to see where they burn the bodies."

"Child, no you don't." Bok's voice was soft, his head shaking gently. "There's nothing there. And anyway, it's probably been cremated already."

It? "Don't call me child, Dr. Bok. Who came into my room while I was sleeping? Who took him? Who took Jojo?"

Bok said a guilty nothing. Gwendolyn looked at Sarah who turned her head away.

"You?" and Sarah shook her head.

"You?" and Bok looked down and shook his head.

"Don't do this to yourself, child. There is nothing to see." he said.

"I'm going. You're right. Nothing. And I'm going to go see." She turned around and left; she knew where to go. Sarah was in position to form a hopeless attempt to slow Gwendolyn down, and she silently queried Bok as Gwendolyn approached. Bok looked down, slowly shaking his head. Sarah stepped out of Gwendolyn's way as the girl walked briskly out of the office.

Sarah said to Bok, "Shouldn't we go with her?"

Bok said, "If she insists on this, it's something we won't help her with. Hopefully she'll get through it." They both remained and watched her storm out of the office.

Gwendolyn made the trip to the sickening smokestack in less than fifteen minutes. As she approached, she saw that the building was indeed attached to the power plant. It was part of the same complex. There were large, open utility doors, doors one could drive trucks though, in both sections. As she got near the power plant she looked into the deserted building, which she had never really done before. She saw lots of machinery but saw none moving, though there was a minor current of smooth mechanical sounds throughout the place. The kilowatts coming to life there seemed to be doing so with in stillness, with hardly a sound. She remembered there was a nuclear power engine below, and she shivered as the probable radiation surged through her body, poisoning her future on this depressing day. Her fear of cracking the nucleus in the eerie near-silence reinforced the steepening of her approach gradient toward Jojo; she broke into a run and closed in on the grisly building next door.

It was difficult to see inside the building because of the sunshine surrounding her. There were native men moving things off a truck parked just outside the near side of the building. Nobody acknowledged her as she entered through one of the large doors. Her eyes adjusted, and she was dumbfounded. Two men were carrying a dead woman through a door off to the right at the far end of the room. Behind them was a pile of grey cloth or plastic wraps, empty and stacked on the floor—the now-familiar body bags she had seen before. Between Gwendolyn and the men was another stack of over a dozen such wraps, stacked in alternatingly oriented layers like a sturdy woodpile. Each of these obviously held a body. *So many dead people today.* It was surreal, and Gwendolyn felt she was watching something out of a medieval horror romance.

Another man, a native quite old, was working on these closer body bags, arranging them, untying the ties, moving them around. He smiled cheerfully to her, showing about half a mouthful of brown and grey teeth. His smile contorted his dried skin as he leaned toward her over the grey bags in solicitous but uncomprehending friendliness. She quickly found that he was one of the natives who did not know any English at all. She resolved to determine whether Jojo had been cremated but decided she would get no help from him.

Gwendolyn glanced around. The center of the room held some kind of long, unused metal machine, and the rest of the area was littered with stacks of boxes, some cabinets and a few tables. In the corner to her left was a table with tools of various types on it. More tools were stashed in the other corners. The only bodies in the room were right in front of her, in the fifteen or so body bags between her and her new friend. Gwendolyn ignored whatever arranging the man was doing and tried to move a body off the top layer. She budged the bag with some trouble, then changed her mind; she stopped and asked the man for help through the universal mechanism of helpless eyes reaching out. The communication succeeded. The man seemed unconcerned with delaying his own work, and through an impromptu sign language they coordinated their efforts. He enthusiastically helped her move the body from the top of the stack to an empty area on the floor a little ways away. For his diminutive stature he was incredibly strong and fast. At Gwendolyn's pantomimed behest the process continued until four of the wrapped corpses were spread on the floor.

All these bodies were far taller than Jojo, and were she in full composure, Gwendolyn could have proceeded much more quickly and efficiently by making use of such an observation. Instead she fumbled with the flaps, opening the first container to look within. When the stiff flap suddenly gave way she was staring straight at a pathetic woman whose dried eyes and mouth were open. Seeing the texture of the face, the dry skin, the thin, wiry hair, she recoiled with a start. The woman's body had already attracted a layer of dust, and her expression, despite the position of the eyes and mouth, was... nothing. Not horrific. Not placid. Nothing.

At that instant a shiver traversed Gwendolyn's body. She had a momentary inkling that a human being is more than a collection of chemicals and mechanical structures and linkages. Something was missing from this body, something more than chemical. Fire—what the Greeks called fire, maybe. *There is more than this.* She gasped and recoiled, but within seconds she shook it off. It was no more meaningful than the nightmare she had a little while ago. There are no spirits, no ghosts. This woman is here. She is dead. That is all. *What am I doing? I need to find Jojo. Why do I call him Jojo? No.* Gwendolyn quickly closed the flaps and moved to the next body bag, oblivious to the worker standing watching and indeed, oblivious to all the world.

She exhausted the sequential search of the first four corpses and, leaving them there, turned her attention to the original stack. She walked over and, with the help of her new worker friend, lifted another cadaver and carried it over to those on the ground, placing it clumsily supported by portions of three of the original four. As she went back to the pile a shock of excitement went through her—she noticed a splash of color in the dismal grey and black morass. Projecting between two wrapped bodies was a fragment of Jojo's blanket. It was visible only as a corner, beneath the layer below the single corpse she had just removed. She shrieked excitedly. The smiling man's eyes were happy that she seemed to be pleased. She pointed to the blanket, unable to speak, and he nodded. Before he could move she was trying helplessly to lift the top body bag off the stack. His help arrived, and they moved four corpses, yielding Jojo, eyes closed, head and upper torso uncovered by the unfolding blanket. He had obviously just been dumped on the stack as it accumulated without any particular attention to wrapping him in a body bag like the rest. She bent down and picked him up, kissing him on his cold and dirty forehead. The confused man watched as she turned to leave with him. She twisted with her burden and nodded a well-comprehended thank-you over her shoulder. She effortfully carried her burden outside with the intention of finding a burial spot and giving Jojo a grave.

Gwendolyn's only experience with death outside the mission was ten or eleven years prior. Her cat up and died one day, and she insisted on burying it. With much labor she had dug a shallow hole in the soft loam of her moist Vermont backyard on a beautiful spring day. Her parents, declining to assist, watched from seats on their porch as she constructed the grave in the garden. As she stumbled clumsily with Jojo today, she relived the day when a beloved companion had died, against all logic and justice, leaving her crushed and cheated and alone.

A child that seems small when his feet align with yours seems almost your height when held with his upper body even with yours; Jojo's feet dangled along below Gwendolyn's ankles as she walked. His toes dragged on the ground, and they caught when she bent or twisted. She was unable to carry him horizontally, and so her only option was to carry him in a tight hug, much as she did early in the morning. The human body, shaped as it is, does not come with convenient handles and stiff structure designed for leverage and ease of balance; wrap it all in a blanket, and all you have to work with is friction. Gwendolyn stumbled along with Jojo, squeezing him hard with muscles aching from this morning's labor, trying to keep him from crumpling to the ground.

Before she got far she realized she needed a shovel. She wanted to go back to the building and try to find one, but was reluctant to put Jojo down. Since she had no idea where to bury him, she walked in a straight line almost to the base of the dirt hills. At the foot of the dirtpile she started to climb, with the intention of burying him partway up. But she decided a burial place on the flat ground at the bottom would be more secure from the elements over time. She made sure she was well off the path where people walked and drove trucks. There she laid the boy down.

Gwendolyn unwillingly separated herself from the boy and walked back to the horrible building, often turning to look back protectively at him. When she entered, the friendly worker stopped his efforts and looked at her solicitously. She pantomimed a shoveling motion as she glanced around the room. He seemed to understand and stood pensively. Gwendolyn glanced to Jojo's body and back. The man was still motionless, then he suddenly swung his index finger up in a burst of energy, turned and disappeared. After a moment he came back with a pickaxe. Gwendolyn had never used such a thing before but, thinking of the compaction of the ground, she realized it was a better choice than a shovel. She accepted the pick, and the worker again lifted his fingers and disappeared, leaving behind only the mental image of his upthrust index finger beckoning her to wait. She stood with the pick on the floor and waited. The man returned with a shovel and gave it to her, pointing to Jojo's body and nodding.

Gwendolyn thanked him wordlessly, picked up the tools and turned toward Jojo. She stumbled away clamping the unwieldy implements much as she had squeezed Jojo. Not realizing how much simpler it would have been to use her hands for a change, she ambled away, shifting her clasped arms as the handles slipped about. She progressed slowly, wavering laterally, leaning, tugging the ever-shifting tools and scrambling maladroitly, but she got back to Jojo presently.

She paused for a moment near the body, kicking at the ground to see how difficult the digging would be. The ground was quite hard. She stood resting for a moment and looked around the mission. The only people visible outside were a few individuals far away, walking near the cafeteria and residences. After taking a few breaths she grabbed the pick, lifted it over her head and struck the ground. It bit heavily into the packed dirt. She started to pull it out, but it was stuck surprisingly tightly. She discovered that rocking the handle by leveraging her weight against it broke up the dirt. She raised it above her head again and took another swing. She repeated the process again and again, to the exhaustion of the muscles from the soles of her feet through her back, neck and arms.

Her work in breaking the tough dry ground was absurdly inefficient due to the combination of her body size, her inexperience and her physically dissipated state. She struck the ground a few dozen times, loosening the dirt in an area almost the length of poor Jojo's body, then threw the pick aside and collapsed as an aching mass of bones and throbbing muscles. She discovered the amazing speed with which the body starts to develop blisters on tender skin. She sat on the ground, then allowed herself to topple, the side of her face on the dirt just like Jojo—facing Jojo in fact, who also happened to be on his side. Mindlessly lying in front of the dirtpile, she was fatigued on varied scales from many factors: her travels in Europe, the overnight airplane ride. Dearth of sleep. Mental stress. Physical exertion. Jojo. Cecilia.

Gwendolyn lay limp, knowing that she had to get back to work and dreading the pick's weight. It required so very much power expenditure. She could not conceive of swinging the tool again right now. Determined to push forward, she stood up and picked up the shovel, her conscience eased by a created-on-demand fiction that moving small scoops of already-loosened dirt was just as important as swinging the pickaxe. She started moving clumps of earth around with the blade of the shovel. Her back resumed aching after only a few scoops, but it was small discomfort compared to her recent activity, and she persisted, trying to pile the loose earth into a line along the long edge of the prospective hole.

As she lifted a shovelful of earth, Gwendolyn was startled—she heard the sudden crunch of the pickaxe hitting the ground behind her. Shocked, she turned around and saw the implement lodged deeply in the dirt. The hard ground crackled dully as the pick broke it into clumps. Her eyes followed the blade as it traveled back to the sun and returned violently to the earth with another raspy thump. Her gaze climbed up the handle to a set of bony fingers and beyond. She froze in astonishment. The tool was driven by a nun, a woman only marginally taller than the pick and perhaps not as heavy! The nun—old, thin, dressed completely in a black robe—had appeared from nowhere. She broke the pick out of the ground and lifted it over her head again.

The surprising and incongruous tableau at first prevented Gwendolyn from seeing the two other identical nuns standing to the side of the active woman, and she stood dumbfounded, almost falling over. The nuns generally were a peripheral part of the scenery at the mission; she had never talked to one. No—she had never seen any workers or volunteers talk to one. No—she had never seen a nun talk to another nun. They weren't living, interacting participants at the mission; they were a silent constituent of the background, part of the scene like potted plants. Not even real. Existing in some spiritual plane orthogonal to earthly reality. And now they were here, corporeal entities so tangible they could get dirty breaking the hard ground. Gwendolyn was seeing an energetic, determined actor working under the hot sun, wrapped in her black habit in the middle of the almost-lifeless field.

Gwendolyn stood motionless and mindless. She had often seen the nuns praying at the edge of the cafeteria, food in front of them. She sometimes watched five or six of them in a slow procession from the eating place back to their cathedral. In the lines, they walked in a peculiar leaning-back posture, arms folded inside their habits, which made them look stubborn and fat. They always arrived at the cafeteria hunching forward and down, but left bloated-looking in that peculiar determined, slow procession. They never said a word, and they never varied in their routine.

They were all old women, all native. Nun number two said something in a foreign language then curled her lips in determination and said, in English, "I will dig" as she took the shovel from Gwendolyn's unbelieving hands. She stepped forward and continued Gwendolyn's work of piling the loose dirt as nun number three stood still and nun number one worked with the pick.

The nuns were far more efficient than Gwendolyn. None was even three quarters her size, but their productivity was prodigious. As she stood, Gwendolyn's hands suddenly hurt; painful streaks of red crisscrossed her palms and finger joints, reinforcing the pain from the irritation of the cuts she had acquired in the early morning. She sat on the ground and concentrated on the pain, nourishing its growth. Just as she verged on tears she had a sudden awakening: *If there are tears to be shed here, they're for Jojo. My little scratches and blisters don't count.* She composed herself mightily, got up and walked over to nun number one, timing herself to the cycle of the woman's effort. She broke in, putting her hand on the pickaxe just after it went into the ground. The nun withdrew with an obedient smile, downturned eyes and a bow of the head. Gwendolyn continued the work, delivering her unwieldy and inefficient blows, then breaking the ground clumps as nun number two watched between her shovel thrusts. Gwendolyn savored the increasing pain on the contact points of her hands and offered it up for Jojo. Nun number three had slipped away unnoticed.

Presently Gwendolyn's exhaustion prevailed. She put the pick down on its head and leaned on it, breathing and sweating. Nun number two, who had been following the pickaxe with the shovel, dropped the shovel and gently moved Gwendolyn from the heavier tool. She lifted up the pick and continued Gwendolyn's work. Nun number one grabbed the shovel and resumed moving the loose dirt. The two worked like synchronized steam engines, and the dirt flew.

Gwendolyn walked over to Jojo's body. There was an air of unpleasantness about. She gently tried to straighten the uncomfortable-looking boy, wrapped the blanket around and under his head, and covered his exposed face. She sat watching the two women digging at their furious pace. No conversation passed between the three.

Then nun number three emerged from an unspecifiable direction with another pickaxe and shovel. She put the shovel on the ground as far from Gwendolyn as practicable and started working with the pick. Gwendolyn sat and watched with the feeling that she was seeing a noisy three-piece machine. The nuns, flapping black wrappings slapping wildly, tore into the ground at an unyielding pace with motions remarkably well coordinated. She glanced over at Jojo, then she stood up and started moving dirt with the unmanned shovel. The work was crowded and even dangerous with the four long-handled tools being wielded, but she fit herself into the nuns' rhythm, basically following one pickaxe and clearing the dirt in time with it. As the hole got deeper the second pick became too dangerous for four active workers, and Gwendolyn rested more than any of the others. They continued working for the better part of an hour. At the end of that time they had created a passable grave over a yard deep. Gwendolyn collapsed and lay on her side on the ground, panting and thirsty, savoring the plateau of accomplishment. She closed her eyes for a brief moment of calm and rested, breathing deeply and letting her head tumble down onto her shoulder and arm.

She remembered the reason for all the effort. She looked over at Jojo and saw the nuns in a triangle kneeling around the body, eyes closed, hands pressed together in foldless prayer. Their mouths moved in uncoordinated unison but emitted little that was audible; only occasionally did they murmur a phrase or two of Greek or Latin or Hebrew or some such venerable religious language. Gwendolyn remained motionless on her side as she listened to the praying. She observed the tableau, with the nuns in dark silhouette against the red brick of the cathedral in the distance.

The nuns paused expectantly in their prayers. Somehow knowing their expectations, Gwendolyn, as Jojo's proprietor, approached him and opened the wrap to comfort the eternally sleeping child she had come to love. The nuns remained in position, habits forming puddles of black on the brown dirt as they knelt erect with bowed heads in silent meditation. Their eyes were closed.

Jojo lay on the open blanket, back twisted and bent, limbs haphazard. Gwendolyn placed him supine and tugged at his arms, positioning them across his front. She then straightened his legs and moved them together to the extent possible, and smoothed his clothing. He looked like a child sleeping awkwardly in the sunshine. The nuns resumed their prayerful activity. There was some rock or obstruction under a fold where his shirt was tucked into his pants, and Gwendolyn reached inside the shirt to rid him of the uncomfortable intrusion. She felt a smooth section of a round shell, perhaps two fingertips wide, which she clutched between those fingertips and pulled out, smoothing the clothing with the other hand as she withdrew. She looked at the dirty whitish cup in her finger, confused. It was not a coin or piece of jewelry or seashell. The dusty object's scalloped edges were smudged with brown marks which were even more dusty, the smudges violating the concave surface.

She flipped it over and was startled. She dropped it immediately. There, on the ground, was a perfect, if filthy, brown eye, glaring straight up from an unseen face in the ground. In fact its position—it had landed next to a little hill and some small depressions—made it quite easy to see a face in the dirt. The orb menaced her, troublingly strange and simultaneously familiar in some chilling way. Without thinking or further pause, something drove her to destroy it. She stood and smashed at it with her shoe, stamping it into the dirt, disturbing the deep meditation of the nuns.

The tenacious organ survived the punishment. It flexed up in the dirt and continued staring at her. She attacked the alien thing in many ways, but nothing at her disposal—shoe, pick or shovel, could break the ocular menace. The hellacious iris still bored hauntingly into her psyche from the shallow hollow it had dug ever deeper in defense against her repeated assault. Nun number one was undisturbed by the ruckus, but the other two occasionally peeked over from their praying posture. Gwendolyn shuddered in disquiet and frustration. But then she got ahold of herself. She gouged the threatening fractional orb from its tunnel and pocketed it in anger—if she could not destroy it she would control it.

Gwendolyn wrapped Jojo's body in the blanket. As she moved to pick it up the nuns all joined her, making light work of setting the poor boy into the grave. Gwendolyn and nun number two picked up shovels, and the others waited while Gwendolyn poured the first portion of earth onto the boy, then nun number two started filling the grave alongside her. After a few minutes nun number one nonverbally insisted on taking Gwendolyn's shovel; nun number three relieved nun number two. It was not difficult work, and this was not for relief of exhaustion; the swapping clearly was intended to assure full participation in this part of the ceremony. The shovels changed hands a few times, and everybody transported dirt with both of the tools. With a few scoops to go, the nuns stopped working, and nun number one handed Gwendolyn her shovel. Gwendolyn placed the last bits of loose dirt on the pile and patted it down with the shovel blade as the nuns retreated, leaving Gwendolyn to do the finishing work. The girl lost herself in lovingly packing and arranging the earth above Jojo.

Noticing some odd sounds, she looked up to the head of the grave. Two nuns were working, banging and scratching on the dirt as nun number one watched. Gwendolyn's view was blocked by the billowing habit of nun number two whose back was to her. She stepped around and shuddered with what she saw. From nowhere they had conjured up a crucifix, a sturdy and ancient artifact of polished dark wood mounted with an awful stone statue of Jesus, gruesome and battered and bloodstained. The statue had obviously been painted many times during its apparent thousand year life. Red blood on the chest and around the rusty tacks holding the hands and feet to the cross was illustrated in delicately conceived streaks. The whole thing projected almost two feet from its root in the ground.

The gory talisman reached into Gwendolyn's personal inner core as fragments of her parents' indoctrination over the years asserted their primacy. She felt dizzy. She had always been nervous around religion and had only been in a church once. Secretly as a teenager she went to a service and a youth gathering with a friend. It had seemed harmless enough, but she knew from her upbringing that religion was an unsavory thing: parasitic and abusive of its believers at best; a malevolent menace at worst. Here was the most powerful symbol of the greatest of the religions. Right here, marking Jojo's grave. And it was a macabre symbol of torture and death; she remembered many sermons from her father explaining how many killings that symbol is responsible for.

She was torn. These gentle and goodhearted nuns were probably just the simpleminded and obedient followers of dogma instituted by faraway puppeteers. They certainly had helped her, but she was uneasy with their symbology and the implicit claim it staked on Jojo. After some consideration, she decided that distasteful as it was, leaving things alone would be less troublesome to her than uprooting the cross would be to the nuns. They would see it as a blasphemous attack on their sacred idol, whereas she saw the crucifix only as a creepy and offensive, but essentially meaningless, statue.

She noted that this—uprooting the religious symbol—is the exact sort of situation Kingman had cited many times over the years as the sort of thing that makes Christians kill in the name of their god, though she resisted believing it could lead to violent behavior in these peaceful women. She put it out of her mind. Jojo was dead. These women were helping to bury him. If it helped them to believe there was some sort of ghost they were sending to a fabled paradise, let them be happy with it. It could not harm the poor child now. Even Kingman had never hinted that Christianity could damage anybody after they had died; only on this side of that border was the religion dangerous.

When the crucifix was firmly in place, all the women stood over the grave looking down. Nun number one said simply, "We failed him." Gwendolyn was puzzled but stood silently. Then she nodded to the nuns and clumsily picked up a pickaxe and turned with the intention of taking the tools back to the building, one at a time. Nun number one touched her hand and said, "You may come," as nun number two took the pick from her and picked up a shovel. Nun number three picked up the other pick and shovel. Gwendolyn turned and obeyed nun number one's clasp. They walked with nun number three toward the cathedral as nun number two went toward the crematorium with a shovel and a pick.

As Gwendolyn trudged toward the cathedral, she was afflicted with a mysterious trembling. Tears of exhaustion and despair welled in her eyes. Unnoticed to her at the moment, the sinister false eye traveled along in her pocket as she shifted effortfully along.

Come Hell or High Water

How many layers of mystery?

I t was approaching evening as the nuns led Gwendolyn toward the cathedral. As cathedrals in Europe or America go, it was not a large one, but it was easily the largest building in the mission, with the possible exception of the power plant-crematorium complex, and that comparison depended on the definition of 'large.' Gwendolyn wearily trudged along, sandwiched between the nuns, impatient to be at the nuns' destination, but thankful for the slow pace due to her drained state.

The group walked along the gently varying slope, traversing one third of the length of the mission complex. They approached the large red brick building with the two towers. The shape of the cathedral was that of a large cross lying on the ground, and they were to enter through a pair of massive oak doors at the foot of the cross. Nun number one gave two strong tugs on the thick, heretofore-unnoticed, knotted rope that hung down from a hole in the masonry above, and Gwendolyn could hear the faint sound of a distant bell somewhere on the other side of the dense wooden doors. She was uneasy; she had not been this close to a church in years, and the prospect of going into the dark and unpleasant place was disturbing. They waited in silence.

As Gwendolyn's eyes roamed the ancient curve-topped doors, the nuns' eyes were stone still, aimed to eight o'clock in devout patience. The women seemed to use every spare second to launch silent prayers or engage in personal meditation. As her eyes happened to rise above the nuns' shoulders, Gwendolyn noticed Dr. Phineas Boseau far away in the direction of the executive residences, waving and walking excitedly toward them at an increasing rate. He was followed by Aloysius Fink, who was moving at a slower rate. Beside Fink was Sandy Crittenden, and Gwendolyn realized she had not seen Sandy since before she went to Europe. As Dr. Boseau gained ground over Fink he transitioned into a trot, then a run, all the time waving and now almost audibly calling Gwendolyn's name from a distance. Fink walked steadily behind, giving the impression of a smoothly traveling buzzard moving beside a nondescript woman. Dr. Boseau gave up on signaling with his fingers, took off the hat he was wearing, and waved it as he ran. All this was a movie projected on a faraway screen to Gwendolyn: two dimensional, dimly performed, sub-reality. Irrelevant.

There came a creaking. The door opened slightly, and the two nuns started through. Just then, the third nun arrived empty-handed and stood behind Gwendolyn, who took one last glance at Dr. Boseau and went inside followed by nun number three. Within, another nun essentially identical to the three Gwendolyn knew closed and bolted the door behind them. As they stood in the gloom Gwendolyn mused on the fact that she was within a holy place for the first time in almost a decade. Nobody gave another thought to Boseau, Fink & company.

They were in an alcove elevated above the bulk of the building by a half flight of stairs. The girl's eyes were drawn upwards into the huge space beneath the high roof. The building's main illumination was provided by many colored-mosaic windows high up on one side of the building. She could see a huge crucifix on the wall at the far end of the large room, lit by several small electric spotlights; this instance was far more artistic than the blood-curdling model on Jojo's grave. In fact, the smooth and bloodless sculpture was mysterious and even strangely compelling, and looking at it she perceived an inkling of how some people could draw comfort from such a strange symbol. The darkness, compressed by the spotlights, leaked motionlessly throughout the building, gathering itself in corners and all the unseen spots.

Throughout the silence burbled a noticeably quiet thread of indistinct, incongruous sound as though the moribund building was teeming with many kinetic but unseen spirits far off in the permeating gloom. The noise was like innumerable mixed and blurred voices occasionally punctuated by a doubly equal number of bumps or footsteps. The sounds, not being the mournful sorts of things Gwendolyn would expect in a church, seemed to decorate the quietude more than displace it; this sourceless and not-unpleas-ant noise no more banished the silence than the spotlights banished the darkness.

Everything was surreal in the twilight of the building. Overall, the lack of sound matched the murk: imperfect but overpowering. The total combined effect—the lights, the darkness; the noise, the silence; the stained glass, all centered on the crucifix—was one of beauty and even peace, not suffering, menace or abuse as Gwendolyn expected upon entering a Christian church. She was also surprised that the distinctive odors sourced of dusty hymnals and polished wood, impressions long resident in her memory and bound to the concept of church interiors, were absent. *Funny how I remembered the aromas so much more than the dark or the quiet.*

The stained glass windows, high on the wall, ran above a multileveled set of balconies near the junction where the arms of the building joined the main column. The space reminded her of some modern buildings, like a hotel with an atrium surrounded by rooms and walkways stacked one above the other. Gwendolyn's eyes traveled down to the floor level at the foot of the steps before her. It was a scene from a completely different world; it had the form of a bazaar in a bustling primitive city, but it was deserted. Rather than benches for obedient congregants, the area was broken into small compartments, haphazardly arranged open alcoves, irregularly shaped quasi-rectangles with only two or three walls each.

The contrast of the majestic beauty of the palace above with the visual cacophony of the floor below made Gwendolyn remember her first and lasting impression of Paris: the feeling that she was in a beautiful and divine place built by some great, long-gone civilization of cultural giants, its remnants overrun and infested by generations of peasants—brutes who, not understanding the essence of their appropriated home, crawled over the magnificent locale like crabs, mindlessly desecrating its artifacts and adapting things for their vulgar needs. This lovely Xanadu was now populated by creatures obliviously scurrying through the juxtaposition of sublime and persistent elegance with the mundane features and detritus of their quotidian lives.

Nobody was visible and the sound level did not support the idea that there were people in these compartments below; it was clear they were empty. She wondered who they served. She wondered where the noises came from.

Nun number one turned to Gwendolyn and said, "You are Gwendolyn. You may call me Brendan." She turned her head downward slowly, lodged a bony finger in the direction of nun number two and said, "Paul." Then she moved the trembling digit toward nun number three and pronounced her

"Bridget." Brendan then pointed to the nun who had opened the door and said "Joan." Gwendolyn nodded to each of the women in turn.

Brendan turned and stepped down into the church, instructing the girl to follow by the curve of her back and the twist of her body as she moved. Gwendolyn followed, and the other nuns walked behind. Brendan turned and indicated that Gwendolyn should enter an alcove to the left. Inside she saw some mats and blankets on a small platform bed. The nun said, "You may rest." Gwendolyn just then realized how tired she was. She asked for some water, at which Paul disappeared into the gloom, and came back with a pitcher of crystal cool water and handed it to her. The girl poured and drank a cup with greedy haste, the first touch of the water hijacking her consciousness, purging everything else from her mind as it spiraled down her throat, banishing the dry heat and dissolving away the layers of dust it encountered. As she poured a second cup she became aware that the nuns had withdrawn. She walked to the bed, emptying the glass and putting the pitcher and glass on the floor. Curling up some blankets for use as a pillow, she lay on her side. As her eyes drifted shutward, she saw four shrinking shadows lazily merging with the darkness outside her little alcove.

GWENDOLYN OPENED HER eyes after an unknown-duration sleep. She was more groggy than refreshed, and very thirsty. The room, once she remembered where she was, seemed to become exactly as before. It was suffused with a low light, the reflected light of reflections from invisible sources outside the room. Stirring and sitting on the edge of her bed, she rubbed her eyes and smoothed her hair. Remembering the pitcher, and seeing it completely full, she poured and drank a glass of water, then another. Without wondering, she broke off a piece of soft bread from the small loaf she found next to the water. Now she walked to the open side of the room, smelling the fresh bread in her hand. She ate from the bread, assuaging hunger that had lurked below her consciousness. The stained glass windows high up on the far wall showed only motionless dark reflections from candles. *So it's nighttime, or at least evening.* She bit a mouthful, and as she stood chewing she turned to look at the crucifix; it was far to her left, lit by spotlights. She saw candles burning around the periphery of the altar now. Noticing the absolute stillness of the frozen candle flames made her aware that the bustling noisy spirits she had heard earlier were gone, and the place was totally quiet save her chewing. She stared mindlessly at the crucifix and candles as she finished her ration of bread, slowly biting off small pieces.

She was curious about the huge cathedral, the stacked asymmetrical balconies and the haphazard ground floor with all its fractional rooms. She walked farther into the building, looking into the open-sided alcoves. None held a cot like the one she just awoke on, and all were deserted. As she walked along she saw some rooms with books, old books, many Bibles. Generally the little areas were disorganized and individually different; most held miscellaneous items, and none were cluttered. She saw rooms with small lamps, none of which were burning. Some held boxes, others had chairs. Occasionally a small table or a shelf or some other random piece of furniture was present.

She walked deeper toward the crucifix, then turned out toward the building periphery. As she progressed she saw more lamps and more Bibles, and a few incongruous items: colorful children's books and school primers. She reached the wall and continued around the corner of the building's cross junction, keeping to the periphery. Still she saw and heard nobody. This section of the building was organized into sections with regular church benches, and there were some small doorless rooms along the wall. Walking by the first of them, she looked in. There lay Brendan and Paul on the bare floor, asleep. She proceeded on to the next door and was surprised to find a large room. It had benches against the walls; on top of, and beneath the benches was a myriad of golden artifacts: crosses, chalices, many smaller items as well. *There must be a thousand pounds of gold right here in this one room!* A steel platform with tools and miscellaneous disorganized signs of work in progress scattered about it sat in the middle of the room. Apparently the tools had been applied in breaking pieces from gold items: there were a few statues and containers on the table, all broken or with small fragments cut out. To the right her view was blocked by a protruding wall separating the near corner of the room from the central portion. On the shelves on the far wall were a dozen or so metal bins full of broken pieces of multicolored rock ranging from pebbles to baseball-sized or bigger. She peeked around the little wall and saw a dark stairway. She felt the gloomy air as she leaned in, trying in vain to see something below; all she could make out was steps disappearing into the darkness. It looked like the entrance to a haunted cave. She stepped back.

Gwendolyn was confused, and in her groggy state, she was unable to reconcile the spare church and lifestyle with the presence of what appeared to be millions of dollars' worth of pure gold artifacts, artifacts that had been attacked and rent to pieces smaller than a silver dollar. And where the nuns would find rocks around here or why they would have them in the church was unfathomable. *And what is in the basement?*

This section of the building was divided vertically into several floors, and just then she heard noises like footsteps, impatient footsteps, like those of running children, directly above her head. Suddenly she felt a wave of shame, a feeling she was violating some kind of sacred privacy. The brush with the spiritual chilled her; her aversion to religion, so effectively inculcated during her upbringing, gripped her with a form of claustrophobia, and she felt trapped and confused. She left the room and quickly navigated her way back to the church entrance, zigzagging through the partitions. She got to the heavy wooden doors and tried haplessly to loosen the bolt. She was struggling mightily when Paul appeared at her side. The nun nodded with a thin smile and unbolted the door—there was a simple trick to it like that in a child lock. She bowed her head as Gwendolyn nodded "thank you" and pushed her way into the night air. Gwendolyn heard the door close gently behind her, the bolt slowly sliding back into position. She found herself on the steps looking at the middle of the night in the mission. The stars were the only break in the darkness. There was no moon. She was cold.

She suddenly remembered Jojo as she started along the path toward home. Shivering from the assault on her psyche as much as thermal considerations, she walked along looking at the beauty of the stars and could not help thinking that some god must have created it all. Otherwise where did it all come from? But Jojo was dead. Why Jojo? So many stars. *No gods.*

Just then she was stopped by a shooting star born directly over her head. Its whiteness seemed to traverse a band of colors as it arced leisurely across the sky for four or five very slow seconds. After it disappeared over the dirtpile, Gwendolyn marveled at how something could be so singular and bright, yet simultaneously so flamboyantly silent. She looked at the notch on the dirtpile where the meteor had vanished behind the hill, half expecting to see a trail of vapor or smoke, but there was no trace of anything. It seemed so close that she could not help but imagine it rolling around on the ground, bouncing and throwing off brilliant white light among the patients in the camp where her illusion placed the end of its arc.

Fully awake now as she approached her building, she felt her chin stiffen as she remembered and redoubled her earlier commitment: whatever the resistance, she was going out to the camp to work with those suffering people for the rest of her stay here. As she quickened her pace, the ghost of Jojo's innocent smile came to her mind and prompted tears. Shoving her hands in her pockets, she hurried through the chill. Her left hand grasped some sort of object; she pulled out a strangely shaped, curved thing and looked at the fake eye. Its irregular edges gripped the folds in her hand, and the iris stared grimly at her. A surge of revulsion compounded her extant shivering. Impulsively Gwendolyn closed her hand over the counterfeit organ and threw it violently off toward the dirtpile. She saw it arc in a tight curve and hit the ground not nearly as far away as she wished. She sped on her way.

In her room, the first thing she did was to attend to Pyratticus Julius; somehow he had been unceremoniously flung into the space behind her bed. She straightened and patted the octopod's six painful-looking tentacles, then sat on the bed leaning against the wall with the forlorn beast on her lap, feeling as lonely as she ever had in her life. Her eyes drifted away from the wall and out the window to the static stars and the spot in the dirtpile where the meteor had disappeared. What was she doing here? *There are thousands suffering here, and I didn't even help Jojo. Not even him.*

Pyratticus Julius seemed to share her melancholy; his tentacles drooped limply as always. Gwendolyn thought about how she yearned for Alitisha, how she missed her family. She was alone. Sarah was a robot, and Sandy Crittenden was probably always acting as required for her professional deportment. Bok. Bok—the man was no saint at all, far from it. *On the contrary.* She wanted nothing to do with him. She thought of the sisters in the cathedral. Her only encounter with these strange and usually peripheral nuns, for all their convenient, if cold help, was awkward; their deadpan personalities and the confines of that strange church puzzled her mind. Who was in there? Was that gold? Had she imagined it? How could it be there? Lonely or not, she was glad to be out of there. And she had only been in there because of the worst thing that had ever happened to her. *Why am I here?* She sat listlessly until she heard stirring outside in the morning. It is impossible for us, as for her, to know whether she and Pyratticus Julius slept or just sat through the dark night.

Suddenly Gwendolyn had a stroke of memory, and a bolt of energy pulsed through her body. She jumped up, placed Pyratticus Julius carefully on his shelf, arranging his tentacles for comfort, then went to the bathroom and quickly cleaned herself up. Grabbing some bread and a banana, she rushed outside before any of the other sponsored volunteers were awake.

Gnawing her breakfast in the morning air, she went past the empty staging area near the native workers' dormitory and continued by Bertha Martha's factory, where a truck was just pulling out laden with foodstuffs. She walked past the schoolhouse, picturing the children who must be starting to stir upstairs, a thought that had her smiling weakly until Jojo's face came to her mind. She picked up her pace, but then started to lose her nerve for her mission. Searching for a distraction she decided to walk a full circle around the cathedral, which she did. Examining the outside walls as she orbited, she noticed that the highest windows in the rear would have a view over the dirtpile and into the camp, and filed the information in her memory for curiosity's sake.

Gwendolyn had had enough of comfortable schoolhouses and boring clinics and floor scrubbing, all of which she could have done in California or Vermont. She was here to make a difference, and she was going to get her hands dirty. Gathering her resolve, she looped back toward the workers' staging area and hovered in the quiet. Eventually, one at a time, five or six small trucks of various shapes rolled up. The drivers got out and began talking with each other, laughing and joking. As time progressed male native workers started arriving and gathered in small, shapeless and slowly evolving groups. Two regulars approached together. Gwendolyn walked by the nearest trucks, looked inside and saw food and supplies. Without saying a word she climbed in the back of one and sat on a box, watched apathetically by those gathered outside.

Eventually the laborers all climbed aboard the trucks, and the drivers started the engines. Her truck was filled with workers who cheerfully exchanged chitchat in their native language as the truck bumped around the dirtpile and out into the camp. They climbed the gentle slope approaching the eastern edge of the dustbowl, the part farthest from the mission buildings. Around the dustbowl Gwendolyn could see that the fence was not a mere region of tangled and deadly barbed wire. Here, it was a two layer heavy-gauge chain link fence topped by doubly sloped barbed wire.

Gwendolyn was finally, and for the first time, among the needy patients she had come to help. *This is what I came for. Those ones in the clinic don't count.*

Looking out the rear as they traveled, she noticed she could see the top of the cathedral, including those windows on the upper floors. The truck stopped at the far edge of the camp. Nearby was a sideless tent above some empty chairs and tables. Gwendolyn saw a gate to the outside world a bit farther away. The gate was closed, and beyond the fence she saw an impromptu encampment of people who had obviously been living outside for a while. Some were up and about; most were lying on mats on the ground. There was also a militia jeep with a few sleeping members who stirred for a momentary peek as her truck disturbed their slumber.

The workers in the truck jumped out, Gwendolyn in their midst, rejecting multiple offers of helping hands, yet receiving quite a few gropingly cheerful assists anyway. She walked a few steps and looked around, seeing hundreds of patients in her vicinity. All were lying down except a few who sat up. Surprisingly few were children, and all were horribly thin and misshapen. A truck was just pulling away. It had delivered closed containers that were now standing near the edges of some tables under another tent with no sides.

Some native workers from Gwendolyn's truck collapsed its canvas roof, unloaded boxes and dragged them into this tent and another not far away. One man took a red container from the truck, an enclosure Gwendolyn had not noticed although it had served as her bench. He went to the gate in the fence and opened it. As a crowd watched, he delivered the crate to a groggy and heavily armed man from the militia. The man lazily stumbled away, carrying the container back to his truck, followed at a respectful distance by a cloud of onlookers. He jumped inside, and the vehicle drove a few hundred yards away, then stopped. By now the worker had returned, and the gate was locked again.

Some of the mission's native workers opened the containers that had been in the nearby tent. They pulled out bowls, placing them along the tables, then unpacked small containers of food substance, apportioning the material into the dishes. The whole operation was quite efficient. Many of the patients rose and entered a well behaved queue that had started growing outside the tent. Each was served a dish of food and a helping of nutrient-infused water while walking through in an orderly fashion. They returned to where they had been lying to eat their daily portion. With the exception of Gwendolyn, everyone from her truck was busy serving food or guiding people. She watched the line of patient patients; though individuals progressed forward, the line itself quickly reached stability; individuals condensed on the rear of the line exactly as fast as those at the front left the tent with their food.

Nowhere in Gwendolyn's sight was there any argumentation, squabbling or fighting. She watched those in the queue walk by, each patient passing within a few feet of her. It was clear that the exertion of just standing was a strain, but she detected no discontent, no boredom. Just even, vacuous existence. By and large they were smudged with dry dirt; many seemed to have desiccated greyish skin, a strong contrast to the vibrant golden brown of the workers.' Their lethargic eyes yielded to psychic gravity, just as the leathery skin of their faces surrendered to physical gravity. As they passed Gwendolyn, their gazes scanned across her, an uncurious and blind exhibition of their lack of interest. These people could not aspire to the state of ennui, so far above their reach was even that condition. The patients did not really see Gwendolyn, and she did not see the individual patients—she saw them merely as a collection of identity-free unfortunates; thus she perceived the queue progressing only in an abstract sense.

The children seemed more alive than the others. Their eyes engaged Gwendolyn's with a passive, plaintive curiosity. She looked at the hundred or more people lined up and estimated that it would be hours before all those destined to flow through the queue would be fed at this rate. There was an ocean of mats on the ground, all occupied save those whose proprietors were in the line at any given instant. All in all, there were certainly many hundred people destined to eat from this tent. And this was only one small portion of the camp itself. She shuddered at the immensity of the problem, then her eyes turned to the fence and those swarming masses outside the gate. They were lined up several deep against the barrier, watching the feeding, and there were many more on the ground out there. Gwendolyn noticed, within easy view, a number of adults who could be dead for all she could tell. In fact she saw one man prodding a supine woman for her attention and getting no response. Gwendolyn glanced at the militia truck sitting contentedly a quarter mile past the fence. The silhouettes inside were clearly dividing up the offering from the mission, some kind of food that the shadows were shoving into their heads.

Gwendolyn consciously avoided making any estimate of the number of people outside the camp hoping to gain entry. She could understand their desire; they could see, just as well as she could, the feeding going on inside the camp. She stood immobile, becoming depressed and mentally crippled by the magnitude of the mission's task. And the starkness of the boundary between its task and the rest of the hopeless Swazizibian world. The precipitous barbed pale stood right there, only a few feet from her. She wondered how even a man like Bok could possibly draw the line between those inside and those outside. For all her examination they were indistinguishable, with the possible exception that there were more children, moving faster, outside than inside the mission camp.

Gwendolyn had been stationary for many minutes, and she could not bear to stand amidst this anymore. Just as another truck drove up and swapped full and empty food containers, she started walking down along the fence toward the mission proper. The crowd outside extended quite a distance as she traveled; at every point there were sets of eyes on her from without. She passed another feeding station. The line was just as at the first: ten or eleven dozen miserable listless creatures awaiting a baseline helping of food. She felt no larger than an insect walking along the fence of the giant camp in the huge continent on a planet so filled with distress. *But where am I going? I can't just walk away from this. I knew it would be difficult.* She decided that she had to go into the mass of suffering people, that walking along the edge was wrong. She had to be in the middle of things.

Stepping down the gentle slope of the ground leading away from the perimeter fence and toward the center of the camp, she soon found herself among people who looked more desperate than those lining up for breakfast servings at the tents spaced through the camp. These people were too weak to stand up. She stopped at one mat where a sickly mother and a baby boy were together. Their eyes were mostly closed as they lay facing each other, the mother's arm on the boy's side. Gnats were wandering on the greyish-brown skin of the little boy's face, an indignity that pained his mother through her milky eyes. She lifted her hand occasionally in a fatigued attempt to scare away the flies, but her efforts, efforts robbing her of the ability to shoo away the vermin landing on her own body or those hovering within the confines of her open mouth, never lasted more than a few seconds.

Gwendolyn stooped down, and her eyes said, "Let me help you." The woman's motionlessness seemed to convey grateful acceptance of the uninterpreted foreign silence. The girl energetically put both her hands in motion shooing the flies off both mother and child. Looking at the flies now hovering aloft, she felt the satisfaction of accomplishment; this small kindness was but one tiny example of why she had come around the world to this place.

She continued in peaceful movement, helping someone in need. But after a few minutes an ill-formed darkness gathered in her mind. The ugly thought matured and crystallized, and she realized she had a tiger by the tail—a toothless tiger but an unappeasable tiger. A tiger with far more patience and stamina than she had. Or any human, for that matter. And there were thousands of such tigers in the camp. And outside the camp... And they were here before she was. And they would be... Her hands revolved in damped ovals as she squatted in growing despair. How about the rest of Africa? The world? *What am I doing?*

Here is the thing about a swarm of insects: it cannot be dissuaded. Bugs will not be discouraged, frightened or bought off. They do what they do, and they do it mindlessly. They respond only to the most immediate of dangers, and they have no concept of mercy. If you are shooing them away, the vermin will retreat into a holding pattern of disorganized loops, always monitoring you through their determined compound eyes. They will hover relentlessly, and they will come back at every opportunity. This will never pause. This will never end. If you stop to rest they will land. If you stop to eat they will alight. If you stop to scratch your leg they will renew their assault. If you sleep... *This is hopeless.*

She held steady for a few more minutes, then carefully avoided the mother's unseeing eyes and stopped circulating her hands. She stood up, turning away as she did so, stretched out her tired wrists against opposing palms, shook her shoulders and walked briskly on her way—to where was not important. She refrained from glancing down but knew that flies were crawling on the mother and her small son before she had attained erectness. As she stepped carefully on her way she rationalized her failure by actively noticing that the same was true for all the woman's neighbors. *She's no worse off than the rest of them.* She did not look back to see that the mother had sensed her departure and resumed her own futile pursuit of relief for the baby.

Gwendolyn kept walking down toward the center of the natural tilted bowl comprising the camp. She looked around as she walked unceasingly, seeing mats and occasional tents without walls stretching all the way to the dirt hills and the fences. As she traveled, gloom accumulated within her. Eventually she came to a region where she saw some native workers and a volunteer ministering to the weak patients, walking around and delivering food at their mats. By now Gwendolyn was near the center of the camp, and she turned to resume her journey toward the mission proper. She stepped up her pace, avoiding seeing patients to the extent possible, avoiding seeing them as people.

The patients were very close together in this part of the camp, and most seemed hardly able to move. None could stand, she could see that. The workers' concentration gradient was greater than that of the patients, as the work of delivering nourishment to this section was slowed in inverse relationship to the health of the patients. The inmates seemed to be in increasingly worse shape as she progressed in her slightly aimed walk toward the power plant. She remembered how the disgusting but descriptive nickname 'ghosts' arose in her mind in conjunction with these poor souls when she saw a few at the clinic, and tears welled in her eyes as the world shrank around her. She had transitioned from concerned, through depressed, to crestfallen in just a little while.

Some workers were loading a dead body onto a truck a hundred yards lateral to her. The realization of the obvious struck her in a shock, and she stepped up her pace. She started to feel trapped within the huge camp. She walked in zigzag patterns, maneuvering around sick patients, always keeping the power plant smokestack in view, navigating as directly as possible to approach it. She was increasingly frustrated by her slow progress among the dense patients.

All at once, Gwendolyn felt physically compressed by some sort of invisible straight jacket. She had an urgent need to escape from the camp. Her heart pounded. She began gasping for breath. She felt a shiver of heat; she tore off her blouse and dropped it on the ground or perhaps on a patient, leaving herself in her bra. She had to get away from the endless ocean of piteous sick patients. She had to get unsurrounded by the ghosts. It would be too difficult to continue walking toward the gate to the mission proper; she decided to fight her way to the fence and follow it down along the edge of the dustbowl. She broke into a hyperventilating trot as she jinked along her way, avoiding seeing patients. Finally she arrived at the fence, and she stopped, clasping it tightly. She pressed her face into the metal links and breathed huge gulps of air from outside the camp. She looked at the beautiful barren scrubby dirt outside the mission's perimeter, imagining the abundance of space and freedom extant out there. Only peripherally did she notice the encampment of hopeful natives up to her right, a set of blurred patches, some of which displayed indistinct motion.

The girl walked down along the slope following the fence, still avoiding looking at the camp inhabitants. Eventually she got within sight of the path into the mission proper. She paused now for a look toward the center of the camp and could see many workers serving food to very, very sickly patients. The workers were carrying heavy-looking packs on their backs from which they served the food. In the distance she saw a truck collecting another body; two workers were carrying a drooping corpse toward the vehicle.

As Gwendolyn neared the exit of the camp she heard a whistle behind her. She turned and saw the closest five or six workers place down their packs and close them securely. As she stood and watched, they merged at a collection point. A truck arrived holding a dozen others, and they all climbed aboard. She would later learn that this was the lunchtime break, and that the workers she had been with in the morning would come to reinforce those in the more intensive-care part of the camp after lunch. It was quite well organized, whether by Sarah or Fink or Bok, a fact that did not strike her.

Now she felt a bit better, having been distracted from her troubles by the whistle and the activity of the healthy workers. Several trucks passed her on the way back to the mission proper. She felt the pull of the familiar region; she jogged down to the path, out the silly little gate and up the slope. Once she had made the turn near the power plant she slowed to a walk. She savored being outside the camp; she basked in the oxygen-saturated air and the freedom from the impinging and oppressive misery of the camp. Her relief was such that even the oily black smoke from the chimney of the hardworking crematorium escaped her attention. She progressed along the path toward her room lost in thought, getting some confused or interested looks from workers along the way, which she ignored.

Gwendolyn was eager to see Pyratticus Julius; her animal confidante was often able to put things in perspective for her. When she went through the lounge, it was lunchtime and many of the sponsored volunteers were eating. Gwendolyn walked through cluelessly in her bra and pants and thought about the contrast between the bland paste given to the patients and the fine Italian chicken parmesan, high calorie hamburgers and warm breads she saw the volunteers eating. Ice cream. There was nothing new in this, but today the contrast seemed poignant. Everyone was looking at her, but nobody commented on her apparel or its sparseness. As she walked through, one of the women dallying over her lunch called out in a disinterested tone, "Dr. Bozo was looking for you."

"When was that?" she asked as she continued toward her room. The woman said Boseau had been there about an hour ago, and he had gone into Gwendolyn's room in her absence. Gwendolyn flushed as she walked toward her room, her hand shaking on the doorknob. She felt violated and enraged, and it brought to mind the incident with Jojo's body. *What is wrong with these people here? Why does Bok allow this sort of thing?* She wished she could go somewhere isolated for a long afternoon walk, but that was not possible at the mission; there was nowhere to go, and furthermore, now she had been tipped off that if she walked around outside she was likely to be accosted by the clown-doctor.

Gwendolyn went into her room and felt a flash of anger when she saw Pyratticus Julius tangled with himself on the floor below his shelf. She picked up the poor beast, stuffed him roughly, feet sticking out, into her small backpack and left the room with it, wishing there were locks on the doors.

In her days of wandering the campus of the mission, Gwendolyn had discovered a small isolated room that had probably been forgotten by everyone. She filed it in the back of her mind in case she wanted to get away from everything, and soon thereafter she had started doing just that. She had gone there only a few times; today was a day when she certainly needed her own private real estate. She went downstairs, doubled back into the lower hallway then walked to a small staircase almost hidden at a junction. She climbed up eighty-eight steps to the empty room she called her 'crow's nest,' a small rectangular box whose windows were little things high enough above the floor that she had to strain to look out. The room was possibly intended for some equipment, maybe a telescope or a radio during the military days. She never knew why it existed, and she certainly never asked anyone about her secret hideaway. For today she asserted full occupancy of the crow's nest.

She and Pyratticus Julius sat in the corner on the floor. The room was not dark because light entered through the little windows, and she could see some points of sky light through the soffits as well. She felt depressed while she contemplated the mission silently with Pyratticus Julius. There were several truths, and she tried to reconcile them with each other and with the picture of her noble task, doing the work of the angels. *There are thousands suffering from starvation here. There is an endless stream of potential entrants, and we turn most away. Some of the children (the schoolhouse) are happy and well cared for, and we can't stop flies from eating the others.*

She felt dizzy, and Pyratticus Julius was of no help; he seemed as confused as her. She scooted deeper into the corner with her friend clutched to her breast and continued with her thoughts. *Volunteers from abroad and foreign employees are very well fed. Bok feeds his dogs steak here. Bertha Martha thinks she is running a food factory. Nobody ever seems to say things are improving for anybody.* Gwendolyn bit her fingernails as she followed her circulating mind's swirling morass of questions seeking answers. *What does Fink have to do with Jojo's death? Who are those nuns? Was Alitisha right—is this all a waste of time? Where do they send people when they're healthy?*

The room was spinning, and as she tried to penetrate to the center of her spiraling questions the centrifugal force of her whirling confusion threw her more and more forcefully into the corner and away from any answers. She lost consciousness under all the pressure.

She stayed asleep till evening. Waking up slowly at dusk, she gathered herself and Pyratticus Julius and made the dark journey down the hidden staircase. Gwendolyn felt she was climbing down from a lonely lighthouse on an isolated rock, a lighthouse circulating a worthless beam that was never seen, a beacon that served to give no guidance to a dark world.

Cat O' Nine Tails

What is the reciprocal of one hundred years?

A fter this initial shaky start in the camp, Gwendolyn settled into a routine working in the dustbowl every day. Over the next few weeks she evolved into a capable and effective worker in the difficult situation; she learned to control her emotions to some extent and made numerous practical decisions every day. She experienced no more panic attacks or claustrophobic frenzies during this time. She rode out to work with the same group of workers most mornings and got to know them a bit. It still tore at her heart to see the conditions in the camp, but she increasingly resisted temptations toward useless measures—no more swatting at flies. Over time, this tormented her to a diminishing degree. She also learned to dull her anguish over the seeming hopelessness of the mission's task. After the first week or so, she was neither happy nor melancholy while out with the patients; she was simply doing the work she came here for. The work itself was monotonous, and the proximity to the pitiful people out there was a burden, but one she had chosen.

Though she often felt depressed outside work, Gwendolyn did not visit Sandy Crittenden for any sort of professional help, and she did not seek diversion by taking part in any of the enrichment activities offered by the sponsored volunteers. She felt lonely when she was not working, and only at these times did thoughts of Alitisha or Jojo creep into her mind. She read a couple of famous but seemingly plotless classic books with no memorable characters.

Being an extra helper in the dustbowl and not part of any one work team, she could move around, assisting with logistics where she saw the need: moving bundles, feeding people, picking up refuse, cleaning up after the more helpless patients. For some intuitive reason she followed an unperceived rule: she stayed on the far end of the camp.

Early one morning she woke to an unusual amount of activity outside her room. She heard Sarah Greenwater's voice excitedly barking orders. Unhugging Pyratticus Julius, she went to her door and opened it to look out. She saw Sarah in animated and gestureful discussions with the women who served breakfast. Some of the other sponsored volunteers were also awake and watching the commotion from their doorways. Gwendolyn put on a robe and came out to Sarah, who was similarly undressed. Sarah greeted her and told her that Dr. Bok had to leave right away, and that she was in a hurry to gather some provisions from this kitchen for his trip.

Now, Director Professor Dr. Florian Q. Bok had only arrived onsite the evening before last; he usually stayed the better part of a week on his visits, though of course the duration was subject to fluctuation; with ever changing schedules and circumstances, the important man could be called upon at any time to seize an opportunity or respond to a crisis elsewhere. Sometimes he was summoned to consult with governments and intergovern-mental agencies. So it was unprecedented but not inconceivable that Bok would leave so soon after arriving. But it was definitely odd to have Sarah in the lounge dressed in her robe, banging things and barking out orders at dawn, waking up sponsored volunteers as she raided their food.

Sarah gathered her bundles and said to Gwendolyn, "I'd better get back to packing him up." She quickly disappeared out the door. Gwendolyn heard her patter down the stairs, then through the window she saw her trot straight across the ground toward the executive residence. Gwendolyn got some breakfast and sat down to eat. After a short while she heard the quiet disturbance of a small airplane engine sputtering its intransigence from the far end of the runway. Hearing the motor she could not help thinking of Colonel and Bourbon and their incongruous presence in airplanes, fine hotels and the mission, majestic animals thriving as they gleefully traveled through a world of privileged and misfortunate humans. Really, though, they were just stinky animals overpowering the confines of a small plane. She wondered if they were traveling with Bok. Her mind tightened as she thought of their cheerful, portly, disturbing owner. She frowned.

This day was bright and clear as Gwendolyn walked to the trucks for her day in the dustbowl. On her way she saw Bok, Aloysius Fink and Sarah Greenwater riding along the runway in an open truck. Bok was driving with determined focus; the others had equally grave expressions on their faces.

Gwendolyn was surprised to not receive a friendly wave as they passed within range, though for her part, she could not bring herself to initiate a greeting to any group holding Fink, and maybe even Bok. There were bundles of suitcases and boxes in the rear, loosely superintended by Colonel and Bourbon who were snapping at the air and, in contrast to their driven master, enjoying the ride and loving life. *I guess that answers the question about the dogs.*

She boarded her truck for the trip to the day's work. When the vehicle arrived at the top of the dustbowl, Gwendolyn jumped off. She still felt a knot in her stomach near the gate every morning, seeing the people across the line dividing those who get help from those who don't—the insiders from the outsiders. Even after weeks of visits she was still bothered whenever she thought of the limitations of the camp; something in her wished to walk over and somehow let them all in the camp, though this was mostly just a distant feeling after the weeks in their proximity. This desire pushed her toward contemplation of the immensity of the problem she purported to alleviate, but she had developed an ability to suppress this line of thought and cope well enough to work every day. And to a lesser extent, sleep every night.

Today she wandered through the upper portion of the camp and stopped at a number of mats, smiling at the patients when she found it possible. She was in a section of the camp where the patients could all sit up, and though they were incredibly gaunt and bony, most could stand and even walk. By and large they had horrible dental problems, and many had severe skin conditions. Gwendolyn did not touch any of the patients except where there was no choice, and of course she never got to know any of them individually. Even when she was certain she was in the same spot as the prior day and working with the same people, the individuals were undifferentiated in her mind. This included the children, except for a few boys that made her think of Jojo, incidents that started to make her cry until she gripped herself.

Over the weeks an understanding formed somewhere in her brain: the condition of the patients degraded along the slope back toward the mission proper. She saw very little of this in the mornings as she rode to her work; the truck traveled along the edge of the camp and the gradient of health pointed not only away from mission buildings, but outward from the camp's center to all the curved edges of the camp's periphery. So as it happened, the worst patients were never visible from the truck or from where she typically spent her time.

As this morning wore on, Gwendolyn felt a nagging thought surfacing, an idea that had marinated invisibly, probably for days: she was not contributing fully by coming to this part of the camp and working with the healthier patients. It troubled her and increasingly distracted from her work. And though she was uncertain why, she felt strange today. Maybe it was the weird encounter with Sarah, or Bok's hurried departure. Even the weather seemed strange—there was a long, straight line of clouds near the horizon far to the south, and she felt none of the normal mild gusts of wind.

For whatever reason, eventually she decided to go back to her room and clean her clothes instead of staying at work in the camp on this day. The long string of workdays without a break let her justify taking a little time off from her unassigned work here, and she hitched a ride back in the early afternoon on one of the trucks carrying back refuse. She disembarked when the truck stopped at the crematorium. As she walked away, she saw the driver pile the refuse on the ground inside the open doors exactly where she had found Jojo's body. Up until now she had never wondered where the trash goes, but now she found herself oppressed by imagined pictures of bodies and trash all mixed, undifferentiated as they were fed to the flames.

She walked toward home dominated by gloomy memories of finding Jojo's corpse. She went into her room and took a short, depressed nap. Later she did her laundry. As usual, Gwendolyn did not eat dinner in her lounge area, but, with her normal longing for variety and company at a distance, she went to the open cafeteria to eat dinner alone. She was sad, something that happened often at dinner, and went to bed early that night clutching Pyratticus Julius.

When she awoke the next morning, Pyratticus Julius had migrated to the floor. She readied herself, had some breakfast and set out for her workday after placing him perched on the shelf. The sky was unusual today, filled with many kinetic-looking clouds, and strangely, there was no wind at all. At the staging area where workers boarded their trucks, some of her crew were on edge about something. They tried to communicate it to her, and she did her best to understand. But since their continuing refusal to study the rudiments of English manifested itself in a communications gulf, Gwendolyn was unable to fathom the issue. She figured it was probably some superstitious trivia; workers seeming agitated was not such an uncommon occurrence. Despite their discomfort, everyone got aboard the trucks and went to the dustbowl.

Throughout the morning large turbulent clouds formed and transmogrified almost directly above the windless dustbowl. Later, increasingly dark clouds gathered far to the west and invaded a growing portion of the sky. Gwendolyn floated to different stations, helping feed patients and doing her normal miscellaneous things. She straightened mats. She doled out food. She moved a baby within reach of its mother. The sky darkened, and by early afternoon the western clouds had vanquished all the cotton-like clouds overhead and extended almost to the eastern horizon, thus covering the whole sky. Gwendolyn was inside one of the sideless tents serving food.

Then it began raining.

Raining.

Since she had come to Africa, Gwendolyn had never seen rain. She had heard nobody mention rain, and the ground cover did not suggest familiarity with water from the sky. Even the volunteers' slang—dustbowl—did not contemplate precipitation. The tents were all sideless, and most of the camp was completely unprotected from above. Even in the mission proper, few windows had panes. They were present just on the buildings with air conditioning: the executive and sponsored volunteer residences, administration building, and a few others like the schoolhouse. The cathedral was airtight for all intents and purposes. Everything else in the mission had open holes for windows.

Gwendolyn conceived that the rain could cause real problems out here in the dustbowl if it became a serious storm. Everyone's first reaction to the precipitation was immobilization: when the light rain started, it surprised everybody fully. After a bit, there was a ruckus as the rain went from a drizzle to a light shower. The native workers shouted to each other, nodding and pointing. There was only one other volunteer in eyeshot. She was stunned, standing outside her tent looking up into the rain, mouth gaping open, holding her ladling spoon. Patients in line also seemed surprised, if a bit less attentive to the distraction than the workers—they retained a greater interest in food than did those serving them.

It was not cold, and the main inconvenience to the patients from being wet was that the coating of mixed dust, sweat, accumulated bacteria and other material that tended to cover their skin would become a layered, flowing shroud of paste that was offensive and slippery. Despite the excitement everyone settled down and resumed working, patients and many workers getting wet. The ground was not soaked; it had been so dry that as yet the rain did not make a visible difference because water was sponged in as quickly as it fell. The decrease in airborne particles meant the dustbowl, for the first time in anyone's memory, failed to earn its nickname, though one could still not see across it due to the rain.

For a while Gwendolyn filled dishes with food and distributed water. She thought about the weaker patients in the camp, those who could barely move and certainly not stand up. Their exposed bodies would be getting drenched until the rain let up. The weather was warm, and perhaps it was not a real problem, but she felt some wind now, and with the still-darkening clouds, she wondered if the rain may intensify. Uneasy, she stepped away from her more or less redundant position; the hole closed up behind her quickly. She started walking down toward the mission proper. Everyone was wet, and now outside the tent she was no exception. She looked at encampments outside the fence; she saw little movement as people mostly huddled in the sparse grass. She craned her neck back and to the right as she walked, and she could see the militia sitting in the shelter of their truck outside the intake gate. The rain was annoying, but by no means could it be considered a downpour.

She walked toward the dead center of the dustbowl and followed twin gradients: decreasing ability of patients to help themselves, and increasing amounts of water just starting to flow along the ground. Now all the patients around her were in a sitting position, huddled against the rain. She continued slowly moving toward the center, and then a third sibling joined the gradient of misery: with disorienting celerity, the wind kicked up in chaotic bursts. She felt the gusts whipping her back more and more as she continued down the slope.

She walked on as the rain intensified and the patients lay waiting out the storm. Soon she got to where many were lying down, and she saw that she had been right—they were totally exposed, the water hitting their faces and bodies. She looked to her left and right and saw hundreds of patients beleaguered by this moderate physical increment of affront to their normal condition. She continued walking down.

Without warning a huge surge of lightning lit the sky in a fractal, multicolored flash, its sharp tendrils dividing and multiplying as they filled the sky with shimmering incandescence from all directions. Seconds later a burst of thunder converged on the camp, seemingly from everywhere at once. It scared the foreigners, and it drove panic into the souls of the natives, patients and workers alike. It was almost certainly true that none of the local inhabitants had ever encountered a thunderstorm; they were incredibly rare in the region. Gwendolyn was startled and frightened by the unexpected explosion as well. The sudden surprise brought to mind safety guidelines she had heard: one should not be the tallest thing around during a thunderstorm, which she certainly was—all around her were lying down—and one should not be near anything taller than himself because lightning can somehow jump from the taller target. As always in a situation defined by contradictions, her mental equipment became immobilized and shunned responsibility to make decisions. She blundered on.

The workers were more visibly terrified than the patients, whose energy output was typically pinned near its peak just to handle daily survival, and so they could not really show their distress. Many workers ran for the trucks, and they put up the canvas tops as shelter from the wind and rain. There they huddled, head in knees, relying on the false security of the thin cloth protecting them from the gods, or an angry mother nature, or whatever was assaulting them with the terrifying lightning.

The rain abruptly intensified wickedly. Now it was as though buckets of water were being dumped in clumps onto Gwendolyn's head and back. Those patients unable to roll onto their side took the brunt on their fronts, and a woman right next to her feet gasped and coughed as the water filled her nose and mouth. Gwendolyn, struggling with the gusting wind that was thrashing the rain into her own eyes, squatted and repositioned the woman on her side. When the woman started to tilt back, Gwendolyn wedged some folds of her mat under her ribs and fumbled with them as they slipped out of position, then caught herself—she realized that this was just another example of a now-familiar situation: a palliative measure taken which was wholly ephemeral, if not completely symbolic. She jammed the folds under the woman one last time and quickly stood back up. She caught glimpses of many patients in similar distress through the interstices of her storm-induced blindness as she moved along.

The wind remained turbulent, and its intensity continued to grow alarmingly. The torrent of rain persisted. When she noticed she was up to her ankles in water on the sloping ground, Gwendolyn became truly frightened for the patients lying on their mats. She had trouble standing and controlling her pace, as the average wind direction was still in her direction of travel, but its angle jumped randomly. She could see no farther than thirty feet, and even that was not reliable. She saw agony whenever a window opened up in the mist, and she heard nothing except the wind. She stopped and crouched, leaning against the wind, to gather her thoughts. These people were in trouble. Not the gradual, planned-for trouble the mission was designed for but stark, imminent danger of being killed by a simple rainstorm that should be no more than a nuisance. She scanned her field of view, seeing only fluctuating shades of grey. She was alone. The patients were in trouble. She had to help them through this. She had no tools. The wind was hammering her. A seed of panic took root in her.

Gwendolyn closed her eyes and swayed against the wind, trying to overcome the power of the fear that had started to grip her. Scrunching in the storm, she breathed slowly. This loosened her body enough that a few tears crept out the seam between her eyelids, and her heart slowed slightly. Thinking a bit more clearly now, the pungency of the terror was marginally attenuated by her knowledge that Bok was a smart man. He had planned for such a catastrophic occurrence. He may not be as warm and cuddly as she once thought, but he was a practical man, and he would certainly be coordinating efforts to mitigate the effects of what was, after all, just a thunderstorm.

She heard a crashing sound through the rain and looked behind her, to her left. The metal-ribbed canvas top of a truck had been torn off, and it was bouncing and spinning along the ground in a scene that would have been more horrifying had she been able to see the destruction being wrought on those below. She was in no danger, and it was just a peripheral event that lasted until the rooftop disappeared in the fluctuating fog ahead of her; the picture of the twisted, deforming metal beams slashing and crushing the sickened patients eluded her mind. Looking back to find the truck, she saw the workers it formerly sheltered scattering through the disorder.

She heard nothing but the wind and rain. She felt water touching her bottom as she squatted on the sloped ground. It was inches deep here and rising at an alarming rate. All of the patients' indistinct faces in this section of the camp seemed likely to be underwater soon; many may already be. She froze in helpless dread at the thought, then looking to her side she saw arms and a chin desperately thrashing back and forth in the water. She jumped over and grasped the head and shoulders of the genderless patient, who coughed and gasped for breath. His head slumped forward in exhaustion as he became an ancient man, gasping and breathing in heavy gulps. Gwendolyn made a few encouraging words that he undoubtedly could not hear, and groped for something to prop up his head. She found the edge of a mat below the water and rolled it up, helped by the current of the water as it ran down the slant of the ground. She jammed it under the back of the helpless man's neck, made one last soothing sound, stroked his face and stood up against the wind and rain.

Anguish assaulted her as she drove forward, all the time ignoring everything around her. She had the now-familiar feeling of having performed an explicitly meaningless act of compassion. The propped rug was destined for failure. *In fact, it's probably unrolled by now and that poor patient is doomed. Maybe he's dead already.* She was possibly not incorrect about the timing, as her mental processes were now proceeding in slow motion, just as her walk was. There had perhaps been enough time for that patient to drown, even in the interval between when she started and finished that thought.

The torrent and the wind continued, and continued varying. Gwendolyn pressed on with frayed nerves. She was becoming tired, dragging her feet through the deepening water. She could barely see irregular rectangles and formless human objects on the ground in front of her as the wind and rain snarled at her back. She navigated clumsily over the bumpy ground, sometimes stepping on a slippery and pliant thing that must be somebody's arm or foot, causing her no end of anguish. But she forced herself forward. Fear bloomed up from within her with a fury. *I'm panicking. This happened when I was here before. No. This is much worse. I have to escape from this mess.*

Something dull and generic bumped against the back of Gwendolyn's heels and legs several times in quick succession. She stopped and turned, trying to look, but the wind and rain hitting her face grudgingly revealed only an indiscernible spray of water and churning mist. She paused and surveyed the ground on her sides to the extent possible, and saw only grey representations of human forms, visible simply as a variation on the overall shade of indistinctness filling her field of view. None of the native workers or volunteers were in visual range either. As she progressed, the banging of objects sporadically repeated on her legs.

When she arrived at the area where the ground bottomed out, the water deepened, wetting her up to the middle of her shins. She trudged onward and climbed the slight slope toward the dirt hills and the mission proper. Finally, with her feet dragging through the water of the newly formed lake, she could see where the path to the mission led up from the camp. Water was funneling down the slope, and the level approached a foot in depth as she scrambled up and out of the dustbowl. The rain, wind and wind instability were all at their heretofore peak and probably still increasing. Exhausted, she crawled up the slope of the path on all fours. Then she stood in the storm and tried to look back, shielding her eyes as much as possible. But the fragments of vision she got only delivered formless and changing grey shades chaotically whipping across her field of view.

Looking around, Gwendolyn could see no activity in the mission. She was frightened, fatigued, depressed; she felt beaten. She had an impulse to find shelter, but also some component of a masochistic drive to avoid hiding from the storm while so many were suffering, and she sat on the wet ground in the rain and wind. She was still stunned by the suddenness of the storm and surprised by her quick descent from concern to panic amid the patients. As she sat, tears mixed with rainwater and spiraled down her cheeks.

She thought about the man whose head she had propped out of the water. She recalled the grabbing or bumping on her legs. Had she not killed these people? She had to admit that at some level she knew she was abandoning that man to drown. Could she somehow convince herself she did not know that lifting the man's head and allowing him to clear his lungs once was a useless gesture, delaying his death by a few minutes at most? These people were so starved, how much could they weigh? Couldn't she have carried him out, or at least dragged him? But those she would drag him over—would she not be helping to kill them then?

She was tired, but as she sat in the driving wind and rain, which was still escalating, she knew she was in no danger; she had not been physically imperiled when she was out in the camp either. She was not even cold in the rain. *I lost my nerve, that's the simple fact of the matter.* But the whole thing was hopeless. *How many patients does Bok have here? Five thousand? How does the idea of dragging them out, one by one, scale up to that quantity?* Granting she had the energy and strength to bring a patient across the camp, up the slope and into the mission proper, all doubtful, what about the other four thousand nine hundred ninety-nine? She could go back, maybe several times. She could, with superhuman exertion, pull perhaps a dozen people out. She would have to choose each from the set of those who did not drown while she attended the prior patient. Maybe she could have selected some children.

So what?

Where would that leave her? And the world? A dozen more anonymous patients alive at the end of the storm, that's all. A dun-colored shroud of lethargy was descending over Gwendolyn's psyche, and she felt herself becoming immobile as it enveloped her and constricted around her limbs. She felt her joints lock in her seated position. She stayed there, with the rain washing over her body, her mind's blankness punctuated by spasms of guilt, for a long time.

Something within her burst, and Gwendolyn was enraged. She stood up, feeling her legs and back groan as she straightened and marched along the mission in the buffeting rain and whipping wind. All the doors were closed. Windows, where they had panes, were also closed, though a few on the side facing the dirtpile were broken. There was now a stream at the bottom of the dirtpile as the water that was collected on the hills rushed down and turned toward the power plant. From there it would undoubtedly run down into the camp and settle with the rest of the rainwater, cultivating the newborn lake that was the lower central portion of the dustbowl.

She was determined to find Director Professor Dr. Florian Q. Bok. Why were his emergency plans invisible? Where was Aloysius Fink and for that matter, Phineas Boseau? Why did she not see all hands—all employees and volunteers from the mission—ministering to hundreds or thousands of recently saved patients laid out safely, if uncomfortably, on the grounds of the mission proper, between the buildings, on the floors inside, wherever? Was it too late to do something? The mission must contain the better part of a hundred people who could help, considering the native employees living in the barracks she was passing right now along with the volunteers. She attempted to step up her pace in her agitation, but her legs served as leaden weights being dragged along in her exhaustion, rather than an energetic propulsion system. She had to settle for slow progress.

Just as she happened to get within sight of the cathedral she noticed something she had never seen: the large front doors were wide open. She saw the tail of some sort of filthy sheet of fabric waving violently out past the ends of the open doors. It was receding inside. She ran toward the church building. As she approached, she could see inside one of the doors, and it was being held open by a line of diminutive, wet, black-clothed nuns and what looked like two native boys, perhaps ten years old, struggling to help hold the heavy doors in place against the whipping of the wind! Her angle around the nearer door now allowed her to just see a bit of the interior of the building.

She peered through the rain into the building. The inside of the cathedral was lit brightly, much more brightly than when she was inside. She could not see the floor because of the elevated alcove, and the haphazardly arranged walls of the little compartments broke any meaningful holistic view of the building's interior; however she saw a half dozen hyperactive nuns scurrying all around. She was surprised to catch an instantaneous glimpse of what appeared to be some girls and a few more boys inside. There was shouting and raucous motion, with nuns and children hustling back and forth. *Somebody is doing something at last. Maybe Bok and Sarah are there with them. Maybe I was wrong.* The doors were closing now, and her view inside was shrinking as the nearer door sliced into it. She accelerated her pace, calling out to the slowly closing doors, but no matter how hard she worked, she could feel her own feeble voice strangled by the storm as it left her lips.

She fell face-down in the wet dirt. She did not linger—she was up and sprinting, mud dripping off her face, as soon as her skid stopped. Gwendolyn called out to no avail as she sprinted the final distance, but the doors were tightly shut before she got up onto the porch. The rope attached to the bell inside was thick and heavy, but it was being buffeted by the wind and jostling around, keeping it mostly out of reach. She intermittently screamed and pounded on the doors as she tried to catch the rope. No response came. With a few minutes of effort she captured the rope and pulled it with all her might. Between the bursts of wind buffeting her ears, she could hear the bell ringing inside the church. It was as from something a thousand years in the past, sound delivered in small glimpses as fragments muffled by the heavy oak threaded their way to her ears through the buffeting wind and rain. She pulled again and again. She pounded and kicked on the door, surprising herself with how tiny a disturbance she caused in the massive wooden obstruction.

Nobody was coming for her. The door was going to stay closed.

She leaned against the door and slid her back straight down and there she sat, feet extended, listlessly showered by the rain. She watched the kinetic, statistically unchanging tableau of the weather against the mission buildings and deserted pathways with a numb detachment. Occasionally her eyes detected something worth following. Twice she saw a native worker appear, moving through the storm, and enter the extinct-looking worker's dormitory. She also saw one regular volunteer walking along, fighting the air and rain. She made no attempt to communicate with either.

The rainstorm continued unabated. As Gwendolyn sat she heard an engine through the noise of the storm. She looked to her right and saw a truck pulling out from between two buildings. It fishtailed out onto the path and bounced away toward the power plant. It was moving rapidly, even recklessly; its tires slipped and wobbled on the slick dirt as it traveled along the trail. The black truck became invisible in the grey rain before it turned out of sight on the path to the camp. She found it interesting, in a detached way, that someone was hustling such an energetic machine out to the camp.

Eventually Gwendolyn tired of her passive stance sitting against the heavy wooden cathedral doors. She wondered what the nuns were doing inside. But she really wondered what Bok was doing about the crisis. She stood up and hustled off the porch and down to the path. She felt her anger steeping to a boiling point. She turned toward the administration building and walked briskly in that direction. The wind and rain was still at its most intense level so far, but she was protected from noticing it by her furious concentration on finding Bok.

She got near the administration building and saw a woman bundled in heavy coats or towels enter the executive residence. She ran forward, feet splashing and calling out, but the woman disappeared inside. Gwendolyn found the door locked when she arrived. She pushed the doorbell button and waited as the rain flogged her. She repeated the process several times, and her anger notched higher each time. Nobody was going to answer. The building looked deserted; had she not seen the woman enter, she would have been able to believe she was outside an empty edifice. In fact, the whole mission had a abandoned feeling for her, regardless of what was going on with the vast and pathetic crowd over the dirtpile.

The affront of the woman entering and disappearing, shutting her out, increased Gwendolyn's agitation. She now craved violence, and she looked for something with which to attack the door. There was a bench not far away. She went over to examine it, but none of the metal slats were loose enough for her to work them free. She forayed over to a shed near the runway, incidentally noticing there was no militia jeep or truck visible outside the gate. Opening the hut's door, she was presented with the wealth of miscellaneous tools and junk within. Her attention focused quickly on a long steel handle from some sort of large tool. It was a bar that had a square opening near one end, with the far end capped by an irregularly shaped knob. Below the square opening the bar flared out toward a convenient handle. She grasped the implement, at first underestimating its heft, then picked it up with both hands and slung it over her shoulder. She made a beeline to executive residence. Upon arrival she pressed the doorbell button and without hesitating, lifted the tool and swung it at the metal bar across the middle of the building's door, bending it and breaking it free. It fell to the ground. Gwendolyn lifted her steel bar and swung it like a bat at the glass. It bounced off the windowpane and jumped backwards out of her hands; she was knocked her off her feet. She sat for a few seconds then crawled over and retrieved her weapon. *I guess that's not glass.*

Gwendolyn was growing more determined. She stood up, came back to the door and, with a much better grip on her weapon, repeated her last blow twice in quick succession. She sensed and ignored motion inside the building as she again raised the steel bar and swung it at the door's glass, taking aim at the right edge, near the frame. This time the entire panel dropped inward, intact, with its frame bent. She threw down the tool, reached through the empty window and opened the door. Withdrawing her arm, she stepped inside.

Standing a few feet inside was Sarah Greenwater. Her hair was wet around the edges, and she stood wide-eyed and gaping-mouthed. She was looking at Gwendolyn as though the girl had gone postal. Gwendolyn walked steadily and slowly to her and asked, "Where is everybody?"

Sarah delayed and then said, "What is going on? What are you doing here? There's a storm outside. You should be in your room. You can't be here."

Gwendolyn could not believe her ears and clarified her question. "Where is Bok?" The physical activity of dominating the door had had a positive effect on the amount of negative energy she had available, and she seemed quite imposing to Sarah.

Sarah stepped back and said slowly, "He's not here…" She looked blankly at Gwendolyn. The girl shrugged in frustration as she walked around Sarah, who turned and called after her, "But you can't be in here."

It was true. *I don't doubt it. Fully against all rules and propriety. A scandal, surely.* Gwendolyn walked along the hallway, peeking in all the unlocked rooms. The doors that were ajar or open led to small offices, closets or empty rooms. She found a stairway at the end of the hall and climbed up. Looking down the hallway from the second floor landing, she noted that it seemed much like the first floor except that the hallway was shorter and ended in a door. She continued climbing and found the penultimate floor had a locked door at the stairway, with no windows in it. She climbed the last flight and reached the top level, where she found a closed but unlocked door on the landing. She went through and was immediately stunned by what she found.

Gwendolyn walked into the single room comprising the entire top storey of the executive residence building. There were contiguous windows around the periphery, and she could see the dirtpile, the power plant, the cathedral and much of the dustbowl. Bertha Martha Larssson was in her wheelchair facing the far right corner. She was alternately looking out the window and managing the mouth-driven stick on her chair for some purpose, obviously a purpose other than steering the stationary chair. Aloysius Fink and Phineas Boseau sat on a couch looking at a huge electronic screen Gwendolyn could not see. At each man's side was a can of beer on a small table, the condensation indicating low temperature and perhaps recent liberation from the refrigerator that Gwendolyn subsequently would notice in a corner kitchen area. Next to Fink's beer sat a GVCD. A collection of stacked electronic equipment was nearby, and its mass of cables rose in the middle of the room and disappeared through the ceiling. There were several other chairs and small tables around the room, as well as mostly empty shelving built into the wall below the windows. A few lonely and dusty books were positioned at various points on the shelves. A telescope with some electronic apparatus sat in the far left of the room, pointed out the window at the camp, which was largely visible over the dirtpile.

Dr. Boseau looked over at Gwendolyn when he heard the door open. Bertha Martha turned also, but her neck did not have the range to bring Gwendolyn within her view. Fink's single eye was fixated on the screen, and his jaw had an angry grind in process. Boseau started opening his mouth, but just then a roar came from the screen. Fink's body violently jerked, and he knocked over a can of beer as he lurched forward, his face contorted in anger. He cursed, and Boseau shrunk quietly into the sofa. Fink gesticulated less-than-pleasant motions and snarled at the screen as Boseau sat in apparent dread.

Gwendolyn looked out the windows. The weather could not be the reason for Fink's sudden conniption—the storm was fluctuating but basically unchanging. Fink glanced up at her and then looked down at the mess of beer draining into the fine carpet. His expression revealed that his anger had not abated from whatever offended him. She walked toward the sofa, and he stood up, wiping some beer from his thighs. He was soon to be standing in a small lake of beer as the liquid approached his feet.

Gaining an angle onto the screen, Gwendolyn saw that Fink and Boseau were…

Watching a soccer game!

Bertha Martha had twisted her neck to see the commotion, but since she had to adjust her wheelchair, which required a series of manipulations with her tongue, she missed some of the activity. Sarah arrived at the top of the stairs and stood quietly, still dripping.

Fink barked, "What are—" but Gwendolyn walked right up to him so closely she could unwillingly see the tiny gap at the bottom of his eye patch. He pushed the damp intruder away.

"Where is Bok?" she demanded, flipping his hands off her shoulders and stepping back in. "What the hell?" she swore uncharacteristically, and possibly for the first time in her life. "Don't you all know it's storming out there? You have people being killed in the dustbowl, and you sit here WATCHING A SOCCER GAME?" Her voice reverberated around the hard windowpanes. "Where is Bok?"

Fink was startled by the girl's assertiveness. He stood spluttering in anger and surprise but unable to put forth English syllables. She put her hands on his chest and pushed him. The seat caught the back of his legs, and he fell onto the sofa and landed in a seated position, stunned. He clenched a fist and adjusted his posture to bolt upright as he sat next to a visibly horrified and cringing Boseau.

Bertha Martha rolled up in her wheelchair and stopped abruptly. The fat on her face still shaking from the suddenly terminated motion, she spoke in a calm voice, "Gwendolyn, please help me to my apartment. We will talk." Before Gwendolyn responded, before she had decided how to respond, Bertha Martha started her wheelchair toward the elevator that Gwendolyn had not noticed. Its doors opened, and the wheelchair rolled into it as Gwendolyn stood frozen. Bertha Martha entered and executed a perfect wheelchair pirouette. She sat facing out, stick in her mouth, watching Gwendolyn imposingly through the open elevator door. Gwendolyn glanced down at Fink and Boseau, then looked at Sarah. She decided her best chance of finding out what was going on was to follow Bertha Martha. With one more glance back at the sports spectators, she went into the elevator, where Bertha Martha sat in stillness, stone-faced, lips pursed. Once the girl was in the compartment, Bertha Martha said, "Three," to which Gwendolyn responded by pressing the button for the third floor, leaving Fink and Bozo to their soccer game, well removed from the human devastation outside.

She rolled the wheelchair to Bertha Martha's room, easily following nonverbal directions. The woman thus had herself delivered to Room 309, and the door popped open as the chair approached. Gwendolyn wheeled the chair inside, and the door slowly closed. The studio apartment had a large living room-bedroom combination with kitchen equipment off to the side. She saw, through an open door on the left as they entered, a large bathroom with custom equipment within. Bertha Martha said, "Please heat some tea. You are soaking wet." Gwendolyn's anger, and even her worry for the patients, had receded to some extent, and upon hearing this she felt tired and a bit cold. She found tea for steeping and started heating some water in an old-fashioned kettle over an open flame. She was distantly troubled by the continuing storm outside, but it faded to a background concern for now.

As the water heated, Bertha Martha suggested that Gwendolyn dry off. She went in the bathroom and got what water was available from her hair and clothes out into a towel. Bertha Martha invited her to sit, and she did so after folding another towel and placing it on the sofa. As she sat it struck her with guilt that she was concerned with her own delicate comfort on the soft couch while those poor patients were facing disaster; her exhausted mood, not high to start with, sagged, and she sat looking at the floor.

After a while Bertha Martha indicated with a nod that the tea water was ready. Gwendolyn got up and made two cups of tea. Under silent direction she put some honey in them and placed one of them in a specially designed cup holder configured to hang on the wheelchair. She took her own cup over to the sofa and sat down. That first sip of the tea tasted heavenly, relaxing and wonderful. She closed her eyes and forgot where she was as it coated her throat.

Bertha Martha sipped with consummate expertise at the dangling cup. In contrast to Gwendolyn, that woman was not susceptible to falling under any spell from a pleasant warm drink. "Dr. Bok is not here at the mission," she stated.

Gwendolyn was thoroughly enjoying her sweet, hot beverage, and it consumed her full attention. As the N-th sip of tea was greasing her throat she started to hear Bertha Martha's voice seeking delayed entry into her mind. The warm liquid had the girl transfixed, and so to her the sound was like one spoken in slow motion by someone wrapped in cotton a mile away. Her subconscious was working to protect her from sensing anything except the beauty of the tea. Nonetheless, some part of her evaluated the statement and summoned her full awareness. *Not here? What? Oh, yes. I saw him leave yesterday morning.* Was that just yesterday? She had to check herself because Bok's departure seemed so far in the past.

"He left, he said, for an urgent meeting that came up back home in Switzerland. That is the mission's position."

"But... what are we going to do?"

"Do, my dear? Whatever do you mean, 'do?'" Bertha Martha's face approached as neutral an expression as Gwendolyn had ever seen, and the older woman took an unhurried sip of tea from the hanging cup. The expression was not actually neutral; an observer would judge her either angry or pensive, with the eyebrows together and her lips pinched into a pucker. She was taking the position of a seasoned teacher facilitating a pupil's discovery of truths that Socrates posited were within students since before birth. She was trying to be impassive.

"The storm. The patients are being killed by the water. I was out there. It's horrible. And it's just a little bit of water, just a few inches."

"They told me that they tried to warn you many times not to go out to the camp. I understand you insisted on going out there every day." The teacher was stern.

"They knew this would happen? What, they didn't want me to see it?" Gwendolyn was confused. "Oh, I hope this storm stops soon."

"This was well before any storm was coming. You were directed to stay over here with us, away from those people. It's not a pretty sight on the best of days, and volunteers are assigned elsewhere for good reason. As for the storm—it will proceed for only another hour or two."

Gwendolyn was shocked. How could she know how big the storm is? *They have weather predictions here? And they didn't prepare for this storm?* Her face showed her astonishment.

Bertha Martha took another sip of her drink. "Until a few days ago nobody saw any storm coming. Even then it was just a developing possibility, unusual but not unknown. They hardly ever actually materialize. It was assumed to be a standard false alarm until the night before last. And of course, I can tell you that none of them wanted you exposed to a storm like that out in the camps. But trying to reorganize things just to shelter you from being out there was, I suppose, not a sufficiently high priority. There is much to this mission besides worrying about Gwendolyn Dressel-Meier's moods." She sipped her warm tea and motionlessly requested more.

Gwendolyn was dumbfounded, and had there been less surprise in that package of statements, she would have found a way to be hurt, but she did not. Questions raced through her mind as she instinctively refilled Bertha Martha's tea. What was Bok's business that had him rush out the morning before the storm hit? Even if he were an impersonal, hardened man and not the warm and sentimental person he pretended to be, wouldn't he want to be here to direct some sort of mitigation of storm damage? Wouldn't that be the practical thing to do, if for no other reason than to avoid criticism later? If a storm was expected, why weren't the patients evacuated to somewhere with shelter? Was Bertha Martha in some kind of position of authority here? Why was she speaking almost as though she were?

Gwendolyn was mentally dizzy from the whirlpool of emotions she had traversed that day. Since leaving her room that morning she had experienced in a variety of sequences unease, neutrality, sympathy, depression, alarm, surprise, fear, despair, fury, astonishment and confusion. She strained to process Bertha Martha's bizarre information dump. "But Bok told us there was no electronic communication with the outside world. He took our GVCDs."

"He took your GVCDs. I was not there to hear your introduction, but I strongly doubt that he said the mission was isolated completely from communication with the outside world. The man is a wordsmith, if nothing else, and he can smoothly stimulate misunderstanding without making any individual statements that are false. Did you talk to your own parents on a phone from the mission? And what are Messrs. Boseau and Fink doing right now?"

Gwendolyn was silenced; Bertha Martha was correct. She was so accustomed to having no instant electronic communication that she had not even connected the dots, forgetting she had talked to Winifred and Kingman from Sarah's office before her trip to Zurich. She nodded dumbly, nonplussed from visions of Fink and Boseau rooting for their favorite teams and drinking beer while patients drowned.

Silence.

"So, you knew the storm was coming. Why didn't you prepare to help those people?"

"Gwendolyn, I want you to know one thing. I am here as a factory manager. That is my job. It helps these people. Only because of my special situation do I live in the executive residence with Dr. Bok, who makes all the decisions. I am not consulted on such things. But for my specific handicaps and funding from the Swedish government, I would not be here at all. This is not my show. Make no mistake, I make a serious contribution to the productivity of the food preparation here, but like everyone else, I am here with my own constraints. It is something you should think about. But

I am wandering, talking about myself. I think you bring that out in me. I feel some unusual kindred bond with you." She smiled to the extent she was someone who smiled. "I will say no more this evening."

Gwendolyn listened, only fleetingly distracted by the preposterousness of Bertha Martha's opinion of her own effectiveness as a manager. Gwendolyn started thinking about today. About her stay here. About how effective her own efforts were at bringing lasting relief to anyone.

Then Bertha Martha belied her last sentence. "Before I tell you a bit more about Director Professor Dr. Florian Q. Bok, I will take an opportunity to give you some unsolicited advice. As you make your way in the world, choose to be involved with something you can control, or at least truly contribute to. I imagine your upbringing and schooling has given you to understand that corporations are evil, and that for-profit work is a low and parasitic form of existence."

Gwendolyn nodded.

"Sucking money out of the people and dragging down the economy." Again Gwendolyn bowed her head twice. She sipped some of her own neglected tea. "Rather than the reverse, rather than for-profit work being the engine that supplies the resources for the rest of the people, the government and all, whose major responsibilities are therefore to decide how much of the profit-seeker's money to help themselves to, and what to do with the proceeds." Gwendolyn agreed, though this was unfamiliar phraseology, seeming to be a step toward inverting what she had heard from everyone else throughout her life.

"Then why doesn't your government send dollars to all of its citizens every year?" Gwendolyn did not understand the question. Bertha Martha was not making sense. Maybe the old invalid was a little crazy. Gwendolyn looked quizzically at her.

"Why do people write checks to the government every year for their taxes? Why do they pay money to the authorities each time they buy something new? Why does the money not go in the other direction?"

Gwendolyn did not answer at all. The question was obviously a cartoon representation and a ruse of some kind. It was leading somewhere her mind would disallow, somewhere forbidden. The woman was about to trick her.

Bertha Martha let out a breath through her mouth, flapping her lips to create what would be a raspberry if she had employed her tongue as well; as it stood, it was a passive and exasperated noise, not an expression of contempt. She continued, "I will not go into the theoretical and overwhelming historical evidence, but your worldview is distorted in this respect. I will not mention that I worked for a very profitable company that alleviated suffering around the world with several products in a way that is hard to replicate. You may read from any number of authors on this subject, authors you have never heard of. I would suggest some if it were plausible to imagine you were interested. So if you are, please indicate that."

She took a sip of her tea and paused quietly. Gwendolyn could not help pretending to wonder to herself which of them had the distorted view. She did not interrupt the woman by expressing interest in doing her own research.

Bertha Martha nodded with a smile and spoke. "I suspected as much. Let's talk about a practical matter now. Though it is not true at all, for the sake of argument let us grant that those in control of any establishment—company, governmental body, school, charitable group—are always out to use the machinery of their organization to abuse, mistreat, extract advantage of, the common people. You will see where I am leading with my assumption."

Gwendolyn did not see; she was confused. She listened although she believed little of what she heard this woman saying now, especially the part about people outside of companies wanting to cheat everyone else, just like people inside them. The older woman continued, "A profit-seeking corporation is dependent on its own objective success to survive; a government is dependent on its ability to force compliance, and a charitable organization is dependent on convincing outsiders that it is good and that they should sacrifice their interests to it so it can continue in its mission.

"Now before I give you advice I want to be clear: I am not referring to the worst of all worlds, worlds that have happened for centuries and are still dominant: monopolies, huge corporations or charities colluding with government to extract the productivity of the population and divide the benefits as they see fit. This happens all too often, and I can give you references to read on this as well, if you want it."

Gwendolyn did not want it any more than she desired the earlier-proffered resources.

"Here is the advice you did not ask for: You can choose to be involved with an organization that can consistently thrive only by objectively doing something judged worthwhile, or you can choose to be involved with an organization that can thrive in steady state by deceit or bad dealings. If you choose the latter, and if has chosen to be an evil group, you must understand that you are complicit in willing blindness, degrading and robbing yourself.

And the worst part is this: the clients of such organizations are the real suckers. They cooperate in degrading and robbing themselves. The organization flourishes by either forcing or misleading them into giving away their family's hard-earned money. Do you know any charities that rely on tricking people and misusing their donations?"

Gwendolyn did not answer, but her mind was involuntarily captured by memories of Kingman's speech in Zurich.

Bertha Martha continued and broke up Gwendolyn's reverie. "And one other thing: do not misunderstand me, young lady. So long as there is human nature, so long as there are rogues and thieves, so long as there are statistics and fluctuations, there is a need for government and a need for charity among us all. Charity in the linguistic meaning of the word, independent of the organizational meanings. I am in a position, a configuration to know this better than most anyone. These needs will not go away. And they must be paid for, they should be paid for. There are thousands, maybe millions, of people around the world working with the best intentions in nonprofit and government organizations. All I am saying is that these systems can become corrupt over time. The temptation is great. And you should grasp that the source of their power, their subsistence, is necessarily allocated from the directly productive portion of the economy."

The woman looked at Gwendolyn with her lips pinched into almost a kiss. Her expression was serious as she checked for some signal from the girl. Gwendolyn was resisting the perceived sophistry and getting impatient. She did not say anything. But Bertha Martha had more to say. "In that for-profit world, with the conspiratorial exclusions I mentioned above, this process of thriving while abusing those who supply your financial support cannot happen except temporarily. But in the other parts of the economy, in government, in charities, it can and does happen. In steady state.

"Which is worse—to be cheated by someone at arm's length or to be cheated by someone who tricked you into asking them to cheat you? I will say no more on this." Gwendolyn's attention was still strong enough that she could note that Bertha Martha was stating this last clause for the second time today.

Gwendolyn had no interest in what Bertha Martha was babbling about, and it seemed unrelated to the storm. Nonetheless, she felt a glimmer of an incipient hint that there was some speck of wisdom in what this old lady said, though it seemed buried in convolutions and the biases of a strange and mildly demented woman.

She got herself another cup of tea and re-refilled Bertha Martha's. When she sat down, she used the break to come back to the present situation, "You all knew a storm was coming. Why didn't Bok order some emergency measures? Why did he let such a thing happen?"

"You say we knew a storm was coming. Certainly Dr. Bok knew, and Sarah. It is unlikely that anybody else was informed ahead of time, though I don't think telling us would have changed much.

"As for Dr. Bok, you have to understand some things about the man," Bertha Martha said without expression. "He is a master at some things, very creative and beguiling. He could sell the proverbial ice cubes to Eskimos. He can set up what we eventually learn to be the most breathlessly cynical enterprise and run it with vigor and success, promoting it as the most humane and caring undertaking in human history. But he is not at home with people. And he is not a detail man. He cannot run this operation without the carnivore Aloysius Fink and the lapdog Sarah Greenwater to take care of organizing and controlling the actual work. And the last thing that Florian Bok could ever do is face the patients. Even that name, patients, his name, is a disguise. We are not at a hospital. We are not a university headed by the distinguished professor. The mission is not a mission. We may as well be a railroad, with the patients as the material moving through from the entrance gate to the crematorium in slow motion. We are a mission, a hospital. We are a university headed by a professor."

At the shock of this brightly painted image of the mission, a paroxysm seized Gwendolyn. She felt faint, and her mental processing churned furiously to accept what she must—the information illuminating Bok's orientation—and to reject or at least bury the horrific and cynical caricature of the mission's function, a mockery she somehow worried was not too absurd an exaggeration.

Bertha Martha sipped tea with a stone face, as though she had just commented on a flower arrangement or a new hat a friend was wearing.

How could this woman sit there so well composed and make such charges? Gwendolyn gasped for breath as her heart pounded. Eventually she righted herself and forced her concentration to the task of reconciling the words and what was real, at least about Bok. Her mind would not cooperate, and its blank screen facilitated little progress in the task.

Bertha Martha answered the girl's oxygen-starved silence. "Have you dealt with Dr. Bok regarding anything where he had to make a decision concerning the health or welfare of one of his so-called patients? Allocating resources, say, or improving the food composition? Or is your interaction with him confined to hearing how the mission is doing great but general things in the world, how it is working closely with your father's Worldwide Transformative Foundation? Why is it important that you go home reporting a good experience here?"

Gwendolyn had figured out that Bok was falsely avuncular. The man was shallow enough to feed steak to dogs within yards of starving people, people he could not possibly care very much about. This much made sense. But she had never pictured the man as anything less than a master in full control of the mission. Whatever her flaws and mental diseases, Bertha Martha had a penetrating intellect. Early on, though, apparently Bok had even been able to pull the wool over her eyes, no small task. Could a man so capable also be an awkward bureaucrat, a man passively piloting the place along whatever course unfolded in front of him, rather than the all-powerful puppeteer controlling the mission's destiny down to the tiniest detail? Could he really be afraid to confront those under his own protection?

Gwendolyn thought of her interactions with Bok. It seemed he had sought her out every time he was onsite. He was always solicitous, always asking about her father, with whom he had had more recent contact than she did. The man always smiled at her below his thinning white hair and thick glasses.

"Have you ever heard of him going out to the dustbowl?" Bertha Martha's voice sounded.

The image of Bok out there among the common Africans, with cane and white suit, was preposterous.

A burst of intense rain struck noisily at the window. Gwendolyn lurched for the opportunity to pursue distraction. She wanted to steep in anger but failed to summon the emotion. A surge of tears welled from her eyes. She cried, "But shouldn't we do something? How can they be watching a soccer game? A soccer game, of all things?"

Bertha Martha stayed on track. "First you must understand Director Professor Dr. Florian Q. Bok and the mission. You must go through the process."

Silence. Gwendolyn squirmed motionlessly.

"Do you have the experience of seeing Dr. Bok feeding a patient? Or binding a wound?"

Gwendolyn had to admit she had not. She had started having questions about the man when she met the dogs. She began personally disliking the man when Jojo was killed, but this took things further. She reluctantly listened, and no inconsistencies arose to combat Bertha Martha's portrayals. The elder woman pointed out that Bok came to Swazizibia for about a week every month. That justified his claim that he spends one quarter of his time at the mission, supervising and working at the ground level. In fact, he spent almost the whole time here in the executive residence or the administration building, working far from any needy patients. He took his meals in the buildings and never even went to the workers' cafeteria. He was simply marking time here for the log books.

Gwendolyn was unable to lodge a question she had suppressed thinking about. *What about those dogs? How can he bring dogs here? And feed them steak?* She knew the answer—she knew there was no answer.

Proceeding on the subject of Bok, Bertha Martha said, "He had just arrived here less than three days ago. Overnight the next night it became clear that a hundred-year storm was forming in the region. The projections were not very clear, because we are not in an area where any worldwide news service is interested in providing detailed weather updates. But it was pretty certain that the fossil river bed—that's what the area you volunteers call the dustbowl is, you know—was likely to be flooded suddenly. It's been discussed theoretically, in a disinterested and academic way, many times in the past.

"Now, one could argue we have the manpower to move some fraction of the patients, perhaps all of the ones at real risk, and place them on the higher ground on this side of the mission, or outside the mission fence, or even in buildings in the mission area. Maybe just doubling them up at the far side of the camp, which is more elevated, would be enough. It would have been a heroic effort; thousands cannot move, and each pair of workers would need to move many dozen. But with almost a thirty-six hour warning we could have managed something."

Gwendolyn listened intently. She was agreeing, and something within her lurked, hoping time would turn back and they could follow Bertha Martha's prescription.

"Florian Bok judged it was not worthwhile to fight the storm. And believe me, he had zero willingness to witness its reality. He scurried out as quickly as he could. The only thing that kept him here till daybreak was the fact that the pilot had, as normal, gotten drunk after arriving here, this time drunk enough that Dr. Bok, who is pretty tolerant on these things, felt he could not allow the man to fly his precious dogs away. Sarah had to go into the women workers' dormitory where he spends time, er... visiting, and drag him out and start to sober him up enough to keep Bok and his precious damned animals alive on the flight back to the capital city."

Bertha Martha sucked in a few efficient sips of tea and drained her container of the last drops of the sweet, lukewarm drink. Gwendolyn had a feeling of almost complete disorientation one gets when he realizes he is suddenly placed in some world foreign to all he knows, standing on bedrock that morphed into quicksand under him.

After a long pause during which she resisted, Gwendolyn was forced to ask a question. "But what about you? All that about being complicit in degrading yourself. How can you participate in all this if it's true?" The girl was confused. Her emotions not knowing what to do, she cried, disappointed, furious, miserable—or with some other unspecifiable mixture of feelings controlling her actions.

Bertha Martha answered calmly, "Will you please refill my tea?" Gwendolyn, trembling, filled her cup and reset it on the wheelchair's fixture with some trouble. The woman continued, "I have no illusions. And you should not either. Florian Bok has no illusions, and certainly Aloysius Fink and that god-awful Phineas Boseau are not kidding themselves. As for Sarah, she certainly must have started with a pleasant fiction, but she knows what is going on as well."

She sipped, and Gwendolyn listened silently. "I am here because I have nothing else. I am not saving anybody's life, but that is the façade we work under. Yes, I am degrading myself by participating here. But at least I run an efficient factory. That is all; it is its own reward. I was being squeezed out of any meaning in my home country. I come from Sweden, as you know, and Sweden is one of the most comfortable and advanced civilizations. Though in theory I could have continued a consequential and productive life, as I told you before, that does not really happen in practice. I was being degraded there as well. I was headed for being warehoused; nobody wants to see an invalid who can remind them of their own frailty. I frightened people when they looked at me. I could see it. My dear, can you please help me with something?"

Gwendolyn agreed to help, and she attended Bertha Martha on a necessary trip to the toilet. Bertha Martha's bathroom had good and complex equipment; Gwendolyn had to strain surprisingly little as she moved the obese torso between situations. Gwendolyn tried to avoid looking troubled about her own distress in this unpleasant task, but did not succeed until a particularly noisy burst of rain at the window reminded her that hundreds of people were probably filling their lungs at this very moment, helpless in six inches of water or less. That gave her some subjective perspective, and stiffened her up regarding her current task.

When the nasty little chores were complete, she brought Bertha Martha back out into her living room, and the woman continued holding court. "How many patients do you believe you have saved, Gwendolyn?" she asked in a serious tone.

The query caught her by surprise. *You can't measure things that way here.* She avoided the question. "Shouldn't I get out there with Mr. Fink and Dr. Boseau? It's so... horrible. They've got to be dying out there. A few inches of water, and these people can't sit up to get out of it. It's so... pointless. So wasted. If they could just sit up. The ones at the near edge of the camp, especially."

"And if they sat up and survived, what then?"

Gwendolyn had no idea what this meant.

"What happens to them if they get through the storm?" Bertha Martha pressed, and Gwendolyn shifted restlessly in her chair.

"But Bok—it's his responsibility. How can he just leave? How can they watch sports upstairs? Aren't we going to do anything?" The rain pounded. Except for her underwear and socks, Gwendolyn's clothing was dry.

Bertha Martha sipped her tea and turned a grim expression, unjustly classified as a species of smile, as she looked down and shrugged. "Well, if it's any consolation to you, there will be plenty of room in the camp to admit more patients from the outside now." Her face dropped as though she was about to cry.

Gwendolyn felt sick. She drank the last little bit of tea from her cup. She slumped in her chair, turning toward the window.

Conversion to the Past Tense

How long does a very bad day last?

It was morning. Gwendolyn lay on her side on a sofa with a large, soft blanket covering her. Weak, diffuse light seeping in through the window provided an uneven grey illumination to the colors on the walls. Looking around, Gwendolyn could see the place was not her room. It had a kitchen and a large bed and a dining area and some other furniture, all inside the same open area. There was an electronic screen on one wall. Not recognizing her location, she was disoriented on several scales, and the screen brought to memory some old story where such things spied on the inhabitants of apartments. She turned away to huddle under the blanket. She could not remember what the story was but did recall that it told of a dystopian world, one where the mundane and the absurd and the ominous swirled together in a menacing potpourri of obstacles and subterranean threats.

She saw an empty wheelchair, then it came into her mind that she had been talking to Bertha Martha. She was in Bertha Martha's apartment. She looked at the bed again and saw that indeed, the woman was there asleep, an odd-looking, breathing mountain under a blanket. It was pre-dawn, and out the window she could see the glow of the still-occluded sun soaking into the fabric of the cloudless eastern sky over the dirtpile. Gwendolyn started to remember her conversation with Bertha Martha. That led her to the nightmarish events of yesterday. Could these be real? All that must have been a horrible dream. It did not take long for her to reason that she was here, and she could trace the entire course of yesterday backwards. It was not a nightmare.

What world was this? Things were all so simple just twenty-four hours ago. She was making sacrifices for the good of people in real need, and her small individual efforts were amplified by the professional machinery of the mission to deliver help to these people in their desperate plight. But the events of the past day and the seemingly emotionless revelations from Bertha Martha—these things, combined with her own prior doubts about Florian Bok, seemed to prove that she herself did not really know anything. She was in a surreal world, one where the mundane and the absurd and the ominous all combined together, one where it seemed the very ground could be melted away without warning, and the dark maw of nihilism lurked nearby, threatening with every footfall.

Gwendolyn sat up, keeping the blanket warmly around her shoulders, and wondered what her obligation to Bertha Martha was; as a visitor, was she expected to get the woman cleaned up and fed in the morning before work as repayment for her hospitality? She thought about how Bertha Martha told her that Phineas Boseau's job was to take care of her needs here. *I must have fallen asleep, and he came in here and moved Bertha Martha from her wheelchair to her bed.* The girl shuddered with the realization that he had come in while she slept. He obviously covered her, and he likely rearranged her sleeping body—she did not remember lying down across the sofa. Then as she moved, she noticed something strange. She dropped the blanket and saw that she was in a ridiculously large and flowing dress, shiny warm velvet, comfortable in spite of its elegance. An evening gown, obviously brand new, one that could fit someone of Bertha Martha's girth. She had a pang of revulsion. Her movements provoked another discovery: she was in perfectly dry but hugely loose and ill-fitting underthings. She fought her tendency to concentrate on the creepiness of the obvious, and swooned as her autonomous nervous system squeezed the blood from her brain in an effort to starve the onslaught of mental images attacking her. She lost consciousness.

THERE WAS SUN on Gwendolyn's face. Her memory asserted itself and gripped her psyche in layers. Her exhaustion and psychological defense mechanisms had combined to stimulate a deep slumber, and whatever woke her left her groggy. She lay perfectly still, remembered yesterday's storm, and recalled where she was. Cracking an eye, she looked out the window to what promised to be a beautiful day. She could not see the ground, just the dirtpile and the sky, but surely nobody would guess there had been a disastrous storm that must have wiped out dozens, hundreds of people—her memory intensified—a storm that incited her to effectively kill at least one patient in her own personal distress. She thought of the man whose neck she propped up as she passed by him. And there were others she should have somehow saved. Many others. Tears of guilty pain arose in her motionless eyes, precluding tears of grief for the victims in the catastrophe. After she suffered quietly for a little while, her mind went to the larger tragedy, and her silent tears broadened their base.

Strangely, in the midst of all this, manners came to mind again. She was, intentionally or not, Bertha Martha's guest. The woman was sleeping across the room. Would polite protocol require that she stay and take leave formally? She looked over and saw Bertha Martha lying under her blanket, making noise, breathing roughly. The blanket rose and fell irregularly, but she was otherwise motionless. It was still early morning, and she seemed asleep.

Gwendolyn only had to consider courtesy for a moment. She shuddered at the thought of approaching that mass of protoplasm, in whatever shape it assumes lying down. *Does she lie down to sleep?* How would someone wake her gently? To shake her would certainly start Bertha Martha's whole body oscillating, undulating... and the woman was, after all, maybe crazy at best or horrid and heartless at worst. Yesterday she said some pretty nasty things about processes in which she was a full participant. Gwendolyn quivered squeamishly and ruled out any absurd overlay of polite societal customs on her situation.

Her thoughts returned to the cataclysm of yesterday, to the ongoing tragedy of Swazizibia. She wondered if she could withstand the sorrow, the anguish of being here. There were two choices: engaging the tragedy, which was bad; or worse—holing up like a sponsored volunteer and avoiding it. The tears resumed their tracks down her cheeks. She felt a crescendo of sympathy for herself.

Then she sat up and mentally slapped herself across the face. *This is life, this is the world. For a comfortable person from America to caterwaul about how badly she feels, how horrible it is to have to be near others who actually are suffering, is unacceptable. To feel sorry for yourself because you have to witness people's misery; to complain because you must see them die—please!*

To sleep in a sheltered room and have three meals available, to be a part of an operation that feeds dogs steak—all this while people are perishing just over the hill; to pass by drowning people. These are things she would not deny she had participated in.

I have to grow up. I must get a grip on myself.

With newfound resolve controlling her thoughts, practicality set in, and Gwendolyn realized today would be a busy day; the mission certainly had to deal with the horrors and wreckage of yesterday. She decided to get back out to the dustbowl right away. Standing up in her ridiculous dress, she rooted around and quickly found her own clothing. She slipped out of the borrowed clothes, defiantly crushing them beneath her feet and curling her toes into the soft velvet. Bertha Martha's sedate quivering and heavy sporadic breath continued, seeming more pronounced. Gwendolyn wanted to get out of there quickly, so she fluffed her hair in front of the low mirror in the bathroom and went to leave. She tried to open the door, but it seemed locked. Then she noticed a large button for handicap access, one Bertha Martha could obviously not operate, and pressed it. The door opened, and she left. Her last act was to turn and glance at the older woman; she could see her eyes and flowing face under the blankets as the door swung shut. She turned and hurried toward the stairway just as she realized that Bertha Martha was sobbing; the side of her face was lying in a pool of tears. Gwendolyn shuddered with a combination of emotions that propelled her faster on her way out of the building. She rushed home.

As Gwendolyn crossed the lounge area in the sponsored volunteers' area, the native women were working, preparing to prepare breakfast. She went directly to her room and opened the door. It seemed an ordinary day; inside her room Pyratticus Julius was on the shelf looking undistressed. She picked him up. She sat on the bed, eyes closed, hugging the stuffed octopod and rocking back and forth for a minute, then she got up to shower and clean up for the day. On her way out to see the state of the dustbowl she took a handful of breakfast components.

It was early—much earlier than the time when workers gathered at trucks to be taken to the camp for food duty. She decided to walk to the dustbowl and see the extent of the destruction. She had never walked there, though it was not much more than a mile from her room to the center of the dustbowl, even with the walk around the dirtpile. In fact, she had never heard of anyone walking there. But there was almost no real barrier—one could easily walk straight over the hill and defeat the feeble border of barbed wire on the side of the dirtpile. And the gate across the path the trucks traversed was a joke. It was a swinging section in a short chain link fence, normally fully open, sometimes ajar. But the whole thing was absurd. The gate crossed the path and was contiguous with a fence that joined the corner of the building next to the power plant—the building Gwendolyn refused to name in her mind—the crematorium. But it extended perhaps fifty feet down a small slope on the other side of the path and ended abruptly in space. Anybody who found the gate closed could simple walk a round trip of a hundred feet or so, admittedly with a minor climb, and just proceed on by the gate. In fact, the only things stopping the patients themselves from walking over to the mission proper were ignorance, habit, and lack of energy.

Gwendolyn started to walk toward the camp as the sun climbed toward its position of authority over the day. The morning was commencing with beautiful weather; it was an average day again. She shook her head as she walked past the quiet cathedral and went by Bertha Martha's factory, where hustling workers were already preparing food, dancing to the music as if nothing had happened yesterday. *Maybe nothing happened yesterday! Please, please.* She knew better but quickened her steps; she had to see the extent of the problem.

She saw only a few signs of activity along the mission, due to the early hour. Only the muddy remnants of the rain in puddles and some streaks of brown from the bottom of the dirtpile betrayed anything abnormal; also the ground, usually parched, was moist everywhere.

Gwendolyn walked briskly and came to the power plant. She followed the path as it curved toward the dustbowl and went down the gentle but slippery, muddy slope and through the open gate. As she walked around the end of the dirtpile, she was increasingly anxious in anticipation of seeing the camp. She broke into a trot, and soon was at the edge of the dustbowl. The camp was in an oblong basin running mostly south to north, and her eyes swept the expanse of the dustbowl. From her distance it looked like the encampment of an undisciplined army of thousands. Over the near half of camp the ground glistened with water or moisture where it was visible. Water trickled down the slope of the camp and lingered in a sort of shallow lake at the bottom of the dirtpile. Missing from her view were the twenty or so tents that were normally present at various points in the camp. They must have all blown away and were probably on the ground somewhere.

As Gwendolyn surveyed the scene, the amorphous patches populating the dustbowl started taking on specific shapes and meanings. In front of her eyes they acquired detail. She observed the closer portion of the ground, and the blobs separated into two distinct classes. Some of the inchoate patches attained full focus as twisted mats or miscellaneous debris from the camp: clothing, pieces of tents, mats. Others emerged from the meaningless flotsam and morphed into human figures in front of her eyes, as though in a bad movie. Grey and gaunt, contorted and hopelessly still corpses.

She looked around the whole dustbowl. Far in the distance, near the top of the camp, she saw motion like that of insects. Turning her gaze back to the region near to her, she observed that the frozen corpses had grown fully clear, and they were lying scattered among the rubbish. The twisted human figures were located independently of the mats and other debris: some were partly on the rugs, others under them. Bodies were scattered on the bare ground, alone or in small groups. Some patients were on their backs or sides, and some were face down on the wet ground or in shallow water.

Gwendolyn was strangely unaffected and distant. She was not queasy, depressed, dizzy or weak. She remembered seeing video of a tsunami on the far side of the world from the turn of the century, and this destruction reminded her of that. *And it's right here with me. Those old scenes made me cry for days. I'm right here right now. What's wrong with me? But... what if this storm didn't happen?* She was reaching for something and not finding it.

She walked forward into the placid lake, her feet splashing as she approached the closest patients. Their facial features had fully materialized, and she was stricken with how many had their eyes open. Most of the deceased had gaping mouths, as though they had died trying to get one last breath. She zigzagged among the bodies remembering yesterday's wind and water. The storm had made it difficult to stand and see and even breathe, but all this death seemed unjustified for what amounted to just a rare single-thunderbolt rainstorm and small gale. These people should not have died. It was not their weakness that doomed them. It was Bok's dereliction. She had a flash of guilt. *It was my panic and unwillingness to pick some and save them.* She stepped around a mother and baby. The mother was clutching the child whose face was buried in her chest. Gwendolyn could not help wondering if she had lingered over them yesterday, but then walked away from the heart-wrenching scene with unemotional detachment; the flash of guilt did not last, perhaps because it would be impossible for her to sustain such emotions in a situation of this scope—if she wanted her heart to keep beating long.

She trod with rambling progress, passing by the faces of the dead. Occasionally she saw a sign of life at some distance, but she thought of the vastness of the ocean of bodies and fought any impulse to seek out or stop for anyone. She came upon another mother and baby. The mother was curled in a semicircle and had piled up a mass of mats to close the circle. The baby lay face up in the circle, his head on his mother's thigh. Something was captivating about the baby, but Gwendolyn could not identify it at first. Against her own will, her detachment melted. She knelt near the baby, and she saw what she already knew at some ulterior level. This baby was alive! The poor emaciated thing had been saved by his mother's makeshift cradle. She brought her face close to his and looked at his face and chest. She saw that he breathed. Suddenly he cried a weak, muffled-sounding cry. His skinny arms waved in the air, and his eyes closed and opened. She recoiled in surprise and stood up.

Her impulse was to pick up and comfort the poor baby. She knelt down again and looked at him. His eyes were dry, and his voice was weak. He gripped her heart, and she reached down and stroked his face. This surprised him, and he stopped crying for a few seconds before resuming as she gently petted him.

Something made her stand up. With some distance between their faces, she became remarkably unemotional. She thought about the thousands of patients, so very many of whom were now dead. She had a vision of helpless souls scattered in the misery, silently and hopelessly dying in the morning air like faint candles winking out one by one across the whole dustbowl, unseen and not even forgotten. She thought about the fact that she, and all the workers at the mission, had slept sweetly in their sheltered rooms last night. A picture of the determined Bok transporting his ebullient dogs to the plane the day before yesterday flashed across her mind. She saw images of Aloysius Fink and Phineas Boseau watching a sports contest as lives were extinguished by the storm. Perhaps Bertha Martha was right to talk about the uselessness of the project; she was certainly right about Bok. *But then why is she here?* Gwendolyn felt hopeless.

Gwendolyn straightened herself upright. She felt a hesitation but quickly and willfully overruled it and forced herself to walk away from the crying baby immediately. She had an odd and twisted sense of having achieved a milestone; she would never have imagined she had the ability to voluntarily walk away from a baby in distress, a doomed infant, even twenty-four hours before. She became ambivalent as she continued on her way, though, and it troubled her. Her mood darkened further.

She walked an irregular path up the hill of the camp. As she progressed she saw motion on the mats; she was occasionally passing living patients. She continued up the slope and encountered some patients sitting up. After a little more distance, most people around her seemed to be alive. She looked outside the fence at the encampment of people who had been hoping for entry to the mission. Those people, sitting among the scattered thin grass and the rocks on the relatively flat slope, seemed to be awake and alive.

In an involuntary reversion to her normal personality, Gwendolyn felt a stab of guilt twisting her stomach. She thought of that living baby back among the dead, and hot strings of pain launched from her gut to her extremities. A spear charged to a thousand volts pierced her heart and enflamed her from fingers and toes to head. She turned and looked back through the many hundreds of patients, nervously hoping to see where she had abandoned that child. She was more than halfway through the dustbowl, and her scan may as well have been for an individual pebble on a rocky river bed. She thought about mounting a search, retracing her steps, but she quickly sensed the magnitude of impossibility in such a folly. She considered her dim prospects for finding the baby, along with the probability of having to see others who were alive but imminently dying. Finding it all overwhelming right now, she turned and continued on her way up the slope, quietly sobbing to herself in guilt for all her decisions on the matter, past and current. She had the subconscious wisdom to add sobs for her future decisions, a process that continued till she reached the far edge of the camp, where the patients were finally alive and her attention was distracted.

Two covered trucks drove up just as she reached the top of the camp. Both vehicles had some food for the patients and they were loaded with individuals sitting on the crates. A half dozen or more native workers jumped out of one truck, followed by Evelyn, the regular Gwendolyn had worked with in her janitorial-duty phase at the mission. Evelyn nodded to her as she climbed off the truck, then the newcomer's attention and motion froze as she saw the disastrous tableau beyond Gwendolyn. From the other truck stepped down six regulars Gwendolyn had seen around the mission, and Tammy Van de Bunt, the woman she remembered from their first day onsite. A larger third truck, also laden with food, arrived just then, and ten or so native workers climbed out. Gwendolyn saw that the last to emerge was the driver. It was Jumo, the actual, if not titular, manager of the food processing plant Bertha Martha imagined she ran.

Every one of the new arrivals quickly started looking toward the massive devastation between them and the mission proper. All mats were covered with mud. Most of the patients were splattered with it, and the dun coloring smeared into a homogenous mass as in the distance. Gwendolyn saw Jumo's eyes momentarily survey the entire camp, then he quickly motioned for the crews to listen. They stood huddled in the curve formed by the three trucks, and Gwendolyn scooted over and eavesdropped. In the background two more trucks drove up and dropped some bundles. Jumo talked to the lead driver, then swung his arm in a big curve, indicating direction and dismissal. The two trucks proceeded to split up and travel along the perimeter of the camp, still carrying most of their cargo. Gwendolyn thought about how hard it would be for trucks to travel into the camp; the nominal arrangement of jagged paths among the mats and tent locations had been destroyed in yesterday's disaster, and if a truck were to enter, it would have to be preceded by someone walking to clear the way of patients and patient remains. Unless... *No.*

Jumo assigned Evelyn to take one native driver and half of the volunteers, which he indicated with a sweep of his hand, and go down to the far side, trying to identify those alive and in need of help. He had evidently planned for the trip; he brought out packages from his truck and opened them, exposing backpack-like bundles of sticks with orange flags attached. He gave one pack to each of Evelyn's crew and told them to place one in the ground near anybody who was alive but may be mistaken for dead. They were not to dawdle or try to help any of the victims, just mark them. Jumo then divided the native workers and the remaining volunteers into two groups. One group was to set up food service. The normal areas for food were not visible after the storm had blown the tents away, so they would have to do without tables and such.

Evelyn and her command were listening. Jumo looked up and, surprised that they were still there, motioned them on their way with a sweep of both his hands. He returned to the other group as the band climbed into the truck.

Jumo instructed the food-setup group to make two stations. One station should be a hundred yards into the camp, and it would serve the ambulatory patients. He shooed that team on their way and turned to the remaining group with their assignment. They were to walk into the camp with bundles of sealed food containers, which they would drop throughout the camp as preparation for ministering to those in the vicinity who could not move. There was some interactive discussion in the native language that seemed to indicate some disagreement, but it settled after a while. Gwendolyn could see that Jumo won the day, and everyone was going to follow his plan. She was included in none of this, as she had stood behind Jumo silently.

Jumo used the familiar sweeping-hand motion to start his charges on their way, then he turned around and saw Gwendolyn. She was always happy to see him. They had sometimes exchanged greetings as she walked by his factory, and he was always easygoing, joking. He was the only person in Swazizibia with whom she felt she had any mental bond. She felt he was a friend, though their acquaintance was quite casual.

Today he was all business. He gave her a quick nod then turned, ran to his truck and jumped in. She impulsively ran to the other side and hopped into the passenger seat before he started moving, surprising him. He showed his teeth in a big, stressed, grimace of a smile as he turned the wheel and said, "Difficult times, Gwendolyn." She was relieved to be in normal human company for the first time in what seemed like forever, and she relaxed a bit amid the destruction as he drove. He took the truck along the fence in the direction Evelyn's group had gone. Gwendolyn noticed him looking at some orange flags and shaking his head.

She said, "Are you in charge?"

"Mr. Fink is in charge. Nobody is in charge. After our first few batches of food were getting ready I just run out of the building and get as many people as I can find to come out. The workers were almost ready to come here anyway. I wake up all my people very early in the dark, and we prepared much food today. I see you walk by, you know." Gwendolyn flushed at the thought that he had noticed her.

"They're still making more at the factory, but Mr. Fink come by and stopped the workers. I wait till he was gone and then make sure they are still working. Anyway I brought as many here as I could find."

"What about yesterday? What happened?"

"I don't know. After the rain started I come out in the camp. I work all yesterday afternoon and all last night, you know. I can not get my friends to come help me because the storm frighten them. They believe the gods are angry. I move many people to up the hill in the rain and in the mud, but the job is so big. So big. So many." He closed his eyes sadly and turned his head down, shaking side to side. The truck accelerated slightly and drove blind in the interval. "The volunteers did not want to come because they're forbidden. Yesterday I am alone, but today they come, all the ones I found. I do not let them tell me no. I should have make them came yesterday."

He shook his head again and closed his eyes as he accelerated down the hill over the bumpy ground. Gwendolyn saw that his eyes glistened when he opened them. She also noticed the man looked downcast for the first time in her experience.

"I know some of them. I've been working out here for a few days. You're right. You'd think they are under threat of death for coming to the camp to work with the actual patients."

Jumo shook his head again, looking at some orange flags. Gwendolyn asked him why, and he said that there were too many flags. He was sure the volunteers were flagging many dead people as alive, and maybe he should have switched the groups' assignments. The native workers would have done a better job.

"How can you know that?" She did not see any sense in it.

He answered her, "I have never be to Switzerland. I will never go. But I know that you people have a lot to learn." He assumed Gwendolyn and the rest were all from Switzerland, which he did not distinguish from Sweden, or even the United States. He almost echoed Bok's words from the orientation for newcomers. "Here in Swazizibia you can learn the value of life, and it is very small. Famine. Bad men with guns. Sickness. War. Now weather." He shook his head. "You cannot understand it, your world does not have these things." He was somber, even pensive. Jumo stopped the truck. He got out and went to the nearest flag. He knelt down by the person the flag signified. He picked up the flag and brought it back to the truck, saying to Gwendolyn, "All these flags. I need you go check all of them. Take down all next to dead people. Your girlfriends are too nervous for this job."

Gwendolyn was horrified. She retreated to the corner of the door, sat mutely in the truck and shook her head in fear. Jumo's face became ferocious, and he leaned it right up to hers with a terrifying scowl. "You must do this. We must separate living from dead. We must burn the bodies before we have disease. There are hundreds, thousands. Do you want the ghosts, your precious patients, wallowing among rotting, worm-infested bodies, stinking and spreading disease? We do this right. It is less important than getting food delivered here," he misspoke. "You must go. NOW." With that last word he made a sudden shake of his head, then he glared at her from a few inches away.

Gwendolyn felt compressed against the cab wall by the onslaught. Turning and fumbling for the door handle, she gasped, "I want to go with you. I want to help prepare the food."

Jumo's face turned to anguish. "We probably already made enough for the whole day. You cannot help us there. We do not need so much food now.

All the workers will come here to help. You must do as I tell you. I need you use judgment." He gave her a menacing glare. "Take a pack of flags if they missed some."

Gwendolyn had not thought about the practical aspects of having fewer mouths to feed. Beaten, she opened the door and got out of the truck. She listlessly took a bundle of flags and slung it over her shoulder, then stood uncommunicatively looking at Jumo, her mind frozen. Jumo said matter-of-factly, "If you collect too many to carry, drop them in a pile with one standing up and go on. Go behind those girls," and he swept his arm again indicating a volunteer in the distance as the truck started moving. Gwendolyn nodded and started turning toward the devastation. Jumo stopped the truck and called out, "Gwendolyn." He said, "Do not mark any dead bodies. It will delay us. This is very important for disease." She managed a melancholy nod. Then he said, "You must not mark those that will be dead soon. Do not fail." He gunned the engine and drove off as soon as the tires bit in the slick dirt.

Gwendolyn, who had been staring at her feet in sadness, was stricken into terror by the last unexplained command, and the truck was gone by the time she looked up. Who was she to decide who would be treated as the unwitting dead—those that are dead but don't know it yet? She was not a doctor. Her experience in walking through the camp earlier today convinced her that she could not tell a dead patient from a living one. It seemed there was a continuum from healthy to dying to dead. But it was not so easy to know the difference between the locations at that one end of the spectrum. And now Jumo was telling her to detect that precise spot where she should declare someone hopeless. What if she got it wrong?

She was back to the old Gwendolyn, the Gwendolyn that existed before today. The Gwendolyn that walked away from the baby this morning had disappeared. She stood still, faint, paralyzed by indecision and fear. She watched Jumo mercilessly shrink in her view and realized she was on her own. It occurred to her that maybe her best choice was to refuse to engage the situation—drop the flags in a bundle somewhere and walk away. That way she would not be responsible for encountering a living patient and deciding not to tag him.

She gravitated toward this null plan and started back up along the peripheral path the truck had driven, avoiding the bulk of the camp. She controlled her eyes; if she was not careful she could catch a glimpse of somebody who was actually alive but had been passed over for dead by the other volunteers. She still had the backpack of flags, for dropping it somehow seemed too much of a decision for her.

As she traveled, a more difficult thought sprouted, as yet unformed. She fenced the troubling menace outside her consciousness, but it persisted deep within, and grew in its vague intensity, pounding for entrance to her awareness. Something about this camp. Something about... *Oh yes. No.* Her defenses folded, and the battle was over. The horrid invader came welling into her brain. It trapped her consciousness like an icy prison. There was no way to stay free of the knowledge—she already had made decisions about who lives and dies. Yesterday. Today. She could have picked up that baby. She could have dragged one or more patients to the edge of a hill, as Jumo had apparently spent the day and night doing. The rain only piled up a few inches of water. The wind was inconvenient, but not really that bad. Once the tents were blown away it was not objectively dangerous. Yesterday she pretended to help that one man, then sentenced him to death because she did not want to be troubled. Yesterday she went back to the mission proper and sat down while patients died. All this she knew.

Now her mind wandered more expansively to her whole mission at the mission, and she surrendered to questions and doubts. Why was she here, exactly? Was Florian Bok a villain? Should Fink be in charge of anything? What about Sarah? Is there anyone good here? Maybe Sarah was an accomplice, but Sarah had good intentions and was not in command; if she wanted to help people she had to fall in line. Why was Sarah here anyway? *Why am I here?* Gwendolyn felt depressed, and her lackluster pace slowed.

She was near the fence, and above the center of the camp now. Just momentarily, she glanced up and away from her feet. To the right, through the fence she saw nothing but wilderness. She looked left and saw a mixture of patients lying down, sitting and standing. Some were eating at their mats, and some were standing near the workers receiving food and water. She tried to limit her eyes from looking, just like she used to do when she was taking a practice test for school, uncovering the answers one at a time, but she espied many patients lying down. Some were lying prone, face in the mud.

In this region of the camp there were no flags, and most patients were alive; those who had died were easily distinguished. Maybe she could continue walking uphill and would soon be where there were none at all who died yesterday. She could avoid thinking about death, her responsibility, and her contribution to saving patients—or at least the latter's mirage.

No, she couldn't.

Gwendolyn suddenly felt compelled to face the brutal, awful conditions around her. She sadly walked off the peripheral pathway and turned back toward the most afflicted area of the camp. Her intention was to carry out her assignment, no matter how difficult. There were no flags installed in the local area. She headed down to the region where she saw flags, not making eye contact with any of the patients, and she did not stop till she got to a region where most were dead. She stopped at the first orange flag she came to. The indicated patient was clearly alive among the corpses, though she looked very bad. Gwendolyn was surprised at how detached she felt, but she had no pity or any other feeling for the woman; the patient just existed. Gwendolyn left the flag there. She started a pattern of traversing down the slope, making sure to check to the left and right in a way that guaranteed there were none immediately behind her that were unchecked. She numbly progressed, and the first five or so flags seemed to be accurate—that is, they signaled that here was a live person who must be treated differently from the surrounding bodies.

Then she came across a flag at a patient that seemed to be dead. She was unsure, and prodded the patient, who did not respond. She felt for a heartbeat and did not think she could feel one, but the flesh seemed possibly warm. She felt at the mouth and nose, searching for breath. *What I wouldn't give right now to have been a girl scout and know how to tell if someone is alive!* After several minutes she was completely unsure. She had an upwelling choke of what should have been tears and sobbing, but she was overdrawn—she had no tears left. Soon she realized the day would be quickly consumed if she progressed at this speed. Besides, it would not make much difference in the scheme of things if she mistook someone so very close to death that careful examination yielded no sign of life. So she picked up the flag and carried it away. The process repeated, with less depth in the investigative stage, several more times as she walked past more than 150 flags in the next few hours. Sometimes she left them, a few times she removed them. As the time wore on she became more skilled in her evaluation, eventually satisfied with a visual examination accomplished without even bending her aching and exhausted back. By the time she reached the end of the camp she had picked up over twenty flags, though she was pretty sure that they would find some dead patients by some of the flags she had left. She dropped all her flags there near where the path goes to the mission proper.

Gwendolyn looked back over the expanse of destruction. Distant in the middle and far ends she saw the outlines of workers and volunteers feeding patients. Some more trucks had arrived, and they were setting up sideless tents to replace some of those destroyed the prior day. The desolate camp glowed grey in the radiant sunshine. It was a gloomy and depressing sight, but Gwendolyn felt none of it. Her only sensations were a simple dissipated ennui and a creeping loneliness. She took a few steps up the path, and just then several tanker trucks entered the camp. She continued walking, then turned and watched them as they stopped along the fence a short distance inside the camp. Nobody got out. She walked toward the power plant and somehow got the idea to find Sandy Crittenden. Sandy had always been willing to act like a friend, and if Gwendolyn ever needed to talk to someone, now was that time. She sped up and quickly got back to the mission proper. As she passed lateral to Jojo's grave, she saw that the crucifix had fallen over. She surprised herself by finding that now she felt the thing was too beautiful to be left bleaching on the ground. She picked it up. *Anyway, whatever function it had in consecrating the grave must be complete by now.* She lingered a moment meditating on Jojo before leaving with the heavy sculpture dangling from her hand.

She stepped up her pace further, envisioning a visit with Sandy. As she walked, she found the crucifix strangely comforting, though she had not noticed or thought about it since Jojo's burial, and she had found it bothersome then. Today it seemed to have the opposite effect from the one it had when the nuns assaulted the burial site with what she saw as a gruesome talisman. Now the heft of the object resonated with her movements, riding at her side, hooked in her hand as she walked along.

She thought she should take the cross back to the nuns in the cathedral. So when she reached that point on her journey, she climbed the front steps and pulled the rope to ask for entrance. She heard the faint bell through the thick doors and waited. She pulled the rope again. There was no response. She stepped back and looked up at the front of the church, then pulled one more time. The cathedral may as well have been deserted. She was disappointed but had actually begun to enjoy carrying the cross along, so she wandered with it. She walked past Bertha Martha and Jumo's food plant. It was empty and perfectly still.

Gwendolyn looked toward the end of the mission and saw some people among the buildings near the residences. Here was life; here was some scrap of normalcy. She walked that way. As she got near the building where Sandy had fashioned her little office, she heard motors behind her and turned to look. Two huge front-end loaders appeared from between buildings, turned onto the path and trundled away from her. She walked on. *They must have been in one of those buildings I never wondered about.* It looked like Jumo was driving the trailing vehicle. Turning and continuing to Sandy's office, she found it empty. The building was not usually populated by many people, and without Sandy it was deserted today.

Gwendolyn was disappointed. She really needed somebody to talk to. Never thinking that maybe Sandy was off helping someone else deal with their own emotions, she decided to seek Sandy in her usual places. The cafeteria looked like a normal day at this very late lunchtime. A few people were eating, and she saw two nuns praying in the corner. She walked right through and went to the regulars' dormitory. Most of the doors in the hallway were closed. In the rooms with doors open, occupants sat inside or lay on their beds, glancing up as she walked by. She approached Sandy's room, and the door was closed. She knocked, but no answer came. She paused and then knocked again, loudly, and ignored the several heads that popped out of doors along the hall. She heard Sandy say "Go away," in a voice like a little girl's.

"It's me. Gwendolyn."

"Leave me alone" was the reply.

It had never occurred to Gwendolyn that Sandy could have mood swings of her own—she was a psychologist, for goodness' sake. How could she have problems? The girl stood perplexed. She had come to Sandy in the hope of getting help with her own mental torment, and something was wrong with Sandy. Sandy could not help her. Crestfallen, she turned and walked down the hallway, starting to tremble and almost cry. Then she stopped. She needed human contact. Truthfully she had not expected solace when she banged for the nuns at the cathedral door, but she had held out high hopes for her visit with Sandy. She hesitated for a minute, then turned back to the room. She opened the door and saw Sandy Crittenden lying curved on her bed facing the wall. Sandy was clearly weeping. Something gentle rose in Gwendolyn. "Sandy, what is it?" She leaned the crucifix against the wall and sat on the bed, putting her hand on Sandy's hip as she lay.

Sandy paused, about to throw the hand off, but lay still and closed her eyes.

Silence.

Eventually, Sandy spoke through her tears, "Sarah just told me about the storm, what happened. Do you know there are probably a thousand dead patients out there now?"

Gwendolyn believed it. It had to be more than that. She sat silently and telegraphed nothing.

Sandy cried a bit more then said, "And they're going to burn the bodies all right there. Right in the camp. Now. Today." She continued sobbing. Gwendolyn realized she had a full day's head start over Sandy in dealing with the emotional impact of the deaths. Had she not been in the dustbowl when it turned into a huge puddle, had she never seen the patients' situation out there, she would have assumed the rainstorm was nothing more than a nuisance. She numbly thought about Sandy's pain. She sat still, her hand on Sandy's pelvis.

After a few minutes Gwendolyn asked, "Where is Sarah?"

"I don't know," through sniffles. "I was with her a while ago, and she had to go work on something with Mr. Fink. I don't like that man. I've never told anyone, but except for Dr. Bok, the western guys here give me the creeps. I shouldn't say that, it's not fair. I'm not allowed to get the creeps from people." She blubbered, "I'm the psychologist." She buried her face in her pillow. "But I'm not perfect" muffled its way out.

Gwendolyn, of course, knew exactly what she meant and went farther; she had already added Bok to her own version of that list. Her mind revolted to different levels when she thought of Bozo, Fink and Bok. After last night, Bozo's creepiness quotient had risen, but he was still far, far behind Fink. She said, "Maybe you should say it, maybe not. But you're right. These are weird people." Sandy turned over and faced Gwendolyn on the bed.

Sandy rubbed her nose; she relaxed with the validation and said, "Everyone knows it. It doesn't matter what they say. People can't be fooled. Everyone that meets them gets a read. In Fink's case it's instant and unambiguous. Dr. Boseau gives a more mixed first impression. Nobody figures him out very fast, but nobody really likes him even from the start. I do this for a living. I know."

"I know what you mean. I've lived through exactly that." Gwendolyn held back from mentioning Bok; maybe he had a better veneer, and even a professional like Sandy could not penetrate it. People can be fooled, whatever Sandy said about it.

"What are we talking about? Those people. They are dead."

Gwendolyn was now to be the steady one—strange, after all her tears and all the people, including Sandy, on whose shoulders she had cried in her life. In the silence they heard irregular grinding and shifting of engines cascading along on the far side of the dirtpile, not three hundred yards away. It must have been the front-end loaders. Sandy looked over toward her window, then went back to focusing on empty space a foot from her as her face dropped.

"Sandy, what can they do?"

Sandy agreed, but sobbed nonetheless. She said that just one day ago she was comforting volunteers here in the dormitory and in the lunchroom, volunteers who were on edge about the patients out there, volunteers far from their families. Volunteers bothered by a lightning storm. She was dissipated.

"Were you up all night worrying?" the girl asked.

"No, I wasn't." Sandy felt guilty about that, too. "I slept like a baby. All day I told people not to worry. I said it for no reason other than it seemed the right thing to say, and logical. But I was so wrong. I was tired and never once really thought about the plight of those people; I'd been denying it all day. I slept just fine. I thought it was just a thunderstorm. And besides, I knew Dr. Bok had things under control, and if he needed our help he would come for it."

"How could you know? How did you find out?"

Sandy was getting composed, sad but composed. She sat up and wiped her eyes on her arm. "We all should have known, or at least checked on things. We're here to help people. Anyway, I saw Sarah this morning. I told her some volunteers were worried, and she told me about the devastation. She swore me to secrecy, though I don't see how that will last. I asked if she'd been out there, and she said she did not need to. They knew what the conditions were. Somebody must have gone out there last night; she seemed to indicate they figured it out overnight."

Gwendolyn's mind went to the window view, the telescope. To Sarah's lies.

Sandy continued, "She said Dr. Bok is not here. I thought I saw him the other day, but she said I was wrong, it must have been someone else. What the hell? Someone else? Anyway, I never really know when he's here. I haven't talked to him since just after we arrived. Sarah says he's arranging to come here now because of this horrible storm."

It was only because of Gwendolyn's special status as Kingman's daughter that she always knew when Bok was around; he always made a point of seeing her, conversing with her, stroking her. Just now she realized that the rest of the volunteers probably never saw him at all. Gwendolyn thought about how things had turned around. She was the young girl asking this older woman about things just three days ago. She decided not to compound Sandy's anguish by telling her Bok was here the day before yesterday. But she could not let Bok off the hook and was unwilling to help Sandy like the man. Something in the girl stiffened. She retreated psychically.

"Bok won't be back before all the destruction is cleaned up. The bodies will be burned and the ashes buried before he comes back."

"Do you know when he arrives?"

"No. I know he won't be back till we're back on a more or less normal footing, though."

"But..."

"He'll stay away. Trust me. I know."

Sandy looked quizzically at Gwendolyn. She waited, looking at her, expecting some explanation the girl was uninterested in giving. Sandy noticed the crucifix for the first time, and her eyes bounced quizzically between Gwendolyn's face and the statue, again prompting for a reply.

In a sudden burst of impatience Gwendolyn forced herself to confront the fact that Sandy would do her no good; if anything, she felt worse for the visit, and now with Bok's mention, angry. She stood up as she said "It was knocked over at Jojo's grave. I'm going to give it back to the nuns." Sandy, who may not have even known who Jojo was, made a thin, wan smile and swept a tuft of her colorless beige hair from in front of her eye. Gwendolyn stood for a moment, then nodded and left with her crucifix. The older woman clutched a pillow and sat against the corner of the wall, staring hollowly. Her mood had improved from sobbing to listless.

Gwendolyn felt bound to two tasks. First, she should give the crucifix back to the nuns, and second, she should participate in whatever nasty chores were scheduled for the dustbowl today. Hearing the grinding and sputtering of the earth-moving equipment over the hill the whole way, she walked back to the cathedral and pulled the rope to no avail. She dismounted the porch and walked around the building in what she knew was a futile pursuit. There was nothing to see; all the windows were high above the ground, and the large solid door in the back that opened onto a long-ago-disappeared porch was closed, locked—it had probably not actually been opened in years. She thought she heard some noise from two windows very high up in the back of the building; her imagination formed it into the distant traces of happy children playing on a playground. *I am indeed going crazy here. Who am I?* She felt constrained and stressed by the thought of going back to the dustbowl, but driven there.

She went back around to the front and pulled the string once more, expecting no response. She stood delaying her trip to the camp as the immediate prophecy was fulfilled. She started to turn to leave, but knowing they heard the bell and ignored her, a wave of anger arose in her, and she thought *If they want their damned cross they can pick it up.* She threw the superstitious charm down on the porch.

She quickly walked to the edge of the camp. Standing on the ledge at the foot of the dustbowl, she was presented with an amazing tableau. Except for the period of the storm, she had only seen the dustbowl in a static situation: the biggest motions had always been the slow progress of small trucks delivering food or picking up refuse, volunteers walking, and some few of the patients moving around. But today the place was jumping with activity.

Gwendolyn stood looking at the camp and did not know where to focus her attention. She saw five piles of earth next to excavations distributed across the nearer half of the camp. Front-end loaders were maneuvering furiously at the largest two of them. One was quite close-by. The machines were working like bulldozers, fashioning holes and ramps. Workers were scurrying along emptying litters of corpses at the edge of each of the trenches. Hundreds of more or less parallel cadavers were accumulating near the holes.

The ground on the near portion of the camp was littered with mats and debris, but significant regions were devoid of patients. Some workers were walking along behind a slow-moving truck, lifting the rubbish from the ground and tossing it into the back of the vehicle. Gwendolyn saw two other identical operations in process and could see that, despite the mess, there had been quite a bit of progress in cleanup today. A tanker truck sat beside the nearest hole. Some workers seemed to be doubling up the bodies there, shrinking the pile by layering corpses atop one another.

Far across the camp Gwendolyn could see normal daily work. Workers were feeding and attending to the patients. For those faraway patients on the other side, the day's activities were probably almost back to routine, with the possible exception of grief at having lost so many friends. Gwendolyn walked down the slope and onto the dustbowl. She decided to bypass the heavy destruction at this end of the camp and work with the living patients. *They need the help.* She skirted the edge of the dustbowl, walking up along the fence; she kept her eyes in front of her and only occasionally looked into the camp or outside the fence. She hurried as she passed into less-severe destruction. It seemed that the people outside the camp suffered less; the encampment looked pretty much like it had before the storm.

She spent hours working with the patients. First she lent a hand with the feeding and the normal activities. After a while, this was complete, and she pitched in helping to clean up wreckage and debris scattered about lower down toward the mission proper. She worked diligently, far more diligently than most of the native workers or volunteers. She encountered Jumo twice; he was energetically toiling with cleanup duties and directing others; he slowed down only for a brief nod to the girl each time they met.

Gwendolyn was working in the lower middle of the dustbowl as the first hints of dusk surrounded the camp. She was just above one of the burial pits and saw that the corpses beside it were stacked tightly at least four-high. Workers were still gathering dead patients and bringing them to the piles on litters. The digging was apparently complete; neither of the front-end loaders was moving anymore. *I guess they're almost ready to bury them.* She felt a heavy sadness and decided to proceed back to the mission. She walked down, giving a wide berth to the locations where the dead bodies were gathered now. Eventually she stood on the little ridge near the path to the mission proper, but she could not leave. *I can't run from this.* Turning around, she looked at the closest burial hole. The stack was three, four, even five cadavers deep. As they brought stretchers with more bodies, the workers contorted in an effort to avoid contacting any portion of the corpses, giving her the impression that there was a supernatural prohibition against interacting with the dead.

She went down and walked right up to the pile of bodies. Insects abounded in the early evening air. She could start to smell death, so oppressively close to her now. Just then a front-end loader came driving up on the left, wobbling side to side, the driver waving his arm and shouting impatiently to the workers around the bodies. The workers scattered as the heavy equipment bounced along in slow motion, tracing an arc like an old woman's car veering left to enter a parking space on the right in a crowded parking lot. The machine stopped and quivered in place perhaps forty feet from the edge of the bodies. Gwendolyn instantly recognized the heavy bone profile of the man at the helm, eye patch or no. Aloysius Fink grimly and assiduously focused his attention on aligning his nervous, reigned-in mechanical creature into just the proper orientation as it chugged and struggled against his control in chaotic bobbles. The man's physical and mental stress was visible in his savage eyebrows as they strained to meet at the bridge of his nose, resisted by the increasingly knit skin on his central forehead. His one eye glowered down at the corpses with more than enough intensity to make up for its missing twin. Gwendolyn saw his back teeth tightly clenched as his concentration forced his lips together at the front, curling them open to show his molars.

Gwendolyn broke her eyes from this dark caricature and glanced at the loosely organized stack of bodies destined for bulldozing. Her eyes jumped to the surprised workers, standing watching from well out of the way. She looked at the dead people again. Fink was fine-tuning the machine's planned approach and carefully orienting it to attack the center of the array of bodies.

Aloysius Fink dropped the shovel and slowly drove straight forward. The huge contraption bounced on its massive tires in response to the impact of the scoop as it crept. Just then Gwendolyn saw a flash of movement in the pile. The motion was infinitesimal, just a quick flicker of a shadow down near, or on, the ground. She screamed, "Stop," at the top of her ability and put up her arms, but Fink continued forward. She ran closer to the pile of bodies, waving her arms back and forth. She saw Fink's unquiet and overworked single eye glance over, but his profile was stable, and the machine continued on its path without interruption

Desperate, she ran out onto the pile of corpses, stepping on and between body parts, waving and yelling, her glance bouncing between her path in the heap and the eye of the horrible machine's master. The bodies bent and twisted her ankle and caught at her limbs as she struggled forward. The workers watched in surprised horror as she stumbled in the midst of the morass of dead people. She fell just as she attained the center of the mass of the cadavers, her hands twisting as they rolled off ribs and penetrated to stopping points, one on the ground, one on some unidentified bone of one of the patients. She was down among the bodies, right in the path of the machine. Her ankle throbbed painfully.

She closed her eyes as she smelled the combination of wet musty rags, human waste and incipient deterioration of flesh. Bugs beclouded the world; the oppressing buzz and hiss of all manner of flying insects tormented her ears and made her skin itch. Her nose had stopped just short of a man's chin; one of his eyes stared straight past her into the late afternoon sky while she stared right at the filthy and leathery skin of his neck. She felt sick and closed her eyes, yet holding her head off the bodies. In her misery, for a timeless instant her reptilian brain determined that if the bulldozer broke her to bits and threw her into the hole, that would be just fine. But she recovered, stood up and started making her way toward the edge of the pile.

Fink had popped the front-end loader out of gear and was waiting. He jumped down with exaggerated motion, yelling an abusive string of unintelligible sounds. Gwendolyn stumbled out of the morass, irregularly alternating her gait between that of traversing a shallow river of slippery rocks and one of crossing deep snow with a crust of ice on top. She got to the edge and hopped down onto her painful foot. Over the noise of the front-end loader's anxious engine, she told Fink she saw one of the patients move.

She could see that Fink fought the impulse to climb back on his machine; in fact his upper body had started such a motion, but in mid-turn he checked it and turned back. Gwendolyn realized he only listened to her because of who she is—Fink was obviously under orders to accommodate her to some extent. But he did not believe her. And 'to some extent' was an uncomfortably elastic clause in such a situation.

"Which one?" he growled. Against his desires, he looked over to the haphazard stack and forced his single eye to make at least a perfunctory, spurious survey of the pile of bodies. He looked back to the girl.

"I don't know. It was someone on the bottom, right about there." She pointed to the region where she had seen the motion. Fink glanced over, this time without turning his head in the least. The workers stood talking, disagreeing among themselves, looking at the dead and pointing. Gwendolyn could not understand what they were saying to each other. She focused on looking for more motion.

"They're dead," pronounced Fink as he turned to follow his eye patch back to the vehicle.

"One of them is NOT!" she screamed at her loudest, stamping her foot and shaking her head one cycle, both hands in fists lunging straight down toward the ground.

Fink started walking back. "Dead enough," he said without looking back. He had exhausted his patience and climbed back on the front-end loader. Gwendolyn stood paralyzed by rage as he started the machine moving forward toward the pile of bodies. Recovering, she ran over and jumped onto the side of the moving vehicle and tried to push him off the seat.

"Dead as—NO. YOU WON'T!" she shouted into his face as the machine swerved and bounced.

"What difference at this point does it make?" he scowled as he shoved her off the vehicle with his big filthy boot. She fell on her side, hitting her elbow painfully on the dirt. As she lay stunned on the ground Fink corrected the motion of the front-end loader, pushing it into the corpses nearest the middle of the irregular array, bulldozing them into their neighbors, distorting and shoving the whole mass along. The scoop was wider than the height of any single body, and some corpses rolled into the shovel as others bent and dragged while Fink forced everything toward the hole. Heads and feet lagged as bodies rolled over and piled up, some caught with their midsections impaled on the scoop's fangs. As everything went forward, Gwendolyn was sure some of the bodies would be cut in half or torn asunder from the strain, but to her relief she was subjected to witnessing no such ghastly occurrence.

She stood frozen and watched the macabre progress as Fink's machine achieved victory over the first pass of corpses and shook the last few patients off the shovel's tines like so many dead leaves. He backed up all the way to the point of his old-lady's arc and repositioned the machine for the next pass. Before moving, he signaled and yelled something to the driver of the tanker truck that Gwendolyn had stopped noticing on the other side of the hole.

The man started spraying whatever was in the tanker truck onto the corpses in the pit. *Disinfectant? What would it be?* Just then Fink started his next run at the bodies. He took on the farther mountain of cadavers and drove many of the bodies into the hole. The spraying man shifted his stream to this new delivery. Now thirty or forty percent of the dead from the stack were in the trench. As Fink backed up again the tanker man put down the hose. He lit a torch and threw it into the hole. Immediately red and orange flames flounced up from the mass grave in a curling, rolling display, stark against the darkling heavens. With the help of her senses of sight, logic and smell, Gwendolyn identified the material in the tanker: airplane fuel.

Just as Fink started his third approach, Gwendolyn fleetingly saw a tiny animal's tail disappear under the bodies where the machine had cut a channel. She only saw it for an instant, and though she could identify its color—grey—she could not say whether it was warm-blooded or cold-blooded; mammal, insect, crustacean or reptile. It did not matter. It was vermin, and she shuddered. Fink proceeded to bulldoze all but a few of the bodies above the creature into the hole. The man across the hole had picked up the nozzle again but was not spraying. Gwendolyn stood and watched as

Fink made a cleanup pass, and all the bodies on the far side of the original chasm were now in the hole. The flames had subsided, and the pit was a simple burning mass. Fink backed the front-end loader up again and came forward into the cadavers, trimming off the bodies on the edge of the remaining stack. As they started toppling into the grave the tanker man sent a stream of airplane fuel in, resulting in another fireball rising dramatically into the air. Fink's profile was etched against the brilliant orange flames. Gwendolyn could see glare through the gap in his molars as he clenched his front teeth. Feeling weak from stress and fumes, she backed away from the scene. Her eyes arced over the camp; nothing much had changed. Patients were being fed, workers were piling bodies near the holes. But many of the workers and patients alike were watching the activity here at the flaming pit.

Standing in the midst of all this as the sky darkened, Gwendolyn felt hopeless as a general despair about the world gripped her. She had been depressed and ineffective before, but this dark mood was singular. She felt she was realizing what the world is, for the first time. How big and how full of tragedy. Her melancholy asserted motor control, turning her away from the patients and corpses in the camp and sending her walking slowly back through the accumulating gloom toward the mission proper. She rubbed her sore arm as she began the trek.

She remembered nothing until she was abeam the cathedral, when she noticed that the crucifix had vanished from the front porch. By now there were multiple fires in the camp, and orange incandescence swept down over the dirtpile, coloring the whole mission scene with flickering flashes dueling with silently snapping shadows.

She wandered throughout the mission area, walking by the buildings, past the executive residence, all the way to the south end of the complex. She continued walking aimlessly in the mission for a long time, turning as necessary to allow her to keep moving in the confined space. Her spirits lifted from depressed to numb, and her mind went through all the doubts she had had about her efforts here, but she experienced them from a distance. She thought about how her work here generalized to her whole life and to the entire world. Nothing was resolved; she was left with puzzles. How can people do good? Why is there a need? Is it really possible? Why is there so much suffering, and why is it so unevenly distributed? What happened to Sandy? Sandy Crittenden, a pillar of strength.

What are we doing here? What is anybody doing anywhere? Is it wrong to try—is it against nature? *Should I just somehow find a way to accept*

things as they are instead of always trying to fight everything? Gwendolyn
thought about history, and how incredibly tiny the lifespan of even a great
historical figure is. One of her favorite characters in American history came
to mind. Maybe Benjamin Franklin was eighty-four years old. Maybe he
did things to make the world better. But in the scheme of things, he died.
Hundreds of years ago. The world went on. And, by the way, one could say
that even this great man was corrupt; he certainly took advantage of being
both a politician and a self-dealing businessman, locking up contracts with
his government, and once he got going he never had to worry about starving
like these poor patients. What does it mean to be a great person?

She considered her father, Kingman. He had grown up anonymous,
not rich, not famous. Driven all his life, he quickly made his mark. He had
always told her he wanted to help people, and that is what drove him to
construct one of the world's most celebrated and prestigious charities. He
and her mother had dedicated their lives and worldly fortunes to helping
people; that's what she had been told since babyhood. Fair enough. But this
mission: Florian Bok. Bertha Martha. Fink. The storm. All this had planted
some seeds of doubt in her. Everything she had seen here was consistent
with Bertha Martha's analysis. And Kingman was essentially a partner here
now, a teammate of the Wholesome Globe Project.

If Florian Bok was in fact a charlatan or worse, a demon, it is
preposterous to think that her father did not see through it. After the last few
days Gwendolyn was uncertain that the sun would rise tomorrow; she did
not know whether sugar would taste sweet next week. But she was certain
that Kingman Dressel-Meier never had the wool pulled over his eyes by
Florian Bok or anybody else. Ever. *And that speech in Zurich.*

As orange flames occasionally flickered up into the sky, she walked on
and thought about her mother and brothers, all mindlessly ambling along
whatever path her father chose, never questioning. None of them ever
seemed to spend time at places like the mission. She had heard the reasons:
better leverage, wasting effort at a low level… maybe that was justified.

Bull. There are no expensive masseurs here. Could she really be a blood
relative of these people? Why did the picture of Cecilia Strong seem to lurk
at the periphery of her mind? What happened to Jojo? And what was Bertha
Martha trying to tell her before?

Questions, questions.

So here she was. She had been here for many weeks. She occasionally
got her finger into a dike for a little while, then moved it to a different dike.

And she had seen the best in the world at this business. Not just her father—that whole conference in Zurich. These were the cream of the crop in the Cash and Charity Industry. And, excepting the small fraction who walked out in protest, they had all cheered Kingman as he admonished them to stamp out individual help from one person to another who needs it. They accepted it when he judged it not even moral. All her life she had idolized her father, imitating him in many ways. In Switzerland, she didn't understand the whole idea that people helping people directly was immoral, but she had given her father the benefit of the doubt at the conference—throughout her life, he had often made pronouncements and decisions she did not understand.

But everything seemed uncertain now. Even her own father made no sense to her. Or worse: maybe he made perfect sense. Whose world view was right? His or hers?

The earth could swallow fifteen hundred patients with a not-really-impressive rainstorm here. What happens to the patients when there are no rainstorms? Quadruple amputees are allowed to consume resources while believing they are creating productivity. Sponsored volunteers, rich people from the advanced countries far away, fund themselves to come here to do… what? Attain bragging rights back home for their sacrifice? Progress in yoga? And Florian Bok and maybe even her own father preside over all this. *Why?*

Nobody knows how slowly she walked or what she was thinking about, but it was profoundly dark as she made her last orbit around her dormitory. A flicker of orange brightness lit the sky behind the dirtpile just as she opened the door to her building. Upstairs, the sponsored volunteers were in the lounge. She walked through without acknowledging anyone and went to sit with Pyratticus Julius on her bed. She was uneasy, and the unpredictable light fluctuations in the sky outside did nothing to settle her. She needed to quiet her mind.

On an impulse she left Pyratticus Julius and went out to the lounge, an act that surprised the others due to its rarity. Of the other sponsored volunteers, she knew Sonja the best. She sat next to her as Sonja played an old-fashioned children's board game with another volunteer. Gwendolyn engaged in strained, perfunctory small talk and watched a few rounds, then Sonja offered her the seat at the game. She declined.

She was nervous and very tired, and at a convenient point, she asked Sonja for her sleeping pills, pleading exhaustion and stress. "Sure. Take what you want. They are in the little brown case on the shelf in my room," was the answer. Gwendolyn got up and easily found several full bottles of barbiturates in the little treasure trove that was the brown container. As she fumbled trying to open one of them, Sonja came in with a smile. She took the bottle from her, opened it with one motion, and held up the container in one hand and the lid in the other. Then she pulled out a flask-sized bottle of expensive bourbon from under her bed. Breaking the seal on the brand new container, she raised it to her lips and took a drag, her eyes watering as she exhaled the hot volatiles with a satisfied "Aaah." The alcoholic steam forked around Gwendolyn's neck and head, and she felt flushed. "Here. Do you want to sleep? This stuff is better than drugs any day." She took another drink as Gwendolyn stood watching. She replaced the cap and handed the bottle to Gwendolyn with a robust shake of her head and a smile and said, "Take it. It is yours. I have plenty more. It will add to the pills." She went back to her game in the lounge, leaving Gwendolyn standing in the volatile aromatic cloud with an unbalanced pair of bottles in her hands. Gwendolyn decided to preserve her options; she pocketed the drug container and carried away the whiskey, waving superficially to Sonja and the others as she proceeded to her own room.

Sitting cross-legged on her bed holding her fuzzy invertebrate, Gwendolyn was tense. She watched passively, exhausted and depressed as flashes of orange lit up the unseen side of the dirtpile like silent little explosions and bounced off her wall. Her mood was glum and her mind blank as she slouched there holding the liquor in one hand, a few tablets in the other, and Pyratticus Julius in both. She sniffed the whiskey and quickly gulped some down her throat. Any other day, the shock of the flaming fluid attacking the lining of her throat and vaporizing to assail her nose and lungs would have sent her into a coughing fit. But tonight it was as though she was observing an acid eating the tissues of some laboratory specimen; she felt the pain only as a neutral signal from a distance. When the violence within died down, she looked up at the flickering wall and took another drink. She lay on her side with Pyratticus Julius in a tight hug and closed her eyes. The disquiet leaked away from her depleted mind slowly, and even the flashing orange of the fires over the dirtpile became unnoticed. But as she lay, she eventually reached a state where the normal meaningless banter of the other sponsored volunteers in the lounge dominated her environment. She tried to ignore it, but there was something about the sporadic bursts of laughter, especially Sonja's, that grated on her attention whenever it arose, jerking her from her repose. *I can't even get peace and quiet in my own room. This place is hell.*

Craving isolation, she decided to go to the crow's nest for solitude. She left her room carrying her friendly critter and the liquor flask. She went across the lounge and picked up a bottle of water, nodding to Sonja and a few others as she swallowed the sleeping pills that were still in her hand and washed them down with water. She and Pyratticus Julius proceeded downstairs and climbed up to the crow's nest. The mission was mostly dark at night; there was only light from the windows in a few buildings, and there was an eerie variety of orangish glows in the camp this evening. Looking out one of the crow's nest's small windows with Pyratticus Julius, she could see the burial sites over the dirtpile. They all still glowed. Occasionally one of the tankers drove up to a burial site and aggravated the fire with jet fuel, provoking the brilliant flashes that had followed her all night. They were keeping the fires hot rather than letting them wither under the chill of the mass deaths. The flashes were strangely unfocused and intriguing as she watched.

She looked up at the stars, which were now out in force. She had never had an interest in distinguishing one from another, and she had an unusual sense of regretting that now as she let herself drop down, sliding against the wall, watching through the tiny opening as the stars seemed to move in soft curves. She sat against the corner and pulled the bottle of barbiturates from her pocket. She put a few of the pills into her mouth, intending to swallow them with water, but as she picked up the water bottle, unbeknownst to her it became the whiskey. She mindlessly gulped the liquor. It burned this time, and she had to put forth some effort to retain the pills as she coughed and hacked under its assault. The tablets went back down with a few sips of water. She remained against the wall with her pet for a long time, watching the small windows dance high on the walls above.

She stood and twirled clockwise as she traversed the periphery of the crow's nest in a counterclockwise circuit with Pyratticus Julius. When she stopped and looked outside, she could see the top of the executive residence, and she wondered if Bertha Martha was watching the fires through the telescope. What was Sarah doing? Hiding in the building? She drank another portion of the burning liquid.

Gwendolyn twisted and dropped to the floor again with her pet. She had visions of her happy childhood. Playing in Vermont on the tire swing Kingman had had installed. Being chased and swung around by her brothers. Throwing sticks for her little dog, Moose. Yes, she had almost disremembered Moose; she was a toddler when he met an unfortunate end at the front bumper of the flaky woman who lived down the road. She had heard the stories about Moose many times, and they had become her earliest memories, retroactively fabricated or authentic, and more likely the former.

Playing schoolgirl games with Alitisha. Sleepovers. Poor sweet Alitisha. *Alitisha still doesn't understand anything. Do I understand anything?* Picking strawberries together in the woods behind her house. Arguing over whose pony was prettier. *Those days are gone. That's not the real world.* Despite resistance from her psyche, the pleasant memories softened her melancholy. Now she was becoming sleepy after the exhausting tension of the long day. A long sojourn. A long life, over twenty years. Realizing she might doze off to sleep, she placed Pyratticus Julius snugly on her lap. She sat quietly watching the dancing shadows, getting drowsier by the minute. She drifted off.

In the middle of the black of night, the dark shock from a terrible but unknown dream ejected Gwendolyn from deep sleep. Not really awake, she looked around the room and took a drink of water. She picked up Pyratticus Julius from the floor and put him on her lap. Moving him uncovered the sleeping pills. The chill of her nightmare was still with her, and suddenly, on an impulse and deliberately resisting any urge to stop and think, she took a handful of the drugs, forcing them down with two gulps of water abetted by a determined strain of her neck muscles. She had an uncomfortable bloat in her stomach and immediately almost lost some of the pills in two or three nearly productive burps, but everything stayed down. She sat, awake. *Nothing.* She put the bottle of drugs into her pocket and told Pyratticus Julius to relax, things will be all right. Pyratticus Julius seemed doubtful. Doubtful about so much.

Gwendolyn Who?

Gwendolyn awoke three-quarters face-down, with stones cutting into her cheek and vomit on her arms, face and clothing. It was almost dawn, and without moving she could see the sky was permeable to grey light invading from below the dirtpile. There was no trace of fire. Her mind was empty until she saw Pyratticus Julius just beyond arm's reach. He was on his side, most of his legs twisted to the right. Two were bent under him. He was expressionless as ever. Gwendolyn thought about yesterday, about the mental anguish she endured all day.

Just then the girl was wracked with a dry heave, her face dragging across the gravel of the roof she found herself on. Nothing came out, but she tasted bile as it climbed then subsided. Her tongue was coated with a sort of dry felt fuzz, and she had just now added a few cuts to the abrasions on her cheeks. Her head was pounding, and her stomach was burning. She reached for a water bottle, lying on its side in her view, two thirds empty, and she sat up. She took a mouthful of the warm liquid and let it soak for a bit, then swished it around and spit it out. She repeated the process, then drank the rest of the water. She recovered Pyratticus Julius and lay on her other side on the rocky surface. With the partial comfort supplied by her stuffed animal, she lay motionless for a long time.

The day grew sunny and hot as she lay still. She was sweating and scratched, and the stench from her adventures was oppressive. She sat up dizzily and said to Pyratticus Julius, "We've been to hell and gone right through," though with the painful condition of her body she was far from convinced they had completed the whole circuit. She remembered her actions in the middle of last night, and mused on her good luck. *Or my incompetence.*

As she rose to her feet and straightened her body, a tentative burst of dizziness engulfed her, but just at that exact instant, the cocoon of Child Gwendolyn cracked and fell down discarded. She stood steady as a rock. The lines from her favorite old verse came to mind:

> *You author your story. The future's at stake.*
> *You're sure to construct it. Which path will you take?*
> *The wind or the feather? The golf club or ball?*
> *In living your life the game's winner take all!*

The puppet or puppeteer? The hammer or nail? The cannon or fodder? That's the world. It crushes people and I can't change that. Here stood the filthy and disheveled, newly hatched Adult Gwendolyn. Her head and body were shot through with pain of several simultaneous varieties. Her mind was alive. As if animated by an enlightening vision from outside, she ephemerally developed a glimmer of proto-understanding of many things she had heard and seen in her lifetime. All was not what it seemed. The mission. The Glowing Circle. Good works had become incidental, almost orthogonal to the actual business of the organizations. The Foundation. Her brothers—the absurd idea that Marshall or Hunter had ever helped anybody more than a goose egg, more than she had helped anyone here. She started to grok some people here at the mission. For sure, Florian Bok was far worse than a fraud. Sarah Greenwater: nothing. Boseau: a clown. Bertha Martha: a waning and cheerless aging woman keeping herself busy. This is all real. *This is life in the 'how-things-really-are.'* Her glimmer of insight disappeared as suddenly as it arose.

Cecilia Strong's face mysteriously hovered in the distance of her mind. As she stood looking around the mission from her vantage point, her thoughts went to the larger Charity Industry, as Cecilia called it. The meeting in Zurich. *This is the world. Maybe Bertha Martha actually knows something.*

She felt a foreign thought: maybe she should get out of this world. Perhaps it would be best to just be a profiteer. Possibly, it would be most honest and efficient to become a predatory banker, or an avid polluter who inhales clean air and money, and thrives by fouling the world and poisoning beautiful children to make profit. She could fit right in. *I killed somebody yesterday—was it yesterday? And the day before.* But she was kidding herself. Gwendolyn was never, ever going to become an industry tycoon, a banker, a lawyer, a grocer. She was going to stay in the world she lived in, the world she had thought she knew. If that world was not what she had always believed... well, so be it. *I will adapt.*

At this point she had not wondered exactly where she was. Now she noticed that she was on a roof. She walked over to the ladder protruding over the side of the building and looked down to see a window of the crow's nest beside the ladder's track as it descended to the ground. Through the oblique slant of her view, she saw a half-full bottle of bourbon on its side in the crow's nest. Somehow she had gotten on top of the building just above her secret hideaway.

Gwendolyn straightened up and sightlessly surveyed the mission again. She yawned. Filthy and stinking in the hot sunshine, she shook out her hair and clothes. Knowing it was empty, she picked up the water bottle and did her best to suck out any available drops. Inexplicably feeling strong, though still shot through with pain, she closed her eyes and thrust her hands into her pockets as she turned her face right into the sun. Her hand encountered the bottle of barbiturates, still partly full. She pulled the topless container out, scattered the pills onto the rooftop at her feet, then tossed the bottle over the building's side. Next she picked up Pyratticus Julius. She quickly fixed him up so his legs were more or less parallel. This was the first time in her life that she did not pretend to worry about hurting him while combing his tentacles.

Gwendolyn had some idea of what she wanted. She swung onto the ladder, ignoring the hammering in her brain each time her position changed, and carelessly climbed down the building's side past the crow's nest window. She neared the end of the ladder and jumped the last few feet to the ground, a blunder that caused blinding pain in her stomach and head. *Serves me right. What did I expect?*

Crossing the lounge on her way to her room, she passed many of the sponsored volunteers as they were eating breakfast or relaxing over their coffee. They gawked at the disorganized walking mess as Gwendolyn traversed the room. She had no interest in conversation with any of them, and the feeling was sufficiently mutual that it left her unmolested; she went to her room without making eye contact, provoking only a trail of quizzical looks and shrugs. She quickly got out of her clothes and indulged in a long cold, then hot shower. Standing in the streaming water, she enjoyed her first creature comforts in a weeks—with the exception of the day she buried Jojo, she had been forcing herself to take quick and lukewarm showers during her tenure here, a small token of discomfort she offered up in light of all the suffering just over the dirtpile.

Gwendolyn had undergone a molting of something inexplicable. She felt the subsiding painful remnants from last night's exploits and simultaneously experienced a sort of waxing of unfocused certainty and strength. For the first time since arriving at the mission she had taken care to bring her luxurious body wash, shampoo and makeup into the bathroom. *No washing my hair with a bar of soap today.* She smiled in the relaxing hot shower, recalling how Winifred had overridden her objections and insisted on putting the luxuries in her suitcase back in Vermont. She stood enjoying the limitless heat of the nuclear-warmed water and let her mind wander, almost forgetting where she was. Her sicknesses dissolved away in the steam, and after a while she was ready for the day.

The voracious girl collected the biggest breakfast she had eaten in Swazizibia. She ate alone, and something about her demeanor protected her from the usual peppering of small talk in the lounge, the anticipation of which usually prompted her to eat her breakfast outside. She sipped sweetened coffee, another vice that she had curtailed for this sojourn. She lollygagged over a few cups, her mind attracted to the future.

After a while Gwendolyn cycled back to the present, and in a move unthinkable even two days ago, she decided to seek out Aloysius Fink. She refilled and covered her cup of coffee, then walked toward the administration building. When she arrived there, she gained entry without trouble and walked to Sarah Greenwater's office. She found Sarah at her desk, talking on the phone. She sat down on the corner of Sarah's desk, to the older woman's discomfort. Sarah considered challenging her, but something dissuaded her. She abruptly ended her phone conversation, saying, "Yes. I'm quite sure." She looked at Gwendolyn expectantly.

Gwendolyn sat silently.

Sarah stumbled motionlessly through the clumsy quiet, then said, "Hello, Gwendolyn. Are you doing well enough? We're all exhausted after the last couple of days, no?"

Gwendolyn said, "Where is Bok?"

Sarah smiled sweetly. "He's on his way here. In fact, that was him I was just talking to. He'll arrive back here around suppertime."

Suppertime. Before today Gwendolyn would have found it difficult to measure time here in Swazizibia by specifying breakfast, lunch and dinner hours. Now she understood Sarah without a pang of stress over it.

"Why did he go away?"

Sarah sat nonplussed, not knowing what to say.

"I would like to see him after he has his dinner. Please plan on it."

Sarah continued her look of confusion, then gave her answer, "Uh…"

"He'll be happy to talk to me. Let him know I'm leaving tomorrow. I'm going home. I assume you can make arrangements for that. Please do so. Geneva should be fine. If you can get my father's foundation's airplane to take me from Cairo, so much the better. But if not, please book me to Europe. If you can't do Geneva, route me to Stockholm or Paris."

Sarah was not stuck on protocol or position power, but she was unaccustomed to getting orders so unambiguously from anybody except Bok or Fink. She stuttered something that Gwendolyn did not hear. The girl leaned down with a determined grimace and asked, "Were you busy the past couple of days? I didn't see much of you." and Sarah nodded mutely. Gwendolyn stood and left the room, certain that Sarah would make the travel arrangements. Sarah sat looking out after her.

Gwendolyn roamed the various floors and hallways in the building looking for Aloysius Fink but did not find him. She decided to walk out to the camp and see how things had progressed. Along the way she passed a number of workers walking between buildings. It seemed like a normal day; if only the clocks were set back it could have been three days ago. Presently she walked by Bertha Martha's factory, and through the open door she saw the sour invalid scolding a patient Jumo for some sin, undoubtedly a violation of protocol; perhaps a perception of decreased productivity. Jumo noticed Gwendolyn outside and smiled slightly, too subtly for his tormentor to notice, during his dressing-down. Gwendolyn could not help smiling, possibly for the first time since working in the schoolhouse—which, by the way, she was now passing. She did not slow down as she walked by.

As she traveled, she marveled that until two days ago she had never even thought of making the short walk from the mission proper to the camp. She continued on, and as she passed the crematorium she noticed that there were three or four bodies waiting to be cremated. *I guess things are back to normal; probably a little light today, what with the decreased population out there… maybe it makes sense that business is down.* She was strangely unfeeling. She shrugged and continued on. She proceeded through the imaginary gate and continued along to the rim of the dustbowl.

Gwendolyn arrived at the ledge at the bottom of the camp and was surprised at what she saw. Nothing. It was as though there had never been a disaster. The entire near half of the place was a blank—it held no bodies, mats, tent wreckage. No pits, no piles of bones, no ashes. The area looked as though it had been graded for a suburban Vermont shopping mall. The only slight motion she noticed was that of a few normal food delivery trucks far across the camp.

She looked more closely at the other side of the dustbowl. The activity there was that of an average day. Native workers were feeding ambulatory and immobile patients. Gwendolyn could not help contrasting the quiet with yesterday: no grinding of diesel motors, no scraping of the ground, no Aloysius Fink framed by the menacing flames of the pyres, barking orders or killing people with his bulldozer. She looked at the intake gate at the far end; she could barely make out a cloud of activity as new patients were being ingested. She could tell even from this distance that the man at the center of the table near the gate was Aloysius Fink. Something about his posture, the dark silhouette dominating the table, gave him away.

So she had found Fink. He was half a mile away. She had wanted to talk to him earlier. She intended to let him know she was on to him. But… it did not seem important enough now, and besides… *what if I'm NOT onto him?* What did she know? *No. I know his game.* She set out across the camp.

She walked in the sun across the well-packed ground. *You'd never know we just had a flood. And a bunch of mass burials.* She resolved that Fink was a snake. She had seen him torture children. *He did something to Jojo, too. I know it.* In a demonstration of emotion-driven but quite practical thinking, she convinced herself that had she a gun, she could go right up to him, shoot Fink dead, and walk away with impunity; Bok's need of her father's favor, the lack of a controlling legal authority and Fink's lack of friends would all work in her favor. *Yes, he's vermin. And Bok employs him. And Daddy supports Bok.*

Shooting Fink—that was just a daydream. But without thinking, when she saw a tire iron in the back of an unattended truck, she grabbed it and continued up the slope, walking toward the group. As she approached the table she saw some familiar-looking volunteers handling papers, tattooing wrists and transcribing serial numbers. They were processing people into the camp under Fink's direction. Central among the helpers was Sandy Crittenden. Everyone at the table was occupied, but as Gwendolyn walked up behind Fink, Sandy noticed her and stood up, saying, "Gwendolyn. How are you holding up?" She seemed composed, recovered from yesterday. She glanced down at the crowbar.

Fink turned his head over his right shoulder to look at the girl. The sight of the cold-blooded, one-eyed carnivore bulldozing bodies, dismissing the difference between the dead and the probably-not-dead superimposed itself on his face. In a not-consciously-planned flash of action, Gwendolyn swung the tire iron around toward his head. He saw it coming and managed to get his arm up and his head down. Instead of crashing into his teeth or nose, the bar traveled up the ramp of his arm, and he got only a glancing blow that bruised his arm and took a bit of skin off the top of his head. He howled in pain and instantly stood up, grabbing Gwendolyn around the torso with one arm, pinioning her upper limbs. He put his other hand on her head. The grip bent and twisted her neck severely. The tire iron continued its motion, yanked itself out of her hand with a painful jerk that transmitted to her neck, and arced to the ground behind her.

Sandy and the others stood horrified. Fink instinctively started to compress Gwendolyn's neck, and he could have killed her. But just before her spine was damaged, he somehow overcame his angry instinct for action and loosened the pressure. He released her, and she dropped into a disorganized heap on top of the steel bar. Fink put his hand up to sample the blood on his head and probe for damage. The gasping girl knew that if she were anonymous, if she were just a regular, she would be dead. *Like so many he bulldozed yesterday.* They stared at each other wordlessly, she on the ground panting and he towering above, rubbing his head. Sandy stepped between them and helped Gwendolyn to her feet. She started leading her away. Gwendolyn shook her hands off and walked away alone. The frozen crowd of onlookers slowly melted back to its business. When the girl was partway back down the slope, Fink drove by her in a truck, doing nothing more serious than yelling a string of obscenities.

Gwendolyn calmed down remarkably during her walk and over the span of the afternoon. She spent most of the day avoiding conversation in the sponsored volunteers' lounge. She ate a full lunch, then killed time sipping a drink and reading pages of some of the books that were lying around, instantly forgetting the events in the stories. Over this period, she passively came to classify her whole visit to Swazizibia as part of her past. She thought about the future, but that familiar spot in her mind seemed foreign, strange; its pictures were far less formed than they usually were in her reveries.

A few sponsored volunteers tried to strike up a conversation out of curiosity about Gwendolyn's odd demeanor, but it was useless. Dr. Boseau came in for a while and sat, laughing and talking to some of the others. This was an event that normally would have sent her into her room, but today she ignored him easily. He tried to bring her into the conversation, however even the animation of the tip of his nose did not distract her from her mixture of contemplation and mindlessness. Eventually he became uncomfortable in her vicinity and left. Afterwards she had a suspicion that he had come to talk to her, but being uninterested, she did not pursue the thought.

The engine was audible from the lounge as Bok's plane arrived. Gwendolyn waited a while, somehow without the torment of boredom today, then went to the executive residence and rang the bell. Sarah met her and said that Dr. Bok was just asking when he could see her. They took the elevator up to the floor below the top and stepped into Bok's living quarters. Director Professor Dr. Florian Q. Bok stood trimming his stately white beard in a hallway mirror, but he immediately turned his attention to the newcomers. Colonel and Bourbon appeared in a doorway and trotted toward Gwendolyn.

Bok smiled warmly as he turned and silently warned off the dogs, who disappeared back around the corner. He stood proudly following them with his eyes, then turned back to Gwendolyn and said, "Come in, my child. Have a drink and don't let's be strangers." He poured two glasses of Scotch and dropped two ice cubes in each. He held one out to Gwendolyn and looked at Sarah and said, "Sarah, my dear, won't you have a drink too?" as he shook his head below the threshold of perception. Sarah made an excuse about having to do some chores and left as Gwendolyn walked forward. The dogs reentered visibility, and they kept along the far wall.

Gwendolyn took a drink of the whiskey and liked it, which surprised her. She had stolen sips of similar drinks many times and found them bitter and offensive; on balance, last night was not so grand either, so far as her drinking experience went. She swirled her glass, the ice circling smoothly in the liquid. She spoke up, "Director Professor, I understand this place now."

Bok was surprised and showed none of it. He took a sip.

"I will be leaving tomorrow if you have a plane to take me to the capital, which you do. I am hoping Sarah has made arrangements to get me to Geneva, or Paris if that's not possible. I will stay at one of the Worldwide Transformative Foundation's apartments there until I can make arrangements to get home. I believe my contribution here is done, and I am certain my education here is complete."

Bok was a smooth man. He knew when to probe, when to push. He did not know exactly what was in her mind, but he went along with the conversation. "Of course, Gwendolyn. And please, call me Florian if you will. I think we know each other well enough now."

They knew each other well enough. Too well, maybe.

She did not nod, but stood quietly and took another swig of her drink. Then she asked, "Why do you do it? Why the mission? You won't change things doing what you're doing here."

The man considered her carefully. He drained his drink and hesitated, looking the girl up and down, considering. He seemed about to speak, but then refreshed his whiskey and held the bottle forward. She declined his gesture. He took a big drink, concentrating his attention fully on the liquid. She stood. Again he looked at her for a long moment. Deciding that Kingman's daughter was ready to be informed, he said, "But that's exactly it. It has to be hopeless."

Gwendolyn's psyche had come a long way in the past two days, after the weeks of calibrating the man, thinking about the problem of the mission, and unconscious mental gyrations. But his answer still surprised and confused her. She looked at him quizzically. He drained his glass. "Never-ending, or what's the point?" He smiled cordially and took a sip of brandy; having completed his whiskey he was returning to the snifter from which he was apparently drinking before Gwendolyn arrived.

Bok's answer was baffling. It was illogical and seemed to do the exact opposite of making sense. But Gwendolyn could detect that it contained an embedded kernel that told her something. She surmised that it would take her a while to absorb the man's statements and distill whatever meaning they held. She stood up "Make sure Sarah gets me out of here early tomorrow." She belted down the rest of her drink and savored the pain in her throat as she left. Colonel and Bourbon peeked out of the back room, then followed each other as they trotted cautiously out into the hallway in search of some attention.

"Boys, boys. Come to Daddy," Bok said.

Commandeering the Juggernaut

Did you see that?

Arriving in Geneva, Gwendolyn went directly to the Worldwide Transformative Foundation suites downtown. Many of the employees remembered her. They had watched her grow up, enjoying occasional visits from Kingman's cute and vivacious daughter. So the only trouble she had in obtaining a residential suite was the repeated pestering of old women who remarked how tall she had grown, and how she had bloomed into such a beautiful young woman. These ladies kept trying to pat her hair and pinch her cheeks when they were not stroking her arms. She survived it all in good cheer.

She went into her room and sat down to relax. Normally her first thought would be to call Alitisha on her GVCD. Somehow that did not come up in her mind, though, perhaps because she had not touched the device in months. After she got settled she called her father, who was in Spain at the moment, and told him about her decision to come home. He already knew and asked, "Is everything all right, sweetie? I know you had your heart set on a longer stay." Gwendolyn asked him not to call her 'sweetie' since she was now a grown woman. She found he knew about the disaster at the camp. "It's a shame," he said. "I really wish we could do magic, but we have to do what we can. What can we do?"

"We do what we can," she complied mechanically, and the words evoked Bok's face. Perhaps Bok had enchanted her father; it sounded like one of his lines. "I'll tell you this," she continued, "Maybe you were right that I should have stayed home, maybe you were wrong. But I've gained a lifetime of insight from the trip."

Kingman laughed with presumption, "I knew you'd come around sometime." He sensed that his daughter may finally be headed for the trajectory he had always hoped for: joining him in the organization.

She let the implied insult to her judgment slide. "I have a favor to ask you."

"Anything, sweetie. Oops." He smiled slyly, which she ignored.

"Please make sure I have access to cash for a while. I'm going to do something I always wanted to. I'm going to drive across the country alone. It'll take a few months. Expect me to be buying some outdoor gear, doing some backpacking. Maybe generally bumming around."

Kingman's only reservation was the nervousness a father would have picturing his daughter among the barbarian masses in the wilds of the countryside. Knowing her level of tolerance for interference in such things, and in light of the Africa experience, he decided not to mention it. "Sure thing, honey. Whatever you need. Don't carry much cash around. This isn't the eighteen eighties. And we'll get you a car, whatever you want. You may have to stop at a few Foundation offices as you drive along, though, for legal cleanliness." He was referring, somewhat dishonestly, to the need for her to be doing official Foundation business to use Foundation money. She ignored the reference to the speck of legitimacy embedded within the Foundation's layers of fraud. She knew his motivation.

"Good catch on the car, Daddy. I'd not even thought about it, never been without transportation in my life. No stops at the offices, though. I'm not going onto a schedule. I'm not checking in, and you won't have a trail of reports following me and flowing back to you. I'll be fine." Kingman said nothing. He knew the prior limits of his influence over Gwendolyn and was starting to sense the new ones. "Also Daddy, I want you to arrange for Stambridge to confer my degrees. Sociology and political science, remember? And one more thing. Have them expect to prepare a Ph.D. diploma for me too. They can have the first two ready when I'm done with my trip. It'll be over in plenty of time for the spring graduation ceremony. As for the Ph.D., they should award that in a year or two. I'll let them know when."

"But honey, I thought you weren't interested in graduate school."

"Correct."

He sat confused for a few seconds before he understood what she was saying. She impressed him as having a whole new way of expressing herself. Just as he was starting to understand her drift, she helped him. "I'm sure you can take care of this. Let them know that I'll choose the doctorate's domain later, in plenty of time for them to print the diploma and update their records. Tell them the degree will be in something innovative, interdisciplinary. Something not right out of their standard list of programs."

Kingman grumbled a bit mentally, and some of it leaked out into a few words. But in thinking about it, he knew she was correct. He could arrange it. Any problem was one of hassle, not capability. Anyway, if he truly were not able to execute, his daughter would not believe it. That would be asking her to accept that he was unable to turn on the charm, wield the purse, or use whatever tool he found necessary to encourage the university to accommodate this modest request. He acquiesced, "Okay, sweetie. I guess we can do that." She nodded, and they finished up with a few family niceties.

GWENDOLYN SPENT A little over a week with Winifred in Vermont enjoying the bucolic solitude, but quickly became bored and restless. Then over her mother's protests, she traveled to Boston. She stayed in one of the Worldwide Transformative Foundation's suites and invited Alitisha to room with her. It was a treat for Alitisha to leave her dark little apartment for a while and live in the luxurious penthouse with Gwendolyn, and she enthusiastically jumped at the invitation. Alitisha had not gone back to school this year, and she had taken a job in a fabulous hotel downtown, not far from the Foundation's office and suites.

Gwendolyn dearly loved Alitisha, and they had great fun in Boston together when Alitisha was not working. As the days evolved into weeks, their conversations about everything important seemed to drift onto separate planes. They had no problem having fun and reminiscing, but some sort of newly formed mismatch in the girls' drive levels and world outlooks made Gwendolyn feel they had little, other than their childhood, in common anymore. Both were vivacious and practical, but in completely different ways. Alitisha's energy was always optimistic, maybe foppish or even Pollyannish, focused on the near future. Boys. Fun. Gwendolyn's thoughts were far ranging and restless, generally more troubled. They were less innocent than even a few weeks ago, and when she envisioned the world there was always darkness chewing at the periphery. The two were growing more distant, and it was a psychic separation felt far more pungently by Gwendolyn. After staying in Boston for a few weeks, she firmed up her travel plans. The girls said goodbye to each other, and Alitisha went back to her small apartment.

Gwendolyn set out on her targetless vacation. She traveled the country, expecting… she was not sure what she expected. Without an itinerary, she found herself wandering along small highways in flyover country, seeing interchangeable towns populated by indistinguishable yokels in an endless progression across the hills and the expansive plains. Whenever she stopped, it quickly seemed important to get back on the road, despite her lack of a goal. Boredom combined synergistically with her strong and genuine disinterest in the lives of those she met, spurring her forward. She often saw a food bank or a rescue mission, and they made her smile in some distant way as she thought of Cecilia: people toiling away to make the world a better place. Once, she stopped to help serve dinner in a small town's version of a soup kitchen, but she left after less than an hour, feeling it was somehow just a waste of time. She returned to the highway.

She stopped in some mountain parks for adventure and hiked some easy trails through scenery as wonderful as any in the world. Somehow, the awesome beauty of the icy waterfalls among the cliffs, the green trees against the snow and the rock faces, the majesty of the peaks—all this registered on her retina but not in her emotions. She felt isolated so far from the crowds of the city. *Who cares about the mountains? They're there. I've never understood, and I guess I've been right.* And the cheerful people she saw in these naturally beautiful places seemed nothing more than ebullient clowns happily marveling at nature's simple existence, or captive peasants escaping their dreary lives for an afternoon of fresh air. The people were even less interesting than the beauty of the scenes. How different it would be, how much more fun, if only she were walking the scene with Alitisha. But not that Alitisha. An imaginary Alitisha compatible with what Gwendolyn needed her to be—whatever that was.

The whole trip, as it turned out, served up nothing but the doldrums; she slowly understood that it held no fascination for her. She was starting to realize that without people—real people, not strangers—she was bored, unmotivated. Whenever she was on the highway, her mind drifted to Alitisha: how could she wake Alitisha up, renew their bonds? After less than two weeks and two thousand miles, she had not made significant progress toward her nonexistent goals for the trip, and the tediousness of her journey subdued her. She did not feel driven to push on the rest of the way to the ocean. She felt as lonely as she ever had in her life.

Gwendolyn made a U-turn and headed back to New York. She told Kingman she was coming to work for his Foundation as soon as she could drive back. She outlined her expectations for her new office at the Foundation, requirements he readily acceded to. Now, with a destination in mind, her energy level and outlook picked up markedly. During the solitary drive, she developed some increasingly clear pictures of how the Foundation should direct its efforts to grow and control the future.

There existed no next-generation leadership at the Foundation. Marshall and Hunter, of course, worked there. But the boys were not visionaries like their father. Though each aspired to take over the organization someday, it seemed an unlikely fit to anyone but himself. The boys' real strengths lay elsewhere, somewhere yet to be discovered.

Each little element in the organization that was the Foundation had its reason for existence, some valid and some merely historical. All pursued the purpose of extracting life-giving cash from the outside world, fighting the laws of economic thermodynamics. Keeping this complex machine running properly was done by a staff organized hierarchically, with two chiefs of staff, each in charge of approximately half of the organization. These officers reported to the boys, with dotted-line responsibility to Kingman, who showed more interest in their projects than their actual bosses did. The chiefs of staff managed the day-to-day activities sufficiently well that the boys were able to concentrate on recreational activities and Kingman was freed up to conceive strategies, organize publicity and steer the long-term future of the Foundation. The organization was very successful; it supported the livelihood of a massive number of people in New York and Washington, and it provided a fine lifestyle for the Dressel-Meier family.

Gwendolyn had neither the talent nor the interest for the sort of gear twiddling and dispute mediation that governed the days of the chiefs of staff, and she was not inclined to take a job where she could demonstrate the lack of engagement shown by her brothers. She was familiar with the Foundation; she had visited the main offices in Manhattan many times, and of course she had taken voyages abroad under the Foundation's auspices. But she had always been the daughter in the family, outside the administrative machinery. That location—outside the prison of the organization chart—was where she resolved to stay as she started working there. She saw the Foundation as an incredible and powerful tool, and she felt she had a right to join in without resigning herself to a position where she would be bogged down with banal quotidian errands.

So it came to pass that one morning Gwendolyn stood in the Worldwide Transformative Foundation's crystal-encased lobby in midtown Manhattan, admiring her new environment before reporting to work. She stepped into the executive elevator, and it climbed to the top floor of the Grand Buffaloon building, slowing as it passed the last eight floors, which were also occupied by the Foundation but serviced by the workers' elevator. It was precisely ten o'clock in the morning when she walked past Marshall's office, leaving him incredulous; Kingman had neglected to mention to the boys that Gwendolyn was coming to work, though he had made sure her office was set up.

Here was the Marshall's little sister Gwendolyn, whom he was more accustomed to seeing in blue jeans or an evening gown, dressed in full business attire and striding to her waiting office. As Marshall jumped to follow her, he saw Hunter standing in own his doorway, the morning sun streaming through the open door onto the plush burgundy carpet. The brothers exchanged 'pinch-me' glances, then followed their sister. She went toward her new corner office, one neither brother had noticed being rearranged. In fact, neither could name the vice president who sat there two days ago. She walked into her room, silently passing the ladies at their desks outside Kingman's adjacent suite. She put down her purse and sat straight-backed in her chair, ignoring the large parcel from Stambridge on the desk and picking up something smaller. As Marshall approached she swiveled the chair away, toward the window, and wedged her high heels into the heater mechanism where the window met the floor. She locked her knuckles together, threw her arms behind her head, and leaned back against the desk, looking down through the frame of her thighs at the busy streets below, then back up, unconsciously perturbed by the fact that she could see taller buildings from the window.

By now Hunter had joined Marshall inside the door of Gwendolyn's office. Even with the bright sky, she could see reflections revealing the boys' shock at her silent, assertive arrival, and maybe at her stridently immodest-to-the-world posture.

She sat for a spell, placing the solid gold 'IDIC' stick pin she had picked up from the desk onto her jacket lapel. Then she spun toward the brothers and said, "Let's take this place to the next level. For starters, I want to meet Florian Bok in Montreal next Monday. Can one of you arrange that for me?" She sat, investigating the faces of first one, then the other of her stunned brothers as they slowly grasped the identity of their father's true successor.

Epilogue: The Night Before New

Where can we climb from here?

T he mind of the distinguished and widely esteemed Dr. Gwendolyn Q. Dressel-Meier was, for just a few minutes, wandering lazily after the past few intensive days. Her eyes imbibed the magical panorama of synergy between nature and man below, then her gaze arced over the hills and back down to the city with its shadows growing in the incipient twilight as the sun receded into the ocean. Though she rarely visited the place, she had loved this luxurious top floor vantage point for as long as she could recall. In fact, this was her favorite spot in the world, it having graduated from runner-up, behind the home she grew up in, sometime in the last half decade. She craned her neck to look across the bay and picked out the Campanile partway up the hillside, illuminated to an orange glow against the dark green trees. Ignoring the happy chattering behind her, she let her view pan back to the city and the waters beyond, then she looked lackadaisically at the headlands across the Golden Gate. *Nothing but scenery over there.* She brought her eyes back and traced individual cars crawling in the streets. Down in North Beach she saw a queue of tiny people as they awaited entrance to a soup kitchen—a line of business that was thriving.

Suddenly her mind did not sweep back to her old friend Cecilia Strong. She was unstricken with the realization that tonight was the first Thursday of the month; no picture of Cecilia ladling mashed potatoes or leading prayers at this very hour on such a Thursday evening pried its way into her consciousness. Missing was any pang of emptiness for a discarded best friend, any conscientious sorrow for the turn she had chosen for her own life. No, it had been years since she had contemplated Cecilia, whose Saving Arms, though itself a large charity organization, stood largely outside the universe of tera-charities that formed Gwendolyn's operating habitat. In the absence of the sudden and wrenching consideration of her old friend and their days together, Gwendolyn's eyes contentedly walked along the streets following the cars, whose headlights were just starting to glow attractively against the grey concrete of the metropolis.

"I told you there's no shame in changing your mind, baby." Dr. Kingman Q. Dressel-Meier laughed as he walked up, threw his arm around his daughter's shoulders and took a slow sip of cognac. Behind Kingman, over at the dinner table, everyone was merry. And with good reason. Good reason beyond the genial cheer engendered by the drinks that had been flowing among and into the participants throughout the happy gathering.

Gwendolyn was engaged in watching the streets, and her father's words penetrated her reverie only slowly. At first she did not grok the reference, did not get the humble and perhaps ironic admission from her father. Then she remembered the last time she was here with him. She was such a child; nine years ago, was it? They had argued as he tried to get her to change her mind about going to Africa. *It all seems so trivial, that argument about a few months of time... but that trip was a real turning point for me.* She would have preferred her father avoid the throwback to diminutive nicknames, but she smiled and lifted her drink in salute. "Well, I imagine sometimes it all comes out okay when someone doesn't change her mind, eh?" she smiled.

Tonight there was no tension between them; this meeting was an unambiguous celebration as the whole group contemplated the event that would legally materialize at midnight. Her drink tonight was Drambuie, and she took a sip. Who knew she would take the place of her mother as apostle of that sweet nectar? *I wonder when I first tried this stuff. You know, I think it was at Mother's funeral.* The wonderful syrupy sting of the liquid, the panoramic view of just this phase of sunset in San Francisco, the consummation of many months of work—all these wove themselves into a perfect moment as she stood at the window of the restaurant at the top of the 'Mowk' Perkins hotel with her father. He winked, his grey beard twitching on his cheek, and they sipped in tandem. A quick instinctive glance from Kingman verified that it was too early to see his reflection in the window, and he smiled to his daughter and ambled back over to the table with the others.

Tonight was to host the ripening of Gwendolyn's most creative and ambitious endeavor, a pursuit that took years to bring to fruition. That cheerful tribe drinking at the dinner table behind her, privileged to begin with, was about to lock in everyone's position in her new enterprise with the stroke of a clock. A room full of slowly formed millionaires was about to be instantly transformed into billionaires through a magical synergy: a coherent alignment of America's powerful and privileged within and outside the government. The ink was to dry at midnight.

This exceptional woman had spent the past six years as head of the Worldwide Transformative Foundation. In the year after her trip to Swazizibia, her first year at the Foundation, Kingman recognized a genius and seized the opportunity to start harnessing Gwendolyn's creative energy to propel the organization. She always ignored her job title—in fact, for the first few years she never could remember it—and the spirited girl asserted herself across the whole range of the Foundation's activities. Kingman worked with her, filing down her quills and knocking off her rough edges, helping refine her technique. After a few years this bundle of energy was established as a seasoned and powerful executive. Kingman withdrew from day-to-day operations and appointed her executive director. Of course to this day he technically still held final authority, authority he had never once invoked to overrule his daughter.

At the time of the power transfer Kingman was offered the position as head of the United States government's financial 'watchdog' department when a colleague who owed him a favor retired from the job and bequeathed it to him. He held that office for almost four years before he felt finished with his work there, and then he retired with Winifred to their life estate on a small Caribbean island the Foundation had purchased for the purpose.

The job at the financial agency had been, historically, a sinecure. But unsurprisingly, Kingman looked at it differently. Completely invisible to the general public, he was energetic and productive in the position, and he gained admiring praise from banks, government contractors and other captains of industry, as well as from the tax-free segment of the economy—charities, universities, public pension funds and so forth. His main thrust was spearheading reforms that simplified and lubricated financial transfers; he also gave priority to raising barriers to witch hunts targeting hypothesized malfeasance by executives. Kingman was quite successful, and his work inside the government was in no small part responsible for the ambitious enterprise his daughter was launching tonight with the elite group at the table.

Kingman, as many in the room tonight knew, had always had a soft spot for top American universities. Whether anchored in memories of his unfulfilled childhood wishes to attend one or arising in practical considerations related to huge tax-free endowments, he felt a need to spend time among the academy's elite. He had long cultivated relationships with them, and they got special attention during his tenure inside the government. His first tangible accomplishment was to deliver legislation making it a felony to disclose demographic or financial information regarding any American university's faculty, admissions history or student body without unanimous written permission from the university's board of trustees and both senators from the university's state. Disclosures involving compensation of university officers or admissions decisions were singled out for especially serious punishments, mandating time in a federal prison for the first offense.

Kingman followed up that early success by taking a central role in delivering the coups de grace that dispatched many of the threats the Lobby For Good was originally founded to combat years ago. Congressional attacks on universities and other tax-free entities failed during his tenure. Cascades of executive actions and legal rulings, often combined with aggressive government-backed countersuits, assailed the assailants of the elite universities; Kingman orchestrated these things from within the government, and Gwendolyn's Foundation provided tactical support and resources to the universities from outside. Many private individuals and a number of organizations attacking universities were successfully bankrupted. Threats died away over the course of two or three years.

While he held his influential position, Kingman's creativity provided the solution for another longstanding problem. For years, activists had been creating pressure to cap the pay of nonprofit officers at six times the salary of a member of Congress. This ongoing nuisance had significant support in Congress, but it was fought by the not-for-profit lobby. Over the course of time, Gwendolyn and the Foundation marshaled many university economists who provided economic analyses demonstrating that putting any sort of cap on university or other nonprofit officers' salaries would be counterproductive. But it was difficult to get a final resolution. Kingman solved the problem brilliantly. His big insight was to find a way to keep everybody officially happy, and he delivered legislation rectifying the problem. The ordinance stated that Congressional salaries were pinned to those of nonprofit officers; the government levels automatically tracked increases in the compensation of the highest-paid nonprofit leader in the United States. There were muffled complaints from some quarters, but critics were careful to avoid confrontations on the subject, as they had gotten what they purportedly wanted; in fact, the new law used a multiplier much lower than the original value of six sought by the activists.

The tropical island of Kingman's active retirement was outside the jurisdiction of any nation, but informally protected by its proximity to another land mass that housed a small U.S. naval base. Through a clever series of transactions executed while inside the government, Kingman had managed to have the United Nations legally declare the island itself an oceangoing vessel rather than a landform for certain purposes. The laws of the sea could thus be invoked in case of trouble, a special reassurance to Winifred given the presence of pirates in the region and the regular proximity of Navy vessels.

This island was, of course, physically a land mass. Kingman, never one to sit still too long, harbored thoughts of creating a financial center for confidential banking on the maritime island, but as yet the only actions he had taken were to build an extremely secure vault in the subterranean rock and store valuables there for a few friends and potential future friends, with only informal verbal tracking. Kingman's dearth of overt curiosity seemed to fill a need for these comrades, and he felt that the lack of documentation, which was highly appreciated by his clients, complemented his actual control of the entrusted material and fostered a genial environment for evolution of his future dealings with them.

"Let's drink to Gwendolyn!" Brandy was old Dr. W. Spencer Beaverbrook's drink these days, and the warmth of the drink infused, if it did not sharpen, his slurred and sweet baritone as it rose from the table behind and caressed Gwendolyn. The others around the round table smiled and took a drink in unison.

The room held many of the owners of the nascent company about to conclude its initial public offering. IDIC, Incorporated, named with initials that used to be an acronym but now symbolized only themselves, was the offspring of Gwendolyn's creativity and thousands of hours of hard work. It was the only member of a new legal business classification which would come into existence at midnight, the long-anticipated result of Kingman's work on, and work in, the government.

Most of the university presidents who had launched the Lobby For Good so many years ago were here, as were a few other charter IDIC owners. Absent participants included the elusive pair of Drs. Wilbur Buffaloon and Bob Gaines, as well as Stambridge's president, who had a problem getting home from China. And those owners in active employment in government offices were, of course, missing. The most prominent of this group were Dr. Victoria Hull and some members of the judiciary, for whom there were good reasons to cherish the innovative privacy-of-ownership features of the novel organization. Highly placed executives in some of America's largest industrial companies and most prominent influence-peddling firms were missing as well. Marshall and Hunter were also owners, but in order to keep things moving smoothly Kingman had forbidden them to participate tonight; these grown men were obediently waiting in their limousines in the parking garage beneath the building, undoubtedly playing games on their GVCDs or doing something equally productive as they bided their time. Kingman required that they remain nearby in case a need for super quorum or some odd complication arose unexpectedly; the two were not here at the reception because their father refused the responsibility of supervising them, and Gwendolyn would not even consider their attendance without his guarantee of their good behavior. Unlike the cases of the other absentees, Kingman had not bothered to put in place power-of-attorney provisions for his sons; it was simpler to have them stand at the ready downstairs.

The new firm was to produce no product, create no intellectual property. Its sole output would be position papers written, or at least signed by, any of the small group of elite individuals comprising its current owners. At midnight these proprietors were to shed a portion of their equity, retaining overwhelming and non-proportional control of voting stock.

"Let's drink to IDIC's structure and rules," said a still-energetic Dr. Athena Sterling Munghorn, retired president of Stambridge University as she raised a glass, obviously not her first of the night. Kingman joined the others around the table as they happily indulged in another round of liquid camaraderie. Gwendolyn followed in a damped symbolic gesture, careful in wariness of alcohol's effect.

IDIC's most valuable asset was not the luminaries comprising its ownership, but a legal lock on a figurative piece of paper. The company was formed to capture value from Gwendolyn's years-long work in cooperation with the United States government. The result of all this effort was that the company had gained effective ownership over a small piece of new real estate on federal tax forms. Starting next year all Americans would be presented with a choice when paying taxes. The last line on the tax form would be a new surcharge, instituted to help citizens meet their moral obligation to sacrifice for the less fortunate. It would represent a donation from the taxpaying individual to one of several recipients. IDIC was to be the first choice listed.

In anticipation of recalcitrance on the part of the common population, the whole process had already been legally adjudged a voluntary contribution rather than a tax, a ruling resting on the fact that the citizen could choose where the new surcharge would go. Gwendolyn had obtained this preemptive legal ruling, along with a few others involving IDIC and its public offering, in order to protect her new baby from endless legal wrangling. She took advantage of a new approach to legal protection that Kingman had conceived and nurtured through its birth. The new system was called 'Smoothing the Basis.'

Kingman was an innovative man, and following his initiative, over recent years the legal community had taken a cue from medicine's idea of preventive treatment. The concept is this: it is far better to preclude a lawsuit than to experience one. A mechanism was put in place for use by interested parties with sufficient assets, a mechanism by which they were able to probe new laws for weaknesses and inoculate them against challenges by potential future litigants. The idea was to get a regulation declared completely valid either as written, or as modified by a judge. Once an interested party was qualified as eligible to enter the process, the steps were simple. The plaintiff-defendant paid a steep filing fee and submitted a pro forma lawsuit simply asserting that the law was invalid, optionally adding a few specific objections. No in-court arguments were necessary, though the plaintiff-defendant was required to be on call to answer questions from the judge. The judge could accept the law or tailor parts he considered invalid. Though it had not happened in practice, the judge could strike down the entire law as well. Once a judge had ruled in favor of the regulation, no legal objections could be entertained in the future. Integral to this process was an implicit, or sometimes explicit, trip through one or more Supreme Court justices. This system of handling disputes offered an increase in efficiency when compared to the standard legal process from past centuries; it enhanced the judicial system by allowing it to handle battles before they grew into gigantic contests.

Conceiving and creating the framework for Smoothing the Basis marked Kingman a true pioneer in the country's evolution toward the widespread practice of preventive law. The new approach dispensed with the trouble and expense of weighing contradictory evidence and often disingenuous arguments against each other during lawsuits. It also obsoleted the practice of an attacker concocting endless related assaults on different portions of a new law in the hope that one of them will stick and the law will be overturned. With Smoothing the Basis, one ruling validated the entire law permanently.

The Worldwide Transformative Foundation was an early adopter of the new practice, seeking and receiving several judgments during the process of launching IDIC. The rulings in the Foundation's favor were all signed by the appropriate Supreme Court justices; judges had instituted only extremely minor, almost cosmetic, modifications along the way.

Smoothing the Basis was mostly applied to incipient or recently passed laws. Critics—and there were many—nicknamed it 'Smothering the Baby.' On the other hand, the process had numerous supporters. Proponents of the new system pointed out its long family history: across the world today, and throughout most of history, a much simplified form of this process has always been the way things work. The only exceptions have been a small, ephemeral and changing subset of the world's democracies. All but the most elite Americans felt that their country was a longtime exception, and for this reason the whole process seemed strange to most citizens at first. However, the process was clearly efficient, and many respected intellectuals were pressing for extension of the system into criminal law, noting the massive cost Americans incur by waiting for actual crimes to be committed before adjudicating cases through the existing court system. These intellectuals pointed to well established asset forfeiture laws as a first baby step toward the efficiencies they advocated.

Rulings in these new Smoothing the Basis cases were binding for all future challenges. It was now becoming well demonstrated that all challenges to a Smoothing the Basis ruling indeed would fail. Dismissals were very quick, and recently some judges had assessed harsh penalties against pettifogging malcontents filing suits against the Smoothing the Basis rulings.

As a result of Kingman's and Gwendolyn's hard work in the operational and legal realms, IDIC's position as the first choice on the tax form had completed Smoothing the Basis and was now secure. It had been a horse-race, however: in a display of greed more reminiscent of profit-seeking companies than decorous charities, several influential nonprofit organizations had mobilized to fight for their own positions on the tax forms. The Smoothing the Basis ruling came just in time to quash their assaults.

So, on the tax forms, IDIC had the first-choice position. In fact, the donation from a taxpayer declining to make a choice would be directed to

IDIC as well. There were two other choices the citizen would see: 'Worldwide Transformative Foundation' and 'Unspecified.' In the case where the taxpayer selected 'unspecified,' the default machinery Kingman had set up would direct the money to the Worldwide Transformative Foundation.

The amount of the new tax surcharge was minimal. It applied only to United States citizens, and for many taxpayers it amounted to less than one percent of total gross income. Of course, all income earned directly from the government or from any tax-exempt charitable organization was exempt. Anybody who failed to file tax forms had the charity selection made for them, and liabilities accrued for coercive collection. IDIC was electronically connected to the governmental computing apparatus, and the Foundation had already done preliminary work to have the mechanics of steps like garnishing wages in place at the birth of the new system. Gwendolyn had personally been very careful to supervise the testing of the automated transaction processing systems accessing citizens' accounts.

The structure of the surcharge also recognized practical limitations: any individual who could demonstrate that his income or wealth exceeded a threshold set to match the top few percent in the nation was exempt from the charge. There was good reason for this. During the negotiations and compromises inherent in crafting the legislation, an argument was made that high incomes tended to be difficult to verify, so they were most reliant on voluntary cooperation. Since it is absurd to rely on voluntary cooperation in collecting taxes, those in this category should be exempt. Further, it was pointed out that once an individual had accumulated sufficient wealth to place him in the top tier of either wealth or income, he or his ancestors had undoubtedly paid more than their share of taxes during the climb; it was self-evidently wrong to subject the wealthy to the ongoing surcharge. In the end these considerations won the day over simplistic cries for 'fairness' or 'taxing the rich' from the self-appointed guardians of the common man.

Midnight tonight would solidify the complex business arrangement between IDIC and the United States government that would give birth to the new tax forms. In return for the guaranteed revenue stream from the tax returns, each year the luminaries in IDIC, or individuals they selected, would generate important thoughts, and if in IDIC's sole discretion it was warranted, they would deliver recommendations to governmental departments of their choosing. There would be no charge to the receiving organizations for the work of this highly competent and esteemed group; in fact, Gwendolyn characterized these reports as acts of generosity on the part of IDIC. The decision of which reports to write and where to distribute them was left in the hands of IDIC's cadre of notable leaders.

In addition to the cash flow from the new portion of the federal tax forms, the company had a few other income streams. Some were in early stages of development, but one large source of funds was ready to go. As of midnight IDIC would be under lucrative, binding and automatically renewing contracts with the Worldwide Transformative Foundation and the Glowing Circle. IDIC's sole responsibility, in exchange for eight and one third percent of the gross receipts of these nonprofits, was to think about the current public climate and create a report to be delivered by an IDIC corporate officer in an annual briefing to the charities. The work would identify suggestions for the organizations regarding how they should direct their efforts in the near future, and if it seemed appropriate, the report would give advice on longer-term strategic directions.

There was one modest income stream ready and awaiting IDIC's birth. Gwendolyn had developed this other tributary for strategic and networking reasons. She had contacted the heads of many large industrial and financial companies. The corporations were chosen as those most entwined with large government contracts whose leaders were within a decade of retirement age. Her plan was to receive donations from these corporations and employ their executives within IDIC upon their retirement; their salaries would be paid from the companies' prior donations. IDIC pitched the program as sort of a 'scholarships for college' program at the end, rather than the beginning, of high-powered executives' careers—a reward for decades of hard work. Everybody involved wins, as the executives would be encouraged to deem it appropriate to write unsolicited reports urging that government agencies increase their business with their former employers.

The new company was to exist independently of the tax system, its only direct link being the funding from the federal tax forms. All IDIC compensation, dividends and distributions were to be tax-free, since all income streams were either from tax revenue itself or involved the tax-free portion of the economy. This was a new feature resulting from success Kingman had as head of the governmental financial watchdog agency. He used his position to finally implement a long-standing goal of his: once money left the for-profit economy, it stayed outside the tax system. This eliminated the illogical taxation of money from tax-free origins. For instance, the salaries of government and nonprofit employees were now free of income tax, a change rectifying an injustice long perceived by many in those positions.

Compensation of those working in IDIC was thus tax-free, and similarly, equity gains in IDIC were protected from taxes. They were not profits. The company was a nonprofit organization, and gains were classed as a new financial entity called 'equity bonuses.'

IDIC's separation from the country's tax infrastructure was a key selling point for investors; it had dual benefits of increasing their returns and freeing them from the nagging hassle of tax accounting. IDIC planned to distribute most of its income to its owners as equity bonuses, apportioned in accordance with the seniority of their stock series. Investors could also see that there was essentially no downside risk to the business operations of IDIC: all contracts stated that the work product was 'opinion only,' a legal phrase certified, through Smoothing the Basis, to protect the IDIC corporation from legal jeopardy due to any sort of flawed analysis undertaken by the principals or subcontracted out to others.

So in summary, tonight IDIC would become a totally tax-free entity that would collect and distribute three streams of income, and it was devoid of any meaningful obligation to deliver a valid work product. Gwendolyn's brilliant concept was to create a public company with essentially zero expenses whose profit is guaranteed by law. Its conception and materialization hinged on the self-dealings of powerful individuals whom the public perceived as selfless, and Gwendolyn optimized the design to monetize the current positions of this privileged and publicly trusted elite.

The inclusion of presidents of the most prestigious universities as IDIC charter members was Kingman's contribution, and it added a clear marker of altruistic goodness to the endeavor: Americans had historically looked to their universities for moral, and not just intellectual, leadership. Kingman was also responsible for the significant cadre of judges at all levels, including federal Supreme Court justices, who were participating in IDIC, albeit with a higher level of anonymity than most of the others.

The whole thing was a truly synergistic product of the father-daughter team, and a wonderful exploitation of the psychology and very human nature of individuals who have spent many years as trusted public leaders. It was the culmination extensive missionary work with a wide range of government officials. The Foundation had provided electoral support for friendly legislators at strategic times in their struggles, and occasionally helped out during an errant legislator's ethics investigation or criminal trial. Judges, too, had found it convenient to build relationships with the Worldwide Transformative Foundation for reasons similar to those of the legislators.

It would be an exaggeration to say that membership was open to everybody except the common taxpayer.

Timing was good for Gwendolyn's initial public offering. The overall U.S. economy had peaked years ago. There was a period of solid stock growth as large companies shed significant albatrosses in the guise of large work forces, pleasing the investing class and driving up values for several years. The economy drove smaller companies out of business, and both the average size and average profitability for U.S. corporations climbed through the period. However, this process had slowed down in the past few years, and corporations were experiencing many difficulties in executing their daily tasks, filling orders and meeting their financial goals. Consumer markets seemed to have somehow stagnated and started to contract. Corporate equity values were dropping.

Another factor working to Gwendolyn's benefit was that the amount of control individuals were granted over their financial lives was increasingly limited by a wide range of regulations, especially constraining the small investor for his own protection. Investors large and small had few good choices regarding where to put their money. There was one last thing working in IDIC's favor: for whatever reason, the American public at large had not cut back on their voluntary funding of charities even in the face of their own decreasing employment and increasing economic distress. In this environment investors would be seeking the sort of income stream unique to IDIC.

Dr. Florian Q. Bok raised his glass and said with perfect, if a bit Swiss, diction, "Here's to privacy in this great country." Everyone laughed—all present tonight were public owners, and Bok was one who would be promulgating his participation quite loudly. But the privacy feature was what allowed IDIC to be born; it had given government participants a way to be involved without attracting attention and the resulting sophomoric criticism from outside. Without this tool, Kingman would have been unable to create incentives to those inside government and form the legal topography necessary for an IDIC to exist.

Gwendolyn could not help cracking a smile as she thought about how old Bok would not have dared set foot in this great country before Kingman made some adjustments in the government bureaucracy, changes that forgave his bygone infractions, or misunderstandings, as Bok characterized them. Her mind wandered to wondering how the Swazizibia mission looked these days. She had not asked him about that in years.

Florian Bok had run the Wholesome Globe Project since its inception almost a decade and a half ago, and he regularly boasted that he had serviced almost 120,000 Swazizibian clients in that time. To this day the camp ran much as it had when Gwendolyn was there, though Bok had grudgingly expanded its capacity by a factor of two. She smiled as she mused that the power plant never did blow up or spring a leak. If Gwendolyn visited, the only changes she would detect are the size of the complex, the absence of Bertha Martha, who had passed away, and grey hair in Sarah, Aloysius Fink and Jumo. And one more thing: much more money was available to Bok now, and he had convinced the government to station the army around the camp, banishing the militia. This changed only the uniforms and not the transactions, but all in all Bok felt it was a change for the better.

Gwendolyn thought about the ever-kinetic Dr. Florian Q. Bok and his activities over the past decade. A single project could never contain his energy. The man was the only current billionaire in the room. He was at the forefront of economic development in Africa; when a new strain of super-high-calorie corn was developed which was particularly suited to the African climate, he got the Wholesome Globe Project involved. The organization provided an infusion of seed money for the development and production of the new food. He licensed the intellectual property from the inventors and formed a company to exploit the opportunity.

It was possible to grow the new corn in many places, but several locations in Africa, including one region splashing irregularly into southern Swazizibia, were found to be many times more productive than anywhere else. These were places where almost nothing else could grow, yet the new plant could be cultivated there almost effortlessly. Scientists did not yet know why this was true.

Florian Bok had wasted no time in expanding his little company. He retained his position with the Wholesome Globe Project, loudly proclaiming that he could never bear to abandon those under his care. The foresighted man negotiated contracts with almost twenty African nations securing the right to exploit their land suitable for growing the new product. It was a revenue sharing arrangement, and most of the governments agreed readily. Only about one percent of the region's area housed villages; most was wilderness. Bok agreed to allow the settlements to remain in place until he used up all the other land for his project.

The company grew dramatically in its early years. Its first large market was fuel. Due to the corn's high energy density, engineers were able to process the grain into a concentrated liquid well suited for powering aircraft, trucks and large earth forming equipment. Almost simultaneously, a ground corn powder itself became something of a boutique food constituent in the advanced countries. The new grain had a pleasant flavor that made it popular in the United States and Europe; connoisseurs reported a taste found nowhere else. It was a sensation for which there was no existing word, and best efforts to communicate the taste always ended up unsatisfactorily approximating it as a cross between vanilla and cinnamon. The product attained the status of a stylish foodstuff sold at premium prices. The high calorie density became a drawback in the west, but Bok's scientists found a way to inhibit all but a few percent of the food's energy content without impacting its taste, texture or flexibility. Retail sales of the corn took off in the West after that strain was released. Over the span of five years Bok's company went from zero to tens of billions of dollars of annual revenue.

Bok had many enemies who regularly tried to coerce him to change his company's path. The critics pointed to his two executive roles and the fact that Bok and the Wholesome Globe Project together controlled the new company and thus the supply of the corn. They attacked his monopoly on the product and his contractual control over all the best land for its growth. The faultfinders asserted that it was unseemly for the Wholesome Globe Project to be working with profit-seeking corporations, and they relentlessly pushed Bok to grow the highest calorie strain and feed it directly those people starving in the surrounding area, including his own mission's inmates.

Ever patient in the face of these pressures, Florian Bok resisted by educating decision makers in governments and western media about the issue, and he consistently fought off the assaults. The good doctor explained that while it may seem obvious that we can solve hunger problems by growing corn and feeding it to needy neighbors, he wished the world were so simple. But it is important to understand that economics is very complex. The best way to help the hungry in Africa was to command the maximum possible income from the advanced countries for the spicy new grain—the important thing was to get a steady and increasing stream of cash, which could obviously increase the financial resources available to the Wholesome Globe Project and thus lubricate their existing, well established efforts to alleviate hunger. Directly shipping high-calorie corn to places like the Wholesome Globe Project would not supply any versatile cash for the purpose, only transient calories.

The African governments were the first to support his logic, and soon the western intelligentsia concurred: if the government leaders of all those African countries thought this was the optimal way to handle this internal problem, who were comfortable westerners to question them? So attempts to force Bok to divert the new grain to the neighbors of the farms were regularly beaten back. The supply to the western world was never really threatened, and the Wholesome Globe Project impressed the world with its swelling bank balance, much of it theatrically earmarked for the benefit of the needy unfortunates camped just a few miles from the easternmost CornSPICE® farm—unfortunates who could actually see the farm's northbound freight trains kicking up dust in the distance six times every year at harvest season.

Gwendolyn's smile had been static as she thought about Bok tonight. Now she looked down from Bok and twirled the drink in her hand. She thought about the others in the IDIC charter group. Dr. Wilbur Buffaloon had been a continuing friend of the Foundation over the years, and he had afforded Kingman and Gwendolyn many contacts in industry and government. They repaid him with an offer to participate as a charter member of the core IDIC group. Buffaloon only accepted a single share of stock, an infinitesimal ownership, to secure a position as a charter owner, which carried some benefits. But he did acquire an option granting him the right to purchase a large helping of an ultra-preferred series of stock at a price of one cent per share at any time.

Major T. Rathbone, a seeming outsider, was present here tonight. Rathbone was a friend of Wilbur Buffaloon, and the head of the largest single government contractor in the country. He was a retired Air Force lieutenant colonel who had taken over the company that built communication infrastructure under his purview while he was in the military. The company was now owned by Wilbur Buffaloon, who had developed a trusting relationship with the man. The corporation had been a source of funding for the Foundation for several years. As a gesture of appreciation, Gwendolyn had invited Deputy Rathbone to be charter member (the man went by his Air Force call sign, Deputy, rather than his forename, Major, or his rank).

There were over a hundred owners who were government employees and needed anonymity; they were divided between the three branches of federal and state governments, with the plurality in the federal judiciary. A comparable number of industrial executives had similar constraints on their public participation. None of these people were here tonight. And no spouses were present this evening; Gwendolyn insisted that attendance be limited to the core group. The only participant who mentioned a spouse with hard feelings was Dr. Wanda Worthington of Cornwallis. "But he'll get over it."

Everyone heard a rumble of throat-clearing, and they all looked to one end of the large table. "Lord, think back even just one decade!" exclaimed the white-haired and distinguished Dr. Napoleon Burnside Turnbull. "Kingman, your Lobby For Good, I have to say... I was wrong. Who would have predicted anything so successful in failure? Tail wagging the dog, perhaps?" He sipped from his tumbler.

Deputy said, "What's all this talk about dogs?" as he smiled.

Gwendolyn walked over to the table and took her seat as Kingman answered Dr. Turnbull. "Well, looking back, I expected the Lobby to go big back when it started, bless Hunter's heart." Most around the table chuckled. "And I guess it did once we freed up Hunter's energy for skiing and womanizing." He was not smiling, but all the others were, save his daughter.

Napoleon Burnside Turnbull's friendly tease arose from an unlikely history: at its inception, the Lobby For Good was to be an appendage to the Worldwide Transformative Foundation, added to Hunter's responsibilities. As it turned out, Hunter did not have the capability to lead the new initiative, and it quickly foundered under him. Within a year of its launch Kingman reabsorbed the whole effort into the undifferentiated protoplasm of the Foundation, reorganized, and gave Hunter an assignment with a group cataloging wildflowers on the different continents. Shortly thereafter, the Lobby efforts succeeded so compellingly that the Foundation slowly morphed; the Foundation itself became largely what Kingman had originally envisioned for the Lobby For Good. All the 'normal' Foundation programs, still vigorous and strong, became subservient to the successful new thrust. Of course, the Foundation retained its premier position in the charity world, mediating monetary flows between its leading organizations, individuals, corporations, and government bodies. But Kingman's and Gwendolyn's real efforts went into sculpting the governmental environment to a more felicitous fit with the goals of large tax-free organizations—first and foremost, of course, the Worldwide Transformative Foundation. In summary, the Foundation had achieved great success in the legislative and government realm—the areas for which the Lobby For Good was originally designed— over the past eight years.

Dr. Wanda Worthington slurred, "Yes, we all appreciate Hunter's effort, and even more, his cooperation in leaving." Laughs ensued, and a good-natured smile even came from Kingman. "But let's fess up: The creativity powering tonight was Gwendolyn's."

Gwendolyn, her normal combat-quality aplomb deserting her, blushed. She said, "Well, maybe I baked the cake, but tonight we'll have final proof that you put the cherry on top, Wanda." She lifted her glass toward Dr. Worthington and took a small drink.

It appeared she was correct. From all indications, Wanda Worthington's contribution was set to pay off well. While Gwendolyn had been formulating and revising her plan for the new company, Wanda was prompted by a happy accident to propose an enhancement to the project. Cornwallis University's largest benefactor was killed in an unfortunate mishap as he piloted an experimental rocket he built. His will named Cornwallis as sole beneficiary, and the university came into control of his carefully guarded 'value from randomness' algorithms and machines.

Dr. Worthington had been a big believer in the rectitude and value of the technology since its first personal demonstration to her: it was used to choose her as president of Cornwallis almost a decade ago. She had an inkling that the technology could be employed in driving up the perceived value of IDIC's stock. Gwendolyn hired experts to analyze the situation, and they validated Dr. Worthington's intuition. Financial engineers designed a version of a proprietary random algorithm for stock value enhancement, and Gwendolyn promoted the technology as an innovative form of equity instrument whose debut would be in the IDIC initial public offering.

The IDIC offering was structured such that new buyers of common stock in IDIC were to own a value that fluctuated with a stochastic component on top of whatever market value existed; the common shares came with a feature that randomly reassigned a portion of the benefits of owning stock between those holding it. The prices of individual shares would vary relative to each other in a lossless random way. That is, the company's common stock came with a built-in lottery—individual shareowners could be wildly rewarded with equity taken from other owners of the same class of stock, or they could lose money. The algorithm was biased to condition the fluctuations: in each random event, losses were small and widespread, while gains were concentrated and large. The public loves a lottery, and most simulations predicted that the gamble-on-gamble aspect of owning IDIC stock was certain to increase both the price and the velocity of transactions in the common stock. The preferred layers of stock, those owned by the charter equity members, did not participate in the random feature.

Kingman stood and pronounced his admiration. "Yes, Dr. Worthington, your idea was a brilliant insight. And who knew it could come from one with your history? You're certainly the incarnation of the saying that a man makes his own luck!" Dr. Worthington smiled at him. Kingman turned toward his daughter and continued. "I like to think I had something to do with this whole thing too, contributing to the mechanics of the deals. Humor me as I muse that my tireless arm-twisting with legislators and judges was crucial." The happy tipsy man looked at his daughter. There was an odd pause as he caught a glimpse of a strikingly handsome and distinguished man holding forth in the reflective wall of window situated a dozen feet from where he stood. Then he went on, looking away from the ghost twenty-four feet from him. "But you're right about Gwendolyn. I don't think anyone else in the world could have conceived and crystallized this whole deal, this beautiful masterpiece blooming tonight. Here's to my daughter, Dr. Dressel-Meier the Junior!" Glasses around the table tinkled among bright murmurs. Gwendolyn's participation in the activity was limited to increasingly reddening, a rare occurrence these days.

In a little while right here, Gwendolyn's lonely sobriety would be put to good use—midnight was coming. She would soon meet with a select group of investment bankers. The public offering would relieve each charter owner of a few percent of his holdings in the company, and, assuming the initial stock sold as projected, each would realize a staggeringly huge cash gain while retaining most of his equity; no new stock was to be issued, and of course all transactions would be tax free.

The charter members continued cheerful conversation through a seven-course meal centering on Rack of Lamb and capped by Baked Alaska. They enjoyed drinks and small talk as they verbally contemplated the events to come. Each envisioned life over the next few days in pleasant anticipation of assuming his rightful place among the super wealthy.

Just before eleven o'clock the group's drinks were refreshed and they obediently, if confusedly, lined up along the window at Gwendolyn's request. Four minutes before the clock strike, the maître d' escorted five black-suited and slick-haired gentlemen into the room. They represented the primary investment bank and three partner banks handling the logistics of tonight's initial public offering. With these representatives was the Foundation's chief financial officer, who held a position that Gwendolyn had established in recognition of the complex dealings the organization was now engaged in. She gestured for the newcomers to hurry over, finger across her lips in a 'hush' gesture. The outsiders stood with the others at the window in silence as the Foundation CFO came to Gwendolyn, tugging her away and engaging in quiet whispering. Everyone stood still, facing the windows without a clue why. The group's silent anticipation was heightened by the concentrated inaction throughout the room.

Kingman stood near the corner, a position that allowed him to examine his appearance from the front and side at once. The room's lights, not very bright to start with, dimmed to his disadvantage and caused him some consternation. Suddenly a massive starburst of bright red, orange and blue streaks of incendiary brilliance lit the room. Just then the crowd was startled by the shock of an explosion perhaps fifty feet outside the window. The glass slammed against its frame, then rattled and banged with the detonation's memory as gouts of multicolored flaming material hit the window, actually melting the outer layer of the glass and deforming the steel in some places. The explosion was followed by another, starting a chaotic and colorful series of fireworks all placed at different heights over the street below. The rockets were launched from the bottom of the hill atop which the hotel perched. Were anyone to look closely enough, he could see the fire department heavily staffing the ground below. Further examination would show that the police had closed all the roads within several blocks for the celebration.

Once everyone was acclimatized to the fireworks, the waiters brought around fresh drinks, proffering Gwendolyn's guess for the newcomers' preferences: Scotch. Her guess was correct, or at least the bankers did not spurn the drinks, though later all four asked for a different drink for the next round.

When the fireworks were over, Gwendolyn called the meeting to order. "Gentlemen, as you know IDIC will be a publicly held company in just a few minutes. We will offer six percent of our stock and expect your participation. We will entertain final sealed bids from you individually and apportion the stock accordingly; I have the contracts here missing just a few numbers and our signatures." She nodded to her financial officer who tapped the folio he was holding. "I assume you have already accessed all our public filing information. We have some private financial information we will share over the next few minutes, for your eyes only please. We ask for your commitment in moving our stock quickly and effectively. We have only a brief interval, but let me review the history of IDIC company…"

Gwendolyn had come a long way from the ingenuous schoolgirl who was so impressed with her friend Alitisha's understanding that paying tuition would be easier if her father saved his money instead of spending it. Now she was working with the best lawyers and accountants, dealing at the frontier of law and finance, structuring this innovative and complex transaction. She powered directly through her persuasive presentation without entertaining questions; the investment bankers were paying furious attention, taking notes, but forbidden from automatically recording anything on their GVCDs.

The IDIC principals watched from their table in detached, alcohol-enhanced relaxation. Most were familiar with only one financial detail—they were to be fabulously wealthy—and had left the rest to Gwendolyn. Kingman did not pay attention; he had every confidence in his daughter. Instead, watched the shifting tendrils of smoke from the remnants of the fireworks drifting outside. He lit his old-fashioned pipe and relaxed with his drink, admiring something that caught his eye in the smooth glass of the window.

Gwendolyn opened the floor for questions and had a lively interchange with the investment bankers, occasionally deferring to her financial officer. When the questioning had dissipated she offered them one more reason they should want to serve as agents in the IDIC financial scheme. "There is one final piece of information you should have. This is not represented in any of the disclosures we have filed, nor what I just showed you." She looked over at her nameless financial officer, who looked down at his lap.

"I have learned that the American Generosity Enforcement, or 'AGE' Act, will be moving out of committee in Congress and is expected to go through quickly. Fifth time is a charm, I suppose." Her thin smile received no counterpart as she paused; the bankers lived in a world free from any sort of humor. She went on, "This bill has had many incarnations. I believe the current concept is the most powerful of all, as it targets top-line financial exchanges. You undoubtedly know that the President has often voiced support for the bill, which should surprise nobody based on her history. IDIC is in a good position. The bill will radically lubricate our access to cash, helping citizens fund good causes through IDIC on an ongoing basis. I cannot go into the details without consuming the entire night, but I can assure you that IDIC and the Worldwide Transformative Foundation have antici-pated this event for years."

Being investment bankers, they all knew of the law, some form of which had been proposed in Congress almost every year for a long time, though they were not aware that Kingman molded most of its language. The law imposed a fee of two percent on commercial, industrial and retail transactions. The tax was designed as 'superior' and 'two-sided': that is, it was computed on the total including all other taxes, and it was assessed on both sides of a transaction, for an aggregate of four percent. The destination of the fee was to be under nominal control of the individuals spending and receiving the money. After committee negotiations, the only surviving full exemptions were for employees and retirees of government and nonprofit organizations, though persons above fifty years in age enjoyed a steeply discounted rate in personal transactions.

The publicly stated argument for the fee had always been: Americans are a generous people, and they need tools to decrease the administrative hassle of finding and supporting charitable organizations; they would choose to give more if it were easier. There was, of course another interpretation of that statement that penetrated to the ulterior: Americans would give more if forced to at gunpoint.

Opponents alternated between describing the proposed law as tyrannical confiscation and calling it a 'tax on everything.' The critics warned of what could be approximated as a four percent tax on the nation's GDP, but proponents countered that argument by pointing out the exemption of employees of government and tax-free organizations. Armed with charts showing the radical growth of these sectors in the face of the overall contraction of the economy, supporters argued that the predictions of doom used flawed mathematics, as only that shrinking portion of the economy concerned with producing or handling new economic content would be impacted. However, ostensibly to address this concern, Congress resurrected a feature that had been stripped from the legislation during final negotiations: an additional exemption was restored for their own side of transactions, for banks and corporations whose revenues put them in the 2000 largest companies worldwide.

IDIC was lined up to supply the infrastructure for the AGE act and direct the cash flows, pocketing a percentage of the revenues. By default, AGE funds were to be directed to the Worldwide Transformative Foundation. Those executing a deal could select other pre-screened recipients on a transaction-by-transaction basis. The participant would designate the target by supplying its eighteen-digit identifying number. No commercial inter-change was too small, and provisions were made to allow a grace period during which things like vending machines could be fitted with keypads or other human-entry devices. The law precluded any form of automated entry of charity identification. For instance, it would be illegal to present a menu to a buyer or seller, or to read a charity identification number directly from his GVCD. The human party in the transaction must enter the identifying number without mechanical or electronic help, or of course, accept the default.

Gwendolyn summarized for the bankers. "The legislation is finally poised to pass and become law. IDIC stands ready for another upside to its revenues, and we are happy to sense the proximity of consummation of years of work by the Foundation and many others."

Just then her GVCD summoned her. She glanced at it and gestured with her forehead to the Foundation's financial officer, who took over the conversation. "... invite you to participate in what we anticipate to be a fairly regularly occurring process of stock offerings structured to put you in a very good position... your bids... sign paperwork... "

Gwendolyn went toward the far end of the room and seemed to speak to the darkness outside the window. She came back just as the banking was being finalized, and closed the meeting with a businesslike parting ritual. Along with the bank officials, her CFO left in possession of the old-fashioned paper contracts complete with ink signatures,.

After they were gone, Gwendolyn sat down. Dr. Napoleon Burnside Turnbull turned to her and said, "It seems you were in quite an animated conversation over there, Gwendolyn." He took a drink. Whiskey, it appeared. Gwendolyn said nothing. She was relaxing for the first time in months and playing a game.

"Well?" Dr. Turnbull's eyebrows communicated.

Gwendolyn relented. "Who knew? It was Victoria Hull. She was asking me to run with her."

Everyone sat frozen. Kingman dropped his pipe. The sounds of the bouncing smoking tool and dumbfounded silence ricocheted around the table as those present tried to disentangle the confusing words from the influence of the alcohol on their brains. Run with Victoria Hull? Run what? Was it possible? Kingman was the first to see that it may be real. The others were mostly just confused, wondering if they heard right.

Kingman asked, "What about Taffington?"

Gwendolyn answered, "Victoria said he's performed his last act of insubordination. She's dropping him, and she needs somebody else. Taffington's out."

It made some sense; Kingman knew that Taffington was a compromise choice, and that the man had always had friction with Victoria Hull. Yes, that part was believable. It was easy to cite recent instances where the current U.S. Vice President openly contradicted the President. But Gwendolyn? Running for Vice President?

Silence.

Everyone started to understand what Gwendolyn had said. "Well?" Dr. W. Spencer Beaverbrook's face was cantilevered forward over the table. But more silence followed. Gwendolyn just sat smiling. It had been a long, exhausting evening that felt like the sprint at the finish of a marathon culminating an ironman triathlon. She wanted to savor her position as suspense dispenser.

Deputy, star-struck, asked, "What did you tell her?"

Gwendolyn feigned a leisurely search for her drink. A waiter, equally as curious as the charter IDIC principals, quickly supplied her with a new cordial glass of Drambuie and stood transfixed. She took a sip and savored the hot sweet vapors as she exhaled. Then she said matter-of-factly, "I told her I'm not old enough. Check the Constitution."

Kingman had many talents, and one was that he could enjoy a pleasant alcoholic haze as much as anyone, but dispense with the fog at will. He exercised this unique skill now; as he fast comprehended Gwendolyn's words, he created and wallowed in a fountain of regret at his own lack of foresight. With all the legislative initiatives and rulings he had worked on, why, why... He took a drink.

There was a short and stunned pause, then the happy ebullience of Dr. W. Spencer Beaverbrook's voice broke the silence. "Oh yes of course. The Constitution. To the Constitution! Letting us keep our fearless leader a little longer!" Raucous laughter erupted across the whole group, and even Kingman's tension dissipated. They downed their drinks with smiles all around.

Gwendolyn cheerfully told the group, "I suggested Clif Rockington. Maybe she can get him to kiss the babies that are scared of her." She sipped her cordial and joined the laughter.

Just then someone shouted, "It's midnight!"

HUNTER AND MARSHALL were having another nightcap in the elder's limousine in the basement parking garage as the elevator doors opened and the IDIC principals emerged. The newly minted billionaires walked, many unsteadily, to their own limos. The happy rich drunken men all hugged Gwendolyn, and she exchanged warm kisses with the air over the shoulders of the two women. All went to their limousines, and the family lingered chattingly for a few minutes before scattering to their own vehicles.

Gwendolyn sat in the dark comfort of her limousine, exhausted, contented, but high strung, and glad to be free of the old men. Kingman's vehicle drove off, as did Hunter's. Just then Marshall appeared at her window holding a box. "Here, this stuff is from your office. When we moved I wasn't sure you wanted it in your new room since you're never there." He was talking about the main office in New York; Gwendolyn rarely visited her office there, now that she was spending most of her time in Washington, D.C.

She nodded wearily and accepted the box, putting it on the seat beside her. Marshall disappeared into his limousine, which vanished up the ramp. Sitting in the shadows with the months-long crush of activity behind her, she realized she was lonely. She thought about friends she had in the area, but realized that even on a normal night it would be too late to visit with Hilda Stumpf, president of Stambridge University down the peninsula, or her old friend Alitisha, now the Dean of the School of Service there. Anyway, Dr. Stumpf was out of the country.

They drove up the exit ramp, and the chauffeur pulled into the middle of the San Francisco night. Gwendolyn was not ready to wind down yet, so her only instruction was to drive. At the bottom of the hill, they traveled not very many blocks and came to the soup kitchen she had noticed from the window at dusk. The place was not serving food in the middle of the night, but there were people sleeping on the sidewalk and in the neighboring alley. The proprietors always provided cots and blankets for the indigent to use; these days the city did not try to assert control over such things, so long as there was no violence. As Gwendolyn drove up she saw two quasi-uniformed volunteers among the thirty or so homeless people asleep all around the place. One volunteer was keeping watch, and the other looked like he just could not sleep.

What are those two thinking? They're never going to get those people off the streets, especially in this economy. The car was stopped at a light, and Gwendolyn was not a dozen feet from one of the haggard and exhausted-looking, but wide awake, volunteers. He rubbed the bags under his eyes and yawned in the false privacy of the night as Gwendolyn watched him from the actual privacy of her limousine. She was transfixed by his drawn and tired-looking facial features, his cheap shoes. *This doesn't look easy for him.* At the same time he disinterestedly glanced at the dark glass of her vehicle. The light changed, and the driver started accelerating, but she barked out "Stop!" and the car bounced to a halt.

She looked at the people sleeping around the area, and her mind was not even attracted to the clients themselves. But the volunteers! That man looked so exhausted, and he didn't look rich enough to even own a car himself. Why was he here? What would make someone do this? How often did he do it? From the looks of him he had not gotten enough sleep in years. *I guess they're some kind of do-gooders.* Just then the man stood and ran his hands unselfconsciously through his hair. He walked back and forth on the sidewalk, swinging his arms in a stretching motion as he yawned, all the while ignoring the limousine. Then he walked over and said something to the only other person who was not sleeping. It was the other waking volunteer. She was sitting on her mat. Her back was to Gwendolyn, but she revealed her face as she turned to answer the man.

Gwendolyn was fascinated, wondering what they were saying. She stared at the woman. Her face was, if anything, even more chiseled and wrinkled and fatigued than the man's. Gwendolyn cracked her window, and she could hear their conversation. "I know. I'm always starving around this time. You'll get used to it. And no. How would it look to them if one wakes up? We can get some breakfast in about four hours when they eat." Gwendolyn saw the listener nodding, then both workers surveyed their sleeping charges. Neither seemed to wonder why a fantastically expensive limousine had stopped in front of the seedy building. Gwendolyn could not know it, but both the man and the woman were approximately her own age, though either could pass for mid-forties. The man walked away from the woman yawning, and Gwendolyn heard him say, "Yeah, well I'm gonna have to take it on the run. I gotta get to work early."

I'll never figure those people out. The newborn billionaire shook off the strange mood that had somehow gripped her, wagging her head actively. She instructed the driver to get moving, and they drove up the hill in front of them. She looked back over her shoulder as the encampment shrank in the distance. *And you know, I used to be one of them.*

After tonight's energetic meeting Gwendolyn was too tense to contemplate going back to her hotel anytime soon. She had the chauffeur drive back and forth along the waterfront a few times. She rested her head against the seat and enjoyed the display of bright lights jostling along their colorful paths in the wonderful city. They drove across the bay and back to the city so she could admire the copper-lined beauty of the downtown buildings at night from the bay bridge. Still untired, she instructed the driver to start a loop around the whole south bay, driving along the hills so she could enjoy glimpses of the sparkling civilization below as they cruised down the peninsula.

Twenty miles south, Gwendolyn mindlessly opened the folded flaps on the carton Marshall had given her. She reached in, unable to see in the darkness, and felt a velvety softness recognized instantly by her inner brain but confusing to her consciousness at first. Within seconds she became aware she was feeling Pyratticus Julius, who lived under her desk in New York. She flipped on the lights and admired the furry octopod, whom she had not fondled for a long time, smiling as she remembered his eye patch. The creature was silent, motionless. *He hasn't talked to me in years. We were so close.* As she noticed the brass medallion anchored in the eye patch, a fog of gloom enveloped her.

She pulled out the token and saw the engraving of the beautiful city with the words 'Build And Trust Your Own Mind' announcing the dawn of a new day. 'TYOM CECILIA 9' was inscribed at the bottom. She had stuck the coin in the eye patch years ago, when it churned to the top of a closet at work along with Pyratticus Julius; she had combined them as remnants of her immature years, obsolete but not quite forgettable. Somehow they seemed to belong together.

Now a tear welled up in her eye as she thought of her old friend Cecilia. It spawned a twin in her other eye as she imagined Cecilia's warmth and then her disappointment, the stark assessment Cecilia would make about Gwendolyn's chosen path in life. She turned over the coin, and the words 'Truth—Persistence—Integrity' jumped out at her. She imagined her actions over the past half dozen years with an annoying miniature Cecilia on her shoulder, whispering judgments into her ear at every turn. Gwendolyn's tears escalated to a flood; she knew that living up to just one of the three virtues would never satisfy the little woman. Exhaustion from the evening of stress at the end of the intense season of business dealings finally overwhelmed her. Gwendolyn lost physical control and sobbed wickedly in the back of the vehicle. In a little while she recovered a tad of composure and tucked the coin back into the eyepiece. She bathed in her melancholy as the suburban lights drifted by below and the stars shone brightly above. At that moment she saw a shooting star, blurred through her watery eyes, seeming to travel straight down from the heavens, disappearing over the dark golden hills across the bay. A pang of distilled regret gripped her as she thought about this meteor and the one she had seen over the dirtpile in Swazizibia, the one that beckoned her into the dustbowl so many years ago. She rolled down her window.

Gwendolyn took a few deep breaths, and for a long time she felt the air in her hair and gazed down at Pyratticus Julius. A tear from her eye kissed his silly smile on its way to his belly. She contemplated a world long gone, a Gwendolyn of the past. Another tear followed. Pyratticus Julius was in her hands, but he seemed years away. As the car sped down the smooth road she saw her hands straighten the octopod's six legs one last time. Somewhere near Stambridge she tossed the critter into the darkness. Somewhere near Cecilia's apartment she rolled the window back up.

THE END

Appendix: The Old Poem

The Torch or the Timber?
Mixed Metaphors
for
Perusal by Prospective Peak Performers

You know how the world works—you've learned that, all right,
And nothing's so new it seems shiny and bright.
You have your routines and for any new door
There's something quite like it you've been through before.

If time's taught you anything here's what you've learned:
In pushing your limits you're sure to get burned.
Life's lesson in hand now, you've carved out a niche.
You're prudent or boring. It's hard to say which.

Well, you can get by if you want to that way,
And most people do, stringing day after day.
But not Peak Performers. They're people who note
That life's to be lived, not just passed through by rote.

Confronted by weeds in a garden they tend,
They'll get mostly flowers and fruit in the end.
Each challenge is new. Every chore yields a chance
To find a reward that's unseen at first glance.

They gather these treasures, though sometimes through tears.
With many small gems they're enriched over years.
They swing hard. They strike out a lot of the time,
But no one recalls. The home runs are sublime!

In battle these people will focus their will
On growing a bit as they fight for each hill.
When body blows come and they're knocked to the floor,
They climb right back into the ring for some more.

It's tempting to think Peak Performers are blessed
With brains and abilities—none but the best.
These gifts are their tickets. It's got to be true,
They have a head start. They're not like me or you.

But here is the secret: they have no such pass.
Yet somehow they rise to the top of the class.
They're born like us all and they muddle along,
But one day decide that just muddling is wrong.

And then they start choosing to choose their own way.
It's not a bad plan. You can do it today.
Though making a change brings a measure of strife,
It's never too late to reorder your life.

You author your story. The future's at stake.
You're sure to construct it. Which path will you take?
The wind or the feather? The golf club or ball?
In living your life the game's winner take all!

www.ingramcontent.com/pod-product-compliance
Lightning Source LLC
Chambersburg PA
CBHW021116260626
47169CB00005B/1312